Shellfargon

by

K McVere

In the year

**of the Holy Serpent 5023
when
a momentous
religious epiphany occurred**

in a graveyard known as Myrtle's Bedrest,
east of Mudflat Village,
west of Greenburg Valley,
south of Bitterroot Forest,
north of Duke Dono Castle,
several days ride from Walrat Island,
but,
a stone's throw from Blueglennen the capital,
in the county of Tweetham,
which all belong to Wolfern Province,
in a country called Curl,
made up of Delphinids,
unlike
Lacertidae from Vespa 1 & Vespa 2,
both species separated by a body of water
called the East Serpent Sea
there are those who fight the NeverEnding War
for control of a planet
known as

Shellfargon

Earth Ship Conference: Year 5091

Crystova Moth, one of the delegates of the Earth Ship Conference stepped out of the shuttle door and into the chilly glass-and-metal framed docking canopy. The docking canopy was lit by hundreds of glow-worms. No. Not glow-worms. Here in this sleek steel contraption lights were lit from a foreign source. She wasn't sure what the material might be, but it wasn't anything like material used on her planet to illuminate city streets and homes at night.

The source of her people's illumination came from the sea – iridescent creatures' swimming inside glass globes hung from street lamps. When in motion the glow-worm bodies radiated a powerful blue light, which penetrated the darkest corners of the old castle, a castle she and the townspeople called Duke Tower.

As the last delegate to emerge from the shuttle, she discovered with annoyance she was also the last to enter the starship hatch. She represented the province of Wolfern, which happened to be the biggest of the provinces in the country of Curl, and even of more import, she'd been born and raised in the capital city of Wolfern Province, Blueglennen. The delegates should have been seated in the shuttle by the size of their provinces not by their surnames.

It felt like a slap in the face to have been left behind. She should have behaved more like the representative from North Victoria. He'd been a complete ass the entire trip blathering about his connections with the Delphadorturo of the country of Curl, Earl Raker. Crystova had her doubts Delphadorturo Raker, the Supreme Commander of Curlecon Forces even knew the delegate from North Victoria.

Debating whether to make a dash up the ramp, the memory of her elevated position as ambassador of the entire province of Wolfern stopped her from making a bigger fool of herself than the polyps undulating toward the starship's hatch. Watching the other delegates jerking forward, two steps at a time, as they tried unsuccessfully not to trip over their own feet was hilarious. They were so eager not to be left behind they reminded Crystova of polyps running from a predator. Only instead of running away, the polyps were committing suicide by running into the mouth of the metal monster, a metal monster which had been circling their world for months generating hysteria and doomsday fantasies.

The ship's officers of the Starship Albion who were leading the way seemed oblivious to the anxiousness of their charges. What a sight to see – the cream of Shellfargon stumbling over themselves to keep up with their colleagues, their heads swiveling madly from side to side, up and down, awe blazing from their big eyes and open mouths. Crystova had to admit the sweeping steel buttresses and heavy glass in the docking port was like nothing she'd seen before.

Some of her fellow delegates might have been curious about what was beyond the massive metal frames and glass, but she suspected most of the delegates couldn't have cared less. Knowing them too well, she believed all they wanted was for the ship and its occupants to sell them more technology, so they could make more money. Setting a brisk pace, the ship's officers marched the line of polyps out of sight.

She considered running after them, but something stopped her. She sensed she would never experience such an extraordinary time in history ever again. With that thought in mind, she had an overwhelming desire to take in everything and store all the wonders of this place in her long-term memory to record later. Her observations would be, not just detailed reports for her superiors at the university or to allay Governor Saurus' fears but for posterity's sake.

Since she had been forbidden to bring a cellphone or any technologies sold to the natives of Shellfargon by the Starship Albion, she had only her photographic memory as a way of recording her observations and the events of this incredible day.

Instead of hurrying after the polyps, she lingered near the shuttle studying with furious intensity the newly built structure made of materials from Shellfargon. The dome and three sides of the canopy were constructed of glass and heavy metal ribs. It was a gigantic docking port attached to one side of the starship which showed her a moving image of dark space and a sight she had never seen in all her born days – her planet Shellfargon, so many thousands of miles below them.

Shellfargon was so beautiful, so delicate, just the way the elders recorded her home in their illuminated manuscripts— like a fragile eggshell rotating in dark space. She could see the oceans and seas and rivers. Those enormous swathes and ribbons of blue were the original home of her people – the Delphinids.

Millions of years ago her ancestors from the sea chose to return to the land where they were created. The Delphinids evolved over millennia and were capable of surviving on both land and sea. On Shellfargon the blue sea was interrupted by gigantic land masses. There was her country of Curl in the Northern Hemisphere, Bojenlac in the Southern Hemisphere, New Dala at the far western half and the faintest of impressions of the other side of the world where Vespa 1, Vespa 2, and Angland lay.

Extraordinary that she and her ancestors had never stepped onto Lacertidae land. In fact, very few Delphinids in all the years of the NeverEnding War had ever seen a Lacertidae up close or spoken to one face to face. All the fighting between the two bitter enemies took place in the depths of the Serpent Sea in underwater ships Earthlings erroneously called submarines and Shellfargons knew as living creatures called bowriders.

Bowriders were the guardians of the oceans, seas, and rivers. Shellfargons, whether Delphinids or Lacertidae, paid bowriders to fight for them. Some bowriders were lizards, a few were whales, still others belonged to the deadly descendants of the sharks but most bowriders were from the serpent class, the class that ruled all the waters of Shellfargon.

It wasn't until the introduction of the starship's technology that both sides were fascinated witnesses to the fierce fighting happening in the depths of the Serpent Sea. Most people were shocked and sickened by the horrible mutilations and deaths. Remarkably, in the last few years, fewer and fewer bowriders were commissioned to fight the enemy.

Crystova wished she wasn't a pessimist. Yet, she had a feeling the fighting would never really end. Old grudges and profiteers with loads of money needed the war. The rest of the world didn't realize what was really at stake.

A cough reminded her of her mission and she glanced at the woman waiting for her at the hatch. She was used to sitting inside a noisy smelly old train powered by steam, even familiar with elevators which went all the way up to the thirteenth floor of Duke Tower where the Governor of Blueglennen had his private apartments. But this space ship, this gargantuan dock was overpowering in its vastness, smell, and cacophony of sound.

Then she saw the delegates from Vespa 1 & 2 coming down the ramp onto the dock heading for the shuttle she'd just left. She glanced at the starship Albion host waiting to greet her. Crystova had been told the inhabitants of the Albion called themselves Earthlings. Her host was female, and she was waiting patiently near the hatch ready to escort her into the ship. Part of her realized she was experiencing culture shock.

Here were creatures she'd never seen before other than in the imaginations of Shellfargons. When the trembling began, she was ashamed of herself. She used an old trick - repeating a mantra from her favorite poet silently to herself – to calm her nerves.

Crystova Moth as the representative of the most northwestern of the provinces of Curl – Wolfern Province had never seen her enemies up close or the strange woman representing Earth. There were seven other Delphinid representatives from Walrus Island, Moorland, Textus, New Enreich, North Victoria, South Victoria, and Hemway.

As far as she knew she and those seven were the last continent to agree to the meeting between the earth ship and the planet of Shellfargon. All the delegates from Curl had long since disappeared down the hatch. She was the only Delphinid to witness the departure of the Lacertidae as the earthlings escorted them to their shuttle.

Growing up she'd only seen images of Lacertidae in newspapers printed on parchment. And if the paper wanted to include an image of the enemy, artists were hired to sketch or paint the enemy based on reports from overseas. Since the earthlings on board the Albion introduced Shellfargon to a thing called broadcasting, the medium allowed Curlecons to see Lacertidae up close, every hour of every day, as the war droned on and on, and each side spouted hate and fear. Even with this new communication system, the NeverEnding War continued. The leaders of Curl and Vespa 1 & 2 were discovering fresh grievances in order to prolong the war.

Unlike the very faintest of grayish blue in a Delphinid's skin pigment, Lacertidae were multicolored with hues of green, gold, brown, and red in their outer shells, a shell which was harder than hers yet breathtaking in its vibrancy. They had two legs and two arms like her. They walked upright like her. And instead of having two heads like idiots believed, they had one head, some noble, some not so noble, all bald.

In fact, it would appear they had no hair on their bodies at all. They'd long since lost their whiptails but Crystova was reminded of their ancestry in their dress. They wore long flowing silk cloaks, slashed in the back and streaming behind them as they moved. The cloaks represented the ancient Lacertidae's whiptail and the colors of their ancient desert lands.

Another delicate cough, a reminder from the Earthling that she, Crystova, was being a rude guest. Crystova turned to the Earth representative. She was an attractive woman with skin the color of midnight. The structure of her skin was far more delicate than cither a Lacertidae or a Delphinid. The most compelling part of her face was her eyes, her eyes transmitted intelligence and charisma, a dangerous combination.

What disturbed Crystova the most was the fact her copper eyes were hard to read. What was this woman thinking? Was she happy to see an alien species on her ship? Or was she annoyed at being assigned to babysit Crystova? It was obvious this woman was no pushover.

As if the woman could read her mind, she stepped forward and offered her hand, "How do you do Dela Moth. I am Shehili Swana, an ethnographer assigned to your lovely capitol. We are late for the opening ceremonies.

Come with me. I will be happy to fill you in on what you missed during the tour. I have been assigned to Wolfern Province and have been asked by your Delphadorturo to establish myself as a tourist in your country. No one outside of this delegation will know my true history. As an ethnographer, it is my task to determine whether or not the legend of Shellfargon is true."

"Which one?"

"The assumption your planet will break apart into a million pieces because the center is a hollow cavity filled with air."

"Why do you care? You can't test our planet. Our leaders would never allow you to drill or mine or deface so much as an inch of soil."

"An inch?" Dela Swana remarked with a grin. "So, you've been studying our language."

"Yes," Crystova admitted. "I've been learning what I can from the news and from recordings from your ship. As I'm sure you know the university has been given permission to access your ship's historical files."

As her guide stepped closer to Crystova she couldn't help but admire the dress Shehili Swana wore. The colors reminded her of the Lacertidae, a remarkable mix of black, brown and red. Throughout the dress, from the shoulders to the hem, the seamstress had woven thin strands of yellow braid.

While appreciating the dress, Crystova listened in growing alarm to the ship's representative explain the ship's intentions. "On this ship we have technology which can determine the construction of your planet. But that's not important. What I, as an ethnographer want to learn, is so much more than sonic scans can tell me. I'm interested in the origins of your species, the history of your culture, your language, your religion. You fascinate us Dela Moth. We want to learn from you."

"No, you don't. You want to plunder our precious resources and leave us with nothing."

"You're wrong," Shehili Swana said her copper eyes so unusual and unflinching. "When Albion first arrived in your solar system, we were short of food and other critical supplies. We made trade agreements with your country and the Lacertidae. Your continents provide us with the food and supplies we needed and in exchange we provide you with our technology. We've honored our agreements. Now, we have a new emergency. The threat is real and not just to our ship. Other lifeforms have discovered the rich bounty in this solar system and are making their way here. Based on past encounters with them, they are no respecters of life."

Crystova snorted, "Of course. Manufacture an emergency so the ignorant natives will give in to your demands. Well the citizens of Curl and the Delphadorturo are too intelligent to be fooled by tricks. All these months while you've been lording over us in space, you've ignored the most important part of being a Delphinid. Our elders warned us this day would come. They predicted our planet would be plundered. Shellfargon is not for sale. The center of Shellfargon is holy and will never be sullied by foreigners. Tell that to your captain."

"Captains," Shehili corrected her. "We have three captains. They all must agree to any major decisions made aboard this ship. Before the captains decide whether to stay and fight or to leave this solar system, the ship's ethnographers need to learn more about your planet and to train your people to protect yourselves against the dangers coming your way.

They have permitted a few of us to return to your planet, study your culture, understand your concerns, learn from you, and show you how to protect yourselves. One of the captains of this ship is my father and he agrees with me – the best chance we have is to stand and fight with your people.

The other captains insist we must leave this solar system. We have until 5095 before the threat to your planet and our ship materializes. As an ethnographer, I have trained all my life for this day. I am ready to walk on Shellfargon soil and live among you. It is imperative the citizens of both continents know nothing about the coming danger. Your people will be told that we are just tourists living on temporary visas who want to visit your art museums, your shops, and your holy places."

"We don't need interfering outsiders telling us what to do," Crystova said taking a step backward prepared to return to the shuttle even if she had to sit among Lacertidae.

Shehili Swana stepped back toward the airlock rubbing her arms and shaking her head, "I'm so sorry you feel that way, but your own leader, the Delphadorturo Earl Raker agrees with my father and has already provided me and the other ethnographers, engineers, and scientists with temporary visas. We plan to do what we can to help you fight off the coming invasion. Even if the Albion does choose to leave this solar system, we will leave behind our technology. No matter what you say or do next, it is inevitable we will be seeing each other very soon.

I am posted to your beautiful city and will be living inside the castle grounds. In three-days' time, I will shuttle down to your planet and arrive by train. As I understand my orders, I will be living in the inner bailey of Duke Dono Castle in the City of Blueglennen. My home will be the corner shop on Merchants' Row near the Valley Long Watchtower. The shop also faces Wolfern Promenade.

And you live at Bishop Cottage with the other faculty, am I correct? Your people call it The Cottage. It's right off the plaza as I understand. You can see the plaza from your dormitory. And from my map, your room is between Bishop Garden and Duke Tower University? Have I read the map correctly?"

When Crystova did not respond to her overture of friendship, Shehili finished by saying, "I understand this is a lot of information to digest. It must seem as if we're invading your city. I can assure you that all we want to do is trade with you and resupply our starship with enough provisions to get us to the next galaxy. We've already agreed to supply your country with the necessary equipment in the off-chance you need to defend yourselves. We're not interested in sticking around.

We've already talked with your leader the Delphadorturo. There will be four ethnographers assigned to each major city. Just four. Against two-hundred thousand Blueglennen citizens, four tourists are hardly a danger to your people. We're ethnographers who want to study your planet and your culture. You've been briefed on what's at stake and signed a state's secret act. If you reveal even the smallest tidbit of information about our conversation or what takes place at this conference today, you know what will happen to you."

Unable to speak, Crystova nodded her head in mute acknowledgement. She'd read the secret's act and knew if she spoke to just one person, she would end up spending the rest of her life in prison. Perhaps she was on the wrong side of history? Even though he'd been newly appointed as Delphadorturo of Curl, she'd already determined Earl Raker to be an intelligent and caring leader. The threat to the planet must be serious if he was willing to send Curlecons to prison.

Chapter 1

Kimberly Lemon, the proprietor of a tiny bookstore snuggled between a cheap diner and an expensive laundry is preparing her shop for a new market, a market she sincerely hopes will bring her customers who are fed up with the hoopla of modernity. Her clientele will be the kind of people who love the eccentric, as well as, the quaint. She also hopes to lure collectors eager to dig through her menagerie of stuff searching for rare manuscripts and artifacts. If she believed enough in the products she sold, if she envisioned hundreds of shoppers coming through her door every morning, then she might just, yes, she might just, crawl her way out of this terrible economic hole.

So, she sat at her little table in her private quarters separated from the shop (but never far from her thoughts) by a dark and narrow hallway with only her lovely new curtains as a barrier between her and the public. She squeezed her eyes shut and held tightly to her cup of tea and imagined loads of customers walking through her shop door. They would be tourists and collectors, the young and the old, the rich and the middle-class, all of them eager to buy her stuff. She even pictured customers beyond Tweetham County. They would be in foreign dress. They would sift through every nook and cranny exclaiming over the simple charm and rustic interior of her shop, then they would buy up all her stock and she could eat a few good meals and sleep content in her own bed another day.

A cramping in her fingers clenching the cup signaled the end of her wish fulfilling exercise. There would be no rush of customers pouring through her stock and scooping up everything in sight. People were scared these days choosing only to buy what was absolutely necessary. Even tourism was down, more like a trickle now. Since last year, the sound of the castle's iron gates lifting and the drawbridge lowering no longer heralded the arrival of eager tourists. Not even locals from Mudflat Village, those poor desperate people with only a few coins to spare bothered to walk across the bridge to sell their wares. They were much worse off than her and yet found clever ways of making a few seastars. Bartering wouldn't work for her though. The rare items in her shop were useless to Mudflat villagers.

Even the new homeowners from Greenburg Valley living in their fancy thatched cottages with their own private wells no longer stopped in after spending a delightful hour drinking coffee and eating pastries at Antonio's Cafe. Greenburg residents used to love sifting through her merchandise searching for bargains or reminiscing about the good-old-days when people wrote letters. Letters used to be paper and ink sealed in scented envelopes carried away to the far corners of Shellfargon. Those birthday cards, legal documents, and private letters used to be sent off at the end of the day either by foot, horseback, wagon, or locomotive along with the castle day trippers. No longer. Now information travels by ghostly signals no one can see but technicians claim are coded into tiny packages then scrambled and unscrambled by machines.

Maybe the lack of customers has more to do with the starship hovering above their planet bestowing trinkets upon us primitives? Their fabulous gadgets: computers, cellphones, and music makers were one of many ways the humans were trying to bribe the planet to give up its resources. Kimberly wasn't fooled. She could smell a Shellfargon trench-mouth even through a thick wooden door and human trench-mouths were no different. The ship's salespeople were cleverer than the Curlecon ones, but both the human and the Curlecon were the same kind of repulsive bottom feeder, ever so eager to steal a poor delphinid's last seastar. Her favorite response to their toothy smiles and greedy eye-bobbing was to toss the slops bucket near their fancy shoes.

At their most outraged, the sweet smile would disappear and the foulest of language would dribble out of their mouths the way her slops would dribble down the cobblestoned street. Kimberly, prepared for the inevitable sputtering temper tantrum would begin with a hasty apology and angelic expression followed by the words, "Oh, so sorry sir. Forgive me, sir. The mistress will be so mad." Sometimes her apology placated the average sales-shark. But when her slop's bucket was nowhere near the door, she resorted to the ragged pitiful-purse with a few coins in the bottom excuse. "I'll give you all I have if you'll go away sir. I have three tinpieces left. Will that do?"

Once he realizes she can't afford his poor-quality products at outrageous prices, he'll step away from the door and move on to the next shop, claiming his ancient cellphones with their rusty batteries and even rustier reception are brand new. Many a trench-mouth and sales-shark can be seen toting reused and abused computers, which, of course, are destined to die on the day you have an important video conference. Oh yeah. She'd been one of those stupid suckers who believed all the hype.

Never again. Never again, not from the ship's trench-mouths and not from Blueglennen's best junk dealers. The trench-mouths and sales-sharks are a daily sight on the streets of Duke Dono Castle as they slither down the streets of the bailey pestering shopkeepers with useless junk all the while claiming their products are made from brand-new parts, having never been used before. She couldn't help but groan at the changing times. Nobody cares about quality anymore or thinks about how the old ways used to bring people closer together. Her people used to love getting their news from parchments wrapped in colorful satin ribbons or old books covered in dead croc skin. Now instead of accepting parchments, birthday cards, and books from the postal carrier Blueglennens received their mail from a tiny impersonal device.

Even the shopkeepers were keeping themselves to themselves. Everyone was terrified of the day the economy collapses and life returns to the savage days when bands of thieves used to roam the backroads. Instead of joining together to help each other out during the difficult times, the shopkeepers were hiding inside like spiders hoping an innocent customer might stumble into their webs. It might have been funny, but Kimberly wasn't laughing. She was too hungry to find the hoarding amusing. She might just have to find her own sticky trap.

Kimberly's neighbor, Queenie Oppfield, the proprietor of Queenie's Diner next door, an eating establishment Kimberly smells everyday through her vents and hears through the thin walls between the shops has never entered Kimberly's Bookworm Emporium. When the two of them meet on the street, Queenie Oppfield enjoys announcing to anyone who will listen, "Books give me indigestion. I don't have no use for them things. They be a waste of time, let me tell you, honey. I don't see how you can stand to be holed up in that place all day. You'd be better off coming in and having a nice thick steak. Put some blush in your cheeks for sure."

Years ago, after several months of trying to make Queenie understand her delicate digestion and restrictive diet (a barefaced lie necessitated by hardwired survival instincts) all while Queenie loomed over her like a Nordic Goddess with her white hair pulled into a tight bun on top of her noble head and her hard blue eyes glaring through her prescription glasses magnifying her eyes to twice their size, Kimberly soon realized nothing she said or did would convince Queenie of her delicate constitution and repugnance for meat. The one and only time Kimberly made the stupid mistake of giving in to Queenie's demands, the aftermath turned out to be the most excruciatingly painful and embarrassing ordeal of her young life.

Shortly after that ordeal, both women had an unspoken agreement to never cross paths or share pleasantries. Even if Queenie wasn't outside, it had become Kimberly's habit to step outside and cautiously survey the cobblestone walkway like a spy in a dime-store novel, and if Queenie happened to be leaning against the wormlight's iron post smoking and chatting with her best friend Beatrice of Castle Laundry, Kimberly would quickly close the blinds, switch off the lights, then turn the shop sign to Closed: Please Come Again.

And if she was lucky enough not to be spotted, she would tippy-toe toward the Cathedral of the Holy Centipede (formerly the Cathedral of the Holy Delph) where she would navigate the twisty, narrow, dark and dank passageway between the Cathedral and Duke Tower. Since the passageway ran underground and took her straight to the courtyard of Duke Tower, Queenie and her friends might assume she'd stepped out for lunch or to the post office. Many people knew about the famous fountain in the center of Duke Tower courtyard and the lovely Bishop Garden beneath Court Key Tower. Unfortunately for her only Duke Tower residents were allowed in Bishop Garden.

But beyond the courtyard fountain she could weave her way between the wrought iron tables, statues of old dead guys, and the potted plants, eventually, arriving at the Cetacea Steps. At the Cetacea Steps it was a matter of minutes to run up the carved stone blocks and search for an empty spot on Rampart Walk. Along the Royal Plaza there was rarely an empty table or bench during lunch where she might sit and enjoy her fried-fish sandwich. Nobody under forty climbed the Cetacea Steps to sit on the wall, so there was always a bit of space available to squeeze herself between giggling students and let her legs dangle off the edge of the wall. The best part of sitting on the wall was the spectacular view.

Unlike most Blueglennens, she didn't mind being up high with nothing to hold onto if she stumbled. She much preferred the wind in her hair and the sun on her back to the press of people down in the plaza shoving and elbowing others in order to get the last chair or squeeze themselves onto a crowded bench. She hated the feel of cold stone on her back and her elbows squeezing her breasts together just to eat. It was much pleasanter sitting up high feasting her eyes on the view.

From Rampart Walk she could see the gorgeous Greenburg Valley with the Siren River running through the meadows like an inky blue ribbon. The ribbon disappeared for a short time just outside of Mudflat Village determined to make its way through Bitterroot Forest. From her vantage point she could even see the tops of the crooked spooky trees of Bitterroot Forest. They looked like revolting mushroom-tops spoiling in the sun. Once clearing the forest, the river ran beside the castle and off toward the east. If she wanted to, she could turn around and watch the river continue toward New Enreich and the capital city. But she didn't want to spoil her lunch by thinking about how the politicians in the capital city had betrayed the nation.

Just a few days ago, she'd been up on the Rampart Wall and seen the trail guide, Dialmere Seely, sitting astride her gigantic seahorse calmly escorting a group of quaking tourists through the spooky and dangerous wood. Every time she watched Dialmere, without fail, Kimberly would suck in her breath anxious for Dialmere's safety as the young woman rode confidently on the back of her seahorse, her short plump body and even shorter legs dangling over the sides of the beast while her strong fat hands held onto his mane expertly maneuvering him sedately up the treacherous path. Unlike the tourists Dialmere preferred to ride bareback. From the wall, Dialmere looked more like a plump child in imminent danger of falling off a monster seahorse's back than a young woman brave enough to venture into the Bitterroot Forest. Like her cousin Guinevere Goodbody, in both looks and temperament, Dialmere Seely was a passionate animal lover and formidable enemy.

And then of course from Kimberly's vantage point she could also see Mudflat Village with its thatched and patched roofs and the thin spirals of smoke from their makeshift chimneys. Ever since the Great Abyss, she had developed a terror of becoming a Mudflat villager. She hated the thought of being so poor she'd end up sleeping on a dirt floor and having no other recourse but to bathe in the chilly Siren River.

Yet from what she could see Mudflat villagers seemed more content than Greenburg folks or Duke Tower residents. Many a time in her life she'd witnessed Mudflat villagers on their lunch breaks sitting on their rock walls, with their tin lunch-pails beside them, eating thick sandwiches made of krill and cheese finishing off the whole lot with foamy beer. Always they'd be laughing and dancing and enjoying themselves. Since today was as sunny as the day before, she imagined Mudflat villagers were doing exactly what she planned to do: eat her one good meal of the day and enjoy the fresh air and sunshine.

Once she climbed out of the darkness of the passageway and stood on the landing facing the plaza, she walked between the massive columns holding up Duke Tower and out onto the plaza. Of course, the faster route would have been down Merchants' Row passed Queenie's diner to Wolfern Promenade, a left onto the promenade, another left to the Royal Plaza. Once in the plaza clogged with people, she would have been forced to elbow her way to a window and wait in a long line to buy lunch then search hopelessly for a place to sit. With the university on her right and the shops on her left she might have found a quiet spot to sit and contemplate Duke Towers, but only if she left her shop in the wee hours before the drawbridge opened, and even then, she might lose her spot if she dared to stand up and collect her food.

She could have paid a professional chair sitter to hold a place for her at Antonio's Cafe. But that would have made lunch even more expensive. Only the very rich could afford a chair sitter. Maybe if things worsened, she could hire herself out as a chair sitter? The original purpose for the plaza had disappeared long ago. At one time the plaza had been a farmer's market, a place where Blueglennens met and celebrated the holidays. Now the tables, chairs and benches choking the plaza were not just for sitting but for the rich and famous to be seen. According to the trend setters, the allure of the plaza had more to do with exposure than sustenance. It was a place where the famous could sit and watch and be noticed, also where the hopeful could be admired and the beautiful or talented could find a rich patron. Parking your butt on the Rampart Wall was considered childish and dangerous.

What annoyed her the most was that some people had no appreciation for history. Duke Tower and the Royal Plaza, indeed the entire bailey, had been designed by master crafters who appreciated clean lines and beautiful stonework. On the bottom floor of Duke Tower, what had once been a shelter for fine art where people sat, and contemplated paintings and sculptures was now boxed in with glass partitions where the royal guards and the local constabulary moved between their offices and the prison cells. The enclosure was meant to keep an eye on the rabble outside and for the worst of them to be kept inside. On the second and third floors of Duke Tower were private apartments rented out to visiting dignitaries. On the top floor was the Governor's apartment where he enjoyed a splendid view of the river and the valley.

A new history was being made now in which the plaza had become the property of the rich and the dangerous ramparts belonged to the young and the poor. A sad day indeed. It was a good thing her grandfather wasn't alive to see what had happened to his beloved bailey. He would have hated Governor Saurus and his royal knights the most. He would have been alarmed at the return of the medieval dungeons beneath Duke Tower where political prisoners were kept. Even now she thought she could smell the noxious fumes of desperate people wafting up to her through the cracks of the stone slabs.

Kimberly chose the underground passageway for a good

reason. It might have taken her longer; yet, what was ten minutes compared to an uncomfortable encounter with Queenie's cheeky grin and stony blue orbs? There were days though when she missed walking down Wolfern Promenade, arm and arm with a friend, admiring the shops and sampling the delicious food offered by the Mudflat vendors.

Now the promenade was deserted but for a few vendors. In the past, she'd have been pushing her way through hungry customers to get to the plaza. Although, the tenacious and fabulous cook Honoria Graceland, mother of a knight, was one of only a few who managed to get her way. Most weekdays her wagon could be found parked against the stone walls between Unique Boutique and Pop's Market near the drawbridge. Kimberly knew the reason why she out of so many had been allowed inside the bailey. The first time Honoria set up the Wagon Wheel Café in a strategic location at the crossroad between the train station, Mudflat Village and the drawbridge, her business soared while the merchants in the bailey suffered. The castle merchants tried to do the same and the Governor realizing the danger gave her a special permit.

It wasn't just the Wagon Wheel Cafe she missed. She missed admiring the beautiful gowns in Unique Boutique's windows and sampling the delicious chocolates at Pop's Market. She hated having to skulk about the bailey like a criminal just to avoid Queenie. She'd done nothing wrong. That long-ago day when Kimberly humiliated herself in front of her fellow citizens, when she made the stupidest of decisions to step into Queenie's Diner and see if she couldn't make friends with her nearest neighbor, also in the futile hope she might add Queenie to her list of customers, began badly and went downhill from then on. She could see herself once again sitting at one of the wobbly pressed-wood tables near the wall furthest from the Bookworm Emporium, a wall, not only crusty with past meals boiled in lard but sweaty with steam from the kitchen. The only advantage to the table was its proximity to the exit.

Of course, Queenie spotted her straightaway. With a triumphant smile breaking across her face like a tsunami generating ever more waves in jowls and neck, she stomped over to Kimberly's table and announced to anyone within five miles. "Well, I'm honored indeed. Look at you, sitting here like a frightened bird ready to fly away. Don't you worry honey, we're gonna put some meat on them frail bones of yours," she said as she slapped a menu down upon a spotlessly white-cotton tablecloth cross-stitched with cavorting and ruminating mammals upon a lush meadow.

Unable to focus her eyes on the menu, Kimberly looked up

and up at Queenie and asked nervously, "What would you recommend?"

Queenie nodded her noble head once and picked up the menu, touching her thick finger to her thick nose, "I know just the thing for you, Lemon. Be prepared for a treat."

Fifteen minutes later, Queenie returned with a plate, no, more like a trough, brimming with brown gravy and big chunks of meat floating from edge to edge, the meat desperate to find some means of escape. From far away, Kimberly heard Queenie say, "Enjoy Love." As she stared mesmerized at the trough before her where a sea of brown and black with nary a green vegetable sat in front of her solidifying as it cooled, she took hold of her spoon.

The food continued to cool waiting for her to do something. It wasn't alive. It had died, that poor creature which had lived once upon a time on Shellfargon had been hit over the head with a hammer, gutted, and chopped into tiny pieces. It was long since dead and existed now only as bits and pieces swimming in gravy.

When she looked back on that terrible day, she had to thank all the gods, ancient and old, and even the newest one - the Great and Holy Centipede - for helping her through the ordeal. Without their benevolent eyes looking down upon her, making sure she chose the late evening hours when the diner was nearly empty (other than the usual drunks) and having the forethought to swallow a quarter cup of stomach protector, she might have cut loose, not only through her mouth, but through the other end as well. Thank the Great and Good Centipede for small mercies the ordeal wasn't longer. After thirty minutes of hell, sipping and chewing and smiling at Queenie who stood behind the counter polishing silverware and nodding her head to a polka tune on the radio, Kimberly only doubled over in agony once, moaned under her breath twice and puked four times on Queenie's spotlessly clean uninspiring white floor.

The next day Kimberly attempted to apologize and received a chilly rebuff, so she tried to apologize through the mail, not only for her rude departure but because she'd forgotten to pay the bill. Thereafter Queenie pretended Kimberly didn't exist. Queenie sent the card and money back. For several months, Kimberly seriously considered selling the shop with the expectation of finding a friendlier and more profitable location than Merchants' Row.

Unfortunately, when the Great Abyss hit, everyone, including Wolfern Province suffered. It turned out to be the greatest catastrophe in the entire history of Shellfargon and the terrible timing meant the value of Kimberly's shop plummeted when she seriously wanted to sell.

Few had the extra seastar to buy tooth paste much less a book shop. Everyone was desperately trying to keep their homes and businesses. To save money, Kimberly moved out of her tiny flat and into the backroom of the Bookworm Emporium, even cancelling her memberships at the Beautiful Body Gym, DVD's Cheap & Fast Store, and the magazine "In Your Face" which she loved for its biting articles critiquing the idiots in Delphadore. Those greedy stupid bankers and politicians were the reason Delphinids lost their homes. As a result of their colossal failure an entire generation of Delphinids were traumatized for life.

Most of the world is familiar with the famous castle where the Delphadorturo and Supreme Commander of Curl lives. But what they don't know is that Silver Crest Hall used to be a special gathering place where ancient Delphinids worshipped Muibo, the River God. She'd always wanted to visit Crest Hall and see the monuments and museums in Delphadore. But after the Great Abyss, she knew she'd never get to walk the streets paved in blue stone or tour the royal rooms. Only dumb luck or wagon loads of seastar would ever make a visit to Delphadore possible now.

To survive the Great Abyss meant sacrifices but she refused to sacrifice once-a-week lunch with friends or forego house parties for chats and sodas, tea and gossip. Instead of taking her annual vacation to Valerian City, Kimberly chose to take mini-trips around Tweetham County revisiting the watering holes of her youth. Being poor meant life had become damned dull. She spent most of her time in her private living quarters reading manuals on plumbing, electricity, and furniture-making while venturing, on occasion, to try her hand at home improvement. Sometimes, her attempts resulted in disaster and made her situation even worse.

Earlier in the morning, after breaking through a wall of dark paneling with the expectation of letting more light into the back room, a room which faced a narrow alley, she discovered what was on the other side. To her dismay a brick wall separated her from sunshine. Kimberly spent more time walking up to the brick wall with her finger to her mouth wondering what the hell she was going to do than attending to her bookstore.

Unable to stand the ugly sight, she postponed her plans for wooing new customers. The day before she'd had the brilliant idea to wear a handmade billboard and stand on the castle bridge. Her plan was to get the attention of travelers as they walked up the hill from the train depot. She'd planned to wave and shout hoping to persuade a few to drop in at the Bookworm Emporium for tea and cookies. Maybe that's why, before breakfast, she decided to tear off the dark paneling. She'd erroneously believed the teardown would only take twenty minutes tops and she'd still have plenty of time to lure customers into her shop before lunch.

By the afternoon, her headache had reached epic proportions. Fortunately, in a serendipitous moment (which seemed to be occurring quite often lately) the shop door chimed and in popped her old boyfriend Caleb Lanternlighter. From the safety of the shop door, he shouted, "Hay there Kim, you in back? I've brought you some crystals. Did you know crystals have magical powers? They might attract more customers." For several seconds she panicked worried Caleb might have a heart attack if he saw the destruction. Then she remembered Caleb wasn't her boyfriend any more. She relaxed and dropped her hammer on the bed. With a nonchalance she didn't really feel, she wandered into the shop sweeping aside her new burgundy velvet curtains.

The discounted curtains had been bought from Beatrice Bottom's Castle Laundry, curtains which some foolish housewife had attempted to wash in her machine on rough cycle in hot water. Kimberly transformed the coarse material into its former vibrant softness using the right combination of liquids to rejuvenate the material. Before the transformation she bought a reliable dye and turned the purplish gray mess into a rich burgundy, her favorite color. Now, whenever she swept the velvet curtain aside on its brand new tinpiece pole she felt as regal and majestic as the Queen of Seagrass.

And seeing Caleb standing there with his box of rocks made her smile too. He was such a good man, a little absent minded at times and prone to a tantrum or two. But for the most part he was a trustworthy, solid, kind person and true friend. Something in her expression alarmed Caleb. Infuriating how he knew her so well. He was a keen-eyed clairvoyant, his expression telling her he already suspected she'd done something crazy. Maybe the cobwebs in her hair or the dust coating her former white shirt were all the evidence he needed.

"Okay there, what's the problem? Is it something I can fix? Let me try, Kim. Don't do it yourself."

With a sigh made up of a bit of annoyance and a bit of triumph, Kimberly accepted his kind offer and made herself busy at the counter restacking neat piles of pamphlets she had decided would be of interest to historians, pamphlets from Wolfern Province's medieval days before the castle had been built, a time long ago when Blueglennen had been a village with a mere fifty residents.

Some drifter from the east, a poor royal had tried to dupe a few of the townsfolk of their worldly goods with the intention of making off with the prettiest female in the village. Kimberly's grandfather tried to tell her about the famous event without blushing. His feeble attempts to avoid the most outrageous parts had been hilarious. Blueglennen residents persuaded the royal to marry the pretty young female and work off his debt to them by cleaning out all the privies in town. His comeuppance had been funny. The fact he happened to be the ancestor of Duke Dono wasn't funny at all.

The resounding silence in the back room caught her attention. Kimberly considered slipping out the front door and escaping to Antonio's Cafe, the beverage shop on the corner of the Royal Plaza owned by Antonio Furness. She would so much rather sip a hot coffee at Antonio's Cafe and watch the world stroll by her table, then wait for the blowup in the backroom. She counted to five sure there would be a blow up any second. Whenever Kimberly thought about Antonio, her heart beat so fast she thought it might burst out of her chest. Her heart continued to beat madly sounding a lot like the boots hitting the floor and the person in those boots heading her way.

When Caleb burst out of the backroom she was prepared. What she was not prepared for was his next move. He stomped toward the front door. Before departing he murmured, "I'll be right back. Don't despair. I'll fix this."

Years ago, Caleb had decided to make himself her unofficial handyman. Why she wondered did he continue to fix her problems? She'd made it perfectly clear last month that their relationship was over. Yet she suspected, Caleb Lanternlighter continued to hope she would come to her senses one day and take him back. Two weeks later, after much hammering and sawing and swearing, Kimberly could sit at her small collapsible cherry-wood table sipping her morning tea and biting off a piece of biscuit. The pièce de résistance was the fabulous view of the alley. And just a mere three feet away was a duplicate red brick wall along which a multitude of blue, green, and yellow bins were lined up ready for the weekly garbage collection.

When she ignored the garbage bins, she found herself delighted with the view. Now, she had real light as opposed to artificial light illuminating her itty-bitty room. Every passing hour the light pouring into her room would change from a hot white to a comfortable yellow and finally to a cool gold. Her bits and pieces and bedraggled furniture looked brighter for the light. The golden light and warmth seeped inside through the magnificent bay window having traveled hundreds of miles from the sun down between the red-brick-walled alley into her private quarters. The best part was that the bay window added two square-feet to her apartment.

As a bonus, beyond the narrow brick passageway and the garbage bins she could also admire her neighbor Lynora Reason's shade loving potted plants which were artfully arranged on her balcony, trailing streamers of green, orange, and purple vines. The potted plants were suspended from the wall by spiked hooks driven into the brick. Come grow when Delan Reason brought her prize roses and Cherry Blossom tree outside, there would be beautiful blooms to admire. All the lovely plants and flowers would bring her many days of spiritual delight.

Even at night she had the pleasure of a healing white bath from Shellfargon's moon called Una. Every month she could look out her window and admire the view as if it were daylight. The priests of the Church of the Holy Delph would plot the movements of Una and argue about her purpose. Some believed the Holy One gave the Delphinids the moon to guide them from the sea onto land. Others believed Una circled the planet and protected the inhabitants from the Evil One. Since the end of the Old Religion, amateurs had taken on the duties of the priests recording the moon's movement and its various degrees of illumination.

After nearly a year of negotiations between the starship and the inhabitants of the western and eastern halves of Shellfargon, once the Supreme Commander of Curl's intelligence forces ascertained the UES Albion to be friendly, followed by the Holy See of the Lacertidae determination to form a separate peace with the starship, Delphadorturo Earl Raker welcomed the aliens of the Albion to Shellfargon. The first step the starship Albion did to confirm impartiality was a worldwide broadcast of Una orbiting Shellfargon. The Lacertidae received the same transmission at the same time. Oddly enough, the knowledge their bitterest enemy received the same transmission made Curlecons more receptive to the starship aliens.

The world of Shellfargon was expanding so much anything was possible now. Cheered by the thought, she began to make plans for the coming grow season. This grow, she might buy a planter box and plant miniature shade loving evergreens, perhaps a Grunoldy Boxwood which would give her color all year long. Although orange was not her favorite color. No. She dismissed that idea with a shutter, a Grunoldy Boxwood tended to stink in the heat and attract the worst of creatures – cats. She hated cats. Cats scared her to death. But a maple, perhaps a Fire Maple in miniature with its glorious tawny leaves and silver bark might thrive in the alley. The multiple slender limbs rising from the roots wouldn't block the view but rather provide Kimberly with privacy. Yes. A Fire Maple would be perfect.

As she admired her imagined view from the window,

superimposed over the depressing backdrop of a fallow sky, she ignored the dark clouds threatening more rain and the pools of dirty water swimming with dead bugs between cobblestones, as well as, the constant drip, drip, drip of the old pipes and instead she imagined a sunny day in grow and pink blossoms on the trees and red and white roses bursting forth from her new plants. She smiled. Her happy moment vanished. A face popped into view pressing itself to her glass. It leered at her suggestively. She shrieked. Her tea lapped over the rim of her cup and spilled onto her bright yellow bathrobe.

When the face resumed its normal shape, she shook her finger at Alexandra and tried to scowl in a menacing fashion. Alexandra only chuckled and waved. Kimberly watched Alexandra spin around on her long legs and head back down the alley to the brand-new door leading to Queenie's Diner. Queenie had reluctantly added the backdoor after the Merchant's Row shopkeepers complained her garbage bins which she parked in the front of her shop ruined the quaintness of the cobblestoned street. Not only were the bins an eyesore, they kept the customers away wafting the sour smell of old milk and rotten meat into the air.

Curiously, when Queenie discovered Caleb had added a picture window to Kimberly's alley wall, she immediately decided she needed a backdoor and hired a carpenter, the very next day. Kimberly's first sweat season was miserable. She couldn't even open the side windows a crack without a plume of flies attempting a break-in. They were so eager to commit suicide, they tried squeezing themselves through the tiny crack she permitted herself so that she might get just a bit of fresh air. Nor could she breathe when a breeze blew the foul odors of rotten garbage into her private sanctuary. And then one morning she had a brilliant idea. She found some screening material and bought two tiny fans. After some maneuvering, she managed to set them up on her window ledge to blow the smell of rotten food and flies toward Wolfern Promenade. So far, no one had noticed.

As Kimberly watched her friend disappear through Queenie's backdoor, she had a sense of inevitability. Kimberly had already gone through a hundred such transitory friendships with people seeking temporary work on Merchant's Row. Ninety percent of Merchant's Row staff came from the university. The students were all working toward degrees that would take them well away from Blueglennen, possibly even out of Wolfern Province altogether. Their positions as clerks, babysitters, dog walkers, cooks, cleaners, and waitstaff were temporary. A woman so fashionable and assured as Alexandra would eventually realize she had nothing in common with a poor dab of a creature like Kimberly Lemon.

Kimberly's new friend Alexandra was meant for bigger things. She would graduate from Duke Tower University and go off to some exotic location and do exciting things. Alexandra S. Montague was tall and slim with beautiful black hair and dark brown eyes. Her dark hair set against her translucent skin made her look so pale and ethereal.

Even with all her vast intellectual powers, Alexandra hadn't a clue why her presence at the diner resulted in a sudden uptick in customers, especially the male customers who chose greasy food over delicate melt-in-your-mouth pastries, pastas, and delectable fish salads. Antonio didn't care whether the men congregated at Queenies, Antonio's Café was so popular he could afford to lose a few customers. Antonio had his own secret weapon anyway – his sister was a fabulous chef and his adoring fans loved him despite his egotism and numerous affairs.

When Queenie's elder sister Frances retired as waitress and Queenie hired two young attractive waitresses from Duke Tower University, word spread throughout the land, from the student body all the way to Greenburg Valley. The old customers still showed up for greasy breakfasts, but now, Queenie kept the diner open after the supper crowd went home to accommodate young university students willing to finish off bloody steaks and oozing baked potatoes filled with butter. The only dish everybody agreed was out-of-this-world was Queenie's scones stuffed with rich heavy cream. They called her scones Una-A-Moona.

The sight of Alexandra reminded Kimberly to dress. She had less than fifteen minutes to prepare for the day. Daydreaming had become a bad habit. Glancing at her new book, *For Successful Entrepreneurs Only*, Kimberly wondered if she was really cut out to be a business person. Her math skills were atrocious, and she hadn't the heart to mark up her merchandise or pretend something was on sale when it wasn't really on sale. By the end of the day, Kimberly's profit was a puny 16.95 in seastars and none of her friends had popped in to visit, not even during high tea. She would have been better off reading her new book instead.

What was most disappointing had been Crystova Moth's cancellation. She'd called to cancel lunch due to several student counseling sessions. And even Caleb called to cancel the minor improvements he planned to do on the shop shelves. He claimed he couldn't come over because he'd been offered work from Queenie's cousin who worked in the kitchens at Bonebridge Castle. It seemed Queenie's cousin, while she'd been outside smoking in the alley had admired the bay window and asked the name of the craftsperson. So now Caleb would be too busy to work on the old wires above the book shelves and she'd be forced to buy more bioluminescent glowworms to hang from the ceiling in the darkest areas. She didn't begrudge him his good luck. She wished him all the best. After all, she couldn't afford to pay him much. He'd accepted her small payments for months now with his usual good cheer.

Kimberly wondered if Queenie had bribed her cousin to hire him just to spite Kimberly. If Caleb were out of the way, then Kimberly's little shop would fall apart and attract fewer customers. If that were true Queenie was in for a surprise, because Kimberly was delighted by Caleb's new job. She'd known for a long time how gifted he was as a craftsperson. For years, she'd watched him sifting through old barns and huts discovering treasures and transforming them into beautiful, practical, everyday pieces.

Today it seemed as if everyone had cancelled on her. Even Alexandra failed to show up for tea. The day Alexandra had slipped inside the bookstore and sat down in the far corner pretending to read a moldy book about insects of the Wild Brunosphere, Kimberly suspected her appearance had something to do with the shrill shriek of Queenie's voice and nonstop monologues. Kimberly soon discovered Alexandra chose the shop because she loved the smell of books, thought the window seat was homey and preferred the quiet.

Further along in their friendship (for Alexandra spoke little) Alexandra admitted another reason for her visits had to do with the overzealous young males who pestered her for dates and ignored her hints to get lost. But the most compelling reason for her frequent visits was her love of books. She loved to talk about books and writing and current events. What both women agreed was that the Church of the Holy Centipede's intentions were to milk every seastar from their poor delusional parishioners. Alexandra even admitted to having doubts about Saint Delph.

Kimberly and Alexandra shared this most terrible of revelations privately but knew if they were to admit such a thing to anyone else, they would be shunned by the townspeople, possibly even branded traitors, maybe even imprisoned in the dungeons of Duke Tower. Well, maybe not imprisoned. After all this was the most rational and civilized period in the history of Wolfern Province. People were no longer tortured or imprisoned for questioning the church or publicly humiliated on the streets for not attending mass. Yet, as a merchant Kimberly would be shunned by the Delph faithful and then she would have no customers at all.

As if Kimberly had conjured Alexandra out of thin air with the power of her mind, she appeared at the shop door and knocked politely on the glass to get Kimberly's attention. Kimberly closed the register and made her way through the tables and shelves overflowing with inventory. Like old familiar friends she did not see the stacked piles of books, papers, journals, maps, manuscripts, the trinkets and relics, all somewhat dusty, some downright ugly, a few broken or missing parts, others pristine, still others quite exquisite but more often than naught stained, splotched, and cracked along the seams. When she opened the shop door the cold humid air hit her in the face. Her nose compared the fresh outdoor air with the stale air circulating in her shop. She hated leaving the door open. It wasn't just the bugs she wanted to keep out but the nosy neighbors. Perhaps she'd have to buy incense? If she wasn't careful, she would end up as dusty, dry and stale as her inventory.

"Hey Kimberly, sorry I couldn't make it over today. It was insane in there," Alexandra nodded her head in the direction of Queenie's diner. "It must be the sudden cold spell. Everybody wanted to stock up on hot scones and coffee."

Kimberly glanced over Alexandra's shoulder and saw Queenie leaning against her favorite lamppost puffing on a cigarette. Queenie ignored them. Kimberly looked up into Alexandra's eyes and noticed for the first time her friend was embarrassed. Curious, she waited for Alexandra to speak. "I wonder if you wouldn't mind doing me a favor."

"Sure."

"Well, you see my mother just called and said if I didn't want my college funds to dry up, I'd better appear at my grandfather's dinner party tomorrow. So, I guess I've been coerced into going to this stupid affair. It means I have to pick out something exceptional, something chic but understated. At least that was my mother's instructions."

"How can I help?" Kimberly asked, puzzled why Alexandra sought her advice at all. She would have thought someone like her would be the last person a stylish female would go to for advice on fashion. Kimberly studiously avoided glancing down at her clothes. Yes, the simple brown slacks and cheap red cardigan sweater were a bit shabby. The sweater had been worn so many times the elbows had elbows. But her clothes were comfortable, and she preferred comfort above all else.

Alexandra chuckled softly under her breath, "You know Kimberly you are so funny, your face is like an open book. No, you're right. I didn't come for your fashion advice. I came for your companionship. Would you please come with me to Dela Swana's boutique and be my bodyguard?"

Kimberly choked back a peel of laughter which ended up coming out of her nose as a sort of horsy snort. The sound made them smile. How could Alexandra justify Kimberly as an appropriate bodyguard for anyone? The image of Kimberly fending off a raging mob set her off again. Kimberly's bark of laughter bounced around Merchant's Row startling the birds congregating on the cathedral ledges. Alexandra covered her mouth and nose and tried valiantly to suppress the giggles bubbling up inside. Kimberly joined in and soon they were drawing curious stares from passing pedestrians, which made them laugh the more, until Kimberly who could no longer speak and with tears streaming down her face gestured wildly for Alexandra to come inside.

Kimberly shut and locked the shop door and pulled down the blind then turned to face the young woman. In the interim, Alexandra managed to sober up and was busily applying the hem of Queenie's Diner apron to her streaming eyes.

"Oh, that was good, that was just what I needed. I wish you could come with me to the dinner party. I think I could endure the boredom if you were with me."

"Please, not as a bodyguard."

Once the second wave of hilarity subsided, Kimberly motioned for Alexandra to follow her to her private quarters. She pulled cups from the shelf above the sink and plugged in the tea urn. "So, if I understand you correctly, you want me to go with you to the boutique as moral support? I suppose I could manage. Are you giving yourself enough time to pick out a dress? You said the dinner party is tomorrow."

Alexandra waved away the thought, "Oh, don't worry about me, I'll find something, I always do. No, picking out a dress isn't my problem. I can do that in my sleep." Embarrassment passed across her face for a second as she confessed. "My biggest problem is when to stop shopping."

"I see," Kimberly responded lamely feeling an overwhelming need to protect this smart sweet kid. Addictions were so insidious. They could take over a person's life and create so much misery for the afflicted, as well as, family and friends who cared about the person. Being brave enough and self-aware enough to admit you have an addiction is the first step, a very difficult step. The least understood of addictions happens to be shopaholism. Kimberly had never had that problem, maybe because she preferred eating over owning new clothes.

"Ah. It's. Well. I've never been in Dela Swana's boutique. The

Unique Boutique is too rich for me. I can't afford her belts much less an evening gown."

Alexandra rushed toward Kimberly with her slender hands pressed together and eyes bright, "Yes. Precisely. You're perfect for the job. You could care less about fashion."

"Well, that's not exactly true. I like clothes, I just don't like to spend a lot of money on something that I'll only wear once."

"Remember the day you told me about stumbling upon a collection of Coral? How you drooled over each embossed leatherbound volume, how you opened one after the other of those small precious books to gaze greedily at the onionskin leaves and gilded edges. You had to make a choice between your wedding dress and the Coral. I remembered your story because you chose some old dusty books over a wedding dress and marriage which I thought was insane."

Kimberly wanted to tell Alexandra she had it all wrong, her change of mind all those years ago had more to do with her feelings for her fiancé than any decision about buying the Noble Coral collection. It was a one-of-a-kind collection which included all of Coral's beautiful plays and sonnets. Just knowing she wanted the books more than the wedding dress made her realize Todd wasn't the man she wanted to spend the rest of her life with, especially when she was honest with herself and admitted his habit of sniffing before speaking made her fuming mad. Each time he sniffed she longed to slap him.

Once she accepted the truth, she cancelled the wedding and bought the Coral Antique Collection. Hiding in her attic room to reread the plays got her through the worst of her family's outraged disappointment.

Alexandra glanced at her watch and set down her tea cup, "We have an hour before the boutique closes. Do you have time to come with me now?"

Surprised and suddenly nervous, Kimberly wanted to back out hoping she'd find a good excuse not to go. What did she have to worry about? For months now, she'd been walking by the boutique on her way to the plaza, admiring the beautiful clothes in the windows and appreciating the perfumed smells wafting through the open door on warm days. The boutique smelled exotic, foreign, interesting. Most women would be tempted by the sight, sounds, and smells. She hadn't been. Instead, she'd been terrified.

Without quite knowing how Alexandra managed to manipulate her out of the Bookworm, then herd her like some elegant sheep dog down Merchant's Row, all the while, guiding her delicately across treacherous cobblestones in the event she tripped and came to her senses, Kimberly found herself in front of the open doors of Unique Boutique. She clutched her handbag for comfort and did her best not to let Alexandra or passersby see how terrified she was at the idea of entering the building.

It was ludicrous! Silly. What was the matter with her?

Alexandra grabbed Kimberly's elbow and led her through the glass doors and into the carpeted room. The bright silks and chiffons hit her eye like a kaleidoscope of color. All those textures rubbing up against each other, sometimes intermingled: cotton, straw, feathers, bangles, beads, faux diamonds or maybe real diamonds, opals, rubies, gold, and silver. All those colors running riot: bright reds, dull reds, brilliant blues and oranges, yellows next to purples, blacks and whites, various shades of every other color. And in her ear, she could hear a pulsing rhythm which reminded her of waves beating against a distant shore. In syncopation, drums were thumping to the beat. The music was oddly soothing.

And the walls. The wall directly behind the counter glowed and pulsed as if it were alive. The strange light fixtures added texture and life to the rest of the shop. When she turned to her right and looked up at the opposite wall, the sight made her head swim with all those colors and shapes and oddities spread out across the stone. There were exotic masks hanging from hooks, some of them painted in black with white circles around the empty eye sockets and the mouths, other masks were made with bright red, blue, and yellow paint cut in the shape of animals or hybrids. And nary a wall carried the Centipede Emblem. Ah hum. She might get to like this place after all.

Then Kimberly spotted the Great Centipede behind the stone and wood counter, in a brilliant green jade outlined in gold filigree. Yuck! Yet the artwork was so fabulous. It wasn't the artist's fault the symbol horrified Kimberly. And what about all those masks and headdresses from foreign places? It made her long for the money to be able to travel and see those countries and mix with the people. On the racks, she saw fabulous hats, belts, shawls, and ponchos made from plants she recognized such as hemp and berseem. And there were materials she couldn't place, probably, from far off places she could never afford to go.

Her cheap brown loafers stepped onto a heavy blue and gold Vullusian rug and she thought she could detect the scent and taste of spices in the air. Was that cinnamon? Was that other one vanilla? That was orange for sure. Wow! She was overwhelmed and overawed. Did Alexandra expect her to be a talisman against this place? Was she insane? Or more likely, was she such a shopaholic she knew that by choosing Kimberly, she could pretend to be responsible and yet, get her own way?

The woman who stepped into the showroom from the dressing rooms was as exotic and beautiful as the merchandise. She stood as tall and regal as a foreign princess and carried herself with pride, her warm brown eyes with flicks of copper sparkling. Her eyes rested upon Kimberly and for a split-second registered dismay, then her professional demeanor returned, and she looked at Alexandra with a soft smile, "Hello. How are you today, Dela Montague?"

"Good," Alexandra said, trying to appear disinterested in her surroundings. "Yep, I'd say I'm good." Then as Shehili Swana paused to adjust the hem of a beaded skirt on a mannequin, Alexandra cleared her throat and wandered toward the proprietor as words rushed out in whispered urgency. "I need something to wear for a dinner party tomorrow. Something elegant, something spectacular. It must be understated but gorgeous. You know, a Dinwire perhaps or Finorini. And I'll need shoes and a cape to match."

Alexandra glanced at Kimberly and with a slight frown added, "Do you have anything inexpensive yet elegant?"

Shehili Swana listened patiently. Kimberly relaxed. The proprietor was a professional, courteous and intelligent, not like the monster she'd imagined, hucksters who lure hapless star-struck young women into financial ruin. Her opinion went up a notch when she thought she recognized humor hiding behind the solemn expression. Humor was so important. Without humor life is a colorless hellscape. Besides, humorless people worried Kimberly. It just didn't seem natural to be consistently neutral about everything in life.

Babies, even a day old were already wired to smile. If a grown Delphi never smiled, not even once, or never chuckled or laughed or even snickered, she worried about their mental health. So, if a foreigner like this woman Shehili Swana could smile, even just a tiny smile, she could relax knowing they had something in common – a sense of humor.

The woman looked like a model herself, albeit different from the usual thin, scrawny wretches Kimberly was familiar with in the pages of Curlecon magazines. She had the dignity and bearing of a model and just the right taste and style to accentuate her good features and disguise the less flattering ones. Over a tight-fitting white cotton camisole, Shehili wore a black silk sari adorned with graceful white lilies down the sides of the legs and the small of her back.

Around her neck she wore a startling silver pendent in the shape of a writhing snake. The snake's eyes were made of jade. Shehili's sandals made Kimberly shiver in sympathy for the woman's poor feet. It was freezing outside. Even though the silver sandals were impractical, they had been made by a genius craftsperson and contributed to the overall look of someone who appreciated beautiful clothes.

When Kimberly looked up at Shehili Swana and saw her smile, Kimberly realized all these months of avoiding the boutique had been for naught, no predatory salesclerk would bully her into spending her last seastar on a Finorini. As usual, her terror of being seduced into spending her last tinpiece on something she couldn't afford had been irrational. The room was devoid of celebrities and an entourage of sycophants which was another ice breaker. If celebrities shunned the place, then the clothes had to be well made and reasonably priced. And the fact Dela Swana and her clerk weren't pressuring customers to buy something or following them around meant the owner believed in her merchandise or the boutique had an excellent security system.

Kimberly could get used to this shopping thing. It was soothing to be able to wander the store looking at the merchandise without some clerk breathing down her neck or a security guard demanding to see her identification. While Kimberly wandered, she watched Alexandra and Dela Swana interact observing with a smile the way Swana herded Alexandra away from the high-end stock. Yet, like the stubborn shopaholic she was, Alexandra managed to find her way back to the most expensive gowns in the boutique. As she started pulling a few off the racks, her eyes devoured others just beyond her reach.

Unfortunately, the proprietor was busy assisting other customers and couldn't rescue poor Alexandra from her poor choices. This must be my cue, Kimberly decided and hurried toward Alexandra intent on rescuing her while her friend examined a strapless silk gown dyed in shades of blue and green adorned with pure silver filigree. Kimberly had to admit Alexandra would look stunning walking down the blue carpet in such a gown. Although, Kimberly nearly fainted at the price: 30,362 seastars and 99 tinpieces. Send us a Knight, Holy Centipede! We need an intervention. The 99 tinpieces annoyed her so much she nearly spit.

From the corner of her eye, she saw a hand reaching toward the dress and without thinking slapped the offending member. Someone yelped. Kimberly turned to face Alexandra with the faint hope she might be able to persuade her friend to check out the cheaper bargain gowns at the other end of the room. Instead of looking up into Alexandra's face as she expected, she found herself looking down in shock at Bishop Little's wife, Clarice Little.

How could she have mistaken Alexandra who is tall and willowy for Clarice a middle-aged plump matron with a perpetually sour sneer? Clarice's small head overwhelmed by a thick stack of hair, forced into schoolgirl curls, and dyed bright yellow barely reached Kimberly's nose. Ironic, how the woman fit the name. Maybe, she'd chosen Bishop Mark Little because she was little and thought she could dine off the imagery for years?

"Send for Us, Centipede. I'm so sorry, so sorry. I thought you were someone else."

Clarice rubbed her wrist where Kimberly's hand had made contact. She noticed in dismay the imprint of her hand, marking her crime in accusatory shades of pink and red. Civilized people didn't strike out at other civilized people. Kimberly wondered if the painful sound of Clarice's tearful shriek, so close, might have burst an eardrum. The shriek was followed by a furious demand to no one in particular, "Call the constable. Immediately. I want to press charges. How dare you? How dare you strike me? Have you any idea who I am? You miserable tramp."

A soothing voice interrupted Clarice's tirade, "I agree. It is a dress worth fighting for Delan Little. Indeed, I can understand why a person might fight over such a ravishing example of modern art. The gown is by Don Twanks. It's his most recent creation. Of course, you must try it on immediately, Delan Little. Come with me Madame, I've prepared a modest tea in your favorite dressing room where you may try on the gown in privacy and decide at your leisure whether it's to your liking." While Shehili escorted Clarice Little toward the backrooms, Kimberly searched for her friend. She felt an overwhelming urgency to leave the boutique straight away before she ended up in shackles in Duke Tower's notorious dungeon.

When she cornered Alexandra standing before an array of colorful silk and satin evening gowns, Kimberly noticed her thin arms were already burdened with several furred capes, one was trimmed in gold silk, the other in blue. "Alexandra," she whispered urgently. "Are you crazy? You can't afford anything in here. Do I have to wrestle you to the ground? Please, don't let it go that far; we would look so ridiculous thrashing about on the floor."

When Alexandra masterfully ignored her, her eyes rooted on the gowns as any good addict would be in the throes of a high, Kimberly unnerved, sought support from the proprietor. With relief she saw Shehili Swana sweep aside the silk curtain separating the individual dressing rooms from the showroom floor. A brown-skinned young woman wearing a chic tight-fitting gold and green skirt and matching blouse which displayed an unnecessary degree of midriff followed Shehili out onto the showroom floor. Something about her appearance and demeanor screamed boutique assistant. Kimberly congratulated herself for being able to recognize that fact even though later she would hate herself for being such a snob. Anxious to be gone, Kimberly watched as the two carried on a fierce whispered conversation.

There were times when she wished she could read lips. This was one of them. She had no doubt the women were discussing Matron Little and devising plans on how to keep the grumpy bitch from calling the Knights and sending them all to the dungeons. The assistant listened attentively to the instructions she was given then marched purposely behind the counter. Kimberly hadn't noticed the wall of glowing rocks until that moment. When the assistant continued moving forward Kimberly gasped. Was she insane? Did she think she could walk through walls? Then the shop assistant vanished.

Transfixed by the sight, Kimberly moved away from her friend and closer to the counter in order to figure out how the illusion was done. The trick had nothing to do with the crystals on the wall, the trick had something to do with the ceiling lights and the way the lights played with the shadows. Maybe the illusion needed the voices singing, along with the syncopating movement of the crystal rocks to trick the eye into thinking there was no door? She had read about these magic rock walls, that the Cavenymphs came from the caverns of New Dala.

When the explorers came upon the Cavenymphs, they soon discovered the rocks were intelligent sentient creatures just like Delphinids and Lacertidae. Merchants of New Dala tried to capitalize on the discovery and sold a few hundred of the Cavenymphs to children as if they were household pets. When a nymph bit a child in retaliation for being tossed off a bed, the Cavenymphs were pulled off supermarket shelves and returned to New Dala. A group of people eager to protect the little fellows marched and protested their inhumane treatment by poachers and soon the Cavenymphs were excluded from sale in the country of Curl and put on the Rare Species list.

When New Dala realized many tourists were eager to see the little fellows in person, especially to hear them sing and sway in chorus, the economy of their country changed overnight. And a few years back, a young man from Curl standing politely behind the roped area watching the Cavenymphs serenade the tourists found himself suddenly the unwitting new attraction. At the conclusion of the song when he followed the others out of the cave, the entire wall of Cavenymphs began to cry and like mourners at a funeral flung themselves off the wall and at him.

Unable to go far since he was upholstered in Cavenymphs from his back to his shoes, the New Dala officials tried to pull the Cavenymphs off his body and soon discovered their cash crop would not let go. Officials, believing the young man was a foreign agent intent on undermining their economy by luring their valuable merchandise away, decided to arrest him. They charged him with espionage and held him in custody indefinitely. To their dismay, they soon discovered the Cavenymphs refused to be returned to the cave wall and instead insisted on being arrested with the tourist. Attempts to remove the little fellows from the tourist's body led to several deaths. The public, upon hearing the tourist's plight, protested and the hapless guards were ordered to stop hurting the tourist and the Cavenymphs.

Eventually scientists concluded the Cavenymphs had formed a strong lasting bond with the young man from Walrat Island and were worried the nymphs might die if separated from him. After much debate the government of New Dala granted the Cavenymphs equal rights as citizens and forever after they were given special permission to travel abroad. New Dala was relieved when most of the Cavenymphs, immune to the young man's charms preferred to remain at home. But the ones who formed a bond with him were given permission to leave and embark on the long journey by steam ship to his home on Walrat Island.

A New Dala law was quickly passed and implemented which required a strict set of criteria before Cavenymphs could leave the country. Other countries soon established their own immigration laws for these newly acknowledged sentient beings. The bond had to be mutual and both parties had to adopt each other. Unique passports had to be created for the Cavenymphs, as well as, the few tourists who discovered they were the recipients of the Cavenymphs' affections.

And an agreement had to be made as to the Cavenymphs unique identifier as a species. The Cavenymphs chose to identify themselves as nymphs having selected the name after consulting with the young man who just happened to be an ethnographer from the alien ship orbiting the planet above Shellfargon. He claimed the Cavenymphs reminded him of a wildflower called the Woodnymph or Single Delight which back on his planet had five or six white star-shaped flowers on the outside and a soft green center protected by sharp teeth.

The fact the boutique's assistant walked through a wall hadn't been as impressive as the idea hundreds of Cavenymphs had chosen to immigrate to Blueglennen because they bonded with these women. It was very rare for so many Cavenymph to bond with two people at the same time. How had the assistant shipped them across the sea? Had she slept in the cargo compartment to allay their fears? She must have, because if she'd transported them in boxes, they would have chewed their way out and returned to New Dala.

Kimberly Lemon tried to count the number of Cavenymphs and lost count at one hundred. They were only as big as the palm of her hand. There had to be at least three hundred, each one a different shade of white. What an exotic sight! All those creatures resembling crystal flowers illuminating the wall while simultaneously sending pulsing music through the air. That's what she'd sensed when she stepped into the shop. She had assumed the music was coming from an audio player. They had been so quiet, not making so much as a peep or a growl when she and Alexandra first entered. And they continued to slumber during the squabble between Clarice and herself. There was a rumor Cavenymphs preferred congenial surroundings.

Someone crept up behind Kimberly. The stealth and suddenness nearly made her jump out of her brown loafers. Shehili Swana grinned and nodded toward the wall, "You look like a child seeing Santa Claus for the first time. I assure you they chose me and came willingly with me to this country. No need to call the constable and have me deported."

"Who's Santa Claus?"

"Long story," Shehili Swana said with a dismissive wave of her hand.

"I was just trying to count them and stopped counting at one hundred. They're amazing. I've only read about them in magazines. Did all of them choose you the first time? I'm trying to picture how you looked covered from head to foot with Cavenymphs. Did they have to climb on top of each other? Could you see to walk? Even if you had managed to walk with hundreds covering you like barnacles, there wouldn't have been an opening big enough to get you all through."

They both laughed in unison. With each new gust of laughter, one would encourage the other to keep the laughter going until finally Shehili stopped to wipe her eyes and Kimberly used the hem of her sweater to do the same. Shehili tucked her silk handkerchief up her sleeve and said, "Well. What a sight that would have been. Where are knights when you need them, huh? I wished I'd had a few back then, a couple of strong gorgeous ones able to carry me covered in three hundred Cavenymphs."

Another gale of laughter hit them and when Alexandra poked her head out from among a carousel of blouses, they both sobered up. Shehili smiled and shook her head and then stepped back to get a good look at Kimberly, "We haven't been introduced. How do you do? I am Shehili Swana the proprietor of Unique Boutique."

Kimberly returned her smile and said, "My name is Kimberly Lemon and I own the bookstore two doors down from you."

"Well, how nice. So, we are neighbors. Odd that I've never seen you before today."

"Oh, well. You have so many exotic beautiful things here but they're too rich for my empty wallet. To tell the truth," Kimberly leaned forward and tried to speak softly so Alexandra couldn't hear. "I'm here supporting my friend Alexandra." Kimberly stopped herself just in time realizing she had almost given away Alexandra's secret. To avoid making the situation worse she changed the subject. "What happened to your shop clerk? She seemed to walk right through the Cavenymphs."

Shehili shook her head with a tiny smile and an admonishing finger, "Don't you get us started again. The nymphs parted for her. They like to congregate near the Safe Room door."

"Safe Room?"

'It's the panic room. I came to Wolfern Province aware kidnapping is big business here. Since the merchandise is of the highest quality and my stock of jewels kept under lock and key, I require a room where Ufeeza and I can go if someone attempts to kidnap or rob us."

Unbeknownst to Kimberly, Alexandra had been watching the two women closely and smiling in triumph assuming she had been instrumental in their newfound friendship. It seemed as if they were hitting it off and wouldn't notice the number of garments she carried as she slid unobserved toward the white silk curtains and into an empty dressing room. As Alexandra tenderly deposited the gowns and capes on the cushioned chair next to the full-length mirror, she could hear Clarice Little talking nonstop to the clerk and between clinks of what must be cutlery and crunching of expensive biscuits, Alexandra whipped off her nasty, dirty apron and threw off her cheap black skirt and even cheaper white blouse with its ugly puffed sleeves. She hated the uniform as much as she hated her family's power over her.

Yet, Alexandra had to admit, a little humiliation now was better than being poor and starving for the rest of her life. She would only have to bare this terrible poverty for two more years, then she would be free to go where she pleased and buy whatever she desired. She was confident the Great Abyss would be over soon. And once it was over, there would be all those scrumptious careers awaiting people like herself.

Two years, that's all it would take. Two years and then she would finally be free! Free from the intolerable bigotry of her family and their insipid conversations which always revolved around shopping expeditions, scandal, the lazy-poor who were always mooching off their betters; and of course, how to convince the poor to give up more of their rights so her family could get even richer. Blah, blah, blah.

"I suppose you'll have to go back to where you came from, hum?" Alexandra heard Clarice say and thought Clarice was talking to her.

Alexandra opened her mouth to respond, but luckily, not before the salesclerk answered, "I don't follow you Delan Little. What do you mean?"

Alexandra stood facing the full-length mirror and listened unashamedly. Sensing trouble, she grew concerned for the sales clerk. She heard Clarice whine, "Help me with these buttons. I can't reach them. Yes. Good. That's better. You haven't heard? I'm not surprised. But it won't be long now. Mark my words, my husband is a powerful man and when he comes up with a great idea, nothing can stop him. Nothing at all.

Don't stand there with your mouth open. You look foolish. You know perfectly well, once the new zoning laws go into effect, everything will change around here. The castle bailey is a hotchpotch of tiny shops and flats. It's overcrowded and unsanitary. There are too many merchants, too many weekend farmers, and all too many foreigners.

The faithful all agree something must be done to put a halt to the overpopulation. Don't be surprised when you and your mistress are sent packing. You'll go back to where you came from and the rest of these merchants will be sent down to Mudflat Village where they belong. There will be no more trash inside the castle. Only decent law-abiding folks will remain inside the castle walls."

Upset, Alexandra could no longer stand silently by. She threw open the door to her dressing room and knocked imperiously on Clarice's dressing room door. A moment later the door opened tentatively. Alexandra saw the salesclerk's stunned face, "Yes, Madame, may I help you?"

Unable to control the shaking of her body, Alexandra grabbed the doorknob and threw the dressing room door wider stepping inside the room without asking. The salesclerk tried to squeeze herself against the mirror to make more room as Alexandra put her hands on her hips and glared down at Clarice Little, "I heard you say there's going to be new zoning laws passed by your husband and the council. What do you mean? What do you know?"

The color returned to Clarice's waxy face and a fiery light burned in her eyes that Alexandra found repulsive. The woman seemed to relish the idea of being able to torment Alexandra and the salesclerk more, "My husband and the Council Elders are planning to tear down all the shops on Merchants' Row to make room for the Holy Days Housing Project. The shops will be fumigated and renovated to be future sanctuaries for Centipede pilgrims.

They will be coming to Blueglennen from all over the world. And they will purify the putrid air of your filthy low-life establishments. There will be no more drunks sleeping on our pews, no more unhealthy food smells wafting into our church, and more importantly no more filthy animals roaming inside and eating our offerings. Our church's pilgrims will join us in worshipping the Holy Centipede and the Centipede's Holy children. The merchants of Greenburg Valley are eager for the pilgrim's arrival. They agree with us that Merchants' Row belongs to the church not to a bunch of lowlife squatters."

"Squatters!" Alexandra said. Just for a second, she thought about wringing the bitch's neck. When she heard her words repeated by Kimberly Lemon and Shehili Swana, she knew they had overheard Clarice's astounding declaration.

"The merchants of Blueglennen have been here longer than the church," Kimberly said in a voice Alexandra had never heard before. "In fact, the former church elders and the merchants agreed to share the castle together and share the expense of rebuilding after the great fire of 3535. But now the mutual friendship between the church and the merchants is gone. And that's because of your husband's appointment as Bishop of Blueglennen. He turned against us.

With your husband bribing his cronies on the council, he reversed years of cooperation between us. Now we're enemies which we never were before. We used to share the burden. We used to share the taxes to keep the water flowing and the pipes clear and the walls safe from crumbling. You'd still be living in the dark if it wasn't for us. You'd be lighting alter candles with flammable oil and dragging water up from the river if it weren't for us. I keep wondering why your husband spreads his lies and why you keep repeating them. You and I used to attend the same school. You were raised in Mudflat Village. You know our history. We've always accepted new people into the city. Well, most of us anyway.

Now I know why your husband is spreading fear and failure throughout the city. He wants to throw us out on the street. He wants only church people in the bailey and the rest of us, where will we go? I know something is going on in the valley. Every day I see a new home or business in foreclosure. Your husband is up to something, something bad, something that stinks worse than Mudflat Village sewers. It's more than just zoning changes. He's trying to drive us out of Blueglennen, maybe even Mudflat Village to make way for more development like Greenburg Valley. Am I right, is he? Who will take our place? Not just your fake pilgrims, I'm sure. Maybe speculators with money?"

"He can't drive us out," a quiet composed voice said behind Kimberly. "Not unless we give him permission."

Everyone turned to look at Shehili Swana. Without a word Shehili left the dressing room. Curious Kimberly followed her out onto the showroom floor wondering what she might say. When Kimberly heard the swishing of silk and glanced over her shoulder, she was not surprised to see Alexandra dressed in an expensive strapless silver, blue, and gray silk gown. She looked amazing. The cost of the dress must be amazing too. The salesclerk followed Alexandra out leaving Clarice to fend for herself. By the time Shehili Swana reached the far corner of the shop, the clerk had joined the three women behind a corral of furs.

"What can we do?" Kimberly Lemon said.

"I don't know. I'm not familiar with your laws. Can he change the zoning codes and throw us out?"

Kimberly looked about her as if the few shoppers who were busy sifting through the clothing racks might have answers. Unfortunately, her knowledge of zoning laws was nil. She had so many questions. Should she go to the sheriff and accuse the Bishop of a crime? What crime? How could the Bishop overrule the mayor or the city council? Wasn't the city council supposed to warn people first? Or perhaps someone even higher up, someone in the legislator could overrule the city council?

She felt like such a fool. That part of school had always bored her – until today of course – now a sting of urgency sliced through her brain. If he could rezone Merchants' Row that meant all the shopkeepers would be forced to leave. Her grandfather, if he wasn't already dust by now should be rolling over in his grave, if he had a grave to roll over in.

She would end up homeless. Homeless! The idea of wandering the streets of Blueglennen or Mudflat Village begging for a bed for the night or horror of horrors having to sleep in some dark alley behind a refuse bin made her stomach turn over. She must look wild with worry the way Shehili and Alexandra were staring at her. She looked down at the carpet instead while her arms hugged her midriff. She tried to think.

A few moments passed in silence. She appreciated their thoughtfulness. Then, as if she really had been ruminating, words began pouring out of her mouth unbidden; that night she would remember her reaction and she would squirm for being all atwitter over something others would consider a minor problem, "It takes time to change the laws. It has too. People can't just willy-nilly throw people out of their homes without going through the proper channels. I'll ask around and discover how this process begins. But the merchants have a right to know what's going on. Perhaps we could meet in private, all of us, the merchants I mean. Maybe someone on this street is more familiar with zoning codes and the law than me."

"Where?" Alexandra asked absently as she dug through a table of satin and silk kerchiefs, her mind obviously distracted by her chief addiction – clothes.

"I don't know. The plaza will be full of people, not a good place. It has to be somewhere private, a place where the Bishop and his kind can't overhear us," and when she thought of the Royal Plaza, Guinevere Goodbody popped into her head, Guinevere standing on a box holding an adorable terrier pup in her arms attempting to educate the masses on the proper treatment of four-legged-creatures. As she continued to fret, she realized she was standing by the fur coats all by herself. Shehili had left the impromptu meeting to escort a late arrival to the fitting room. Alexandra had disappeared with an armful of scarves, hats, and feather boas.

Kimberly glancing at her watch, gasped and headed out of Unique Boutique. Like a dart from a child's toy, she flew across the cobblestones, bumped into an obstacle and paused in disbelief. The obstacle she'd hit happened to be the front door of the Friend for Life pet store. In dismay, she read the sign in the window: ***So Sorry We're Closed: Come Again.***

No. She couldn't give up. Determined to save her bookshop,

she was behaving in a way her grandfather would have despised. She raddled the doorknob hoping she had been mistaken about the sign. And when rattling the doorknob didn't work, she tapped on the pane of glass in the top half and shouted, "Guinevere, I need to talk to you. Guinevere, please open the door."

When nothing happened, she stepped back and moved toward the display window where three terrier puppies were tumbling over each other in mock fighting. Their eyes were huge in their furry round faces and Kimberly should have been distracted and entranced. She was not distracted or entranced; she was still seeing herself shivering in a dark alley staring up at the cold moon. She stuck her nose to the glass and peered inside.

Someone was moving about in the back of the shop. She thought she saw a head full of long golden hair appear for a fleeting moment and then disappear. It couldn't be Guinevere. Guinevere had short thick black hair to match her short thick body. Kimberly with her nose still pressed to the cold glass rapped on the window more urgently. She saw a light pop on and the halo of someone's body behind the counter. Yes, yes, that must be Guinevere. Faintly Kimberly heard her say, "I'm closed. You do know how to read don't you?"

"Guinevere, it's me. Please. I must speak with you," Kimberly shouted through the window seeing the dark outline of someone standing near the door. A larger shadow seemed to menace the smaller one. Kimberly turned in time to see a lady in a black hat with ostrich feathers pause in her march down Wolfern Promenade. She was probably intent on meeting her husband at the Royal Plaza. The officious looking female stopped on the street corner under the wrought iron lantern. As darkness descended the worms inside the globe began to swim, their bioluminescent bodies casting a blue light down on the outraged pedestrian. The woman watched Kimberly with a suspicious air as if Kimberly might break in and steal the cute puppies.

Kimberly did her best to ignore the woman. Nothing happened. Guinevere did not appear at the display window or open her door or beckon her inside. Kimberly stepped back and looked at the windows on the second floor. Did Guinevere still live in the apartments above the shop? She waited for some sort of sign.

From behind Kimberly heard Shehili escorting her last customer to the door. Kimberly turned and waved at Shehili who nodded and smiled back. She made an odd gesture, clenching her fist and then lifting her thumb in the air. Puzzled by the gesture, Kimberly watched as Shehili stepped inside, closed the twin doors and drew the bolts into place. When Swana lowered the shades, which were embossed with the name of the boutique in gold filigree upon a silk surface, Kimberly was ready to admit defeat. Only for tonight though. Absently, she noticed that one side of the shade read Unique and the other Boutique. Very swanky.

Without quite understanding why, Kimberly remained rooted in front of Guinevere's shop unable to leave her spot for fear of missing Guinevere, the urgency inside her belly growing every second. While she waited for Guinevere to appear, she admired the boutique's doors and the shades and then turned her attention to the display window with the mannequin dressed in a tight-fitting red shimmering evening gown.

The mannequin had her hand on her slim hip and seemed to stare right over Kimberly's head in such a haughty fashion that Kimberly wanted to break through the glass and throttle the creature. The gown, like the ones inside the shop, was strapless. She could never, in her entire life, wear something like that. Never in a million years. She would constantly be worried about the gown slipping off her chest and exposing her breasts to the world. Ugh!

Another minute passed and in surprise she saw Alexandra slipping around the corner of Unique Boutique using the staff exit which faced Wolfern Promenade. She could be seen from the lantern's blue haze clutching several packages in her arms. When Alexandra saw Kimberly standing in front of the pet shop, she appeared surprised and embarrassed, then as if she thought herself caught in some smarmy indiscretion jerked her head in acknowledgement and sheepishly hurried away, practically running down Wolfern Promenade toward the drawbridge. Kimberly assumed Alexandra was on her way home, most likely on her way to some tiny student apartment in the village.

Kimberly stepped away from the shop toward the wormlight's glow and watched as Alexandra's tall slim form disappeared across the drawbridge and into the night. Then she glanced at the brick wall facing Wolfern Promenade which belonged to Guinevere. She stepped toward the old crumbling castle walls in the back and noticed a gap between the wall and the shop. Perhaps she could squeeze through the gap, climb onto the pile of stones, and call through the vent which seemed to be where the smoke from a chimney poured forth its black dust rising slowly into the cool air.

Or, she could...she and the woman on the street corner exchanged looks. The woman in the feathered hat gave Kimberly a determined stare and when Kimberly glared back and said nothing, the woman in defeat scurried away. Giving up for the night, Kimberly headed back down Merchants' Row rounding the corner too fast and nearly crashed into a child making his way onto the promenade. The two of them collided. Kimberly smacked her chin into the stranger's forehead. They both cried out simultaneously.

Kimberly stepped back nursing her chin, "I'm so sorry. Are you alright?" Then she saw the person standing in front of her. Guinevere wore a long brown hooded cloak and sunglasses. Why was she wearing sunglasses at dusk? "Oh, Guinevere, I'm so glad to see you. I must speak with you urgently. You have to help us."

Guinevere sighed. For an anxious moment Kimberly thought Guinevere intended to run away. Why ever for? "Can it wait Kim," Guinevere asked in a resigned voice. "I have urgent business elsewhere."

"Please. It won't take a moment. Can you spare me at least ten minutes?"

"We can't stand under this street lamp. Do you want the constable to arrest us?"

"Oh, of course. Well," Kimberly started to say, then annoyed shot back. "Screw him. He knows better. We have every right to stand here and talk to each other. Holy Shark, who gives a damned?"

"What's so important it can't wait until tomorrow?"

"It concerns you too," Kimberly said her annoyance rising at Guinevere's assumption she had nothing better to do then accost people with her boring personal problems. Maybe Kimberly's reaction had more to do with her suspicion Guinevere might be right after all. No. Stop over-thinking. This is important, just as important to Guinevere, in fact more so for the whole damned Merchants' Row. The words burst forth and Guinevere threw back her hood in frustration and stopped Kimberly from saying anymore, "Wait. I'm not following you, say again."

"I told you, "Kimberly said suspecting Guinevere hadn't been listening in the first place. "Clarice Little told us her husband plans to set in motion a new zoning code which will, it will, well, we'll all be thrown out of our shops. That's what's going to happen to us all, very soon."

Guinevere's expression made Kimberly even madder. It was as if Guinevere disbelieved her. How dare she? Kimberly brushed past Guinevere choking on words she knew would only make matters worse. So, this was an example of how the neighborhood would ultimately greet her discovery. Clarice had nothing to fear. People were all the same, they would burrow under the ground like good centipedes and ignore the facts until they had to finally face them, and then it would be too late, their lives would be forever ruined. Well, let them go under, she was damned if she would bother them ever again. She would fight on alone. To hell with them all.

After taking a few steps down the street, Kimberly heard a shout and turned and saw Guinevere standing under the street lamp, "Come by for coffee before opening and we'll talk," then Guinevere with a swirl of her cloak disappeared heading for the university.

As soon as Kimberly entered the Bookworm, she ran to her private quarters and began dialing. This news had to be in person by phone. No texting tonight. No indeed. Voice to voice. She would weed out the disbelievers straight away. Time was critical. Through the new bay window moonlight shone down upon the refuse bins casting them in a glittering silver halo. Nothing should have been saintly about a couple of refuse bins. But in her present state of mind she felt her eyes misting up.

While she sat at her desk by the wall with her small desk lamp illuminating her phone and her telephone pad, she looked around her sanctuary. She saw her little table set beside the bay window with a clean linen cloth draped over the legs and her mother's blue glass vase filled with dried flowers set in the very center. Her gaze traveled to her bed cot in the corner covered in her grandmother's quilt and the pillows protected in matching pillow shams and the bookcase beyond the foot of the cot groaning with her own private collection of books. Then she saw the picture of her grandparents sitting on the nightstand next to her cot.

The sight moved her so much she nearly wept. What would they think now?

E4 Shellfargon Year 5092 FQMP WK 1: UES Albion 4
Visa Successful 5092-5095. Reporting from Wolf Province/City of Blueglennen. Initial Observations Confirmed: Delphinid bone structure resembles ours: Upon closer examination epidermis suggests blue/gray pigment. In heightened emotional state, pigment darkens, and texture roughens. Flight/Fight? As Delphi age, melanin drops. Newborn calves are blue/gray. Dead Delphi exhibit complete depigmentation (albinism). Condition unrelated to burns, infections, fungus, or melanocytes. Symptomatic of natural aging process.

Extra eyelid protects eyes while in full sunlight. A slim fatty fold surrounding eyes suggests further protection against infections while swimming or under water. Evolution of former marine species includes eyelashes to prevent

irritation and infection against airborne particles.

All Delphinids have thick hair covering their heads and as with our species includes various textures and colors. Calves are born with fine downy hair atop which grows much faster than our children's. Remainder of epidermis includes fine downy hair follicles.

Henceforth species will be referenced as Delphi male/female/child/elder.

Chapter 2

In the early morning hours before dawn, Guinevere slipped inside her store. With practice she locked the front door and tippy-toed toward the back. Too late. Within seconds the terriers began to bark shrilly, and Duke flapped his wings frantically from inside his cage. Guinevere lifted the sheet and greeted him with her usual question, "How are we this morning Duke?" a question which had become a habit, not a sincere inquiry. The damn creature would live longer than her which was maddening. The knowledge made her feel subservient which she hated as much as she hated annoying and thoughtless people.

Imagining this creature, half bird / half reptile gorging himself on nuts and bugs for another fifty years, this pampered poop dumped at her doorstep nearly ten years previous by some rich noble, most likely a bastard because bastards preferred exotic and useless animals while noble bitches preferred cuddly useless pets. Worst of all, he would live to be one-hundred years old. An insufferable thought, still not as bad as idiots who neglected pets or dumped them off on her. Although she had to admit the idiot who dumped The Duke off might have had a good reason. His insistent chatter and rude commentary would drive anyone to violence.

Guinevere held her hands together in mock prayer, "Oh please great one, send Duke a brand-new owner, someone rich and stupid. Oh, please great one. I promise to smile at someone at least once a day."

Duke chimed in, "Oh please great one. (cough) Oh please. (cough, cough) Please. Oh. Great one. Great please. (cough) Oh please."

She shouted over him, "How are we this morning Duke?"

"(cough) Murderous thank you."

Guinevere carried a pup under each arm, set them down in the back room and watched the plump balls of fur for a moment as they sniffed the stone-flagged floor, then she turned back to the window display and retrieved another two. She cuddled the last one under her chin reveling in soft gleaming fur and sweet puppy breath. Duke squawked and coughed and continued to berate her until she brought him a dish of seeds and fresh water. When she set the tea kettle on the front burner of her two-burner portable cooker, she groaned reminded of Kimberly's request from last night. She had no time for gossip or petty grievances. She had the cages to clean out and the floor to sweep. As predictable as sleet in Fallowsec, someone rapped on her display window.

Guinevere threw back the bolt and opened her door, just a crack, barely enough to keep the intruder from entering. She looked through the crack prepared to send Kimberly scuttling back home. She gasped. A white-hot anger spread from her head down to her toes. How dare the little twit. . . Guinevere stifled the urge to wrap her fingers around Kimberly Lemon's long skinny neck and throttle her soundly.

What in a virgin birth did she think she was doing? Once she calmed down, Kimberly's apologetic expression registered for the first time. Still pissed she tried to do inventory of her menagerie in her head. Through the haze of murderous rage, Guinevere acknowledge Kimberly's sudden chagrin, the way her angular face seemed to sink further into her skull, the wide mouth drooping, the big violet eyes lowered as she glanced over her shoulder at the party of people waiting patiently for Guinevere to open the door.

The only reason Guinevere didn't slam the door in Kimberly's face was because she recognized Harold Zany of Zany's Music towering above the rest of the group. He looked like an old favorite bloodhound she'd had as a child, his large liquid brown eyes so sad and resigned, resigned she assumed to the fact he would never have that elusive badger between his jaws.

What Guinevere liked most about Harry Zany were those days when he was at his most relaxed and could be mischievously cheeky. Once she got to know him better, she discovered he had a scrappy side like her. Instead of fighting with his fists, he used humor as his weapon of choice. And loyalty, Guinevere appreciated loyalty more than all the jewels in Duke Dono's mythical coffers. Harry was loyal from the crown of his thinning scalp to the bottoms of his brown loafers.

For Harold's sake, Guinevere opened the door a bit wider and stepped outside. Kimberly grew a little taller and a little less embarrassed at this tiny victory. She spoke quickly before Guinevere could slam the door in her face, "I know this is an imposition, but I had to let the others on Merchants' Row know the truth. I notified everyone in the Merchants' Row Alliance even Sylvia Paleone and Luella Morrison."

"You didn't call me," Queenie said with a snort. "Beatrice called me. I wood int a come otherwise."

Kimberly's ivory skin turned as white as new snow. In a faint voice, Kimberly finished by saying. "They didn't seem impressed with my news. In fact, Sylvia called me a liberal anarchist and a traitor to the true religion."

Guinevere hated to see animals suffer, even human animals. With an annoyed flourish, she threw open her front door, and stood aside, her jaw rigid fighting to hold back what she really wanted to say to these people. For years they'd ignored her. While she expressed her concern about abandoned cats running loose in the castle courtyard and the packs of homeless dogs searching for scraps in the village, these same folks who were pouring into her shop at this very moment had been known to smirk at her while she stood on her block of wood in the Royal Plaza telling the world about the daily animal cruelties going on under their very noses. They didn't think she'd seen them smirking. But she had. She'd seen them smirking.

They had a lot of nerve tramping about in her store exclaiming over the animals after so many years of neglect and derision. Here they were milling about in her shop looking like a herd of confused seahorses, only an hour after sunrise, dressed in smart fancy clothes, smiling, nodding, acting as if she'd invited them to a party, "I'll give you an hour and then I'm opening the store. Go on now, we can talk in the backroom. And remove the mud from your boots before entering my private quarters."

Guinevere's little back room looked even smaller with eleven people packed inside. Three of those assembled weren't merchants and she had to wonder why they were here with the other alarmists. Maybe they were spying for the Governor? The ones who hadn't bothered to come were elevated in her estimation. Now that she'd moved the absent ones to a different category, she saw them in a new light. They were superior individuals with taste and good breeding. Since one of them was Dela Swana, she would have been rakcd to tears to see such an elegant person among this rabble.

Blueglennen rarely saw such exotic people as Shehili Swana. The castle and the inhabitants of Mudflat Village and Greenburg Valley were as provincial and backward as a frozen pile of seahorse shit. Guinevere, even though she didn't know the woman well, appreciated Swana's unique situation, since Guinevere too had come from somewhere else and had been forced to reside in a small community like Blueglennen. She too had experienced the mistrust of Blueglennen citizens for outsiders. It took nearly three years before some of these same people warmed up enough to give her the time of day.

Unlike Guinevere, her cousin Dialmere Seeley didn't give a seahorse shitpie what Blueglennens thought of her. But she didn't have to live in the castle bailey either. Like Guinevere she'd been born at Fort Bravado in the north. Everybody assumed her people lived in caves and ate with their fingers.

Guinevere had no illusions about Luella Morrison's reasons for not joining the Merchants' Row Alliance. After all, Luella had the backbone of a centipede. Oops. Another blasphemy. Stop it girl. A long time ago, Guinevere had been a member of the Church of the Holy Delph. Unlike the new religion, she had worshiped Saint Delph, a deity, not a bug. The Church of the Holy Centipede gathered momentum and a flock nearly a century ago. Back then most people thought of it as a usurper religion created by the prophet Chuck.

Chuck had been a Blueglennen citizen, some minor noble stripped of his fortune and devastated when his leader Duke Dono fled the country leaving his people to fend for themselves. Years passed and the people (a bunch of helpless boobies) starved while lords from other regions fought over the carcass of what had once been a powerful kingdom. When Chuck fell into a newly dug grave to escape a marauding band of cutthroats, he told everyone willing to listen that he'd had a vision, a vision of a great centipede promising to bring Blueglennen food, shelter and protection.

His announcement turned out to be unfortunate for him because a warlord in the north had just pillaged the countryside near the castle. His soldiers and knights were on their way to sack Blueglennen. The warlord arrested all the nobles, tortured them and left the capital of Wolfern Province in ruins. The castle had once upon a time been a respected and noble estate. Chuck's followers, oddly enough, decided Chuck's death was a sign from the Holy Centipede and embraced his crazy ideas in the desperate hope his vision would come to pass, especially the part about peace and prosperity. Always with the peace and prosperity. Why don't people wise up? Hucksters always promise peace and prosperity.

A few of the merchants milling about in her back room began to break off as if they had changed their minds about the meeting. Good, she thought, now go home. She finally woke up to the fact that everyone seemed to be waiting for her to set the meeting in motion. That's when Guinevere blew up, "What the hell are you looking at me for? I didn't call you here. She did," pointing accusingly at Kimberly Lemon. "And I'm not serving you any coffee or crumb cake because I'm too damned busy. I got animals to feed. So, go on you bunch of confused seahorses, go do your thing and I'll be in the front listening."

"I'll feed the animals," a man offered as he stood near her metal storage unit where she kept her supplies and extra cages. He looked familiar.

Kimberly pushed her way through the crowd to stand near Guinevere, "I'm so sorry Guinevere. I don't know who this man is. I didn't invite him."

A voice could be heard from somewhere near the storage units, "I did Kimmy. He's a friend of mine." Everyone turned to watch as a woman with long shiny brown hair squeezed her way through the crowd to stand facing Guinevere. Kimberly introduced her friend to the group, "This is my friend Crystova Moth from the university. She's currently researching the original language of Curlecon. She teaches at the university."

Over the years, Guinevere had noticed Crystova Moth coming and going from the castle bailey traipsing over the drawbridge to the train station. Then she remembered. This was the one who liked to drop in and admire the puppies. The last time Crystova had been in her store had been about a year ago when she bought a Curlecon wolf-shepherd mix, a cute fellow with a prankster's benign disposition. Guinevere had warned Professor Moth about the breeds rapid growth and disposition. Sure enough, the wolf-shepherd mix grew and stopped growing around a hundred and fifty pounds. He looked more like a young seahorse than a dog.

Crystova dismissed Guinevere's warning and cheerfully paid for the pup and the food. It took her two trips to get the dog and the big bag of food to Bishop's Cottage. Guinevere loved to see the professor on her nightly strolls as she tried to control the awkward juvenile. For a while their progress through the streets of Blueglennen looked more like a dog taking a Delphinid for a nightly run. But the juvenile eventually grew up and it was a real pleasure to watch the two strolling here and there and everywhere. Sometimes Crystova would pop into the store for a new collar or a toy which was much appreciated since most of her customers never returned.

Guinevere had trouble remembering Delphinid names but no trouble with animal names. Once people passed her rigorous test as dog lovers and she found them acceptable she was ready to boot them out the door. The more time she wasted chatting with people the less time she had for her animals.

Guinevere broke into Crystova's speech, "Henry. That's what you call him. Nice solid name."

The professor smiled delighted Guinevere remembered her dog's name. Little did she know Guinevere had long since forgotten the professor's name until today. Suddenly suspicious of the professor's presence she wondered about her real motive for crashing the party. When the merchants had filed into her shop, Guinevere had seen Crystova Moth devouring the terriers with a covetous eye. Oh no, she'd better not, Guinevere thought, not with that wolfshep at home. No way would she allow Crystova to adopt one of her babies and take her baby home to a crazy dog that would gobble them up in two bites. Guinevere hated to say no to an animal lover, but she couldn't risk the pup's safety, not even for all the seastars in the world.

Crystova addressed the room in a temperate tone which for such a soft-spoken woman carried far further than most people expected. She sounded better than any Coral'ean prancing about on the stage, her enunciation precise and her voice as clear as the chiming of the clock tower. "This is Professor Adam Honeysweet, he teaches Curlecon Law at Duke Tower University. Kimberly, when you called me last night and explained your reasons for arranging this meeting, I thought of Honeysweet. He might be of some help to you and your neighbors."

Professor Honeysweet nodded politely and waited one brow lifted as if his brow had something important to say. All the women agreed that he was handsome in an intelligent way, nothing florid or overtly sexy, yet sexy indeed, with his lush dark hair and green eyes. Wow.

Guinevere acknowledged defeat and jabbed her finger at the storage closet, "The dishes and bags of food are in there. You know the difference between bird feed and dog nuggets I hope?"

He grinned wickedly and said, "I'll muddle through I'm sure."

While they had been solving the problem of the animals, Queenie Oppfield had made herself at home at the head of the tiny table in the center of the room. Beatrice, a plump matronly woman with iron gray hair pulled tight into a bun, pulled up a chair next to Queenie. Bill Anders and Billy Bill Anders of Anders and Sons pastries ignored the other women present and ungallantly squeezed their heavy bodies into the two remaining chairs.

Don Tumble of Hadal's Delight, the high-end wine and cheese shop two doors down from the pet store, considered saying something rude to the father and son but held his tongue. It would be a waste of time. Those two cared only about their own creature comforts, if they had their way no one would get to eat the shop pastries but them.

Harold Zany managed to find a comfortable spot near the propane burner and turned off the kettle which had begun to burp and steam in an alarming fashion. He leaned against the counter and crossed his arms watching the people morosely. He anticipated a wasted hour. These people had as much organizational skills as a herd of cats. Or was the phrase – a basket of cats? Let's see, a herd of buffalo, a gaggle of geese, a murder of ravens, a pack of dogs, and a swarm of bees. What about cats? Didn't cats congregate sometimes?

Harold glanced at Tanny Bright his technical advisor, and on occasion, emergency music store clerk. She'd spent most of her childhood listening to his selection of music, her folks too poor to give her money for her own collection. Now she worked in the laboratory of Duke Tower University as a Space Age Science Technician (SAST) through Wolfern Institute of Technology (WIT). He was pretty sure she made more money than the whole collection of merchants in the room, probably even Governor Saurus. Yet she didn't dress as if she had oodles of money.

She dressed more like a blacksmith in heavy work boots, blue jeans, and leather smock. Her blue jeans were covered in a twinkling array of tiny silver droplets from a series of tests she'd been doing recently on her newest experiment. The droplets congregated just below her knees and went no further, probably because she covered most of her body in a heavy protective apron. She never forgot her goggles but sometimes she'd forget her helmet.

Tanny was brilliant at pretty much everything she set her mind to and as a graduate student working on her third PhD was already on her one hundredth invention. This most recent invention was keeping her up nights and driving her to distraction. Every time she stepped into the music store, he'd see a fresh burn on her arm, or notice her fingers black with ink, or smell singed hair from her flowing black locks.

Feeling Harry's eyes on her, Tanny looked down to see if she'd forgotten to take off her apron. Relieved she had remembered, for once, to leave the gloves, goggles, and apron at the lab she debated whether to stay in the room with these folks. Being around people made her itchy. Wouldn't she be serving Curlecon better by going back to her laboratory and testing the weapon-deterrent-machine (WDM) one more time? If she could figure out how to reverse the dangerous radiational pulses emitted on initial exit she could finally patent it as an antidote to global annihilation. Maybe she should call the device the weapon-interference-machine (WIM)?

No. Come on. What a stupid name. Wait. What about weapon-intelligence-trapper? That would make the machine WIT? Holy Delph that sounded even lamer. No. Wait. She worked for Wolfern Institute of Technology. What about Weapon Intervention Technology? Nice. No. Better yet the name Weapon Intervention Throttle sounded imposing? Oh, no, dear delph give me patience – the name sounded unintentionally funny.

Come on woman, she told herself, get serious. Think. The board at WIT would laugh you out of the room. The device not only repulsed dangerous particles rather than throttle them, the device rearranged the molecules to their original state. It should be something like Weapon Intervention ... Thwarted, Tidal-wave, or Trap. Hell no. It had started out as a virtual reality game. Yes. Weapon Hologram Intervention Portal (Whip). That sounded cooler. She just had to figure out how to contain the dangerous pulses which would prevent the anti-weapon from turning into ash in her hand. She might even end up a pile of ash herself if she didn't get the prototype working correctly.

On the other side of the tiny table someone Tanny Bright had known since pre-school watched the merchants and hoped not to be seen. When everyone first arrived, Valcinda Moorland had tried unsuccessfully to get Tanny's attention. Familiar with the distracted look on Tanny's face Valcinda shrugged philosophically. Tanny didn't possess a mean bone in her entire body. Tanny wasn't being rude. She was just deep in thought for the millionth time, probably coming up with another amazing invention which would make life easier for all Shellfargons.

Unlike some of Tanny's contemporaries, Valcinda appreciated the young inventor's quirkiness. Even though Valcinda was equally as smart and gifted, she never thought of herself as being in the same league as Tanny. She had discovered her vocation early and like a beam of light zipped through school and college with the intention of owning her own business and preparing children for the 51st century. Her business catered to after-school play groups and the selling of toys and crafts. Still Valcinda Moorland, Caleb's younger cousin, who owned and operated the Children's Playhouse worried parents and schools were not doing enough to prepare children for the most dangerous days ahead.

The Children's Playhouse stood next door to Guinevere's pet store. Valcinda bought the store from her aunt and uncle. Her cousin Caleb was a silent partner who would occasionally drop in to fix a toilet or put up a shelf or glue a broken toy back together. Valcinda with her sheen of long black hair and pale complexion kept her head lowered, as was her way. She preferred to remain quiet and attentive placing herself in the best location so that she could see everyone in the room and yet remain invisible.

The best spot to be invisible was near the lockers. Unfortunately for her, the lockers were along the far wall beneath the heating duct, a monster which periodically groaned and gasped and clanked as if laboring under a heavy load. Everyone was used to the old plumbing and heating systems in the bailey. The fixtures were as old as the first people of Wolfern. She hoped the meeting would end soon or she'd end up looking as if she'd just gotten out of a sauna.

Frank Darknight, the grandson of Arthur and Eleanor

Darknight of Pop's Market which sold fresh fruits and vegetables seemed particularly bright-eyed and excited by this impromptu meeting. He had recently returned to Curl from some exotic place across the sea and rumor suggested he had plans to leave again soon. What did his grandparents think of his comings and goings? Would his grandparents finally sell the store and retire to Greenburg Valley?

Kimberly had her doubts about Frank staying in Blueglennen just to take over the store. He seemed wildly out of place in this hick town. Why had he come? Wasn't he usually in bed by now? Why hadn't he abstained like Luella Morrison and Sylvia Paleone? Kimberly Lemon refused to budge from her spot by the threshold. If things got ugly, she'd have enough time to run out the door and lock herself inside the Emporium. She tried not to appear as if she wanted to bolt. When Professor Honeysweet moved toward her with a bowl of food in each hand she blushed and stepped aside to make way for him, "Sorry."

"No problem. Go on with your meeting folks."

"I have nothing to do with this meeting," Guinevere reminded him with a stern eye and pressed lips. "This is all Kimberly's idea."

An unexpected dignity started in her belly and moved to her chest. Kimberly straightened her shoulders and turned to look at the assembled group, "I know this is an imposition. But what would be far worse is if I didn't tell you what I discovered yesterday. It has come to my attention Bishop Little and the Governor plan to rezone Merchants' Row for church business."

"What? Did I hear her right?" Queenie asked loudly in an angry voice.

"You heard her," Beatrice said slapping her arm. "Now listen."

Kimberly resumed, "It's my understanding that they plan to turn our shops into accommodations for pilgrims during holy days."

"Their holy days you mean," Don Tumble said. "I'm Church of Hadal. I don't hold with these upstart religions. Ninety-nine years old for Serpent's sake."

"You mean the gods of the ancient ones?" Harold asked with interest.

"Yes, as a matter of fact, that's exactly what Hadaleans worship, the old gods of the trenches and the abyss."

"Are you serious?" Bill Anders Senior said his eyes widening for a moment in his soft doughy face. "I'm Church of Curl myself, have been since I was a babe, and everyone in my family for seven generations have been Church of Curl." No one in the room was in doubt as to Senior's feelings about the pagan religions of Curlecon. It was writ large upon his face, disgust mixed with triumph. Anders's tone and expression implied that Tumble was no better than a pagan priest or worshiper of the evil one.

Kimberly cut them off before the two men started bickering, "The religious wars have been over for nearly five hundred years. Our new constitution includes religious freedom. So please. Let's stay on track. We're here to make sure that our shops remain open and prosperous. We don't have much time. We must fight to save our shops. First, we must find out if the Church of the Holy Centipede can rezone Merchants' Row. Does anyone have experience with zoning codes?"

Crystova appeared right behind Kimberly holding a terrier in her arms, "Adam might know. Let me ask him."

Guinevere frowned as Crystova fondled the terrier puppy. She opened her mouth to remonstrate with the woman. "Listen here, you've agreed to feed the animals not to..."

Kimberly spoke over her, "Excellent. Thank you, Crystova. Come on folks. We don't have much time. We've got to know more about Bishop Little's plans and if it's true the church is trying to push us out of our shops. If they are, we've got to come up with a plan to push back against rezoning Merchants' Row. I suggest we all think about this today and meet again on Saturday night with some concrete news."

"Where?" Don Tumble asked.

"I don't know," Kimberly said.

Queenie interrupted, "Somewhere larger than this room I should think."

"How about the plaza?" Anders Junior suggested.

"Don't be ridiculous," Don said impatiently longing for the sensibility of his wife. "You want to discuss this topic with the Governor's knights milling about? Why not just meet in the Governor's penthouse?"

"Well, by now the Bishop probably knows about this meeting since Kimberly called Luella. You know how Luella loves to gossip," Anders Senior said in defense of his beloved first born.

Adam popped in for a moment cuddling one of the terriers and turned his brilliant blue eyes on Kimberly. Kimberly made herself look up and up at him and tried not to blush or twitch or so much as acknowledge how all the hairs on her body were standing straight up in amorous attention.

"I understand you need someone with civil law experience," Professor Adam Honeysweet said to her and to the group, his eyes roving about the room with an intelligent friendly expression. "I know just the fellow who'll suit this situation. I'll talk to him tomorrow.

How's that?"

"Sounds like a plan," Queenie said hitting the table with her fist. "I'll give my brother a ring today. He works for the Sheriff's Office. He might know what's going on." Queenie made motions to rise from her chair pausing only when Harold spoke up.

"We could rent the private rooms at the Pub in the village," Harold suggested having been thinking longingly of a pint of something stronger than tea while people had been squabbling about religion.

"Excellent idea," Guinevere said hoping they would all leave now.

"Would you mind reserving the room Harold?" Kimberly asked.

Harold leaned back with a frown. He had been thinking about beer not actually planning to contribute to Lemon's hopeless plan. "I suppose I could," he said reluctantly, and everyone waited because he seemed to have something else on his mind. "I volunteer Billy Boy to come along with me since he's such a good friend of Hugo Atwater."

No one was surprised Billy Bill Anders Junior knew Hugo Atwater, the sole proprietor of Wolf Inn pub. Billy Bill's florid chubby face looked up from a deep contemplation of the table's scuffed wooden surface in obvious confusion. Billy Bill's body worked on autopilot and the brain in sleep mode. Evidently, Harold had been annoyed by Billy Bill's daydreaming and wanted to remind him that he was also a part of the discussion. Yet Kimberly was heartened by the worried expressions of the group; they were alarmed enough at her news to take the information seriously.

Kimberly hadn't realized how tightly wound her body had become. She made herself relax. She began by unclenching her teeth. "Then we'll meet this Saturday at Wolf Inn pub around five o'clock and be finished before they raise the drawbridge. Thank you all for coming at such short notice. I also appreciate your willingness to listen. We need each other. This is too big to be handled alone."

"Should we say anything to the absent ones?" Beatrice asked probably thinking about her neighbor Luella Morrison of Luella's Confections.

Guinevere answered before Kimberly could open her mouth, "You just heard Kimberly say Luella and Sylvia accused her of being a troublemaker. They've probably already run hot-foot over to the cathedral and told the Bishop about our meeting. I bet there are church wardens on Merchants' Row as we speak just waiting to count heads as you all leave the shop. So, think about that, huh? And consider carefully whether or not you want to butt heads with Bishop

Little and his people."

"Bishop Little's cozy with the Governor and all the Duke Tower Set, you know," Don Tumble reminded everyone as he leaned against the metal storage unit with his arms crossed looking every bit the high class gentleman with his smart clothes, long blonde hair tied back with a black silk ribbon and his handsome face looking so smug with male confidence.

Strange how Kimberly had grown indifferent to his charms. When she bumped into him on the street or he popped in to browse through her map collection, she remained cordial yet aloof. Her body now responded to him the same way it responded to Billy Bill Junior with discomfort bordering on revulsion. How strange? Perhaps her new distaste had something to do with Professor Adam Honeysweet?

Beatrice rose from her seat, her customary expression petulant. Ignoring the room, especially Don Tumble behind her, of whom she had an ongoing feud, and without a word to anyone she marched out of the shop. Queenie jumped up to follow her. Kimberly wished Guinevere hadn't been so rude to Beatrice. It was difficult to read Beatrice. She kept her own counsel. Kimberly sensed an iron will beneath the matronly façade. Nothing ruffled her calm not even insults.

Don Tumble was relieved the old battleaxes were gone. He smiled at the young ladies, his biggest smile for Valcinda Moorland. She was as slim as a model and her face and bearing reminded him of an ancient woodcut of the huntress Twilight with her long black hair flowing behind her as she rode her great seahorse through Bitterroot Forest, her face fierce with exaltation. It was unfortunate that at the moment her face was pinched with annoyance. He willed her to look at him. He was sure he could get a smile from her. When Valcinda continued to ignore him, he glanced over at Kimberly Lemon.

Kimberly was watching Professor Adam as he crossed the room to refill a bucket with water for the animals. She reminded Don of a shy deer all browns and reds. He admired her breasts most of all and wondered what lay beneath the plain wool skirt. From the little he could see of her ankles in her clomping big shoes, she must have very fine legs to match her very fine breasts. Now the face, well, parts of the face were good like her high cheekbones and full lips. But her eyes, her eyes were an odd color, violet or purplish, and those dark thick lashes made the whole effect creepy. Now if she had brown eyes and fatty folds like everyone else, she'd be a stunner. Ah ha.

Forget Guinevere. She was too much like her cousin Dialmere Seeley. Both loved animals more than Delphinids. Both were short and plump and angry all the time. He did admire their close-cropped silky black hair which framed their pale faces and accentuated their lovely chins. But he'd already had a run-in with Guinevere. His chest began to hurt remembering when she'd punched him so hard, he'd fallen onto the cobblestones and nearly brained himself on a lamp post.

It was a shame Alexandra or Evelyn hadn't been invited to accompany Queenie the warrior troll. A real shame. He had been frequenting the diner lately chiefly in hopes of talking to the two attractive waitresses from the university, one brunette, the other blonde. He admired most of all their youth and innocence. They were equally shy which he found endearing. Then he remembered his wife and looked about the room realizing belatedly he and Kimberly Lemon were the only people left in the backroom. Kimberly had her head poked round the wall staring into the shop front watching Adam, Guinevere, and Crystova tend to the animals.

The strong smell of men's cologne warned Kimberly of Don's closeness. She ignored him and hurried out into the front room pausing long enough to speak to Guinevere and the others, "Thank you so much for letting us use your shop for this emergency meeting Guinevere. I'm sorry I didn't warn you about the others. I really hadn't expected everyone to show up or almost everyone. And Crystova thanks so much for coming. Professor Adam I really appreciate your advice. You've been very kind."

"Not at all," Adam said as he watched the terriers tumble about in their glass enclosed cage in front of the display window. He straightened to his full height, a few inches taller than Tumble and turned to face her with a brilliant smile, she suspected a smile he habitually wore, "I'm all for revolutions especially peaceful demonstrations and civil disobedience. Power to the people. Liberty for all. Etc. etc."

"Brilliant," Don Tumble said in an acid tone. "An anarchist in our midst."

Adam measured Tumble with an intelligent eye and his smile grew fierce, "What is thy name, that in battle thus Thou crossest me? What honor dost though seek Upon my head?"

Tumble had not expected such a response and stared hollow-eyed at the Professor. He suspected he had been insulted by a passage from Coral. What an elitist snob, he thought trying to cover up a sneer and a twinge of embarrassment. Little did he know, Honeysweet's passage came from the starship Albion's collection of literature from a playwright called Shakespeare.

Kimberly Lemon studied Guinevere's floor as if the floor had done something particularly amusing. The shop owner stood behind the counter counting the cash in the cash register and pointedly ignoring them all. Crystova Moth, alarmed, dropped her bucket on the floor which shattered the quiet and made Guinevere look up from counting. Crystova called to the professor urgently, "Adam, don't you have a class this morning?"

Adam nodded soberly, "You win, my dear lady Moth. Time to sheath my sword," he looked as if he now regretted his quotation from Shakespeare's Henry IV. Crystova made a point of walking to the door and opening it waiting patiently for Adam to follow her out. Adam turned to face Guinevere who never looked up from her counting then glanced at Kimberly. Kimberly nodded and smiled, "Thank you Adam for all your help."

Guinevere belatedly looked up and said, "Okay folks. Get your butts out of my shop. I've got work to do."

Adam nodded coldly in Don Tumble's direction, then spun neatly on his heels and followed Crystova out onto the street. The door closed behind him. Kimberly stepped over to the display window to watch her friend Crystova stroll beside Professor Adam toward Wolfern Promenade. She noticed Shehili Swana standing in front of her shop pulling candy wrappers and a soda can from her potted plants which were attractively positioned on either side of the double doors. Kimberly had always wanted to learn the art of topiary so that she could grow some fancy boxwoods in front of her shop door too.

"They're not for sale, Kimberly. They haven't been weaned yet," Guinevere said as she closed the cash register door with a snap. Guinevere must have assumed Kimberly was eyeing the cute puppies. She turned to face the room in time to see Tumble walk away his expression stormy. Now Kimberly understood why she disliked Tumble so much. He imagined himself some sort of great lover and believed women should bow down before him. Too bad, so sad, so he was miffed because the only two women left in the room were ignoring him.

Once Kimberly knew Tumble had left the shop for good, she approached Guinevere tentatively, "I know you're still annoyed with me. I don't blame you. I should have asked your permission before bringing the entire Merchants' Row Alliance in here."

Guinevere looked up with a steely eye and said, "Yes. You should have. Next time I'll leave you out on the street or call the constable."

Something moved from Kimberly's gut upward burning a path to her throat. She had not felt such anger in a long time and the words spilled out of her unbidden, "There won't be a next time Guinevere. If the Bishop gets his way, we won't be neighbors. You'll be somewhere else, and your shop'll be some pilgrim's private sanctuary, a sort of holy day hut. And I'll end up homeless mooching off my friends and begging door to door." Unable to bare looking at her a second longer, Kimberly stormed out.

By the time she reached the street she felt like smashing something or hitting someone. Then she saw Shehili standing with her hands on her hips holding a bag of trash with a look of quiet contemplation as if Kimberly's face told her all she needed to know about the disastrous meeting. Kimberly wondered if Swana's support might change a few minds and hurried across the street eager to disabuse her of the notion the meeting had been a failure.

Shehili waited for Kimberly then opened one of the doors and gestured for her to enter. The first think Kimberly noticed was that the boutique was lit only by the Cavenymphs perched on the wall behind the counter. The shadows in the rest of the shop made her task much easier. Shehili couldn't see her face. She turned and said, "I know you're busy, but I just wanted to update you on the Merchants' Row meeting."

"Why?"

"Well," Kimberly began and then stopped. She'd assumed Shehili had a vested interest in fighting Bishop Little and the zoning commissioner. "I guess I thought you had a stake in this fight too."

The woman shrugged her elegant shoulder and brushed past Kimberly dispensing with the trash bag behind the counter. Feeling rebuffed, Kimberly turned to leave the shop. Shehili chuckled and Kimberly turned around in time to hear her say, "I'm not a citizen of Curl, Kimberly. I'm just a tourist. How do you think I can be of any help?"

"Oh, I didn't know that. Well you're right. It's not your fight. I suppose it won't be a hardship to pack up and leave and resettle your boutique in the big city, maybe, in the east, some place like Delphadore, maybe close to Silver Crest Hall and the Delphadorturo."

"I chose Blueglennen because of the university. There are more young people in this town than in most. The young tend to be more open-minded and eager to buy exotic things. I would regret having to leave. But if I must, I must."

"I don't see why you can't fight with us. After all, you're a merchant too."

"I'm a foreigner here, Dela Lemon. If I protested over the rezoning of my shop the Governor could have me sent back to my ship."

"Part of me understands. You're probably right," the phone rang and Shehili moved toward the contraption on the counter.

"Well, have a good day," Kimberly ended lamely glancing one last time behind her before leaving the shop. Shehili Swana nodded goodbye and then answered the phone suddenly all business.

Kimberly hurried toward the Bookworm realizing belatedly all the other shops were open for business. Odd, how she felt as if she had failed, even though she had managed to get all these diverse people together. Her thoughts turned to the two people she respected the most who seemed oblivious to the coming plight of Blueglennen.

At that moment her plans appeared hallow, tawdry even. What did she think she could achieve? She was a nobody with no money and no influence. The church and the city council were capable of chewing her up and spitting her out without breaking stride. She considered backing out, maybe, telling the others to let the church go ahead with their rezoning plans. She could find another shop, maybe take her own advice. She wasn't doing so hot right now. So why not? She barely made the rent. If the shop hadn't been grandfathered into the lease nearly fifty years ago, she would have had to pay the same rent as the other shopkeepers. They had more to lose than her. And here she was ready to give up when her neighbors were risking so much more.

Life could be capricious sometimes. Two people were waiting beside her shop door, the same shop door which rarely if ever had customers. She paused by Queenie's Diner uncertain how to proceed. Bishop Little turned in time to see her stop and stare in dismay. His wife Clarice continued to press her face to the glass of the Bookworm display window and Kimberly heard her say to her husband, "There's nobody inside, honey. She must be sleeping. I heard she sleeps in the backroom now. I've never wanted to enter such an evil place."

There was no other option but to move forward. Something alive and feral crept up her stomach and into her throat. Blindly she moved toward her shop and elbowed Clarice out of the way, "Do you mind? My shop opens in ten minutes. Coming through."

Astonished at her uncustomary rudeness the logical half of her stepped aside to watch in amazement as this new Kimberly, a more assertive Kimberly nudged Clarice Little out of the way and opened the shop door and shut the door in the woman's smug face. From fathoms deep in a part of her mind buried for decades, a thought emerged and refused to budge. No matter what happened, she would not let them win. No matter how much they tried to bully or manipulate her, she would not let them win. Her grandfather gave her the shop because he knew how much she loved books and old things. He had trusted her to keep it going. She wouldn't betray him.

Kimberly paused for a count of twenty before turning on the

shop lights and opening the cash register. A creepy crawling along her spine told her the Littles were still waiting outside. They would not go away. She would have to face them alone. For some strange reason she wasn't afraid. Two days ago, she would have been nervous and obsequious to the point of making herself nauseous. Not today. Today, she felt nothing but contempt for them.

On any other day, the shop would have been open by now. She didn't care. It was still her shop. She could open late if she chose. She straightened a few piles of newspapers and magazines and blew off a layer of dust from a pile of maps on a center table. She looked around for something more to do and realized how childish it was to make them wait. She had standards of etiquette even if they didn't.

As she moved toward the door, she shoved timid Kimberly into the basement and forced a smile. Bishop Little smiled sweetly back, the sweetness never reaching his empty brown eyes. Unlike her husband, Clarice was outraged. She stood beside him with her cheeks navy blue and eyes flickering hot revenge. Kimberly suspected she'd be paying a social price for embarrassing the woman. What more could they do to her? Run her out of town?

As Bishop Little escorted his wife inside, Kimberly turned to watch them maneuver their way between the book shelves and tables. Her ancestors had chosen the best wood in the valley to furnish their shop. They had chosen the best craftspeople to build the wall-to-wall shelves and the free-standing shelves as well as the cashier counter. The furniture had been made from the strongest trees and the glass cabinets from the best artisans. Every piece of furniture was as familiar to her as her own face. Holy Legs! It dawned upon her that the contents of this room included priceless antiques.

As the Littles wandered about the shop, all Kimberly could see from her vantage point was Bishop Mark Little's head bobbing along and occasionally see his head lower to hear what his wife had to say. Since she was two-inches shorter and the standing bookshelves hid her from view, he appeared to be talking to himself. The sight of them so soon after the meeting made her very unhappy, even nervous. Why had they come? What did they want? Had Sylvia Paleone or Luella Morrison run to the church to snitch on her?

The doorbell chimed. Kimberly stiffened wondering if Bishop Little had invited his clerics as well, hoping to intimidate her. When she saw her friend Crystova Moth enter the shop with Professor Honeysweet close behind, her relief at the sight of them nearly made her relax her guard. She tried to keep her expression neutral. Her grandmother used to say she couldn't keep a secret because her face expressed every thought. Crystova recognized Bishop Little and glanced at Kimberly with a questioning look. Kimberly tried to stay calm but must have signaled her nervousness because Crystova nodded as if Kimberly had spoken her thoughts aloud. Oh crap.

Professor Honeysweet watched the occupants with an air of perennial curiosity and wandered around the shop with his hands behind his back. Crystova's voice sounded unnaturally loud, "I've come for those old maps you said might be of interest."

"Oh yes, of course. Let me get them for you," Kimberly said relieved to have something to do other than watch the Littles wander around the shop pretending to be interested in her old books. Since the Littles had never set foot in her store before today, they had plenty to keep them busy. Kimberly made her way to the nook which held her collection of old-world maps. She and her grandfather built the nook in the corner facing the room. With Caleb's help, the bookshelves were bolted to the floor and attached to each other, so no one could inadvertently bump into them and injure themselves or make a spectacular mess.

On the front piece, she stored her special books. While customers waited to pay for purchases, they could thumb through the maps and books. Lots of customers enjoyed the latest scrolls which held mysteries done up in the finest of parchment paper. On the other side of the nook she stored her writing tools, paper, account book, receipts and labels for those times when she needed to sell merchandise quickly. She used the top as a place to put her cash register, brochures, and business cards.

The red velvet curtains behind her concealed the threshold to her private back hall and added a touch of elegance. The huge potted Getal plant in the corner added color with its bright- yellow and red leaves. The sight of her decorating achievements gave her a renewed sense of courage. She compared the shop today under her management to what the shop had been like when she had been young, and her grandparents had been alive.

When she was a kid, her grandparents had conducted their business in the back of the shop using the large gleaming wood counter as a barrier between them and the customers. Her grandfather spent most of his time hiding out in his comfortable chair and reading all day. Her grandmother liked to do her knitting or crochet work behind the counter with the glowworms burning brightly even on the sunniest days.

Back in their day, they kept a price list on the board by the door with a cash box beneath and customers used the honor system dropping money into the cash box before leaving. Sometimes customers insisted on correct change which annoyed them into apoplexy. It was no wonder her grandparents barely survived. They were too trusting and too lazy to make the business thrive. And then she reminded herself how she had had no luck making the business prosper either. She could have done more. She could have diversified. She still had dreams of making the shop into something more than just a quaint place to keep products made of paper.

So, when Kimberly moved past the display window with its hardwood seat inset between the bay alcove, with the seat covered in a cheerful yellow cushion and several attractive pillows artfully arranged, she remembered those children who used to come to the shop after school and grab the comic books or magazines or old newspapers and sit on the window seat facing each other and read or giggle softly behind their hands. She remembered the first time she had seen the tableau standing outside on a freezing chill's day and how proud she'd been to come up with the idea. The children sitting on the cushioned window seat were far better advertising than a placard or a bunch of old books gathering dust. When people passed, they saw the children reading and giggling – a living illustration of a nearly extinct pastime.

Nowadays, what made her sad was that fewer children were dropping by to sit and read. She looked over at Clarice running her fingers along the shelf proudly showing her husband the fine dust on the tips of her white gloves. Kimberly shoved her anger aside. She couldn't afford to make a scene. She'd already alienated Clarice, no sense in making her husband mad. With half her mind on the task at hand and the other half aware of the Littles, Kimberly went behind her booth and pulled out the package of maps she had tied together with red ribbon.

Crystova moved toward the counter and leaned forward to eagerly examine the maps, "Excellent. How much do I owe you Kim?"

Kimberly hesitated and Crystova afraid Kimberly would brush off payment whipped out her pocketbook and started pulling seastars out of her coin purse. "Ah, yes, hum," Kimberly had to think fast having anticipated offering the maps to her friend for free. Since Crystova's research of the lost treasures of the Curlecons required her to provide proof of her legitimacy as a historian in the field of medieval Curlecon culture, the university would require proof of her research. A number popped into Kimberly's head. The amount she came up with would be a reasonable sum, "I'll take three grays for everyone, that'll be ten blues and five grays."

"No. These are rare, Kimberly. If I were some random customer, what would your price be?"

As she stared blindly out the window, she did her best to

remain calm. Poverty was a daily humiliation, but she knew her friend's intentions were good. Crystova Moth was the kindest and gentlest of women. "Okay. I'll accept ten seastars for each one. That's five blues."

Crystova handed her a yellow seastar and when Kimberly attempted to hand her back change, Crystova would not accept the money. More than anything else Kimberly hated feeling as if others felt sorry for her. She wasn't homeless, yet, or begging on the street. She had her pride. Before she could retaliate, Crystova moved away from the booth. Kimberly recognized that her old friend was on the hunt for something special. Crystova navigated easily through the cramped aisles. Exuding delight, she rummaged through a pile of papers and Kimberly closed the cash register with more energy than intended.

When the coins rattled around inside the tray everyone but Crystova looked up in surprise. With the change clutched in her hand, Kimberly walked purposely up to Crystova with the intention of thrusting the orange seastar into her friend's hand or coat pocket or wherever she could thrust the money without doing her friend bodily harm. Her friend's long golden-brown hair was her crowning glory. At that precise moment, with a graceful flick of her head, the shining folds of her hair slipped like silk strands across her shoulder. Kimberly approached so swiftly some of Crystova's hair hit her in the face. She backed up and smothered a giggle.

The exchange brought her back to her senses. Her prickly pride seemed silly now. Crystova, immersed in the junk on the sales table wasn't even aware of what happened. When she turned around in the act of showing Adam something in her hand she bumped into Kimberly, "Oh sorry. Didn't see you Kim."

The orange seastar was equivalent to fifty grays. And those fifty grays in one piece of orange paper after being disturbed floated to the ground. Kimberly bent down to retrieve the paper embarrassed. Crystova stepped on the money with the toe of her high-heeled boot then knelt to pick it up. She flattened the crumbled paper then examined both sides.

The front of the paper included the orange seastar with its monetary value printed in all four corners. She flipped the paper to look at the other side. The face of the former ruler of Curl, Justinian the fifth had a place right in the center with smaller images of wolves in the corners. Justinian seemed to be snarling at them. Why would modern day Curlecons want to see such a rogue every day, Kimberly wondered?

"Look what I found," Crystova announced and handed

Kimberly the piece of paper. "Someone must have dropped this on his way out."

"No, that's your change," Kimberly told her trying to thrust the money back into her hand.

Crystova held up another bundle of old maps and asked, "How much for these?"

"Everything on that table is for sale, only one gray each."

At the thought of a sale Crystova's eyes lit up. She turned back to the table searching for more treasures while Kimberly wandered back to the cash register admitting defeat.

While the two women played seastar-shuffle, Adam made his surreptitious way toward the Littles. As Kimberly glanced toward the back of the shop, she saw Adam deliberately bump into Bishop Little and say, "Oh, so deeply sorry old chap, didn't see you there. Interested in old romances, are we? The romancers of the middle ages were outrageous flatterers, now weren't they," Adam struck a theatrical pose reminiscent of the worst of ham actors and began to recite from memory a particularly bad bit of prose. "Your eyes are orbs of love smoldering with untouched fires."

Adam relaxed his pose and laughed, his attitude inviting Bishop Little to join in the joke. Little watched Adam curiously as if Adam represented a creature from the netherworld, perhaps one of those dangerous lovekins who entrapped souls and made them do stupid things. Unlike Adam's easy address and smiling countenance, Bishop Little tended to smile half-heartedly as if he believed breaking out in a genuine smile or showing a lighter side would make people think him weak. After all, he was a man hell bent on sniffing out evil and had no time for frivolous chit-chat.

But Little did something quite unexpected, he broke into a jovial smile and Kimberly had to readjust her opinion of him. He nodded his head as if he now remembered Adam, "We met at the Governor's Ball last season. Yes. You are that professor fellow, the one from down under in that place called Walkmeback."

"Whalesback," Adam corrected him. "Yes. That's me. And what brings you here Bishop Little?"

"Oh, I'm here to assess the value of this shop. I'm thinking of buying it or more precisely the church is thinking of buying this property."

There it was, out in the open, the church's intentions for all to hear and in her presence too. The man had no decency or delicacy for sure. To so casually talk about buying someone's shop, a shop which had been in the family for generations was cruel and stupid. How dare he act as if her livelihood was unimportant compared to his ambitions.

Before Kimberly could order the booby to leave the premises, Adam responded, "So, it's true. You plan to buy up all the shops on this street and turn them into some sort of spiritual retreat for pilgrims. Have you ever considered the possibility that the merchants won't sell?"

"Don't be silly. In these hard-economic times people aren't foolish enough to turn up their noses at money. They'll realize soon enough the real prosperity is down in the valley," Little said coolly as he looked the tiny shop over with a sneer.

Kimberly could no longer contain herself, she marched to the front door and opened it wide listening to the bell chime the alarm, "You see that sign by the door, Delo Little. Read it carefully. This shop belongs to me. I pay taxes on this property and this property has been in my family for six generations, a hell of lot longer than your church by the by. So now I'm telling you to leave my establishment immediately. Pronto, sir. And be warned sir, I will not sell this place to you or anyone else."

The wooden placard on the wall written in gold script read: *This establishment has the right to toss anyone out without notice for any reason what-so-ever, amen.*

The Bishop seemed amused by her fiery attitude. His amusement made her all the madder. He rocked on his heels and nodded his head sagely and said, "I'm sorry you feel this way, but you are under a terrible delusion. The city council has assured me when the new zoning laws go into effect, the shops up and down this street will become part of church property. It is just a matter of time. Don't be foolish, Dela Lemon. If you wait too long, you'll forfeit the compensation we're offering to you and everyone else."

"Get out of my shop. Now," Kimberly said, her voice steady though she could barely hear him because her heart was pounding frantically in her ears. "I mean it. Get out of my shop and that goes for your wife too." She held the door open and stood her ground waiting for them to leave, wondering if he would try to call her bluff. She didn't think the sheriff's deputies would toss the Bishop out.

When Kimberly looked around the shop, she encountered Crystova looking back at her with embarrassment. Suddenly, Kimberly felt an overwhelming sadness. What else could she do? The man was a trench-mouth in robes. Pretend he hadn't threatened her? No. She refused to be bullied.

Adam stepped toward Bishop Little with a forceful air as if he'd been tossing people out of bookshops all his life, "You heard the lady. I suggest you leave or I, as a concerned citizen, will be forced to throw you out."

From the corner of her eye, Kimberly saw Queenie. Queenie was standing by her favorite lanternlight, smoking her morning cigarette, and sipping her morning coffee, all the while watching the drama unfold with relish. She was only a few steps away with front row seats. Kimberly and Bishop Little were the actors on the stage, there for her personal entertainment.

A few merchants, witnesses to the scene appeared shocked. Although, Diane Tumble seemed to be ignoring all the drama, as she swept an already pristine cobblestone in front of Hadal's Delight and ignored her husband Don Tumble as he fussily tried to find the perfect spot for his A-Frame Chalkboard announcing the bargains for the day. The raised voices finally caught Don's attention. He paused in his work to watch the activity across the street with his arms crossed and his brow lowered in worried speculation.

As Kimberly watched the Littles stroll up Merchants' Row with their arms linked as they headed toward the drawbridge, she had a momentary foreboding. He seemed so sure of himself that man, too cocksure for sure. When Harold Zany whistled and gave her the thumbs-up, Kimberly felt a fraction better. She closed the shop door and turned to face the two-remaining people in her home.

Crystova had wandered away from the front door to examine a piece of dubious art, stuffed ravens pinned to a piece of drift wood. The artist had tried to capture a representation of birds in flight but one of them looked as if he were falling off his perch beak first. Kimberly had set the taxidermy on a pedestal near the old alcove. Caleb had found the monstrosity in Greenburg Valley at a street fair.

"Wow, that was a nasty one," Adam said glancing behind him with a lifted brow. "What an obtuse fellow. So now we know what we're up against. I must get back to the university. My students are probably writing each other's essay answers. I promise, Dela Lemon, at the first opportunity, I will speak with my friend and find out what recourse we have. Do not despair. We will find a way."

"Thank you so much Professor Honeysweet. I don't know what I would have done without you."

"You would have done the same whether I had been here or not, I expect. I'm just glad we could be here as moral support," he said, then he turned to search for Crystova. "Ah, I see she's busy with her research. Tell her goodbye for me. Until Saturday then."

At first Kimberly assumed he was trying to ask her out on a date, and then belatedly remembered the Merchants' Row Alliance meeting at Wolf Inn pub. "Oh yes. Thank you for volunteering to help."

"I love a good fight," he said in parting as he swept out the door and up the street, a gust of wind blowing his long hair behind him and the hem of his dark cloak flapping about his heels.

From the recesses of the shop Kimberly heard Crystova say, "How much for this leaflet on the goddesses of old Curlecon?"

"Two grays," Kimberly said absently moving toward the red velvet curtains. "Would you like a cup of tea Crystova? I've got some orange spice on the burner."

Crystova appeared in the cleared space between the cash register and the door. She stared out the bay window at the tight group of four talking earnestly amongst themselves. She looked unhappy. Kimberly had noticed Queenie marching across the street with her cigarette held aloft and Beatrice following close on her heels. They stood with the Tumbles probably gossiping about her and Bishop Little.

She and Crystova didn't need to speak. They had known each other for a long time. Kimberly was familiar with Crystova's distaste for confrontations. Her deep-seated convictions were to be kind to others and avoid unpleasantness. In the past, Kimberly tended to agree, but not under the current climate. These were strained and perilous times. Today the Church of the Holy Centipede had revealed their intentions and threatened her home and livelihood. There was too much at stake now. He'd come into her shop determined to scare her. His wife had probably told him all about what happened at the boutique, exaggerating her part as the innocent victim harassed by bullies, so he decided to confront the little chit who thought she was better than his wife.

Kimberly slipped through the curtains unnoticed and entered her private quarters with the intention of pouring herself and Crystova tea and serving biscuits from the tin. Out of sight of her friend a cold clammy terror settled on her shoulders. She would not lose her shop or her home. She would do whatever she could to keep her home. Shaking with cold and anger, if he had been here, she would have happily wrung Bishop Little's turkey neck.

E1 Shellfargon Year 5092 XGMP WK 1: UES Albion 4
Confirmation: Detective Inspector, Duke Tower Sheriff's Office complete. Visa 5092-5095. E2 assigned to my team. Recent intercept Albion target identified as Gov Saurus. Albion messenger unidentified. Five second delay on message. Arrived successfully to source. Waiting developments. Majority of knights loyal to Delphadorturo. Three potential insurgents at Duke Tower. Motivation may be

profit. Two natives at Wolfern Institute of Technology (WIT) candidates for future Curl version of our ancient Manhattan Project. Authorities unaware. Continuing observation and assessment of the young people.

Chapter 3

Sylvia Paleone, a political and religious rising star in Wolfern Province, with brown hair and large brown eyes, busty and long-legged, every heterosexual male's fantasy (especially with respect to the banality of her mind and conversation) as owner and operator of For the Soul Relics & Religious Treasures called the morning meeting to order. She bent her head reverently and clasped her hands in prayer. Sylvia's store manager, Mary McGirdle sat directly opposite Sylvia with her elbows resting on the table and her hands clasped, not for prayerful show, so much as a way of propping up her tired shoulders and alleviating the creak in her neck. It was a simple step from positioning herself for comfort's sake to positioning herself for the morning office ritual of thanking the great and Holy Centipede for their continued prosperity.

Mary McGirdle closed her eyes against the harsh light spewing forth white heat from the decrepit old overhead projector which happened to be directly in her line of sight. She strained to hear Sylvia's blessing over the ominous croaks emanating from the projector. Even though she had heard this particular blessing every morning for the last three years, Mary was concerned she might miss something important because sometimes Sylvia would add a special request to the morning-prayer.

Mary was not disappointed. Just as Sylvia finished the routine prayer and added "and great holy one would you please," all the while with Mary McGirdle and the part-time clerk Joanie Fitzhammond straining to hear and anxious to know Sylvia's intentions for the day, since they were expected to do everything in their power to make her prayers come true, they were preoccupied and therefore startled when the door flew open and bounced against the opposite wall. Luella Morrison, a rotund mole of a woman with large red-framed glasses perched precariously on her long pointy nose stumbled into the room apologizing, "I am so sorry, everyone especially you Sylvia. So very, very, sorry. I know I'm late and I'm prepared to do penance for my sin. Please forgive me" and with obsequious urgency plopped herself down on a stool in the corner and bowed her head.

When her heart returned to its normal rhythm, Mary rested her clasped hands against her forehead feeling the veins throbbing just beneath the surface. Garl-damn-tit to every lov'n shit-swats, she thought to herself. Sylvia went nuclear when anyone interrupted her or had the bad taste to ask impromptu questions for which she didn't know the answer. What really stoked Sylvia's shit-hole was people making a fool of her, even if she was responsible for making herself look like a fool. Mary sniffed the air.

Something else was wrong. What was it now? Barely perceptible came a sucking back down the throat of what might have become a full-fledged giggle. Oh, Centipede and his one hundred wives. Mary stiffened, suddenly afraid she might have spoken the words aloud. If Sylvia had heard her invocation, if she thought for one moment Mary was a heretic, Mary would be out the door so fast her false teeth would fly out of her mouth. And most definitely, she would be left without so much as a tinpiece and maybe even run out of town in a fast wagon to nowhere with a nice doorknob-shaped tattoo embedded on her left cheek as a going away present.

Yes, Sylvia Paleone had a few flaws, but she could be a good boss at times and did in fact pay Mary well and even gave her bonuses on the Day of Ascension. And above all else, Sylvia was the embodiment of the church's ideal — she was a faithful wife, a protective mother, and a believer. Most important of all, more important perhaps than all of Sylvia's other virtues must be her undeniable prettiness. It was an unconditional truth that beauty was a sign of the Holy Centipede's favor. Was it not true, Chuck the prophet, had been an extremely handsome young man when the Holy Centipede visited him the first time and announced his four edicts upon the people? Yes indeed. Mary suspected Luella's passion for the church sprung from her secret desire to be granted one important wish — beauty, not beauty in the Holy Centipede sense of beautiful soul, no, Luella's desire was that the Holy Centipede bestow physical beauty on her. Poor thing.

"Sit down Luella. Quickly please. Time is short. Now then, I will start again," Sylvia announced. Mary could hear the suppressed rage trembling in Sylvia's throat. "Oh, great and good Centipede, we thank you for this day's bounty and pray that others less fortunate will seek out your goodness and mercy. It is our profoundest hope unbelievers will come to accept you as their one true divine protector and choose your path to righteousness. Thank you sweet one for your continued benevolence which shines down on us.

And great holy one, would you please shine your light into the dark heart of Kimberly Lemon. Please bring her the blessings of your love. She is in dire need of salvation. Bless you and your children and your sainted wives."

The women sat with their shoulders forward, their hands clasped in prayer and bowed the requisite three times to honor the Holy Centipede, his one-hundred wives, and his two-thousand children. Joanie was the first to jump up from the table moving with speed toward the door and the fresh air beyond, well, fresher than inside the hot stuffy inner offices of Sylvia's world. At least in the shop, Joanie remembered she needed the money desperately; and even her wretched part-time employment meant she could pay rent and feed herself at least three out of the four weeks of the month.

Jobs were scarce these days and the lovely job she had had in Ork working as a copywriter for Muffet and Toomie had been heaven compared to the drudgery she experienced here at For the Soul Relics. Ironic how a place catering to trinkets honoring a silly Centipede conjured up by a handsome charismatic fool could be so soul-crushing an experience for Joanie. Mary, on the other hand, loved her job and loved every little shiny object and every delusional customer who came into the shop.

Unlike the others, Joanie considered the whole morning ritual a repugnant necessity and Mary McGirdle's obsequiousness to the wishes of Sylvia a sad commentary on the state of affairs in the world at large. Greed at the top of the capitalist food chain had created inequality for thousands of average people and greed had also contributed to a growing religious fanaticism. As if the world weren't crazy enough already, new religions were springing up right and left and up and down, depending on your perspective, while people were slavishly following these tyrannical religions to such insane ends, hundreds of converts accepted the most bizarre of revelations and predictions.

The World Enders were the most prolific of religious movements having been around for centuries even before the NeverEnding War began eighty years ago. They insisted the government of Curl build spaceships and explore new plancts, because the sun would turn supernova any day now and when the sun did explode everyone on Shellfargon would end up a pile of ash. The World-Enders seemed rational compared to the newest religions. Even though scientists assured Curlecons the sun would not go supernova any time soon. When they admitted the sun would eventually die out in three billion years, the news validated World Enders position.

As Joanie prepared for the day, thinking: shit, three billion years is a fucking long time and I feel like I've been working in this hell-hole for three billion years, she forced herself to begin the onerous job of dusting the religious objects on the shelves and the tabletops. With her mind free to roam, she ignored the fearsome unknown and kept her sights on the past. As a child, she had loved to read about history, about the Curlecon Civil War nearly three-hundred years ago.

The southern half of the country of Curl had become bitter enemies of the women's movement. They believed women were already cherished and had all the rights they needed. They thought talk about giving women the vote and allowing women to leave their husbands was blasphemous and an abomination against the Great and Glorious Delph. In the south, women were considered children, their brains were thought to be too small and reptilian to be of any use in the outside world. Women were only good for breeding future Curlecons or washing dishes.

Southern Delphinid males believed women were frivolous irrational creatures and especially dangerous to society if not controlled by a strong male. Northerners, on the other hand, were beginning to realize women were capable of doing many things, according to examiners women really did have bigger brains then convention claimed. After a series of tests which took decades, the medical and scientific community concluded women did have brains and were capable of intelligent thought – with a caveat. If inebriated or sick women lost brain cells and never grew them back. When women demanded a comparison test be done on men, the government stopped funding the programs.

Some women even had the imagination to invent new useful everyday machines which benefited the north and gave birth to the Industrial Age. Women had a few significant figures in history to thank for their status as semi-equal citizens – one of them being Noble Coral considered a literary genius and called the Peerless Singer of Nova. Also included in this limited and exotic collection of female intellectuals was Guillioma Clickmellow whose theories about the universe continued to prove useful.

Then came the collaborator of the portable communication device referred to a few years back as PCD which now everyone calls a cellphone offered by UES Albion for sale and improved upon by Guillioma Clickmellow for Curlecons and Vespas. Someday Joanie hoped Barbara Crusthammer could prove to the world Shellfargon wasn't some gigantic eggshell too delicate to puncture. When that day dawned inventors could use the starship's databanks to build an infrastructure and method of travel other than smelly seahorses, bumpy, equally smelly wagons, or overcrowded steam-powered railroad carriages.

Three hundred years ago during the Curlecon Civil War, men killed men so that half the world's population would remain subservient to the other. The North won yet women remained slaves only permitted to vote if their husbands signed a declaration of emancipation while men voted in local elections every year and chose the Delphadorturo and Supreme Commander every eight years. Just eighty years ago, women were still fighting to receive equal rights under the constitution: the right to equal pay, the right to raise their children without the interference of Delphi males and the right to own their own businesses. Then Frank Velt came along as the thirty-fourth Delphadorturo and persuaded Curlecons to allow women to own their own businesses.

Thousands of female entrepreneurs began applying for business loans all over Curlecon. For years now, men were proven wrong (at least in the north) because the south refused to accept women entrepreneurs. Joanie suspected the rise of this new religion was in response to women entrepreneurs, a means by which men hoped to set back the clock by brainwashing women into joining the Church of the Holy Centipede in order to take away their independence.

Joanie imagined herself a northern soldier dressed in green fighting eye to eye with those silver bellies of the south. She pictured herself and Mary McGirdle with bayonets pointed at each other, she would be wearing the green and gold jacket and the white pantaloons of the north and Mary, of course, would be dressed in the colors of her beloved south and Joanie would aim her bayonet at Mary McGirdle's middle, the most conspicuous and largest part of Mary and just before plunging the bayonet into Mary's soft belly, Mary would step back and say, "This here is foolishness. I have no quarrel with the likes of you."

And Joanie imagined herself saying, "Perhaps you don't. But I take exception to your way of life. I take exception to meat cooked in its own fat, your smearing of the Curlecon language into something alien and misleading, your repetitive dull music, and most importantly, your obsession over living in the past. What's so great about the founding fathers? They were a bunch of stinky gray backs who treated women like children. There is nothing honorable about the old south or those old farts. So, get over yourself and start living in the present."

Of course, knowing Mary and her passion for all things southern, the fight would resume. And because Joanie, a newly converted pacifist could see herself all bloody from numerous wounds dying in agony on the battlefield and Mary moving on to her next target realized she'd be wasting her breath. Confiding in Mary or appealing to her better nature was useless. Frantically, Joanie tried to think of something more cheerful, something pleasant like visiting her sons in the east and her grandchildren. But thinking about her sons reminded her of the painful fact they had little in common with each other.

Once a year she would hear from them and usually the conversation lasted a mere fifteen minutes, at least fifteen if she asked questions, otherwise, the conversation ended within five and there would be the usual excuses to end the conversation due to time constraints. For years she blamed herself, she'd chosen the military as a vocation and her job required her to travel. After her husband left her, her family took over the raising of her sons.

Yet on furloughs they seemed happy to see her. Maybe they'd been pretending. She must have been a frightful mother to have raised sons so selfish and cold. It only dawned on her recently that without their father beside her giving her respectability, they had no reason to talk to her. She was just a dumb animal who happened to have given birth to them, whereas, their father had been a supreme being endowed with strength and cunning and joie de vivre.

Oh. If only she had had girls. She would have given anything to have had a parcel of daughters like Mary McGirdle. It just didn't seem fair that someone like Mary McGirdle with all her foolish talk and southern snobbery would have the good-fortune to have such loving thoughtful children. When she realized she was fast becoming maudlin, Joanie brushed away the tide of self-pity threatening to drown her.

She turned her thoughts to the book waiting for her at home. It was the newest novel by P.D. Picture, a historical piece of fiction set in the dawn of the NeverEnding War. It had received three prizes for its writing style, historical accuracy, and compelling insight. Joanie couldn't wait to get home and climb into her comfy sweats with her favorite hot tea by her side and sit before the burping coal stove reading P.D. Picture's latest masterpiece.

As Joanie Fitzhammond imagined a tableau of herself this evening in her tiny flat in the attic above Wolfern Promenade sitting in her favorite rocking chair with its well-padded cushions protecting her bottom and backside, wearing her comfortable sweats and bright yellow bathrobe, with a cup of steaming orange and green tea at her side, she shivered in anticipation.

Above her shoulder would be her casement window with a breathtaking view of the castle ramparts, turrets, and Duke Tower. And on such a cold fallow night, there would be a moon in the sky turning the black sky white and a series of blue-lights twinkling inside the Governor's suite, and she would be all cozy and warm from the little iron coal stove in the corner of her room. Beyond her rocking chair would be her cot and nightstand and, on the nightstand, would be her green lamp and from the lamp there would be the pale glow of a dim glowworm bulb lighting the pages of P.D. Picture's latest masterpiece.

As she sipped her tea and turned the pages of her book, she would know that below her tiny flat was Harry Hanson's local publishing firm, the Shellfargon Seed, a weekly news magazine in which Harry Hanson pumped out articles and editorials during the daylight hours. His pieces were sometimes honest enough to annoy the Governor but sadly tended to be cruel barbs at local people who had offended Harry for not recognizing his literary talents. Lately though, Joanie had noticed a change in the magazine. There were much more frivolous pieces and less criticism of local authorities especially Governor Roger Saurus.

Secretly, Joanie had been writing articles of her own. She kept them locked away and wondered when she'd have the courage to present them to Harry. Under her present circumstances, Joanie couldn't afford to antagonize her employer. If Sylvia were to discover the source of the incendiary articles Joanie would most assuredly lose her menial and mind-numbing job.

Yes, her menial and mind-numbing job. Well, maybe she should say her job was laboriously boring. She had very few serious responsibilities beyond cleaning the floors, polishing the brass, dusting the fake relics and arranging them to best advantage in their glass cases. But on occasion, there were moments of excitement, especially when Mary had to run an errand for Sylvia. Her job improved several degrees when Mary assigned her cashiering duties or the delivery of a package to a bedridden Church of Holy Centipede member. It was pure bliss when Joanie could get away for a few precious minutes.

And just as Joanie heard the swift tread of Mary's feet on the tiled floor and turned with the dust mop clutched in her hand, Mary McGirdle moved to the shop doors to sweep them open. Joanie's throat tightened in self-loathing when she recognized she was being a catty, small-minded woman today. Mary had given her this job when no one else would. She and Mary came from military families. They shared a history together as sisters-in-law. Their husbands had been twins and as twins they had been very close.

When Mary's husband Brian got the crazy idea in his head to fight alongside the Sea Serpents in proxy for Curl, Brent, even though he should have known better just had to follow him. Her husband Brent had chosen to go along with his brother not for patriotic reasons or religious reasons but to protect Brian from his own recklessness. They had already fulfilled their five-year tour of duty. This time, in their late twenties with young children at home, the men had chosen to reenlist for altogether different reasons, wildly ludicrous reasons.

No Curlecon had ever seen real combat. The Sea Serpents fought the NeverEnding War in proxy for both the Delphinids and the Lacertidae. But Brian had gotten the lamebrain idea into his crazy head the only way to finally win the war was for a Delphinid to man the bowriders.

For the last ten years, Joanie's thoughts continued to play and replay the fight between her and her husband. She had done everything she could to persuade him to stay home. He had ignored her arguments. It was revelatory when she finally figured out her husband loved his brother more than his wife and children. The boys considered Brent a hero and thought of their mother as a traitor for choosing a different branch of the service.

Throughout their marriage, Joanie had insisted on keeping her maiden name. It was only after her husband was reported missing in action, presumed dead, that she hyphenated her name. But when Mary McGirdle offered her the job at For the Soul Relics and Religious Treasures, Joanie dropped the McGirdle knowing full well Sylvia disliked favoritism even though she promoted favoritism in her own life.

The McGirdle family had shared holidays and birthdays and special occasions together. They had been a family for fourteen years and even though Joanie found excuses not to attend future family gatherings after Brent's death, these days, Joanie was forced to acknowledge, without Mary, she'd be in some serious shit. Mary also treated her like family even though Joanie had been away for so many years on special assignments.

Unlike Sylvia Paleone who treated everyone as brain dead, Mary had a big heart and when Sylvia was absent from the shop, Mary would talk to Joanie and Luella with her usual artless exuberance. Mary loved to gossip, and Luella was an avid audience member. There were days though when Joanie missed her old job. She'd been paid a lot, paid for the risky work she did. Today, her savings were gone, and her military benefits cancelled, reduced to subsist on a tiny pittance Sylvia Paleone called a living wage.

Mary could be annoying, especially when she regurgitated Sylvia's stupid thoughts. Yet she was also family and had stood by her during some dark times. After reaching this revelation, Joanie felt like being charitable and do her best to recognize the little kindnesses in life – for kindnesses were truly few and far between these days. So, when Mary McGirdle turned, and saw Joanie's face, Joanie realized Mary's blush had something to do with Joanie's expression. Joanie had to conclude her recent thoughts were reciprocated in the contours of Mary's affectionate smile. It was a good way to start the day, much better than praying to an imaginary centipede.

At the opposite end of the castle proper, Antonio Furness prepared his small staff for the coming day with the usual instructions: keep the customer happy and thereby keep your job. As he looked at his crew languishing about the place as if they had recently rolled out of bed with their mutual expressions suggesting to the public they would prefer to slip back under the covers, Antonio sighed. He couldn't do much about their attitude – but. He scrutinized his waitstaff carefully finding fault with Angelina's wrinkled blouse and Daniel's baggy pants, neither of them conforming to his specific instructions.

Blouses must be tight and skirts short. Shirts and pants must be tight, the form-hugging the better. He had been perfectly clear about his dress code to the new hires, all staff signed waivers agreeing to abide by his instructions. Yet Angelina and Daniel continued to flaunt café dress code as well as policies and procedures. Rebels my ass, just because they were the best-looking ones, they thought they could be insubordinate.

With his black hair tied severely back in a ponytail in a dark ribbon made of wire and silk and his body clad in his habitual style, chic and manly: a midnight blue sweater, elegant gray trousers which accentuated his height and physique, and the usual calf skin boots with the extra inch of heel, one of those peculiarly androgynous items of clothing which either gender might enjoy wearing, the toe especially, so pointed, now pointed to the ceiling as Antonio perched himself or more accurately posed himself with exaggerated ease on one of the red leather stools along the coffee bar, Antonio knew himself to be the most exotic of the specimens in the room.

The knowledge of his extraordinary sensuality always gave him a thrill. He kept his body in perfect condition, lean and muscular, his face freshly shaved every day, his skin preserved over the years by careful exfoliation and masturbation. But what set him apart from all the other sensual males was his boldness in flaunting his one and only weakness, a slight case of myopia. He had a new pair of eyeglasses for every day of the week and today he wore his favorite silver framed eyeglasses which made his hazel eyes pop.

He knew by combining a lean physique, beautiful hair, and

stylish eyeglasses he presented the epitome of the modern man: handsome, athletic, and intellectual. He had noted with some pride how women would give Daniel Rottweiler the once over and he, Antonio Furness, not one, but two or three backward looks. Years ago, he had recognized how women were more likely to appreciate a combination of sensuality, good looks, and intellectualism over mere beauty.

Antonio having spent his miserable youth watching lesser males snatch the best females for themselves, eventually grew out of his pimply, toneless, and average body into the unique specimen he commanded today – but – at a price. The girls he had known in school had more often than naught mocked him to his face or shown their disgust in other ways. Hiding in bookstores or in his room or in the back seat of the class had become a habit with him, up until the last part of his schooling when he grew more than six inches and his voice changed dramatically from a squeaky soprano to a baritone.

The most transformational moment came when he stepped into that fashionable men's store before graduation day and the clerk sauntered up to him giving him an appreciative up and down eye and said, "My, my, aren't you a long drink of water." Unfortunately, Antonio Furness' first love Lucidana, whom he loved in secret with a furious passion was never privy to the astonishing transformation of his body.

After Antonio's father refused to kill the local game – a Hairy Horned Hog, his father's career as a Lieutenant Governor of Walrat Island ended and the family had to settle in Blueglennen to escape embarrassment. And really, what did Lucidana matter now, when he could have his pick of females at this time in his life. She was probably plump and red faced with a litter of children clutching her skirts. No never mind, he shrugged, her loss.

Antonio had been up since dawn in anticipation of the long crowds queuing up for their morning wake-up drink and sugar high in the form of his delectable pastries. His staff, on the other hand, mostly good-looking students from the university straggled in one by one and propped themselves on any available surface before the morning rush, girding themselves for the usual long speech reminiscent of Fidel Hasbro, the chancellor of Duke Tower University, in length, dullness, and repetition.

Daniel Rottweiler listened with half an ear to Antonio's boring morning sermons, his real concern finishing a ten-page analysis of Coral's Tragedies. Unlike Sylvia Paleone's sermons, Antonio's sermons were borrowed from the greatest lover in history Charley Silver Surfer, the most daring of lovers and aficionados of good-taste, especially good-taste in clothes, women, and food. Daniel could have cared less about how to seduce seastar out of an unsuspecting customer. He had more important concerns – how to stay in his dorm room without strangling his roommate and how to pass Coral's Tragedies without failing the rigorous and stimulating philosophy class of Dr. Zalinka.

In the other room a high-pitched scream of pain pierced the night. There was a brief scuffle, a chair overturned, a groan followed by a whimper then the man began to sob. Victoria recognized Scotty's mad laughter. Victoria bored with the whole procedure (no one was paying any attention to her anymore) had wandered into the back part of the armpit of an apartment and after careful examination of the bathroom, no bigger than an elevator, and the bathroom's porcelain sink and stained and torn countertop, noting that the surface was relatively clean proceeded to prop her hip on the edge of the counter and lean toward the smudged glass of the bathroom mirror. With delight she surveyed her blonde hair cascading in perfect ringlets down her back then moved in closer to appreciate her new ripe cherry lipstick. With horror she drew back from the mirror. No fucking way.

With a sick feeling in her stomach, she leaned in closer and scrutinized a spot on the tip of her nose. Her mumbled "fuck" was drowned out by another piercing scream from the occupant of this tasteless, stupid apartment. The feeble light from the single bare bulb above the mirror left the contours of her face in shadow but the zit, the fucking-pus-filled-putrid zit seemed to grow and grow as she turned her head one way and then the other. The dark hallway echoed with fists meeting flesh and the bubbling wet screams turned to feeble moans.

The sounds seemed to cling to the shit colored papered walls all around her. Victoria mumbled "idiot" under her breath before returning to her most pressing problem. Her irritation with Scotty grew as did the zit. She would have to rid herself of both. On the other side of the bathroom wall, a body was hurled, and the medicine cabinet shivered in sympathy. Victoria threw the door open and stood on the threshold glaring at Scotty. She ignored the mess on the floor near her right foot. "Is this really necessary? Now? Just shoot him or something. I'm tired of the noise."

Scotty whose face was red with exaltation (he really loved his work) and exertion (he wasn't getting any younger) paused to stare at her absently, then scowled, "Get the fuck back in the bathroom or put some fucking clothes on."

"Who's going to notice?" she shot back. "You're the only one able to see me. His eyes are swollen shut. He's probably dead. I'm sure he's dead."

"Let me do my job, Vicky. You mind?"

Victoria stepped back into the bathroom with a shrug. Dumb ass, she thought to herself. She stared at her naked image in the mirror and smiled. An idea was coming to her.

Victoria spent the better part of the afternoon cleaning up after Scotty while Scotty took his problem to the other side of town. She had come prepared with enough plastic gloves and cleaning liquids to do an entire hotel. The dead guy's home had been the only occupied apartment left in the building. He had been one of the stubborn ones, refusing to accept the money the landlord offered if he moved out the same day. So, Scotty had been hired to persuade him to leave. Unfortunately, Scotty loved his work too much and now they had to cover their tracks, hide the body, and leave town.

Victoria had persuaded Scotty to stay one more night in town. She chose a swanky hotel, convincing him no one would look for them in such a fine place. The guards were probably searching the train station or asking coachmen if they had been seen in the vicinity. After all, Scotty had made a lot of noise and there must have been a few curious neighbors wondering what was going on across the street. No one called the knights though. No one even bothered to shout out for Scotty to stop beating the guy.

Now, after having had some peace and quiet in order to think, Victoria Lemon pulled on a new pair of plastic gloves and surveyed the hotel room with a practiced eye. The idea had come to her while in the shower. Scotty was a clinger. He would follow her to the ends of the earth and never give her any peace. She hated clingers. Her plan was brilliant and without a moment's reflection, she stepped out of the tub with her shower cap still protecting her blonde ringlets, her plump naked body still wet from the spray and marched into the adjoining room where Scotty lay sleeping.

With her wet washcloth still clutched in her hand she wrung the excess water out onto Scotty's bare back. Not so much as a twitch. She was not surprised having watched with disdain mixed with revulsion as Scotty spent the rest of the night finishing off the expensive whiskey his boss had given him, followed by early morning hours of noisy and nasty barfing. His favorite tools were still in his open black leather valise. She chose one of the smaller knives, one she knew he had recently sterilized.

Now where the fucking hell was his heart? Annoyed she hadn't paid more attention in anatomy class she tried to imagine where his heart might be. She couldn't remember dissection, only high school assembly and standing before the Curlecon flag with her hand over her heart making up her own words. She giggled remembering her limerick. Stop that, no time for reminiscing, time to get down to business.

If Scotty lay on his back his heart would be on her right. Since he was laying on his stomach his heart must be on her left. As she bent over him, his nasty breath struck her in the face and made her want to gag. She sucked in air and with both hands plunged the knife between his shoulder blades. She knew she could never penetrate through bone. A gun with a silencer would have been perfect right about now. Scotty's body jerked once. Desperate to finish the job, Victoria began stabbing and stabbing and stabbing until she was sure he was good and dead.

Once she stepped back into the shower, she nearly screamed at the cascade of icy cold water hitting her breasts and stomach like a thousand sharp needles. She forced herself to stand under the faucet until all the blood had spilled down the drain. And here she was again, twenty minutes later wearing only the plastic gloves she used to color her hair and searching the room with the intention of wiping away all evidence of her existence. The night clerk had been asleep behind the counter when she and Scotty entered the hotel lobby.

And Scotty had been drunk. She had been forced to drag him toward the elevator and pinch him to keep him awake long enough to get to their hotel room. No one had seen them go up or enter the room together. The room was in Scotty's name and Scotty had used a stolen credit card. All she had to do was clean her prints off anything she'd touched.

When she heard the maid tap on the door across the hall, a thrill cascaded from the top of her head down to her toes. The idea she might get caught made her wet with excitement. She stood still and allowed the orgasm to flow over her. In the afterglow, she paused to appreciate the moment. Victoria could barely distinguish the words between the occupant of the hotel room across the hall and the maid. From the thump and rattle of the maid's cart and the maid's voice receding as she entered the room across the hall, Victoria guessed she probably had another fifteen minutes before the maid knocked on Scott's door to deliver fresh towels and make his bed.

With five minutes to spare, Victoria opened Scotty's hotel room door with her hair covered by her hood, her blue silk evening dress hidden by her ankle length chill coat. She trotted down the hall toward the service elevator carrying her overnight case. She met no one in the elevator or in the lobby. She heard the clink of glasses and silverware as the hotel personnel prepared the swanky tables in the dining room for the business lunch crowd. Scotty's choice of hotel failed to impress her. After last night his male bravado and posturing had been a real turn off. He had reminded her of a dumb thug in one of those bad mafia movies. Where were all the real men? She had yet to find anyone worth keeping.

The last ten years had gotten tougher and tougher for her. In the past, when she was still young and firm, she could seduce a guy real-easy and even if she wasn't his type, she knew how to give the best and longest blowjobs in history, well, according to the last jerk she had opened her mouth for, she had been the best. Times were tough. She figured she had a few good years left. Ignoring the honest voice which knew Scotty chose her because he was a bedwetting drunk and blind to a few extra pounds and a few extra years, Victoria headed toward the train station.

As she climbed into a private berth which would take her north, she had a moment of regret. She brushed the regret and the flutter of panic in her gut aside and concentrated on what she knew — men were fucking idiots, smelly, noisy and worst of all infantile. She was better off without them. There were other ways to make a million. She reread Antonio Furness' email and smiled.

Read your blog about those godless traitors who want everyone to kiss the Lizard Lips and get equal pay and equal rights and how they should be thrown out of the country and dumped in the swamps of New Dala. You've got Paleone excited. She and the Bishop are ready to anoint you into the church's mysteries for Centipede's Sake. Holy Children! Everyone's talking about Sour Lemon and her mad talk. Hear about Merchants' Row and the church's plans to turn the shops into sanctuaries for the pilgrims? Better talk to your niece. She's being stubborn and stupid.

Furness had been such a pig back in the day, skinny, pimply, with his thick ugly glasses and quivering voice. Even at twelve, she had known she could wrap that slug around her pussy without any trouble at all. He had spent plenty of money convincing her he was the greatest lover of all. Butthole. She had known he'd had a crush on her niece Kimberly and with a few lies and some manipulation managed to convince him Kimberly thought he was too repulsive for her finicky tastes. Furness pretended not to care but Victoria was no fool, even now she could read between the lines, especially the part about "better talk to your niece." Was he nuts? Victoria had a better idea how to get rid of her niece.

Kimberly Lemon threw back the bolt on her shop door and stepped out on the cobbled street to breathe in the morning air. She tried to catch Diane Tumble's eye. As usual, Diane was in too much of a passion to stop sweeping and pay attention to people and her immediate surroundings. With renewed energy Diane swept the clean cobbled street in front of her shop as if an army of loathsome bugs were attempting to infiltrate her sterile, overpriced shop.

Turning her back on the brown gothic façade of the Cathedral of the Holy Centipede Kimberly looked down Merchants' Row enjoying the familiarity of the shops and the shop owners: Zany's Music, the diner, the launderette, the child center, and the pet store. The only shop no longer resembling the shop of Kimberly's youth stood at the end of the row closest to the promenade and Harry Hanson's newspaper business. Unique Boutique looked too fancy for the row.

Though she tried to ignore the cathedral behind her, Kimberly's guppy brain circled back to it. Several thousand years ago, according to her grandfather, most Curlecons worshipped the divine god Muibo, Lord of the Elements. Her grandfather's grandfather had been a Muibonite until the Duke fled Blueglennen and the pagan worshipers returned, worshipers like Don Tumble's ancestors who believed in the god of the ocean's underworld Hadal. During the Religious Wars, former worshippers of Muibo were burned at the stake, and Hadal worshippers were tortured. All seemed hopeless until religious leaders came together from each religious sect asking the princelings in the east to intervene and pass laws permitting Curlecons to worship the god of their choice without fear of punishment.

When she was a child the cathedral had been an inspiration for her. She had loved to step out on the stoop and look to the north at the old place. Yes. It had been a haunted place, full of mystery and possibility. The ghoul in her imagined monsters lurking inside. Mostly she just wished someone would turn the beautiful place into a fancy hotel. If she had had the money, she would have created a museum downstairs, and in the priest rooms she would have fancy overnight places for rich people. The cathedral had been neglected for nearly a decade, after the last priest of the old religion had died and the cathedral had been sealed up and left abandoned. Then Bishop Little showed up and nothing was the same.

When Kimberly heard someone hailing her, she spun around

to watch as her friend Professor Moth hurried toward her, her long shiny brown hair flying behind her. As usual, Crystova had an intricately designed fashionable handbag slung over her shoulder and Kimberly suspected the contents included a plethora of papers to be graded or notebooks or special research documents. On her other shoulder, she carried a smaller purse where she kept her personal belongings. Around her neck she wore a silk scarf, a wildly attractive scarf in multiple colors which accentuated her lovely hair.

Kimberly waited patiently for Crystova to reach her and when Crystova thrust her coffee mug in Kimberly's hands, Kimberly waited patiently for Crystova to drag something out of her handbag. "We must talk Kim. I've discovered – wait, not out here," Crystova caught herself and looked around fervently as if she expected spies on every corner. It was still early and most of the shops had yet to open. Diane Tumble had already swept her front stoop spotless and reentered Hadal's Delight. There was no reason for Crystova's extraordinary behavior.

Crystova brushed past Kimberly and swept into the shop dropping her heavy handbag gratefully on the window seat, then her jacket and gloves followed. Only after Kimberly shut the shop door did she announce, "If I'm right, this find will be a historic moment in Curlecon history. And I suspect," she paused looking at the walls of the shop with intense interest.

It was a good thing she'd known Crystova most of her life otherwise she might have wondered if Crystova was having a nervous breakdown. Her eyes were brilliantly lit from some intense intellectual gyrations, the excitement making her pale skin rosy. Kimberly could hardly stand the suspense, "What Crystova? What do you suspect?"

She looked at Kimberly and said as calmly as possible, "I think I know where the illuminated manuscripts of the first peoples of Curlecon are hidden."

"What? I'm sorry. I don't follow."

Plopping herself down on the window seat, Crystova dug through her handbag. When Kimberly realized she was still holding Crystova's coffee mug with the black stenciled imprint of Antonio's Café artfully drawn on the silver surface, she set the mug down on the counter more worried about the state of Crystova's mind than whether the coffee might spill over her accounting books. When Crystova continued to dig into the cavernous innards of her handbag, Kimberly eyed the mug nervously and finally unable to help herself moved the mug to the end of the counter, so that if its contents spilled, the coffee would fall onto the dry worn floorboards rather than her accounting books or her special collection shelved on the other side.

"Ah ha, here we go," Crystova said behind her. Kimberly turned in time to see Crystova unroll a mildewed parchment yellow from age, rather thin, the back covered in sheepskin. "You won't believe what I found in Lucie's pawn shop. I still can't believe my good luck. It cost me just one yellow."

"You mean lecherous Lucie?"

"Why do you call him that?" Crystova asked absently. "He's always been a perfect gentleman around me."

"Ask Sophia some time. Or Alexandra. Or. Never mind. A yellow seastar for that, ah, thing. That's still a lot of money," Kimberly said as she stared in horror at a lump of greenish goo, something undefinable but nasty on the skin side of the parchment. "You could buy an Albion cellphone and still have change left for a movie and dinner."

"He had no idea," she said setting the parchment tenderly on the empty seat beside her. Kimberly wanted to cry at the sight of the mildewing object resting on her lovely window cushion.

"I asked him where he found it and he claimed a guy from Old Town found it in the dump. I know I should have been honest with him. It's just. All I had was a yellow. I didn't want to walk away without taking it home with me. You understand?"

"Crystova, are you seriously feeling bad about finding a bargain in Lucie's pawn shop? His stuff is overpriced junk. It's about time someone got one over on him."

Even Kimberly knew the parchment came from a much later period, certainly not the founding of Blueglennen which according to archeologists and historians took place a thousand years ago. Nothing short of stone or precious metal would have survived in the country of Curl because the first Curlecons were a nomadic people with no known written or symbolic language.

Anticipating Kimberly's inner thoughts Crystova said, "For years I've believed the first peoples were sophisticated enough to have constructed their own written language. And when Eric Fontaine wrote his groundbreaking work on the evolutionary nature of our species, as well as the Lacertidae, which even now our government suppresses as heretical, I have often questioned the Lacertidae insistence their ancestors were the only civilized communities rich with written language, art and monuments.

I've often wondered if Fontaine spread the lies about our backwardness. The Lacertidae have such beautiful poetry and gorgeous gardens. It doesn't make sense that they would accuse us of being barbarians. Remember the one about our ancestors and their grooming habits and how they grunted their way toward communication while Lacertidae were building monuments and creating language and memorializing their achievements on stone tablets."

"I've never taken the Lacertidae boasts as fact," Kimberly said placing herself behind the counter safely in her nook with the wall at her back and the counter separating her from the customers. "Our ancestors were just as civilized as theirs, the only difference between us is the way we worship Shellfargon. We have always believed in preserving our planet for future generations. The Lacertidae from early on had no such reservations.

Look at what they used to do – they buried their queens hundreds of feet underground in fancy tombs. They built and still build monstrous skyscrapers which block out the sun. They blow up mountains and dig craters to mine for minerals. We don't do those things. We don't do them because we have always followed the word of the Holy Delph. I know, very few people buy into the Holy Delph anymore. Yet, he was right about Shellfargon. Shellfargon is too precious to be gutted like a fish."

The discussion was intriguing and if Kimberly had more time, she'd be eager to listen, yet her thoughts kept returning to the pile of bills in her drawer. Even though she was distracted by money worries, she detected a note of admiration in Crystova's voice when she talked about Lacertidae language, art, and monuments. Were the Lacertidae superior to Delphinids?

The disappointment in Kimberly's voice must have registered with Crystova at last. Crystova lifted her eyes from the parchment and looked directly at her, "Do you think I'm a traitor because I admire Lacertidae architecture and language? That's silly. Appreciating another culture isn't a sign I'm a foreign agent. If that were true, then all delphi who watch Albion movies or listen to their music are traitors.

Maybe we've never built gigantic monuments to dead queens, but our culture has a long and rich history. Our history has been passed down through the centuries orally in songs and stories. Unfortunately, if you've ever noticed how gossip spreads, you've probably noticed the story changes a lot by the time it reaches the last person. So, what's wrong with me wanting to find evidence ancient delphinids carved songs in stone or wrote poems on a tablet?"

"Nothing. But if no one has been able to find anything in the last two hundred years what makes you think you can?" Kimberly asked fed up with fanaticism in all its forms, even academic fanaticism.

Kimberly stabbed the parchment in her lap and said, "Because Duke Dono mentions in this paper his ancestors built the castle walls, the great hall, the tower and the bailey on top of an ancient mound overlooking the Siren River, which many historians believe is where an ancient temple stood, a temple erected by the first people of Wolfern Province. He had his stonemasons start at the outer wall of the ancient temple, shore up the wall with mortar. It even mentions where. It's the wall overlooking the river.

That wall is where the Cathedral of the Holy Centipede stands and. Well, this is just conjecture at this point. Part of your wall might be even older than the castle.

You see, when they began the other half of the wall, they went to Old Town and dug out more stone for the remaining three walls. And I suspect inside the walls of this shop are where we will find proof the first peoples of Curlecon developed a written language around the same time as the Lacertidae queens. If I find a stone tablet or parchment with ancient writing, I'll be able to prove whether our oral history is accurate."

Neither of them had noticed Valcinda Moorland and Caleb Lanternlighter outside the Bookworm Emporium. Caleb had propped a ladder against the shop wall right next to the bay window and Valcinda was holding the ladder while Caleb climbed to the top. The glass behind the window seat was old and thick, yet, Kimberly watched the cousins with concern wondering if they'd overheard Crystova. Crystova followed her line of sight turning on the window-seat cushion to stare at the cousins. Valcinda smiled gaily and waved; Kimberly waved back.

"Caleb offered to fix the lights above the shop placard," Kimberly explained.

"Kim," Crystova began in a serious tone, then glancing over her shoulder lowered her voice. "I know you think my theories are wildly impractical, but if I'm right, this would be the most astounding discovery in history."

Doubtful Kimberly looked around her shop most particularly at the walls. Without meaning to do it she mumbled under her breath, "Oh no. Oh no."

As if Crystova had read her mind, her friend said in a tone reminiscent of a zookeeper calming a skittish dorphen-colt, "Hold on there, Kim. I'm not asking you to demolish the walls. With the technology the ship's granted the university, I'm sure I'll be able to locate any artifacts which might be hidden inside these walls without resorting to demolition."

"Why my place in particular? The moat-and-bailey castle was built six hundred years ago. Every shop on Merchants' Row and along Wolfern Promenade and the plaza is made of the same stone. The artifacts you're looking for could be anywhere."

"No, not according to Duke Dono's parchment. The old temple stones were used mainly in this corner of the battlement walls and I know that the shops along Merchants' Row are the most ancient. The stone from the plaza and the stone from Duke Tower are not from the temple but came from the old quarry."

"Again, I say why my place?"

The look which passed between them surprised them both. They had always been careful not to ruffle the fragility of their friendship. In the last ten years, neither of them had ever said or done anything to annoy the other. Would their friendship survive this moment? Their disagreements in the past had been impersonal more about abstract concepts and ideas. But now, now, Crystova threatened to damage her very home perhaps even her livelihood. It was sad how easily friendship could end over something as silly as money.

When Crystova walked toward the counter and laid the parchment over Kimberly's accounting books setting her coffee mug on one end and her purse on the other with the mildewed paper spread open for Kimberly's examination, Kimberly thought about her precious accounting books so callously mistreated. She debated whether to say something. As a precaution Kimberly held onto the coffee mug just in case Crystova's hand hit the mug and sent it flying.

Kimberly followed Crystova's finger as her finger rested on a tiny map in the far-right hand corner of the parchment. Kimberly could distinguish the castle walls, the inner and outer bailey, the watchtowers and the moat design albeit up-side-down. Crystova's beautiful manicured fingernail, painted a rich plum, pointed toward a barely discernible symbol written on the lot marked E11. Crystova explained in a whisper, "The shape you see signifies a holy shrine in ancient Curleconese. I believe Duke Dono never had a chance to tell his successor about this secret before fleeing the country."

"And you're assuming E11 is the Emporium," Kimberly whispered back with an air of disbelief.

Her heavy sigh brushed the hairs of Kimberly's bangs and made Kimberly momentarily ashamed of herself. For the first time in years, Crystova was fired up and Kimberly had no reason to doubt her research skills. Kimberly heard her say, "I need more than just a secondary source to confirm my findings. I can't move forward based purely on this document. So, don't worry, I'm not going to sneak into your shop one night and start breaking through the plasterboard."

Lester Lucie's shop, Electricity Solutions and Security, squeezed between the Bridgekeeper family holding and a weekly newspaper called the Shellfargon Seed, believed he was situated in the best location of all. Long ago he'd coveted this apartment. He knew enough about the Bridgekeeper family and Harry Hanson who owned Shellfargon Seed to anticipate some major seismic shifts coming soon for both. The first seismic shift turned out to be a bust, but he'd figured out another way to get the holding and the other apartment might prove fruitful for Lester's nascent business.

The Bridgekeeper family had been drawbridge technicians for hundreds of years. The gift of the apartment had been granted nearly three hundred years ago. They'd been given the choicest flat near the gate with excellent views of Greenburg Valley and the train station for obvious reasons. It made sense for the drawbridge technicians to live close to where they worked. The Duke tower lords had been promised the Bridgekeeper holdings until the last Bridgekeeper died. In the past, each generation of Bridgekeeper boys and girls learned the maintenance and operation of the drawbridge – until Governor Saurus.

When Governor Saurus was elected by the nobles of Wolfern Province, his first act was to fire the Bridgekeepers and replace them with his own lackeys. An over exuberant lackey oiled the chains so well he shortened the time between drawbridge operations. Ironically Saurus gave the man a medal. Though Saurus tried every trick he could think of to remove the Bridgekeepers from their gifted holdings, he failed. Since the Bridgekeepers still lived in the gatehouse apartments, they were the first to see how Saurus' men performed their duties. They tried to warn the governor. Every time they went to Duke Tower to speak to him, the governor sent them away.

During a grand ball the governor discovered he'd made a colossal mistake by refusing to see the Bridgekeepers. The lack of maintenance and sloppy operation of the drawbridge resulted in the deaths of several early arrivals who'd been waiting on the other side of the moat. They were crushed beneath the weight of the massive bridge. If they had been Mudflat Villagers, no one would have cared. The poor were always in the wrong place at the wrong time. But the new arrivals weren't Mudflat Villagers. Instead they happened to be wealthy nobles from Delphadore. News spread of the disaster and soon everyone in the country of Curl knew about the tragedy.

Even with so much at stake, Saurus refused to reinstate the Bridgekeepers. Eventually Sophia's father and mother gave up and became tinkers traveling the roads to make extra money. They left their youngest daughter Star with her sister Sophia. The two fended for themselves, barely. Once the parents left Blueglennen, Saurus sent his lackeys to Sophia for instruction on the proper maintenance of the bridge. So now there were two Bridgekeepers left in the gatehouse apartment with very little money and no protector. And the two were attractive young women of marriageable age.

Somehow Saurus with his continual bungling managed to make Lester's future much brighter. And then there was the Shellfargon Seed on the other side of him. The location was a dream since the apartment abutted the renovated and terribly expensive Wolfern Promenade Condos. The condos used to be the suites of the nobility. The only suite still untouched belonged to Timothy Finstickel who had the best spot of all allowing him views of the Siren River and the Eastern valley. Lester had no plans to tackle the condos. He wasn't that ambitious. No, he only wanted a few extra slices of pie. Harry Hanson's Shellfargon Seed apartment looked out onto the Royal Plaza and after the renovations property values in the bailey soared.

As Lester kept an eye on the Bridgekeeper daughters, he also took great interest in Harry Hanson. Over the last few months, he'd noticed some peculiar comings and goings of people he'd never seen before. He had to wonder if Hanson was up to something. The Shellfargon Seed, a weekly newspaper catering to Duke Tower residents, Mudflat and Greenburg happened to be the place where people purchased advertising. Since Lucie was an independent electrician and owner of a thriving pawnshop, as well as, Harry's close neighbor, he'd assumed Harry would give him some great advertising deals. He didn't. "I got to make a living same as you Lester," he told him.

Too bad for you Harry. Lester never forgot a slight. And that was why he kept a close eye on Harry's "guests." Maybe one day he'd discover something he could use over the guy. It would be a pleasure to wipe the smug smile off his face. Still his apartment and his business on the bottom floor provided the best of both worlds – immediate proximity to the drawbridge and a prime location in a fashionable neighborhood near the Royal Plaza.

Most of Lucie's traffic consisted of local citizens from Mudflat Village pawning their precious possessions and wealthy buyers from

Greenburg Valley who were obsessive bargain hunters. Lester Lucie also moonlighted as an electrician for the village and the valley. After a decade living in New Dala, when he returned to his hometown, he was dismayed to discover Blueglennen already had several trusted and reputable electricians. He improvised his business plan and added a few extra words to the marquee. The security part of his business turned out to be his biggest money maker.

Though he did his best to hide the growing bald spot on the top of his head by brushing his thinning dark hair to the side, there was little he could do about his eyebrows. They were hairy centipedes perpetually frowning. They could have disappeared into the folds of his forehead if they had the courage to move. Lester's squat short body had once been well muscled under a layer of plumpness. Now the muscle was gone, and the fat remained.

He still had his charm though. He could still make women smile with his jokes and his flattering words. He especially liked the women who found him repugnant. The more difficult the conquest, the sweeter it was when they fell at his feet begging. He had very few regrets. He'd slept with a lot of women as a young rutting male. He especially liked blondes with foul mouths.

Victoria Lemon came to mind. No. He shuttered at the thought of her skinny body and wide face with the vacant brown eyes. She attracted men. Yeah, she had the notorious mouth but there was something missing, a dark cavity in her soulless body. He favored sweet-tempered, stupid blondes with dirty mouths and breath stinking of stale cigarettes. Victoria, even young Victoria in Form Two turned him cold and always had. She reminded him of a snake with tits.

He spit into his empty coffee cup and turned his thoughts to his favorite contemplation, the lovely lady of his dreams. He hadn't seen her in nearly a week. What was she up to? Maybe he should make an excuse to borrow a cup of sugar from the Bridgekeeper family.

As if he had conjured her from his thoughts, his favorite bush entered his abode with a shake of her platinum locks and robust biscuits. Sophia Bridgekeeper was the eldest daughter of a long line of Bridgekeepers, a family which had served the royals of Duke Tower for centuries, well, up until Duke Dono fled the capital. Even though there was no reason for the Bridgekeepers to patrol the parapet in search of enemies or draw the bridge to protect the great hall or the bailey, the Bridgekeepers had a living for life at the behest of the late Governor, a distant cousin of the old Duke.

In her sweet voice Sophia said breathlessly, "Morning Lester. Here's your paper. The boy left it on our stoop again."

Lester stepped forward to accept the paper and held Sophia's hands between his own for longer than necessary. Sophia blushed and stepped back. Lester was disappointed. There was something different about her today. She was lit from within. As she masked her unease with aimless small talk, he studied her closely. As the seconds ticked by, an irritating itch developed right in the center of his forehead.

"Did you hear about the Church of the Holy Centipede, what they're up to? Merchants' Row is beside themselves."

Talk dirty baby, Lester urged her wishing Sophia would look into his eyes and hear the voice in his head. Come on baby, talk dirty to me.

"Well, Kimberly, you know, Kimberly Lemon, she's not going to just sit by and let the church take her shop. She's getting organized. And there is the potential Dad says of maybe our trust being broken and where would we be? Yeah, where would we be? So maybe there is something to what she's doing. Although I hate to see the church and the merchants angry with each other, I agree something must be done. And Caleb is real concerned for Kimberly. He wants to help and if it means tearing up the shop to do it, he said he's more than willing to put his muscle to the job."

There was a long silence and Lester tore his eyes away from Sophia's amble breasts reluctantly and began to really pay attention to what she was saying. Sophia looked chagrined. Had the little minx said something she shouldn't have, he wondered? "I'm not following you, honey. What did you say?"

"Oh. Wow. Look at the time. I got to go. Bye Delo Lucie. See you later," Sophia said as she backed toward the door and threw it open. Fresh cold fallow air hit him in the face and sobered him up right quickly. She was in love, Lester realized, the little minx was in love with that Caleb fellow, the one always busy doing small favors for everyone in the bailey even in Old Town where the poorest of the poor lived in mud huts and had pigs for pets.

What a stupid sod. As poor as Caleb was, where did he get off thinking he was better than everybody else? Where did he get off going around doing nice things for people? As far as Lester was concerned, Caleb wasn't all that good looking either. So maybe people liked his open honest face and his generous nature. So, what? There was more about being a man than being nice.

Lester had been the youngest of fifteen children. By the time he was a teenager, his mother had been a grandmother three times over. She had been his father's first wife. By the time Arthur met his father's third wife, Arthur's pity for his mother turned to loathing.

Her kind of womanhood made him physically ill, her groveling ways and pious attitude made him want to hit her.

Perhaps her groveling and piousness had disgusted his father too? And then the laws of the land changed and people like his father were considered criminals and men could no longer have more than one wife, so his father moved to New Dala. Lester refused to follow his younger siblings and parcel of nieces and nephews and aunty-mothers to the promised land of milk and honey and freedom. He chose to break away from his strict life and drink as much as he wanted and fornicate as much as he wanted. He traveled east drinking and fornicating along the way and discovered he had a gift for luring women into his bed.

Unfortunately, age crept up on him and nowadays he was lucky to snatch a slobbering kiss from a reluctant widow. Well, there were always the sweet innocent young things who dropped into the shop, the ones he might have a chance fondling if he was lucky enough. He sighed knowing full well he didn't have the courage to fondle the young ones because young ones usually had fathers or brothers or someone ready to defend their honor. The Governor's Knights were another deterrent. There was no law forbidding him from daydreaming though.

Lynora Reason threw open her thermal curtains and the sun nearly blinded her. She narrowed her eyes against the light and determinately unlocked the Bojenlac doors which led onto a tiny terraced balcony. So, what if the balcony looked out upon the rooftops of Merchants' Row and beyond the Row, the castle rampart and the machicolations where the knights of old used to pour oil down on invaders. She still had a view beyond the battlement to the rooftops of the Mudflat Village and beyond the battlement various bits of nature and a gorgeous sky in all its splendor.

Ignoring the cheeky wave from a knight on duty as he sauntered across the rampart toward the River View Tower, she stepped onto her balcony and took in a deep relaxing breath of fresh air. She knew the drill. The knight would hide out the rest of the night in the cozy heated gatehouse peeking through the arrow loops, probably nodding off every so often, in the full knowledge Duke Tower Castle hadn't seen an invader in three hundred years. Besides, there was no one stupid enough to storm a castle wall when he or she could simply bribe one of Saurus' personal bodyguards or the few mercenary knights he owned.

Even though the knight temporarily obscured a portion of her view, Lynora could still appreciate the mountains in the distance, the wide swath of brown mushrooms signifying treetops of the Bitterroot Forest and the silver waters of the Siren River curling around the castle on its way by Mudflat Village. The river she knew would be gently moving the ice-cold water from the mountains down through the valley and beyond. The river quenched the thirst of the villagers and the animals who came down at night to drink. The Siren also supplied the townspeople of Blueglennen with tasty fish. She'd forgotten the name of the fish but remembered the blue ones were very tasty.

She stood upon her balcony and breathed in the fresh outdoor air. Her apartment had become stale during her trip abroad. She returned to her apartment and crossed the stone flagged floor to open the casement windows which faced the Royal Plaza, so a nice cross breeze would blow the staleness away. Even with the cold air circulating through the rooms, she felt hot. In sweat season, she rarely spent much time in Blueglennen. To do so meant a miserable three months of intense heat not only from the furnaces in the restaurant below but the heat from the cobbled plaza and the limestone walls. Only during chill did she appreciate the conductors of heat. Because of them she had no need to buy fuel for her little burner.

With the lights off, the sunlight from the windows and the open Bojenlac door were enough illumination. She unpacked her heavy trunk with the sounds of Blueglennen wafting up to her from the open windows, the parade of people milling about in the plaza below, the school bell notifying everyone in a three-mile radius of the ending of classes for the day, the shrill voices of children as they made their way home. It wasn't until she'd finished unpacking her belongings and arranged the presents for her friends that she became aware of the quiet.

Once settled in, she strolled out onto the balcony with a cup of coco and examined her cherry blossom tree. She observed the buds on the limbs with pleasure. She had come home just in time to see them bloom. It was a shame the apartment didn't include a balcony facing the plaza. Only Duke Tower boasted a balcony because a long dead king declared the nobility must always be higher than the peasant. Such antiquated thinking made her teeth hurt.

Delan Lynora Reason relaxed and rocked as she sat on her cushioned chair enjoying the momentary quiet. She sat in the concealed beauty of the white branches of her tree and the fancy flowered iron rail of her balcony. The rail protected her from the possibility of an absurd freefall onto hard cobblestone or a worse death, a painful fall into a blue trash bin. She chuckled at the thought and set her cold coco on the little stand beside the chair telling herself she would only close her eyes for a moment. The feel of the last rays of the setting sun on her face were delicious.

It had been an aggravating trip home to be sure, all those miles traveling by pleasure cruise from New Dala to the mainland trying to avoid a strange old man who insisted every time they met, whether in the banquet room at the dinner table or on the top deck, on holding her hand. Once docked at Walrat Island she escaped his attentions by sneaking onto the ferry to Wolfern. She'd endured a miserable twenty miles of bumpy road in an uncomfortable carriage to get to the village of Twofold Hill. Thankfully the Delphadorturo pushed for a railroad through the center of Curl which she happily boarded and which happily whisked her the remaining hundred miles to a train station in Abbyville where she boarded a coach driven by four seahorses to Blueglennen. Yes, indeed, this trip had been rougher than the others.

She woke to the sound of trash bins colliding. She rubbed her tired eyes, blinked a few times and leaned forward to peer down into the dark alley holding onto the cold black wrought-iron of her balcony rail. The coldness of iron brought her back to her senses. The moon was on its way over the forest and would soon bathe the night in white light. Unfortunately for her, the light did not penetrate the darkness below.

It sounded as if someone was pulling a heavy trash bin down the alley. The bin kept bumping into other bins as the person in charge cursed and fumed. By the time the bin was under her balcony, she froze, fearing the curser might spot her spying on him. Her tree obscured her view of the man but through the intricate wrought iron design of the balcony floor, she thought she saw a tall man in a hat and long coat. She couldn't see his face just the top of his head. There was no place left for the man to go because the alley ended at a brick wall. The interloper changed course and retraced his steps heading back to Wolfern Promenade.

It was obvious. Lynora's lips curled in disgust. Some drunk who thought he could dig his way through brick decided he would steal someone's bin. As his progress improved, he began to hum. When she recognized the tune, all her irritation vanished and suddenly the rude person changed into an eccentric genius.

E2 Shellfargon Year 5092 FMP WK 1: UES Albion 4

Assigned as Knight to E1 Duke Tower Sheriff's Office. Visa Successful 5092-5095. Rampart patrolled constantly, replaced every shift. Knight's Captain reports to Raker then Governor. Deaths of knights from previous year appear natural according to report by retired D.I. Knight Bracewaddle.

DTK1 drowned while saving Mudflat Village child who fell into Siren River.

DTK2 death from renal failure related to skin cancer prevalent for Curlecons stationed in deserts of Vespa 1 & 2. DTK2 never stationed overseas. E3 has been granted disinterment and autopsy from E1. Testing skin samples from deceased. Will send follow up report.

DTK3 death due to massive organ failure after collapse of old tree on trail. DTK3 protecting Delphadore dignitaries in Bitterroot Forest. Entourage unharmed. Gov ordered Forest Mgmt clear cut woodland. Savage animal attacks ensued. Gov rescinded order. Bitterroot notorious for plethora of dangerous predators. (DO NOT DROP ALBION TECHS ANYWHERE NEAR FOREST). Dialmere Seeley, reinstated as tour guide. No further attacks. Seeley & Goodbody cousins. An evolutionary adaptability?

DTK4 drowned in moat. Known to have been drunk at time of death. E3 checking alcohol blood levels. Curfew ordered by Gov. At twelve bells each night drawbridge raised, gates locked. Reason? Gov claims attempt on life.

DTK5 declared missing. Last seen drinking with friends at Wolf Inn. No one assigned to locate deserter and bring him back for court-martial.

Chapter 4

When Kimberly looked up from her book and saw Victoria enter the shop, a cloud of foulness entered the room. Kimberly's body responded to the sight of her aunt with cowardly fear and trembling. A flight or fight reptilian instinct kicked in and as she stood poised between the two conflicting desires, a thought made her lean forward and watch Victoria as she would watch a rabid animal approach. The only way to combat a mad dog is to remain perfectly still and vigilantly watchful, she said to herself drowning out the other voice that shrieked "Get the hell out stupid."

Kimberly anxiously surveyed her aunt for any signs of imminent attack. Victoria did not disappoint. "Get that asshole out of the townhouse. I came all this way across the world expecting to find my room ready for me – only to discover," Victoria Lemon began as she tossed the townhouse keys onto the bookshop counter. "My key doesn't work in the damn lock and guess who answered the door, yeah, that smug idiot Antonio. You remember the one, the one you masturbated over in junior high. I used to think you were nuts. What a retard," she said with a shallow grin and a long pause. "The both of you."

They exchanged looks. Kimberly knew if she gave in and looked away Victoria would make her life miserable. It wasn't until later Kimberly realized during the quarrel, she'd been clutching her pen as if it were a knife, ready to defend herself if necessary. In a voice she hardly recognized, Kimberly said, "I could no longer afford the taxes and insurance on the townhouse. I leased the townhouse to Antonio four months ago."

Victoria tossed her blonde curls off her shoulder with contempt, contempt for Kimberly, the shop, and everyone in Blueglennen. As Victoria's predatory eyes took in her surroundings, her eyes widened when she noticed the red velvet curtain behind Kimberly, "Grandpa may have given you the shop, but the townhouse is entailed to the surviving family members, not just you, nerdiness. That means the townhouse belongs to me as well." Victoria stepped past Kimberly and threw open the red velvet curtains.

"What's back here?"

Kimberly opened her mouth to speak and nothing came out. She wanted so much to follow Victoria and keep an eye on her and her thieving fingers. Instead of having the courage to follow, Kimberly remained frozen in limbo behind the counter hoping a customer would come in and rescue her. The rat-tat-tat of Victoria's heels on the old cedar floorboards grated on Kimberly's ears. Those sharp stiletto heels were probably gouging holes in the wood.

She imagined her aunt throwing open cupboards and searching inside tins for spare change. And then a strange thought popped into her head as she waited anxiously for Victoria to grow bored – while growing up together, only three years apart, Kimberly could not remember even one time when Victoria had shown emotion. She'd never seen her cry. Normal people cry. They cry when they're sad or they're hurt. Not Victoria.

Kimberly tried to remember if Victoria had ever shown normal human emotions. It was an effort to relive those painful days. She never did figure out why Victoria hated her so much. Was Victoria incised because people mistook them for sisters and she hated people thinking she was just-a-kid?

Yes. There was a time when Delphinids greeted each other according to class and family position. Maybe she wanted Wolfern society to return to the old ways? Or did her anger and jealousy stem from Grandpa's obvious preference for Kimberly? He insisted Victoria call him Grandpa instead of father. For a tiny moment she felt pity for her aunt.

Kimberly thought she remembered Victoria laughing a lot when she was younger. Or had it been laughter? Perhaps what everyone took for laughter had really been Victoria's mockery. No, there had been a time when they were young, Victoria, eight years old and Kimberly, five years old when they would play down by the Siren while Grandpa fished. They used to have fun. They used to be friends. It had been the two of them all the time, playing together and reading together.

They treated each other like family in the beginning, just kids playing. But as they grew up, Victoria began to pull away. Kimberly thought Victoria's coldness had to do with her new friends. She'd started running around with older kids, wild kids, kids who smoked and drank and notched their ears with fishing tags. Victoria's friends considered themselves rebels.

Kimberly saw them as oppositionists. No matter what the issue, if the majority of people were for it, the oppositionists were against it. Aunt Victoria joined the group for a totally different reason though. There was a boy in the group she really liked. And when Victoria liked something or someone, she made sure she got it.

Did other families experience fear, the way Kimberly feared Victoria? Did other families wait anxiously for the cutting remark or the unprovoked blow? Or did other nieces and aunts treat each other like friends and want to see each other all the time, go to lunch together or spend holidays together? When one of them was in pain did the other empathize? Why did Kimberly no longer care whether Victoria lived or died and much preferred her aunt dead? The first time she thought about wishing her aunt dead was when her aunt beat her senseless over a favorite dress.

So, Kimberly no longer felt guilty about wishing her aunt dead. Was she an unnatural niece or was she just in an unnatural situation? How could she tell? Other people talked as if family members were awesome and family was the only defense against a hostile world. But all Kimberly had ever known was the terror of displeasing Victoria, having to watch for signs of her displeasure, and having to hide her most treasured possessions because she feared Victoria would steal them. Victoria also lied to everyone. Even if there was no reason to lie, she would lie anyway and watch Kimberly to see if Kimberly would correct the lie.

The bell startled Kimberly out of her reverie and the first thing she saw was old Timothy Finstickel in his dirty mustard colored mackintosh and brown knit beanie with the beard even longer and dirtier than the last time she saw him. She watched him wander toward the jumble of old magazines in the darkest part of the shop. Unfortunately for her, he came in once a week to look over the new merchandise and spend nearly an hour browsing, making the place uncomfortable and uninhabitable for others, eventually buying one or two cheap items, and finally, thankfully, he would leave, leaving of course his usual reek of unwashed body as a reminder of his presence.

Oh yes, a good start to a fabulous day.

It seemed as if Victoria had been in the backroom for nearly the entire morning. A person's perception can stretch time into infinity or snip it in half when the circumstances were different. Like now, with Victoria riffling through her belongings in the backroom (she should go back there right now and tell her off) and Finstickel muttering to himself and smelling up the place.

And now, of course, why not, make the day perfect, little Star Bridgekeeper popping in, all eighty pounds of dark hair and pale white skin and large brown eyes and skinny, oh so, skinny legs and arms. She looked as if she would break in two, her neck so incredibly fragile.

Not now honey, not now, Kimberly tried to warn her with her eyes. Star had other things on her mind, too busy dumping her school bag and coat and scarf and mittens on the window seat to look up and see DANGER, DANGER written all over Kimberly's face. "I've had it Kim. I'm not going back to that place, never ever again. I hate it. I tell you I hate it and you can tell my sister and she can drag me back to school and I'll just run away again."

Kimberly made herself move from behind the safety of the counter toward Star. "What's wrong at school?"

Star gazed up at Kimberly with her big brown eyes and incredibly long eyelashes which made Kimberly weirdly protective and obscenely jealous all at once and said, "Dela Browning won't let me pray before we pledge allegiance to the flag."

There was nothing more disconcerting than young religious fanaticism. Fanaticism defied Kimberly's understanding. The young are supposed to be self-involved and destructive. Well, maybe not, just because Kimberly had reached a stage in her life where religion smacked of brainwashing didn't necessarily mean everyone else had come to the same conclusion. And just because Star's peers were more interested in sex and drugs and music, and Star had dreams of becoming the next Blueglennen saint, was no reason to believe Star was crazy. Someday, she would grow out of her enchantment with the church and its ridiculous God of a Thousand Legs.

It must be natural for the naïve to be the most easily indoctrinated. And the younger the convert the easier the conversion. Of course, Star would be fanatical about religion at this stage in her life. The rise of the Church of the Holy Centipede founded by Bishop Mark Little's grandfather and the restoration of the cathedral with all the new people congregating at the Holy Church of the Centipede meant Star had a community of people who shared her views. In other words, people who believed they were special and everyone else pathetic pagans who would end up in hell.

Fortunately for Kimberly's continued sanity there were many religions in the country of Curl. Yet the centipedes did have a lot of pull in the local government and were tight with Governor Saurus. She didn't think Governor Saurus had gone so far as to join. Yet? And if he did would he demand all Blueglennens follow the Church of the Holy Centipede?

What annoyed her the most was Star's determination to convert Kimberly. Star's older sister Sophia, older by at least ten years remained her usual innocent sweet self, her main goal to find a husband and have a dozen babies. Kimberly, as surrogate parent while their real parents were away reminded herself again to remain patient with the sisters. She had to admit, even when she was Star's age, she had never been as fervent, as devoted, as loyal to anything.

Attuned to the sounds coming from the backroom, Kimberly knew when Victoria appeared behind her even before Star stopped talking. The only sign of discomfort Star allowed herself was the widening of her eyes and a slight flush of her cheeks. Kimberly refused to look at Victoria, even when Victoria moved to face the two of them with the light shining through the picture window creating a weird sort of halo over her head. As if the Evil One had entered the room, the former spitfire teen shut down completely and began gathering up her coat and gloves.

"Why are you leaving? You just got here?" Victoria asked with a frown never having had much success interpreting social signals.

"I told her she could put her belongings in the backroom for safe keeping."

Star glanced at Kimberly warily and with a brief nod and a handful of belongings disappeared behind the red velvet curtain.

"Shouldn't she be in school?"

"Did you find what you were looking for Victoria?" Kimberly asked tired of being afraid. Oddly enough having someone to protect gave Kimberly courage to challenge her aunt. Why? Didn't she love herself enough to think she was equally worthy of defending? Victoria gave her the lizard eye. It seemed as if Victoria had become an impenetrable block of granite, unmovable, a monster which could stretch out its thick arms and snap her neck in two. How did Victoria do it? It was a brilliant trick.

One moment she appeared to be a living breathing social creature and the next she became a block of stone. And this transformation occurred within seconds. There had been others like her; Kimberly had become unusually sensitive to the type. It did not matter if they had learned the art of civility by mimicking normal people; she could always sense them even if everyone else remained blind to their tricks.

It was something in their eyes, something predatory like a wolf, no, not a wolf, wolves had a sense of community and sharing – these creatures knew only how to take. And some of them enjoyed humiliating and overpowering people they sensed were weaker. Then there were the socially challenged ones who could turn on a person without provocation. In order to make a sale, Kimberly often had to hold back the scathing words she really wanted to say when customers suddenly and inexplicably turned on her, but with her own aunt she had no such tether.

So why didn't she go all out raker?

Kimberly looked around the room and realized the only people in the shop were Finstickel browsing in the dark corners and Star in the back rooms. Kimberly looked Victoria in the eye. Of course, Victoria didn't flinch. Not once. "I want you out of my shop now. Go. Go Victoria before I call the constable, and have you thrown out. The shop belongs to me and as the executor of grandfather's will,

I have the right to sublease the townhouse to Antonio."

She returned to the safety of the counter and reached down for the aerosol can she kept ready. "If you have the money to pay for a lawyer you can contest the lease. Under Blueglennen law an accuser must prove a contract is unlawful, not the defendant. That means you'll have to pay the filing fees and convince a lawyer. Good luck with that."

When Kimberly set the aerosol can on the top of the counter, Victoria's eyes narrowed. She recognized a threat when she saw one. Kimberly continued, "But you won't bother finding a lawyer, convincing a lawyer, or paying a lawyer, you'll probably find some stupid schmuck to do your dirty work."

Kimberly glanced in the direction of Tim Finstickel who was still fingering the sales items and changed the conversation, "It won't matter. By the time you go through all the trouble of seducing some horny lawyer, you'll get bored and move on to your next victim. Besides," Kimberly paused for effect. "We both know how you feel about courts. You prefer the dark. The light might get you noticed. You can't sneak behind my back anymore and lie to my neighbors, and steal my stuff then pawn them without one of my friends telling me. It doesn't matter anyway. Love to disappoint you. There's nothing valuable here."

While Kimberly had been talking Victoria had been inching her way toward the door. Kimberly remained behind the counter and instead of rushing to catch Victoria, she leaned over and pressed the keypad and punched in the password which would open a little box inset into the counter. With satisfaction she heard the little door click open.

Without calling attention to what she was doing, Kimberly grabbed hold of a wooden handle no bigger than her middle finger. The box and its contents could not be seen by customers in any part of the shop. It was attached to a series of cables which ran under the floor and up the wall and connected with the deadbolt on the door. Just as Victoria reached for the door handle Kimberly shoved the handle down. The device kept would-be-thieves and other unpleasant persons from entering the shop during the day.

Years ago, Caleb had come up with the elaborate security system as a way of protecting her after several shops on Merchants' Row were robbed. It had been intended to keep dangerous or unpleasant people out, not lock them inside with her. Was she crazy? Would Tim Finstickel panic and destroy the place? She glanced at the security mirror in the back. It was mounted in such a way she could observe the customers browsing the sales table while working at the cashier's counter. She saw Tim Finstickel with his head bowed absorbed in the collection on the table. He was oblivious of people, as usual.

After twisting and jerking the doorknob for several seconds, Victoria realized she was going nowhere. When Victoria gave up and turned those blank eyes in Kimberly's direction, unnerved, Kimberly shut the box quickly, effectively locking all of them inside. Now who was missing a few pages in her book? Kimberly Lemon. If anyone were to find out what she had done, there was no knowing what penalties or fines the knights, or the governor might throw at her.

Kidnapping? Extortion? Sure. Kimberly was so desperate for a sale she trapped customers inside until they bought something. Oh yeah. She could see the headlines. She felt hysterical giggles percolating in her stomach, threatening to undermine her attempt to appear tough. One look at Victoria's dead eyes extinguished Kimberly's amusement.

Only she knew the password. Even if Victoria overpowered her, she would not be able to get into the box or get out of the shop. Kimberly waited for Victoria's hissy fit. She did something in character when she stepped forward menacingly. Only the pedestrians strolling by outside checked her forward motion. Victoria's shoulder's relaxed.

Kimberly spoke first, "Whatever you have hidden under your cloak set it on the window seat. When I'm satisfied you have nothing more, I'll let you out." Kimberly set the aerosol can with the lethal pepper spray on the counter.

Just at that critical moment Star threw open the red curtains and said, "I noticed you have a pot of tea on the burner Dela Lemon, do you think I might have a cuppa?" A cuppa! Good Mother Earth why did the child try so hard to be different? Because she wanted people to be impressed with her accent? Because she assumed sounding foreign would give her more cache with her peers? No, stupid girl. It does the opposite, it makes people think you're a lame-brain.

Then Star sensed the growing tension between the women. Like a frightened rodent she froze by the curtains clutching one of the folds as if the soft fabric were a blankie. Inwardly Kimberly groaned knowing Victoria would never expose her true nature to the general public. Then Kimberly realized there was a way to save face for them all. "Star I need your assistance. My aunt is interested in travel, would you find her a book on foreign travel. And Victoria those items you said you wanted to return, go put them on my bed?"

From somewhere in the dark recesses of teenage sullenness,

Star said, "Why doesn't she look for a book on her own? She can read, can't she?" But instead of stomping back into Kimberly's quarters, she stepped through the curtain and moved toward Victoria.

So many painful memories were resurrected by the tableau of the two women, Victoria and Star, as Star moved past the older, much taller and stronger female. The sight threatened to bring on a nasty migraine. Star had no idea of the danger only inches away. Stupid girl. Stupid girl. Shut up. Shut up. You don't want to piss her off.

Kimberly clutched the aerosol can and moved quickly to step in front of Star, in a futile attempt to shield the child from Victoria's wrath. When Victoria's rigidity collapsed, Kimberly started shaking in relief. She gently pushed Star down the nearest aisle to hide her trembling hands. "I thought you wanted to work for me today? Or should I call your sister and tell her you've changed your mind?"

As Kimberly motioned for Victoria to lead the way beyond the red velvet curtains to Kimberly's private chamber, Kimberly heard Star's hefty sigh and her boots retreating in sullen heaviness. Victoria's neck and cheeks were red, her eyes glittering, a dangerous sign. She was on the verge of a tantrum and her tantrums could be deadly.

Kimberly kept the can out in the open. In a voice she hoped was quiet enough not to be overheard, she whispered, "I want to save face for us both. It's just you and me now. We're all that remains of the Lemon family. But remember this – I'm not afraid of you anymore. Even though we share the same last name, that doesn't mean I'll let you bully me or hurt anyone in Blueglennen. I will do whatever it takes to protect what I cherish. There's no percentage in making a scene. Put my stuff on the bed and I'll let you leave quietly without a fuss. No knights. No publicity."

Without a word, Victoria plowed through the curtains and within five minutes returned with her fancy expensive embroidered blue cloak draped across her arm. She walked to the door and turned to watch Star. Star held out the travel book. Kimberly rushed to the secret box and said, "Hold on Star, let me wrap that up for my aunt." Uncertain what to do Star paused midway between them with the book still outstretched. Kimberly punched in the password, heard the click of the door, pressed the lever and everyone heard the bolt draw back.

Even Tim Finstickel with an armload of magazines popped his head around a library shelf searching for the location of the odd sound. When he saw the three females, he lost interest and returned to his research.

Looking bored, Victoria left the shop. It was a good sign. She'd decided to move on and find a new victim. Star still had the book in her hand. Kimberly took the book then saw Star's expression of terror. Without thinking Kimberly brushed a long black strand of silky hair away from Star's pale face and padded her on the shoulder, "Thanks. You're going to make a wonderful assistant."

"You mean I don't have to go to school anymore? I can work here?"

"No. I just said that, so my Aunt Victoria wouldn't call the school or your mother," Kimberly fabricated out of thin air, knowing full well Victoria could care less about Star's education. Star visibly pouted at the news. Her reaction surprised Kimberly. She'd assumed Star came to the shop to escape the girl gangs she claimed tormented her enthusiastically and often. It was obvious the girls from the academy hated her because she was so delicate and beautiful and strange. The boys, of course, acted like fools around her.

Yet the child obsessed over the church and the hope of one day becoming a saint. The way she talked to people in such a condescending manner wasn't the path to sainthood. Kimberly wondered if doing good works or helping a charity was a part of the Church of the Holy Centipede. She debated whether to ask Star then changed her mind. She'd ask someone else, because if Star got going Kimberly would never hear the end.

Saved from any further discussion on the topic, the women watched as Tim Finstickel, in all his smelliness, dumped his choices on the counter and began counting out change. He dropped what he considered proper payment on the gleaming cedar countertop and pulled out his tattered dirty bag and began stuffing the magazines and maps inside without a by-your-leave. Sad to see the old nobility ending up like this one. Her grandfather had told her all about Finstickel's family line. She didn't care. Rich inbred royalty wasn't her thing.

"Hold on Finstickel. I need to look those over before you take off. This isn't a flea market, you know." He glanced over his shoulder with a distracted frown, his eyes not even registering her presence.

Star, bored now, probably because the dramatic parts were over wandered into the back room, assuming she could get herself a cuppa without asking permission. After Finstickel had been taken care of, Kimberly pointed the large arrow to lunch hour on her sign and flipped the front piece to face the customers. She supposed she would have to call Star's sister now. Star would never forgive her for such a betrayal.

Or perhaps she could be clever and figure out a way to get Star out of the shop and onto the street and headed in the right direction

– preferably school. She pulled out her loose change from her cardigan and came up with five grays and seven coppers. Tucked away in a secret compartment were two reds all she had left to pay the bills. The five grays and seven coppers were the equivalent of two cups of coffee at Queenie's Diner or one of Antonio's famous chocolate crumb cakes. Before she could march into the backroom to persuade a sullen teenager to share a crumb cake, Alexandra appeared at the shop door and tapped on the glass, her dark eyes smiling mischievously.

At the sound of the chiming of the shop door bells, Star swore under her breath realizing there would be another delay and they would never have a chance to have a cuppa which meant Star would never have a chance to persuade Dela Lemon of the error of her ways. She had to convince her friend of the real danger, the possibility she might lose her soul to the Evil One. Star liked Kimberly but mostly wanted to save her soul. Bishop Little told them if they saved one hundred souls in their lifetime they would be on the road to sainthood.

When she heard Kimberly talking to a new customer, she frowned down at the assortment of things Kimberly's aunt had dumped on the bed. She picked up the pretty gold wristwatch and tried to count the number of tiny stones embedded in the face of the clock. At that precise moment, Star heard her name called followed by someone marching down the passageway toward her. If Kimberly were to catch her snooping, she would be so mad she would never listen to Star's carefully crafted testimony to the awesome powers of the Holy Centipede.

Before Dela Lemon reached the backroom, Star had stuffed the watch in her skirt pocket with the expectation of returning the pretty thing once Kimberly had finished with her customer. Star looked up in time to see the ironic twist of Kimberly's mouth at all the stuff on the bed. Star feared Kimberly thought she was prying and tried to separate herself from the bed and its contents. It only took two strides to reach the burner where the tea pot sat quietly steaming. She lowered the flame just the way her mother did to prevent ruining the brew or burning down the house.

Dela Lemon brushed past Star, set the tea pot on the counter to cool, grabbed a set of keys and her outdoor jacket and said, "Come on Star. I'll buy you a yummy torte at Antonio's. You don't mind if

Alexandra joins us? Let's go."

"But what about our cuppa?"

"It's too fine a day to be cooped up inside. Let's go before all the good tables are taken."

With dawning suspicion Star wondered if Dela Lemon intended to dump her off at her sister's work or march her back to school. She knew she couldn't hide out in the shop much longer. Resigned, she gathered up her belongings and followed the two older ladies outside blinking as the sun hit her face. She had always hated the light preferring cool dry dark rooms. She fumbled in her school case for her sunglasses and popped them on having to sprint after Dela Lemon and her friend Alexandra Montague.

Alexandra Montague had the longest legs Star had ever seen. Star hoped one day to be as slim and stylish. Yet the woman could be irritating. Star wondered if Montague was laughing at her. Whenever Star talked about the church Alexandra would cover her mouth to hide a smile. She wasn't a believer. But she seemed kind, as kind as Lemon, although Kimberly lacked Montague's fashion sense or height.

While watching the two women striding ahead toward the congestion of Wolfern Promenade, where pedestrians from the village and those from the bailey collided at the juncture to the Royal Plaza, she had to hold back a giggle. Dela Lemon's hair fell to her shoulders but in untidy strands as if she'd forgotten to comb her hair this morning. And her cardigan, much loved, the pockets baggy from all the stuff she kept in them: small books, reading glasses, bits of paper, the whole ensemble of baggy pockets made her hips look huge. Her pants did nothing to improve the image. They were old brown corduroys fraying along the hems with a patch on the right buttock. It made Star uncomfortable to feel pity for Kimberly Lemon.

Why had Lemon bothered to bring her navy-blue pea jacket if she insisted on carrying it over her arm? And those shoes, since when did anyone wear dusty old loafers anymore, especially purple ones? If someone were to help her with her clothes, maybe pick out a cute dress or stylish shoes, Lemon would look so much younger and prettier. She couldn't be that old? She had to be younger than Star's sister? It was hard to tell. Why did she care anyway? It was Lemon's soul she hoped to save, not her fashion transgressions.

Lemon didn't seem to mind how frumpy she looked next to the elegant Dela Montague. How odd. Elegant Montague reminded her of something else. The fear percolated to the top overtaking all others. What if they encountered the Serpent Six? Star hated to see nasty Poppy with her even nastier friends pointing and smirking at

Lemon. Star glanced back at the cathedral clock and groaned realizing belatedly that school was in recess for lunch. The popular kids would be sitting at the little tables on the plaza sipping their expensive coffees and munching on fancy pastries. They would see her with Lemon and Montague and think she was an even bigger loser.

Star saw Lemon stop and turn around. Lemon called out to her with a big smile gesturing as if to say hurry up. Montague paused beside Lemon and waited patiently for Star to reach them. Lemon grabbed her arm and Montague the other and the three of them plunged into the promenade, wading through the press of people. Some people were leaving the bailey, others were fighting their way toward tables.

Really, Star thought, why didn't the Governor schedule different shifts for lunch breaks? Someone should do something about this tangled mess of people. Star disliked crowds. Nobody respected the rights of petite people. From in front of her and from behind her all she could see were people's torsos. Although Lemon's affectionate squeeze and friendly smile made the moment less terrifying. "We're almost there," she told Star. Star forced a facsimile of a smile.

Once they were through the crowd and onto the plaza, Star took a deep breath. It was Lemon who managed to grab an empty table in front of Antonio's Café just as a couple of white- haired ladies rose to their feet. Star couldn't help but admire Lemon's forceful attitude today. Usually she was so quiet and bookish. Before the Governor's daughter Poppy Saurus entered the Delphadore Academy for the Gifted, Star had been the most popular girl in school. Roger Saurus' daughter, rumor said, had been going to a fancy private girl's school across the water in Angland. And Poppy made sure to remind everyone she'd traveled.

So far Montague hadn't spoken. Maybe she didn't like children? With her back to the plaza, Star felt brave enough to look around. There was no one she recognized sitting at the café tables. She figured Poppy and her friends were across the plaza over at the Green Monkey finding new ways to torment outsiders and a few gifted ones uninterested in joining their group. Star began to relax. Then she noticed a boy a couple of tables over watching her.

Boys were so disgusting always ogling people and trying to paw them with their dirty hands. Delo Lucie's leering face popped into her head and she nearly gagged. At least this boy was her own age and a talented violinist too, and even better, he didn't run around with Poppy's crowd. But all her old friends had chosen Poppy over her and that old pain had yet to dissolve. Only in prayer or at church services did she forget her humiliation and loneliness.

She liked to watch people. The plaza was the perfect place to people-watch. When she was one of the cool ones, she used to enjoy poking fun at the poor dumpy village people when they tramped across the drawbridge and into the plaza. You could always tell the village people – they wore clothes made by their parents and mixed up their pronouns and used double negatives and smelled of horse sweat and manure from squelching through the bogs they called streets.

They still rode those dirty ponies instead of the magnificent seahorses. A decent person couldn't leave the bailey without putting on galoshes for fear of being hip deep in horse manure. She wished the Governor would build a walkway over the village straight to Greenburg Valley and the Siren River. That way the castle people wouldn't have to be subjected to the revolting smells and sights of Mudflat Village.

And Star could always pick out the tourists, they were the ones gawking at the Duke Tower gargoyles. Every day the gargoyles leered menacingly down at the people from the tallest gutters and the highest points of the fortified walls. Too bad the gargoyles didn't suddenly come to life and fly down and eat all the tourists. Instead of eating the tourists, the gargoyles seemed to be posing as the tourists took endless pictures of them.

It was insane how the tourists seemed to have an endless supply of digital space for their silly pictures. They spent hours recording the watchtowers and the knights in their flamboyant dark blue and gold threaded uniforms with their rifles slung over their shoulders. They spent too much data on pictures of fancy shops along the plaza selling overpriced trinkets and pastries. What was worse was the constant snapping of boring artwork along the promenade. Why bother with a mess of stupid statues of old dead men in funny clothes who had never done anything important except fight in battles and hoard their gold?

During grow and sweat, every Wednesday at four o'clock the old guard known as the Duke's Own would put on a show for the tourists stomping around and marching and flinging their swords in the air. It was so medieval, so corny. Star sneered at the thought of all these foolish people bent on earthly concerns when their souls were in imminent danger of eternal hellfire. While Star had been twisting around to watch the parade of people, Lemon ordered a torte for Star and a coffee for herself. Star would have preferred Lemon to ask her preference first before ordering. But it was too late now. Bishop Little frowned when she mentioned sweets.

Remembering her manners, she said, "Thank you, Dela Lemon. You shouldn't have."

"I hope it won't spoil your lunch. You are planning to run home for lunch, aren't you?"

"No. There's no one home. Father and Mother rode to Greenburg Valley for the apple cider festival and Sophie is off with Caleb. Oh. Sorry. I forgot."

Dela Lemon's brows crinkled as if she didn't understand. Star relaxed. Lemon wasn't worried about Sophie. That was good to know. "I thought you and Caleb were a couple?"

"No. We were once, but now we're just good friends."

"Well, they went over to the orchards to see if they could find some old pieces of cedar. Caleb's going to make Sophie a fancy poster for her bed."

"Caleb loves to do nice things for people."

"He's still going to burn in hell. Don't forget that."

Star looked up in time to see Lemon raise her palm as if to slap Star's cheek. Dela Montague leaned over the table and grabbed Lemon's arm before she could strike Star. Lemon dropped her hand in her lap, her cheeks and forehead blotchy with embarrassment and rage. Star leaned back in surprise. When the ugly look on Kimberly's face receded, Star still didn't understand what had made her so mad. Then Lemon threw back her chair and rose to her feet and stared down at Star with steady cold eyes she'd never seen before and said, "You spoiled stupid child. You aren't fit to lick the dirt from his boots. You hear me. Get out of my sight. Get out of my sight before I."

All eyes were on them and the heat of embarrassment ran straight up Star's stomach to her ears. She was burning, burning all over. In that moment she hated Lemon more than she hated anyone in her life. But she knew her emotions were wrong. Lemon was one of the damned and the damned were to be pitied. She forced herself to stand with dignity and pushed in her chair, oh, so, carefully saying in a loud and clear voice, "I'll pray for you Dela Lemon. It's obvious you can't face the truth, but I'm right – Caleb Lanternlighter is going to hell. And so are you. But you can prevent damnation by joining the Church of the Holy Centipede and asking for his forgiveness."

When Star made herself look into Dela Lemon's eyes all she saw was pity. Star's first reaction was shock. She'd expected anger or maybe humiliation not pity. Then she got angry. How dare Kimberly Lemon pity her? She had no right to feel sorry for her. All her composure vanished. She pushed her way through the crowd. "You're a witch. You're evil," she screamed. The words rang through the plaza, echoing off the stone blocks and inside her brain. She began to run, desperate to find a quiet place to be alone.

It wasn't until Star found herself curled up on one of the front pews near the altar in the cool dark vault of the cathedral, she remembered she'd screamed out the words she'd been thinking in her head. She remembered now. She had called out to anyone who would listen and told them Dela Lemon was a witch and she was evil and going to hell. People turned to stare in annoyance and some in wonder and surprise. Some people laughed. She remembered how Poppy and her friends watched with eager eyes. Star hated them all. She hoped they'd all go to hell and burn in hell's fires for eternity.

Alexandra gave Kimberly time to calm herself. People who had watched with open curiosity turned back to their table companions and the usual chatter drowned out their voices. Kimberly appeared ashamed of her outburst, "I nearly slapped that silly foolish child," she said off-handedly staring down at her cold coffee.

Alexandra shrugged, "Don't worry. She'll get over it. She'll probably never bother you again. Why should you mind? The kid is clearly shy a few dresser drawers."

"I prefer shy a few pages myself," Kimberly said in response, forcing a chuckle through her throat which sounded lame even to her. The silence made her uncomfortable. "That metaphor is too simplistic. There is more going on in that girl's head then just this newest obsession with the Church of the Holy Centipede."

"Why waste mental energy wondering what a teenager is thinking? I remember those days," Alexandra began as she watched the people wandering in front of them. It was easy to spot the tourists. They were sipping their coffee or eating their sandwiches as if they had all the time in the world. Now that Alexandra had experienced how the majority lived, she was much more aware of the gulf between those who had plenty of time and money and those who had no time and very little money.

There had been moments when she had seriously considered returning to New Enreich and giving into her father. She'd given up the chance at a prestigious college education paid by her parents plus a handsome private income, so she could make decisions about her future career without her family's interference. And what had she really accomplished?

When she lifted her cup to her lips, she saw her hands and

winced: broken fingernails and dry sore hands. Hum. The semester was barely started. She could call her mother and by tonight she could be home and in her old bedroom with three closets all stuffed with designer clothes and accessories. And then she remembered the echoing hallways, the way her footsteps rang out on the polished tiled floors, the way the servants would abruptly disappear terrified of being fired for inadvertently crossing her path. Her friends could have cared less about the real world, about the world where ninety percent struggled to put food on the table and hold onto their homes.

Alexandra remembered her petty concerns back then, how spoiled she'd been, spoiled and isolated. She'd sensed early on she was cut off from the real world, from humanity but had no idea what to do about it. And then she was introduced to Freidman's letters to his wife. His letters described the harsh realities for the poor and the homeless. A larger world opened for her and she had no regrets leaving home and joining the real world, this Blueglennen world.

"Alexandra. Albion to Alexandra."

Alexandra smiled and shook her head, "Sorry, what was I saying?"

"I think you were going to say something about your own teenage angst."

"Well, I'm not Star. I'd already figured out religion was just a means the status quo used to brainwash people into being docile little pets."

The venom behind the words was so unlike Alexandra. Before Kimberly could pry more information out of her, a man stopped at their table. Fear like a small quake beneath her feet shook her body and unsettled her stomach. Fancy coffee and fear didn't mix. Had he seen the fight between her and Star? Was the fight why he was here? She knew who he was and couldn't figure out why he scared her so much. People said he liked results. She waited numbly for him to speak first just like one of Alexandra's docile little pets.

"Good afternoon ladies. And how are you this fine day?"

Alexandra did not know Detective Inspector Burhani Hawk well, but she had heard the rumors – that he was from the starship Albion and might be ex-military or special forces. What did it matter? He was from another world. He was a foreigner, a hired gun. He reminded her of the family's personal body guard. He'd stood seven feet tall, a well-muscled man, sleek and fast with an imposing head and penetrating eyes.

When she was a kid Rufus seemed to be everywhere. Her mother loved to reminisce about her diaper days when Rufus watched her constantly. Her mother claimed Rufus wasn't stalking her, he was protecting her. Kidnapping was big business in New Enreich at the time. Years later, she learned Rufus died protecting her mother and her from intruders who broke into their summer home in Angland.

When Alexandra realized Kimberly was turned to stone like a plaza effigy, Alexandra forced herself to look up and up at the man. She hated talking to strangers. Too bad kid, her grandmother would say, you wanted independence and adventure.

"We're well thank you and yourself?"

Kimberly managed to mumble something like, "Good."

The dark man sat down in Star's vacant chair and leaned toward them his brilliant white teeth flashing and his keen dark eyes examining them both with interest. "I am well. But I do not think Star Bridgekeeper is feeling very well. Why is that?" Alexandra continued to look into Burhani Hawk's eyes while her brain tried to get used to the man's skin color. Shehili Swana had the same dark skin. Yet Burhani seemed scarier. Maybe it was his imposing height and large shoulders? She knew the members of the starship were a diverse group of people, some were white, some were brown, others were dark skinned. Yet to see the people from the starship up close was so weird an experience. She looked down at her hand. She'd always thought the slight bluish tinge of her skin was normal. She couldn't say that anymore.

Kimberly remained uncharacteristically subdued. The silence was getting uncomfortable. Burhani Hawk didn't seem to mind the silence. He seemed to be enjoying the view as he patiently waited for someone to answer his question.

Alexandra was forced to be spokesperson, "Star is, what, fourteen, fifteen? It's a volatile age for Delphinids. You must know since you've been studying our species for years."

When no one spoke, Alexandra grew angry and with a shrug said, "Who knows what a kid might be feeling at any given moment?"

"Interesting, "D.I. Hawk said all the while ignoring Alexandra and openly scrutinizing Kimberly's face. "Which one of you is going to hell?"

His question surprised them both and for the first time Kimberly looked up and into his eyes, no longer intimidated. Alexandra never had time to warn her as she replied, "We're all probably going to hell, all of us in this square and beyond. Are we really sitting here discussing an insignificant incident? Don't we all have better things to do?"

Hawk ignored Alexandra which for many reasons personal and not so personal irked Alexandra no end. Like Rufus his attention was locked on the problem, the problem happened to be Kimberly.

Why? No one would mistake Kimberly for a criminal, just as no one would mistake Alexandra for a dwarf. There was an undercurrent of intrigue surrounding D.I. Hawk which Alexandra found offensive. No matter how attractive he might be, he was still uncomfortable to be around.

She suspected Hawk had been sent by someone to bait Kimberly. Alexandra looked around and even went so far as to stand up to look over the heads of people and finally she spotted him. But he wasn't down below amongst the press of common people, no, the Governor was up on the last floor of Duke Tower on his balcony seated at his table having lunch and watching the crowd below. Alexandra sat back down.

Kimberly wondered if Victoria had something to do with Hawk's sudden interest in her. Last year, the Governor hired Hawk to oversee his knights and his deputies after the last Detective Inspector's unexpected demise.

Some people in Blueglennen suspected the Governor had been a party to the poor man's "early retirement." No one credited the story he'd been drinking heavily and while smoking burned down his house. Yes, she had to admit he had been a foolish man. He'd told people he hoped to restore the rights of Blueglennens to vote for their local representatives. The right to vote ended when she was a teenager. Now, the governor chose Wolfern Province's two representatives to Delphadore.

And here sat a man who represented all that was wrong with the province of Wolfern today. Blueglennen, as the capital city of a once proud state, now had been reduced to cowering under the yoke of a man like Saurus. And here was a man from the starship Albion, his puppet, prying into honest people's personal lives, gathering information for the Governor, intimidating honest citizens. She didn't care if the scorn she felt showed on her face. She was sick of being afraid.

"You want to know what happened here. Well, I'll tell you and you can trot on back to Saurus and tell him how the big bad criminal chastised a child for accusing a friend of going to hell. That's right. Star, under the unhealthy influence of the Church of the Holy Centipede is under the delusion anyone not associated with the church is headed for damnation. Well, I let her know a good and kind man like Caleb is in no way headed for hell.

And I would do it again, sir. I, unlike some people, am loyal and I will not stand by and listen to some little twit speak ill of someone I respect. So, there you have it. Now if defending a friend from a lie is against the law, then arrest me. I can't keep track of all the stupid useless laws the Governor keeps thinking up to keep our cheeks to the stone. But let him know this newest one which prevents Blueglennens from immigrating to other provinces is abhorrent and such a law will only further cripple us as a nation."

Her speech seemed to amuse Hawk. Throughout her diatribe he watched her closely and listened carefully and when she was finished, he pushed back his chair and rose to his feet probably trying to intimidate the women with his height. He put his hands in his sleek black leather trench coat and nodded his handsome head and sauntered off without another word.

Alexandra watched the detective inspector make his way through the square. Instead of heading for Duke Tower, she saw him head for Unique Boutique. Kimberly was no longer interested in Burhani Hawk. She was staring down at her hands and from the trembling Alexandra guessed she was trying very hard not to cry. An unfamiliar emotion washed over her. Alexandra crossed her arms and hugged herself tight attempting unsuccessfully to banish the feeling. How unpleasant. She had been raised to believe public emotion was unsightly and rude, an invasion of the private into the public. What had been a cheerful break from a monotonous morning had turned into a Coral drama.

"What an ass," Alexandra said, attempting to lighten the mood. "Too bad. He looks mighty tasty." When Kimberly did not respond, she sighed and sat in silence for a few more minutes. When a dark shadow crossed their path once more, Alexandra became instantly alert wondering if Hawk had returned with a few of his deputies or maybe the Governor's knights.

She relaxed when she realized the tall man towering over them wasn't Burhani Hawk but the proprietor of Antonio's Café. He was staring down at Kimberly with an odd expression on his face, an odd mixture of annoyance, concern, and something else – unrequited love? Hardly. More like resentment. Odd. Very odd.

"Ladies. How are you? I see you haven't touched your torte. Shall I warm it up for you Dela Lemon?"

The sun was shining in her eyes, which gave her an excuse to continue to stare down at her plate. The plate was gorgeous made from the finest red stoneware with gold etching around the rim. The chocolate torte decorated with an artful weave of rich caramel and whipped cream reminded Kimberly once again of a childhood deprived of such treats.

"No, that won't be necessary. It's kind of you to ask though." Kimberly lifted her fork and forced herself to take a bite. She'd paid for it after all and she refused to let good money go to waste. She let the torte slide down her throat. It might as well have been sandpaper. But she pretended to enjoy the cake and made herself nod and smile. No one was fooled, not even Antonio.

He leaned down to pour her a fresh cup of coffee from a silver urn, "Your aunt dropped by this morning. I thought you should be warned."

Kimberly's forehead and cheeks turned pink and her lips nearly white. "Yes. She dropped by the shop. You know she has no legal right to throw you out of the townhouse. It is leased to you, unless in the last few days, private contracts are no longer permitted in Blueglennen?"

Antonio tossed his beautiful brown locks away from his face and chuckled, a chuckle both Kimberly and Alexandra thought forced, "Don't be silly, Kim," then he leaned down. His glasses which he'd tucked in the pocket of his stylish shirt were in imminent danger of falling into Kimberly's cup of coffee. "I hate to rush you ladies, but we really need this table soon."

The women searched the area wondering who wanted this table so badly. There was no one waiting. The truth dawned on Kimberly. Antonio's face was no more than a few inches from Kimberly's nose so when she gave him the stink eye, he was the only one who saw it. "I'll leave when I've finished this overpriced coffee and this tasteless torte. I am after all a paying customer."

Antonio was too tall to maintain such an awkward position for long. He stretched and straightened and stuffed his eyeglasses back into his shirt pocket and left with a parting shot, "Maybe, you're not so different from your aunt. For a moment you reminded me of her."

With a flip of his noble behind, Antonio sauntered off obviously pleased with himself. Alexandra leaned forward. "Shall we forget the tip?"

Star woke to the sound of someone walking down the cathedral aisle. She peeped over the pew and saw someone in a long black vestment carrying a valise. It must be one of the Bishop's priests. She could barely see the person in the gloom. The priest wore a hood, no, a sort of tall pointy hat made of paper and cloth like the pictures she'd seen of the old Duchess. There were sparkly stones embedded in the material. Maybe, what she was seeing was one of the mysterious and elusive priestesses of the church.

The stones winked at her from the sunlight filtering through the stained-glass windows above her head. She watched the person set the valise on the alter before the image of the Holy Centipede, a life-sized rendition of the Holy One all green silk body and golden eyes. Careful not to make any sound, Star tried to sit up. The priestess whirled around and saw her for the first time. All she could see were its eyes, eyes terrible in its fury. The figure swooped down upon her, but she was too fast for it. She squirmed away and began to run down the center aisle.

A tiny hard rock hit her between the shoulders. Another rock hit her in the head. She stumbled and corrected herself and tried to reach the massive cathedral doors in time. Arms wrapped themselves around her and a hand, a big smelly ugly hand, covered her mouth. She recognized overpowering incense. The smell made her cough. She was lifted off her feet and carried away. She struggled but the kidnapper was too strong.

Her kidnapper carried her down a series of stairs to the catacombs below the cathedral and then through the tunnel leading to Duke Tower. It had once been a secret passageway for the Duke and his family three hundred years ago. It had long since been neglected. It was wet and dark and smelled of nasty things. She heard the nasty things squealing and clawing about on their pointy feet. She struggled the harder to get away.

She didn't want to be left alone down here. Her kidnapper who grew impatient dumped her on the ground and when she tried to rise and run, he swooped down on her again. It must be a he, a strong and smelly he. Help me. Help me. Oh Momma. She felt a sharp pain on the back of her head.

Star woke and tried to open her eyes. They felt so heavy. Her arms felt heavy too. She made herself lift her arm, so she could touch her eyes to see if they were open. They were open, yet she was still in the dark. She tried to stand up and hit her head on something pitiless. It wasn't stone. It was plastic. She sat back down on the cold plastic beneath her. Her shaking fingers explored the walls. The walls curved. She hit the walls with her fists and the sound of her blows echoed inside and outside.

She fell forward when the container she was inside nearly tipped over. She sat down and screamed. The screams bounced off the container and inside her ears. And then she knew. She knew where she was. She tried to lift the lid of the garbage bin, but the lid refused to open. She sniffed the air and smelled old paper. She felt around on the bottom of the cart using her fingers as eyes and tried to understand what she held in her hand. It must be an envelope.

It was so hot. She gasped for air. Where was the air? Carefully she rose up an inch at a time and explored above her head. She tested the edge of the lid. Someone had taped the edges to keep out air and light. But she should have been able to tear away the tape and break free? Why couldn't she break free? Her heart hurt. Her head ached. She opened her mouth desperate for cool air, air of any kind. She began to claw at the walls calling out in her head for her mother, her father, for Sophie, even Dela Lemon.

She had been praying. She remembered falling asleep on the front pew, closest to the life-size statue of the Holy Centipede, close to where the altar stood before the holy image, where the priests kept the candles and the incense and the holy book. She had been praying and she had fallen asleep. She touched her face and felt the tears rolling down her cheeks and her neck. And then her body felt so heavy and she began to sail away.

The sound which erupted from Kimberly's mouth reminded her of the gasp of a frightened mouse. She'd been aiming for a sophisticated chuckle. Why couldn't she have taken acting lessons? Now that skill would have come in handy at times like these. She could have pretended an indifference she did not really feel. In the quiet of the Bookworm Emporium, Kimberly contemplated the shop with a quizzical eye wondering if all her problems could be solved by simply walking away. She could take her few personal belongings, lock the shop door, and walk away. Once the tiny payments stopped arriving at the bank, the bankers would foreclose on the business. Once the business was no more, then someone else would snap this little gem up for a song.

Like hell.

She knew full well the church would end up getting the property. The Bookworm would be gutted, the merchandise burned, and priests in hoods dancing around the pyre naked would be celebrating the end of radical degenerate ideas ruining the pure innocent minds of the townspeople. She had to hold her head for a moment. She felt as if she were clinging to a spinning top.

The doorbell jangled. She looked up. A groan escaped her lips. The person who entered never noticed. Tim Finstickel slipped inside. He avoided her eyes and scurried toward the back of the bookstore, his scent hanging in the air for a few nauseating moments. Holy Centipede! Did the man need a bath urgently or what? The Finstickel family had once been prominent members of society until Duke Dono fled the country in 4692. Without the Duke's favor, the family dispersed or faded into obscurity. Soon their fortunes declined. Yet, they managed to keep their Blueglennen home – the palatial apartments at the end of Wolfern Promenade.

The apartments were located right next to the Highway Watchtower and the magnificent windows overlooked not only Greenburg Valley below the castle mound to the southeast, but to the north views of Duke Tower and the plaza could be appreciated. Kimberly had been told a visitor, if standing in the middle of Finstickel's apartment could see through the massive floor-to-ceiling windows the plaza, the Cetacea stairs and rampart, Duke Tower and Bishop's Garden. Then when the visitor turned, he could see Mount Lordbuster in the distance and closer to the castle the road east, a winding gravel road paved in yellow rock.

A long dead former Sheriff of Blueglennen used the Finstickel family's only asset as a means of saving himself a few seastars. No one bothered to post a knight on Highway Watchtower any more. Why bother when the Finstickels were always in residence and the unofficial and unpaid watchers of the capitol city? Evidently the Finstickel apartments no longer include running water. Why else would he smell so bad? Finstickel was the last of his family. He'd never married. No surprise. Females preferred marriage partners who talked to people not to furniture.

In an effort to forget the unpleasantness of the morning, Kimberly sat down at her counter and concentrated on the bookshop's accounting problems. She had to figure out how to pay for next month's property taxes and the fire insurance payment. They were small compared to the other merchants' expenses yet her sales for this month were dismal. Perhaps she could do without chocolate? No more little coffees and cakes at Antonio's. That small economy would hardly be a hardship.

How about cutting out vegetables this time? She'd already eliminated meat. Maybe she could grow her own vegetables? From somewhere nearby she heard water running. Closing her accounting book, she turned toward the sound of running water and realized someone had gone into her private bathroom. She threw back the velvet curtains and hurried down the passageway wondering who had dared to come this way without a by-your-leave. She paused at the closed door of her bathroom listening to the sound of splashing inside.

Beyond furious she rapped smartly on the door, "Who's in there? This is a private facility. Get out or I'll be forced to call a knight. Do you hear me?" She banged on the door several times but whoever the interloper was he or she refused to come out. Kimberly had her suspicions and the idea of that man sitting on her toilet or using her bathroom shower made her skin crawl. "I'm going for the knights this instant."

She turned to her bedside dresser. Her purse was not in its usual place. She searched the room, frantic now. Had he taken her purse? All her disposable income was in her purse. She didn't make enough money to have a regular bank account like normal people. When she had tried to open a savings account, the bank clerk had informed her in a pitying way she had to come up with at least 200 seastars just to open a savings account.

Some people would think such a sum paltry. Not Kimberly. It was one yellow seastar more than she could afford. So, the absence of her purse in its usual place paralyzed her for a moment. She thought she might faint. When she didn't, she made herself move. She checked under the bed, in the dresser drawers, in the clothes closet, and then under the stairs. Still no purse. Then she realized the last time she had had her purse was at the café. Glaring at the bathroom door she hesitated. She couldn't call the duty officer because her cellphone was in her purse. All her money was in her purse.

As she left the bookshop and hurried down Merchants' Row, she knew her habit of keeping the shop keys in her sweater had been a mistake. She would keep them in her purse from now on. Because if she had left them in her purse, she would have known hours ago she had left her purse under the table at the café. By the time she trotted down Wolfern Promenade and into the plaza she was nearly out of breath. She went directly to the café table where they had sat and instead of finding her purse, she found a young couple sitting close together sharing an iced coffee. They were so close they could have been conjoined twins.

"Did you see a purse under the table?" she asked them.

They glanced up at her sleepily with drowsy love-soaked eyelids and shook their heads in the negative, annoyingly in unison, then returned to their mutual admiration of each other. Kimberly wanted to smack the love right out of their heads. She rushed into the café and was grateful Antonio was not in his usual spot paying court to the ladies while sitting seductively on his stool sipping his cappuccino and waving his eyeglasses around like a baton.

Instead she noticed the pretty blonde waitress just finishing up with a customer. She hurried over to her, "I believe I left my purse under the outdoor table. Did someone find it? It's made of brown imitation leather and has a gold chain for a strap."

The waitress smiled, "Oh yeah. One of the guys brought it in. Antonio recognized it and he said he'd deliver the purse to the customer personally."

"Well, I'm that person and he hasn't. Is it still here?"

"I'll take a look in the back. Just a wave."

The minutes seemed to stretch until she wanted to vault over the counter and go searching for her property in the backroom herself. When the waitress reappeared carrying Kimberly's purse, Kimberly's legs began to shake in reaction. Kimberly fairly snatched the purse away from the poor girl and belatedly turned in time to say to her, "Thank you so much. I'm sure you know how important a woman's purse is."

The waitress smiled, "You bet. I once tore an old boyfriend's apartment apart looking for mine. I'm glad no one stole it."

By the time Kimberly returned to the shop, she discovered whoever had been in her bathroom was gone. There was evidence that someone had used her shower and her sink. The floor was wet too, and the towel was dirty and soaking wet. She rushed back into the shop searching for the monstrous criminal who would do such a thing and discovered soon enough the bookstore was empty.

When she left the shop, she locked the door tight and double checked to make sure the door was locked at least three times; and as a further precaution she checked to make sure her purse was dangling from her shoulder, moving the purse closer to her hip to reassure herself. She felt violated. How could someone do something so nasty? How could they invade her privacy and use her personal belongings, her bar of soap, her shampoo, even her brush and comb? She would have to have everything sterilized immediately.

She wanted to find him; she wanted to face him and scream at him and tear his face off. She hurried back to the plaza and down to the end of the promenade staring up at the Finstickel apartments. It had to have been Tim Finstickel. No one else would have done such a thing. She stood before the massive lobby doors, suddenly unsure of herself. The glass inserts showed her a palatial interior with an expensive tiled floor, and in the distance a grand staircase leading to a second-floor landing. She tried the door.

It wouldn't budge. To her right inserted into the stone façade was a speaker. She pressed the button below the speaker. When no one answered she stabbed the button numerous times. Then she grabbed the metal doorknocker above her head and using it like a stone to pulverize wheat into chaff made such a racket several heads popped out of the upstairs windows to see who was making all the noise.

"I'm looking for Finstickel," she called up to one woman. "Have you seen him?"

"You must be joking," the middle-aged woman snorted. "I have better things to do then keep an eye out for the likes of him. Go away, Dela. You're making poor Michael's head ache."

Several apartments down, a door opened, and Crystova Moth appeared holding a cookie in one hand and a book under her arm. When she recognized Kimberly she smiled, "Hi there. What's up?"

"I'm looking for Finstickel."

"He's down there at the juice bar," Crystova said using her cookie as a pointer. "He's at the end table in the sun. Looks like he's drying his clothes on the empty chairs."

The woman leaning out of her second story window laughed, "Oh my. Yes. There he is using the chairs as his own laundry line. I'm surprised he hasn't been booted out yet."

Without another word, too angry to speak Kimberly stormed toward the juice bar and surprised Finstickel reading a book and sipping a pineapple-passion fruit smoothie.

"How dare you use my private bathroom to take a shower and wash your clothes," she began. "You had no right. My private quarters are not for the use of the general public. You are from now on barred from ever entering my shop again. Are you listening to me Delo Finstickel? Delo Finstickel, do me the courtesy to look up and pay attention when I'm speaking to you."

Delo Finstickel continued to stare down at his old magazine. Every so often he would sneak a sip of his smoothie, but never did he, ever, look into her eyes or so much as acknowledge her presence. She was sure he heard her though. Oh yes. Of that she was sure. Her voice must have been louder than she intended because she had drawn a small crowd.

It was the hottest part of the day and most people were inside out of the burning sun working, studying, napping or, watching something on the internet. Sane people didn't sit in the full glare of the sun with the heat fairly frying the tops of their heads. A knight strode up to them and that was when Finstickel started gathering up his belongings especially the underwear drying on the chair closest to him.

His socks were draped on the chair close to where Kimberly stood. On the other chair his shirt, once upon a time, white, now a smudgy brown lump was drying in the sun mocking her. The shirt seemed to say: "You see. I can use your soap and your sink and leave my filthy cooties all over your bathroom." One side of the shirt was already dry.

"Is there some difficulty here?" the knight asked trying to maintain a pleasant demeanor as his eyes roamed over the two and then the objects drying on the backs of the juice chairs. He carefully avoided staring at Finstickel sitting at the table in only a pair of trousers. Finstickel's face and neck were brown yet his chest and arms were white as the underbelly of a cave dwelling rat.

Kimberly faced the knight. He looked about fifty. He had kind eyes. She suspected due to his lack of ferocity the Governor's people had posted him to the worst possible duty for a knight – keeping an eye on the tourists, the university students, and the teenagers who liked to hang out at the juice joint in the late afternoon.

"This man came into my bookstore and used my private bathroom to shower and wash his clothes. Look at his hair. The back of it is still wet."

"When did this happen Dela," the knight asked pulling out his notebook. "And why didn't you call us immediately?"

"It happened about ten or fifteen minutes ago," she began and for the next thirty minutes standing in the full sun with sweat dripping off her forehead she tried to explain what had happened in her shop. Finstickel mumbled something barely discernable with his pointed nose and muddy brown eyes continuing to examine the table as if fascinated by the contents upon it. Occasionally he took a sip of his smoothie. Once while the Knight was interviewing her, she saw him get up, flip his socks over then his shirt and sit himself back down. The knight ignored him.

"I'll need to go back to your bookstore and see the evidence of this major crime," the knight said with a straight face. Kimberly stepped back realizing she had been wrong about him. His eyes were not kind. He'd just been humoring her, thinking she was as crazy as Finstickel. No doubt he had encountered similar petty squabbles between people like Finstickel and herself and had simply lumped her in with them. The knight didn't know her. And when he did get a good look inside the Bookworm, he would still assume she was as crazy as Finstickel.

Only eccentrics were interested in products made from paper or parchment. No one read books or magazines or maps anymore. There was no need. The internet provided all the reading materials and maps a person could want. Her shop was a dinosaur, out of step, and out of date. Even collectors no longer bothered to keep printed materials – not unless they were radicals or anarchists.

"It may not be a major crime to you, unless of course, you find Finstickel in your bathroom one day using your shampoo and your toilet paper. Then maybe you'll feel different." As she tried to defend herself, she noticed Finstickel move his feet. She feared he would try to run away. That's when she noticed her jewelry box under the table.

A wave of nausea came over her. She felt as if she'd been violated. "There has been a crime," she told the knight and pointed down at her jewelry box. "That's my property. My grandmother gave me that jewelry box when I was ten years old."

The knight paused in his notetaking and bent down to look under the table. He looked up into Finstickel's face, "Is that your jewelry box?"

Finstickel pretending innocence moved his chair back to look under the table, "I've never seen that thing before."

The knight got on his knees and pulled the jewelry box out from under the table, his face contorting as he tried not to breathe encountering Finstickel's foul smelling feet for the first time. When he was standing erect and his skin returned to its normal color, he said to Kimberly, "Give me your name and address, Dela. Since Finstickel claims not to know anything about the box, I will have to place the jewelry box in evidence until you can prove ownership."

After careful thought, trying very hard not to cry she looked into the knight's eyes and said, "Yes. It is my jewelry box and I will prove it. Forget about the other crime. My jewelry box is more important to me."

The knight flipped his notebook shut and stepped back, "As you can see Dela, the man is a paying customer and has every right to sit at this table and sip his smoothie."

"And dry his socks and underwear on the chairs?" she asked as she brushed by several other customers who had come over to watch the spectacle.

Before she returned to her shop, she made a detour to Caleb's place in the village. He had a tiny house at the end of a shady wood. His garage door was open, and she could hear him banging around inside the dark interior. She stepped inside and called his name.

Caleb appeared around the corner with a hammer and a chisel and smiled when he recognized her, "Hi."

"Hi yourself."

"Is something wrong?" he asked suddenly concerned.

"Yes and no. I need a lock for my bathroom door. Do you have one lying around?"

"I'll do you one better," he said giving her a reassuring smile.

"Don't stop what you're doing. It can wait," she said feeling suddenly guilty.

"No problem. I'm just doing a commission for the Knight's Guild. It's not due for another month."

Two hours later, Kimberly had a brand-new lock for her bathroom door, one which bolted on the outside which she could keep locked during the day. In addition, Caleb replaced her old private backroom doorknob with a locking doorknob which meant people like her Aunt Victoria and Finstickel couldn't make themselves at home in her private quarters. She insisted on paying Caleb. She knew she had to keep their relationship as business-like as possible. He would only accept small payments from her over the course of a year and nothing she said could make him change his mind. She was extremely grateful and, in her gratitude, wanted to invite him for supper one night then realized he had someone else in his life now.

By the end of the afternoon, Kimberly had added up the numbers in her accounting book with disappointing results. It was a relief to be interrupted several times during the day from her dark thoughts to greet curious tourists browsing her store with wondering eyes. They acted as if they'd stumbled back in time. She heard a woman exclaim over a calendar, "I remember having one of these. I remember wishing the calendar could talk, especially when I missed an important meeting. Now they can!"

By evening Kimberly managed to come up with a few economies which could get her through the rest of the year. Eventually she found the courage to go into her bathroom and start scrubbing away signs the intruder had taken his pleasure there. Once the bathroom belonged to her again, physically and psychologically, she showered and put on a new face and decided to step out like a normal person and reenter the Delphinid race.

Kimberly joined a few of her neighbors as they moved down the street toward the plaza. She spied Crystova sitting on a bench with a friend and joined them. She sat facing them on a stone pedestal which faced the River Tower and listened to the two university professors discussing literature and art and politics. Occasionally, she was prompted to join in, but she preferred to listen.

She'd finished her ice cream and was looking for a trash receptacle for the remains of a napkin and disposable spoon when she heard a woman scream. The fancy wrought iron sconces along the plaza walls were ablaze illuminating the blue tiles and the ivory stone squares, the tables, and the patrons. The patrons were milling about the plaza, some were sitting, some standing and still others eating. So, when a small woman, no more than four-feet six inches tall came running through the plaza screaming, her face a mask of terror, everyone turned. They could see her clothes were torn and bloody.

A man twice her size chased her through the crowd and nearly caught up to her before she managed to pull herself up the Cetacea stairs. The stairs led to Rampart Walk and the River Watchtower on the other side. The stairs were narrow and steep, and she had to struggle to climb each one. The man who was nearly seven-feet tall and three-hundred pounds carried a heavy baseball bat. At one point, he swung at her. The bat missed her heel by inches and struck the step instead. It was as if the crowd was watching a play on a stage. Nobody moved. All eyes were on the two actors playing their parts. The man was in a murderous rage and the woman was beyond terrified. It wasn't real. This couldn't be happening. Not here. Not in Blueglennen.

In shock Kimberly stood and watched anxiously waiting for the Governor's soldiers to come rushing out of the tower or the knights on duty to rescue the woman. But the soldiers did not come. The knights were missing. Where were the knights? Every eye was locked on the tableau above them. Kimberly made a sound. It wasn't until later, she realized no one could hear her over the woman's screams as she stood upon the parapet and with one look back at the mad man with the bat threw herself off the rampart.

Everything went black. Later, Kimberly was ashamed to remember how she'd fainted and her cry when she landed heavily on the stones of the plaza, grazing her elbow and her cheek. For a split second, she'd felt sorry for herself. A stranger helped her to her feet and set her on the bench vacated by Crystova. Crystova, she learned had run home to fetch her boyfriend in the hopes he could save the woman. There had been plenty of able-bodied men in the crowd close at hand. Kimberly had seen plenty of them posturing themselves in front of the ladies. Why hadn't they stopped the man? Why hadn't she used her cellphone and called the knights? Where had the knights been anyway?

All around her people were talking. She listened in a sick haze.

"Did they find her? Is she alive?"

"Are you crazy? She plunged fifty feet down to the valley below. Some guys from the village fishing by the river heard her screams and turned in time to see her throw herself over the wall. They found her on the rocks near the river."

"Where were the knights? Couldn't they hear what was going on? Why didn't they do anything?"

"The knights were busy in the village. They're looking for a missing girl."

"What missing girl?"

"I don't know. Some school girl."

"Who were those people? Why was the man chasing the woman with a baseball bat? Were they on drugs?"

Kimberly jumped up wanting desperately to do something, anything to expunge her sense of guilt. She stared angrily at the people milling about, some of them taking pictures of the tower and the stairs. "We did nothing," she heard herself say. "We just stood and watched and did nothing. What's the matter with you? Aren't you as ashamed as me? We're all cowards. We did nothing."

Empty faces stared back at her. She pushed her way through the people, wanting only to get back to the safety of her shop. A hand tugged on her arm and she whirled around ready to do battle if necessary. When she recognized Honeysweet she stopped and turned to face him, "Were you here? Did you see what happened?"

"No," he said. "I was in the village having a drink with friends. I heard what happened. Did you know her?"

"No."

"I did," and when he said that she looked closely into his eyes and saw the sadness looking back at her. "She'd been in one of my classes last year. Her name is Deletha Child. She has a little boy about five years old. She wanted to go back to school and become a nurse. She wanted to help people."

"Did you know that man, that monster? Was he her boyfriend?"

"No," Honeysweet said. "No, he wasn't. I'm sure he wasn't. At least from what I heard on the way here. Deletha had been at Wolf Inn pub having a drink with some school friends and she was on her way home when the man accosted her and insisted on buying her a drink. She refused, and he chased her down. Maybe he'd never been rejected before. I don't know. Someone else said she took a stick to his needle-chub. That he became crazy when she tore a hole in his new silk upholstery."

"He had a chub?" Kimberly asked in shock. "I thought they were dangerous. Too many horses have been injured pulling a chub, the back wheels are too high and the whole under carriage is flimsy. On our rough roads people end up in ditches or down ravines and worse seahorses are crippled or die. Who did he bribe?"

"Some people still have permits to buy them. There's a local shop that still sells them in Old Town. It's expensive and not worth the cost. Young guys get a kick out of being up high, above the crowd. It makes them think they're special."

"Was he rich?"

"No. I don't think so. I don't know. You look unwell. Let me escort you home, Dela Lemon."

As they moved away from the plaza toward Wolfern Promenade, as the soldiers and the knights began to trickle into the keep from the only entrance along Bishop's Gate, and as the curious were pushed back, Honeysweet and Kimberly heard people talking about the tragedy. Someone had recognized the man and Kimberly heard his name for the first time – Cartel Hills. Cartel Hills had been arrested. There had been plenty of witnesses to Cartel's murderous rampage, but would anyone come forward and say so? Hardly. That would mean the witnesses would have to confess they did nothing to save Deletha Child.

Kimberly wheeled about and began pushing her way back toward Wolfern Promenade, back to the knights. She had to do something. She had to do something to wipe clean the shame pressing on her mind to the exclusion of everything else. Honeysweet called out to her but she ignored him and kept on moving toward the press of knights clustered at the far end of the Royal Plaza, as far away from Duke Tower and the Cetacea Stairs, and the place where the man was being led away to prison by D.I. Hawk and several deputies, the man who had taken a baseball bat and tried to bludgeon a young woman who felt the only thing she could do was jump off Cetacea Rampart to escape a beating.

When she got close enough to the cluster of knights to speak, she heard one of them say, "Yeah, she was half Lacertidae, you know. A little Delphinid, a lot of Lacertidae. I think the nut-job is a half breed too. They deserve each other." One knight, a very handsome knight broke away from his peers in disgust and seemed to be looking at her expectantly. She opened her mouth to speak. Nothing came out. He moved to touch her shoulder.

He was too beautiful, disturbingly beautiful, and this day was not meant for beauty. This day had become foul and dangerous and something in the recesses of her mind warned her, the ugliness was far from over. She brushed past the strange knight and pushed her way through the gawkers milling about doing nothing constructive. Once she was free of the crowd, she began to run toward home.

E3 Shellfargon Year 5092 TQMP WK 1: UES Albion 4
Placement within Duke Tower Coroner Hall. Visa Successful 5092-5095. Former coroner removed from position. Sent to Delphadore. Staff unwilling to reveal reason for dismissal. Coroner Van Creek's records impeccable. Surgery pristine. Equipment state-of-the-art.

Several records missing: DTK2's post mortem report and samples. Granted permission to disinter and examine body of DTK2 on E1's orders. Mindful of unforeseen diplomatic difficulties, I seek permission from UES Albion (Captains 3) to proceed with exhumation and examination. Will await signatory permissions.

Examination of Star Bridgekeeper postponed on orders of Governor Saurus.

Chapter 5

Just as Kimberly sat down to drink a hot cup of tea to calm her nerves, she heard someone bang on the shop door. The day which initially had so much promise was now a nightmare. She was afraid to open the door. What could be worse than what had happened to poor Deletha? Yet a nuisance of a thought surfaced – what further indignity would she experience before the day was done? Was it Finstickel on the other side of the door demanding to use her bathroom because he was descended from Duke Dono? Oh, get over yourself. Of course, he wouldn't. The man was crazy but not crazy enough to be noticed by the Tower Knights. She must be calm and take stock of the day.

The reminder that Deletha Child, unlike herself, could never again take stock of her day or answer her door brought the nightmare back in all its horror. Her gut reacted, and she had to run to the bathroom before the contents of her stomach ended up on her dining room table. The poor, poor woman. How could she be so selfish about her trivial concerns when she'd just witnessed a young woman's death?

As she threw on a robe and tucked her feet into her slippers, the knocking continued, getting louder and more urgent. She hurried to the front of the shop wondering if Star had witnessed the tragedy. A trickle of dread slid down her spine, somehow, she just knew the person on the other side of the door was going to tell her something dreadful. Before opening the door, she peered through the glass. Nearly shaking with relief, she quickly drew back the bolt allowing her two visitors inside. Sophia rushed in and whirled about to face her as Caleb carefully shut and bolted the shop door behind him.

"Star is missing. We've been looking everywhere for her. Antonio said he had seen Star with you this afternoon. You were with some lady and you and Star quarreled. Is that true?" Kimberly took in Sophia's youth and stature, annoyed at how tall and manly Caleb appeared standing beside her. Unfortunately, she and Sophia had never clicked. They were such opposites.

Sophia had no time for books or learning nor was she interested in debating politics or philosophy or science. Sophia preferred to spend her time flipping through fashion magazines, gossiping with friends, sitting on the couch, or laying on a beach towel near the river. Kimberly had known Sophia all her life and Sophia's vegetative habits, knowing smile, and shifty eyes now appeared alarmingly sinister.

When Caleb went to stand beside Sophia and put his hand on her shoulder, Kimberly wanted to cheer. So, he had finally made his choice. He had finally come to his senses. It was odd though the twinge of regret she felt mingled with relief. She sincerely wished he would have found a better partner, someone as thoughtful and eager to please as himself.

After a minute of tense silence, Kimberly realized she had to say something. "Star showed up at the shop earlier today upset about the kids at school. She wanted to talk. My friend Alexandra came by and we took Star to Antonio's Café for a treat. It was my intention to persuade her to go back to school. Before I could convince her, something she said upset me and I spoke my mind. She was offended and rushed off in a huff."

As Kimberly related the events of the day, in the back of her mind she thought, *I'm standing in my shop in my bathrobe and slippers and I'm defending myself as if I have already been accused of something heinous. Why? I wish that little twit had had someone else to torment with her silly schoolgirl dramas.*

What annoyed Kimberly most was Sophia's expression as if she had already made up her mind about Kimberly and the decision would not bode well for her. If she was so sure Kimberly was at fault, why did she continue to stare at a point midway between Kimberly's waist and her neck, never actually connecting with Kimberly's face? It was Sophia's way but at this moment in time, Kimberly really needed to know what Sophia was thinking.

The logical part of Kimberly realized she couldn't read Sophia's mind or gage her thoughts by her facial expressions. Since Governor Saurus rose to power, Blueglennens were getting better at hiding their true thoughts. What concerned her the most was the fact powerful emotions bring out buried jealousies and insecurities. We are never far away from our origins. We may be the dominant species, but we still think with the primitive part of our brains.

Unable to suppress an inward sigh of resignation, she anticipated this situation would soon spin out of control. An angry relative fearing for her sister might latch onto a sacrificial lamb. Since she was the last person to see Star and she'd admitted to quarrelling with her in public, she would be the most likely suspect if something happened to Star. She suspected there were quite a few innocent people in the dungeons, prisoners waiting in their damp, cold, dark cells for rescue which would never happen because the people walking in the rich air of freedom and sunlight had forgotten them.

Why had her thoughts immediately gravitated toward prison? She hadn't been accused of anything. Yet. Star was probably hiding somewhere nearby. She'd probably fallen asleep after a cathartic bout of tears. And when Star returned home, everyone would go back to their everyday lives apart from Kimberly. If this situation spiraled out of control, nothing would be the same again. Didn't these people realize hysteria was not the answer? What happens in the next few minutes might change everyone's relationship forever? Kimberly had an unhappy suspicion Caleb and Sophia were similar in their view of the world – prone to ignore unpleasant truths until there was no way to avoid them.

That was probably why she had done everything she could to get them interested in each other. It was Caleb's lack of inner certainty, his desire to please everyone without exception and then to be upset when those same people treated him unfairly which Kimberly found so exasperating. She had been a coward resigned to sharing her life with a man she did not love, just to avoid the potential pain of being rejected by someone she really could love.

For years, she had continued to ignore the signs of discontent between them. She suspected his reason for siding with Sophia had more to do with his fear of being alone than any conviction Kimberly was responsible for Star's disappearance. Maybe he really believed Kimberly had done something terrible to Star?

"Why didn't you insist she go back to school straight away or go home?" Sophia asked in a voice Kimberly could barely hear. Even in the best of times, Sophia tended to speak in whispers and when she was upset, she was positively incoherent.

"She told me your parents were gone. It was close to the lunch recess anyway. I thought I could persuade her to go back to school after she had a treat at Antonio's. Feel free to search the shop and my private quarters if you don't believe me. Star is not here, nor have I taken her prisoner."

Caleb spoke up for the first time, "We don't think that, Kimberly. We're just concerned for Star."

She turned to him and smiled, relieved to find his expression still the same – open and friendly and pleased to see her. His blonde hair, as thin and fine as a young child's, looked a bit damp around his forehead and temples. It was obvious he and Sophia had been scouring the castle grounds for Star. "Let me help you look for her," she offered.

"What did you and Star quarrel about?" Sophia insisted her frown deepening.

"Nothing, nothing really. It was stupid. Star claimed one of my friends would be going to hell for not believing in her church and I reacted instead of remembering she's still a child. It was silly."

"Why did she call you a witch, if there was nothing serious about your quarrel?" Sophia stepped away from Caleb assuming he would side with Kimberly. "When she called you a witch, that was a serious accusation, you know. She spends a lot of time here in this gloomy, dusty place and it's not healthy."

"And you think letting her be brainwashed by those cultists is healthy?"

Caleb reached over and pulled Sophie closer to him and with a neutral expression said, "Sophie, you know Star. She's going through a tough time right now."

"What does that have to do with her disappearance?" Sophia asked pulling away to look up at him, her expression mulish. Kimberly recalled with misgivings the first time she had met Sophia. She had known within a few seconds she and Sophia would never be friends. In public they were cordial, in private Kimberly rarely thought about her. Now she wondered if Sophia's anger had more to do with jealousy than Star's disappearance. Perhaps in Sophia's mind, old flames should hate each other, and the way Caleb offered to fix leaky faucets reminded Sophia she didn't have complete control over him.

Kimberly tried to allay Sophia's worries even though she didn't deserve it. "I know you're upset but keep an open mind. Star is going through a painful period in her life. You told me Poppy took all Star's friends away from her. I think they were never really Star's friends in the first place and she is well rid of them. Yet she's reminded daily of how her friends have deserted her and when we were at the café, she saw Poppy and her will-o-wisp friends sitting at a table at the Green Monkey laughing and teasing each other. It had to hurt. Because she's young, she lashed out at the closest target. She chose to hurt one of my friends. I don't want to say anything more about it."

When Caleb attempted to put his arm around Sophia's shoulder, Sophia brushed him off and marched to the door, "I can't hold this off any longer. Mom and Dad won't be back until tomorrow afternoon. I'm in charge. I must go to the knights and tell them about this. They've been searching in the village, but I think they need to look here inside the bailey. They have the equipment and the power necessary to find her."

Kimberly watched the mixed emotions playing across Caleb's expressive face. She decided to put him out of his misery, "Sophia's right Caleb. The town should be aware of what's happened. Even if Star is discovered safe and sullen, it is better than the alternative. Time is crucial."

When Caleb nodded and hurried after Sophia, Kimberly was relieved. By the time the two of them made their way to the Department of Justice and Sophia announced her concerns about Star, Kimberly would be dressed and ready for the knights and their questions. She had no illusions about the way the knights of the Department of Justice worked. They much preferred the obvious to the subtle and politics rode beside them every minute of the day.

She was poor and with her continual reliance on special services an irritant to the despot currently ruling the capital. With her organization of the Merchant's Alliance she might even become dangerous to the church. She was already a threat as an unbeliever and an agitator. She would be a perfect target since she was without a protector, poor and a pain in the ass.

In her private quarters, as she sat at her little table near the window, she parted her curtains to peer out, with her fingers rubbing the soft velour fabric of her window like a child seeking the comfort of a much-loved blanket. She noticed absently how the moonlight attempted to penetrate the thicker darkness of the alley. She craned her head to catch a glimpse of the moon and stared and stared at its face. She felt empty inside. How odd. She should be afraid right now, the way she used to be terrified of her grandfather's displeasure when she had misbehaved.

A light moving down the alley startled her. She drew back and quickly turned off the lamp behind her then parted the curtains and peered out as people entered the alley. She recognized the familiar dark blue uniforms and heavy boots of the Governor's guard, but they were also wearing armor-plated chest shields and leggings and carrying flashlights. The flashlights panned back and forth, flickering and bobbing, as they searched every inch of the alley, every brick and every object. They searched behind, inside and under the trash bins as well as all the crates and old boxes left near the bins.

Did they really believe they would find Star stuffed in one of the trash bins behind the shops? Did they really think she was such a fool as to dispose of the child's body so close to home? Star might have been slender and small, but Kimberly was no Sea Serpent. To accomplish such a feat, she would had needed an accomplice to assist in lifting Star's body into the garbage bin.

The trickle of fear sliding down her spine made her hands shake. She let go of the curtain allowing the blue folds to swing back into place, thus effectively shutting out the night and the men searching for the missing girl. By morning the news would be all over Blueglennen and she suspected she would be the prime suspect. The knock on her shop door confirmed her worst fears.

On trembling legs, she rose to her feet and walked across the uneven floorboards, down the dark hall, and through the red velvet curtains into the shop. Standing outside her door stood D.I. Burhani Hawk with several of his knights in tow. He said something her ears refused to hear. She invited him in and while the knights searched her shop and her private quarters, she sat on the window seat with her back to the street where several people had converged.

A brief glance had been enough to tell her the merchants who didn't attend the meeting were chief among the eager onlookers. She recognized Sylvia Paleone and Luella Morrison. The knights hadn't bothered to inspect anyone else's shop or home, only hers. No one could miss the implications.

What had Sophia told them? Caleb must have said something; he must have defended her to the police. Yet she knew him well enough to know authority unnerved him. He much preferred peace to confrontation. In the beginning she had liked him for his gentleness. Now she would have wished for someone stronger and braver, someone willing to support her, perhaps even defend her. She had only herself to blame. She'd pushed him aside.

Near dawn, she was not surprised to find herself sitting at a scratched worn wooden table across from D.I. Hawk and one of his other men, a man who preferred to take notes and look up at her only to glare suspiciously at her answers as if he already knew she was guilty. Typical Blueglennen justice. The room was lit so bright, Kimberly winced squeezing her eyes shut against the blinding whiteness. She felt as if she was at the mercy of the sun's full rays. Her eyes began to tear up. The light in the room dimmed and from the corner of her eye she noticed D.I. Hawk walking back to his chair. Thoughtful or premeditated?

"Now Delan Lemon. May I have your first name please," he asked.

"It's Dela, sir. Dela Kimberly Lemon. I'm unmarried. Or better yet why don't you call me Delphus Lemon since my status is neutral and I'm a citizen of Curl."

"I see," he said his lips manufacturing a smile while his piercing black eyes scrutinized her face. "I am mistaken then in assuming Caleb Lanternlighter is your husband or former husband."

"We have always been friends," she said and hesitated.

"From what I understand you were more than just friends."

"Yes, we were and then we weren't. Our relationship changed recently."

"Five years is a long time. You make it sound as if you were only lovers for a few weeks."

What did her relationship with Caleb have to do with Star Bridgekeeper?

"We have known each other fourteen years. For the first few years we were strictly friends. A year ago, we ended our closer relationship."

"When he switched his attentions to Sophia Bridgekeeper?" D.I. Hawk asked in a gentle voice. Kimberly had no trouble figuring out his gentle interrogation was a trick used to fool his victims into thinking he was on their side. Some people might be fooled by his act, not her. She must not say anything foolish or risk incriminating herself. No flip remarks about Star's neediness or the Centipede cultists brainwashing her.

"No. A year ago, we were no longer lovers. We were friends. I was the one that suggested a relationship change. He agreed. We've remained good friends. He continues to drop by. Sometimes, we'll watch movies together or go for walks or ride out into the countryside, but our relationship is nothing like it used to be. We'll always be friends. We have so much history together; I can't imagine not having him as a friend. I hope we are still good friends when we're old and gray. Caleb's been seeing Sophia Bridgekeeper for the last few months. I was relieved. I mean. I was happy to see Caleb dating again."

"According to Dela Bridgekeeper their relationship has been a long one, nearly two years long. She believes your jealousy ruined her and Caleb's relationship."

Kimberly lifted her head and stared into the man's eyes and gasped. "What? That's insane. Have you asked Caleb? He'll confirm the timeline. The two of them have been dating for only a few months. I wanted Caleb to find someone. I knew he was miserable. He just doesn't have it in him to be alone. He's the kind of person who needs someone to love, someone he can take care of and watch over. Ask him? He'll tell you the truth."

The more she thought about Sophia's lie the more anger churned in her belly, an anger she did everything she could to hold back. Her body trembled with the effort. For the first time in a long time, she imagined herself beating the vapid little twit senseless.

D.I. Hawk watched her closely. His intensity reminded her of a Bitterroot badger watching and waiting for signs of weakness, "I, of course, will check out your claim Dela Lemon. Now then. Let us move on to the day of Star's disappearance. At what time did she show up at your shop?"

Four hours later still playing with a cold cup of coffee, Kimberly answered Inspector Bracewaddle's questions which simply regurgitated D.I. Hawk questions. Bracewaddle's questions lacked creativity which was good because she didn't have to think too hard about the answers. An hour ago, D.I. Hawk left presumably for a nice leisurely lunch in the plaza. Kimberly, on the other hand, was given a stale sandwich and limp salad smothered in some ghastly vinegar. Her throat refused to swallow the stuff.

The nightmare continued and the hands of the clock hanging from above the door wobbled slowly forward. The only sound in the room was Bracewaddle's pen scratching the surface of his notepad as he wrote or doodled or did whatever he did to pass the time. She thought about asking for a book or a notepad, so she could doodle too.

The fear and anger had long since settled into the pit of her stomach and the rest of her felt only an overpowering weariness. She wanted to sleep. She wanted so much to go home and make herself a nice cup of tea and sleep away this hellish day. She had never been inside the Department of Justice offices, the glass enclosed rooms next to the Department of Safety. Some wits liked to call the place the Department of No Return. She wished she hadn't thought of that just now.

Duke's Tower comprised a central courtyard jutting out into the plaza with the offices of the licensing bureau, city trash collection, city post office, water analysts, and a myriad of other service departments side by side. Further back in the central hub was where the sheriff and his knights controlled the barracks.

In a small corner of the first floor someone had assigned D.I. Hawk and his inspector an interrogation room and adjoining office. The least dangerous prisoners were kept in the glass-enclosed box where anyone entering the room could see the prisoners in their tiny holding cells. Kimberly had not been assigned a cell yet. Perhaps because she was a woman, they continued to keep her in the airless, windowless, interrogation room.

The floor above her was where she believed the Department of Safety resided. The Governor had more than doubled his police force since the uprising twenty years ago. She knew the fourth-floor rooms belonged to the Lieutenant Governor. The fifth floor used to be the penthouse suites belonging to the old Dukes. For nearly a century the suites had belonged to Duke Dono's family until he absconded with all the wealth. The suite overlooked the bailey and Bishop's Garden. Now the fifth floor belonged to Governor Saurus. She'd never been to the fifth floor; yet rumors suggested he'd changed the apartments to fit his needs.

In the old days, the rooms were used for fortification with

windows only wide enough for arrows and walls five stones thick. Lavish carpets from foreign countries separated the apartments from the lower orders. Saurus chose to gut and redo the rooms to fit his idea of luxury. He needed thick warm curtains to keep out the chill and large fireplaces big enough to stand in. His enemies called him the thumb sucker. Saurus should take a lesson from another guy who bled his subjects dry to pay for his comforts and lavish lifestyle.

A thousand years ago, the Wolfern Napalo had strutted his way across the seas and landed on the shores of the Lacertidae. His inept attempt to dominate the east failed miserably. When he returned to Blueglennen, he survived long enough to end his days in his own dungeon.

Years ago, she had seen glossy pictures of the Governor's penthouse and had been more impressed with the views from the balconies, one facing the plaza and the other on the Siren River side of the castle, than with the opulent furniture and priceless paintings hanging on the newly painted stone walls. She shivered at the thought of all that space, the coldness of stone and concrete and plaster, the dizzying heights where one would feel so small and insignificant. She preferred the warmth of wood and velvet and those colorful and richly textured carpets from Bojenlac.

When she heard the doorknob turn, she looked to Bracewaddle for confirmation. With his head bent and his pen moving feverishly across the notebook, he was too busy finishing his masterpiece to notice. The door flew open and D.I. Hawk strode in wearing his usual black leather jacket which swept the floor as he walked. His boots strode across the room with such swaggering confidence, she felt real fear.

Fear because they made no sound on the stone floor. He moved like a big cat, so graceful and smooth. His jacket was typical Department of Justice issue for knights. The boots were not. Every other officer in the building had the shiny black boots which made such a racket when they hit the tiled floors. For some reason Hawk was permitted to wear his own footgear. What were they made of? Why did they make no sound?

Was it the body that made the man or the man who made the body? She compared Caleb to D.I. Hawk and knew the comparison unfair. Still she was mad at Caleb, so she continued to judge them based on their looks and demeanor. Caleb was strong and sturdy like an ox. D.I. Hawk was lithe and athletic and probably just as strong. Caleb was trusting and thoughtful. No one knew what D.I. Hawk was thinking but he appeared to be suspicious of everyone. So, Hawk won the hottie contest and Caleb won the sweetie contest. There was no question then.

If she'd been Hawk's former love interest, she wouldn't be in an interrogation room, alone, fighting for her life. It made her want to cry.

This afternoon, Hawk had replaced his white silk shirt with a blue one made of expensive cotton. Yes, indeed, he was a well-dressed man. He had the sleek good looks of a model, but she was not deceived. She had spent too much time in this room with him to ever doubt his piercing intellect. His eyes swept the room and settled on Bracewaddle with an uncharacteristic annoyance, then shrugged and turned his full attention on her. She wanted him to glare at Bracewaddle instead.

"I've finished my investigation and sent my report to my superior, Dela Lemon. You may go."

Bracewaddle set down his pen, his shaggy gray eyebrows wriggling in consternation, "But sir. I thought."

"Dela Lemon is no flight risk, Tom," he told the inspector and turned to face her. "I recommend that you stay in Blueglennen for the duration of our investigation. I have interviewed Dela Sea...Alexandra Montegue and she has confirmed your story. We are satisfied with her explanation of the facts. The department no longer feels you are a person of interest. I will escort you to the courtyard."

Side by side they traversed the corridors, the stairs, the numerous offices of the Department of Justice without a word. A quick glance at the forlorn individual trapped behind the holding cell glass like a zoo animal on display made Kimberly flinch with sympathetic pity. Hawk paused at the sheriff's office and the deputy sheriff, someone Kimberly had known most of her life, Danny Wakefield fetched her personal belongings. After she signed for her belongings, Wakefield handed them to her with a relieved smile and a pat on the hand. He was relieved! She stifled the hysteria threatening to choke her.

In the courtyard with the sun shining down on her head, she and Hawk faced each other. His eyes were much lighter than she remembered, almost the color of almonds. She was surprised to see him smile down at her, "I hope you will pardon our zeal Dela Lemon. We are only doing our duty, as you know."

"Yes, of course. I hope you find Star, Detective Inspector," she managed to say before turning toward the plaza. To her left she could see the green beauty of Bishop Garden where the grass and shrubbery were lovingly tended by a troop of gardeners and the artwork by curators. Placed strategically about the garden were magnificent bronze statues by the famous sculpture Radon. She had paid the small cost of the entrance fee many times in her life just to stand before his art, to stand and soak in the passion and beauty of his creations. Now, Bishop Garden would be tainted with the memory of her night as a prisoner.

Her prison cell, four walls, a floor and ceiling made of plastic had been the size of a bathroom, a bathroom furnished with a lumpy cot and a cold plastic chair. Three sides of her prison cell looked out upon the sheriff's lobby. The fourth allowed her a view of Bishop Garden. Now she knew how zoo animals felt. Her only compensation was her knowledge the visitors to the garden couldn't see her through the opaque glass. After most of the staff left for the evening and the sheriff's office included only a duty clerk and the prisoners, she had the dubious pleasure of being able to appreciate the garden by moonlight.

As she hurried home, she imagined all eyes upon her, judging her, wondering if she had really done something as despicable as kidnap and murder a poor, defenseless, young girl. She had known most of these people all her life. As she rounded the corner to head down Merchants' Row, she admonished herself, *Once Star Bridgekeeper returns home, all of this nonsense will die down. It is time to stand up straight and look people in the eye, goof-ball. Do you want people to think you're guilty?* She made herself look up and just in time. Bam. Her face collided with someone's expansive chest. She bounced back and looked up in time to see Professor Honeysweet grinning down at her.

"I was just on my way to find you. Crystova came to my office extremely upset. She said the sheriff's office refused to let her see you. I am glad to see that you are free."

She simply stared at him, surprised by his obvious concern. She turned her head looking about her for the first time and realized there were several people watching, people she knew, Guinevere Goodbody, for example, with her arms clutched to her chest to keep warm in the shady overhang near her pet store. She had been deep in conversation with Valcinda Moorland who had a toddler cradled on her hip.

They both looked relieved to see her and gave her the wave, a gentle dip of their hands as if plunging into an imaginary ocean and the surge upward over their heads symbolizing victory. Only kids did the wave. She was embarrassed at her embarrassment. And even Frank Darknight unloading produce from the back of a farmer's wagon paused to shout out, "Merchants' Row united. See you at the pub tonight." With a cheery expression he disappeared inside Pop's Market.

She had forgotten. It was sixday. In all the drama of Star's disappearance she had forgotten about the meeting at the Wolf Inn pub. Professor Honeysweet had an uncanny ability to read her face, "Don't worry. A group of concerned citizens have been scouring the valley and the bailey looking for Star. By the time we meet at the pub, it'll be too dark to search for her anyway. We'll find her. Don't you worry."

"Are you a member of the search party?" she asked absently, her mind still thrashing about over this new problem. Adam stepped aside. With a gallant flourish and an enigmatic smile, he stayed in lock step with her as she headed for home.

"Yes, as a matter of fact, I volunteered early this morning when I heard the news. If I had known D.I. Hawk had called you in for questioning, I would have gotten up much earlier."

"Don't let me detain you," she told him pausing in front of her shop door to look up at him. "I know how these things go and time is so important. We must find her. I'm going to change and grab a sandwich and help. Unless the Bridgekeepers would rather I stay home? I don't know. I haven't spoken to them. Are they back?"

"No. According to Sophia they'll be back this evening."

"I see. Well, I don't care what Sophia thinks. I want to help with the search."

"Good girl."

"I'm not anyone's good girl," Kimberly said without thinking only remembering belatedly she didn't have the luxury of losing another friend. "I'm sorry, that was rude."

"I like a woman with an independent mind. I apologize for my condescending comment. It was quite unforgivable. I hope you will overlook it and we can go back to being equals."

"We've always been equals."

He sighed in exaggerated gusts and pretended to beat his head, "I did it again. Before I make matters worse, I will say adieu. Until tonight."

By the time he had reached the Unique Boutique, Kimberly had unlocked her shop door and slipped inside. She'd felt censorious eyes upon her wondering if Luella Morrison or Sylvia Paleone had been watching. It was only when she paused before her picture window and peeked out, she saw Diane Tumble glaring at the Bookworm Emporium door. Kimberly was relieved. She'd never been able to figure out why Diane hated her so much, maybe her hatred had nothing to do with her but with her grandparents. Did she care? Diane's animosity was a familiar eyesore, unlike the stink eye looks directed her way from a few of her neighbors on the row.

Kimberly, reluctant to face such hatred full on, postponed the inevitable by slowly consuming a stale bun and sipping a hot cup of tea before venturing outside. As she began to relax, a question popped into her head. Could Diane be hiding Star just to implicate Kimberly? The revelation took such hold of her, she found herself, even in her new terror of the woman, purposely moving toward the wine shop with the clear intention of demanding to know if Diane had Star hidden away somewhere in an attic or vault. The other side of Merchants' Row butted up against the castle's oldest wall, nearly a thousand century's old, often having to be repaired by special bricklayers and buttressed by iron rots. Perhaps the wine shop had a secret room where the Tumbles were hiding Star?

Once inside the wine shop with hardwood shelves filled with wine racks which reached to the ceiling, right and left and behind the massive front counter, even a few tucked into the corners, all filled with bottles of expensive burgundies, whites, and blues, she realized with a moment of anticlimax that Don Tumble and his wife, who habitually stood guard behind the front counter were today missing. Kimberly weaved her way through the attractively arranged kiosks and tables where other merchandise was for sale: fancy bottle openers, corkscrews, wine glasses, storage racks, even something which looked like a knitted sweater for a bottle.

There were buckets, holders, and chillers for wine, bottle tags, label removers and albums, books, media, and educational material on wines, even wine luggage of all things, temperature gauges and cellar monitors. Gracious Centipede! She felt overwhelmed by so many products, her eyes darting madly left and right, up and down until she had to pause to catch her breath. The smells were intoxicating. She rather liked the blend of wood and grape and candles. Lovely. But she would never admit to liking anything in Hadal's Delight. They'd assume her compliment hid a complaint.

There was just no way to win with the Tumbles.

When she arrived at the front desk and pressed her nose to the glass to read the tiny tags attached to their special collection of wines, wine bottles artfully arranged on swathes of fine silk like beautiful models on bedsheets, she heard someone approach. With no time to wipe the smudge off the glass, she scooted backward and arranged herself near a carousel pretending an interest in a set of wine goblets.

The person who emerged from the backroom wasn't Diane. Her initial reaction was relief. Then she grew worried, maybe even now at this very moment, Diane was in the bowels of the wine cellar unlocking a massive wooden door behind which led a dingy dank and dark cell where poor Star lay in chains? She tried to think of something else afraid Don would suspect.

At sighting her, Don's face registered surprise. She'd lived all her life just across the street and had never stepped into the wine shop. So, yes, this was an historic moment. She had a damned good reason to be here today though and said, "I'm here about the meeting tonight. I hope your wife will join us at Wolf Inn pub. It is more crucial than ever we fight this unfair eviction."

Something had changed. She saw the change on Don's face. A few days ago, he'd been just as concerned as everyone else about the possibility of the merchants being forcibly removed from their shops. Now he seemed blasé, almost bored. What had changed? "Ah, I see, you haven't been told yet, have you?"

"Told what?" At that precise moment Diane appeared, glancing suspiciously between the two of them as if she suspected they were having an affair. Kimberly ignored her, now more concerned than ever.

"Whoever said the Church of the Holy Centipede and the congregation and Bishop Little were planning something diabolical were greatly mistaken. I've spoken to the Bishop and he has no intention of driving us out of our shops. You must have misunderstood."

"But his wife-"

"He assured me that his wife had no inkling of what was going on and had simply blown up what was an innocent conversation between himself and the Governor. You see," Don propped his lean hip against the counter and bent toward her. Kimberly noticed how Diane's eyes flicked to the palm of her husband's hand pressed against the clean glass and how she opened her mouth to scold him. She never got a chance to speak.

In a condescending tone, her husband told Kimberly, "Bishop Little is getting permits to build in Blueglennen but not on Merchants' Row. He was telling the Governor about his idea for a church facility where pilgrims would be welcome to stay. It would be a tasteful hostel with a dining hall and rooms for pilgrims to rest and rejuvenate their spirits.

I assure you, he has no interest in Merchants' Row. According to him, the shops along here are too small. You see. There is nothing to worry about. Once you know the truth, it makes so much more sense. And in fact, I can't think of anything I like better, because such an enterprise will attract people from all over the world, people who in the evening might enjoy a fine wine or bit of cheese or," he threw out his final thought without much conviction, "they might even like to dig through some of your stuff."

Kimberly could only stare at them. She forced her lips closed unable to think beyond this surprising bit of news. She wondered how Clarice could have misunderstood. Then she remembered the day Bishop Little came into her shop. No. The bishop was lying.

"Where?" she asked.

Don had his back to her as he opened the cash register. The ping of the drawer opening should have been a comforting sound. Not today. She watched him pull off the paper which held the money together then set each denomination in its proper slot in the tray. The quiet and Don's relaxed movements seemed to lull his wife. Maybe, Bishop Little had changed his mind. Maybe the future wasn't as dire as she imagined. A wave of hatred trickled through the air directed her way. Kimberly stepped back from the carousel and inched toward the door.

Diane's cold eyes stared at her with such an intense hatred, Kimberly began to wonder if the woman was unhinged. An unhinged person might kidnap a child in order to implicate the person she hated? Kimberly spoke without thinking, "Why do you hate me so much? All these years as neighbors and I get nothing but dirty looks from you. You're practically a stranger to me. What have I ever done to deserve your ill will? What?"

The face of the woman before her, the wide cheekbones, the black eyes with twin expressions of sullen displeasure remained the same. Nor did Diane seem in the least bit discomfited by her question, "I don't like you."

"Why?"

Her tweezed black brows furrowed for a millisecond then she shrugged, "I've never liked you. You have foreign eyes."

Don, still with his back to them, took his time counting the money in the cash register; yet, Kimberly could tell from the tautness in his shoulders how very carefully he was listening.

"That's not a good enough reason. There's more. What is it?" Kimberly insisted.

Diane thought for a moment and then said flatly, "Because you're a liberal cry-baby do-gooder and we don't need your kind in Blueglennen. The rest of us work hard. We don't sit around mooning over books and ideas," she stabbed at her chest, "We're the ones that clean up after the likes of you and your grandfather. You're nothing but lazy weevils gobbling up our bread, our very livelihoods."

The fact Diane believed what she was saying didn't surprise Kimberly, as much as Don's lack of interest in contributing his thoughts on the topic. Irony played a hand in this marriage, Kimberly thought cynically. Diane, the spiteful, nasty, sour-faced squib had married just such a weevil as she accused Kimberly and her grandfather of being. Diane couldn't be mad at her weevil-husband, so she deflected all her hatred onto the Bookworm Emporium. It was right there in front of her every day when she woke up. The bookshop was a perfect target for her frustration.

Rumor said Don Tumble married Diane, so he could live off her hard work and money. The fact he was in the shop at this hour was a complete surprise. More often than naught, he could be found down at the pub lecturing drunks and the disinterested tourist about his take on philosophy, literature, and religion. Well, Diane had barely graduated from primary school, so Kimberly shouldn't be surprised. Diane probably didn't even know what the word irony meant or how her marriage and her business were nothing if not ironic. All the fancy gadgets in the shop screamed hypocrisy. Most hardworking people, garbage collectors, street sweepers, farmers, mule drivers and the like couldn't afford to buy anything in her shop, not even the silver corkscrews.

Why would they need them when they could twist the top off their bottles and drink down their cheap wine in a simple mug or tankard? No, the people who shopped here were rich enough to buy expensive wine and pointless accessories as a means of impressing their other rich friends. And most of those rich folks hired other "hard-working" people to do their dirty work.

Her epiphany made her smile. Kimberly's smile infuriated Diane, "If you're not going to buy anything, get out of my shop."

"Gladly, but not before I ask you if you've seen Star. Has she been here?"

"What are you implying agitator?"

"Well, isn't Star a friend of yours?" Kimberly asked. "I mean of both of you. Didn't she work here one sweat?"

"That lasted two days," Diane said her eyes blazing as she moved purposely forward as if to throw Kimberly out. They were of the same height, yet, Diane had the big bones and big muscles of someone who could do damage. "And she went crying back to her entitled parents to whine about how much work she had had to do here. I told you to leave. Maybe, I should call a knight."

Kimberly turned to Don Tumble, "Did Bishop Little tell you where he planned to house these religious pilgrims? If not on Merchants' Row where will they spend their nights? In the village? Nah. At the university? They're overcrowded as it is. In Duke Tower? Hardly. The Governor would be apoplectic at the thought. The Bishop's lied to you. Maybe he offered you something in return for the sale of your shop? What's he promised you? To buy all his wine from you? Well, watch what happens once he gets what he wants. You'll be gone too. All your fancy bottles and expensive la-de-douches. Think on it, think about where he plans to put his pilgrims."

Pretending indifference, Kimberly turned and walked out of the shop, congratulating herself on remaining composed throughout the ordeal. If she'd broken down in front of the Tumbles, she'd never have forgiven herself. Although her silly references sounded childish to her now. She wished she could go back and replay the moment and unsay "expensive la-de-douches."

It took half a second to realize someone was standing near her. She froze and long before her brain could figure out what she was seeing, her body knew. Plunged into sudden panic, she saw from the corner of her eye D.I. Hawk sitting on the bench near the wine shop busily writing in his notebook. He glanced up as she closed the shop door and nodded once in her general direction then returned to his scribbling. Relieved he'd not come to arrest her, Kimberly hurried back to the imagined safety of the Bookworm Emporium.

She found a note taped to her door and after unlocking the shop, she slipped inside and tore open the envelope, all the while moving toward greater security beyond the velvet curtains, a security made up of those things she loved, those things that belonged to her and only her, heirlooms and gifts reminding her of the dignity and grace and beauty of her heritage and her beliefs. Why bother to open the bookstore so late in the day? It was already late afternoon. She didn't need to prove anything to anyone now. The Merchants' Row Alliance would be meeting tonight at the Wolf Inn pub. They would be there. She had something substantial to hold onto, something she'd forgotten. She had neighbors who believed in her innocence.

The note had come from Guinevere Goodbody and Harry Zany. "The meeting of the merchants will continue as scheduled. Harry and I agree the merchants need to make plans. It is no surprise Don chickened out. We'll say no more until tonight. Harry has made reservations for dinner under his favorite song." She smiled at the implied bit of cloak and dagger. For the rest of the afternoon, she sifted through her memory of Harry's favorite music. Hopefully, by the time she reached the pub she would have the answer. If not, she supposed she could wait for one of the merchants to show up and follow them to the right room.

By evening, with the streets lit only by the wormlights' glow and the moon just a sliver of light in the dark sky, Kimberly left her shop wrapped in her comfortable sweater having finally discarded the idea of dressing up for the occasion. This meeting had to do with serious matters, why not dress seriously. The debate continued inside her head for a good fifteen minutes and then she realized the meeting had to appear casual. They couldn't look as if they were attending a board meeting. A part of her was grateful. She hated dressing up.

Rather than search for a knight to lower the drawbridge, most bailey residents slipped through the Bishop's Court Key, a wrought iron gate guarded by a single knight at the northeast tower. The same knights were posted to the Key throughout the years and knew the faces of every castle merchant, student, and resident. Tonight, was different. The line was longer than normal and there were two additional knights on duty. She assumed their presence signaled Star was still missing. As she crept closer to the Key, the mouse in her stomach began to chew.

Kimberly waited her turn. The man at the head of the line continued to argue with the knights over whether he had to have proof of right-of-way. While listening to the conversation and siding with the man at one point (identifications could be falsified) and then siding with the knight (the process deters most citizens from falsifying identification with the new fingerprinting and encryption logo on the card) she spent most the time examining the art work, a beautiful puzzle which she had enjoyed looking at in the past, but now could not appreciate as fully.

To keep her mind off unpleasant possibilities, she did her best to admire the masterpiece tucked away in the corner alcove surrounded by shade loving plants. Placed on the ground in strategic locations were a few floodlights which illuminated the marble statue. An unintentional and disturbing effect of the lights was to create the impression that the eyes were following her.

Was that a satyr or just a man standing in front of a horse? That part on the right must be a man holding a guitar. Long ago with the sun striking the piece with clarity, she had seen the man standing with his foot on a turtle's back strumming his guitar. Tonight, her brain simply accepted her childhood construction and refused to see anything else. That other statue might be a child holding a kitten.

Distracted by the quarrel at the head of the line and annoyed at the lateness of the hour, she wondered why the drawbridge continued to be raised at the close of day, the close of day determined by Governor Saurus which happened to coincide with six of a clock, six of o clock when people returned home from the fields or the forests or the canals, six of o clock when the pubs and the restaurants in the village served drinks and dinner. Eight hundred years ago, the drawbridge and moat were necessary for the defense of the castle; now, the drawbridge was either the Governor's means of impoverishing the merchants or a sign of his paranoia over the possibility of being kidnapped or murdered.

An ancient privilege, not used for nearly two hundred years, meant Saurus had something else in mind. The man reminded her of a dung beetle spreading his arms and legs out and out and scooping up all he could touch, a big dung heap of possessions, so big his possessions ruled him. He can't leave Blueglennen for long or someone might usurp his authority. He can't travel through his own country because he is so disliked he might be assassinated. Instead, he uses his wealthy family and connections to get things done. She glanced up and up and up curious whether the Governor might be watching his subjects below. The lights were out in the Duke Tower Nest – apropos for everything going on in that man's mind.

The man standing in front of her began to fidget and Kimberly tried to peek over his shoulder to see if the knights had resolved the problem. What if there was a fire? Everyone inside Bishop Garden would be burned. She hadn't realized she'd spoken aloud until the fellow in front of her glanced over his shoulder and gave her a frightened horse look as if she had morphed into a dangerous four-legged rodent. "Are you trying to start a panic Dela?"

"No, kiddo, I'm not. I'm just pointing out the obvious. The drawbridge is closed and there is no other way out but the Bishop Garden Gate. Do you know of another way out?"

What was the matter with her? Astonished at her own rashness in talking back to this stranger, six inches taller and eighty pounds heavier, she tensed anticipating a scene just as lively as the one at the head of the line. Instead, the man turned and leaned closer peering at her face in the half light, "Dela Lemon?"

She looked up at him and realized belatedly the man standing in front of her just happened to be D.I. Hawk, "Detective Inspector. How come you're standing in line with the rest of us? Don't you have some sort of special cache?"

Hawk straightened to his full six-feet three-inches and snorted rudely, "Cache. Hum. You mistake Dela Lemon. I am a simple servant of the Governor."

"There speaks a newbie for sure," Kimberly told him in a whisper. "I've seen deputies go to the head of the line, flash their badges and slip out of the bailey faster than a bird snatching a bug in midair."

"I prefer to observe nature in all its painful stages," Hawk said in a sober voice which Kimberly suspected had more meaning than he was willing to reveal. When he turned to listen to something someone said in front of him, Kimberly stood on tiptoe craning her head trying to see over his shoulders.

She caught a few words and a name, "someone should ... Finstickel ... moron" - and realized the man quarreling with the knights must be her least favorite customer. She suspected he only concerned himself with her pamphlets and books as a means of building himself a fort made of paper. No, maybe he used her stuff to keep himself warm? Hawk turned to her once again and even though she could barely see his expression, she was astonished at his continued serenity. "We should be moving shortly. Ah, here they come."

She turned in time to see several deputies moving purposely toward them. The deputies were wearing dull brown uniforms. Attached to their leg straps were the ominous LSR7 guns and clubs. The Lucifer Sting Rays could immobilize a person or kill them dead depending on the button pushed. Their helmets with visors down hid their faces. As the deputies brushed past them, Hawk grabbed her shoulder preventing her imminent fall.

On a pleasant evening of a particularly hot sweat season, there were occasions when the people in the valley enjoyed a stroll up the hillside and around the worn path of the outer bailey, which everyone in Blueglennen called Bishop Key Walk. An attendant would take their ticket or their coin for the privilege of viewing the Bishop's Garden and the beautiful statues. Originally, the elegant flat next to Bishop's Garden was the residence of the old Bishop of Blueglennen, a younger brother of Duke Dono. The Bishop Key Walk had been his private means of reaching his lady loves.

Centuries later, the tale had morphed into romance, no longer associated with hypocrisy and debauchery. No, now the idea of a supposedly celibate priest fornicating with reluctant females or as the plaque euphemistically stated, *cavorting with women of the village*, appears to the modern intellect as romantic. Oh please, Kimberly thought, why are people so easy to fool?

Yes, Bishop's Garden used to be a peaceful place of contemplation and beauty. Not tonight. Tonight, she was the unhappy onlooker as the deputies dragged crazy Finstickel past her, marching him down the path in lock step with their longer strides. The deputies moved so swiftly she barely had a chance to register Finstickel between them wearing his brown trench coat, smelling of old sweat and dirt, his tangled dirty hair trailing down his backside. When had he gotten so dirty? He'd taken a shower in her bathroom only a short while ago?

All three figures began to shrink and expand, disappear and reappear with the moon's light playing tricks on the eye, one moment real, the next a frightening statue resembling a writhing battle between chaos and conformity. A hoarse braying reached their ears. Kimberly realized the sound was coming from Finstickel who found the whole incident extremely funny. When had arrest and imprisonment become fun?

"The line is moving Dela Lemon," Hawk told her helpfully as she returned her attention to her immediate goal – to get the hell out of the courtyard. She watched as Hawk took a few steps forward and as an afterthought glanced at her watch realizing she'd been standing in the same spot for nearly fifteen minutes.

The wind hit her first and she gasped at the sudden change in temperature. It had been humid and hot in the Bishop's Courtyard. Out here on the path exposed to the elements with only the cold stones of the castle at her back and below her miles of jagged rocks where, if she made a misstep, she'd plunge into the swiftly moving Siren River, a river which had plenty of sharp rocks and freezing cold water and would take her poor body all the way west to the sea. She froze and found herself clinging to the wall beyond panic, in catatonic country now. The narrow winding path paved with gravel and lit by medieval smoking lanterns allowed the line of people only room to move single file.

The people behind her began to grumble. Someone grabbed her arm and led her to the bottom of the path where she recognized the rounded turret of the River View Tower. Now that she was down on level ground, she pulled away from her guide and realized she didn't know him. The stranger shrugged and followed the others toward the bridge. By the time she reached the Valley Long Watchtower, she could see someone tall wearing a dark cloak waiting for her under the lantern's light. Her delight at seeing him disturbed her. Was she a masochist after all, one of those foolish females who needed a domineering male to make her feel feminine? The idea made her queasy.

"Dela Lemon let me assist you over this rough patch," D.I. Hawk said and promptly took her elbow and guided her through the maze of broken paving stones. His behavior reminded her of a courtier escorting his lady love through Bitterroot Forest. They navigated the rotten boards which constituted the end of Bishop Key Walk onto firmer ground where a flimsy wood railing separated them from a deadly plunge down into the castle moat. She accepted his help reluctantly and hoped he didn't plan to escort her all the way to Wolf Inn. How would she explain his presence to the others? They would think she was double-crossing them. She had to get rid of him. Then she laughed at the idea this man had any romantic intentions toward her. Hardly.

By the time they reached the drawbridge, a new bridge, built by the Governor's own hand-picked craftsmen made of fancy steel and stone, Hawk, dropped her arm allowing her to move freely. Without a word, he proceeded to walk over the bridge beside her. She glanced up at him and then away, the mouse in her gut nibbling closer to her chest. Not good. Not good at all.

She decided to be blunt with him. "Where are you headed?" she asked in a high-pitched nervous twitter. She sounded like a silly wench.

Once on the bridge, they walked under a series of lantern lights. The lanternkeepers must have recently fed the glow worms swimming inside the globes because the bridge was bathed in a beautiful blue light. She could see his eyes now. He appeared to be amused. "Why do you ask?"

"Are you following me?"

"No. But I could just as easily say you are following me. After all, I was ahead of you in the line back there."

She stopped. He stopped. In concert they turned to face each other. She had to admit he had a legitimate point. Even though she shouldn't be suspicious, she disliked being so close to the detective inspector. She also disliked that due to his height, he loomed over her. She stepped back. "Yes. But we crossed the bridge way back there," she waved half-heartedly toward the bridge. "Yet. Looky. Looky. You are still here."

He shrugged. "We happen to be going in the same direction."

"Oh, and where are you going?"

Hours ago, she had been frightened of him. Why was she no longer frightened? His expression remained uncommunicative. And as she waited for him to speak, she studied him, wondering why she no longer felt anxious around him. The mouse in her tummy was sleeping. He still wore the black leather jacket and had the aura of a very dangerous man.

Yet.

And yet.

Something about the way he stood, so casual, a fraction more welcoming, more open, well as open as was his nature. Did she imagine a crack of friendliness in his bearing? Nah. An angry wasp long past its bedtime zipped by her head. Hawk turned to watch its flight then resumed his scrutiny of her face.

Wait. Lack of suspicion perhaps? Yes. That was what she sensed. He no longer considered her a suspect in Star's disappearance. In fact, he seemed to have concluded she was nothing special after all. The idea he'd already figured her out annoyed her more than she cared to admit. Getting mad would be fruitless now. She should be happy.

How dare he dismiss her as insignificant.

She could be dangerous.

No one really knew what people were capable of these days.

No one really knows what sort of nasty specimen could be hiding behind a sweet smile and a friendly gesture.

While they stood facing each other, neither one ready to speak, several people passed them making their way toward Wolf Inn pub. The pub was in a perfect location, on the corner just after the bridge and outside the jurisdiction of Mudflat Village. The owner made sure visitors couldn't miss the pub (as if anyone could) by placing a huge neon sign above the old mining cave hole which illuminated the street as the boom, boom, boom of heavy bass in its cavern could be heard all over the valley. For the pub was a cavern, not a structure built by local craftsmen.

During the founding of Blueglennen, miners dug through the rock looking for rare blue gems. Instead they found iron ore. By the time they realized all they would ever find was iron ore, they had dug twenty-feet across, half-a-mile east and then a mile down. A mile was all they were permitted to go down according to country and church law. Some claimed the mine went all the way beneath the castle where the miners built a special chamber. It sounded like nonsense to her. Yet Harry Zany, a student of history, claimed his great-great grandfather had been one of the masons who helped dig out a hollow where the old Duke stored water beneath the castle in case of a siege. The mine had been repurposed for water delivery with pulleys and buckets.

The prolonged silence unnerved her. Kimberly gave up and started moving toward the pub, "Well I must go. I'm meeting friends. For drinks. And conversation. You know. Night stuff."

Hawk nodded in acknowledgement with what she suspected might have been a quickly concealed grin. To her astonished annoyance he proceeded to walk beside her all the way to the pub. She kept her temper under control and allowed him to open the pub door for her. Once inside the crowded, hot, smoky, noisy pub filled with old timber beams and walls plastered with posters and rough wire, she weaved her way through the tables toward the bar where at least a handful of barmaids and barmen were busy serving the thirsty crowd.

Someone bumped into her and she turned in time to acknowledge Harry who held two full tankards in his hands. "We're in the corner," he said with a nod of his head to her, then acknowledged Hawk with a crack of his lips which might have been a smile, but no one knew for sure.

"We just happened to be going in the same direction," Kimberly explained to Harry. Harry shrugged and turned carefully in the aisle, holding tightly to his tankards of beer, sometimes forced to lift them above patrons' heads so as not to have one drop spill on the floor. Kimberly followed in his wake, her hair practically standing on end trying to sense whether Hawk followed. She was acutely conscious of predator types. Like a shark, predators were a Delphinids worst nightmare. This man was quiet, efficient, deadly.

It wasn't until she stood behind Guinevere's chair and turned to face the room, she realized Hawk had made his way up to the busy bar. He'd placed himself in a perfect position to see the entire room. He casually leaned against the bar, his eyes traveling from table to table as if memorizing faces. The others had noticed that she and Hawk entered together and looked at her for confirmation. "No. I don't believe I'm still a suspect. There's some other reason Hawk's here. At least, I hope there's another reason. Maybe, he's following another lead."

Professor Honeysweet had jumped up on her arrival and still stood with a chair ready for her. She thanked him and sat down noting happily that most of the merchants she had expected to come were at the table: Frank Darknight, Guinevere Goodbody, Harry Zany, Queenie Oppfield, Beatrice Bottom, Valcinda Moorland, Bill and Billy Bill Anders. No surprise Luella Morrison, Diane and Don Tumble, and Sylvia Paleone were a no show. Seeing Harry Hanson of the Shellfargon Seed among the circle of merchants surprised her though. Beside him sat a woman rather pale and thin about the age Kimberly's mother would be if she had lived, a woman she did not recognize. It was also disappointing Shehili Swana had chosen not to come.

Harry Hanson stood up and addressed her, "I've been told you're the head of this Merchants' Group. I don't want to butt in, but I thought this would be a great story for my newspaper. No? Oh well. Maybe some other day. I see my renter Joanie Fitzhammond is here. Sylvia tells me she's a hotshot stenographer. Don't worry she's not my spy, are you Joanie?"

"Well," Kimberly began looking around the table at the faces watching her expectantly. "It seems premature to be consulting with a journalist. We've just come together to discuss starting a merchant's coalition. I don't think we'd be of much interest to your readers."

Hanson nodded ruefully. Then Kimberly realized what the

newspaperman had really come for and the mouse returned nibbling hungrily away at her stomach. She looked down at her hands, then around the table and finally the face of the woman he had introduced as Joanie Fitzhammond.

Everything Kimberly wanted to know played across the woman's face: embarrassment at being stared at by strangers, discomfort at being at their table without an invitation, and something else. She had an open honest face and her eyes were kind. Also, she disliked her landlord's ruse. He may want to interview the prime suspect in the disappearance of Star Bridgekeeper; yet, Joanie was anything but happy about the way he had gone about doing it.

Most of the merchants had a drink in front of them. Professor Honeysweet anticipating her said, "No need to get up Dela Lemon. I'll be happy to get you a drink. What are you having?"

She looked up into his beaming face and had to smile. He seemed to be enjoying himself hugely. None of the merchants looked as if they suspected her of any wrong doing. She had been worried they might not come, imagining her to be a kidnapper or even worse. But she read on some faces only delight in being out on the town for the evening. On other faces she read an impatience to get down to business. "I'll just have a cup of coffee, Professor. Thank you."

"Are you sure?"

"Yes. Thank you."

She looked up at the journalist. He was still standing. "I have business to conduct Delo Hanson. But you're welcome to stop by the bookshop and I'll tell you the little I know."

Joanie Fitzhammond pushed back her chair and began to gather her belongings. Kimberly stopped her, "Delan Fitzhammond, would you mind staying and recording our minutes?"

"I would be delighted."

Hanson stood for a moment examining the people at the table as if he hoped someone would disagree with Dela Lemon. In an irritated voice she didn't bother to disguise Queenie said in no uncertain terms, "You've been dismissed Hanson. Move on. Go on now." He made a piece of work out of pulling on his coat and slinging his leather satchel over his shoulder. The group waited patiently until he reached the bar and was well out of earshot.

"I see there are only eight of us representing the alliance," Kimberly said and glanced over at Guinevere. Guinevere ignored her and continued to munch away on a plate of vegetables, every so often sipping at a light ale. She seemed to be enjoying herself.

Beatrice Bottom leaned forward and placed her plump arms on the table top and addressed the group with her bright eyes smiling into each face, "We are small, but we are strong."

"As strong as what? Stink on a skunk?" Zany asked popping a pretzel into his mouth. Everyone laughed.

Kimberly brought the discussion back to the business at hand, "Perhaps the others will want to join us when they realize their livelihoods are threatened. The reason I'm so concerned is that I just had an epiphany on the way here. You see, by the time I left the shop, the drawbridge had been raised and I had to go out the Key Gate. There was a problem getting through the line which made me realize that the Governor started this whole curfew nearly a year ago. Since then business has been mediocre after five o'clock. Why would customers want to be trapped inside the bailey or forced to go through the checkpoint at the Key?"

"No, that's not the only reason," Bill Anders said leaning forward to speak to her over his son's huge belly. "We've had a serious recession in this country and people are hurting everywhere. Don't be blaming the Governor for your mismanagement."

No one spoke for a moment. When Professor Honeysweet returned and carefully set down a hot cup of coffee in front of her, he looked around with raised eyebrows. "I see we've gotten off to a good start."

Guinevere used her carrot to stab the air in the general vicinity of Bill Anders, "The pastry guy just insulted your girlfriend."

The professor sat down and with a conspiratorial grimace shrugged his shoulders and threw up his hands, "Thanks Gwen. Thanks a lot."

"I thought I'd move things along," she said grinning slyly.

Kimberly ignored them both and said, "What I want to discuss is how we want to set up our organization. We probably need a mission statement and guidelines and, of course, to nominate people for positions."

She began ticking off on her fingers the positions she thought they would need, "We need a president, vice president, treasurer, and secretary."

Frank Darknight raised his hand, "I nominate Kimberly Lemon as president," and then took a hefty slug of his beer. Even though his cheeks were flushed, he still looked dangerously handsome. Kimberly noticed how the younger women at the tables nearby were giggling and staring in his direction. He seemed to enjoy the attention.

Before she could answer, Beatrice raised her hand and said, "I second the motion."

"Don't we need a mission statement first?" Zany asked.

Guinevere concentrated all her attention on her food and beer. Other than trying to embarrass Kimberly, she ignored the people sitting around the table and acted as if she had more important problems than the current threat.

"I volunteer as secretary," Joanie Fitzhammond said waving her pen in the air.

"Shouldn't the secretary be a merchant?" Queenie asked.

Beatrice slapped her arm, "Nonsense. Okay. Two down and two to go. I nominate Harry as vice president."

Frank chimed in, "I second the motion," and took another swig of his beer.

"I should be treasurer," Bill Anders said with a stern look around. No one seconded the motion.

For the first time, Guinevere looked around the table and said, "Frank is leaving for Walrat Island in three days. What are you doing here Frank?"

"I'm representing my parents. They asked me to come."

"Well," Guinevere began and then seemed to forget what she wanted to say. "I offer up Beatrice as treasurer."

"Why Beatrice and not me?" Bill Anders demanded.

"Because Beatrice is a certified public accountant," Guinevere retaliated in the same stern voice as he, even going so far as to stand up and lean toward him in an intimidating way. Her short stature was no match for Bill Anders' girth; yet, he remained seated and said nothing more.

Two waiters appeared with a large tray of food and drinks and for thirty minutes people at the table were busy collecting their food and drink and conversing on topics unrelated to the current threat. Professor Honeysweet handed Kimberly a plate filled with oysters. "I went ahead and ordered the appetizer for you. Are you sure you wouldn't want something lighter to chase them down with?"

"No. Thank you."

"Oh, look who's here. If it ain't the man of the hour," Frank said gazing at someone over Kimberly's shoulder with a charming smile on his charming face. Everyone turned to watch as Bishop Mark Little and his wife Clarice headed toward the private dining area in the back of the pub. Kimberly studied Frank's face and wondered if the man disliked anyone. It occurred to her, he had way too many friends. It just wasn't natural to like so many people.

"You could call them a cowardice of clams," Zany said to someone.

"They're oysters Harry not clams," Beatrice assured him.

"I know that. I'm talking about them," he said pointing at the

Littles.

"What are they up to, I'd like to know?" Queenie asked glaring in the Littles direction as if her furious expression might stop them in their tracks.

"Having dinner, I suspect," Harry offered helpfully.

Joanie looked up from the woefully empty page of her black notebook, her pen poised and asked the group, "So what is the Merchants' Row mission statement?"

By midnight the group managed to come up with a general mission statement, all agreeing should the Merchants' Row Alliance resolve the present crisis, the Alliance would continue. The mission statement would be to support each shop keeper and fight like hell to prevent a zoning code change. Dues were set at twenty-five gray seastars. After Delan Fitzhammond dutifully printed every name, each member signed the document beside their printed names using Professor Honeysweet's special dark-blue ink pen. The party broke up soon after with the Anders leaving first still ruffled by Guinevere's rudeness.

Guinevere looked at Joanie with a wary eye and asked, "Don't you work for Sylvia Paleone?"

At that precise moment, Fitzhammond had been in the process of handing over the Merchants' Row Alliance document to Kimberly. Like a bad tableau Kimberly and Fitzhammond stood with their chairs pushed aside and a table between them each holding one end of the document. "What is the matter with you, Guinevere?" Kimberly asked having lost her patience at last.

"She might be a spy," Guinevere explained as she jabbed the air with her finger and slowly stood up, all her movements careful and controlled. When she finally stood on her feet, Kimberly noticed how she had to support her weight by holding onto the table.

"You're drunk."

Someone nipped her shoulder and Kimberly turned to face Valcinda and Valcinda whispered in her ear, "One of the puppies died this morning."

"Oh no," Kimberly suddenly felt sick to her stomach. She forced herself not to cry in front of the others. "I'm so sorry Guinevere, so very sorry." Kimberly turned in time to realize Guinevere had moved away from the table and was nearly at the door.

Kimberly and Joanie exchanged glances. Joanie dropped her eyes first. That made Kimberly mad, "Don't worry. Just because you work for Sylvia doesn't mean you're like her."

"If I could afford to work somewhere else I would. But I can't."

"If I could afford to pay you, you could work for me."

They walked to the door together, Harry Zany, Beatrice Bottom, and Queenie Oppfield having left. Frank Darknight, Kimberly noticed had remained behind and was making his way to a back table where a few lovely ladies were waiting for him. When Adam Honeysweet arrived at her elbow and opened the door for the two of them, Kimberly felt extremely uncomfortable. What he said surprised her, "I'm sorry my friend with the zoning board couldn't make it. I'll bring him by your shop one day this week."

"That would be fine," Kimberly said as she followed Joanie out of the pub, only to find herself surrounded by a group of knights and D.I. Hawk. Hawk had changed dramatically. They had been in the pub nearly four hours quarreling over the correct wording of the mission statement and in those four hours something terrible had happened. She could see the mistrust on D.I. Hawk's face. On some faces in the crowd who were just leaving the pub, she saw shock as the knights surrounded her.

"Dela Lemon," D.I. Hawk announced loud enough that people leaving the pub paused to hear. "You are under arrest for the murder of Star Bridgekeeper. I caution you to remain silent until such time as an attorney can be found to represent you."

The annoying gyrating lights from the neon sign above the entrance to the Wolf Inn pub switched off and everyone vanished. Kimberly woke to find herself lying on a hard cot with a candle burning on a stone pedestal near the bed. Her candle had burned down to a mere stub. Gratefully, she noticed several fresh candles placed in a holder.

No lighter. No matches. No electricity.

She looked up at the ceiling and stared at the stones, stones dripping with perspiration. The smell of dank dark places filled her nostrils. And when she finally woke, truly woke, she swung her legs off the cot and realized they had placed her in the old medieval chambers below the tower. She heard herself breathe. She heard water dripping somewhere beyond her prison cell, no other sound, nothing beyond the noises she made, no other prisoners or guards or visitors.

Her bed and the stone pedestal took up only a small portion of the chamber. Beyond her cot, everything was dark as the abyss. The flame shook as she lit a new candle and carried the stub of her candle the few steps to the prison bars. She peeked out. In the days of Duke Dono, laborers had carved these passageways from bedrock, four-feet wide, six-feet tall, and miles long. Every six feet, the laborers had carved a space fit for a prisoner with heavy iron bars to keep them inside. Each furrow had been used to lock away dissenters, enemy combatants, and vicious criminals. Kimberly paced from one end of the bars to the other craning her head, standing on tiptoe, desperate to find evidence she was not alone. The darkness surrounded her from behind and in front and from either end of the underground catacombs.

E4 Shellfargon Year 5092 NDMP WK 5: UES Albion 4
Encounter at Unique Boutique reveals potential conflict between castle shopkeepers and Church of the Holy Centipede. Wife of Bishop Little let slip church's intention to rezone Merchants' Row as pilgrimage hostels. All shops may be confiscated under ancient law citing imminent domain to cathedral. Formerly shops on Merchants' Row belonged to Church of the Holy Delph as cloisters, school rooms, and scriptoriums. Rumors abound of three current shops on Merchants' Row as potential scriptoriums where holy books were copied by priests, a few of the books rumored to be priceless illuminated manuscripts.

In response to E2's query of Seeley and Goodbody. Dialmere Seeley and Guinevere Goodbody are first cousins and animal activists. These female Delphi could be mistaken for identical twins: petite/plump with close cropped dark hair and brown eyes. See video of Seeley mesmerizing injured horse. Without anesthesia horse dropped to ground and slept while she applied poultice to wound. Sending graph of her heart rate and brainwaves during procedure.

Chapter 6

D.I. Hawk glanced out his office window into the lobby where a delegation calling themselves the Merchants' Row Alliance congregated in small angry groups. His face showed nothing of his thoughts or emotions, even when he spotted a familiar figure moving purposely toward his door. Deputy Wakefield prevented her from reaching Hawk's office by blocking her path with his girth.

Shehili condescended to stop, even taking a step back, her face expressing disbelief than annoyance. D.I. Hawk suppressed a grin, amused at her reaction to the native's uncouth behavior. He knew such conduct by an inferior would never have occurred aboard the UES Albion. Today, she was dressed in a fashionable gray pantsuit with matching purse. All business, he realized with an inner twinge of irritation. Instead of leaving, Shehili chose to remain standing by his office window. Unlike the delegation of merchants, Shehili might have been on top of a majestic mountain admiring the view for all the attention she spent on the mob behind her. The mob milling about the courtyard and the lobby were eager to speak to Kimberly Lemon, the murderess.

In contrast, the merchants reminded Hawk of chattering monkeys. Although he had to be honest some of the merchants surrounding the monkeys were doing their best to calm them down. One of the zookeepers was a tall woman well-dressed and slender with black hair who looked very familiar. Yes. He remembered now. She was a university student, a friend of Kimberly Lemon. But no. He'd met her somewhere else. He filed her image away to take out at a quieter time. The other keeper had silky reddish-brown hair. A part of the university as well. Not a threat. And then there was the male, Professor Honeysweet doing his best to distract the menagerie.

They stood near the sergeant's podium, anxiously awaiting news, and every so often, moving in on Queenie and Guinevere before the women could whip the crowd into a frenzy. Honeysweet whispered in Guinevere's ear a little too long and got a little too close. Their air of composure and concern sent off alarms in his head. Were they plotting something stupid? Were they plotting to rescue Kimberly Lemon from the catacombs?

To see Shehili aligning herself with these people made him hot with shame. Had she lost all reason? These people were undeserving of her compassion; they were puerile, unsanitary, tasteless creatures bent on their own self-serving agendas. Yes, he supposed, he had at one time felt a moment's pity for the murderess.

She'd had the bad judgement to befriend a silly child who had aligned herself with dangerous men. And now, he realized angrily Kimberly Lemon had infected Shehili with her crazy conspiracies.

Once he had Wakefield's attention, the man stepped into his office and shut the door behind him. Wakefield wore the uniform of the Blueglennen deputies – brown shirt, trousers, and necktie. The tie-clip made from a cheap mineral dipped in gold paint which he proudly wore every day, Hawk, upon closer examination realized had the letter S engraved in black on the front. The letter S was the insignia of the Governor's family name. Not to be outdone in his slavish devotion to the Governor, the deputy wore a badge pinned to his breast pocket which depicted a falcon perched on a parapet.

To himself Hawk thought the insignia apropos for his deputy, a man closer to sixty than fifty with a receding hairline and a bit of a belly. He conceded for his age the man had energy and a gift for accuracy; yet, as far as creative thinking and criminal analysis were concerned (necessary for a justice system) the deputy lacked objectivity. In Hawk's estimation the man, like the Governor, preferred to hide behind rules and regulations, thereby, avoiding any critical inquiry into the truth.

"I assume they are all here to see the suspect?" Hawk asked watching Wakefield closely without being obvious.

His deputy grunted, his attitude conveying his disparaging opinion of the group; well, to be fair, the man had little respect for anyone who entered the building who did not belong to law enforcement or his inner circle of believers. Hawk had yet to discover if the man belonged to the Church of the Holy Centipede. Yet his beliefs were ultra-conservative, so conservative indeed that the man had had the bad taste once of saying aloud in a roomful of people, "Women belong in the bed servicing men and in the kitchen cooking our meals."

If Shehili had been present, she would have sent him to the Albion brig and left him to dine on bread and water for the rest of his born days.

"Tell them there will be no visitors until the suspect has acquired someone to represent her."

"Gotcha," Wakefield said and instead of promptly doing as he was told, the man stood beside Hawk's desk looking out the window at the merchants milling about the floor of the lobby. His attention seemed to close in on the two males among the group. Hawk waited for Wakefield to say something. When Wakefield continued to frown at Caleb Lanternlighter and Professor Adam Honeysweet, Hawk found himself growing more irritated with the man the longer he stood by the window. He thought better of voicing his opinion. The man was a booby. The lack of discipline and respect for the rule of law from the knights and the deputies in this department made him itch to discipline them.

"Yes, Deputy?"

Wakefield glanced his way and said, "Sorry sir. Just wondering why Lanternlighter is here. He's sweet on Sophia Bridgekeeper, the poor dead girl's sister. So why does he want to see the murderess?"

"I'm aware of Lanternlighter's relationship with both parties. And may I remind you Dela Lemon is a person of interest. She has yet to be found guilty by the tribunal of judges, Deputy. Anything else?"

Somehow, Hawk's tone still hadn't penetrated the thick skull of the deputy. Wakefield glanced at him with one eye cocked in a friendly manner, as if they were old friends sharing a private joke. Unable to ignore the tension in the room any longer, Wakefield jerked to attention realizing belatedly this wasn't a tête-à-tête with one of his cronies. "No. Ah. I mean I have nothing else to report, sir." With a snappy salute he left the office and shut the door firmly behind him.

Hawk had no illusions about Wakefield. Wakefield had an instinctual attraction to hierarchies and did his best to wiggle himself into the good graces of his superiors. Superiors? These people had zero understanding of what constituted superiority; they were no better than groveling primates rushing to pick the fleas off the strongest back. He could see for himself how poor Deputy Daniel Wakefield struggled to come to grips with his numerous biases.

What degree of obsequiousness should he offer toward the new detective inspector? Or should he behave like some of the others toward Hawk – disdainful? Perhaps being insolent would better serve him? Let him dance the fool's dance. Those who chose the latter soon learned to regret their decision. It only took one example to educate the rest of them. Wakefield, slow to see the consequences, vacillated between rudeness and groveling, hoping one way or another to insinuate himself into the good graces of the detective inspector.

Everyone knew D.I. Burhani Hawk had been assigned by the Governor from outside Wolfern Province, upon recommendation by a branch of his more wealthy and influential family members. As a foreigner, a different color, an uncertain background, and someone from another planet, his allegiance to the country or the Governor was suspect. Yet, the attitude down world was to accept the inevitable. For several years, the inhabitants had been terrified of the starship and the aliens orbiting their planet. Then, world leaders discovered the starship personnel were learning Shellfargon's numerous languages. They were also preparing to meet with the planet's leaders.

Before any face to face meeting of world leaders, there had to be one representative from each species assigned to an uninhabited part of Shellfargon. The goal was to ensure there would be no ill effects from a personal encounter between species. Months passed before medical personnel on the starship and scientists on the planet accepted the results of their tests which established that first contact would not be biologically lethal or cause a pandemic. Against his family's wishes, Hawk volunteered to be one of the test subjects. He was glad he had. During the quarantine, he managed to make alliances with different groups. He'd been especially interested in Wolfern Province. It was considered the most volatile and dangerous part of the country of Curl. Still in its infancy as a member of Curl.

Once he'd made connections with certain people, it wasn't difficult to get the assignment as Detective Inspector of the Department of Justice. Of course, Hawk could not be placed properly in the hierarchy. Such ambiguity upset Blueglennen factions. Most of the knights and deputies were disdainful of mercenaries, yet, willing to follow the Governor who chose mercenaries as his personal bodyguards and emissaries due to their communication, security, and military skills. Governor Saurus would have preferred native Wolferns as his bodyguards but because he had been chosen by leaders in the east, Wolferns mistrusted his loyalty.

Wolfern Province history was a long history of betrayals.

With a rough exhalation, Hawk tried to rid himself of his annoyance with these barbarians. A momentary twinge of nostalgia for his ship assailed him. He brushed the feeling aside. He had a job to do. The future of the eighty-thousand people on the UES Albion required him to remain levelheaded and finish his assignment. Saurus thought he'd gotten himself a mercenary. What an idiot the little man was. And the Governor's idiocy was all to the good because if the citizens of Blueglennen had chosen an intelligent and ambitious leader, Hawk would never have gotten in the door. Governor Saurus had been pampered all his life and knew nothing of the danger orbiting his planet. The man was not only a moron, he was a gluttonous greedy bastard who had an addiction for young beautiful women, the younger the better.

A remorseless rapping on his door brought Hawk to his feet. In one bound he was at the door and ready to send the intruder off with a few well-chosen words. The door had been an effective cushion to the cacophony of voices in the lobby. When he saw Shehili Swana's black eyes boring into his skull, he considered sending her on her way and then changed his mind knowing he'd never hear the end of it. He stepped back allowing her to enter his private office in full view of the lobby. The merchants and deputies attuned to the oddity of D.I. Hawk opening his office door to a stranger watched in amazement as Hawk gestured for Shehili to enter.

Shehili in a voice which carried across the quad announced to D.I. Hawk, the reporters, the merchants and the deputies her intentions, "I am representing Dela Lemon. May I have a few words with you Detective Inspector?"

Giving himself time to answer her, he shut the door with a decided snap, effectively shutting out the noisy lobby and trapping Shehili in a sound-proof room surrounded by glass where her traitorous performance would have no sway over the simpleminded. They both knew enough not to stand where they might be observed and have their words translated by someone with special skills in lip-reading and facial language recognition.

Prepared for a fight, he faced her, his expression composed for the benefit of the crowd, and said in a calm voice, "Are you qualified to defend anyone, Dela Swana?"

"I am more than qualified sir. I present my credentials," she said pulling out her passport and certificates of justice with a flourish. With his back to the lobby, Hawk cracked a smile – a crumb of a smile – nearly subliminal to anyone else. She had no trouble recognizing his amusement and with one finger of her left hand lashed back. If she thought a snap of the middle finger would offend him, she was much mistaken. "That is beneath you, Madam."

"When in-country," she said with a shrug.

Had she been on this planet and in this oxygen rich environment too long? With a pettiness he abhorred in others, he took his time reading the documents she presented. The certificates seemed to be in proper order; and of course, he had no doubt about the passport for he had one equally as "authentic" tucked in his jacket pocket.

"Please sit, Madam," he told her gesturing to one of several chairs as he returned to his desk. Once they were seated, the grey frosting on the glass hid them from view. The room had been debugged months ago and several filters were operating to cripple audio or video devices.

Shehili leaned forward and in a voice barely registering as speech said, "What possessed you to come here? I was assigned to Blueglennen, not you. You're supposed to be at Crest Hall assessing the Delphadorturo's leadership. And why are E2 & E3 here? Who authorized these assignments? It's foolish and dangerous for us to be in the same place. If we're discovered, the natives could spin our presence as political or even suggest we're a 5th column bent on the planet's destruction."

Hawk rocked back in his chair waiting patiently for her to finish and doing his best to control his temper. He threw her documents on his desk, "You and I have unfinished business."

"No. We do not. Once again you are mistaken."

"We are here to educate ourselves not enable the natives."

"I've done enough observing and writing of reports. You know, as well as I do, by our mere presence, we are changing events. This is our moment to take sides."

"And how did that work out on Taurus? Hum? Not so bloody well, huh? Our objective is to continue surveying the situation until events reach criticality then intervene."

"By extinguishing their planet? I strongly abject. It is a callous response to an imaginary threat."

"It won't be your decision. We were too soft on Kavell and look what happened. They are thriving and more predatory than ever. Soon they'll reach the outer edges of this galaxy. The ship's consensus agrees that this galaxy will not go the way of the predators."

"You have no problem with Delphinids and Lacertidae destroying each other?"

"The natives of Vespa 1 & 2, the country of Curl and the provinces appear to be perfectly contented with the NeverEnding war. Only a few go out to fight and those few who never return are soon forgotten. Life is as cheap here as it was on Earth. Has anyone objected to the wars? Has anyone martyred themselves for peace?"

"There are dissenters."

"Few. Very few. With the way these Delphinids and Lacertidae breed there will be more senseless wars. Once they're tired of killing each other, they'll find new enemies."

"And how much of the fomenting and interference has been due to us?"

"Enough," Hawk said and moved to rise from his chair. "They've been fighting each other for centuries. We've been here barely two years. We're bringing them technology and enlightenment, a chance to fight the Aviangore."

Shehili activated the chip in her brain mindful of listening devices. Hawk may think he's safe but Shehili didn't trust anyone. Without asking his permission to communicate via thought waves, Shehili ignored the ship's protocol which might have earned her several demerits on the Albion. When Hawk received her thought wave, her rudeness cemented his opinion she was unfit for her current assignment.

We are no better than the Shellfargonites. I've suspected for a long time the reason the war drags on is because of us. The Serpent Sea is riddled with the bodies of the war dead. Our greed for their resources is laying waste to Shellfargon. I know you're still upset that I asked father to broadcast the carnage on television.

And how did that go?

It's made an impression. We can't see the results today. Someday, someday the people of Shellfargon will end the war.

Don't be a fool. They've been murdering each other for centuries. You really think live coverage of Sea Serpent bowriders killing each other for cash will suddenly make the two enemies stop? No. We're wasting our time. We need to be concerned with our survival. You want our ship to end up like the others?

Poor planning and fear created our present problems. We have to be smarter this time.

"I said enough E4," Hawk hissed forgoing the connection, then rose slowly to his feet, his tall figure looming over her. Stifling the urge to hit him, Shehili shut down her chip. It had been her intention to sit patiently and wait for Hawk to compose himself, but when Shehili saw Deputy Wakefield approach she gave up. Pretending to have gotten all that she asked for, she followed his lead and stood up.

When Wakefield opened the door and stepped inside, she turned to Hawk and smiled sweetly, "Thank you Detective Inspector. I will take you up on your offer. I'm ready to see my client. My legal staff is included, I hope? Is this man escorting us to the room set aside for Kimberly Lemon?"

The silence made Deputy Wakefield uncomfortable. He supposed the detective inspector had reservations about choosing him to lead the woman and her legal team to the prisoner. He had the necessary credentials to get through the check points and knew where the guards kept the keys to the lower regions. Perhaps he needed to remind the D.I. of his loyalty to Governor Saurus and the Duke Tower Set. He opened his mouth to speak and stopped just in time. No. Bad move.

The foreign woman in the stylish pantsuit stood patiently waiting beside her chair with her purse slung casually over her right shoulder and her shawl draped artfully on each arm. Her large brown eyes glanced calmly between Hawk and Wakefield. Wakefield put his weight on first one foot then the other. Instinct warned him not to fidget. Perhaps this was his chance to show the detective inspector he could be trusted. He might even hear something important which he could pass on.

Hawk glanced at his watch and asked, "Has she been fed? No? Yes? You don't know? Why not? I see. Well, you may have the honor of carrying a tray down to Dela Lemon along with her defender and her legal staff. Good day Dela Swana."

The woman barely moved her head as she swept past Wakefield without a word. She started toward a group of women unashamedly watching Hawk and Dela Swana. Before Kimberly Lemon's defender had a chance to say anything to her staff, Wakefield announced, "Remain here. I will return to escort you to Kimberly Lemon's cell."

By the time he traveled to the prison kitchen and collected a tray, the afternoon shift of deputies had eaten and were emptying their trays in the bins. Normally he would have been one of those lucky fellows leaving for the day, but because D.I. Hawk was under the delusion Wakefield was his personal servant, Wakefield's routine was continually disrupted. He tried to convince himself the disruption was character building. As he reached for one of several food trays left for the night shift, he decided to take one brimming with meats, vegetables and a tasty dessert.

"What are you doing there, Deputy?" a man wearing an apron asked him. Wakefield was surprised. When he'd entered the kitchen, the man had been sweeping the floor.

"Collecting a tray for a new prisoncr."

"Not that one, man. We don't waste the good stuff on the criminals," he said jokingly and marched over to the freezer. He walked inside leaving the freezer door open.

Wakefield, forced to wait an extra minute or two, glanced around the kitchen wondering where the other staff had gone. It was so quiet, he could hear the ping of the heater kicking on. He noticed that every stove and countertop gleamed like newly polished silver. Through the plate glass window separating the Knight's Eatery and the station kitchen, Wakefield could see the chief cook and his assistant eating dinner at a small table.

He remembered talk of how Governor Saurus bribed the cook from some fancy place back east to come work for him. She made more in a week than Wakefield did in a month. Yet he had to admit, she was a damned good cook. He was grateful for the fine food since his third wife took off with a Coralian actor.

Wakefield frowned and frowned again at the new man for taking so long. The guy strolled out with the tray in his arms as if he had all day and then some. The tray was just like all the others left for latecomers, so why had this fool made him wait? He grabbed the tray and hurried out of the room. The group had shrunk to three women. The others must have gone home. Wakefield was relieved. Once they had spoken to the prisoner, he could go home.

"This way," he said using the tray as a pointer and with his back straight as an arrow, he marched past the Duty Station down the narrow corridor to the old reception hall. The reception hall had been converted into a detainee room and used for prisoners to await the descent down the stairs to the dungeon. There were two knights on duty. They were standing at attention on each side of the reception doors. They automatically barred the way inside the detainee room.

"I have orders to escort the prisoner Lemon's defender and her staff to Dela Lemon's cell. I'll need the necessary pass key."

"Where are your papers?" the tallest knight asked. Wakefield didn't recognize him.

"I was given none. Call D.I. Hawk. He requested I escort these people to the prisoner and provide her with a meal."

While the tallest knight used his com to contact D.I. Hawk, the other knight lifted the lid and examined the food. He used the fork to stab at the dessert. His zeal turned the tasty treat into a lump of muddy slop. The taller knight opened his side of the reception door. Wakefield slipped inside the detainee room.

Before the women could enter the room, the knights padded them down. Wakefield had seen plenty of shake downs before. This one though seemed obscene. The youngest of the group, a tall elegant female with shiny black hair had an air of nobility about her and kept her face composed as did Dela Swana. By the time the knights were finished searching Professor Moth, her cheeks were as fiery as her hair.

Only a little more to go, Wakefield thought as he marched across the tiled floor toward the massive heavy door at the opposite end of the room. The heels of his boots striking the floor ricocheted off the plastered walls. Professor Moth's pointed heels hitting the floor accentuated her fury over being mauled by strangers. Another knight sat at a desk near the heavy door. When he heard the reception doors open, he looked up from his computer monitor and watched the group approach him. Just as Wakefield reached the desk, the knight rose to his feet.

"We're here to see Dela Lemon. I have clearance from D.I. Hawk to deliver this tray and her defenders."

The guard didn't even blink. He turned and unlocked a cabinet which contained a series of keys. When he handed the key to Wakefield, he glanced at Professor Moth's high heeled boots. "She has to sign a waiver before descending the stairs. The Department of Justice will not be responsible for her death."

Another humiliation for the group. Professor Moth seemed to have regained her cheerful demeanor. She smiled and said, "Where do I sign?"

As the group descended the stairs moving deeper beneath Duke Tower, the air became as stale and antiquated as the rooms and the furnishings surrounding them. By the time he reached the final door leading to the catacombs, the tray had become a nuisance. He regretted his decision to intercept the D.I., only having meant to remind the D.I. he would be off shift in a few minutes. It had taken them nearly thirty minutes just to get through security.

He inserted the black iron key into the iron lock. The foreign woman interrupted him with a brusque question, "What is this place? It smells obscene."

Wakefield glanced over his shoulder and while balancing the tray with one hand unlocked the door, "The D.I. ordered the prisoner to be kept down here."

"What purpose does it serve to keep Kimberly so far away from everyone? This treatment is unconscionable," the youngest asked. She reminded Wakefield of a model, tall and thin with her short cropped black hair cut in a fashionable bob. She dressed as fancy as people in Delphadore did back east. He couldn't quite identify her accent. All he knew for sure was that she was a student. She seemed so familiar though, her large dark eyes reminded him of someone, someone important.

He tucked the key back in his pocket and threw open the iron door ignoring the women's critical comments, shocked gasps, angry mutterings, wanting only to deliver the tray to the prisoner and let the guard on duty lead the visitors back to the upstairs offices. Wakefield led the women down the passageway lit randomly by a series of old light bulbs encased in dirty plastic globes. The floor of the passageway was mostly dirt and the walls rough granite. They still had the narrow stairs to descend. The distance between the iron door and landing where the guard waited at his post could only have been about ten feet; yet, the murky surroundings made their trek seem longer.

Just ahead he saw a light illuminating a strange tableau.

Wakefield didn't recognize the guard on duty. Grover Courtney should have been assigned to the prisoner. He was usually assigned to the politically volatile or violent prisoners. Instead of Courtney, some guy dressed in identical clothes as D.I. Hawk, black leather jacket and high boots with a fancy crossbow slung over his shoulder and a dirk in an ankle holster watched Wakefield and the women approach. He was so tall his head nearly touched the roof. He seemed to be in a meditative mood with his elbows resting on a wooden podium and his body relaxed. Behind him was a long dark corridor where the prison cells were lit by individual globes. The light from his computer screen highlighted his strong cheekbones and pale white skin.

As Wakefield got closer to the stranger, he started to panic. The relaxed posture was a ruse. The man's eyes never stopped assessing them. Wakefield heard him address someone from his head set, "Yes, sir. They've arrived."

Now that the group were a mile or more underground with only a few dirty lights for illumination and with the accompanying smells of old dirt, sweat, and despair, the normally gregarious women were speechless with disgust.

Everyone heard the man say, "Twenty, yes. Yes, sir."

The guard's charming smile unnerved Wakefield. He accepted the tray and said, "Very thoughtful of you, deputy."

"It's for the prisoner," Wakefield reminded him.

"Oh, she's had her lunch deputy and her dinner is being prepared. No need to worry. The D.I. tells me you're free to go home and thank you for your service."

Wakefield hesitated suddenly uncomfortable, "Ah. Well. You see. The food's probably cold. Security ruined the dessert. If you'd like I can return the tray to the kitchen before clocking out."

The guard's smile disappeared. His frown transformed his handsome face into a cold piece of granite, "You're dismissed deputy."

Wakefield brushed past the women feeling his cheeks burning. He'd never been so humiliated in his life. One day he would get even with that foreign piece of trash. When he paused at the foot of the stairs and looked back at the group, he saw Bristlecone escorting the women to the murderess' cell. He felt a second's qualm remembering Kimberly Lemon as a child. She'd been a polite quiet little girl always with her nose in a book. People forgot about her strange eyes when she smiled. He felt sorry for her. But there was nothing he could do.

The charm reappeared when he turned to the women, "Ladies. I understand you want to talk to Dela Lemon. I'll show you the way." From a compartment inside the podium, he extracted an inspection wand half as long as his leg. The wand illuminated the passageway for several feet. He handed the wand to Dela Shehili Swana. Either the man was a genius or an idiot for his gallantry could have been used against him. He didn't look like an idiot. He must have figured the defender wouldn't be so desperate as to brain him with the light-stick.

The knight assigned to guard Kimberly Lemon looked familiar to them all. Yet none of them dared acknowledge to the others in their group that they knew him. They all had compelling reasons to treat him as if he were a stranger. Shehili, of course, recognized him immediately, since she'd known him her entire life. Alexandra had seen him in Delphadore at one of her mother's concerts. And Crystova Moth thought she had seen him on the UES Albion. He had been one of the greeters at the Shellfargon / Albion conference.

All of them secretly admired his long thick curly brown hair and his tall lean body and gorgeous face, even as their eyes took in the nastiness of their surroundings. His male beauty could not dispel the claustrophobic atmosphere of being a mile underground, breathing fetid air and the humiliation of having their bodies groped by strange men. The body search had seemed to be the worst of their present circumstances, until they reached the iron door. None of them were prepared for the terrifying darkness, dampness and air of misery.

It was not lost on Shehili, Alexandra or Crystova when the handsome knight paused by a garbage can full of bloody rags and tattered clothes and casually dumped the tray and its contents inside. Kimberly's dinner which the deputy had carried so carefully all the way down into the dank cold dungeon was now a pile of slop oozing down the sides of the garbage can. It was only good for hungry rats now.

Perhaps the handsome knight didn't trust Wakefield or Governor Saurus' Department of Justice? How naïve of them to think Governor Saurus' Department of Justice existed to protect the citizens of Blueglennen? Was Wakefield a poisoner? He didn't look like one. How would they know? Only one of them had ever met a poisoner before, and Shehili would never admit that fact to any Delphinid.

Until the humiliation of a body search, Crystova believed Kimberly's imprisonment was just a stupid misunderstanding which would soon be rectified by justice. Then the guard tossed the tray in the trash bin. Now, her trust in the natural goodness of people was gone. Crystova did not believe for one moment Kimberly murdered Star Bridgekeeper. With the front-page news still fresh in her mind, she saw the photo of the innocuous blue bin metamorphized into something so unnatural, so horrifying.

In stark contrast, Harry Hanson's photograph of the bin and its contents included a school picture of Star on the right-hand side as she smiled into the camera's eye. Surely most people will realize Harry Hanson is a sensationalist and only wants to sell newspapers? Over the years, Crystova had come to the sad conclusion most people were easily persuadable. Since Hanson didn't care about the truth, the article had been deliberately inflammatory and suggestive.

Who had allowed him to take such a photograph, a photograph so graphic of Star's poor little body lying at the bottom of the trash bin? He'd managed to capture her curled up in the fetal position, her hands clutching her throat. The article included details: chains wrapped around the bin and a padlock used to prevent Star from fighting her way out. Poor Star, poor, poor Star, dying by asphyxiation. What a painful nasty way to die.

The evidence against Kimberly was circumstantial. The Department of Justice had no right to drag Kimberly down to this hellhole, no right at all. Her thoughts were echoed by Alexandra Montague, "This is not happening. You can't possibly think this is acceptable," she told the knight.

He turned his brilliant brown eyes upon her and said with uncharacteristic sobriety, "It's for her own protection, Dela Montague."

"Here? Are you kidding me?" Alexandra demanded. "If you want security, why not the Governor's penthouse? No one would dare harm her with the Governor's guards surrounding the penthouse. Instead, you've buried her a mile underground. No, this can't be happening. I cannot believe this is happening in a civilized world."

The sounds of someone moving toward the bars of a cell made everyone's head turn in unison as Kimberly stepped into the light cast by the old bulb on the wall. She blinked a few times before finally focusing on the women standing near her cell door. The light caught the sheen of tears swimming in her eyes. Unable to speak, she lowered her head as the tears began to run down her cheeks. Alexandra reached through the bars and took hold of Kimberly's hand. She held on tightly, "We're going to get you out of here. I'll go speak to the Governor personally. Don't you worry. I won't let this continue. This is barbaric. This is monstrous."

Shehili stepped forward and gently brushed Alexandra aside,

"Hello Dela Lemon. How have they been treating you? It's very cold down here. Do you have blankets? Are the meals adequate?"

In the silence, they could hear the far-off drip, drip, drip of water and nothing else. The thought of being down in this dark damp place for any length of time froze Crystova's vocal cords. When Kimberly spoke, they could barely hear her, "Yes."

"I will have you out straight away Dela Lemon. I promise you. Your bail has been set at 20,000 yellow seastars," she said, then with an elegant shrug of her shoulders continued. "Obscenely high but manageable. Once you've been exonerated the bond will be dropped. And since I am here to offer you my services as your defender, I strongly urge you to say nothing to anyone but me. I will be your advocate. Do you agree?"

Kimberly stared at her in surprise, "I don't understand. What have I done?"

Shehili turned to the knight with a contemptuous lift of a dark brow, "Why has my client been kept ignorant of the charges against her?"

The handsome knight's charming expression vanished for a second and then returned. He resembled one of the statues in the plaza as he looked straight through Dela Swana. When he continued to ignore her question, she snapped, "Contact your superior this minute Knight Bristlecone and inform D.I. Hawk to release this woman into my custody immediately. I have ample grounds now to have this entire inquisition dismissed out of hand. No judge, no honest judge mind you, would accept this situation as anything but a crude attempt to force my client into a confession."

While Shehili reprimanded the knights, the Governor, and most especially D.I. Hawk, Knight Bristlecone ignored her tirade and walked back to his podium with his hand pressed to his ear. They could barely hear his responses. Alexandra squeezed Kimberly's hand and opened her mouth to speak, but before she could explain the reason for her imprisonment, Shehili Swana stopped her, "No. It is not your job. This should have been done by D.I. Hawk or one of his deputies. Obviously, someone has made a serious mistake."

Crystova Moth, for the first time, found her voice, "If she has not been arrested, then why is she here? D.I. Hawk doesn't strike me as the kind of person who would overlook protocol. There must be another reason."

Booted feet marching down the dark passageway interrupted Crystova's speech. Then they heard two sets of heels striking stone and were not surprised to see D.I. Hawk himself coming down the passageway. He paused by the podium to talk to Bristlecone. To their further frustration none of the women could hear their conversation. Hawk couldn't have arrived so swiftly unless he had already been on his way down to the catacombs. The women waited for him to come to them. Alexandra refused to let go of Kimberly's hand. When he approached the group with a bland smile, Shehili suddenly understood everything. She tried not to relax. It would be best if she kept up the pretense of outrage.

Hawk ignored Kimberly's visitors and concentrated all his attention on the cellmate, "Did my officers inform you of your rights under Curl Law and announce the reason for your imprisonment?"

The light-stick cast into ghastly relief the woman's haggard face and her confusion, "I don't understand what you mean. You were there. When I came out of the pub, you and the other knights told me I was under arrest and pushed me into the wagon."

"Yes," D.I. Hawk said with a nod and waited patiently for her to continue. "And?"

"I don't remember anything else. I haven't spoken to anyone until now."

"Are you sure? Are you absolutely sure, Dela Lemon? After all, there was a deputy assigned to you in the wagon. Did he read you your rights and explain why you were under arrest?"

"No. He just sat on the other side of the wagon grinning at something someone was telling him in his earpiece. He ignored me the entire trip across the bridge and into the castle bailey."

"But when you arrived at the station, the sergeant on duty must have read you your rights and explained why you'd been arrested?"

"No," Kimberly said suddenly growing impatient." No, he did not. He was too busy on his computer and just handed some keys to the man who dragged me out of the wagon. By the time I realized where the knight was taking me, I was starting to get lightheaded. I hate dark closed-in places. I threw up. Someone gave me water and I don't remember anything else."

"Drugged? You were drugged?" Shehili demanded glaring up at D.I. Hawk with a look so scathing it should have peeled the ugly green paint off the wall.

"Nonsense. No one would have any reason to drug you here. I will send for a physician and he will confirm Dela Lemon has not been drugged. Now then, let us proceed to the real problem. It seems your arrest was handled improperly. For that I am truly sorry, Dela Lemon. It is my understanding Dela Swana has chosen to be bond for your good behavior." He paused to looked down at Swana and with a critical eye on her said, "Can you assure me you will protect Dela

Lemon from any harm while she is in your custody?"

"Harm? Don't be ridiculous."

"There has already been an attempt on Dela Lemon's life," he announced.

"When? How?" Crystova asked in surprise.

D.I. Hawk's dark penetrating eyes assessed her reaction, "Last night. It happened on the Mudflat Bridge that crosses Poison Creek. It was when Dela Lemon and I paused beneath the lantern's light to talk."

"But that was a wasp," Kimberly shouted out her voice echoing down the passageway.

"I went back to the Mudflat Bridge after our conversation," D.I. Hawk said in a gentle voice. "I found a bullet lodged in the breastplate of the third wolverine statue on the right-hand side and an empty casing shell four-feet away near the pub."

"You mean the one everyone rubs for good luck? The gargoyle with the chipped nose?" Crystova asked in astonishment.

"It's not a wolverine?" D.I. Hawk asked in surprise. "I've done my research and I've been assured the statue depicts a wolverine."

"There were supposed to be ten gargoyles commissioned by Duke Dono to protect the bridge. Below the bridge runs Poison Creek. Dono thought building the bridge across Poison Creek would keep out invaders. The tainted waters and the gargoyles were supposed to be a warning – keep away or the Wolf Soldiers will return and hunt you down. The sculptor Cyclesmen was commissioned to do the gargoyles," Crystova said. "Unfortunately, the tenth gargoyle was never finished because Duke Dono fled after the King sent his soldiers to the castle to put down a peasant uprising.

Duke Dono's murderous behavior culminated in the sacking of the castle. The peasant uprising had been fermenting for decades. What finally enraged the people enough to fight back was the death of a Mudflat Village child. The Duke's priests accused her of being a witch. The Duke ordered her death. She'd barely turned nine when the Duke's guard tied her to a stake and set her ablaze.

Thousands of angry citizens marched across Mudflat Village bridge and circled the moat and the entire castle demanding the Duke's head. Of course, they couldn't get inside. But the siege lasted two months and the Duke's supplies were running low. Those were the days. Back then people had backbone. Not today, today everyone genuflects and prays for someone to deliver them from their oppressors."

"Actually, the statues are talismans," Alexandra corrected Hawk and Crystova in a quiet hesitant manner. "They're not wolves.

They're us, our ancestors, wearing wolf masks. Our ancestors would dress up as wolves and dance around a fire. We thought the masks and hides would protect us against attack. If we smelled like wolves, covered our bodies in wolf skin and wore masks which made us look like wolves, real wolves would leave us alone. The ruse worked. Unfortunately, the practice nearly wiped out the wolf population until we found something else to fear."

"What was that?" Crystova asked intrigued. "Wait. Of course. The Lacertidae."

In a sharp tone which echoed down the dark passageway, Shehili said, "Now, that Hawk suspects someone attempted to kill Kimberly last night, what do you propose we do, just leave her to rot down here?"

D.I. Hawk presented a set of keys from his armored vest. He handed one of the keys to Shehili Swana. "I've arranged for a set of furniture to be moved down here temporarily. You may have the key to the door leading to the basement and will have unlimited access to Dela Lemon any time, day or night, to check on her condition and assure yourself that she is treated fairly."

"But I have agreed to pay her bail," Shehili said in a fierce undertone. "She cannot remain in this cold dank miserable place."

"Until her trial, she must remain down here guarded by my own handpicked knights, Dela Swana," D.I. Hawk stated firmly and without another word strode away his back stiff. He paused to say a few words to Bristlecone. Before he disappeared up the iron stairs, the women could see in the feeble light cast by one of the lanterns a knight carrying a piece of furniture in his arms. D.I. Hawk squeezed past the man without a word. Before the new knight approached the podium, the women could see other knights burdened with furniture and watched in dawning dismay as D.I. Hawk's plans became a reality.

In less than twenty minutes, Kimberly Lemon's cell had become as comfortable as a cave can be when someone rolls out an expensive hand-woven carpet and arranges on its surface a tiny dining area with a small wood table and four chairs, a comfortable bed complete with silk sheets and thick goose-down blanket. Next to the bed one of Hawk's people placed a night stand and added a glow lamp and several books. On the other side of the cave two knights set down a dresser made of wood from the forests of Keldarin and a standing mirror made of shiny paper. Alexandra was intrigued by the mirror. She ran her fingers lightly along the surface wondering how the material was able to reflect her image so perfectly.

All the comforts of home, Kimberly thought. Even more

comfortable than her private apartment at the bookshop. Yet the trappings of comfort were disheartening because the objects suggested she'd be trapped down here for a long time. What was beauty compared to freedom? She was in a lovely cocoon but a prisoner still.

D.I. Hawk had said someone had tried to kill her on the Mudflat Bridge. Yet they only had his word. She'd like to see this bullet and the hole. It could have been there for years and only noticed because he heard the wasp too. She didn't trust him. She didn't trust anyone. And then she looked at the women sitting at the table waiting for her to sit down and drink a nice hot cup of tea. Someone had brought them a tea caddy with fancy porcelain cups and a silver 3-tiered tray filled with cakes. Kimberly's stomach turned over at the thought of having to eat. What if the cakes were poisoned? What about the tea?

As if Shehili Swana had read her mind, she took a cookie off the tray and ate it brushing the crumbs off her lap. Alexandra sipped her tea and Crystova leaned over to spin the bottom carousel unable to decide on which fancy cake to choose. The handsome knight stood on the other side of the bars and watched them for a moment. He noticed Kimberly looking at him and said, "Don't worry. The tea and cakes were made by my landlady Romanova. I asked her to accommodate several more people.

"Doesn't she make the cakes for the Wolf's Inn?" Crystova asked.

"Sometimes. She caters for weddings and dinner parties mostly."

Shehili stood up, "Thank you but time is at a minimum and I would like to speak to my client in private." The knight smiled moving into the shadows. He seemed too nonchalant in Crystova's opinion. Sanguine or an act to lull Kimberly into a false sense of security? "Before you go. What's your name, your full name?"

From the darkness they heard him say, "Gawain. Gawain Bristlecone."

"Thank you, Gawain. We'll call you when we're finished," Shehili said in a stiff tone.

"Not at all, Dela Swana. Your word is my command," he said with a smile in his voice. There was something about his attitude toward Shehili Swana that puzzled Kimberly. He seemed awfully familiar toward her. What was his game?

Soon, Kimberly's thoughts were occupied by answering rapid fire questions from her defender. Shehili was relentless in asking Kimberly numerous questions which amazed even Alexandra having had no experience of the woman outside the boutique. The woman knew Curl Law more than most native Curlecons. Kimberly had to sit down to steady herself as the barrage of questions were thrown at her from every direction. Crystova joined in.

Alexandra sat with her eyes downcast playing with her spoon. She noticed there were no knives. A person couldn't do much harm with a spoon. Dig her way to freedom? Alexandra snorted and for a second caught the attention of the others. When they realized Alexandra wasn't clearing her throat to get their attention, they continued to cross examine Kimberly.

"When did Star show up at the Emporium?"

"I don't know, sometime before the school lunch bell went off, around eleven-thirty I believe."

"Why did you choose such a public place to quarrel?"

"I didn't choose to quarrel with Star. It wasn't really a quarrel."

"Why did she call you a witch?"

"Because she lives in a fantasy world."

"Lived not lives," Crystova reminded her gently. "She's dead."

The silence was like the earth shaking under their feet. Too late Crystova realized her mistake. It seemed impossible that Kimberly could look even paler than usual. In the glow worm's light on the table her veins seemed more pronounced. They waited for her to speak. She looked up from her plate, her eyes shining with unshed tears.

"I had this terrible feeling yesterday. I just knew something bad was going to happen. I should have guessed. But they're wrong. They're all wrong."

"What did you quarrel about?" Shehili asked impatient with unnecessary diversions. They only had a few precious minutes left.

"She insulted a friend of mine."

"Kimberly, you know the prosecutor is going to ask these questions. We can't help you unless you answer the questions fully and credibly."

"I don't remember exactly, something about Caleb going to hell because he wasn't a member of the church of the Holy Centipede. I told her off and she jumped up and did her dramatic bit to call attention to herself as usual."

"Why did Star run away from Antonio's Café?"

"I told you. Because I finally had had enough of her rudeness and told her what I thought. So, telling someone the truth is now a crime?"

"Where did you kill her?"

"I didn't kill anyone. I don't know what you're talking about."

"Why did you kill her?"

"I told you already. I didn't kill anyone."

"How did you get her body in the bin?"

"What bin? I don't understand you."

"I brought Hanson's newspaper," Crystova said.

Kimberly stared at her in disbelief, "No. There's been a mistake. This is the first time we've met since I was arrested outside Wolf Inn pub. No one's told me anything. Star isn't dead. I would know if she was dead."

Crystova pulled the news article out of her jacket pocket and handed the paper to Kimberly, "Just a few minutes ago, I handed this bit of paper to you while Gawain went to fetch cakes and tea."

"Why?" Kimberly asked baffled.

"Your aunt wanted you to have a copy."

Kimberly's stiff body and hooded expression made everyone uneasy.

"Where were you between noon yesterday and five o'clock?" Shehili asked resting her arms on the back of her chair.

"Around noon I was at Antonio's Café with Alexandra and Star."

Shehili glanced in Alexandra's direction, "You shouldn't be here. You're a witness."

"Can I excavate the northeast corner of the Bookworm this week?"

Kimberly with her hands clenched on the arms of her chair and eyes shining with unshed tears turned to face Crystova Moth. From the depths of her belly laughter burst forth followed by gasps. Her response was a complete surprise to everyone. Most people would have been annoyed or angry. What no one understood was how absurd the whole situation was, how impossible to think Star was dead. Without quite understanding why, the women joined in her laughter. Gradually, they came to realize how macabre their behavior must appear to Gawain.

The room grew quiet. Kimberly kept wishing she'd thrown Star out of the bookshop. Then she realized nothing she did would convince Blueglennen of her innocence. Harry Hanson had already accused and convicted her. Recognizing her own inevitable fate, the hollowness in her belly expanded into her chest nearly cutting off her air.

Alexandra's amusement consisted of a protective hand to her mouth and a deep throated tickle of the vocal cords. Shehili chuckled a few times and then grew thoughtful. Crystova threw her hair back with a toss of her head and a flip of the hand. She looked them over as if they had suddenly sprouted horns. Her surprise nearly unnerved Kimberly once again. Crystova was surprised by their reaction. She hadn't been joking. She'd been serious.

"You were serious?" Kimberly asked.

Crystova shrugged, "Well, yes. I was. I suppose my question was in poor taste but it's all absurd. You're innocent and the D.I. will prove it and while you're here, I can keep an eye on the bookshop." As if everyone felt ashamed, the women stopped laughing.

Kimberly stood up and began to pace the floor, "I doubt you'll get a chance Crystova. The police and the knights are probably ransacking my shop searching for proof I killed Star. You said something about a bin. What's so important about a garbage bin?"

Alexandra opened her mouth to answer and Shehili waved her to silence, "I hear Gawain. Our time is up. I will come back this evening and we'll talk further. It was a mistake to have so many here at such a crucial time."

"I was a paralegal at one time," Alexandra reminded Shehili.

"And my third major is law," Crystova said in her defense.

"Yes. But now that I know Alexandra is a witness, she cannot be here. The accuser will want to talk to her and she might unintentionally give away our defense."

"There were dozens of witnesses near our table at the café who saw and heard everything. Even Hawk showed up shortly after Star made her dramatic exit," Alexandra said in her defense as Gawain unlocked the cell door and threw it open with a flourish of his arm.

"Ladies. I'll escort you back to the basement door. Just follow the stairs upward and you'll reach the last door, a guard will take you the rest of the way through the station."

Crystova grabbed Kimberly's hand and squeezed, "I am concerned about your situation, Kimberly. It's not just about my job. I know you're innocent."

"Of course," Kimberly said squeezing back. "I know your interests align with mine. I would rather have you keeping an eye on the shop while I'm stuck down here."

When Crystova glanced at the women preparing to leave, then looked down into Kimberly's eyes, her silky brown hair brushed against Kimberly's cheek and Kimberly had her answer. They exchanged smiles. "You have my permission to hunt for the manuscript. I seriously doubt you'll find it hiding in my walls."

"Now I know you're wrong," Crystova countered, forced to move away as Alexandra came forward to rest her hand on Kimberly's shoulder. Kimberly jerked away in shy discomfort embarrassed by

184

the state of her clothes and the faint whiff of unwashed body. In every way the system made sure to assign guilt or innocence based on subliminal or unspoken clues. Prevent the innocent from bathing and others will judge that person guilty. Lock them away like animals and everyone will assume they're hiding something.

Alexandra didn't seem to notice Kimberly's rude reaction and with a brief smile told her, "If I'm to be a witness, it will mean I can't come down and visit you again. Be sure, I'll do everything in my power to find the real murderer."

"I appreciate your concern Alexandra. Thank you. Thank you all."

"Don't speak to anyone about this case Kimberly," Shehili warned her. "I am officially your lawyer. I will be back this evening to go over your testimony."

As they walked away, Kimberly turned her head to the right and peeked out through the bars. The light from Gawain's wand grew smaller and smaller and soon was gone. She was left alone, alone in the dark catacombs. The hairs on the back of her neck were standing at full attention. She made herself look in the other direction to her left. The long dark passageway beyond her cell must hide other cells just like her own. She hadn't heard anyone in the cells closest to her. Were there other people down here? What was beyond those prison cells? Surely not more cells? Did the catacombs end? They had to.

Looking to the left was frightening because the dim bulb in the passageway made the shadows move. As she peered toward the right again, she saw the fading light return, soon illuminating the entire passageway. Was the shadowy shape Gawain Bristlecone returning? Would Hawk have left his knight with no other defense but the podium a few yards from the iron door? If someone really wanted to kill Kimberly, why would Hawk choose a place that had no exit? He was smarter than that. She suspected there was another way out.

"Would you like some music, Dela Lemon?" Gawain asked with a smile and an inscrutable look.

"Yes, thank you."

When he moved back to the podium, Kimberly turned to face her cell, incongruous in its décor and luxury. She might have been a princess of old, imprisoned in a fancy cell before her execution. Oops. Not a wise choice of words. She sat at the table and stared at the cakes and the tea caddy longing for a good book to occupy her thoughts. She poured herself a cup of tea realizing that the cramping in her stomach had as much to do with hunger as fear.

Even with classical music playing softly in the background,

Kimberly heard a door, a heavy wooden door squeal as old hinges protested their abuse. The sound had come from the opposite direction beyond her cell somewhere in the dark catacombs where the empty cells resided. She got up from her chair and moved as quietly as possible toward the back of the room. She thought she could hide behind the lovely butterfly partition which also hid her bed. And then she realized the futility of hiding and stopped and waited for the intruder to appear at the bars of her cell.

Instead, she heard Gawain's heavy boots striding past her cell. He did not stop. She stayed hidden behind the partition. The sound of his footsteps receding seemed to go on forever. When he spoke, the acoustics were so sharp and clear, he might have been standing right next to her. Yet she couldn't understand what the other person was saying. The one-sided conversation lasted several minutes barely enough time to wonder what the other person had been saying.

"Channel 4. Yes sir."

"Some reading material would be nice, sir."

"You want what, sir?"

"I threw it in the trash bin."

"Yes, sir."

As quietly as possible, she snuck around the partition and crept toward the cell bars. Even though the rocky wall was rough and icy, she tried to squeeze herself into the corner and peer out at the empty passageway without being seen. She watched as Knight Bristlecone strode past her cell without looking her way. He must have seen her. Yet, he pretended not to notice her odd behavior. Who had he been talking to? He was taking orders from someone. Her money was on Hawk.

He returned to the podium like an actor on a stage and she the only audience member sitting in the dark. He picked up the bin holding it away from his body as if it could contaminate him. He passed her cell a second time pretending not to notice her, his back ramrod straight. His co-conspirator must have come from a different direction. Kimberly would have seen him if he'd come by way of the iron door.

Earlier, while sitting on the floor in despair, Kimberly had had the dubious pleasure of experiencing life as a blind person, only able to hear the tap-tap-tap of water on stone, the wind blowing through the catacombs, the comings and goings of Gawain. Before her room had been redecorated and several fancy new lights had been added to the cell, she had sat in the dark and overheard the exchange between Gawain and Wakefield. She recognized the surprise in Wakefield's voice when Gawain told him she'd already been fed.

Why had Gawain lied? She hadn't been fed. She wondered if Governor Saurus intended to starve her until she confessed. But now as her eye roamed over the three-tiered silver tray filled with cakes and cookies, she suspected he or D.I. Hawk planned to kill her with kindness, maybe clog her arteries. She longed for a salad.

Before he appeared at the bars of her cell, she had prepared herself. She stood a few inches away from the cold dank stone wall opposite the fake mirror and saw him approaching in the paper reflection cast by the light-wand he carried. He had his usual charming smile painted on his face which was beginning to get on her nerves. He handed her a book, a thin volume just small enough to fit between the bars. She accepted the book with surprise and a nagging sense of worry. "It's light reading I know, but something to keep your mind off your troubles. And here are a few magazines we keep in the lobby."

"They left a few books on the nightstand. One is a history of Old Town and the other is about precious gemstones along Poison Creek. I'm sure they'll put me right to sleep in no time," she said trying to get him to smile. He gave her an inscrutable look. He reminded her of a magician. If she looked at his hands instead of his face, she'd be able to figure out how his tricks were done.

How long had she been down here? It seemed as if she'd been down in this dank cold place for days. There was no way of knowing. No natural light penetrated the dark, only the feeble lights along the passageway and her little globes in her cell. She missed the sun and the moon. She missed fresh air. The only way she could determine time was by the changing of the guards. She believed she'd been down in the catacombs for two days now. It must be day shift. She heard Knight Graceland exchange a few words with Bristlecone. Bristlecone had the graveyard shift; Graceland had the day and Lively the night. Why did Graceland and Lively have to guard her?

She wasn't complaining. She liked them both. She and Graceland and Moth were fingerlings together in primary school. They'd become close friends. And their friendship didn't end when they graduated. Only when Graceland went off to New Enriech to train as a knight did they lose touch. When she heard someone approaching her cell, she moved toward the sound.

Knight Graceland glanced over his shoulder then turned to smile at her, "Here. I've brought you some oranges." He passed the small oranges through the bars of the cell one at a time. Yesterday, he'd brought her a bunch of bananas. She tried not to cry. Somehow, he knew.

"It will be alright. You'll see. You can trust Hawk and Bristlecone."

"You said that yesterday and I'm still down here."

"It's for your safety," he assured her with his familiar sweet smile. For a knight, Juleus was too trusting. He did have a remarkable instinct for spotting troublemakers though. "Take these. Don't let Bristlecone see them."

Instead of an orange, he slipped a packet of letters into her palm, "Got to go back to my post. They've got vid. Remember."

"Thank you Jule. I don't know what I'd do if I didn't have you and Lively to keep me company."

"Don't cry Kim. Please?"

"I'll try."

With her arms loaded with goodies she went behind the partition and hid them in the bottom drawer of her dresser. She would wait until the night shift to read the letters. There was too much activity during the day shift with Saurus' personal guards tromping back and forth through the catacombs. She returned to the bars of her cell and tried to see Graceland at his post. The light from the ceiling bulb above the podium illuminated his head. He had his cellphone and was busy texting. She wondered if he was texting Crystova letting her know Kimberly had received her letter. The other letters must be from Alexandra, Valcinda and Harry Zany.

Kimberly wandered back to the partition and sat down on the edge of her new mattress, a thick comfortable mattress with a goose-down comforter for warmth. She nearly slid off the bed onto the carpet realizing belatedly that the comforter was made of the finest of silks. Ridiculous. Then she tried to stop thinking, tried to make her mind blank. It was impossible.

The ugliness of it all swept over her like a tidal wave. Falsely accused of murdering a troublesome child and now a victim of someone else's blind rage. Worst of all, much worse was the knowledge she had no privacy, none what-so-ever, not even the privacy of her own thoughts. What kind of people were in charge here? Were the humans on the ship in charge of Blueglennen now? Gawain was not from Shellfargon. His skin was pink. He had thick eyelashes too.

He and Hawk and Shehili didn't even try to hide their foreignness anymore. When she first met Shehili Swana she assumed she was from New Dala. She'd never been to New Dala but had read the people were darker skinned there. But after watching Hawk and Swana closely, reading their body language and listening to their words, she knew they were pretending to be strangers for her benefit, maybe, even for the benefit of her friends. Hawk made no secret he was a foreigner. Or could they be Lacertidae? The idea terrified her. She'd never met a Lacertidae.

How would she know? With all the new technologies, they could have disguised themselves to look like members of the starship Albion. She must be hallucinating.

Then she heard the voices whispering again. For days now, most often during Knight Bristlecone's shift she'd hear mumbled conversations. It sounded as if the voices were coming from the floor. At first, she wondered if her time in the dungeon was making her crazy. But now, she could distinguish words. She knelt on the carpet and scooted over to the corner of her cell. She could smell fresh air. Then as if someone had his lips pressed to a hole, she heard a man say, "Don't despair."

The other voice replied, "It's been months. We've done nothing wrong."

"Remember my darling that I love you. I'll always love you."

"And I love you. But when will this end? I can barely breathe. The air is getting worse."

"He passed me a note. Don't despair. It's good news."

Kimberly lay down on her stomach and searched the rock. Then a piece of slate fell on her head. Elation sang through her body. There were others down here like her. She repositioned herself in the corner sitting cross-legged on the floor with her forehead pressing against the cold cave wall and whispered, "Hello? Who are you? My name is Kimberly Lemon. I'm a prisoner here in Duke Tower."

When no one answered, she tried again, "Please. I know you're there. I hear you at night when the guards change shifts." Still no sound. Disappointed and pretty sure she knew why no one would answer, she leaned back. The other prisoners must wonder if she was trying to trap them into revealing their identities. Kimberly got to her feet and sat on the edge of her bed, listening intently, hoping they would trust her.

"You have a visitor Dela Lemon," Graceland said startling her so much she nearly fell off the bed. She hadn't heard him approach. She peeked around the partition and saw Victoria standing beside Graceland with a self-satisfied smirk on her face as if she were enjoying herself hugely, which no doubt she was. There was nothing Victoria enjoyed more, than other people's misery, especially Kimberly's misery.

How could she have missed the sounds of people approaching? Every other sound in this hellhole reverberated off the walls. From which direction had they come, from the lower rooms of the police station or from beyond the catacombs leading outside the castle? Yes, she suspected the catacombs crisscrossed the caverns. They might take her to the river. Still other passageways might lead to the village or Bitterroot Forest, maybe, even across the moat and Poison Creek to Wolf Inn pub. Graceland probably thought he was doing Kimberly a favor by sneaking Victoria down here.

The women barely looked at each other. Kimberly made herself move away from the partition and sit down on the chair which faced the corridor. She crossed her arms and waited for Victoria to speak. She hoped she appeared indifferent, perhaps even contemptuous. She suspected her face registered everything she was feeling. The mind produced the thought and the thought produced the emotion. No. Wait. Perhaps they worked in unison. Who gave a bumblebee's butt? Victoria looked sideways at Kimberly and smiled with relish letting Kimberly know how much she was enjoying the moment.

The smile disappeared as soon as Graceland glanced her way. "You have twenty minutes ladies," Graceland said with a genuine smile and discreetly moved back to the podium.

Victoria ended up speaking first. Kimberly felt a moment's satisfaction followed by blinding rage which took all her energy to control. "Where's the key to the Emporium?"

"Why?"

"While you're busy here," Victoria said surveying Kimberly's dungeon cell curiously. "I thought I'd take charge of the shop."

"It's been taken care of."

"But I'm family and the shop should stay in the family."

"No. The shop belongs to me. What do you want in the shop? I have nothing of value."

"Don't be silly," Victoria said as she looked over her shoulder where Kimberly imagined Graceland was standing guard near the iron door. "I just want to help out. You certainly can't make any money stuck in here."

"After your recent visit, I took precautions. You won't find anything of value so don't bother."

"I can get a court order. I'm family and the Governor believes in families."

"Actually, you're not a member of my family or in any way a claimant to the shop. I mailed several copies of my will and power of attorney to the two people who will inherit the shop, if I die or am disabled. I even posted copies in the Shellfargon Seed. It's all public record now."

"Who has power of attorney?"

"Buy a back issue and find out for yourself."

Victoria leaned forward nearly pressing her face to the iron bars before having second thoughts about her skin touching something so dirty and decayed. Victoria hissed under her breath saying, "Are you serious? Oh child, child, child. Poor, foolish child."

"I am not your child or your niece or anything to you. We are strangers."

"Wow, you really are delusional. Our blood and especially our DNA will tell a court of law differently."

"Actually, you're wrong. Grandpa told me the truth before he died. After my mother died Grandma Electra traveled to Walrat Island to find me. Grandpa wanted to come but he was ill. She found me, along with you. You were three years old and thought my mother was your mother. My father left his dead wife and child and took off to avoid paying the doctor bills. The midwife took care of us until Grandma arrived. After mother died, the midwife sent mother's letter to Grandma. Mom begged her to come and take us to Blueglennen.

Grandma learned from neighbors how mother took pity on you. She found you when you were just two years old begging for food in the market square and fighting with the feral dogs for food. She brought you home. My father, the worthless bastard, quarreled with mother because he didn't want to feed another child. Mother was stubborn. She insisted on caring for you. Grandma Electra chose to take you along with me to live in Blueglennen.

She believed she was following her daughter's wishes. She and Grandpa adopted you. Then you turned on them and they realized no amount of loving kindness could change your first impressions of the world. Once you turned eighteen and left Blueglennen, they discovered you'd robbed them of their life savings. They managed to survive with the help of friends. Your first two years of life must have been hell. I'm sorry for you Victoria. Until you stop hating the world, no one's going to trust you. Read the will and the power of attorney and you'll understand."

If circumstances were reversed would Kimberly have traveled a mile underground in the semi-dark with a cold wind blowing from some crevice in the earth and with the sound of drip, drip, dripping water in the distance and other sounds less friendly? Would she dare come down demanding the key to the bookshop while surrounded by rodents clawing their way along the rocks? Would she stare like a dumb animal through the bars of her aunt's prison cell, stare with such a fixed look upon her face as if by staring into Victoria's eyes she could will Victoria into giving up the shop keys?

Kimberly knew Victoria wouldn't waste her time unless she was desperately in need of money or afraid someone was after her. Kimberly did an inventory in her head of the layout of her shop and the contents trying to figure out what could be so important to bring Victoria down to the dank dark cold of the Tower dungeons. Had Victoria left a cache of stolen money or jewels in the walls before her last disappearance?

The silence stretched on. Kimberly remained seated in her chair, her hands flat on the surface of the table, the wood beneath her fingers a symbol of something solid, something real. This conversation between her and Victoria seemed surreal, one of a hundred childhood nightmares. It was a shock to figure out at this late date how much safer she felt behind bars than if she and Victoria were standing outside in the open air only inches between them. That was how scary Victoria had become – a monstrous Delphinid capable of almost any cruelty.

Kimberly had often dreamed of one day finding her father, someone she could turn to in times of need. The reality was a horror. Maybe that was why Grandpa Lemon waited until so late to tell her the truth about her father. And then her sweet mother with her kind heart unknowingly installs a viper inside her family's home. All of Kimberly's experiences with Victoria had been chilling reminders her aunt lacked so many things that made a Delphinid, a sentient creature capable of bonding with other Delphinids, capable of empathy, kindness, and generosity.

A long time ago Kimberly realized Victoria had lost the ability to feel normal emotions. Maybe, she'd never had them to begin with? As a soulless Delphinid, she might as well have been a rogue Serpent trolling the oceans and seas killing and maiming for pleasure.

Victoria stepped away from Kimberly's prison cell and without a word headed back toward Graceland. Kimberly waited until she heard the iron door open and snap shut behind her rogue aunt. Several minutes of silence passed without sound and Kimberly remained seated in the semi-dark. She knew there were candles and a few glow lamps in her cell. She knew she could light them at any time. She could even set the furnishings on fire.

But to what end? She would have to run away and they, of course, as law enforcement would have to chase her. She didn't have any money. They had all the manpower and money. Where could she go? She'd never been outside Wolfern Province in her whole life. She was a poor female without any family.

"I see your aunt's visit was short and unpleasant. Cheer up Kim, you have many friends to compensate for lack of family," Graceland said as he walked toward her cell and peered inside. "Many more friends than you know."

"You're a good man Jule. You see the good in so many people. Not everyone is good."

"I've been in law enforcement long enough to recognize a serpent when I see one. But don't let this situation cloud your judgement, Kim." His words were comforting, and she tried to hold on to them through his shift. When she heard Lively take over and Graceland didn't get a chance to say goodbye, she was sad.

Once the iron door shut behind Graceland, Knight Lively stepped up to her cell and slipped something through the bars. "A little something to cheer you up, kiddo." She retrieved the candy bar and chuckled.

"I'm going to weigh a ton if you guys don't stop bringing me treats."

He laughed all the way back to the podium. Her spirits lifted. She felt as if the Holy Delph's angels were watching over her. Stupid, stop tearing up, she told herself. You don't believe in gods and angels. And then she thought she heard someone say, "You do if you're down here."

"Is that you Bristlecone?" she whispered moving toward her chair feeling her legs grow weak.

"It's me."

"I was wondering when you'd slip up. You've been reading my mind. How? Is it something your people are born with or a special spy device?" Kimberly asked pushing back her chair and sitting down. "Whatever it is, stay out of my head."

Bristlecone's laughter echoed up and down the passageway growing fainter as the laughter disappeared down the many tributaries. "You seem teachable Dela Lemon and we have all the time in the world. Why don't we begin with your first lesson in mind reading? Hum?"

"What?"

"I'll show you the brakes first. It's just like driving a car."

"What's a car?"

"I'll show you later. Come now. Let's begin."

"I was joking. I know you can't read minds. The acoustics

down here magnify everything.”

"I was joking too. How about some music? Do you like rock-in-roll?”

"What's that?”

Time meant nothing to Kimberly down in the belly of the earth. The only way she could approximate time was during meals which were personally delivered by Knight Bristlecone. He informed her in a very serious voice that he prepared her meals with his own hands without anyone's assistance. This news which was supposed to make her feel better had the opposite effect. The idea someone wanted her dead terrified her. It was difficult to think straight in the gloom. She found herself pacing the floor a lot.

It had been several hours since dinner and when Bristlecone opened her cell and carried in her dinner tray, she groaned wondering if the man would insist on another "lesson" in defense. Her legs and arms still throbbed from the last lesson. She suspected she had bruises up and down her body. Her world had certainly expanded.

Ironic to be virtually buried alive yet learn new tricks which might one day save her life. One day she might even get good enough to flip Gawain over her shoulder. He was also good at chess. She used to think she was pretty darn good at chess. She used to be able to beat her grandfather at the game on occasion. Now she wondered, if like Gawain her grandfather had let her win.

"You have several visitors. D.I. Hawk will permit them down after you finish dinner. I am to report to him when that happy occasion arrives. Bon Appetite Madam.”

"Who are they?”

Bristlecone glanced up at the ceiling of the cave for inspiration then into her eyes, "I don't know. Friends? Lovers?”

"You don't know. Why? Shouldn't you know?”

"Don't you worry. They've been searched, and their weapons confiscated.”

"Please. Be serious for once. You said several. I'm assuming I have more than one visitor. What if they overpower you?”

He frowned in annoyance and searched her face intensely, "I sincerely hope you haven't succumbed to my numerous charms.”

"What?" she asked. Bristlecone could be outrageously annoying.

"It is a common effect of being held against one's will. Studies prove hostages identify so strongly with their captors they lose their own objectivity. Don't let this handsome face and brilliant mind bring down your defenses. Stay true to yourself."

"I'm not your hostage. I've been arrested because someone's trying to get rid of me and end the troublesome Merchants' Row Alliance. Whatever you're up to stop it. Quit being so silly."

Knight Bristlecone put a hand to his ear and bent his head listening to a voice speaking to him through his earpiece. Kimberly grabbed her fork and knife slashing at the chicken breast with a ferocity Bristlecone should have stopped. Why in the world is he allowing her to have these dangerous weapons? She could stab the guard, kill herself, or pry the hinges off the bars, maybe even dig her way to freedom. Ridiculous. The whole situation was ridiculous.

Without a word Bristlecone disappeared, only the sound of his boots hitting rock a signal he was still nearby. She heard the groan as the iron door opened, the murmur of voices, followed by the sound of several people moving toward her cell. She tried to chew her chicken quickly. By the time they arrived she had swallowed her first bite. She continued to remain seated at her miniature dining table with her matching chairs and candles lit and the smell of incense in the air – all very romantic.

Her visitors were startled by the sight of her and the opulence of her prison cell. She could see the disbelief registering in different forms on their faces. It should have been funny. They had expected something far sinister. Now she realized the genius of Hawk. Rather than instilling pity upon her from those friends and relations who might visit, her environment would instill confusion and doubt. She was surprised to see Caleb among her visitors, but not surprised to see his cousin Valcinda Moorland. They stood close together behind Guinevere Goodbody and Professor Honeysweet. Four visitors at one time! Why not sell tickets?

"Why don't you sell tickets Delo Bristlecone. It could pay for my defense."

Guinevere drew closer to the prison bars, her eyes taking in the fancy partition, the mirrors on the cave walls, the candles, the carpet, and Kimberly sitting at a fine table covered in fresh linen with handsome cutlery held in her hands and a plate of Orange Spice Chicken Marinara on an expensive set of stoneware. "This situation is outrageous. Why are they keeping you down here? We are supposed to be a civilized people."

Kimberly set down her knife and fork and lifted a goblet of wine to her lips. She drank the entire contents without taking a breath then refilled the goblet from the decanter in the iced bucket. Normally she hated when people stared at her and all her life found ways to avoid being the center of attention, yet, now, she had nowhere to hide other than behind the partition. And that would be rude. Instead, she decided to add to the charade. She'd be the circus side show, the horned and bearded lady surrounded by luxury, a grotesque, an oddity.

When Guinevere couldn't get a response out of her Guinevere turned on Bristlecone, "If Kimberly is a murderess why does she get to have a knife? And what about all this stuff in here? Do you really think you can keep her a prisoner forever? We've paid her bond. Set her free."

"That decision is up to my superiors, Dela Goodbody," Bristlecone said between clenched teeth, the charm on vacation. "You have twenty minutes. I'll be just down the corridor."

"Corridor," Guinevere snorted. The petite and plump woman fired back. "You call this a corridor? It's a cave, you monstrous creature." Her thick short hair glinted blue-black in the light. A gentle hand on Guinevere's arm calmed her down. She glanced up into Honeysweet's face and something in his expression silenced her for the moment. Her belligerent expression suggested she had much more to say about the subject.

"Dela Lemon we are doing everything we can to get you out of this place," Honeysweet began. "I suppose we should be grateful that they've made you comfortable but actually this opulence concerns me greatly. The merchants have contributed money to your bail and Dela Swana has offered her services without pay. An extraordinary thing to do, but she insists she will not take so much as a tinpiece. What can we do to help you, Dela Lemon?"

The wine hit her empty stomach with a rush of blood to her head. She held onto the swaying table for dear life and tried to speak in a normal voice, "If I am to stay down here for an undisclosed amount of time, I would appreciate some reading material, preferably from my bookstore."

"I know what she likes," Caleb said from behind Honeysweet's shoulder. Honeysweet stepped aside to allow Caleb to move closer to her prison bars. "Kimberly, I know you didn't hurt Star. I've tried to make Sophie understand but she. Well, I'm going to keep on making her see reason."

"Thank you, Caleb. I'm glad to see you."

"I've been watching over the bookstore. The knights and the detective have only taken a few things just some of your personal stuff but none of the inventory."

Valcinda squeezed through the group in order to see Kimberly better and smiled, "I've shelved all the books they threw around the room and swept the floor. They tracked in a lot of mud and dirt. It's back to the way you like it."

"She even washed the bedroom coverlet and sheets. You wouldn't believe what a mess they made of things," Caleb said as if this news would make her feel better.

"Has Victoria?" Kimberly began and then looked at Guinevere and Honeysweet and realized her private problems were not their concern.

As if Caleb knew where she was going with her cryptic question, he said, "She tried to get in, but I told her you had made me trustee of the shop. She didn't believe me until I showed her the document. I have it right here in my pocket," demonstrating the truth of this remark by padding his jacket pocket.

"Dela Lemon, I hope you'll allow me to help with your defense," Honeysweet said his expression unreadable. "I've offered my services to Dela Swana as investigator. Sadly, she told me she has everything under control."

"She told you to mind your own business," Guinevere, ever the arbiter of truth, interjected.

Honeysweet ignored Guinevere's rude interruption and spoke, "Even though she rejected my offer, I believe she will permit me to nose around and uncover the true murderer."

"Your faith in me is astonishing," she said to him and then looked at the others. "All of you. I don't understand. The evidence seems to point to me, but you don't believe it. Why?"

"I've known you for just a few months," Honeysweet said. "And I am convinced you couldn't hurt so much as a mite."

"You didn't do it Kim. We know you didn't. I've known you forever and in all that time you've never spoken a cross word to anyone or raised your hand to anyone. There is no way you could have harmed Star. No way," Caleb said.

"I remember the first day we met in kinter school," Guinevere said. "Remember the day that bully pulled my hair?"

"Ah no, sorry Guinevere I don't."

"Well, maybe, you don't remember because you were always sticking up for me and all your friends."

"I had a big mouth back then and it got me into trouble," Kimberly confessed.

"You got into trouble because you couldn't stand to see people hurt," Guinevere said in a fierce voice. "That's why I know you didn't do this. Stop being a martyr and let us help you."

"I'm not being a martyr just a realist. The evidence is against me."

"Come on," Guinevere shouted, her words echoing beyond the dim light bulbs and the impenetrable blackness of the catacombs. "Get real. They have a trash bin which happens to be in a place where everyone has access to its contents. They can't prove a thing. So, you raked Star once. So, what. Everyone in Blueglennen has been on the receiving end of Star's hissy fits and she isn't even a dominant member of the castle. She can, could be stubborn at times. Why do you think the merchants have rallied round you? Because they know you. They've known you all your life. Please let us help."

The idea that so many people believed her innocent was overpowering. She did her best not to cry. The wine was to blame. She made herself stand up and move toward the bars. She padded Guinevere's fingers now wrapped around the bars as if she wanted to pull them apart and free Kimberly right that moment. Kimberly was astonished Guinevere liked her enough to brave this dark damp place. More astonishing was the sight of Professor Honeysweet and Caleb coming all this way to talk to her. She'd expected to see Valcinda Moorland because Valcinda had always been a champion of the underdog.

"I am so grateful for all of your support. Thank you all. Thank you, thank you."

Valcinda shoved a box of cookies between the bars and whispered, "There's several letters inside."

"Time's up ladies and gentlemen," Bristlecone announced in a loud emphatic voice that probably carried as far as the upper rooms of the knight's quarters a mile above ground. Guinevere grabbed Kimberly's hand with both of hers and squeezed and pumped it up and down.

Caleb moved forward hurriedly and poked his arm through the space between the bars and padded her roughly on the shoulder. "Don't worry, I'll take care of the shop. Everyone will be okay."

Honeysweet extended his hand and Kimberly whose hand was tingling from Guinevere's overcharged enthusiasm allowed him to take her hand. Then he did something completely unexpected. He bowed and kissed the back of her hand. The brush of his lips on her skin made her body tingle.

Valcinda with tears swimming in her eyes was the last to go and clung to her hand until Bristlecone's voice startled her with "Miss. That's enough, Miss. You must go."

"Get it right alien invader. Call me Dela. And for your information justice has been denied Kimberly Lemon. You're wrong," Valcinda said. "You've got the wrong person."

When everyone had been ushered out and Kimberly resumed

her seat at the table, she stared at the congealing mess on her plate and thought she might throw up. Sometimes people's support could be worse to bear than a stranger's hate. Pity, though. Pity made her squirm. She would rather die than have anyone feel pity for her. What gave her courage was the knowledge her friends and some of her neighbors were convinced she was innocent. She looked again at her plate and picked up her fancy fork and knife and made herself cut a new piece off the chicken and pop the morsel in her mouth. She chased the cold chicken down with a swallow of wine.

Somewhere beyond her cell, something particularly hilarious seemed to be amusing Bristlecone no end for he began to chuckle to himself and the chuckling and thigh slapping seemed to go on forever. She threw down her utensils and covered her face.

Then, she heard someone whispering her name. She ran to the partition and sank down upon the carpet. Trembling she pulled the piece of slate away from the tiny holes and bent her head. "Hello. It's me Kimberly Lemon. I hear you. Who are you? Where are you?"

Time seemed to stretch into infinity as she waited for someone to answer her questions. Then a man's voice whispered, "My name is Charles Thornton. I'm a prisoner. My wife is also a prisoner. We were to be married but the Governor discovered we were incompatible."

Kimberly was so eager to talk to another prisoner, she banged her forehead on the hard cave wall in her eagerness to be heard, "What do you mean? I don't understand."

"We've heard of you," a woman said. "I'm Emily Thornton. My husband Charles has six percent Lacertidae in his DNA. The church and the Governor forbid us from marrying. There is a priest down here who has been marrying couples like us."

"Why did they put you down here? You're not criminals," Kimberly said in a shaky voice afraid Bristlecone might hear her.

"Charles is considered sub-Delphinid, an enemy of the state. Because I tried to tell my story online and ask someone to free my husband from here, they arrested me claiming I was a subversive undermining the war effort," Emily Thornton said.

When Kimberly heard booted feet heading her way, alarmed she hissed, "Stop. Someone's coming." With shaking fingers, she set the slate back in its groove and rose slowly to her feet. Beyond the partition she sensed a presence. She waited for the person to speak. Then the booted footfalls could be heard returning to the duty station. Had Bristlecone heard her? Did he think she might be talking to herself?

E1 Shellfargon Year 5092 NDMP WK 5: UES Albion 4

Young Delphinid female missing. Her disappearance generating hysteria in region. Star Bridgekeeper presumed dead. Bridgekeeper body discovered. Religious and political factions at crossroads. Dead female is a member of Centipede Sect. Merchant accused of Star's disappearance. May be politically motivated. Lemon is head of opposition against Duke Tower and Governor. 2 attempts made to eliminate opposition. Ordered E2 to guard suspect in dungeon below Duke Tower until trial.

Request removal of E4 from Blueglennen Site. Prefer replacement at earliest convenience. E4 too emotionally involved with natives. At risk of exposing our project and undermining our authority with ruling party.

Several new technicians and engineers without clearances have been assigned to Duke Tower Castle. They are spooks with fake credentials. Request further investigation.

Chapter 7

When the door opened, and she could feel the warmth of the sunlight on her face, Kimberly closed her eyes against the painful glare. She felt someone's hand lead her out into the light. She wanted so much to see where she was going. She heard birds quarrelling somewhere above her head. She smelled newly mown grass and the perfume of flowers. She heard their shoes crunching on the graveled path and then she realized where she must be.

Bristlecone urged her forward with a steady hand on her arm. A voice Kimberly recognized with delight spoke to someone behind her, "You bastards. This is unconscionable." Relieved to know the woman hadn't abandoned her after all, a pinch of hope got her moving forward.

Bristlecone guided her to a bench and with his strong arm as security lowered her to a sitting position. She recognized the wooden bench beneath her buttocks. If only her eyes could adjust to the brightness. Her eyes were tearing up unable to adjust to the light. Someone leaned in close. She recognized Bristlecone's curious smell. He smelled of a clean breeze off the ocean. She wished he wasn't so handsome. She should hate and despise him with her entire being. Unfortunately, her body had other ideas. In an uncharacteristic motion, he tenderly set a pair of sunglasses on her face.

She opened her eyes a crack and could see his face leering into her own. He said, "There now. That's much better isn't it? Oh yes. I can almost see your eyes."

"Move away Knight. I would like to discuss the case with my client in private," Shehili ordered.

Kimberly heard the perpetual smile in Bristlecone's voice and knew his constant cheerfulness chafed people's lily white, bluish grey, and coffee colored behinds, even the creamy in-between behinds. Kimberly was sure his mentally deranged cheerfulness was simply a defense mechanism against people's attempts to get close to him. After all his gorgeousness made women behave like idiots. What better weapon did a man have but an imbecile grin and meaningless chatter. Since he refused to be serious, serious subjects could never be brought up.

Gradually, Kimberly's eyes adjusted to the light and she was not surprised to discover that she was sitting on a bench inside the Bishop Garden's courtyard. Shehili sat on a special chair she must have brought with her, a cloth contraption, very elegant with sticks of bright colors running up and down the fabric. At that precise moment, Shehili was sifting through a large picnic hamper and setting up a small table with various delicacies. She pulled out a miniature bottle of something, unscrewed the top, and handed it to Kimberly. The bottle was no bigger than the palm of Kimberly's hand.

"Drink it, it will do you good."

"What is it? I don't like alcohol."

"It's a refreshing drink, not a bottle of whiskey. Go on. Live a little. Try something you've never had before."

She took a sip. The bubbly liquid slid down her throat soothing the rawness inside. In a few seconds the liquid sent wow messages to her brain. "Nice," she managed to say and finished off the contents.

"Yes. A real perk-me-up, aye? Here now, have a sandwich. And try this pickle." Kimberly accepted the plate filled with food, a plate she might add that would have done the Duke proud: porcelain with gold filigree running around the outer and inner rims. Once she'd started sampling the tasty delicacies on the plate, she noticed the engraving on the bottom of the dish. It was of a sleek black starship circling a red planet. How had Dela Swana obtained such rare plates? Only Governor Saurus could afford such expensive cutlery.

The sandwiches had been cut into wedges easily held between three fingers. She bit into one and the creamy paste zinged through her mouth sending another shock wave of goodness straight to her brain. Ghee, this was very, very, nice. She could easily get used to this sort of treatment. Then she remembered. In a few short hours she would have to return to the ass-end of hell for Holy Delph knows how long.

Shehili set her plate on the table between them and brushed crumbs off her fingers and her lap, all while asking Kimberly questions in an undertone. Kimberly answered back in a like manner glancing at Bristlecone standing at attention by the gated entrance to the courtyard. The exit behind Kimberly must be locked. If she really wanted to make her escape, she would have to throw a hooked rope over the parapet and shimmy down the walls. Ridiculous.

"Where were you between eight in the morning and midnight sixteen days ago?"

"What day is it?

"It is the 5th day of Sweatfir. On the Albion this month is called July."

"When was I arrested?"

"Ever-loving-hell," Shehili swore. Kimberly looked up in time to see Shehili throw a biscuit at Gawain. The biscuit hit him squarely in the stomach. Bravo thought Kimberly. Shehili Swana, you can be on my Tortuga Toss team any day. And when you toss a plastic shell instead of a biscuit, you'll probably knock out our opponent's team member. With relish she heard her defense say to her dungeon troll, "You mean to tell me you've kept my client ignorant of the days?"

Gawain remained unmoved by Dela Swana's outrage. "Yes. Take it up with Hawk. My job is to protect Dela Lemon."

"Kimberly. You've been in Duke Tower dungeon for nine days. You were arrested on the 30th of Growthir. I'm asking about the day you and Star Bridgekeeper had lunch in the plaza, the last time you saw her. It would have been the 23rd day of Growthir."

"I was at the Bookworm preparing to open the shop. Around ten o'clock, I unlocked the shop door and it wasn't ten minutes later my first visitor showed up. My aunt Victoria Lemon. Shortly after Victoria arrived Finstickel entered and made his way to the back. He likes to go through my old magazines in case he missed a good one. Then Star Bridgekeeper popped in around fifteen minutes later. She told me she'd run away from school and the reason she ran away was because the teacher wouldn't let her pray before the pledge of allegiance.

My aunt went into my private quarters without permission while I tried to persuade Star to go back to school. When she refused to do as I told her and after my aunt and Finstickel left, ah, it must have been before the lunch bell, Alexandra Montague showed up and asked if I wanted to have coffee with her in the plaza. At noon, the three of us, Alexandra, Star and I walked to the plaza. We found an empty table outside Antonio's Café. I ordered a coffee and a torte for Star."

"Hold on," Shehili said lifting a manicured finger and sighed. "You're going too fast. You're leaving out important details. I want a complete picture. Leave nothing out."

"Well," Kimberly hesitated. "There are some things I would rather keep private."

"You forget. I am forbidden by oath to reveal anything you tell me unless the information will help your defense. Now, let's go back to the beginning. Did Star and the other two occupants of the bookshop, Victoria or Finstickel interact with each other?"

Kimberly hated airing her underclothes in public especially her heated relationship with Victoria. If she mentioned Victoria's thievery and bullying would people slap her with the same immoral stamp? Yet, did she want to end up living underground for the rest of her life? She started over at the point Victoria entered the Bookworm.

Whenever Kimberly hesitated Shehili Swana would tap her

tablet with the stylus and say, "The truth please." Her insistence on the truth forced Kimberly to reveal unpleasant family secrets she'd hidden from even her closest friends.

For the hundredth time Kimberly wondered if Shehili like Gawain could read minds. Ridiculous. According to experienced travelers who'd spent time on the Albion, none of the crew or captains showed any sort of paranormal abilities. Whereas, some Delphinids were born with the gift of finding lost objects and missing people. Some scientists believed these gifted Delphi were using ancient sonar abilities. A few of these people who had proven themselves in the past were asked by concerned citizens to locate Star Bridgekeeper.

Delphi trackers were no match for the starship Albion personnel. A rumor suggested one of the ethnographers assigned to Blueglennen discovered the garbage bin where poor Star's body had been imprisoned.

"So, you suspect Victoria stole a few of your belongings while she was in your private quarters? Yet, you trusted her enough to allow her to leave without insisting she dump the contents of her purse where you could see it?"

"I had no other choice. All I have is hope where Victoria is concerned, hope she won't steal my personal belongings or the cash in my register."

"You say she left objects she planned to steal on the bed? How do you know? Did you go back and check?"

"Yes. I mean, yes, she left the objects on the bed because she told me so. And no, I didn't go back and check. Why would I? Victoria is strong. She could easily overpower me if I tried to search her purse."

"Didn't you say at one time Star had been in the back room? You mentioned she wanted to make tea and discuss religion with you?"

"When she comes to visit, she tries to convince me to convert."

"Convert you?"

"Yes, she's tried to convert me numerous times. It's a part of church doctrine. Their members seek out new converts by going door to door or stopping people in the street. I tried everything I could to distract Star. She gets upset when I tell her no and stomps out in a huff. I wish I'd just stayed in bed that day."

"From what you've told me, Victoria or Star could have stolen the watch. We can use this in court. If we can get Victoria on the witness stand, we can establish doubt."

By the time Kimberly finished answering Shehili's questions, her throat was sore. She'd never talked so much in her entire life.

Shehili offered her another zesty lemon drink, and Kimberly gratefully finished off the bottle before Bristlecone arrived to put an end to the bliss of being out in the sunshine among nature, eating tasty treats, and enjoying good company. If she continued to accept these delightful treats, by the time of her trial, she would have added an extra person to her skeleton, an extra Kimberly Lemon.

Alexandra and Guinevere stood in the reception area of Duke Tower, waiting patiently for the woman to finish answering the insistent machine, a machine nobody had ever seen two years ago, which now seemed to be on every desk, in every business, and kept interrupting their conversation every thirty seconds. Only someone with a bad case of Attention Deficit Disorder could stand to work here for even a day, Alexandra thought while she surreptitiously glanced around the lobby at the people exiting the elevators and still others entering the reception room. If anyone recognizes her from Delphadore, she'll deny knowing them. Yes. She'll pretend to be deaf, no, better to pretend to be blind. Holy Chocolate she could kick herself for agreeing to Guinevere's crazy scheme.

How could Guinevere possibly believe they had any influence over the Governor? He had made himself Governor-for-life and no one in Blueglennen objected. Realistically, he was a dictator, not a duly elected official. They might as well go home. Unless Guinevere planned something completely bonkers. Alexandra wouldn't put it passed the fiery pint-sized woman. She made up in courage what she lacked in inches.

Before the next phone interruption, Guinevere managed to tell the receptionist they were here to seek audience with the Governor. The comment brought an amused smile to the attractive woman's bright silver painted lips. Evidently, the receptionist had more brains than her present duty suggested. Alexandra considered an alternative - sending the Governor a strongly worded letter with her full legal name and seal.

Just as the receptionist put down the receiver, a man walked out of a private elevator reserved for the penthouse occupants exclusively. He paused at the sight of the two women. Dressed in a gray pin-striped suit with his long blonde hair tied back in a queue and wearing – boots, boots, oh-my-sainted-legs, how dare he, the monster, the inhumane monster, boots obviously made from the skin of a reptile, Guinevere realized. How tasteless.

As he crossed the floor, he took a second look at Alexandra and the taciturn expression was replaced with one of joy. "Why Alex! How good to see you darling. It's been ages."

"Ah yeah. Um," Alexandra began, and then she did an odd jerky sort of dance, shuffling sideways toward the glass doors leading out into the plaza. For a second or two Alexandra hovered by the door, hesitated, then as if coming to a decision straightened her shoulders and turned her tall, slim, elegant person around to face the stranger.

Her expression struck Guinevere as comical. Guinevere laughed. Alexandra's expressions fluctuated between embarrassment and annoyance, then resignation to gloom. Just when Alexandra seemed to have run out of emotional cartwheels, she rallied and expressed her final emotion – haughty distain. Alas, this new Alexandra didn't last long either, Guinevere observed. Haughty distain just wasn't her style.

Alexandra's quiet sweetness was missed by at least one person in the lobby. Her haughtiness looked foreign, weird, and even seemed to add years to her face. Guinevere preferred quiet sweet Alexandra. And by the by, who was this guy in the reptile boots, generating so much terror? Guinevere debated whether to punch the guy for upsetting her friend. She knew just the spot for generating the maximum pain.

Alexandra opened her mouth to speak, couldn't think of anything to say and wheeled about to face the door once again. She began hurrying toward the doors and Guinevere watched in growing suspicion as the man followed Alexandra out. They stood in the courtyard among the statues, their expensive shoes elegant against the brick paving stones, eyes latched onto each other's faces, talking earnestly, waving their arms, and having a hell of a row.

Guinevere wanted nothing to do with a domestic squabble. She felt betrayed. The idea that Alexandra knew someone who wore a dead animal on his body appalled her more than her cowardly retreat. She turned to face the receptionist once again and this time the woman removed her earpiece. "I demand to speak to the Governor. It's a matter of life and death."

"You must go through the Governor's secretary Dela. I'll see if Delo Mooney is in."

"I don't want to speak to Delo Mooney. I want to talk to the Governor."

"The Governor is a very busy man."

"Not too busy to throw an innocent woman into the bowels of the earth to rot."

"What?"

"You know what I mean."

Before Guinevere could say another word two of the Governor's knights appeared from behind a door and began circling the lobby then spotted her. With eyes locked on her face, they moved in for the kill. They reminded her unpleasantly of two pit bulls she had seen once who did the same thing when cornering their prey, the prey having been Guinevere's adorable miniature puppies. But she'd taken care of those two adolescent males. Once she paid off their owner and took them home, she had them back to their loveable selves again.

"That won't be necessary," a man said from behind Guinevere. "I'll take the ladies up to the Governor personally."

Guinevere turned to see who was behind her and realized the man wearing the dead animal skins had spoken. He was on the move striding past them in the direction of the elevator. Alexandra turned and motioned for Guinevere to follow. Guinevere glanced at the receptionist and the knights who all seemed to know the man. She gave the strongest knight a disappointed smile. Knight Graceland's gentle expression brightened. His eyes told her he would have accepted her challenge happily.

Good another sparring partner, she thought as she sprinted toward the elevator before the doors closed. Guinevere rode up to the penthouse with Alexandra and Snake-Skin Boots without saying a word. She wanted to ask her friend a million questions; yet, she was determined to keep her mouth shut, knowing her best chance of getting a reliable answer would be when she and Alexandra were alone. Yes, when she could speak without censoring herself, she would wrestle the truth out of Alexandra with one of her biting comments or sneering looks or incessant whining. One of those strategies had to work.

The elevator door opened onto a foyer, elegantly simple, with New Dala tiled flooring and a single table holding a crystal bowl full of letters and invitations. Guinevere feared the foyer would be the only part of the Governor's private apartments they would ever see. A connecting door opened, and a man stepped out dressed in a black suit. He wore a silver stickpin in his lapel.

Guinevere recognized the stickpin's symbolism, a hawk swooping down with talons extended preparing to snatch its prey. Everybody in Blueglennen knew Saurus loved symbolism. The fact he erroneously believes he is the mighty hawk made her laugh.

Alexandra frowned at Guinevere as her new-found friend spoke to stickpin, "Tell the Governor," he paused glancing at Alexandra with a hesitant look. "Tell him, I vouch for this woman and strongly recommend he listen to what she has to say. They are here to speak on Kimberly Lemon's behalf."

The Governor's servant glanced at the three of them with an equal measure of disinterest, turned on his polished heels and marched back through the inner sanctum. Several minutes passed before the doors burst open and instead of getting the brushoff, Guinevere and Alexandra were privileged to receive Governor Saurus in person.

Guinevere was surprised at the sight of him. She'd only ever seen him from afar or surrounded by knights. His head barely reached Alexandra's breasts. Alexandra was tall for a female yet there was something weird about him. Was this guy a body double? In his photos and on television he looked so much taller. And he had a puffy face and bags under his eyes. It was all television magic and lots of makeup. The once handsome face looked haggard with a perpetual bemusement as if he were surprised, he was still Governor, but honestly just wanted to play Parcheesi rather than manage the largest province in the country of Curl.

The suspicion Governor Saurus had no real power trickled up from the fatalistic side of herself she tried to quash. Maybe, the real power behind the Governorship was his advisor, Kick Cheeky? Then she looked down at the floor, doing her best to tamp down on the embers of anger. She noticed, for the first time, that the man was wearing bedroom slippers, fancy silk bedroom slippers. Maybe, he wore lifts to make him look taller? Or maybe he was a body double?

"So Christian, you recommend I speak to these, ah, advocates for the accused?" Governor Saurus asked Alexandra's particular friend who still had not been properly introduced to Guinevere. Guinevere thought such lack of etiquette terribly rude and so unlike Alexandra.

"Yes, Governor. They wish to convey their concerns as citizens of Blueglennen. I know you are a busy man sir but hope you can allay their fears about Dela Lemon's welfare."

The Governor eyed the women the way a cow eyes a butcher. Alexandra's new best friend seemed to have said something which may have upset the Governor. Nothing short of a bullet to the head could ever upset the Governor. No matter how many men and women fought in foreign wars, some dying, some coming back crippled in mind and body, wars the Governor and his cronies continued to conjure up to please their rich backers, the Governor remained indifferent.

No matter how many people were living in poverty at home or homeless, dead or injured, the Governor remained indifferent. All was well in Saurusville where he was ten-feet tall and a mighty warrior and everyone loved him. To see him now, cold and calculating, glancing at the three of them wondering how he could smooch his way out of this predicament made Guinevere furious and even more determined to speak her mind.

"Why are you holding Kimberly Lemon a mile underground in the old torture chambers? Has the clock turned? Are we again living in the dark ages?" Guinevere demanded to know.

"I know of no torture chambers. What is she talking about?" Governor Saurus asked his associate.

"This is the first I've heard of it, sir," the man said bowing his blonde head respectfully still topping the Governor by nearly six inches. The sight made Alexandra want to giggle. And then she saw the Governor's stony face and no longer wanted to laugh. This man was not amusing. He was dangerous. He lacked humor, wisdom, and intellectual curiosity. Such men and women were capable of ruining so many lives because they'd never experienced adversity and had very little empathy. Most of them were spoiled rich idiots. And then she grew nervous worried the stupid Governor might reveal her real identity to her friend.

The Governor was only an inch taller than Guinevere. Oddly, Guinevere seemed to provoke the strongest responses from him. He glared at her, recognizing her as an agitator and animal right's activist, "I will look into this situation. I must go. I have pressing business to attend."

"Wait. We're not finished. I want to talk to you about Kimberly's innocence," Guinevere shouted out. "You can't ignore us forever Saurus."

"Please, Governor Saurus," Alexandra spoke forcing herself to shout louder than Guinevere which she realized too late was impossible. "Your reputation and honor are at stake."

The Governor refused to turn around and moved as fast as his short legs could carry him back to his private apartments. The man called Christian turned to Alexandra and cupped her hands between his own, "I'm sure your friend will be well taken care of. The Governor isn't a monster. He needs us. He may be Governor for life, but he needs our troops and our supplies and most importantly our weapons. Have no fear Alex."

Alexandra had plenty she would like to have said to him;

unfortunately, Guinevere stood only a few feet away and she would rather keep her family history and background private for a little longer. Christian's delight at annoying people had been the overarching reason for his readiness to take time out of his usual schedule and escort them to the Governor's private sanctuary. Christian loved to show off what a fool the Governor truly is; yet, Christian was walking on dangerous ground.

Governor Saurus may be a simpleton, but the people behind him, his rich backers and influential advisors are the most ruthless men and women in the whole country of Curl. As one of the richest men in the country, Christian thought he was immune from any retaliation by Saurus' backers. She had her doubts. With revulsion running through her arm at his touch, she forced herself to remain unmoved for as long as the trip down to the lobby took them. The elevator seemed to take its sweet time getting her into the sunshine and clean open air.

Her revulsion must have finally penetrated Christian's thick hide. He didn't bother to mask his fury and abruptly swung around and re-entered the tower. Relieved to see the back of him, Alexandra looked out at the plaza and all the clueless people sightseeing and stuffing their faces.

What now? What about her friend? What could they possibly do to fix this mess? If only Kimberly had money enough to pay off the authorities or powerful friends to protect her. She wished she could help. Until she reached twenty-five, she had only the allowance her parents permitted to pay for her tuition and expenses.

Crystova Moth stared at the wall then back to her map. She wore gloves to prevent staining the parchment with the oils from her fingertips. Unrolling the parchment had been a chore. It had taken her several months to unroll the delicate fabric. Each inch of open parchment had been sprayed thoroughly with a clear liquid softener to prevent cracking and tearing. She wanted to avoid at all cost having to reconstruct thousands of tiny pieces of dried parchment. Such an undertaking had consumed most of her free time.

Now, time was short, very short. The map held between two pieces of glass lay on top of her computer tablet. She peeked over her shoulder, over the book shelf toward the big bay window where a knight stood at attention in front of the Bookworm Emporium. Detective Hawk had granted her permission to explore the bookshop only after his knights had thoroughly inspected the contents of the shop and private quarters.

The knight on duty was a solidly built young man with wide-spaced black eyes and a sweet expression. He was around the same age as Crystova and yet looked older with thinning salt-and-pepper curly hair. Unlike Crystova, as a knight he spent a lot of time standing at attention or securing the ramparts of the castle. Indeed, he and his friend Knight Lively were the only knights who were not paid mercenaries.

When she first arrived during a duty shift, as if they were strangers, he introduced himself to Crystova as Juleus Graceland. Following his lead, Crystova shook his hand and introduced herself. D.I. Hawk watched them with an intensity they both found uncomfortable. Hawk made her nervous on so many levels. Intelligent ruthless males always made her nervous. She had done nothing wrong but felt guilty anyway. After Hawk walked swiftly away and disappeared around the corner heading down Wolfern Promenade, she and Juleus exchanged silly grins.

"Thanks, Crys," Juleus said. "You read my mind."

"I've known you since kinter school, Juleus. So, you don't want your boss knowing about our friendship?"

"I think he trusts me enough not to let you walk away with the silver. But the less the rakes know the better."

"I agree," she said giving him a friendly elbow in the side. "The rakes can be pains sometimes. Us proletariats need to stick together."

"You've been in school too long, Crys. We're called fingerlings, fingers for short since we do all the work."

"Oh yeah. That's the new talk."

"What's the new talk?" someone asked behind Crystova. She spun around and stepped back in order to look up at the man towering over her. Physically he resembled a menacing troll with broad shoulders and thick arms. Then she looked in his eyes and relaxed. He had a mischievous twinkle in his eye suggesting a humorous and intelligent mind hidden by a shock of thick black hair cut unusually short for a knight.

Undeterred by his fellow knight's towering presence, Juleus introduced the man to Crystova, "Hey Crys. This is my buddy Madas Lively. I call him Mad Ass because he looks scary but he's not. He and I joined the University of Justice the same year."

"You mean we joined the UJ and survived. That makes us heroes by default."

Juleus grinned, his smile transforming his face making him look years younger, "You bet Fingerling Lively, we survived the grueling classes and got lucky they didn't throw us in the brig."

Madas shrugged his big shoulders and searched the streets, "A finger back at you, bro." The whole time the two knights teased each other, they never stopped working, their eyes constantly on the move watching people walking by and keeping a close eye on the mercenaries patrolling the rampart. It was a testimony to their training and level of experience.

"Well, knights, I feel safe knowing you're out here keeping an eye on things. Hawk's allowed me a week to do my research. So. It's been a pleasure meeting you Knight Lively. See you around Jule."

"I'll be here until the glowworms turn blue," Knight Graceland assured her.

Her first sight of the bookstore several days ago had been a shock. Every book had been removed from the shelves and the tables and after being shaken roughly thrown on the floor like so much garbage. The dust stirred up by the Governor's henchmen had yet to settle. There were little bits of paper sprinkling the floor where old books yellow and cracked with age had been badly mistreated. The Governor's henchmen had no respect for the past or for people's property. Most of the Governor's henchmen were mercenaries from other provinces or other countries. Saurus didn't trust his own people.

With Caleb and Valcinda's assistance, they and Crystova managed to put the store back to its former condition, albeit with an added housekeeping touch – polished bookshelves, dust free stock, and a swept floor. Even Adam Honeysweet pitched in by cataloguing the inventory as a way of assuring Kimberly none of her stock had been stolen by the mercenaries.

Hawk had been a curious observer of their activities on the first day of the cleanup, sitting with his back ramrod straight on the cushioned seat near the counter, his hands resting on his knees, his lips curled in an amused smile as he watched them work. "Do you really think Saurus' men would be interested in stealing this junk," he said with a wave of his arm at the paraphernalia on the floor, at the books, pamphlets, magazines, flyers, posters, maps, and rolled parchments in different stages of decrepitude.

Professor Adam Honeysweet who happened to be sitting on the floor with his back supported by the heavy leg of an old table, adjusted the clipboard on his knee and paused before jotting down the title, the publication date, and the condition of a book resting on his lap. Once Honeysweet was finished with his current task, he set the book in the designated spot marked "to be shelved." Valcinda was busy spraying her special wood polisher on the shelves, shelves which her brother had been permitted to repair and stain several days ago. Each section of free-standing shelves stood only as high as Valcinda's nose. It was rather funny to stand by the wall and see only Valcinda's eyes as she carefully shelved yet another book.

The two women were the only people left in the shop. Caleb had a job to finish in the valley and Hawk had grown bored watching them work. He'd left one of his own knights on duty to make sure no one took anything out of the shop. It was lucky he assigned one of his own knights because on that day Kimberly's obnoxious aunt attempted to gain entrance. The tossing of her hair and fluttering of her eyes did her no good. Crystova supposed she could have thrown Victoria out on her own; yet, she had felt an overwhelming urgency to get started on her excavation. She had so little time before Hawk shut her project down.

She still had nearly ten-feet of wall to examine, to tap with her little hammer, to test with her special gold metal detector, to listen with her stethoscope. Earlier she had cut the wall into sections by applying blue tape and when she finished one square, she stuck a yellow posted note in the center of the square making careful note of the tool she'd used to test for clues. She had chosen to use the metal detector first because she had more faith in it than in her little hammer or her stethoscope. Rumor suggested the illuminated manuscripts of the early church scribes had been adorned with precious stones.

The metal detector had been invented by a prospector nearly a hundred years previous, and over the years had been refined. Today the antenna or transmit coil could detect minerals no bigger than the freckle on her left hand. The detector she held in her hand was no bigger than a ball point pen. She held the device between her fingers admiring its shape and colors. She had chosen the device because it was small enough to carry in her purse and because the designer had been a true artist. He had chosen to coat the handle in cobalt blue with tiny, tiny white enamel swirls. The artist had even coated the transmit coils in gold filigree.

Anyone watching her might assume she held a butterfly on the end of a stick. The delicate mesh of wires did seem to resemble butterfly wings. When she moved the electronic detector slowly back and forth between the lines of blue tape on the wall, the current produced an electromagnetic field and any object encountered revealed its image on her tablet. Her detector's transmitter field had picked up an image of the remains of a mummified mouse frozen in time and a mason's forgotten chisel. Her hope was to finally see an image of an ancient illuminated manuscript or two hidden in the walls by the old Delphi priests.

After all, gold is an excellent conductor and should give off a large phase shift and since illuminated manuscripts were heavily laden with gold, the detector would have no trouble finding the ancient manuscripts hidden in the walls. She was ninety percent convinced there had to be ancient manuscripts hidden somewhere in the old priest cells. Well, maybe fifty percent sure.

One had to be here, in this very wall which was a wall shared by the bookshop and the cathedral. Nearly a thousand years ago, this wall had been on the highest mound overlooking Greenburg Valley, one of four walls of an ancient chapel. This wall might have been part of a private meditation chamber used by the Elders of Curl. She was convinced, the Elders created a written language combining nearly one hundred tribal languages into the language of Curl.

A person living today though would have a difficult time communicating with the ancients of that day for the Curleconese language had evolved over the centuries. And she supposed once she found the manuscript, she'd be forced to share her discovery with other universities, notably Dr. Astound since he was one of the leading experts in several ancient languages of Curl. As a younger academician in the world of ancient languages, she hoped one day to unlock the secrets of the Elders of Curl.

A groan escaped her when her butterfly detector passed over the last inch of the last square and found nothing. With nervous fingers she picked at her hair searching for the pencil she had stuffed in the knot on the top of her head. Once she had the pencil between her fingers, she scribbled the acronym for detector in the center of the square. Her lower back ached from standing so close to the wall for so many hours. What time was it anyway? She stuffed her pencil back in her hair, turned off her butterfly detector, and stretched her body to get the kinks out of her back and shoulders.

When she felt someone's eyes on her she turned in time to see Valcinda standing behind one of the shelves watching her. Only her head and lovely large black eyes were visible. Crystova wagged her fingers and smiled, "I left my watch at home. Do you know the time?"

Valcinda glanced around the room with a puzzled expression, "The lizard clock is gone."

"Lizard clock?"

"You know, the wooden one that used to stand in the corner there," she said pointing in the corner opposite the shop door. "It was Kimberly's great, great, somebody's clock handed down through generations of Lemons. She had to wind it every week. The tongue of the lizard rocked back and forth. You must remember it."

While Valcinda had been talking, Crystova carefully tucked her butterfly detector into its box using the tiny key she kept on her bracelet to lock it safely inside. Then she proceeded to stuff the box into her bulging leather bag. Even though she intended to walk the few steps toward the only free space in the room, free from book shelves and tables and coat racks that is, she felt compelled to check whether the clock was indeed missing. Before walking away from the brick wall, she gathered up her belongings and slung her bag over her shoulder.

She nearly stumbled at the unexpected weight. Alarmed she stopped afraid the contents inside her bag might damage the detector. Protectively, she held the bag close to her hip. Not only was the butterfly detector her most expensive possession, she also carried her grade book and the unread student essays yet to be assigned grades. She always kept her bag with her fearful a snoopy housekeeper might try to sneak a peek inside. She would die rather than let her students down by losing one of their final test essays or exposing their grade point average to the world.

The two women stood in the corner staring at the empty space where the lizard clock should have been and then turned slowly one hundred and eighty degrees. "I'll check Kimberly's private rooms maybe the clock is there," Valcinda offered and without waiting for Crystova's permission disappeared behind the velvet curtains.

Crystova walked around the shop slowly peering down at the floor and into corners. Perhaps the clock was underneath a few piles still left to shelve? She even went so far as to lift the lid of the window seat where Kimberly sometimes stored games. She stared in disbelief at three empty compartments. There used to be boxes in the storage spaces, boxes of games and cards and even a few sponge balls and jacks for the younger children to use while they waited for their parents. Crystova heard Valcinda return.

Few people ever heard Valcinda approach. She was light on her feet and seemed to walk on air. She had beautiful shiny black hair and fabulous skin and reminded Crystova of people she had met on her one anthropological trip through New Dala. Perhaps some of Valcinda's ancestors had been New Dala immigrants. When Valcinda walked into the center of the shop, she said nothing just shook her head sadly. She seemed convinced one of the Governor's goons had stolen the big, scarred, ugly old clock.

Crystova found the idea hard to believe. It was so ugly, why would anyone want to steal it? And it was so big. How had the robbers managed to carry the ugly old thing out the front door without anyone noticing? The bottom chamber could have hidden a small child inside and the whole thing smelled of mildewed wood. Why Kimberly kept such a bad example of folk art was a mystery for in all other things she had a discerning eye for quality.

"So where is it?" Crystova asked to no one in particular. "And who took the games?"

"The games?"

"Kimberly keeps, kept games in the storage under the window seat."

As if Valcinda did not believe her, she walked over to the window seat and opened the lid. When Valcinda simply stood staring out the window at the knight on duty and said nothing, Crystova decided to take charge. She flung open the shop door and stuck her head outside and spoke to Juleus, "Has anyone been here before us?"

Knight Graceland turned in surprise, "No. Not since we showed up." He pointed up at the rampart where Knight Lively paced the walk his eye on Merchants' Row. Juleus touched his earpiece and said, "Can you come down? I need to check inside." Lively nodded once and started toward the gatehouse. Graceland didn't bother to wait for his friend and stepped inside the shop looking around the room with concern, "Why do you ask?"

Valcinda spoke up, "The lizard clock's missing and Crystova says the games that used to be inside the window seat are gone."

The tension in the knight's body disappeared. He pulled out a folded piece of paper from the inside pocket of his black leather jacket. Crystova noticed he held a paper with an official seal and a scrawled signature at the bottom. The contents included a list of items. "Yes, D.I. Hawk confiscated the clock and the contents of the window seat. They are being tested for fingerprints and DNA."

"Why ever for? I should think there's plenty of DNA all over this room, probably better DNA in Kimberly's private quarters," Valcinda said, her face registering her disgust with intrusive rakes.

Crystova snorted, "Do you really think Kimberly hid Star's body in the clock or the window seat? How ridiculous."

Juleus Graceland stuffed the paper back in his vest pocket and with a tiny shrug left the shop to resume his post. The women exchanged looks. Valcinda was the first to move – with a sad frown and a shake of her head she returned to shelving Kimberly's inventory. Crystova supposed by returning Kimberly's shop to its former cleanliness and order Valcinda would feel as if she were helping Kimberly in some small way. Perhaps Hawk and his goons had done Kimberly a favor by removing the lizard clock since the smell of dust and mildew were gone.

Today, the shop smelled faintly of freshly stained and

polished shelves with an underlining sweet incense. The incense came from a stick burning in a tiny urn and next to the tiny urn was a duplicate urn set on the corner of the counter near the cash register. The urn looked brand new made of freshly glazed ceramic about as large as a two-year old child. Inside the larger urn someone had arranged dried grasses and flowers. Crystova knew for a fact the set of ceramic urns had not been on the counter when she entered earlier in the day.

"Who brought the urns?" Crystova called out to Valcinda.

Valcinda popped up from behind a shelf and glanced her way, "It's a gift from a well-wisher. I found the box near the door this morning. Juleus checked the contents and read the note."

"Which well-wisher?"

"The notes in the cash register drawer. Go ahead and read it."

Crystova dropped her heavy bag on the window seat and walked around the counter, "How do I open the cash register?"

Valcinda peered at her from around the corner of the shelf in surprise, "You've never used a cash register before?"

"No."

Instead of instructing Crystova in the proper use of a cash register, Valcinda dropped the few books in her hand on the freshly swept and waxed floor and walked over to the cash register. She punched a few keys so fast Crystova had no time to distinguish the sequence. A drawer flew open and inside the individual compartments she found a card, an elegant card written in an elegant script – *I believe in you. Don't give up. Our thoughts are with you.* The gift giver had deliberately left his name off the card but Crystova recognized the handwriting.

Dr. Adam Honeysweet's elegant penmanship was all too familiar. She kept her knowledge to herself. Our thoughts? Hum. Chicken. He could just as easily have declared himself. Instead, he chose to leave the impression the gift came from all of Kimberly's friends.

"Were you planning to take the urn to her?" Crystova asked.

"I called Dela Swana and she recommends keeping the urn here for safekeeping. She said she'd tell Kimberly about the gift. She assured me Kimberly will be released any day now. Did you know Guinevere and Alexandra went to see the Governor?" The last announcement was flavored with wry disbelief. Crystova had entertained the idea days ago and dismissed the plan as hopelessly optimistic. Since Saurus didn't read, the sight of an academic would only make him nervous.

"No," Crystova said, realizing belatedly that Valcinda was still waiting for her response to the news. "Were they successful?"

"Yes. Amazing isn't it? They went to speak with him just this morning. According to Guinevere, the clerk in the lobby was rude and unhelpful. Then a man came in who seemed to know Alexandra and he got them up to the penthouse. They ended up in the lobby just outside his private apartments. He spoke to them for a few minutes, and it seemed as if he was really considering whether to release Kimberly. So, perhaps we might hear some good news soon."

"If Guinevere and Alexandra were at the Towers just this morning, when did you speak to Guinevere?"

"We had lunch at the plaza."

"Lunch? Is it lunch time already?"

"Well, you were so absorbed in your work, I didn't want to bother you."

"How long have you been back?"

"About two hours."

"So, I'm too late for lunch?"

"It was great because we had our choice of tables at the Cher Amie."

Crystova grabbed her bag and started for the door, "I'll go home and whip up something for myself and be back. Will you be here?"

"Oh yes. I'm sure Kimberly will be released today. I just know it. I want everything clean and ready for her return."

"You seem awfully sure of yourself," Crystova said before opening the door. When Valcinda returned to shelving, she called out. "I'll bring back a treat. Any preferences?"

Valcinda mumbled something Crystova had trouble understanding. Feeling peckish she decided to buy an assortment of goodies and left. By the time she returned to the Bookworm, it was nearly dusk. The sun had dropped behind the hills and Merchant's Row had become a gloomy narrow passageway. She balanced her heavy bag on her shoulder and under her other arm held a basket full of treats. She'd bought a loaf of freshly baked bread with plans to spend the rest of the evening working on the wall.

When she got close to the bookstore, she realized Juleus was no longer posted at the entrance and Mad Ass was nowhere in sight. In fact, there was no one guarding the bookstore at all and the door was propped open with light spilling out onto the cobblestones. Concerned, Crystova hurried forward nearly dropping her basket. It wasn't until she entered the shop, she realized Kimberly had been set free. The room was choked with people, most of them the merchants who had come to celebrate Kimberly's release.

She discovered Kimberly had been released on bond. She knew without asking because as she entered, she heard Harry Zany say, "You think I was behind your bail? Are you crazy? These days, I can't rub two tins together much less five thousand seastars."

"It was your idea Zany," Queenie shouted out somewhere close to the counter where Kimberly sat on a high stool overlooking the crowd. She seemed dazed by all the fuss. It looked as if all of Merchants' Row was in the bookshop. Well, other than Paleone, her crony Luella and the Bishops. Even the stranger living above the newspaper, Joanie something, was in the shop busily passing out wine samples. The samples must have come from Don Tumble's shop. What a guy, never wasting an opportunity to sell his product to prospective customers.

Arthur and Eleanor Darknight were sitting on the window seat watching the crowd with bright curious eyes. The Darknights were Frank's grandparents and owners of the only small grocery still in existence in Blueglennen. The couple were so old their wrinkles had wrinkles and their spines resembled hooks. They must be close to ninety by now. Both were barely four-feet tall with a few wisps of hair covering their pink heads. They looked like clams with spindly legs when they walked arm and arm, their progress painfully slow over the treacherous cobblestones.

Old Man Darknight's face reminded her of a turtle with his snub nose and tiny eyes peeping out of a leathery wrinkled face. She noticed Frank talking to a couple of young attractive women. Then she remembered them. They were Queenie's waitresses: Alexandra S. Montegue and something, something Lordbuster. It started with an E. Eve? Ellen? Estelle? No. No. No.

Crystova felt a conflicting rush of emotions, just then, as she pressed her way through the crowd to hand her basket to Guinevere. She told Guinevere, "There's a cake inside and some cookies if anyone is hungry." Yes, she felt relieved Kimberly had finally been released from prison and equally frustrated she couldn't finish her project tonight.

What really burned her butt was seeing Harry Zany and Don Tumble leaning against her wall sipping wine and contemplating the blue tape. The blue tape still crisscrossed the entire brick facade. She hurried over to them worried they might try to peel off the tape in the erroneous assumption the Governor's goons had been the culprits.

"Please, don't touch the wall Harry," she told him noticing Honeysweet on the other side of Don Tumble.

Honeysweet leaned forward and waved his plastic cup filled with red wine in her general direction, "Don't worry Crystova. We haven't touched anything. I've been explaining the methods of research necessary when excavating a site such as this one."

"Seems like a lot of work to me," Harry commented drolly. "When you could just as easily remove all the brick and see if there's anything behind it."

"I'm sure Kimberly wouldn't take kindly to us demolishing her wall."

Harry looked down at her from his great height. With his brown eyes shimmering with a sadness he could not shake, he patted the top of her head gently then turned to admire her excavation. He contemplated the blue tape seriously and said, "If you do find something of value, does Kimberly benefit or does all the glory go to Wolfern Province and Governor Saurus?"

Before Crystova could open her mouth to answer, Honeysweet answered his question, "The shop belongs to Kimberly and since the shop has been in her family for generations, nearly five hundred years I'm guessing, she has nothing to worry about. Any other claimants to an archeological find of this magnitude are long since dead.

No doubt the state would have precedence over whatever is discovered, dependent on the artifact's value, yet, the university already has a permit for this excavation. And if she discovers something of academic significance, I'm sure Kimberly will donate the find to the university."

"You still haven't answered my question," Harold said.

Honeysweet looked puzzled which gave Crystova the opportunity to elaborate, "Actually, everyone will benefit. If I find something of value, the artifact will help us understand our history and ancient culture and end up generating interest all over the world. Tourists will come. Scholars will come. And maybe someday, we'll understand our ancient language and its origins."

"But do the contents inside these walls belong to her?" Don asked staring blearily at the wall in front of his nose. It was obvious he'd started celebrating long before Kimberly was released from prison.

"I don't understand," Crystova said a little too crisply and tried to amend her tone.

He gestured toward the wall splashing a bit of wine over the top of his cup. The drops of wine landed on his shoe instead of the wall. "Well, Bottom's Castle Laundry shares this wall doesn't it?"

Honeysweet leaned forward to stare at Crystova with real concern. She ignored him, "No. It doesn't. Beatrice Bottom's Castle Laundry is set forward at least a seahorse length closer to the street and its wall is actually the cathedral's outer wall.

I researched the archives of the university and the national library in Delphadore and discovered the Bookworm is made up of older stone quarried by our ancient ancestors from the caves near Old Town. This shop is set way back and the stones are from the ancient church which used to stand on the mound overlooking Greenburg Valley.

During the northern invasions, the priests decided to dismantle the Delphi chapel and bring the stones inside the castle fearing their place of worship would be destroyed. They tried to reconstruct the chapel just the way it had been on the mound. All the other shops on Merchants' Row are made from blocks of granite, timber, plaster and brick. They were built to house the priests as private sleeping quarters.

This shop is much larger than the other shops on Merchants' Row, and behind the brick façade of this wall are huge slabs of marble, the same marble quarried at the Blue Mines outside Old Town. On the other side of this brick façade, I've discovered a layer of plaster, a layer of timber frames and finally thick blocks of marble stone."

"What about the alley side? Is that part of the old chapel?" Kimberly asked barely above a whisper. She stood at the farthest end of the aisle close to the back wall. She must have maneuvered her way unnoticed through the people in order to get close and hear Crystova's lecture. Crystova couldn't tell from her expression how she felt about this new knowledge.

The truth dawned on Crystova why Kimberly looked so upset and she rushed to assure her, "This wall extends beyond your private quarters to the end of the alley. The brick facade where your cupboards were built is a new addition and the wall Caleb cut through to make your window is even more recent.

The original chapel wall is along here and includes some of the secret passageway between the Church of the Holy Centipede and Duke Tower. It sounds crazy, I know, but if you look at the oldest blueprints of the bailey, you can see the builders were making do with past mistakes. Nothing is plum. There are no straight lines and sharp corners anywhere inside the castle walls."

Kimberly stood near Honeysweet who made room for her, "We were just discussing Crystova's excavation. We're curious about what she might find behind this wall."

"She seems awfully sure she'll find something," Zany said glancing down at Kimberly with real affection. "For your sake, I hope she doesn't find anything. You don't need any more publicity."

Kimberly glanced up at him and grinned, "Don't worry Zany. The publicity might be a help. Maybe it will overshadow my trial."

Zany padded her shoulder clumsily and made an excuse to move on. Crowds made the street-wise-philosopher nervous. Kimberly looked everywhere but at Don Tumble. Tumble made an excuse to follow Zany toward the front door. Crystova glanced over her shoulder and with relief realized the party was winding down. They would raise the drawbridge soon and some people who lived in Greenburg Valley were afraid of ending up in the bailey for the night. Just moments ago, the room had been packed with Merchants' Row shopkeepers, quite a testimony to their assumption she was innocent.

Beatrice Bottom and Queenie Oppfield were the last to leave. Even Harry Hanson from the Shellfargon Seed had been among the group welcoming Kimberly home. She suspected Harry had ulterior motives. It would be no surprise to anyone when they read about this evening's event in the morning paper. The Anders, both father and son had brought pastries and left a few behind for Kimberly. At five-thirty, she and Kimberly heard the blowing of the horn warning residents they had twenty minutes to reach the drawbridge. They looked around and discovered they were the only ones left. Kimberly stood by the shop door as if waiting to escort Crystova out.

Crystova went with her gut and asked, "May I stay and finish. I'll be so quiet you won't even know I'm here."

For a moment, Crystova thought Kimberly might refuse, "Well, I had planned to make myself a cup of tea and go straight to bed. I haven't been sleeping well."

"Of course. I understand. It's just I have this feeling. It's telling me to press on."

Kimberly shut the door and locked the bolt and pulled down the drape then turned to face her friend, "Well, you're welcome to sleep on the window seat. I'm going to set the alarm, so you'll be locked in. I can make up the couch for you?"

"Thank you, Kimberly. Thank you so much. Don't worry about me."

Kimberly waved her off with a tired smile and disappeared behind the velvet curtain. Crystova hurried toward the wall and dumped her heavy bag on the floor near her feet. With shaking fingers, she rummaged through the bag for her tools. Since Honeysweet opened his big mouth and told the world what she was doing, there was very little time left. Once news got out about the excavation, every history buff and amateur collector would be rushing to Merchants' Row to see what glory they could steal for themselves. She would have to work all night.

Kimberly woke to a streak of light in her eye and her entire body shook in fear thinking she was back in the dungeon and Bristlecone was coming toward her cell with his light-stick. But the light blinding her was normal sunshine peeping through her curtains from her lovely alley window. A window free of shame. She threw off her covers and slipped her bare feet into a pair of warm slippers. Her first thought was to open the curtains and let in more light. She pulled the curtains apart and saw the beautiful flowers growing outside her window sill. Someone had mounted a window box on the sill and filled the box with rich dark earth and beautiful pink, purple, and gray flowers. She did her best to push back the tears – and failed.

After putting the kettle on to boil, she threw on a robe and shuffled down the passageway toward the shop. The newsboy always left the morning paper on the stoop outside her door. But before she got to the door, she realized she was not alone. Her heart nearly stopped before she remembered Crystova Moth had asked to stay. She found Crystova behind the bookshelf sitting on the floor surveying a hole. The hole wasn't very big. There were only about twelve bricks piled neatly against the wall and it looked as if Crystova had swept the plaster away.

Her friend had wiped the cobwebs and dirt off a satchel made of animal skin. She'd used a cloth rag dipped in some sort of special cleaner. When Kimberly appeared around the book shelf, Crystova was in the process of slipping on a pair of gloves. She looked up in time to see Kimberly in her robe shuffling down the aisle toward her. Her hazel eyes were huge, her pale skin even paler from a long night, a long, desperate night searching for the elusive artifact.

Kimberly ignored the dust on the floor and sat down beside her friend. She said nothing as Crystova carefully removed the artifact from the satchel. The first thing that caught Kimberly's eye was the gleam of gold. She held her breath waiting for Crystova to open the satchel, unable to decide whether she was excited or scared.

When Crystova lay the book tenderly down on the satchel like one might lay a newborn on the belly of his mother, they both leaned forward to admire the artwork. The edges were gilded with gold filigree. It wasn't just gold. There were other gemstones inlaid on the surface of the manuscript and until Crystova said "jade," Kimberly assumed the color came from the juice of a plant. Then she realized the colors had been created by using precious and semi-precious stones ground to a pigment.

The spell was broken when someone knocked on the door then urgently pressed the buzzer. Kimberly saw the shadowy outline of a man standing on the other side of the door. It was too early for customers, friends, or neighbors. He must be the law. She turned to look into Crystova's eyes. Kimberly didn't have to say a word. Crystova simply nodded and set to work. Kimberly pulled back the shade and peeked out. D.I. Hawk acknowledge her with a curt nod. He entered the shop without invitation and strode about the room surveying the tidy interior with some surprise, "You've been busy."

"It wasn't me. My friends did all the work."

He turned to face her and said, "I've come to tell you I've appointed Bristlecone as your protector until after the trial."

"I thought I was out on bail," she asked pressing her hand to her stomach to stop the mice from chewing their way through her body.

"Yes. Of course. This is just a precaution. Bristlecone will guard you every moment of every day. Do you understand? Oh, and I'll have someone posted outside in the evening."

"You seem to be under a misapprehension. I'm the suspect."

"Yes. Well. I have a few new leads and want to be sure I have the right person."

The scraping of a shoe spun D.I. Hawk around, "Who's there?" He strode to the wall and down the aisle. Within seconds Kimberly saw Crystova's head pop up from approximately the same area she had been earlier. She moved toward the two worried Hawk might arrest her friend or accidently hurt her. Crystova spoke first, "I found something this morning in the wall. It's a satchel. I haven't opened the satchel yet. Would you like to be a witness to the unveiling?"

"Who are you?' he asked.

"I'm Crystova Moth. I teach at the university. I'm also a friend of Kimberly's. She's given me permission to excavate this wall. Beneath this wall is the original stonework from an ancient Delphi chapel. My research suggests holy men and women left behind a history of our ancient language inside the gap between the marble and the brickwork. I discovered something in this wall. You see the hole here."

"You knew exactly where to excavate," he said his tone suspicious.

"I have tools which can pinpoint objects in the ground or behind walls. Well, my tool can penetrate a few feet beneath the surface."

"Let me see your tools."

Crystova searched the ground near her feet and handed him her butterfly pen.

"Your detector can locate minerals, not clothing or wood. I see only cloth here."

"I haven't opened the satchel. My Rover 2025 can detect gold as small as my pinky. Before you arrived, I'd been in the process of opening the satchel. Would you mind?"

"Bring the satchel to the table near the door where the light is better. May I borrow your gloves? I will examine the contents first."

"You may look inside but it is imperative I extract the manuscript. It is delicate."

Crystova carried the satchel as she would a large piece of glass. The satchel had a fine coating of dust on the leather, dust, Kimberly remembered her friend brushing off earlier. The dust must have fallen onto the satchel as it lay on the floor. When Crystova opened the satchel and pulled out several small rolled parchments made from animal skin, Kimberly managed to hide her surprise. She was grateful Hawk was too busy studying the parchment to notice her reaction to the contents. She kept her thoughts as blank as possible, superstitiously afraid he might be able to read her mind the way Gawain and Shehili seemed to read minds.

"What are they?" she asked Crystova.

"They are very old books Kimberly, older than even the monks who built the monastery here nine hundred years ago. I suspect they may be books from the tribes that lived in these parts, the people the monks wished to collaborate with in order to create a new language. These scrolls might be the primitive language of our ancestors," Crystova's voice quivered.

"Wow."

Hawk straightened and looked down at Crystova, "This is quite a find Dela- "

"Moth. Crystova Moth."

"Unfortunately, I will have to confiscate this discovery until my superiors have looked it over and determined it has nothing to do with the present murder."

Her shock mirrored Kimberly's. All the color drained out of her face and her lips looked as white as the collar of D.I. Hawk's shirt, "But the only way to examine these artifacts would be to unroll them and if you do not have the proper equipment or know what to do, they will be destroyed."

"That is why we need you to come to the coroner's lab and officiate in the examination. Our people will take orders from you."

The color returned to her cheeks and with shaking hands she

returned the scrolls to the satchel, "Would you mind carrying my purse? I must handle this discovery carefully. A dust free container would be perfect."

Kimberly watched Hawk and Crystova leave the shop, Hawk with Crystova's heavy bag over his shoulder and Crystova with her arms cradling the satchel. Crystova took small steps toward the door, reminding Kimberly of a new mother carrying a baby for the first time. Kimberly tried to close the door, but Knight Bristlecone appeared and with a mischievous smile said, "Good morning, Dela Lemon. I hope you slept well."

"Well enough. Have you had tea?"

"Yes. I'm good thank you."

"Then you'll excuse me. I must dress and find something to eat before opening the shop. You can sit on the window seat if you like while you're waiting."

"Don't trouble yourself. I'll be fine."

Kimberly hurried to her sanctuary and quickly threw off her robe and nightgown and surveyed the clothes hanging in her wardrobe with a frown, unable to decide what to wear, her mind circling the strange morning. The day had barely started, and somehow, she had become complicit in a theft of an ancient artifact. Where had Crystova hidden the illuminated manuscript? She'd seen it with her own eyes. The manuscript had been inside the satchel.

Had Crystova put the manuscript back in the hole? No. Hawk would have noticed. It must be somewhere in the shop in plain sight. If she started searching her inventory near the wall would Bristlecone suspect? She stared at her clothes and bit her lip and soon realized she was getting cold. The hangman's noose dangled before her eyes. Why her? Why now? Had the Bishop been after the manuscript all this time? Or worse had someone kidnapped and killed Star because they suspected she knew something?

E2 Shellfargon Year 5092 NDMP WK 5: UES Albion 4

Governor released suspect from dungeon. E1 assigned me to protect her. E4 determined to defend suspect at trial. Trial will be broadcast live around the world. Second search of shop uncovered planted evidence. Evidence sealed and tagged by me. Evidence stored in E1 safe at Sheriff's Headquarters. Indication spooks planted evidence in clock and games confirmed. E3 testing evidence for DNA and potential tampering.

Moth found rolled parchments behind wall of Bookworm Emporium. Artifacts could be eight hundred

years old. Moth claims unwinding the parchment will take years. E1 curious why Moth no longer mentions illuminated manuscript. Parchments may complicate situation down here. Orders?

Chapter 8

Joanie Fitzhammond glanced at the clock and wished the hands would move faster. Almost over. Soon Mary would be back from vacation and her part-time schedule would resume. The extra money felt like a burden, a back breaking burden having to be responsible for the cash in the register and the accounting books and locking up at night; all the while, with Sylvia Paleone breathing down her neck and giving her the stink eye as if she suspected Joanie of stealing one of the cheap relics or sleeping on the job with her eyes open.

In the process of closing, For the Soul Relics and Religious Treasures, Joanie was dismayed to discover Sylvia Paleone was still in the building. When she left her office and entered the lobby, the thought that all the time she'd been counting the money in the cash register Sylvia was spying on her made her skin crawl. To prove to Sylvia her efficiency and initiative Joanie strode into the store room and double checked the safe, the windows and meeting room door.

From the corner of her eye she thought she saw the life-size portrait of the Holy Centipede wearing his royal robes begin to move. She must have made a sound, a stupid gasp of surprise. The portrait swung back and forth several times like a pendulum and then all motion seized. Joanie's initial assumption was that the phenomena had been caused by a small earthquake tremor. Then the logical part of her brain kicked in and she questioned why nothing else in the room was affected.

Sylvia rushed in. "What are you doing?" she demanded, her normally vacuous expression transformed into an ugly mask of suspicion, as if she suspected Joanie of theft. Why would Joanie steal anything in this room with the boss in the next room? Did she really think Joanie was so stupid? Would she need a stapler that bad? A box of paper clips perhaps?

"Just making sure the safe is locked and the windows and doors are secure," Joanie managed to say.

"I've already made the rounds," Sylvia told her in a tone which implied Joanie was a major dunce. In Sylvia Paleone's world she considered herself a stable genius surrounded by idiots.

"I didn't know. Mary told me to be sure to do a once over before leaving."

As Joanie made her way out, she felt Sylvia's penetrating gaze burning twin holes in her back. Tomorrow everything would be back to normal. Tomorrow Mary could deal with the stable genius. Thank you, Holy-Slimy Insect, for that small favor. Odd to be anxious for McGirdle's return from her holiday in South Victoria. Mary's entire family lived in South Victoria. When she returned from a week with her family, Mary would have built up enough reserves to deal with the cruel and capricious Paleone.

It was on that pleasant thought Sylvia Paleone sauntered up to Joanie with her hips swaying and a plastic smile affixed to her face. Without batting an eyelash, she announced, "Thank you Joanie for your service to us in these trying times. You have been a dear soul to volunteer your services for so many months. May your next endeavor be as rewarding."

"I'm sorry, I don't understand," Joanie said in an obsequious manner she later squirmed when remembering. Had she really been so desperate? The woman's remark rattled around in her brain like so many silly ping pong balls, and still Joanie couldn't quite grasp what she was hearing. At first, she turned the assault into a punishment for her catty thoughts about Mary's cousins which was superstitious nonsense. There was no deity listening to her every thought. There was no deity duly punishing her for said thought.

No. There was something else going on here, something very strange.

Why had Sylvia Paleone been hiding in the back room? Why hadn't Joanie bumped into her an hour ago when she'd gone into the room for extra paper for the cash register? How had Sylvia returned from lunch without Joanie spotting her? With her photographic memory, she clearly remembered Sylvia leaving the shop for lunch and announcing to the room in general (because she didn't look at or talk to the hired help – ever) that she had several meetings with church officials and would not return.

How had she gotten back into the shop without being seen since lunch? Joanie had spent the entire afternoon behind the counter staring at the door or dusting the artifacts. And most odd was Sylvia's current behavior. For the last two years, Sylvia's interaction with the help consisted of a dialogue between her and Mary McGirdle. The most recent exchange between Joanie, Sylvia and Mary came to mind.

"Tell Joanie to wipe off the kiosk with the silk cloth not the cotton," Sylvia said to Mary as Mary stood next to her.

And Joanie only a foot away from the women heard Mary repeat, "Joanie, please wipe off the kiosk with the silk cloth not this cotton one. Thanks."

As Joanie's world began to disintegrate immaterial thoughts popped into her head. Sylvia should be out there defending the

Governor, the Duke Dono Set, and her adopted religion by spending her husband's money buying up air time on the Internet, accepting guest appearances on radio shows, badgering newspapers to interview her, and generally searching for other ways and means to attract attention to her causes. For the Soul Relics and Religious Treasures hardly brought in enough money to pay Mary McGirdle's wages much less Joanie's tiny pittance.

So why bother to fire her now? What had she done? And why was Sylvia in the shop this late at night when she could be convincing Curlecons the Church of the Holy Centipede was the only way to heaven? Nothing made sense. Instead of promoting her cause, Paleone chose to hide in the back room and then find fault with the hired help and fire her.

Joanie waited hoping for more information. Sylvia stared at her with an annoyed lift of her carefully clipped eyebrow. And then Sylvia Paleone did something unlike herself. She extended her hand. Joanie, caught off guard, wondered if the woman thought since she'd fired her, her former boss could treat her like a paying customer. Joanie accepted Sylvia's hand and shook it. Sylvia's smile vanished. Once again, Joanie had misread the signs. Sylvia jerked her hand back as if she thought Joanie might bite it off.

"Excuse me, but you still have the keys. Hand over the keys please," Sylvia ordered, her strong square jaw reminding Joanie of a male wrestler. The pent-up rage, glittering eyes, and sneer transformed the insipid prettiness into a ghastly Hollow's Eve mask. It was the most frightening transformation Joanie had ever beheld and she'd seen some nasty, ugly, bloody awful sights in her career. Joanie tossed the keys in her general direction and hurried to the backroom.

Behind her Joanie could hear Paleone grunt when she was forced to bend down and pick up the keys. Joanie also heard the woman scream out, "Where do you think you're going?"

Surprised, Joanie turned around in time to see Paleone's bright blue eyes behind the fake wire eyeglasses harden as if the woman was debating whether to murder the hired help. "I have a right to my personal property. My purse and coat are back here," Joanie told her in a calm voice which stopped Paleone in her tracks. The woman couldn't possibly want her magazines or old leather purse with the worn clasp.

"Oh," Sylvia said and took a step back her beefy shoulders suddenly relaxing. The transformation from pretty, simple-minded female with perfect hairdo, carefully applied makeup, and figure flattering clothes into the beefy, square jawed wrestler had been a warning against underestimating such people. For just a moment, Joanie had been a witness to the real Sylvia Paleone. There would be other moments and someday the fake Paleone would be exposed as a ruthless cruel shark willing to swallow anything in her path.

With that comforting thought, Joanie gathered up her purse, her books, her favorite coffee cup and the silver framed picture of her dead husband. As she prepared to leave, from the corner of her eye, she noticed an oil painting of Duke Dono snug in its ornate frame and thought she saw the eye's move. Subterfuge had never been her strong suit, but with only a few precious minutes left and a desire to confirm her suspicions, Joanie searched through all the cabinet drawers. Sylvia stood by the entrance with her arms crossed waiting impatiently for Joanie to finish gathering up her belongings.

While Joanie opened drawers and pretended to search for nonexistent belongings, she covertly watched the wall straining to hear if there was somebody else in the room. Someone was hiding behind the wall. Someone was watching them through the slits in Duke Dono's eyes. What an ugly portrait and even uglier eyes. The inconsequential thought percolated in her agitated brain long after Sylvia closed the shop door leaving her standing in the dark. The glowworms had yet to be fed. Who was the man watching the room through the eyes of the portrait? Was he Paleone's husband? Hardly. In the two years she worked at the shop, Paleone's husband had been seen only once as he waited outside and continually looked at his wrist watch.

Once out on the street, frightened for her future, Joanie forgot about the mystery visitor. She had more serious problems than who Sylvia was boffing. Joanie hurried down Merchant's Row ignoring the late shoppers and the merchants, brushing past the usual people she bumped into on the street, unable to force even a ghastly smile to her lips or a nod of recognition.

In the few hundred steps it took for her to travel from the end of Merchants' Row to Wolfern Promenade, she saw her future, a future of homelessness and hunger. All the while in her mad dash to her sanctuary, she craved peace and familiar things. She needed the warmth of her tiny flat above the newspaper shop, the little stove, a warm cup of tea, her bed, her books. She needed time to heal and hide her shame.

When Joanie Fitzhammond arrived at the front door of the Shellfargon Seed, she noticed Harry talking to a blonde, a stocky woman with a big chest, the said chest thrust straight at Harry Hanson.

To get to the upstairs flat, Joanie was forced to enter the

newspaper office and pass by Hanson's desk. Behind the desk was a flight of narrow curved stairs which led to the flat above the newspaper office. Before she could get to Hanson's desk, she saw a familiar item squatting on the floor like an obedient old dog. It was Joanie's suitcase, a suitcase which had once belonged to her dead husband. She stopped in her tracks and with the sensation of ice dribbling down her neck, her body knew what was coming before her brain could assimilate the horror of it all.

"You've been smoking in the attic Joanie," Harry Hanson began his eyes rarely connecting with her own. "Sorry, but I can't allow that. The whole place would end up ashes if just one of those cigarette embers landed on the floor. This building is old you know. It wouldn't take much to burn it down."

"I don't smoke," Joanie said in her defense knowing the futility of even one word of protest reaching Hanson's hormone activated conscience. The man was a slimy toad.

"I found a cigarette butt up there. I don't care who smokes, maybe it was one of your gentleman friends," he said holding back a snicker. The blonde with the boobs and the vacant hazel eyes just stared curiously at her. She reminded Joanie of several especially vicious female assassins she'd interrogated in her past life. Joanie averted her gaze pretending to be an unassuming middle-aged woman for her benefit. If the she-devil thought Joanie was a threat, she might find a way to eliminate the threat. Joanie had no safe place now to protect herself from such a person.

Before she grabbed her suitcase, Joanie said, "I have the right to look the flat over to make sure all of my belongings were packed," and without looking at either of them made herself walk between the blonde and Hanson's desk, then up the narrow stairs where she found the door of her former flat open and the sheets thrown off the bed.

Someone had tossed the sheets in a corner. She set her suitcase down and walked slowly around the room, opening drawers and looking behind furniture to make sure nothing would be left behind. It could only have taken five minutes but from the sounds below the two of them were already in the mood to celebrate. They were disgusting. He was a filthy excuse for a man and a slum lord to boot. She'd been forced to pay more for the flat than the market value.

It was too late at night to find other accommodations. She had no place to go. She squelched the fear knowing full well if she thought about her plight, she would end up shaming herself in front of the rabid dogs below. She rushed down the stairs holding her suitcase in front of her chest as a defense against the ugliness. She stepped out into the street with her coat slung over her arm and her suitcase held in front of her like a shield. It was after six o'clock and the drawbridge was closed. She was trapped inside the bailey for the night. Where could she go?

Perhaps the rabid dogs were standing in the office gloating and watching as she paused to consider her situation? She couldn't face them. She couldn't face anyone, especially not the tourists sitting at the outdoor café tables eating dinner or drinking wine. Instead, she wandered down the alley between Merchants' Row and the plaza forced to creep along so as not to run into the stone walls or the garbage bins. It was difficult not to think about the contents of those bins, the smell wouldn't let her forget rotten food, used kitty litter, dirty diapers, and other equally nasty things inside.

Despair ripped through her chest and choked off the cry she wanted to make. Her worst fears had been realized – she was destitute and homeless, one of the invisible to be pitied and spit on and shunned. It had taken less than an hour for the life she had tried to build to come crashing down around her. When she reached the end of the alley, she found herself facing a brick wall.

Tired and scared, she sank to the ground clutching her suitcase. She wept as quietly as possible so as not to wake the shopkeepers or anyone living in the apartments nearby. She could hear a party going on just above her head. There were several balconies above. The one where the party was going on with such abandon had its curtains tightly closed and only small spots of light sifted through the cracks.

It wasn't until the moon shone down on the floor of the alley, she realized she was sitting on a rolled-up moldy carpet. She'd had no dinner but had had the forethought to remove the little food she had left in the flat's pantry and tiny refrigerator. She opened her purse and with the aid of her flashlight key made herself a turkey sandwich. Even though her stomach continued to claw and knot at her, she made herself eat the sandwich. She didn't trust the rats or cats or other noxious predators. If they smelled food, they would try to steal hers. She especially feared the biggest predator – man. Some homeless male might take exception to her use of his territory.

Then nearby, only a few feet from where she sat, a light went on. She tried to figure out the lay of the land in her head and decided the light cast from inside one of the shops must be coming from the Merchants' Row side. As she tried to recall the names of the shops near this end of the alley, a door opened and a woman wearing a white apron stepped out carrying a sack of garbage. She carelessly tossed the bag into the bin.

Instead of returning to the warmth and light inside, the

waitress paused to fish something out of her apron pocket. Joanie watched in dismay as the tall skinny young woman with black hair lit a cigarette and took a deep drag. From the open door, Joanie could hear dishes rattling in a sink, the low murmur of voices talking and laughing, and smell the wondrous odor of fried foods and sugary pastries. The alley door belonged to Queenie's Diner.

A voice floated down to them, startling the waitress into a choking gasp, "Those things will kill you quick, child. They may keep you thin now but wait a few years. You know 400,000 people die every year from nicotine related deaths. 400,000."

The young waitress looked up where she thought the voice was coming from. It was a balcony covered in flowering pots directly opposite the Bookworm Emporium. The woman on the balcony had sounded educated. The young waitress sounded deferential and equally as educated, "I don't believe I have the pleasure Dela. I'm Alex. Who might you be?"

"Lynora Reason, my dear. How do you do?"

"Well thank you. I appreciate your concern for my future health," she said ruefully and took the lit cigarette and threw it on the alley floor grinding the cancer stick into a pulp beneath her high-heeled shoe. Joanie winced at the thought of the poor girl's future bunions after years of waitressing in them. Oh well, wisdom was wasted on the young. The waitress with the manners of a queen and the look of a runway model waggled her fingers at the shadowy figure sitting on the balcony above. She reentered the diner shutting out the smells, the light, and the sounds of people with a purpose, people who had jobs.

Joanie remained as quiet as a mouse and waited with trepidation for the woman to address her, perhaps insist she leave. She could even threaten to call a knight who might lock her up for vagrancy. Time passed slowly. It seemed like hours before Joanie heard the creak of a chair and then watched as the woman with silver hair disappeared through a stylish Bojenlac door covered in silky cloth. The balcony occupant shut the Bojenlac door behind her. Joanie was once again alone surrounded by the stench of the garbage bins. She watched the lights spring on in the rooms where Lynora Reason lived.

Just as Joanie believed she could relax a light sprang on in the apartments on the first floor facing the alley. She'd seen the bay window carved out of the brick façade and wondered who would do such a silly thing. A woman who thought she was invisible to any onlookers threw open her curtains and peered out as if searching for someone. Joanie realized the woman was peering straight at her. She recognized her as the owner of the Bookworm Emporium and instigator of the Merchants' Row Alliance, Kimberly Lemon.

Joanie heard the cranking of a lever. She noticed one side of the bay window begin to slowly open outward. Inside Kimberly seemed to be moving furniture. She could hear the legs of a table squealing in protest. Kimberly crouched down on the floor in order to see Joanie and pressed her face close to the slit in the window.

"I know you're out there, Witless. If you're hungry, I'll be glad to share my roast beef sandwich and salad with you. Come on Witless, don't be proud tonight. I can see you over there sitting on the rug. Do I have to walk all the way down the street and into the alley? Don't make me put my shoes back on. My feet are killing me." Joanie wanted to say something, but she was too ashamed. She cowered further back into the shadows pressing herself against the cold brick.

"I'm sorry I've been gone so long Witless. It's been weeks I know. But I told Caleb to keep an eye on you. I guess he forgot. Alright then, if you're going to be stubborn, I guess I'll just have to come out to you."

Finally, Joanie couldn't stand the suspense and spoke, "It's not Witless. It's me."

Joanie heard the scraping of wood on wood and saw Kimberly pressing her face close to the window slit, "Me? Who is me?"

"Joanie Fitzhammond, Dela Lemon."

"Joanie! Joanie what are you doing out there at this hour of the night?"

The shock and warmth and sincerity in Kimberly's voice broke her. She began to cry, great gasping sobs erupting from deep down inside her soul, sobs that hurt her back, her chest, her entire body. She covered her eyes even though she knew Kimberly couldn't see her face.

Kimberly disappeared, and Joanie was left alone to weep at her leisure grateful for the darkness. When the sobs subsided, and she had wiped her streaming eyes and nose with the edge of her blouse, she heard someone running down the alley. She looked up in time to see a light bobbing up and down as someone wiggled past trash bins and discarded toys and furniture and boxes.

A shoe hit a soda can and sent the can flying against the wall. Kimberly cursed the can. The light continued to bob and weave madly. After a minute or two, Joanie figured out that Kimberly was searching for something. Joanie rose to her feet and without embarrassment asked, "Did you lose something?"

Kimberly's self-deprecating laugh made Joanie smile, "My damned shoe. It flew off. Hold on a sec. Wait. Yes. I think this is it."

Kimberly losing her shoe in a dark alley would have been comical at any other time but only reinforced Joanie's feeling of despair. Before Joanie had time to flee from Kimberly's pitying eyes, Kimberly stood in front of her clumsily trying to slip her shoe back on. Only later did Joanie realize Kimberly had had the presence of mind to keep her distance, signaling her respect for Joanie's personal space, as if Kimberly had transformed the alley from dirt and filth to an extension of Joanie's own home.

"May I come closer?" Kimberly asked.

Joanie must have made some sort of sound which might have resembled acceptance because Kimberly began to move forward. The young woman crouched down in front of Joanie and with her flashlight pointed at the ground spoke in a breathless voice, "Oh Joanie. I'm so sorry for your troubles. Please, please don't cry. Come inside and share a sandwich with me."

"I've eaten thank you."

"Then a cup of tea."

"It's late. I appreciate your thoughtful gesture, but I can't impose."

"Stop it," Kimberly said in a stern voice. "Stop pushing me away. I know what it's like to be alone and scared. I know how frightening homelessness can be. Please come inside and sit with me and let's figure out what we can do to help each other. Please Delan Fitzhammond."

When Kimberly threatened to find Caleb and have Caleb carry her to the Bookworm, Joanie realized how foolish she was being and agreed to follow Kimberly into the shop. And once inside, Joanie followed Kimberly down the long corridor to the private quarters accepting a seat at Kimberly's little oak table with the matching cream-colored cushions tied to the matching Elmherst Revival Nook Chairs.

She even accepted a cookie from the boxed cookies presented to her and sipped her hot tea and stared at the polished wood of the tiny table unwilling to unburden herself just yet. Kimberly sat on the other side of the table and waited patiently for Joanie to finish her tea and cookie. The clock on the mantel above the stove declared the time. It was nearly eleven. Joanie moved as if to leave and Kimberly stood up.

"You can stay here and help me with the shop until you find another job. The merchants need your skills as a bookkeeper and secretary Delan Fitzhammond. We've decided to make our Merchants' Row Alliance permanent. We need a secretary and treasurer. Harry Zany is one of the directors. I've been made

President. There are also dues to be collected and records to be kept and minutes to be typed. Oh, and we've decided to start a newsletter. There's so much to do and I just won't have the time to do it what with the shop and my current situation."

Finally, Joanie grew exasperated enough to say, "But you only have the one tiny bed. I'm not going to take your bed."

"I have a cot under the stairs. If you don't mind sleeping under the stairs, I'll prepare your bed. Help yourself to the bathroom. We'll find accommodations for you tomorrow."

They exchanged looks across the table and Joanie realized Kimberly meant every word and would be hurt if Joanie left. She felt the tears congregating in the back of her skull and her throat beginning to constrict and to save face ran into the bathroom and shut the door. When she came out, she heard Kimberly wrestling with the cot in the hallway under the stairs, stairs which seemed to go nowhere.

Joanie went to help her. By midnight they were both lying in bed in the dark thinking their private thoughts. By two o'clock in the morning Joanie had cried herself to sleep. Kimberly's goodness had been her undoing. The idea the ruthless blonde gold-digger and Kimberly shared the same blood boggled the mind.

Nearly twelve hours had passed since Joanie had stepped into her new life. She had two part-time jobs now which made up for the one miserable job she had had under Sylvia Paleone. This job had much more to offer: a chance for dignity, creativity and autonomy. No one would demand she bow her head and say a prayer before opening the shop. No one would demand she lie about the merchandise and claim the relics had been touched by the holy one before his ascension.

Instead Joanie was encouraged to help the Bookworm customers find what they wanted or recommend a bookstore that might have what they wanted. While assisting Kimberly, she created Alliance membership cards and handed out receipts when merchants paid their first dues. During quiet moments she created two separate accounting programs, one for Kimberly's business and the other for the Merchants' Row Alliance. Without being asked Joanie typed up a letter for the county clerk and offered to deliver the letter to the county making the Merchants' Row Alliance official.

Originally the merchants considered creating a guild but had been told by the clerk of the court guilds were no longer in fashion. He claimed the "mixing of trades" was unheard of with such a disgusted expression Joanie and Harry found it difficult not to laugh in his face. The man acted as if they were suggesting something lewd.

The two ignored the clerk's precious sensibilities and insisted the alliance be recorded in the official records as a limited liability corporation.

Just as Joanie finished recording the Darknight family's recent contribution to the newly established Merchants' Row Alliance, the bell above the Bookworm Emporium jangled and she looked up in time to see Professor Honeysweet enter. He was a familiar face in the bailey. She'd seen him many times in the plaza lecturing for the benefit of his students or giving tours of the castle for tourists. The students and the tourists were transfixed by his stories. He came up with the wildest most shocking anecdotes about Duke Dono castle and the surrounding countryside.

Inwardly smiling, Joanie noticed Gawain Bristlecone's sudden interest in the newcomer, the way he studied the professor suspiciously as if he expected the man to whip out a gun at any moment. From his comfortable position reclining on a chair in the corner of the room near the newly returned lizard clock, Bristlecone pretended to be immersed in the contents of a pamphlet he wasn't reading. With a huge effort the knight made himself relax, uncross his legs, sit straighter. Then he leaned forward with his elbows on his knees and the pamphlet held between his hands. When the professor asked for Kimberly, Bristlecone seemed to vibrate.

"She's with her lawyer, Professor Honeysweet," Joanie informed him.

The beaming good cheer on Honeysweet's handsome face disappeared replaced by a look of disappointment, "Ah. I see. Well, would you tell her I dropped by?"

Honeysweet turned to look at Bristlecone. "Aren't you supposed to be guarding Kimberly?"

Bristlecone ignored the professor and kept on pretending to read the pamphlet. Honeysweet took a step closer to the knight's chair. "Sir. I say sir," he said and stopped moving when Bristlecone looked up. "Why aren't you protecting Dela Lemon?"

"And you are?"

"I thought you knights had dossiers on everyone. For your information, I am Professor Adam Honeysweet. I teach Blueglennen history at the university."

Bristlecone took out a pad and pen from his pocket, "And where can you be reached sir? Your number please?"

"My number? Why do you need my number?"

"Answer the question Professor Honeysweet or answer at the Department of Justice," Bristlecone said. Joanie was amused by their attempts to intimidate each other. Then her photographic memory replayed the conversation and she realized their body language and expressions did not sync with their words. Were they pretending to be rivals? Joanie's lifelong observation of people made her particularly good at spotting insincerity.

Honeysweet appeared baffled by Bristlecone's aggressiveness. "I wasn't trying to tell you how to do your job. Demanding my phone number seems a little excessive. I'm just concerned for Kimberly's wellbeing."

Bristlecone stepped closer. The two men were equal in height and build yet that was where the resemblance ended. Bristlecone, skilled at hand to hand combat could have crushed Honeysweet without breaking a sweat. Especially now. Where was the professor's swagger? Since entering the shop, he seemed to have lost his confidence. His body had curled itself up into a protective ball. His head and shoulders were tucked in like a turtle hiding in a shell. Did they think she was an idiot? Maybe they did. She let them think she was a frumpy old maid without a clue what they were up to.

To keep the charade going her face had to match the impression she wanted to give, so she started thinking about society and power. In a fair society, in a society where laws were taken seriously, and the average citizen had rights, Honeysweet would be safe. But in Blueglennen, in the whole of Wolfern Province, there were only two sets of laws – one for those in political seats of power and one for those with coffers of yellow seastars in the bank. Everyone else had to claw their way to the top or do their best to remain invisible, so they wouldn't end up injured, humiliated, imprisoned, or dead.

While she'd been thinking about power, she'd been staring off into a corner of the shop pretending to keep an eye on a customer in the security mirror. What she did instead was watch as Honeysweet passed a note to Bristlecone. It happened so quickly most people wouldn't have noticed. They were that good. Impressed, Joanie watched as the two men casually moved away from each other and resumed their former positions: a bored Bristlecone sitting on a chair pretending to read and a worried suitor anxiously awaiting Kimberly's appearance.

D.I. Hawk entered the shop and paused. His eyes took in the occupants. Then he frowned. "Where is Dela Lemon?"

Since Joanie stood behind the counter and was the official representative of the Bookworm, she decided she would speak on behalf of Dela Lemon. "She's with her attorney, sir. May I help you? I'm Joanie Fitzhammmond."

"And in what capacity do you represent this establishment?"

Hawk said, annoyed he even had to ask.

"I've been hired by Dela Lemon to assist her in the shop and I'm also the secretary and treasurer of the Merchants' Row Alliance."

Instead of using Hawk's appearance as an excuse to avoid a confrontation with Bristlecone, Professor Honeysweet settled himself comfortably on the window seat as if he had been invited to an impromptu play, his eyes wandering back and forth between Hawk, Joanie, and Bristlecone. Joanie was rather proud of him for not bolting out the door in fear for his life. If she'd been a man, Hawk and Bristlecone would have been a real threat to her masculinity. Since she now knew he was an informant, her good opinion of him vanished. No matter what the circumstances, she would never betray her country to an alien species.

"Business must be doing well," Hawk said nodding in a friendly fashion in the general direction of both Bristlecone and Honeysweet. "I'm pleased. Now captain, I would appreciate a few moments of your time in private. Let's get some fresh air."

Bristlecone seemed unhappy at the news, "Of course sir."

When Hawk and Bristlecone left the shop passing by the display window in a hurry, Honeysweet jumped up from the window seat and in less than two strides his long legs maneuvered him into position beside Joanie near the cash register. His closeness made Joanie nervous. What were his intentions? With his usually merry eyes suddenly serious Honeysweet said, "We must do all we can, to help Dela Lemon, Fitzhammond. She is in danger. I'm sure of it. Why does she have a bodyguard? Tell her I am at her service. Any time. Any day."

The news made Joanie nauseous. Did he really think she was so stupid as to trust him? Dela Lemon was a good kind person and Joanie vowed she would defend her to the death. After all, how many people would invite a stranger into their home while being scrutinized by the law as a possible murderer? With all she had to worry about, the woman still took time to worry about a stranger.

Joanie hated what the vile Hanson was writing about Kimberly in the Shellfargon Seed. The man was a fork-tongued serpent. He no longer bothered to pretend he was unbiased. His editorials might as well have been written by Governor Saurus himself. Joanie despised traitors like Honeysweet and Hanson. One day, they would be punished. That was the only comfort she could drum up.

When she found Kimberly reading Hanson's salacious piece of trash and quizzed her about reading the man's lies, Kimberly said, "It's best to know what their thinking. If I know what they're up to, maybe, I can protect myself against them. He's writing what he thinks the Governor wants to hear."

"Harry Hanson rubbing shoulders with the Governor?" Joanie snorted. "That scarecrow in a bad suit with the lips of a lizard? Never."

Kimberly laughed and set her paper down, "Hanson. You think I meant Hanson. No. He doesn't decide the news. He gets his orders from the Governor and from the town's powerful money men. They'll decide my fate. Either someone set me up or someone is profiting from this situation. My grandfather and I used to play chess. He said to never underestimate the pawn, the pawn isn't as weak as you might think. That goes for our side too."

Joanie had presumed Hanson's innuendos, veiled threats, fantasy statistics, and imaginary judgmental editorials were his own evil genius. Now, she began to see Hanson's newspaper as a toady's way to suck up to money. The Church of the Holy Centipede and the weapons suppliers back east were the real power behind Governor Saurus. Hanson was just trying to cash in.

The silence between Joanie and Honeysweet had gone on too long. The professor with all his nervous energy began to pace about the room, moving from the counter to the lizard clock. And then she saw his eyes roaming about on the floor as if he were looking for clues. She supposed he really didn't need her acquiescence, he must have taken her silence for agreement.

"The authorities believe Kimberly is guilty based on three important bits of evidence: the fight with Star Bridgekeeper, Star's body found in the catacombs in Kimberly's trash bin, and some sort of personal object which links the two females. The fight is public knowledge, so too is the bin. According to the Shellfargon Seed, the serial numbers inside the trash bin were assigned to the Bookworm Emporium. Those two bits of evidence are circumstantial. It's the object linking the women I'm worried about. No one is willing to tell me about it, not even Dela Swana."

Joanie let the traitor pace and pretend. The silence helped her think. An odd man, Professor Honeysweet, odd in so many ways. She watched him. The way he strode about the room, the way his eyes lit up when he talked, and the excitement she detected just beneath the surface made her wonder if perhaps Star's murder and Kimberly's arrest were more of an intellectual challenge for him then a desire to save Kimberly from the gallows. When he tripped over the rug by the door, she suddenly had an epiphany. He wasn't a Delphinid.

The shock nearly gave her away. Desperate, she pretended to drop her pen and dropped down to the floor to retrieve it. He wasn't human either. She'd have known. The folds of extra skin around his eyes looked so real.

Maybe he was a hybrid?

She'd heard of them. Evolution was a fascinating phenomenon. It made her feel so puny and insignificant when she realized nature had other ideas about the world. Once the starship Albion provided the medical world with the powers of DNA, the Delphadorturo ordered that all jobs in highly sensitive areas of the government and education must be tested. How had Honeysweet passed such a rigorous background check?

Maybe that's how Honeysweet was recruited – blackmail?

Joanie shrugged – time to worry about Kimberly's defense. Then she remembered her few miserable hours in the alley and the conversation she overheard between Alexandra the waitress and the unknown woman who lived in the top-floor apartment. What was her name? She introduced herself to the waitress. Reason. Yes. Lynora Reason. The woman's balcony overlooked the parapets where she could watch the sentries on duty.

What a strange place for a balcony, hardly a good place for contemplation. She recalled her hours of despair and thought about how she might have become homeless forever, but for the fact Kimberly Lemon had mistaken her for Witless, the independent alley cat. And then Joanie had another epiphany and gasped. Her gasp surprised Honeysweet. He spun around suddenly vibrating with renewed excitement.

"Do you know what they found on Star's body?" he demanded.

"No," Joanie said and left the security of the counter to stand near the velvet curtains leading to Kimberly's private quarters. "Come with me. I want to show you something."

Honeysweet followed her down the dark corner unaware of the cot under the stairs, the cot which signified poverty. Yet the cot also represented empathy and generosity. Joanie vowed she would never be dependent upon another person again. She would diversify. Perhaps she would return to the work she'd done so well, only as an independent investigator.

She might talk to Shehili Swana and offer her services. She would be the perfect spy. She was a middle-aged, plain woman with little money and no respect. She could blend in anywhere, overhear private conversations, spy on people who would be too immersed in their own more exciting lives to notice her. Yes. As accountant for the Merchants' Row Alliance and clerk for Kimberly, she could still find time to investigate.

They stood before the bay window. The curtains had been tied back against the wall to allow for more light to penetrate the dark room. With Honeysweet towering over her, the room seemed smaller. Kimberly had set a few plants on the window ledge. Staring out the window, they could see a stone wall, and on the wall, flowers cascading down the brick like so many colorful rivulets in blue, pink, orange, red, and yellow.

She had been told that Caleb submitted a request through the city clerk for permission to hang the baskets. The city allowed them to hang the baskets if the baskets did not impede the trashmen. Kimberly, with the help of a few neighbors arranged honeysuckle and some sort of exotic purplish leafed and ruby red lip-like flower in wicker containers. Caleb attached them to the brick wall with spikes. The flowers spilling over the sides of the baskets and along the wall appealed to all the senses and did much to mask the odors.

"Come closer," Joanie urged Honeysweet and peered up at the apartment across the alley where she could see a balcony covered in potted plants and a gorgeous flowering tree. "You see the balcony up there. Well, that balcony overlooks the alley and the trash bins. Think about it. Star was found in the Bookworm trash bin.

The person who killed Star would have had to stuff her in the trash bin and roll it down the alley across the promenade in full view of everyone. If we are to find evidence, we will have to question the shopkeepers and the woman who lives in that apartment. Perhaps, she saw something and doesn't realize she saw something important. Do you want to help save Kimberly and find out who is the real killer?"

Honeysweet moved closer to the table and peered up at the balcony, "We should talk to the occupant first. Can you get away?"

"I'm supposed to be taking care of the bookstore while Kimberly's busy with her lawyer. I'll have to lock up the shop and ask Kimberly if I can break away. She's at the boutique."

"While you're doing that, I'll stop in at the Seed and ask Hanson if he saw anything."

"Don't. That would be a mistake," Joanie said, unable to say more, clearing her mind of any thoughts which might give her away. Hanson was vile enough to make up a scandal involving Joanie and Kimberly.

Honeysweet glanced at her curiously and waited.

"I used to live in his filthy rat hole of an apartment. You couldn't see much out his dirty windows. Besides, his living quarters are on the first floor in the back of the townhouse. He wouldn't have seen anything or heard anything. No. The people who pay attention to what's going on in the streets are people you would never imagine."

As if he had come to a momentous decision, Honeysweet straightened and stuffed his hands in his jacket pockets, "Of course, how stupid, the trash collectors! While you're busy getting permission, I'll stop by All Clean and question the collectors, see if they might have seen something odd on that day." Then he pulled his right hand out of his pocket and glanced at his watch. "We'll meet at Tony's and go together to visit the resident who owns the apartment above. Oh, yes, I was wondering how you knew the occupant of that apartment is female?"

"Oh, I've seen her before."

He smiled and turned to leave, "See you in an hour. An hour okay with you?"

"Yes," she muttered looking for her purse and keys.

Kimberly shifted nervously in the deep leather chair and watched as Shehili Swana poured over the folder she had open on her desk. The Unique Boutique remained closed which wasn't unusual since today happened to be Monday and Mondays tended to be slow. Kimberly hoped Dela Swana would not lose business over this ugly situation. The thought of money reminded Kimberly of Dela Swana's expenses as her lawyer. Strange, Shehili hadn't brought up the subject of money.

Kimberly opened her mouth and before a syllable passed her lips, Dela Swana looked up from her reading and said, "Their case is circumstantial at best. Anyone could have dumped Star's body in your trash bin. And we can easily dismantle the prosecutor's attempts to make something significant out of a difference of opinion in the plaza. After all, if quarrelling in public automatically constituted murder, then everyone would be in prison. No, there is no clear motive. By the way, I'm thinking of hiring an investigator."

Like a signal from a divine spirit, the boutique bell went off and Dela Swana rose from her chair as if she was expecting a guest. Kimberly stood up and turned to face the door, now curious. Dela Swana's nervousness was so foreign Kimberly began to worry. She behaved as if she were waiting upon royalty. The stranger, escorted through the door by Swana's clerk, hardly seemed to rate royalty status. Yet, the clerk bowed several times so low, she nearly brained herself on Swana's desk. Swana made a point of approaching the woman and taking her hand.

"Shard, it is so good to see you. It's been so long," Dela Swana said. Kimberly unused to seeing Dela Swana gush, took a closer look at the woman who would investigate the case on behalf of Kimberly's defense.

The tip of the woman's long curly dark head reached Kimberly's chin. Since Kimberly was considered petite for a Delphinid, this woman would be considered a dwarf on Shellfargon. Her wrinkled blouse and loose-fitting granny skirt hardly seemed like something a royal personage would wear in public. The much worn and loved tennis shoes were an odd choice for the skirt. And the expensive leather case and tight bun seemed more suitable for a high-power accuser to wear in court.

There were other oddities juxtaposed along with the shabby clothes and designer eyeglasses. She did think the eyeglasses were lovely with their purple ear pieces and gold butterflies, until one noticed the lenses. The woman's lenses were as thick as the bottom of a fish tank. It was plain where the woman's priorities rested – clothes were just a means of covering the body and keeping warm, whereas, the feet must be cozy and the eyes at their telescopic best. Indeed, as the woman dropped into a chair next to Kimberly, she held onto her leather case as if the crown jewels were inside.

Dela Swana resumed her seat. Kimberly sat down and waited. The woman called Shard was busy with her fingers as she pressed the numbered pad to unlock the case. She didn't say a word for the longest time. When the locks flew open, she slipped her hand inside and pulled out a purple folder. She snapped the case closed once again using the case as a makeshift table. They waited patiently as she opened the folder and flipped through the pages attached by a clip.

Kimberly, a habitual reader of anything in print, tried to read the symbols on the pages and gave up. She wasn't even sure the words were in a language.

The sound emanating from the tiny woman was a cultural shock to Kimberly's unsophisticated ear. If a cat could speak, the cat would sound just like Shard. The notes sounded very seductive. Her brain tried to wrap around the tiny woman's figure and the sexy voice.

The woman known only as Shard cleared her throat and said, "According to the coroner, Star Bridgekeeper died between noon and three p.m. on the twenty-third day of the sixth month of this solar system. The findings do implicate your client as a suspect. I've asked permission to examine the body and provided my credentials to Governor Saurus' bodyguard. The paperwork has been processed and in due time I shall hear whether my request has been granted. It is my understanding the trial begins in a few days."

Dela Swana nodded. Using her hands as a steeple, she rested

her chin on her fingers and grinned at Shard, "Yes Bristlecone, the Governor wishes to be present at the trial. He pushed the venue forward claiming he has a pressing engagement next week."

"Hum," the woman calling herself Shard - private investigator and medical examiner rolled into one – muttered with a delicate lift of her lovely brow. Without warning she jumped up still clutching her briefcase. "Then time is critical. I shall report back at the end of the day."

Shard glanced Kimberly's way. The look reminded Kimberly unpleasantly of her grade one-eleven teacher's clinical search for lies and deceptions and possible shenanigans. Shard nodded once in Kimberly's direction as if coming to some sort of conclusion, saluted Dela Swana with a brief smile and exited the office.

"Shard?" Kimberly said still processing the woman's uniqueness while the rest of her thoughts let the news of her early trial stew unpleasantly in the back of her mind.

Dela Swana sat back in her chair and said absently, "Yes. Shard Bristlecone. She's brilliant. She's one of our best. We should know more by the end of the day. Now, I want you to tell me everything that happened from the moment Star entered the bookshop to the moment you were arrested for her murder."

"But I've already gone over this with you, numerous times," Kimberly wanted to say and was interrupted by a brisk knock on the door and Dela Swana's clerk opening the door without permission. "Please forgive the interruption, Madame. I mean Dela Swana. The lady insists on speaking to your client." The beautiful clerk with her enigmatic smile ushered the person behind her inside the room and closed the door without making a sound.

Joanie Fitzhammond stood by the door and looked uncomfortable but determined, "I'm so sorry to interrupt you Kimberly. May I take an hour for personal business. I've locked the shop and let the customers know the shop will reopen in an hour."

"Of course, Delan Fitzhammond. It seems ludicrous to have the shop open at all. It's nearly time for the drawing of the bridge. Have the rest of the afternoon off."

"All the new members have signed the log book, paid their fees and accepted their cards. The Merchants' Row Alliance is in business," Joanie reassured her.

"Excellent," Kimberly said avoiding eye contact with Dela Swana. "And I know you have pressing personal matters to attend to." Belatedly, she realized she might have sounded dismissive. "Please, don't worry."

Joanie's forehead, cheeks, and chin were as red as apples. Her

246

eyes avoided looking directly at Dela Swana, "I won't. Thank you. I'll see you later." She exited the room as if alligators were nipping at her heels.

Dela Swana prudently asked no questions about Delan Fitzhammond. Kimberly debated whether to explain Joanie's present troubles and decided to remain silent about Joanie's current homelessness. The older woman's situation had nothing to do with the murder trial.

"What did she mean by this-solar-system?" Kimberly asked remembering Shard's odd remark.

"Shard Bristlecone is from the starship Albion. She's an ethnographer like myself and has passed the onerous tests your world requires in order to live among you and study your culture. On the ship she's a medical examiner but what she really wants to do is solve crimes like a detective. She also dabbles in archeology and anthropology.

Oh, yes, and she is the granddaughter of an Albion hero who saved what was left of our species seven generations ago. He invented the means by which our starship can travel light-years across galaxies even though he suffered from motion sickness all his life," Dela Swana explained her voice barely masking her amusement.

"How can Shard Bristlecone be his great-granddaughter if he saved your species seven generations ago? Wouldn't she be his sixth great-granddaughter? If she was his great-granddaughter wouldn't she be five or six hundred years old? Is that even possible?"

"She and her brother Gawain are test-tube babies."

"What's that?"

Several seconds passed before Dela Swana looked down at her notes and opened with the words, "Shall we go over the events of Star's day and your confrontation with her?"

Kimberly was sure she hadn't made any sound but Dela Swana chuckled anyway. One day Kimberly hoped to learn more about the starship Albion, test-tube babies and motion sickness.

Shard Bristlecone stood in the catacombs where Star's body had been found breathing in the dank air while her flashlight illuminated the weeping gray walls. The sound of several people approaching did not alarm her. The knights had long since trampled the ground and left their individual signatures all over the scene of the crime, so Shard had no real interest in a stray hair or button or other evidence. No. She was here to soak up the atmosphere and gather her thoughts.

One must think like a kidnapper and murderer in order to understand the motivations behind such a senseless crime. No matter how many decades she spent studying other cultures, she would never get used to the death of a child. There were two sets of booted feet approaching from the direction of the Duke Tower. She had entered the catacombs through the church's secret door.

The quickest most convenient route to the catacombs from the alley would be the plaza then Duke Tower courtyard and down the underground steps. But that would be dangerous with all the police in the area. The best way to go without being seen would be Wolfern Promenade down Merchants' Row and then through the cathedral. The kidnapper chose the garbage bin and the cathedral as his means of disposing of the body.

She and the Blueglennen acting coroner disagreed on the time of death. Without a thorough examination she would not be able to convince the fool he was wrong. All he thought was necessary for an autopsy was to stare at the body hoping the body would jump up and speak to him. It was sad indeed when intelligent people continued to hire lay people to do such crucial work. She could figure out the likelihood of a culture's future based on the people in authority. This culture was headed for extinction. Oh yes, right quick.

Shard waited for the guards and knights to leave, confident all Blueglennen police, on the orders of the Governor, had long since gone about the important business of harassing their citizens and had no interest in this place now that they had a murderer in their sights. Dipped in darkness with only her penlight for illumination, Shard used her heightened senses to guide her. The men approaching smelled different from the local citizenry. One of them she recognized long before she saw him.

Gawain stepped toward her first. No surprise. If there was trouble, he would be the first to take on the interloper risking his life to defend his friend. "Planning on strangling me before your boss arrives?" Shard asked as she used her flashlight to examine her little brother's newest disguise.

"What are you doing here?" Hawk asked stepping around his bodyguard to confront her. "I never requisitioned a medical examiner."

"Shehili asked for my help," Shard told him turning her flashlight on the wall where a large letter S signified the location of the trash bin which had been Star Bridgekeeper's tomb.

"I am the senior officer on this planet," Hawk reminded her.

"And I have autonomy, Detective Inspector."

Hawk relaxed, "You're wasting your time. We will be tripping over each other during this case, and that, is a waste of time. Do you have anything interesting to report?"

"A little."

"Indeed? Already?"

She used her flashlight as a pointing stick and directed the light toward the church, "The murderer came through the church. It is the most expeditious means of transporting a body undetected. I have examined the alley and can tell you for a fact the girl was murdered in the church. Dela Lemon claims Star Bridgekeeper spent much of her free time in the church. I can only assume after Star's quarrel with Dela Lemon she found solace in the church which may have been her undoing. There are several possible suspects if the church is involved: Bishop Little, his wife, perhaps even one of the lay people attending church services."

"What would Bishop Little's motive be for murdering one of his disciples?" Hawk asked with a sneer. Shard had long since accepted his dismissal of her methods. And then she began to wonder if Hawk already knew who the murderer was, and angry at the knowledge that he had no power to punish the real killer wanted to take out his feelings on her.

She knew his views about interfering in alien politics. She disagreed. Discovering the truth and exposing malefactors shouldn't just be an Albion law. No matter how painful, the truth was the best means of obtaining justice for all.

"Perhaps Star was a witness to a different crime? Perhaps Star wanted to leave the church and the Bishop quarreled with her. Perhaps Bishop Little tried to rape her, and she threatened to tell the authorities? There are any number of motives for murder: passion, greed, power."

"Bishop Little has an alibi," Gawain offered his big sister.

"His wife?" she asked with a sneer.

Gawain turned his head and showed her his handsome profile as he sought Hawk's opinion. Shard took the news and her brother's devotion to Hawk in stride, "I see." Eventually, Gawain would find another surrogate big brother to admire and Hawk would continue to make himself indispensable to the captains. Hawk, Shehili, and Gawain were perfectly happy to be on the shortlist for promotion. Good for them but she wanted more. The idea of sitting behind a desk as a Science Officer for the rest of her life made her nauseous.

Hawk refused to talk. Gawain took pity on her and said, "Bishop Little, Governor Saurus, and Hawk spent the day of Star's quarrel with Dela Lemon discussing how to deal with the merchants and whether or not to use force to prevent them from fighting the zoning changes. I stood guard by the Governor's elevator the entire afternoon. Until the woman threw herself off the Cetacea Walk. I left my post for only ten, maybe fifteen minutes. I still had the key, so no one could use the elevator anyway. I saw Dela Lemon among the witnesses. She was visibly traumatized by the tragedy."

"Unless there's another way down from the penthouse tower suite," Shard said aloud and got a pitying look for her trouble. She hated to do it, but truth won out. "What about a potty break hum? How about dinner? You couldn't possibly stand guard for twelve hours without a break?" Shard insisted glancing from one of them to the other.

Gawain laughed, "When it comes to deduction you are brilliant big sister but when it comes to surveillance and matters of protection, you are an amateur."

"Enlighten me," she insisted.

Hawk stepped forward, "We're wasting our time down here. Go home Shard and help our people on the Albion." With what he assumed had been a devastating parting comment, Hawk spun on his heels and marched away.

Gawain and Shard listened as he walked away until they were confident of being alone and able to speak freely. Hawk was quite capable of making a lot of noise announcing his departure and then sneaking back to spy on them. Today, his anger with the captains and their decision to add another member to his team reminded him of how little influence he had over the current commanders. He was ambitious enough to want to be the next No. 1, and even though he and Shard disagreed about interfering in alien politics, he had her vote. If anyone could keep the Albion crew alive it was Hawk.

"It constantly amazes me that you would be willing to give up so much to follow that man through the galaxies. One day he is going to fall on his ass and you won't be there to protect him."

Gawain brushed aside her criticism of his hero, "Someone killed the girl. I know you'll find the culprit. Be quick, Shard."

"Really? I'm amazed you agree with me. Won't Hawk be disappointed?"

When her little brother stepped closer and the light illuminated his face, Shard was surprised by the intense worry in his eyes. Her little brother was concerned about someone other than himself. Hum. "I know you'll find the real murderer and when you do, you'll come to me first with the man's name."

"Oh no," she said shaking her head. "There will be no secrets.

You know I abhor secrets as do Hawk and Swana. My duty lies with uncovering the truth and letting the truth be known, first to Shehili Swana, my client, then the citizens of Blueglennen. What they do with the truth is up to them. No secret ops. No slitting of throats or bullet to the brain. Exposure is the best form of justice."

The heated curses pouring out of Gawain's mouth reminded Shard of the day a mutual friend died. They had been with a group of children collecting samples on an uninhabited planet. Well, a planet their elders assumed was uninhabited. Everyone heard the screams on the other side of the knoll and went running.

Gawain was in the lead with only his scythe in his hands which he'd been using to clear a section of tall grass. The team found one of their own covered in gigantic ants, his poor body torn to pieces. Gawain managed to lop off the heads of a few of the Scissor Ants before the others turned on him. He was too late to save his friend but determined to kill as many of them as he could without being devoured himself.

The older members of the team used their firearms and managed to kill the remaining troop. And then a mile away, erupting from an ancient crater, they saw a colony of gigantic ants, thousands of them, pouring out of the earth like a pyroclastic flow toward their dismembered sentries. The Albion team managed to reach the shuttle and get back to the starship before the colony could overwhelm them. But during the trip back Gawain pounded every available object within the reach of his long arms cursing until his voice was hoarse.

The science team which had given them the all-clear to collect samples and had also given permission for the young science club to join the research team, soon discovered Andromeda 828 was a prison planet where their bitter enemy, the Aviangore, kept the Andromeda Galaxy's most vicious prisoners. Even when he was confined to his quarters, Gawain remained unapologetic when he attempted to sneak off the ship to find his friend. He told the captains he wanted to honor his friend by finding his body and bringing the body home. His loyalty was the best part of him. Yet she feared his obsessive nature would be his undoing.

Safe on the UES Albion, a team of scientists studied the Scissor Ants using powerful scopes. They soon uncovered a vast underground prison system beneath the crater. The captains refused to allow Albion crew to go down to the planet to free the prisoners. After a week studying the planet's inhabitants the scientists realized the Scissor Ants weren't native to 828. As history repeated itself for the second time in a century, the scientists watched in horror as the entire colony of Scissor Ants began to die off, dozens at a time.

Helpless to do anything, all the Albion crew could do was record the deaths of the Scissor Ants and the Aviangore prisoners. Until they reached the surface of 828, all Albion scientists could see were thermal images of the prisoners. Those images showed them prisoners who had been outside their prison cells digging new cells deeper beneath the crater. They saw a few prisoners attempting to free their fellow inmates.

Once most of the prisoners were free, they saw fights break out between different factions. Many died. Yet there were still thousands moving about underground. The prisoners appeared to be collectively gathering up supplies and figuring out a way of escaping the planet. Aviangore's return prompted terror, not only on 828, but among members of the UES Albion crew. Some members of Albion wanted to help the prisoners while others wanted to leave the solar system immediately. The captains reminded the crew that if they returned to the planet surface, they could cause another pandemic among the survivors.

Circumstances made the problem irrelevant as the Albion crew watched hundreds of the different species dressed in identical prison clothes climb out of the crater and over the decaying bodies of the Scissor Ants. The prisoners had survived the pandemic while the Scissor Ants succumbed. The prisoners, over the course of seven days managed to collect materials and technology left behind and built several ships. They escaped 828 before the Aviangore arrived.

The scientists agreed the digested remains of the poor kid's body consumed by the Scissor Ants had infected the colony with a deadly virus. Fearing the UES Albion had made another enemy, they left behind a series of orbiting stations disguised as meteorites. Several light years later, the information collected from the fake meteorites captured the frightening image of a spacecraft above 828. It was the size of a red giant and had been orbiting the planet for months collecting data. What surprised the scientists was the sight of Aviangore landing on the surface of the infected planet.

Many biologists were stumped as to how the prisoners had survived the virus while all the Scissor Ants died. Old data transmitted from Albion 1 confirmed 828 had been a barren planet. Obviously, Aviangore's scientists terraformed 828 as a place to maintain their gigantic prison population. They were, after all, Andromeda Galaxy's most aggressive species appointing themselves judge, jury, and executioners of the galaxy.

Once the fake meteorites transmitted video of the Aviangore's gigantic spacecraft and their crew as they descended to the planet's surface, Albion scientists watched as the Aviangore tossed the dead

Scissor Ants into huge piles and burned the bodies while others patrolled the skies for stray prisoners. Even though the Scissor Ants were the aggressors, the Aviangore would see this new pandemic as payback for the destruction of Albion 2 & 3. The Aviangore ship sent a beacon to the farthest regions of the galaxy and Albion's staff decoded the message as: *Destroyer Albion at large. Location 828 Andromeda Galaxy. Caution. Diseased. Deadly. Ransom offered.*

How could humans justify a second near extinction of an alien species, only this time a species who were not Aviangore? How had the virus spread to the rest of the colony when only a handful of Scissor Ants attacked the boy? Shard and other biologists continued to explore possibilities. They were still in the dark on how the transmission process occurred without bodily contact. Now humans had a new enemy as if the old enemy wasn't dangerous enough. What terrified Albion most was the speed with which Aviangore survivors discovered a cure for the human pandemic.

Aviangore ships must have traveled throughout the Andromeda Galaxy inoculating every species they met, or more likely, inoculated only their prisoners. Earlier versions of Albion starships, on first contact with Aviangore, barely survived because the Aviangore were so aggressive. That had been before the pandemic which nearly decimated the Aviangore's entire civilization. It didn't take the Aviangore long to hunt down and destroy Albion 2 & 3.

Now the Aviangore knew there were still humans in the galaxy. Based on their past behavior, it was only a matter of time before the Aviangore found Albion 4. Just as they did with 2 and 3, they would kill any species dumb enough to give humans shelter.

Belatedly, Shard realized Gawain had seized cursing and was leaning down to glare into her face. She heard him call her name, "Shard. Are you listening to me? Shellfargon to Shard. There you are. Now listen to me closely big sister. I am deeply concerned for a friend of mine living in this city. I have reliable information this person I care about very much is in grave danger. Promise me you'll come to me first with the news. Whatever you find out. I want to know first, before Hawk, before Swana. Promise me?"

Shard considered his words carefully. *I am deeply concerned for a friend of mine.* With dread, she realized her brother had entwined his loyalty and love with a Shellfargonite. His loyalty and love were intense, so intense nothing short of death would separate him from the object of his devotion. Now she had another problem to contend with among so many others. "Yes. I will come to you first. It should be jolly fun. We'll arrest the culprit together. Now go away and let me do my job."

Once she was sure Gawain had left the catacombs for good, Shard opened her leather case and extracted a few necessary items: her ultrasound wand, her frequency monitor, her skin, hair, blood, fingerprint analyzer, and a package of chocolate chip cookies. A glass of milk would have been nice. Regretting her shortsightedness, Shard set to work eliminating Gawain, Hawk, and herself from the scene of the crime, for she suspected this dark dank passageway had been the place where Star Bridgekeeper had died a slow agonizing death.

It was when she peeked behind an old door propped against the wall that she found a treasure trove of evidence just piled up against the weeping stones of the catacombs. The words sounded cool, she said them out loud, "The weeping stones of the catacombs." Ah ha. Ah ha. Then she bent down with her wand and illuminated the evidence in all its nasty dirty glory: hundreds of tiny scraps of cotton, several old magazines tied with a black shoelace, a rusty tin cup and a wrapper from a candy bar called ZoLo's Fancy chocolate.

Hawk and his knights had been sloppy. It was so obvious. Why had they ignored this spot?

Professor Honeysweet knocked on Lynora Reason's door. Joanie stood close behind him waiting anxiously. She was curious about the woman who lived in the apartment. All she had to go by was the woman's voice. The voice had sounded like a mature, well read and fun-loving person. When the door opened, and the owner of the balcony overlooking the alley stared at them in curious speculation, Joanie was pleased.

Lynora Reason's eyes sparkled with curiosity as she looked them over. Her mouth curved into a welcoming smile. Yes, intelligence and kindness, two qualities Joanie admired. Delan Reason had silver white hair cut stylishly short which accentuated her tapered chin. Her brown eyes examined them with friendly interest. She wore a cotton-blouse, tan-slacks and comfortable shoes. She appeared to be on her way out the door.

"We're sorry to bother you but we were wondering if you might have a moment to answer a few questions," Professor Honeysweet asked in his buttery sweet voice. "It's about the murder of the young girl last week?"

"Yes, I remember Star Bridgekeeper. So tragic. I knew her grandfather. Please come in. Would you care for something to drink?"

The apartment walls were made of New Dala plaster with little nooks and crannies where books and art were prominently displayed. The floors were tiled and the pictures on the walls were all landscapes. As Lynora Reason escorted them into her home trustingly turning her back on Professor Honeysweet and herself, Joanie felt compelled to say, "We seem to have interrupted you. Were you on your way out?"

Lynora brushed her word's aside, "That can wait. It's my book club. I can be a little late. Come in, come in. Have a seat. I have lemonade or coco if you're not a tea drinker."

"Just water for me," Joanie said glancing around the attractive kitchen with envy. It was bright, cheerful, cozy, and welcoming. The room reminded her of her own kitchen back before her husband had gone off to war. Lynora Reason appeared to prefer the romance of wrought iron furniture, New Dala plaster, and decorative tile. The heat outside barely penetrated the rooms. She could feel a cool fragrant breeze from one of the open windows.

Honeysweet got right to business before Lynora had time to set a glass of lemonade in front of him and a glass of water in front of Joanie, "We noticed your balcony overlooks the alley and wondered if you might have noticed anything on the day Star disappeared. Even the smallest detail might be of help."

Lynora looked up and then toward the Bojenlac doors. They waited. Joanie was relieved Lynora hadn't instantly dismissed their question. She seemed to be taking Honeysweet's question seriously, "Let's see. That was the day after I returned from my trip to New Dala. It was a long arduous journey on the wagon from the train station I can tell you. Hmm. Let's see now. I arrived in the early evening but that's not the day of Star's disappearance. What did I do the following day? Well. I know. Excuse me for a moment."

They watched as she left the room. Joanie glanced at Honeysweet who was in the act of sipping his lemonade. His face registered a smugness she didn't like. She wished she had his confidence in the outcome. Lynora Reason returned within a few minutes clutching a leather- bound book. She slipped her finger under the gold clasp and opened the book setting the book on the kitchen table in order to turn the pages. She paused on a certain page. Joanie noticed the book was an event calendar. With an unpainted fingernail, Lynora searched for the day when Star was abducted. In black ink, Lynora had written "Antonio's 11:30."

"I met a friend at Antonio's before lunch. In fact, I was sitting at a table near Star. My friend was late, so I did what I love to do – watch people. I overheard the argument between Star and that young woman, what's her name? Kimberly, yes, Kimberly Lemon. What

Dela Lemon said to the child hardly seemed controversial. I was surprised at Star's reaction. Anyway, Star blew up and left and then a man sat down and asked Dela Lemon a lot of impertinent questions. She seemed to take it well. Oh, yes, that was the same day that poor woman leaped off the rampart. How could I forget? So much tragedy in one day."

Honeysweet glanced at Joanie and Joanie answered his unspoken question with a name, "You remember Professor. Deletha Child died that day." It seemed crazy to have to remind him of such a tragic event. She'd heard what happened and still felt queasy at the thought of the young woman jumping off the castle rampart to escape the crazed man who wanted to kill her.

Honeysweet responded with his own take on the event, "Yes, it was a tragedy, awful, just awful, but what we're interested in was if you saw anything strange that night from your balcony."

How could he dismiss poor Deletha's death so callously? Was he feeling guilty he hadn't saved her or tried to stop her murderer? Maybe. He'd been quick to pick a fight with Gawain though. But that had been a fake fight. No courage required.

Joanie forced herself to concentrate on what Lynora was saying to Honeysweet, "I spent most of my afternoon in the apartment that day. It's my custom to go outside when the sun sets and sit on my rocker and listen to the bats flying about the turrets. Let me see. Let me see.

Wait.

I do recall hearing someone humming down below my balcony. It wasn't one of the dishwashers at Queenie's Diner. No. I know their voices. The tune he was humming was familiar. Oh, what was it? I know the tune. Come now. What? Yes. It goes – Oh, we'll rally round the rivers, rally round the rivers. For our beloved freedom – yes, how stupid. He was humming the anthem, The Battle of Two Rivers."

Joanie glanced at Honeysweet. He was nodding his head as if he knew the song. Joanie had no clue what they were talking about now. They seemed to have slid off topic. She made herself as invisible as the furniture and listened as Honeysweet exclaimed, "Unbelievable. What a coincidence! Annex Preparatory. What are the odds?"

Lynora Reason padded his hand affectionately and glanced at Joanie, "I attended the same preparatory school as Professor Honeysweet. It's our school song. The Battle of the Two Rivers commemorates Annex Preparatory history when the Lacertidae appeared on our shores for the first time. We were so young then, marching with our seniors and helping to push back the enemy. Even though we were inexperienced, we kept the enemy at bay long enough for a rescue."

The fact Joanie suspected Honeysweet wasn't all Delphinid made the knowledge of his attendance at Annex Preparatory school, an elite prep school for the rich and famous, absurdly serendipitous. She hoped his DNA proved to be more Lacertidae than Delphinid which would make his history at Annex Prep even more deliciously apropos. After years of service to the country, she'd lost a lot of respect for the antiquated institutions perpetuated by those eager to continue the NeverEnding War. Then she wondered if she'd heard Lynora Reason correctly.

"That was eighty years ago. You can't be that old?" Joanie asked in astonishment.

Lynora gasped holding back a chuckle, "Ah no. I wasn't at the battle."

"No," Joanie said feeling the heat rise from her neck to her cheeks. "Actually, I thought," then she quickly backtracked. "I thought you were younger than me."

"So," Honeysweet said to himself. "Someone was humming our school song in the alley the night Star went missing. I thought I heard you say, he, was singing?"

"A man, definitely a man. There have been hundreds of graduates from Annex Preparatory School," Lynora reminded him. "How will you be able to find the man?"

"You didn't see him?" Adam asked hopefully.

"No," Lynora admitted sadly, her honest face unable to hide her disappointment. "It was a moonless night."

"No lights in any of the shops?" Joanie asked.

"Yes. Dela Lemon's window was lit. I saw her draw the curtains around ten o'clock. And of course, Queenie's Diner had long since closed."

There was silence for so long Joanie felt compelled to break it, "Why are we concentrating on the evening? Star went missing long before dark. Her sister Sophia came into the Relic shop and asked if I'd seen Star."

Adam seemed preoccupied with catching the singer and ignored Joanie. He rose from his seat and said, "I think I know how to flush this murderer out. Well, Delan Reason you've been a real help. Thank you and please excuse us."

Joanie remained seated. Honeysweet's eyebrows shot up then he shrugged and made motions to leave. Lynora escorted him to the door. When she returned to the kitchen, she smiled in a friendly fashion and waited politely. "May I offer you some more tea?"

"No. Thank you. I just realized something. I think I know who might have seen Star last. Yet under no circumstances can I possibly ask the woman any questions. I'm going to have to tell Kimberly or her attorney. I had hoped I could have learned something more today."

"You've lost me, dear. What are you talking about?"

"You see I used to work at the For the Soul, Relics and Religious Treasures. Delan Paleone let me go yesterday. No warning. Nothing. Just get out now and be quick about it. It was far from pleasant. As I recall, she was the one who mentioned seeing Star the day of Star's disappearance. I wish I'd been paying more attention."

"Oh my, you poor thing," Lynora Reason said with a sympathetic smile. "It must have been extremely unpleasant. I've been an unfortunate witness to her tirades over the years."

"I'm surprised to hear you say that. I thought everyone in town loved her."

"Most intelligent people see through her fakery. She gives womanhood a bad name," Lynora said offering Joanie a fresh glass of water with ice included. "And there are plenty of us in this town who wish she would ride off into the sunset and find some other place to *improve*. I take it you need to find someone who will be willing to ask her the hard questions. I would be happy to help. My book club is big on murder mysteries and we'll be meeting tonight."

"I couldn't impose on you. You've been so kind."

"Nonsense. I'd be delighted. Maybe, while I'm questioning people, I might be able to find a potential roommate to share my apartment."

"Are you kidding?" Joanie asked in amazement, unable to believe her good luck.

"No. I'm not. Money is tight, and I refuse to give up my trips, so I've decided I need a roommate to help with expenses. I haven't advertised because I don't want strangers knocking on my door at all hours of the night and day. Since I'm rarely home, a roommate would be perfect. I like my privacy though. I don't know. Maybe I should think about this a bit more."

"Yes. I understand. I was living in the little garret above the Shellfargon Seed until Harry Hanson decided the garret would be better suited for his girlfriend. Dela Lemon has been kind enough to let me stay at the bookshop. But I'll need to find a place of my own soon. Since my husband died and my children are grown and gone, I've lived alone. I've grown used to living alone and quite like it. But circumstances require me to find a place toot-suite. I can't impose on

Dela Lemon much longer."

Lynora jumped up from her chair and threw her purse over her shoulder. Joanie took this gesture as a polite dismissal and embarrassed grabbed her hat and with a mumbled, "Thank you so much for your time," she rushed blindly for the front door, chastising herself for being a fool.

Before she had her hand on the knob, Lynora called out, "Hold on, Delan Fitzhammond. Do you have a second, please?" Joanie turned and found Lynora standing in the hall handing her a piece of paper. "Here is my card. Why don't we talk again tomorrow? I don't have anything scheduled until later in the afternoon. Let's get to know each other and see if this roommate thing might work. Would that suit you? We can meet for lunch at Antonio's say noonish?"

On the way back to the shop Joanie thought about how awful yesterday had been and how different thirty-three hours could be. She could see a crest on the horizon which might just push her toward success. Maybe the world wasn't so bad after all.

Shard Bristlecone found what she believed was the last piece of evidence. After spending the better part of the day collecting her evidence, she needed a hot bath, something rich and fattening to eat, and most critically, a long nap. But she had promised to call Shehili with news before nightfall. It was too late to leave by the cathedral entrance which meant she would have to make her way through Duke Tower plaza and hope to avoid Hawk's wrath.

She was lucky. She met no one on her way up the stairs or the courtyard or even the plaza. She noted how there was not a living soul around during this time of night. The knights were patrolling the ramparts or protecting the Governor, while the rest were having fun tormenting Mudflat Villagers. That meant by ten in the evening the bailey was virtually deserted. Perhaps the murderer knew the castle routine? Perhaps the murderer used this route to leave the secret passageway instead of the cathedral?

Before making her way to her motel room, Shard stopped in at the boutique to hand in her report to Shehili. Shehili accepted the document with a bleary eye and dismissive wave of her hand. At least Shard could sleep well knowing she had kept her promise. Some people just didn't appreciate dedication to duty. Big deal if Shehili had been busy entertaining a friend? They were on a mission and the mission took precedence over everything else. Although from the look of her, Shehili appeared to have had a nasty row with her male friend. Who else would she have had a fight with, Shard thought to herself, but the most exasperating man imaginable?

In her hotel room, by three in the morning, Shard had managed to puzzle the evidence into a recognizable form. With a pair of tweezers and a magnifying glass, she had spread the pieces of cotton out on the floor having first placed a plastic cloth on the floor to preserve her evidence. When she stepped back and looked at the finished product, she was dismayed. Had she made a fool of herself? Had Hawk left this evidence as a bad joke?

When she heard Hawk's voice on the other end of the transmission, she began talking without giving him a chance to stop her, "You left evidence for me to find, I'm assuming, because you didn't want the fools in the Tower to botch the investigation. Am I right? Say I'm right Hawk or I'll come over there and ring your neck." The chuckle on the other end of the line tickled her ear. The man was too sexy for his own good. She truly hated him, knowing full well, she was jealous of his hold over her brother.

"I have every confidence in you Bristlecone," he said before hanging up.

She sat on the edge of the motel bed for nearly twenty minutes going over the facts and finally concluding that not even Hawk could be so crude. She stared and stared at the evidence, appalled and astounded. The cotton scraps, when pieced together, assembled into only one thing, a dingy gray pair of men's underwear. The underwear seemed to leer at her.

E3 Shellfargon Year 5092 NDMP WK 5: UES Albion 4

Food delegated to Kimberly Lemon while under arrest tested as rat poison. Found box of rat poison in cafeteria under kitchen sink. Her death would have been extremely painful.

Forensic examination of garbage bin and clues found at scene of murder: particle test indicates child left in garbage bin one week and three hours to date. Fabric found on body is match for male cotton underwear discovered near garbage bin. Evidence suggests Star drugged and stuffed in garbage bin – death by asphyxiation. Sleeping potion used to drug child contains herbs found locally in Bitterroot Forest.

Star postmortem delayed until after trial upon orders of Governor Saurus. Awaiting UES Albion command: do I proceed with examination or obey native authority?

Chapter 9

Using the Bookworm counter as her buttress against the craziness around her, Kimberly Lemon watched Honeysweet pace the floor. On occasion, he would wave his hands in a theatrical manner as if summoning demons. His behavior reminded her of the last Coralian play she'd seen. The actor had played the part of the grief-stricken vengeance-seeking prince gone mad. Honeysweet had no such excuse. He spun on his heels, faced her and said, "Thus I put an advert in the Shellfargon Seed announcing a reunion of the Annex Preparatory Alumni. I'm hoping the true villain who murdered Star comes forth and all this foolishness will end at long last."

Before she could respond, he strode to the door. Thinking he was leaving, she managed a weak wave. Surprised by his return, she watched him carry in a picnic basket and a blanket draped over his arm. "Since you are under house-arrest, I thought I might bring the picnic to you. May I?"

With a shrug, Kimberly watched in amusement as Honeysweet dumped the items on the floor. It was only when he flipped her sign on the shop door to closed did she open her mouth to protest, thought better of it, and waited to see what he planned to do next. Why bother staying open when people only wanted to come and gawk at the murderess? The thought seared its way down her chest giving her a belly ache. Why did she care so much what her neighbors thought?

And why was this man interested in her? His affections had come on suddenly. They'd only met a few weeks ago and she'd spent most of that time in a dark damp dungeon. Last sweat season before the university opened, she'd met him at a party hosted by Crystova. During the party she recalled Honeysweet kept to himself spending most of his time adding food to his plate and flirting with a TA. Was her newfound notoriety the difference between "unassuming, uninspiring, nice girl" and "exciting, perhaps, dangerous bad girl"? Did she seem alluring to him now as opposed to a year ago because of her new-found notoriety?

Yuck.

His current behavior – was this something he did often? How exhausting. Maybe, he wasn't performing? Maybe, this was him. Teachers, after all, had to keep their student's attention and the best teachers were the best performers. They also had to have a lot of energy. She was getting tired just watching him. "Come on over here Kimberly and sit yourself down. I've brought a nice Camperneice and some cheddar chunks and a cucumber to cleanse the palate. The chocolate crackers are scrumptious. How about a little music to set the mood, ha? Where is your music box?"

"Broken," Kimberly admitted as she made her way toward the blanket spread out on her dusty floor.

"Ah ha," he said jumping up with an unnecessary flourish his wild chestnut locks bouncing, his lean tanned body taunt with suppressed excitement. She could see by his expression his mind working to solve the problem of music. "I know, I'll sing something from the Alberto, perhaps Dazinqa's Love Cry?"

"Oh no," Kimberly urged him making a point of grabbing his hand and squeezing the soft cool fingers. "Please, just come sit beside me and tell me all about the Alberto. What is it? A play? An opera? A musical? And who is Dazinqa?"

He obliged her and settled himself cross-legged on the blanket. She pretended to enjoy the cheddar chunks and listened to his lecture with what she hoped was the right amount of curiosity and interest. Soon she wasn't even pretending and discovered she'd missed a crucial part of her education – the experience of watching a fine teacher educate the audience using facts, fun, and verbal stream of consciousness. The performance delighted her. Fascinated, she watched as he debated key elements of opera and interrupted himself to provide her with back ground details which made her feel a part of the discussion.

According to her grandfather, college was expensive and time consuming and only for elitists. To him, history was a much better teacher. Reading old books and pamphlets brought the past into the present and taught a person how to avoid making the same mistakes those unfortunate ancestors had made long ago. She hated to contradict her grandfather, but her four years of college and lifetime of reading led her to the unhappy conclusion, people perpetuated the mistakes of the past because every generation turned out to be lazy and self-involved.

Unlike dating, it was refreshing not to have to come up with something interesting to say. As she munched on crackers and listened to the professor's thoughts on opera and love, she started to relax and at one point almost fell asleep. All she had to do was stuff her mouth with cheddar cheese chunks and chocolate crackers followed by quick sips of the funny tasting wine. Although she soon discovered her part consisted of occasionally nodding her head in encouragement. As she listened to his soothing voice, her body ached to lie down and go to sleep.

Maybe she could surreptitiously slide her body full length

onto the blanket, maybe with her elbow propping up her head and listen. In this position, she could look him in the eye with what she considered rapt attention. While he was deep into his talking points, she had the opportunity to rest her eyes. As if her mind had fooled her body, her eyes closed. A spoon clattering woke her. She opened her eyes and saw the spoon she had been holding lying near a porcelain plate. Embarrassed, she desperately tried to stay awake. Hell, this whole indoor picnic dating experience can't go on much longer.

To her dismay, she discovered that, yes indeed, the picnic could go on even longer. Just above Honeysweet's shoulder she could see a portion of the bay window and observe the morning light in all its sharp and shiny glory. It reminded her of champagne. Over the course of the picnic with Honeysweet's voice as background noise, she watched the champagne turn to chamomile tea and from chamomile tea to lemonade, and finally the dirty brown orange of a puddle of piss. Was she getting mad now?

The pounding on the Bookworm's shop door brought her fully awake. The sound effectively silenced Honeysweet. They both scrambled to their feet and Kimberly managed to get to the door first. Gawain Bristlecone peered inside with suspicion bordering on certainty. His disgust suggested they had been doing something criminal. The intensity of his stare might have bored holes through their foreheads if he had had such a power. Luckily for them, he didn't have the power to kill them with his eyes.

Kimberly was so relieved at the interruption she nearly wrapped her arms around Gawain's torso and gave him a big hug. And then she got mad. What did he think they were doing, plotting the overthrow of the government whilst lounging on a picnic blanket and consuming cheddar cheese chunks? "The Bookworm is closed Knight Bristlecone," Kimberly said doing her best to keep his large person safely on the street.

One big booted foot trespassed upon the threshold and with a charming smile and eyes alight he said, "I am here upon the orders of D.I. Hawk, Dela Lemon," and without ceremony he put his big hands on each side of her waist, picked her up as if she were a troublesome child and carried her over to the picnic area where he gently deposited her near the basket.

"I'll be speaking to the Governor about your conduct sir," Honeysweet said in a sharp tone Kimberly barely recognized. "How dare you treat a lady with such brutality. I seriously doubt your intentions are honorable. There is already a guard posted outside. Knight Graceland has been exemplary in his duties and there is no need for you to be here. This is obviously a ploy to pressure Dela Lemon into pleading guilty."

Gawain circled the blanket on the shop floor eyeing the basket of food, the crockery, the wine glasses, and the crumbs. "What have we here? A picnic I see. How quaint. How typical of your kind."

"Our kind? What do you mean by that comment?" Adam asked cocking his head to one side and narrowing his eyes suspiciously. "When people use the word, kind, it usually means, the other, as in someone who is different, foreign, unacceptable. What are you implying?"

The atmosphere changed dramatically. Adam, it seemed, had gone too far. Adam had all but called Gawain a racist. Yet if he had come right out and said such a thing, Gawain would have been within his rights to challenge the professor to a duel. Gawain circled the blanket his angry eyes warning Adam to tread carefully. Realizing how close he had come to doing himself a serious injury, Adam quickly collected his blanket and basket.

Kimberly helped him put away the dishes. He threw everything in the hamper. With a hastiness and awkwardness unlike his usual fluidity, Adam flipped the blanket this way and that and eventually managed to roll the colorful quilt into a fine mess under his arm. Without a word the professor swept out of the shop with his head held high.

"What do you see in that blowhard?" Gawain asked standing at the window watching the poor man march off into the sunset. Gawain had his legs spread wide as if he thought himself on the deck of a ship. Standing with his arms crossed and his handsome face sneering he watched Adam exchange words with Knight Graceland. Kimberly didn't like this side of Gawain. Doing her best to ignore his ill humor, she flipped the sign on the door to Open and returned to her post on the other side of the counter.

Her silence had been noticed. Gawain grimaced and made himself at home on her window seat with his back to Knight Graceland who finished writing down the professor's complaint in his notebook. Responding to the complaint, Graceland poked his head inside the shop and looked at Kimberly, "Everything okay here?"

Offended at the assumption Kimberly needed protection Gawain answered for her, "We're good here, Juleus. I'm here to take over. Hawk would like to see you and Lively in his office before the curfew."

With an unhappy frown Juleus nodded his head then peeked at Kimberly. In rapid succession, she blinked three times. The exchange between her and Juleus was so quick she didn't think

Gawain noticed. Kimberly had tried to reassure Juleus without tipping off Gawain. Juleus seemed to relax but before closing the door he said, "Goodnight folks. See you in the morning Kimmy." The door closed gently behind him and they watched as he moved past the window. When he tapped his earpiece and waved to someone on the rampart, Kimberly knew he was relaying Gawain's message to Lively via his com.

Alone in the shop with an angry alien Kimberly did her best to act as if she hadn't a care in the world. Gawain had his hands resting on his knees as he watched her face. With very little effort, he had managed to piss off the professor and Graceland. The knowledge tickled him. She waited for him to say something. Instead, he simply watched her as she fumbled about in search of a pen in the numerous compartments behind the counter. There must be a damned pen somewhere, she thought, suddenly scared.

Kimberly's body and emotions were a confusing paradoxical mess. Still sleepy her body longed to take a nap, yet, her brain feverishly replayed the last few hours. Honeysweet's nervous energy and funny stories had distracted her from her present troubles but peace and quiet was what she really craved. It was unsettling to have two men pretend to fight over her when she sensed neither one of them was sincere.

"I saw you nodding off on that blanket. Admit it Kimberly, you were asleep, and I saved the day," Gawain said with a cheeky smile.

Kimberly found a pen in one of the smaller drawers and with relief began to work on her accounting books. It was a depressing job especially now with no money coming in.

"Honeysweet didn't even know you were in the room," Gawain continued. "I saw the tableau – the two of you on the blanket, the professor waving his arms and lecturing and you sprawled on your side resting your head on your arm, your eyes fighting to stay open. The guy is a pontificating nincompoop."

Kimberly ignored him and looked in amazement at the accounting books Joanie had revamped. Her notoriety as a murderess seemed to have brought in new business. While she'd been a prisoner in the bowels of the earth, locals and tourists had come into the shop to buy souvenirs.

"I know people Dela Lemon," Gawain followed up his earlier remark. "It's my job to size up people, to see their potential threat or value. I've studied Professor Adam Honeysweet closely and, in my opinion, he exhibits many of the traits of a narcissistic opportunist. Do you know anything about narcissism?"

Kimberly had no illusions as to the buyers' intentions,

obviously they'd come in to shop and take "mementos" ghoulishly delighting in showing them off after she died by hanging. Perhaps they even thought they might sell them on eBlueglennen and make a handsome profit. Whatever the reason for the uptick in profit, she now had more money this quarter than she had had the entire year. If she is found guilty, what will money matter to her when her dead body is wrapped in a sheet and she is thrown into the abyss?

Strong hands spun her around. Her shoes left the floor as her body was lifted several feet off the ground. She was crushed to Gawain's tight muscular manly chest. Gawain held her dangling in midair with his nose touching her nose. She smelled his sweet breath and his cologne – an orange and honey sort of smell – and he said, "Why are you ignoring me? I've been trying to talk to you. Please listen. Don't be scared. I'm not here to hurt you. I thought we had something going on. I've never been mistaken about these things."

She must look a fool dangling in his arms with her mouth open wide. She couldn't think. He was holding her so tight she could barely breathe. He was going to break her heart, she just knew it.

"May I kiss you?" he asked.

How sweet.

How polite.

Why not?

Just one.

He moved in with studied determination.

Her brain went ballistic firing off electrical currents which coursed through her body like lightning. The room rocked back and forth. If Gawain hadn't held her, she might have slid through his arms in a puddle of delight at his feet.

A voice shouted, "Captain Bristlecone, what do you think you're doing?"

When her butt hit the floor and the pain shot up her spine, she realized she really had fallen, or more accurately, she'd been released from Bristlecone's embrace and dropped to the floor like a sack of potatoes. Gawain stepped back. Her first reaction was a searing disappointment. You see, she said to herself, you see, how even Bristlecone can be shamed.

She made herself stand up. Ignoring the other person in the room, she brushed herself off and looked Gawain in the eye. It was a long way up and her neck hurt as she threw back her head to look into his eyes. He looked angry and embarrassed and something else. Before she could identify Bristlecone's reaction, he turned to address the man in the room. Kimberly already knew who the interloper was, she'd recognized his smooth baritone straightaway.

After having been interrogated by the man, she'd become all too familiar with D.I. Hawk's voice. He tended to enunciate every Curleconese syllable which should have made him sound ridiculous but did nothing of the sort. Oddly enough, no matter what Hawk said, even if he was just reciting the weather channel, his voice sounded sexy. Gawain was gorgeous and sexy but couldn't out sexy Hawk.

Bristlecone vibrated with fury as D.I. Hawk grabbed his arm and ushered him to the opposite end of the room for a private dressing down. She forced herself to push her stool close to the counter and add up yesterday's receipts. She had to reread the receipt in front of her at least five times before her body gradually calmed down. And only when the two men left the shop, did she feel secure enough to break down and have a good cry.

As Gawain walked beside Hawk down Merchants' Row, he shoved aside his personal feelings. Hawk looked scared. Hawk had never looked scared in his entire life. "Come with me. We don't have much time." Hawk didn't speak as they weaved their way through the press of people drinking wine and eating supper in the plaza. It took a few more minutes to reach Duke Tower. Only when they were inside the Sheriff's Office in the evidence room did Hawk speak. "Bring it out Graceland."

Graceland stepped out from behind a metal shelf holding a box away from his chest as if it might bite him. Gawain's heart began to race. "When I came in to put some evidence back in its box, I heard ticking. I followed the sound and opened the evidence box to find this inside. I recognized it immediately. It's Kimberly's jewelry box. Ever since she was a little girl, she's kept her most valuable possessions inside. Her grandfather carved the box out of Bitterroot wood."

In the time it had taken Graceland to explain the situation to Gawain, everyone in the room had built up enough tension and sweat to create their own sauna. "I'll take it," Gawain told Hawk thinking only of Kimberly and what might happen to her if the bomb went off inside the bailey. "I'll take it straight out the door and out of the castle. I'll take it as far away as possible. Far, far from Blueglennen."

"There is no time," Hawk said between clenched teeth. "I've sent for help."

"How long do we have?" Graceland asked sweat pouring down his forehead.

"Not long," Hawk reassured him. "You heard the box ticking

ten minutes ago. We have time. Deputies have been coming in and out of this room all day. Others would have heard the ticking long before this. We have time. Ah, here she is."

Gawain looked over his shoulder as his sister Shard walked into the room carrying her briefcase. His stomach lurched. No. Not Shard. Her eyes were gleaming with excitement as she took in the sight of the box and Graceland's perspiration. From far away he heard Hawk's voice.

"Watch the door, Gawain. That's an order. You want to start a panic?"

"I need all the vests you can find, helmets for us all, and a block of ice," Shard ordered as she began to punch the keypad on her suitcase. Gawain didn't want to leave her. Hawk glanced over his shoulder and nodded his head reassuringly. With dread pressing down on him, Gawain left the evidence locker and went in search of supplies. Most of the deputies were gone for the day. There was only a skeleton crew tonight. Everyone had assignments outside the castle in preparation for the coming trial.

"You think we're going to survive this?" Graceland asked in astonishment. Even though he sounded terrified he remained calm and held the box steadily in his hands. Encouraged by Graceland's demeanor Gawain hurried out of the evidence locker. He bumped into Lively. Lively held onto his shoulders and said, "How's Juleus? What's going on in there?"

"You know?" Gawain asked as he shoved the big guy aside and started down the steps to the kitchen.

"I was in the evidence room when Juleus found the box. He told me to find Hawk and only Hawk and not to use my com. So, I found Hawk and he ordered me to leave the room and keep people out of the evidence locker. Then I got a call from dispatch. They said I was needed in the village, some sort of riot. I went down as far as Wolf pub and realized there was no fucking riot. I came straight back here. Where are we going?"

"Shard needs a block of ice. You can get the vests. Go on, go back upstairs and get the vests. I'll be along." He discovered when he reached the basement that the kitchen staff had left for the evening. As he loaded a block of ice onto a trolley, he realized the Governor was also outside the castle on personal business.

This month, Lynora Reason's book club chose to meet at the

pub. Since Sylvia Paleone had chosen the book, she sat at the head of the table and presided over the discussion. Since she'd been out of town, Lynora Reason had had only a day and a half to finish the book. If only the book had been a nice mystery or a bit of racy fiction.

Oh no. That would have been too pedestrian for Sylvia.

Instead, the book turned out to be a long boring history of the founding of the Church of the Holy Centipede and the life of the first Mark Little, the current Bishop Little's grandfather. Lynora suspected Sylvia had never read the book herself, that her office manager had probably been assigned to read it and summarize the high points. Last night, Lynora struggled through the remaining pages having made notes before her trip to help her remember what she'd already read. To make matters worse, the writer seemed to relish the horrifying punishments nonbelievers would experience once they died.

The wrath of the Holy Centipede included lots of dismemberment and disemboweling.

When her turn arrived to discuss the book, she realized belatedly she had no realistic segue for inserting Star into the discussion. She made her excuses first, "I'm so sorry I can't really give you a considered opinion. As you know, I've been away in New Dala for the last two weeks. I did spend a week before the trip reading the history of the church and made a few notes and have a few questions for Sylvia."

Lynora looked down the table at Sylvia who paused in her whispered conference with Mary McGirdle to acknowledge Lynora. Lynora continued, "If Sylvia wouldn't mind answering some of my questions, I would be grateful. I will have to be honest and say, I had trouble with the timeline. I know the first Bishop Little had his revelation in 5023 before he became a bishop. Yet, the writer mentions Little discussing the purchase of the cathedral a year before. I mean when the cathedral was known as the Church of the Holy Delph. Perhaps the date is a typo? What do you think, Sylvia?"

Lynora could hear Sylvia say to Mary, "I had to. I know it's close to the holidays and you'll be pressed to keep up, but I had to and it's no big deal."

Since Sylvia Paleone continued to ignore Lynora, Poppy Long made motions as if she planned to speak. Afraid she would lose her advantage, Lynora spoke over Poppy and almost shouted the words, "You know dates and times are a funny thing. Time can speed up or slow down depending on how you feel. I'm ever so grateful for my pocket calendar.

It has saved me many times, reminding me of upcoming

events and helping me to recall what I'd been doing just the day before. Why just a week ago, I remember writing down in my calendar how sooty and awful the train trip home had been, and how the smelly wagon nearly threw me onto the muddy road. It was a good reminder to find another way home from the light rail. Don't you agree? That trip seemed to take months. But it was only a day long.

And then to learn after I arrived home about poor Star Bridgekeeper the way I did. It was during lunch with a friend. When she told me, time seemed to stop in its tracks. Then my friend told me she'd seen Star go into your shop Sylvia. So, you must have been the last person to see Star alive?"

Sylvia and Mary stopped talking and turned to look at her with blank faces. Sylvia might have frowned if she could but because of several operations on her face, she had difficulty frowning. Only her jaw gave away her fury, "Your friend is mistaken. Star never came into my shop."

"Oh, but it wasn't just my friend who saw Star. There were several other people on the street. You see they didn't know about the quarrel between Dela Lemon and Star, not until after Harry Hanson put it in the paper. Then they remembered seeing Star go into your shop. And they were outside chatting and never saw her come out. One of them told me she'd asked a knight if he'd seen Star. He said he'd seen the two of you enter the cathedral together."

"Well," Sylvia began looking confused as everyone waited for her answer. She glanced at her hands then at Mary who was furiously scribbling something on her notepad as if her life depended on getting her words right. Perhaps it did? Sylvia didn't even bother to pretend she wasn't reading Mary's script. "I never saw Star come into the shop because I wasn't at the shop the day Star went missing. I was in the village shopping for a new pair of shoes."

"Wow. I guess you don't need a pocket calendar or fancy calendar app on your cellphone, hum Sylvia? You've got your own stenographer and secretary who remembers everything you've ever done in minute detail," Lynora exclaimed eyeing Mary McGirdle with what she hoped passed for an admiring smile.

Poppy Long, nearly bursting a vocal cord interrupted, "One of those eyewitnesses was my little cousin Angelina Schipperke. She works at Antonio's Café. She's a student at the university studying dress design. She saw Star going into the Relic. You see Angelina was on a break talking with Queenie and Alexandra while the two had a quick smoke. My Angelina doesn't smoke."

"Why in the dang blazes would your cousin remember that? Star comes into the Relic every day, why would she remember something so specific, especially on the day Star disappeared? Sounds like somebody wants five minutes of fame," Mary McGirdle said.

Poppy sucked in her breath holding back her outrage. Lynora had noticed before how Mary's accent got more pronounced when she was upset. Lynora wondered why Mary McGirdle was so vehemently defending Sylvia Paleone. Maybe Mary knew something incriminating and was afraid she'd lose her job if she said anything. Lynora tried not to show how upset she felt. Would her book club friend let a murderer avoid justice just to keep her job?

It didn't take long for the book club to break up. Once Poppy started throwing her belongings in her bag, others began to slam down their beverages and look for their coats and books. Lynora could feel the heat radiating off the two seated at the opposite end of the table. She was glad she had the long table between her and the two women or she'd have been scorched.

An hour later, Shard replaced all her tools in her briefcase and shut the lid. Gawain helped her with the straps on her vest. Graceland had left the room several minutes ago. He was on his way to Greenburg Valley to see his mother. Before he even had his vest off, he called his mother and told her he loved her and would be home soon. Hawk had cautioned him not to say anything about the events of this night to anyone, not even his mother. Graceland's parting words made Gawain smile, "All I could think about this entire time was going home and giving my mom a big kiss. And I used to think the academy was a nightmare!"

With Lively's help Gawain was able to put the vests and the trolley back without anyone noticing. Why would they? The nightshift duty officer barely acknowledged their existence, much less their reason for being in the Department of Justice's office for so long. He'd glanced once at Gawain and Lively with dead tired eyes and then back to his book.

"You know that guy?" Gawain asked Lively.

"Hell yes. He's drunk most of the time. It looks like he'd had a few too many before his shift started. I don't know why they don't just retire the old fool."

"I think that's what his boss tried to do tonight," Gawain replied in a grim voice.

"Boss, huh? It just doesn't have the same punch as rake."

"Rake means something totally different to humans. If we don't like our boss, we call them buttholes."

"What's a butthole."

"One of these days I'll tell you. Right now, I'm toast."

"What's toast?"

"Lively, don't you have a wife and kids waiting for you at home?"

"I sure do. It takes a night like tonight to make me appreciate what I've got."

Honeysweet and Lynora Reason sat at a table facing the modest entrance to one of the smaller university banquet rooms. Reason had spent all morning shopping for appetizers and bottled water. Honeysweet had paid his housekeeper to clean and decorate the banquet room. As the two sat at a table guaranteed to provide the best viewing, they pretended to sip their water and munch on appetizers while surreptitiously watching the entrance. They were hoping to see the prime suspect enter any minute now.

The last few hours had been frantic. Honeysweet assumed only the murderer would respond to his advertisement in the Shellfargon Seed. Lynora thought otherwise. She'd been in Blueglennen long enough to bump into alumni like herself many times. Would there be enough room to fit them all? The banquet room they'd chosen was the smallest and cheapest, ideal because it was far from the grand staircase. If the suspect tried to run, he or she would be intercepted in the lobby. She relaxed figuring only a few people would have seen the advertisement. They would be lucky if five people showed up.

Who would have guessed Governor Roger Saurus was an alumnus of Annex Prep? As he entered, Honeysweet and Reason turned to each other in astonishment. The sight of Tim Finstickel surprised Lynora the most and alarmed Adam. Growing concerned Adam watched in dismay as Finstickel made a beeline to the appetizers. It didn't take him long to shovel the food into his mouth as if he hadn't eaten in days. Which he probably hadn't. I bet he isn't even an alumnus, Lynora thought. He probably heard there was free food and came running. Honeysweet jumped up from his chair concerned there would be nothing left.

"Delo Finstickel, I'm Adam Honeysweet and I'm hosting this event," Adam began.

Finstickel ignored him and continued to stuff cream puffs into his mouth. A thin trickle of cream dribbled down the man's chin. In disgust, Adam grabbed Finstickel's right arm to prevent him from reaching for another pastry. "Are you an alumni sir?" he hissed in the smelly creature's dirty ear. The two of them were about the same height six-feet two-inches tall. For one second their eyes met. The creepy crawly slithered up Adam's spine lodging in the base of his neck.

Frozen in combat, the two men eyed each other. Adam realized Finstickel was a loony tune. The muscles in Finstickel's arm tightened. Finstickel pushed. It was no contest since Finstickel had nothing to lose and Adam still wrapped in the mantle of gentleman scholar had to let go to avoid making a scene. When he realized people were watching, he stepped back. The space between them wasn't far enough in Honeysweet's estimation. Finstickel didn't seem to mind. Honeysweet refused to turn his back on the appetizers.

The governor's personal bodyguard surrounded Finstickel. Adam sensing someone behind him turned around to see who had entered the banquet room. The Governor was dressed in riding boots, riding breeches, a buff colored coat and a black felt hat. The boots gave him the illusion of being two-inches taller. Honeysweet had never been this close to the Governor, not even when he was invited to private parties in the penthouse.

Being so close to the Governor was disturbing. He could see every pore on the man's face. The man's skin looked pale and sickly and the folds under his eyes were stretched so thin they were practically drippling down his cheeks. That was what happened to older Delphinids. As Delphinids aged the folds around their eyes tended to lose elasticity every year. The Governor's pupils looked enormous. What was the matter with the man? He must be spending too much time inside in the dark hiding from the public. Or maybe he was just drunk.

"Governor Saurus," Adam began and stopped unable to think of anything else to say. Adam had only been speechless a few times in his life. He didn't want to revisit those embarrassing days of his youth, not now, not here. He blamed Finstickel's craziness for his present inability to speak. Right about now, Adam would so enjoy throttling the idiot with his bare hands, maybe, if he shook him enough, he'd shake some sanity back into his feeble brain. How dare he make a mockery of the AP.

"So, you're an alum of the old Prep, eh?" Governor Saurus began. "I'm surprised sir. Thought you attended Protest Hill."

Adam pretended to ignore the scuffling sounds and grunts

behind him and did his best to concentrate on the Governor's words. He chuckled at the governor's attempted humor, "No. My family has been attending Annex Prep since its founding."

"Unhand that man sir," someone ordered in a deep voice which echoed down the hall. Everyone in the room turned to watch as Bertram Jones of Manning, Manning, Manning, and Jones Law entered the room accompanied by a young woman. "What is the meaning of this? Is this the way you treat your guests, Professor Honeysweet?"

"He had no hand in the matter," Governor Saurus stated. "It's obvious Finstickel's here to feed his face."

The defender's partner a petite dark-haired woman wearing black-rimmed eye glasses scanned the room with interest. Her brown eyes were twinkling as Bertram Jones introduced her to the occupants, "My partner, Mercedes Hepplewhite, Governor Saurus."

Everyone watched as the governor's personal bodyguard, each with a hand under his armpit lifted Finstickel a few inches off the ground and with resigned expressions carried him out of the room like so much garbage. Finstickel's aroma lingered long after he'd left. Lynora Reason and Mercedes Hepplewhite exchanged glances. Lynora's relief dissolved as she realized no one was immune from the Governor's autocratic and impulsive behavior. As far as he knew, Finstickel had been invited to the alumni party. But that didn't matter to the Governor, only his sensibilities were important. So Finstickel must go.

Finstickel made no sound as he was forcibly thrown out.

Bertram Jones' new partner, Mercedes Hepplewhite, stepped out of the room to watch as Finstickel was escorted down the hall. She remained watching until the trio descended the steps to the first floor. When she returned to the banquet room, some of the alumni wondered if she might be Bertram's niece. To them, she looked too young to be a partner, yet, she carried herself with such confidence and composure, she might have been any age. When Bertram Jones introduced her as Mercedes Hepplewhite, the youngest judge in Curl history, only thirty years of age, then boasted to Lynora and Honeysweet that Mercedes offered to help him with a tricky case during her vacation, Lynora wasn't surprised.

Mercedes spent the rest of the reunion attached to her uncle's entourage. Her family and Bertram Jones' family had been in law for generations. Would Bertram's family have had anything to do with Star's death? Why? What would they have gained? Nothing. Lynora glanced at the table where the Darknight family were seated wondering if they had had something to do with Star's death. Frank

Darknight had accompanied his parents, Arthur and Eleanor Darknight, to the reunion. Which one of them was an alumnus? While Adam Honeysweet sucked up to the Governor, Lynora made her way to the table by the window.

"Hello Eleanor. It's so good of you to come to the reunion. I had no idea you were an AP alum," Lynora began.

Frank interrupted her, "We all are. Grandpa and Grandma met at the AP and married after they graduated. The only person in the family who didn't attend was my mother. Before he died Dad taught at AP and Mom graduated from Duke Tower U."

"Frank recently graduated from AP and he's been offered several scholarships to many of the leading universities," Arthur Darknight announced proudly. "If Ellie hadn't fallen and broken her hip, Frank would be attending Bismarck at this very moment."

"Not exactly Grandpa," Frank corrected him in a firm but gentle voice. "I haven't decided where I'll study. Bismarck is a long way away."

"It's in New Enreich. Close to the seat of power, close to the Delphadorturo and Crest Hall," Arthur argued. "That's where you can make your mark in the world, my boy."

"Leave him be, Arty," Eleanor Darknight said playfully. It was obvious where Frank Darknight inherited his gorgeous physical presence and movie star good looks. Eleanor Darknight had once been a model. Even at eighty, her blue eyes were mesmerizing. Why had the Darknights settled for a small insignificant grocery? They could have gone into finance or law.

Arty must have seen her confusion because he said, "We've spent most of our lives traveling, learning new languages, studying foreign cultures. We had an import/export business and a few years ago sold it to come live in Blueglennen. Perhaps you've heard of us? We're known around the world as-"

Frank interrupted him, "Come on, grandpa, let's find some food before it's all gone. Grandma looks hungry."

Lynora watched as Frank ushered his grandparents to a table laden with food and filled their plates. She didn't remember ordering shrimp or salmon. She remembered asking for sparkling water but not in crystal goblets. Where had the goblets come from? And the purified water? And those fancy cakes and expensive fish eggs? She soon discovered where the fancy food and fancy goblets originated when waitstaff from Antonio's café wearing crisp white shirts restocked the platters from hot plates left in the hall. Maybe the Governor thought the simple reunion needed some sprucing up.

As she mingled and met each new alumnus, Lynora chanced

to hear Antonio Furness boast the reunion had been his idea. Professor Honeysweet didn't seem to mind. At least now she could move about the room pretending to be a guest instead of worrying about how much it would cost to restock the bottled water or buy more cream puffs. Acting as host, Antonio with his familiar long brown hair tied back chose to wear his signature tight blue jeans, expensive cotton shirt under a designer jacket. She was damned sure he wasn't an alumnus. For a few minutes she watched him greet new arrivals as if he'd always been the host. Resigned, Honeysweet popped a delicious chocolate torte into his mouth.

Honeysweet's contributions to the reunion were melting in the hot stuffy room. While the guests ignored the sorry looking cream puffs, Lynora circulated. At one point, Lynora met Joanie Fitzhammond near a window looking out on the Royal Plaza. She was surprised and delighted to see her, "I had no idea you were an alumnus," Lynora said. "What year?"

"You dare ask," Joanie said with a mischievous light in her eye and promptly began to lie with a straight face. "Yes, I guess I'm long past caring about my age. I'm a 5046 graduate. And you?"

"5042," Lynora laughed. "We just missed each other. And your concentration?"

"International Languages and Gross Anatomy of the Lacertidae," Joanie offered. That part was true anyway, but she had attended Passquall Institute of Medicine and International Languages not Annex Preparatory. Before attending the reunion, Joanie had researched the curriculums offered at both universities.

"A double major. I'm impressed."

"And you?"

"Primary Ed Form Eleven through Sixteen."

"You were a teacher!"

"Does that surprise you?"

"You seem too cosmopolitan."

"I taught one-twelves for twenty years."

"You deserve a metal," Joanie exclaimed. Their laughter attracted the attention of Alexandra. Dela Montague appeared at Joanie's elbow and Joanie stepped back to make room for her. Joanie had only met Kimberly Lemon's friend once. She'd formed a good opinion of the self-assured young woman.

With her signature wry smile Alexandra said, "I couldn't help but overhear your discussion. You mentioned studying Gross Anatomy. I was surprised, since I understand you have many excellent clerical and management skills Kimberly tells me."

Joanie was angry with herself. Why had she mentioned Gross

Anatomy? It must be because Lynora had asked her to move in and share her apartment. The woman had a real talent for putting people at ease. Joanie had had a talent once-upon-a-time. She'd been good at getting secrets out of enemy soldiers. At least she been good at her job, back in the day, when she had been brainwashed and determined to show her superiors her interrogation techniques. That had been a life time ago, twenty years. She was no longer an interrogator. She would never go back. She would kill herself first.

Her clearances had been revoked, her career ended, her marriage an empty husk, but once she faced what she had become, she knew she couldn't continue any longer as chief interrogator and intelligence officer for Inner Security Guards (ISG). Only her husband's decision to reenlist saved her from accusations of disloyalty. There were a few who accused her of being a Lacertidae mole. The tests proved she wasn't. Yet she was no longer trusted, and she knew too much. They could have killed her, but they didn't. Instead every avenue of employment dried up and she was forced to leave the capital. The company made sure she had no way of supporting herself anywhere on the east coast. She traveled west to find work using her sister-in-law as a base.

Joanie's lack of response prompted Lynora to jump in and say, "What a lovely necklace? Where did you get it?"

Alexandra fingered the cube dangling from a delicate silver chain around her neck. It was a beautiful piece of workmanship. Joanie realized the silver sculpture had been fashioned into the image of a tiny sea creature, a Hummer. They were such ethereal creatures, so soft and gentle, so kind. Ridiculous. She had no idea if they were kind. She didn't speak Hummerese. Her good humor restored she glanced up at the tall thin quiet woman. She was so pale and sad. What was she doing in Blueglennen? She belonged in a chateau.

"It was a present from my mother."

"It's lovely," Lynora said.

Joanie jumped in, "I once possessed a sea serpent. Not a real sea serpent. Where would I put him? But a fossilized bit of slate which had the imprint of a long dead ancestor of the current sea serpents. Three hundred million years ago, sea serpents were only the size of my eye. It was so small and delicate. The baby serpent lay on its side. Its eye closed. Sleeping for eternity."

There was silence for a few minutes as each of the women thought about the enormity of time.

"Call me Alex," Alexandra said with a secret smile.

For the next half hour, the three women discussed fashion and avoided politics and the murder of Star Bridgekeeper. Lynora watched Alexandra and Joanie and eventually decided the women couldn't possibly have had anything to do with Star's death. They didn't look strong enough to lift Star into a garbage bin. They certainly couldn't have dragged the trash bin into the catacombs without being noticed or hold her down while they wrapped the bin in chains. Besides, the person she'd heard humming the AP Anthem had been male.

Reluctantly, she forced herself to circulate the room searching for the prime suspect. When she spotted the New Enreich Accuser Phil Potts talking to Harry Zany she realized this was her opportunity to eliminate two of them. Phil Potts was a gigantic man with the biggest belly she'd ever seen. He was holding onto a crystal goblet filled with sparkling water. On the table next to him was a full plate of delicacies which he ignored. When she got closer, he looked her over with clinical detachment assessing her usefulness. She must have had a similar expression. He looked away, his bored expression dismissing her. Lynora ignored his rudeness. He thought she wasn't important enough to know. His loss.

Harry Zany oblivious to the exchange between Lynora and Phil Potts moved to make room for Lynora. From the moment Lynora and Phil Potts met, they both agreed to dislike each other. It wasn't Lynora's finest hour. She preferred to make friends wherever she could. But Phil Potts didn't need friends it seemed. Her determination to stay and talk seemed to annoy him a great deal. Her assumption she could come up and talk to them without their permission infuriated him most of all. Before he could put her in her place, Zany invited her into the conversation.

"Hello there, neighbor," Harry Zany said in his friendly fashion recognizing his best customer. "Haven't seen you in the shop for ages."

"Hi Harry. Yes, I've been traveling. Just got back a week ago."

"That's eight days in town and not in my shop going through my special collection of old folk songs," Harry teased her. "Don't you want to contribute to the Make Zany a Rich Man fund?"

"Yes, Harry that's my goal in life – to make you a rich man. So. You're an alumnus of the Annex Prep. It's good to," Lynora began.

"Harry," Phil Potts said talking over them. "I must caution you about this alliance with Merchants' Row. I don't recommend it. Your reputation and future here in the city are at risk. I strongly urge you to cancel your membership and ask for your money back."

"If you can promise the Centipede's rezoning plans die a nasty painful agonizing death with every citizen privy to the carnage, I just might. Can you promise me that?"

Phil Potts gave him the fish eye. Lynora was disappointed when Zany looked away first. What hold did this nasty man have over poor old Harry?

"I'm disappointed in you Harry."

Only when Phil Potts walked away did she hear Harry whisper under his breath, "That goes both ways buddy boy."

Before Lynora could find an excuse to slip away, Harry tried to apologize for his friend's behavior, "Potts and I attended the AP together. We were roommates. Hard to break those ties."

"Really?" Lynora said. "And when you end up without a home will you still be his friend?"

The last person to enter the room created the most stir. Sylvia Paleone must have planned her entrance with maximum heat. Every male in the room turned to watch as she cat-walked her way through the doors. She was wearing an expensive tight-fitting business skirt and jacket with her hair beautifully coiffed and her makeup as fresh as if she had just applied it. Form without substance Joanie thought with a mental sneer hoping the expression had not carved itself into her face. She looked around the room studying the reactions to Sylvia Paleone's grand entrance.

Mercedes Hepplewhite looked as if she'd just heard a funny joke.

Alexandra Montegue turned her back on Paleone and looked down at the plaza, more interested in the view. Lynora recalled that the windows looked out upon Antonio's Café. With the sun shining, there must be quite a few people moving about down below. Luella Morrison was practically humping Paleone's leg in her eagerness to get close to the unofficial celebrity. What was her claim to fame, Joanie wondered? Her husband had bought the shop, so she could hire other women to manage it. She'd never written anything worth reading or created anything worth buying.

All her religious artifacts were designed, crafted, and distributed by others – those others being the poor in foreign countries exploited by greedy entrepreneurs. Children as young as eight worked in her sweat shops churning out her cheap religious relics. And here she was, Delan Paleone, the shark hunter mother of morons floating into the room with her imaginary centipede-wings pretending to be a saint. Her stupidity, greed and hypocrisy made Joanie's head ache. The woman didn't even have the mental dexterity to realize her gender and her conservative philosophies were a badly staged piece of ironic bullshit.

As dumb as a mud rug, Honeysweet thought, even though he had trouble looking away from her legs. Both Joanie and Adam shared the same opinion – little did they realize. Sylvia Paleone annoyed Joanie with her roll back feminist ideas. Yes, she had charisma but so does a snake before the snake strikes. All three: Joanie, Lynora and Adam wondered if Sylvia had killed Star. Maybe she killed Star out of jealousy. Star was the prettiest female in the bailey.

Adam tried to imagine Paleone dragging a trash bin through a dark alley and down into the secret passageway. Would she bother? Maybe she'd killed her and had her husband dispose of the body. And to cement her name in the list of suspects Sylvia Paleone announced to no one in particular, "Sorry to crash the party. I'm not an alumnus or whatever you call it from that fancy school back east. I'm here to see the Governor. We have an upcoming ball to arrange."

Adam shouted out since he was the real host, "How about your husband? Was he an alumnus of Annex Prep?"

"No. He went to business school on Walrat Island," she said with a toss of her long hair as she looked Adam up and down suggestively. When she started playing with a strand of her hair, Joanie thought she might retch. Lucky Adam, Antonio stepped in to take charge of Sylvia. Without having to say a word Joanie, Lynora, and Adam communicated their disappointment when they heard her mention Walrat Island. Obviously, they could scratch Sylvia Paleone off the list of suspects. Their attempt to discover the identity of the singer among the alumni had been a failure.

Joanie Fitzhammmond left the banquet soon after Sylvia Paleone's entrance. At least she'd had a few pleasant hours before the silly wench showed up. Paleone had been furious to see Joanie in the room. Joanie might have stayed just to spite her. But she worried Mary McGirdle might arrive as part of Paleone's entourage and Mary knew very well that Joanie had never attended Annex Prep. It had been fun talking to Alexandra and Lynora. She'd even gotten excited about sleuthing just like in the old days. Unconsciously, she hummed the anthem of the Battle of Two Rivers under her breath as she descended the stairs and paused when she remembered the murderer had been humming the tune the night Star went missing.

Before attending the banquet, she searched for the song on the Internet and practiced singing the lyrics until she knew the words by heart. Her photographic memory had always served her well. Then she slipped off her disguise and retrieved Joanie Fitzhammmond.

Sometimes her gift for blending in made her nervous. For most of the afternoon she'd played the part of an AP alumnus. Her training kicked in the moment she entered the room while the real Joanie observed, recorded and stored her impressions of the guests.

In the lobby of the university's convention center, Joanie spied Shehili Swana and Kimberly Lemon below the grand staircase deep in conversation. Joanie thought she might be able to slip by without being noticed. Dela Lemon had excused Joanie from work today to allow Joanie time to move her belongings into Lynora Reason's loft. What Kimberly didn't know was how little Joanie had to move. Joanie's entire worldly possessions consisted of an old beloved suitcase and matching purse. She had one pair of shoes and a small journal which no one could decipher not even the best decoders in the world.

Furniture wasn't a requirement since Lynora's loft had a fully furnished guest bedroom which included a large comfy queen-size bed, a handsome walnut dresser and matching wardrobe. As an extra bonus an elegant gold inlaid vanity was for her use exclusively. The walls had been left white and bare of ornament. Lynora encouraged Joanie to decorate the room. The best surprise was discovering an on-suite bath. She couldn't believe her luck. The loft would be her refuge from the world.

Touched by Lynora's generosity Joanie sensed she was on a roller coaster ride of changes. Forty-four hours had passed and in forty-four hours she had gone from being homeless, unemployed, and hungry to being employed, well fed, and sheltered. Twenty years ago, she had lived in luxury. Twenty years ago, she owned fine furniture, beautiful clothes and all that money could buy. Yet. Twenty years ago, she'd spent most of her waking hours interrogating Lacertidae prisoners and when the Special Ops were finished with them, dissecting them in order to discover more about their circulatory system and the inner workings of their brains. Her children suffered. She had no one to blame but herself for allowing her job to take over her life.

Now two people in Blueglennen knew more about her than even her children. She must tell Lynora Reason the truth. If the truth meant she would be homeless again, she didn't care. She wanted to live with herself. She liked who she'd become. When they agreed to be roommates, she insisted on paying her way. The Merchants' Row Alliance paid her salary six months in advance anticipating problems. Kimberly and Harry knew they needed someone to be their advocate in the event Saurus' guards sent them to prison. She would have authority to sue on their behalf and fight for them in court.

Without anyone the wiser, Joanie slipped away from the reunion barely making an impression on the members. Her ordinariness had been a Special-Ops prerequisite. The best spies often were people who others dismissed as weak or foolish or insignificant. How they differed from the weak, foolish, and insignificant was in their inner unbending core. The best spies were stubborn and incredibly deft at slipping through the cracks of an enemy's defenses. She had been one of the best. And now her talents were keeping her alive and even contributing to a more altruistic agenda.

Finally, she had the chance to do something good.

If Mary McGirdle had seen her, she would have made a fuss and such a fuckus would have brought Joanie Fitzhammond to the attention of Governor Saurus and Accuser Phil Potts. Phil Potts would have taken a closer look at Joanie and perhaps ordered a background check. He might have forced her to work for him or forced her to leave Blueglennen in disgrace. Either choice would have been devastating for her. Why had she pushed aside her natural reservations and lied to her new friends? Why had she come? She blamed her training. Years spent investigating, interrogating, listening, learning, gathering information, and coming to conclusions had kicked in and she felt an overwhelming curiosity to know.

Her photographic memory allowed her the luxury of keeping an accurate count of everyone who came in and out of the room. And now that she had most of the afternoon to do what she liked, she wanted to jot down the names of those she'd met and her initial impressions of them. She wanted to do some further investigating, most assuredly background checks on all the people who showed up even the waitstaff. At present, she would rather avoid Kimberly Lemon and Dela Swana. She turned back to climb the stairs and nearly ran into one of the governor's bodyguards. His imposing height and breadth stopped her in her tracks.

"Sorry Dela. You'll have to wait in the lobby until the governor is finished."

"It's Delan Fitzhammond. I'm a widow."

Joanie looked up in time to see two other knights guarding the east and west staircases. They were guarding the Governor and Sylvia Paleone who stood on the landing in whispered conversation. When a hairy hand squeezed her shoulder, Joanie instinctively stepped down to avoid his touch. She spun on her heels and managed to rush down the stairs without falling. Instead of leaving the convention center, Joanie chose to make her way around the grand staircase to the tiny alcove hidden under the stairs far away from

Kimberly and Dela Swana. The two of them were sitting at a small table. They were so deep in conversation they never noticed her. Joanie made herself comfortable at a tiny table throwing her purse on the extra chair to prevent anyone from sitting near her.

Her hearing had never been particularly good. No one in Blueglennen, not even the Merchants' Row Alliance knew she wore a hearing aid. As a precaution, she'd kept a few of her tools of espionage in a safe house, a house unknown even to her superiors. And when she was forced to move west, the tools of her former trade were transported with her stitched in her clothes. One of them was a tiny microchip, a live-wire-listening device with a range of twenty-five yards. It took a moment to fish the device out of hiding.

While pretending to rub her ear, she inserted the chip inside its compartment. Pushing the hearing aid back in her ear, she did her best to tune out unwanted voices and concentrate on the important ones.

"Star made her family's life miserable too, you know. Not just me. Sophie used to say that Star would insist everyone pray at the dinner table and the family fought a lot about her new religion. So why is everyone focused on me?" Joanie recognized Kimberly's voice.

". . . saw her snooping around," that was Sylvia Paleone.

"How much did she really see?" Governor Saurus asked.

"I'm worried because," Sylvia again.

"Good let's go there." Dela Swana said excitedly her pitch high enough to drown out Sylvia's voice. Joanie had really wanted to know what Sylvia had to worry about now.

"I'll take care of her," Governor Saurus assured Sylvia.

"The Bridgekeepers are not murderers. I seriously doubt anyone in Blueglennen is a murderer. I think the culprit just wanted to shut Star up and made the mistake of forgetting where he put her," Kimberly said ruefully.

"No. I've taken care of her. She's a nobody. I decided a week ago to get rid of her," Sylvia threw out impatiently. "That's not the point and you know it."

"I seriously doubt that. Remember the trash bin was wrapped in chain and locked. Someone wanted to suffocate Star and he or she did a thorough job. She must have seen something or overheard something important. You knew her. Where would she go if she was upset?" Dela Swana again.

"What do you want me to do about this?" the Governor demanded. His hiss at the end of the question squealed through the wires making Joanie's head throb.

"Before she joined the Church of the Holy Centipede, Star

would have run to one of her friends or to her room to mope. She no longer has, excuse me," Kimberly began.

"Block it off. Blow it up. I don't give a shit. You're the big honcho. You hire guys to take care of these inconveniences," Sylvia hissed.

"I keep forgetting, she lost her friends from school when she tried to push her religious zeal onto them. The Bookworm was her last refuge. I was a captive audience and she thought she could drop into my shop any time and do her complaining and moralizing with impunity," Kimberly still ruminating.

"Why sweetheart? You just said the old bat doesn't know anything. No one knows not even the clueless D.I.," Governor Saurus assured Sylvia.

"Our quarrel left her nowhere to go but," Kimberly still ruminating.

"She's an old frumpy maid. She didn't see a thing. It's our secret, sweet cheeks," Saurus said in a pathetic attempt at sounding sexy.

"Star would go to the church first. She'd want to talk to a member or the Bishop," Kimberly offered.

"I've been thinking Roger. We'd better hold off for a few days," Sylvia said, her voice hardening. "Daniel's been."

"Forget the idiot. Cathedral doors or Bishop's Gate?" Governor Saurus asked in a desperate voice. "Come on, sweetheart. Don't lose your courage now."

"How many ways inside the cathedral?" Dela Swana asked.

Joanie had heard enough. She removed the listening device and gathered up her purse then moved toward the doors at a normal pace. No one noticed her. She had a plan now. Why hadn't she realized the truth before? It was so simple. The number of suspects had grown. Sylvia Paleone and Governor Saurus had motives for murder, more so than anyone. Yet she had to be sure. The Office of Planning and Zoning would have the answers she needed.

When Kimberly stepped into the Bookworm, she heard a crackling and realized she had stepped on the mail lying on the floor. She scooped up the packages and a loose bit of paper. Odd. People no longer sent paper through the mail. The internet took care of people's day-to-day transactions: paying bills, emailing friends and family, reading the local or international news, buying products, voting, and so much more. The experts in the tech-cyber world had yet to discover how to send bulky materials through the internet. Feeling smug Kimberly set the packages on the counter and stared at the envelope in her hand.

On the outside of the envelope, a bold neat hand had written Bookworm Emporium, City of Blueglennen, Wolfern Province. She tore the envelope open and pulled out the thin sheet of paper. It was yellowed from age or made to appear old by someone familiar with the process, maybe stained with coffee or some dark nutty drink and left to dry. The paper was so fine when she held it up to the light she could see through its body and out the window. There was nothing on the paper but stains and smells of dirt and damp.

Bemused she carried the envelope and the paper toward her private quarters. She set a towel under the paper to prevent germs from ending up on the table where she ate her meals. She pushed the lamp close to the paper and squinted at the surface, annoyed and alarmed. Who would do such a thing? What was the point? Was it a terrible bacterial agent? Was she dead already? Oh, Unholy Centipede. She backed away from the table and ran to the shop to grab her purse. She fished inside for her cellphone desperate to talk to someone.

In less than ten minutes, her rescuer was banging on the glass. She saw him standing by the door leaning forward as if he had second thoughts. Why had he been her first choice? She had no time to consider. She opened the door and let him in.

"Show me," Gawain said never quite looking her in the eye.

He followed her to the backroom and she pointed at the table, "There it is. I touched it. My skin touched the paper. I might be contaminated already. Should I see a healer? Or am I too late?"

Without touching the paper, Gawain pulled out a pen and pressing a tiny switch then pointed the end of the pen at the paper. The red beam played over the surface of the paper and within seconds, the light began to widen until the light covered the paper entirely like a gigantic mouth devouring the object. The paper disappeared. A few minutes passed. For some inexplicable reason Kimberly no longer felt afraid. When her eye once again recognized the paper on the table, her fears returned.

Gawain appeared relieved. He pulled out a round object and set the object in his eye and like a man of science read the tip of the pen. He no longer resembled a knight, all muscle and swordplay. Now he reminded her of her grandfather when he would take out his old microscope and peer into the lens at a tiny world unseen by the naked eye.

He removed the device from his eye, tucked the pen and the device in one of his inside pockets and turned to face her. "No worries. There's no virus or poison attached to the surface, only invisible ink."

Kimberly remained unconvinced, "What about the stains?"

"Coffee and chocolate."

"Oh."

"Do you want to know what the message says?"

"Well. I guess so. Who sent it?"

"There's no name attached to the message," Gawain said as he made himself at home at her kitchen table. Kimberly sat across from him wondering if she should be a good hostess and offer him a cup of tea.

"The message is brief. It just says: Trust No One."

"Would you like a cup of tea or a biscuit?" she asked.

"No. I've had my dinner."

"Either the sender is trying to frighten me or he's warning me," she said clasping her hands and holding them in her lap for comfort.

"I recognize the handwriting," Gawain offered.

"Well, why didn't you say so?"

"I would rather take care of this myself."

"If you know something, tell me. I would rather know who the sender is, thank you very much."

"Let me talk to him first. Come now. Don't look at me that way."

"Go away."

With an uncharacteristic slowness, Gawain rose from his seat and made a production out of collecting the towel and message. Kimberly held out her hand, "That does not belong to you."

"Why do you care? It's an attempt to frighten you or a cruel joke. Let me find out."

"No. I want my lawyer to see it. She needs to know about this."

"We'll give it to her later. I'm sorry, but it's evidence and I'm taking it to Hawk."

In silence they left the shop and walked side by side down Merchants' Row to the Unique Boutique. They waited until Shehili Swana had finished ringing up a customer's purchase before following Swana into her office. Gawain did all the talking while Kimberly fumed. Shehili's lively brown eyes watched the two of them curiously. Her amusement made Kimberly even angrier. When Shehili Swana agreed Bristlecone should present the evidence to the D.I., Kimberly was astonished. She had expected a different outcome. Whose side was she on?

Once Gawain left, Kimberly voiced her concerns.

"What else could we do Dela Lemon?" Swana said. "The sender chose the rare object as a means of catching your attention perhaps knowing your fascination with old things would make you less cautious. What if there had been poison or a serious bacterial agent sprinkled on the surface by a loathsome killer? You might have died an unpleasant agonizing death and it would have been hours before anyone found you."

"But he knows who sent the message and he's refusing to tell me the sender's name. Aren't we entitled to know the creep's name?" Kimberly demanded.

"Rest assured. I will find out. I promise you."

"I'm relieved to hear that. Well, I'm sorry to have taken up your time."

"Next time please call ahead. I do have a shop to run, you know. And find someone else to be the buttress between you and the sexy, scary, Gawain."

Kimberly ignored her attempt at humor and hurried out of the office mumbling about dinner. On the way back to her shop, she thought about Gawain, the last hour, and Dela Swana's words and she couldn't help but laugh at the situation. The only two people on the street turned to stare at her in surprise and then looked away when they recognized her. Note to self, she thought, try to exhibit fewer examples of eccentricity in public.

Guinevere Goodbody stood with her arms crossed as if freezing cold while she and Harry Zany stood in front of her pet store. Both of their expressions were sober as they talked. The petite plump woman had a habit of tucking her body closer to her heart as if afraid to let herself go. Harry Zany seemed to be the only person she tolerated near her. Through the window of her shop, Kimberly could see the puppies tumbling over each other and heard their attempts to be tough, their growls feeble indeed. Grow up quickly darlings, she thought, I might need one of you to protect me.

Tonight, with the Row gathering up all the darkness and smearing the darkness with damp, the gloom made Kimberly shiver. Unknown forces were doing their best to frighten her and take away her home. She glanced over her shoulder at Goodbody and Zany. They seemed as worried about the future as she was. What had happened to their city? How had this creeping malaise gone unnoticed for so long? It was as if the world had been plotting behind their backs for years, and only now, the forces of greed and hate were creeping out of their hiding places.

≈

Gawain found Wakefield sitting alone at a corner table in the Knight's Eatery. He slipped into the chair facing Wakefield and began talking. Under ordinary circumstances, the sight of Wakefield with a spoon hovering near his mouth and an air of frightened surprise would have been hilarious, especially, when some of the soup ended up on his pressed and starched pants.

Even the sight of Wakefield frozen in such a comical pose did nothing to ease Gawain's growing fury. The idea that this small-minded, pencil-pushing, xenophobic, ass-wiper would dare to threaten such a kind, funny, sweet-tempered woman, no, not just a woman, a lady, a lady of character and courage, made him even more eager to call the man out with pistol or sword. With a supreme effort of will, Gawain managed to keep his temper in check, even though the idea of throttling the middle-aged booby with his air of habitual constipated abstraction would have been so satisfying. He cleared his throat and shook off the anger as best he could. Wakefield watched him nervously.

"Today Dela Lemon showed me a rather rare object. It was delivered in an antique envelope. The paper inside appeared to be very old, an object by the way that would have generated a great deal of curiosity and interest, especially to someone of Dela Lemon's training and experience. The sender knew this, knew she would have trustingly opened the document in the mistaken belief that someone might have needed an appraisal of its value or to gift the object to the shop. And yet, the slip of paper appeared blank.

But, hold on now. I come along, and Dela Lemon shows me the paper, and she's very concerned, very perplexed, and asks for my opinion. I'm wondering if someone sent this dear sweet lady a dangerous bacterial poison. Not possible. She's had the paper in her possession for nearly an hour and her body shows no signs of poisoning. I look closer and detect writing on the surface. Ha. Trust no one. I recognize the script. It's your handwriting. How strange. What justifiable reason would Deputy Wakefield have for sending such an expensive, rare object to Dela Lemon and with such a strange disturbing message enclosed in invisible ink?

Why are you trying to frighten Dela Lemon, Wakefield? I know you. You do nothing on your own. Someone bought the paper and ordered you to deliver the message. Someone wanted Dela Lemon separated from her allies, alone and at the mercy of the authorities. Now you are going to tell me all I want to know, or you and I will be discussing the matter further in a quiet little place of my choosing."

Wakefield glanced down at his bowl. A few seconds passed. When he dropped his spoon, Gawain inched a bit closer. "Speak to me Wakefield. Speak. Or you'll be regretting your silence."

Wakefield attempted a laugh. Gawain was too mad to feel sorry for him. If the paper had been his cowardly way of frightening Kimberly, Gawain would do his best to make the man's life a misery for as long as Gawain remained on the planet of Shellfargon. Instead of backing away, Wakefield glanced around the room. The two of them were the only people at this end of the Knight Eatery. The other knights and detectives were congregated around a vid screen watching a jousting match telecast from New Enreich.

Wakefield leaned in close and looked Gawain in the eyes. "I didn't poison Dela Lemon's food."

When Gawain looked annoyed, Wakefield tried to explain. "You remember when Dela Lemon was placed in the cells by D.I. Hawk and I brought down the tray for her lunch? Well, everyone assumed I had poisoned her tray. I tell you I didn't. Why would I poison her tray and then deliver the food to her? I would be crazy to do such a thing. Everyone assumes I did it and even though they dislike troublemakers, none of them will look me in the eye. They treat me as if I'm a monster. I would never do such a terrible thing. Never.

I tell you, I'm being set up.

The paper. I swear to you I didn't send it to Dela Lemon. That paper has been in my family for nearly two hundred years. Several years ago, I wanted to impress a young lady and like a fool, I took it from the family safe. Well, she left town before I could show her proof of my love. When she returned to Blueglennen recently, I presented the paper to her. She insisted I prove my love by writing on the paper.

I was shocked. It was a valuable antique. If I had written on the paper, the paper would have lost its value. She insisted," Wakefield looked away obviously embarrassed. "I had been drinking, quite a bit. My head still pounds. I was despondent, unable to believe the lady of my dreams would be so callous. And then the idea came to me. I could prove my love to her and still maintain the integrity of my family's valuable artifact."

"Did you give your friend the original document?" Gawain asked.

"Of course not. I told her I would write down her message and drop the artifact off at the shop. I faked the original and wrote the message she wanted to send in invisible ink."

"Tell me her name."

As the two men sat facing each other, Gawain waited. Wakefield's eyes darted desperately from Gawain to the men cheering their favorite combatants. Then his eyes widened. Someone new had entered the room. Wakefield began to sweat. Gawain's back was to the room, but he could guess who was scaring the hell out of Wakefield.

"Tell me now or we'll meet in less pleasant surroundings and I'll find another way to get the information out of you," Gawain hissed under his breath. He pulled back when he heard Hawk coming towards them.

"And what have we here?" Hawk said as he stood with his arms crossed rocking gently back and forth on his heels as if he were enjoying a good joke. "Gossipers? Who is on your shit list now Wakefield?"

Gawain pushed back his chair and stood up. He and Hawk locked eyes. "Wakefield and I were trying to determine who attempted to poison Kimberly Lemon. Wakefield assured me he's innocent. I've been ordered not to talk to the chief cook and her assistant. Saurus insists if I do try to question them, I'll be sent away or fired. He loves his cook, you know. She's the best in the world. Good cooks are hard to find, blah, blah, blah."

Hawk seemed interested and glanced down at Wakefield. Wakefield jumped to his feet and stood at attention as Hawk questioned him, "I remember reading in your report you went to the kitchen personally to fetch a tray for the prisoner and filled the tray with foods she might like?"

"No sir. I never wrote that. I wrote that I was reaching for one of the covered dishes the cook leaves out for the rest of us who can't make it back in time for meals. The dishwasher, a new guy said the kitchen has special trays for prisoners and he went into the freezer and retrieved one for me. Sir," Wakefield finished glaring up at Hawk as if he anticipated a reprimand.

"New guy?" Gawain asked sharply. "What new guy? I've been in the kitchen lately and there are only women working in the back rooms."

"He was sweeping the floor. He seemed to know his way around the place. Are you sure? I assumed he was a dishwasher," Wakefield said in an apologetic voice.

Wakefield watched as the two men exchanged pointed looks and realized he had made a big shitty mistake which might cost him his job. As a deputy and liaison between the knights and the clerical staff it was his duty to make sure he knew everyone in the Duke Tower

Station. What with anarchists and Lacertidae terrorists on the prowl, every knight must verify the credentials of unfamiliar personnel.

Having been pressed for time was no excuse. He should have taken the extra time to check the dishwasher's badge and identify him as a legitimate member of the kitchen crew. A new worry surfaced as D.I. Hawk's contemptuous glare ramped up his anxiety. This could get him fired, demoted or sent to bowrider watch.

"Take Wakefield to the hologram room and have the graphic designer whip up a sample of this unknown kitchen helper," D.I. Hawk ordered. Wakefield's heart sank. He could tell from Gawain's grin his private life would no longer be private. He had seen Gawain in action and dreaded the next few hours.

Several hours later, Gawain, with a hologram reader in his jacket pocket marched toward Merchants' Row. He was determined to find Star Bridgekeeper's killer and Kimberly Lemon's enemy before the trial. He had until tomorrow. The trial would have normally taken place in the Blueglennen Court House. Due to the notoriety of the case and the number of people already attempting to buy seats, Governor Saurus announced on television a new venue for the trial. It will take place in the Royal Plaza with armed knights stationed at all the checkpoints.

Even now as he left Duke Tower and moved through the plaza, there were clerks, knights, and soldiers unloading chairs, benches, tables, even a podium where the judges and the Governor would sit. The long heavy wagons used to transport the furniture remained on the promenade. The six-team draft horses reserved for plowing fields or pulling canon were too large and dangerous to be among the delicate statues and flower boxes. Instead, the Governor ordered Blueglennen knights to carry the furniture from the wagons to the plaza. Mudflat villagers were paid to sweep and clean the plaza stones and arrange the chairs.

The Royal Plaza banners were removed and replaced with the banner of the Wolfern Court. The silk banner stretched across the entire stage, on the surface of its black silk the weaver had created an image of the original founder of Wolfern Province, King Nemphet. The wolf mask covered King Nemphet's entire face. His blazing blue eyes looked out of the empty sockets, his wolf fangs exposed sharp white teeth and his long white beard grew down to his belly.

Around his massive shoulders lay wolf pelts. Between his feet two supplicants knelt. Their heads were bowed waiting for his verdict. Gawain sneered up at the Wolf King. Barbarians. He longed for home. He longed for security, sanity, and clean air unfettered by animal refuse and wood smoke. But before he could go home, he had to talk to Kimberly.

That night Kimberly sat on the edge of her bed and peered out her alley window. She corrected herself, her bay window, which weeks ago had been a symbol of comfort and love, now reminded her of all she would lose in a few days. She struggled to understand the difference. Someone had loved her enough to cut away the barrier of brick and mortar so that she might have a view of the sky and light might penetrate her tiny home. But the memory of her time in the dungeons below Duke Tower made the window seem futile against the dark forces plotting to imprison her for life. One day a barrier is removed allowing light and color into her world, the next she's sent underground to live in the dark.

And now, Caleb loved another and was probably at this very moment proving his love to her by adding light to her tiny apartment, maybe building shelves to hold her hunting trophies or repairing her four-wheeled bicycle to carry her safely to the next village. Kimberly, both paradoxically, sad and happy, sad to lose him as a friend and happy he had found love again, found herself exhaling. The sigh came out of her body with such an unnatural force as if superheated by pent up frustration.

The sound reverberated off the walls. She laughed, slapped a hand over her mouth, and began to cry. After a good long cry, during which she managed to change out of her blouse, skirt, hose, and shoes and into a warm fleece jumper, brush her teeth, and eventually blow her nose followed by a quick wash of face and further wiping away of tears, she paused to stare at her image in the mirror.

If anyone had heard the hiccupping and groaning noises followed by the bout of weeping, sniffling, snorting, swearing, and gasping, the listener might have wondered if Kimberly was giving birth. It had been cathartic. She hadn't let herself go like that in so long. Her eyes were puffy and her nose red. She made herself look in the mirror. The mirror was her enemy. The mirror reminded her of how ugly she was, how unnatural.

Her reddish blonde hair tied in a pony tail had wisps of limp wet strands beginning to curl around her pointy ears. She hated her ears. She hated her long eyelashes. And her big violet eyes made her look evil. She wanted to look more like a Delphi with short lashes and an extra fatty fold around the eye to protect her when swimming. She wanted to look less like a mutant. When she reached puberty, her recessive genes nearly ruined her life. Neighbors who remembered her mother kept remarking on her funny colored eyes and lashes. They kept the rumor alive that she wasn't Grandpa Lemon's granddaughter.

Her grandpa sent out flyers to the neighbors with her mother's wedding picture magnified. Kimberly's father towered over her tiny mother. He had black hair and violet eyes. He had long lashes and skin the color of wheat. He looked nothing like a Delphi. Her mother with her reddish blonde curls, brown eyes and skinny neck looked so beautiful. Under the wedding picture, her grandfather printed a warning: *If I find out who has been spreading lies about my granddaughter, I'll see you in court.*

How stupid to be worried about her looks when she might end up swinging from a noose. The absurdity of Kimberly's present situation and the memory of her conversation with Dela Swana made her anxious all over again. The Governor and his police seemed determined to hang her for Star's murder. Even many of the citizens of Blueglennen believed her guilty.

And yet there were others who were convinced of her innocence. The merchants hadn't abandoned her and some of her friends still believed in her. Now she really knew who her friends were – but at such a high price. If justice found her innocent, how could she face her neighbors and those who believed her capable of such a monstrous act? How could she pretend everything was the same?

She couldn't. Knowing how gossips could be so vicious, she knew they wouldn't stop believing she was a murderess. It made her feel hopeless and alone. But she wasn't alone. She had Alexandra, Crystova, Dela Swana, even the volatile Guinevere. And Caleb still believed in her. The professor seemed to believe in her. Or was she just a cause he could rally around?

She forced herself to think about the other man in her life. She should examine seriously her feelings for Gawain. Imagine being able to say – the other man in her life. She'd never thought such a thing could happen to her. Maybe there was some truth in Shehili's little joke. Was Gawain amusing himself at her expense? Like sailors all over the world, would he tell his buddies about the funny eyed girl from Blueglennen? And what if he really did like her? Was she prepared to live in a steel box far from home?

With unnecessary force she threw back the coverlet and fell into bed, her body bouncing several times. A crackling of papers propelled her out of bed as quickly as she had gotten in. What? Another sinister message? In her bed? Holy Delph she was getting pissed off. She pulled off the bottom sheet and examined the mattress. There was nothing sinister on the mattress. Sleepy but too frightened to climb back into bed, she used the broom handle and poked the mattress from head to foot.

Before she reached the foot of the bed, she heard crackling. It came from a spot where her knee would have been if everything had been routine. Her grandfather had built the sleigh bed for her years ago. She and her grandmother had stuffed the mattress with thousands of materials: rags, dried flowers and lemon grass, even crushed shells. For nearly twenty years, she had slept on this bed and the bed had never crackled. The bed used to rustle, pop, and sometimes squeak. Not anymore. A special ointment concocted by an apothecary eliminated the critters who'd burrowed through her mattress.

The stitching and buttons holding the stuffing inside were secure. Determined to discover if a new set of critters had invaded her bed, Kimberly unbuttoned the outer shield. As if pressing her lips tightly together helped with her squeamishness, she plunged her hand inside. If she found a dead mouse, she would scream. Instead of finding a dead mouse, she found a long thin box. It was large enough to necessitate she use both hands to pull it out. It was a pencil box. She hadn't seen one in years.

Sitting on the floor with her back resting against the bed frame, she opened the box and looked inside. She found what looked like an old-fashioned quill pen which was actually a tiny computer with a tiny screen. On the screen someone had typed a brief sentence. She remembered as a kid sneaking notes back and forth between friends with these secret communiqués. This pen read – *Look in the secret compartment.* It took time to move the bed and pull back the rug. It took time to find the key to unlock the trap door. Her grandfather's safe was big enough for two people to hide in. But it was dark. And the flashlight and batteries were down at the bottom of the stairs.

By the end of the hour, she was ready to wring Crystova's neck. How dare she hide the illuminated manuscript in her family's hidden safe? As she sat at her little table by the window and stared down at the beautiful gold and green cover, she realized she possessed something more valuable than precious metals, more valuable than the entire economy of Curl itself. Unable to resist, she opened the book. A device the size of a door hinge protected by a purple metal plate sat on top of the first page of the ancient manuscript.

With her fingernail, Kimberly unclipped the plate and stared at the blank screen. She searched for her pick and used the pick to touch the screen. Words appeared. It had to be Crystova's doing. She remembered the night Crystova spent searching the wall for artifacts. It looked as if she'd had time to read a bit of the manuscript and take notes. The last note ended with an incomplete sentence. She'd been interrupted, probably by Kimberly. In her haste, Crystova had shut her Scribner inside the manuscript.

Kimberly read Crystova's notes:

The 600th Year of Islabeck. Year 88 of Civil Disobedience. The ruinous war. 65 more dead. 200 injured. Crop failure second year. Disease takes 1000s.

The 3087th Year of Dono. Chapel to be removed from sacred ground. Duke Dono arrests Priest Attuck. Attuck speaks before lords – warns of Devil's blood be

The rest of the hour was spent searching for a good place to hide the manuscript. Her first inclination was to march over to Crystova Moth's flat, wake her and insist she find her own hiding place. The awesome responsibility of protecting such a valuable artifact overwhelmed her. What really pissed her off was the timing. She already had plenty to worry about, she didn't need any more problems. The manuscript's significance, its history, and its hiding place changed her mind. The manuscript belonged to the shop. It had been hidden in the walls of the shop for more than three thousand years. If her grandfather had found it, he would have kept it safe.

So where should she hide it? If she put it back in grandfather's safe, there would be two people with knowledge of its whereabouts. She had a better idea. Make it ugly and hide it in plain sight. By the time she returned to bed her heart was racing so fast she lay awake the rest of the night. She stared at the moonlight illuminating her wall. Every so often, a winged creature's shadow flew by as if flying in and out of her kitchen cupboards. It might be a hawk hunting rats in the night sky.

The day before Kimberly Lemon's trial, on a crisp morning full of sunshine and bonhomie, Detective Inspector Hawk and Sylvia Paleone faced each other across the Relic shop counter in silence. Hawk's question seemed to have turned the usually talkative Sylvia into a mute. He allowed her another minute to gather her thoughts and then without his usual courtesy strode past her, threw open the door marked private, and paused before the portrait hanging on the wall.

"I'll give you another opportunity to answer my question," he said, not bothering to hide his annoyance at her opened-mouthed empty-eyed surprise. Her dumb act only made him more determined to uncover the truth.

As he stepped toward the painting Hawk said, "I noticed the other day an odd rippling of this delightful primitive you have here, a rippling as if the oil rendition of the Holy Centipede concealed something else."

A few minutes passed in silence. Hawk might have been in the room by himself. Sylvia Paleone gave the impression of a terrified mouse frozen near the exit hoping the cat doesn't see her. She looked as if she might go into catatonic shock. With his characteristic composure, Hawk changed tactics. He ran his fingers over the surface of the painting exploring the bumps and cracks. Then he found a hole. It was disguised within the black pigment surrounding the Holy Centipede.

"It seems out of character for you to relegate the Holy Centipede to a storage closet, out of sight of your customers. The commission for this piece must have been expensive. The frame alone would have cost you a purse full of seastars."

Hawk's fingers traveled around the back edge of the gold leaf picture frame. When his fingertips brushed against a hinge on the right and a clasp on the left, he smiled. He turned to face her, curious to see her reaction when he pulled the portrait away from the wall, exposing the hidden door behind. Sylvia Paleone's attempts to school her expression in what she imagined was bored contempt failed. Her look of sick dismay almost made him laugh.

"Last night I collected the blueprints of the castle grounds and discovered to my amazement your shop includes an ancient stairwell, what the old families would have used as a private means of reaching the church without having to mingle with the great unwashed. When I was in the catacombs reflecting on those good-old-days, I got lucky.

I heard someone walking toward me and hid. I watched as the man pulled a stone out of the wall and stuck his hand inside the cavity. A door opened. It was a miracle. I saw a flight of stairs carved into the stones. When the man began to climb, I thought it my duty to follow him. It was a good thing the narrow winding staircase included many places where I could hide. When I saw a light, I realized the man had reached his destination. You two were so busy rubbing up against each other and moaning, you never noticed me. What a shock to discover he wasn't your husband. What a surprise when I recognized your lover."

Sylvia Paleone had the grace to blush. Perhaps, she wasn't

totally immoral. The woman opened her mouth to defend herself when a man appeared behind her. She must have sensed his presence because she continued to look at D.I. Hawk. He was disappointed when she closed her mouth with a little popping sound. They seemed so comfortable together. Hawk tried not to laugh at the sight of Governor Saurus dressed only in red boxer shorts and matching red socks with his hairy chest and big belly exposed. "Did I interrupt an important meeting?" Hawk asked.

The two of them might have been twins with their identical looks of shocked disbelief. They had been sneaking around for so long, they'd convinced themselves they'd never be caught.

Detective Hawk considered his options. The affair between the two idiots made no difference to him. Sylvia Paleone's cultish following probably wouldn't care. Hawk was a realist. The news wouldn't surprise the ruling class only embarrass Paleone's husband and Saurus' wife. He considered blackmailing the Governor into dismissing the Lemon trial. The secret stairs proved reasonable doubt. Saurus, a stupid man was stubborn in his stupidity. All his life, he'd been groomed for his part as a figurehead and he wouldn't be easy to convince.

The silence had gone on too long for the Governor's peace of mind. "You will say nothing about the secret stair to anyone. Do you understand? If you say anything, I'll have you dismissed and thrown out of Wolfern Province."

"You hired me to find a terrorist. I've no interest in your personal affairs. I do warn you though. If I can find the secret stair, I'm sure there are others who know about it," he said with a shrug which seemed to satisfy the half-dressed idiots. Burhani debated whether to tell Shehili. No. She needed to learn a lesson about the consequences of interfering in alien politics.

"I don't care about your alien sensibilities," the Governor said as he threw out his chest. It was all Burhani could do not to laugh in his face. He waited politely for the man to finish. "I'm concerned about security and keeping my castle safe from terrorists. Do the job I hired you to do. Now get out."

Hawk slipped around the portrait and started down the steps. The door slammed behind him leaving him in total darkness. As he paused on the threshold to get his bearings, he contemplated his next move. With regret he wished he could do something for her. Yet. She wasn't his responsibility. He had the Albion to think of and all that remained of humanity to protect. Damned Shehili. She would have to be stopped. Her meddling was going to get them all killed.

A scuffling down below warned him there was an

eavesdropper in the catacombs spying on them. Someone had overheard the conversation between him and the Governor. The acoustics were better than a theater production of Noble Coral's plays. The person could have heard every word. Hawk knew it would be suicide to plunge down the stairs in pursuit of the spy. Although, if he couldn't see his hand in front of his face or even where to put his foot neither could the eavesdropper. He had his hand in his pocket trying to decide whether to use his penlight or his gun.

Instead of springing into action, maybe breaking a leg in the attempt, Hawk chose to fish his penlight out of his leather pocket. He found the penlight easy enough but had to pull off his glove to flick the tiny wheel. Those few precious seconds gave the intruder enough time to dash down the remaining stairs and flee.

The flame burned blue, yellow, and red, the tip illuminating the stone stairs and the stone walls lined with mushrooms. Someone had left the door at the bottom ajar and the smell of damp air reached his nostrils. With measured steps, Hawk descended the stairs. Once in the catacombs, Hawk turned off his penlight and listened. He searched the darker places wondering if the intruder was still waiting nearby. He thought he knew who'd been eavesdropping.

He tested his theory. "Gawain," he shouted, the name bouncing off the walls becoming less recognizable as it traveled into the darkness beyond. "Gawain. If you're here come forward."

When no one answered and when the silence dragged on for several minutes, Hawk turned his attention to the passage leading to the church. He walked toward the stone arch which would take him to the cathedral hall, still on tenterhooks, preparing himself for the possibility of being attacked, while simultaneously hoping he wouldn't have to kill anyone today.

A solid shape separated itself from the darker shadows near the door. Finstickel clutched the cold stone to his chest and with a final look back decided he would take the same route the other mercenary had taken earlier. He'd gotten stiff and sore waiting for these aliens to go away and leave him alone. The knight with the red curly hair who thought he was quite a lady's man, quite a catch would find out soon enough that Delphi would rather die than let their women soil themselves with filthy rats. These interlopers had no right stealing his belongings or stealing Delphi women. They had no right. This was his home, his property, his female. The bailey and the townships belonged to him. He was the true heir of Blueglennen.

Those bastards had thrown him out of the alumni luncheon as if he were a nobody while the real traitor of Curl sat like a lump of ugly with her little beady eyes watching everyone, assessing everyone, probably plotting how she and her scum loving Mudflat Village traitors would take over the country and throw the nobility in the dungeons to rot. He recognized her straight away. She'd forgotten him. He'd been younger back then with more hair. He'd been good-looking and rich too, well above her station. Oh yes. He'd get rid of her for good.

Gawain never heard Hawk call his name for Gawain was busy thinking and moving swiftly through the passageway headed for Mudflat Village to find his sister. This latest news could not wait. The trial would begin tomorrow, and he needed Shard's expertise. Once Dela Swana had all the names of the previous occupants of the Relic shop, then the jury would have to acquit Kimberly. The easy access of the stairs to the location where Star Bridgekeeper's body had been found meant there were far more people capable of kidnapping and murdering the kid, far more with motive and opportunity than Kimberly Lemon.

E4 Shellfargon Year 5092 NDMP WK 5: UES Albion 4
Wish to respectfully disagree with current orders mandated by captains. Imperative I continue as defense for accused Delphi Kimberly Lemon. She is innocent.

E1 Shellfargon Year 5092 NDMP WK 5: UES Albion 4
In catacombs between Tower and church a secret stair leads to Sylvia Paleone's Relic shop. Uncovered affair between Governor Saurus and Paleone. The affair may have nothing to do with murder. Unable to confirm whether Lemon's trial motivated by politics or personal vendetta. Lemon most likely murderer.

E2 Shellfargon Year 5092 NDMP WK 5: UES Albion 4
Artifact left at bookshop confirmed as property of Deputy Wakefield. Wakefield admitted in the attached affidavit that Victoria Lemon blackmailed him into writing the message to discredit her niece's defender and foment

paranoia.

E3 Shellfargon Year 5092 NDMP WK 5: UES Albion 4
Received communique from New Enreich warning retired spook may be living among residents here. This spook belonged to an elite corps called the ISG. Considered ruthless capable of infiltrating any secure location. No time to review security album and identify spook. Must attend trial. Earl Raker greenlighted my request for E21 to review ISG album. I sent images of likely suspects.

Chapter 10

The moment the knights on duty let down the drawbridge, a drawbridge wide enough for four draft horses to enter, the gatekeepers saw a sea of people jostling to get inside the castle. The line of people snaked through Mudflat Village all the way to the train station. An hour later, the Arm of Justice personnel were forced to open Bishop's Gate to allow for more people. Some tourists were reluctant to climb the steep and narrow path terrified of the long drop down to the Siren River.

Those Delphi brave enough to take the path and lucky enough to enter through Bishop's Gate soon discovered their good fortune which included a tour of the gardens, Duke Tower, the makeshift courtroom, and the nobles sitting on a raised dais in their fine gowns. Those citizens pausing to admire a statue, or a living celebrity effectively changed the tempo and speed of the line. What had once been a steady forward progression ended up a trickle of gawking tourists oblivious to those patiently waiting to enter.

Hawk watched with gathering misgivings as the people kept coming, as the lines began to slow until the line reminded him of a gigantic multi-colored slug weaving and oozing its way toward the Royal Plaza. Savor the sight, he thought to himself with rancor, because my friends your destination will be anything but spectacular.

At the train station where tracks crisscrossed through Mudflat Village, tourists, journalists, and locals crawled along unable to get through the congestion. The narrow streets of Mudflat were ill equipped to handle so many people. Many eager to see the trial and unable to book passage on the trains chose to travel to Blueglennen by wagon, coach, or horseback. At first, the knights on duty turned them away. Eventually, a few enterprising farmers, for a price, allowed the travelers to use their fields. Knight Graceland and Lively took charge.

A steady flow of people four abreast were making their way through the narrow streets of Mudflat Village and up the hillside toward the castle. The early birds received a far gentler reception as they greeted the gatekeepers. They were ushered over the Long Valley Gateway into the bailey and told to move on down Wolfern Promenade and find their seats. Unfortunately, for many, the promenade and plaza had become choked with people.

Soon the hillside was covered with disappointed travelers who trampled on private property and tried to sneak into houses to reach the rooftops hoping for a view. More alarming were the crush of wagons, carts, gigs, buggies, riders, and cyclists massing near the train depot as if they seriously believed they would witness the spectacle from the front row like the rich and famous. At last count the lucky ones numbered two hundred and ten. They got to sit on plush comfortable chairs in the center of the Royal Plaza.

By midmorning, the Governor was forced to order the trains to carry their passengers beyond Mudflat Depot and on to the next stop at Greenburg Valley. Inside the bailey, there were plenty of knights on duty to escort people to their seats. Once travelers reached the plaza and all the seats were taken, they were forced to sit behind the red roped barricade on the cold plaza stones.

People were convinced this was the trial of the century. Murders occurred in Wolfern Province, just like most places in the country of Curl, but this one was different because the television stations had been broadcasting the details of the murder and pictures of the murdered child for weeks with panels of experts debating the guilt or innocence of the suspect.

Most people were convinced Kimberly Lemon was the murderer based solely on her pictures. She didn't' look like a Delphi. She looked like a throwback to a primitive time in Delphi history. Kimberly's aunt Victoria had been on the news so much she'd become a celebrity herself. Her stories about their childhood implied Kimberly Lemon was a cold-stone killer. The most damning information came when anchorman Arnold interviewed Victoria and Victoria told the anchorman and the viewers, "I'm pretty sure she killed her mother. You see, shortly after Kimberly was born, a few months later her mother inexplicably died. Kimberly may have been a baby, but she was and still is a demon. And to prove she's a demon, I can tell you for a fact, Kimberly Lemon is an atheist.

Just ask her. She'll tell you to your face she's an atheist. She doesn't believe in the Holy One. She believes the Holy Delph was just an ordinary ancestor like all the rest of the ancestors. He's nothing special. He's made up. She believes our ancestors left the sea because it was too dangerous to live in the sea at the time, that leaving the sea had nothing to do with God's command to go forth and prosper upon the land. It's all about natural selection and believing we left the sea to save ourselves from earthquakes and fissures of hot gases.

Crazy talk, ha? Yes, that's my niece. I tried to help her. For so many years, I tried to help her see the error of her ways. Star tried too. But Kimberly just wouldn't listen. I think because she couldn't convince Star Bridgekeeper of her radical ideas, she killed her."

Another reason the trial was the event of the year was because murder trials were held behind closed doors, never having been witnessed by anyone in the province of Wolfern. In every case of suspected murder, murders of passion or murders of profit were handled by the High Court and the Governor. After a series of railroad derailments, paddle boat fires, and attempts on Governor Saurus' life, he decided to recruit the local militia to protect Wolfern infrastructure. Therefore, whenever an anarchist was arrested only a handful of people witnessed the trial.

This murder trial, Governor Saurus believed, was too important to adjudicate behind closed doors. The public had a right to know. Along with the Citizen Judges, he wanted the public to decide whether Kimberly Lemon was guilty or innocent. It was a radical idea – to broadcast a murder trial all over the world. No wonder there were thousands of eager tourists willing to brave rough roads and terrifying country just for the chance to witness the trial of the century.

Tourists arriving from as far away as Pinswaddle on the Isle of Walrat (Sylvia Paleone's home town) who dared to sneak through Bitterroot Forest were summarily chased off by bands of young Mudflat village children. The dirty children, in their ragged clothes, threw rocks and sticks, and other handy weapons less savory at the terrified tourists who'd already been frightened out of their wits by the unexplainable fog and terrible sounds along the rough path through the woods.

The savvy residents of Mudflat Village and Greenburg Valley who had been camped out all night on the bridge waiting for the drawbridge to open had a perfect view of the goings-on below. They saw the children throwing stones and rotten food at the silly people spilling out of the forest. It was especially funny to see the damage thorny brush, pools of mud, and horse droppings could do to once fine clothes. A cheer rose up from Blueglennen natives who'd had the forethought to climb up onto their roofs to watch the foolishness below. There were also Greenburg residences atop huts, cottages, granaries and barns.

The knights spent most of the morning calming the crowds, disarming men and arresting a few quarrelsome women, even pulling apart two little old ladies beating each other over the head and shoulders with their purses. The knights at their posts atop the ramparts and in the watchtowers periodically shouted out news for those too late to see the spectacle. One knight Juleus Graceland, a verbal genius, entertained the crowds for hours with his insights into the doings inside the bailey.

Juleus Graceland and Madas Lively stood on the rampart wall looking down at the disappointed people dotting the landscape.

There were people everywhere, from the meadow near Bitterroot Forest to the banks of Poison Creek. Graceland cupped his hands on either side of his mouth and called out, "Valley Long is closed, folks. Every nook and cranny, every brick and street lamp are taken. There's even a guy sitting on Duke Dono's head. The statue I mean, not the real Duke Dono. He's been dead for five hundred years." People below laughed.

Encouraged, Juleus continued, "Oh, hold on. They've dragged him off the royal head. He's clinging to the royal ass. But not for long. There he goes. He's off the royal ass. Poor fellow. Now, they're leading him to the Department of Justice. He'll be spending the rest of the trial staring at a smelly old drunk in the cell next to him. Boo hoo."

A man below bellowed, "Can you see the court room?"

"It's being televised, don't you know?"

The man was standing on the banks of Poison Creek. He spread his arms wide and said, "Does it look like I have a television set?"

"What about your cellphone? It's being broadcast on the Internet."

A woman standing next to the man answered for him, "We can't get reception here. I thought Blueglennen was a rich prosperous city. How come you don't have more towers?"

Juleus using his megaphone said, "Don't blame Blueglennen. You're standing in a hole."

People below frustrated because they had come so far and were blocked from entering, began to chuckle. Lively whispered in Graceland's ear, "Go ahead. You're doing great. What else are we going to do up here? Kick people off the wall? You see any climbers?"

Encouraged by the people below and his friend, Juleus turned to study the Royal Plaza and then turned back to the people below, "They've set up a dais for the Citizen Judges in front of the university and a separate platform for the High Court Judge. His chair is made of the oldest oak in Bitterroot Forest. It's engraved with the beasts of the forest. Above the High Court Judge's chair is the Wolfern Banner.

I don't need to describe it to you. If you're not from Curl, you can look it up later. And next to the High Court Judge is the witness chair. It's smaller but made of the same wood. Facing the High Court Judge is the tables for the Accuser and the Defender and a little desk for the scribe.

Right now, the only people filing into the plaza are the tourists who've come to see the show. I mean the trial. They keep stopping to admire the plaza and all the fancy chairs for the public and tripping over each other's feet. Looks like some guy just fell and an old lady fell on top of him. Okay. They're up and brushing themselves off. Whee, that was exciting."

Long after the trial, people would regale their family and friends with anecdotes from Graceland and his often-funny commentary about the goings on during the spectacle. Many who couldn't remember the names of the accused or the victim remembered how Graceland amused them with his minute by minute narration of the trial.

Blueglennen citizens from Mudflat, Greenburg Valley, and Old Town had been waiting since the night before with their blankets and candles and camp stoves to keep them warm. Their blankets came in handy when they discovered only paying guests were permitted to sit on the lushly upholstered chairs arranged up and down the Royal Plaza. The chairs had been arranged in rows with an aisle between. The chairs went all the way back to the Green Monkey which delighted the owner who doled out drinks and snacks and made a fortune.

Knights in their finest armor were stationed a foot apart along the stone walls of the Plaza, also on the Cetacea Stairs and the rampart. They were most heavily concentrated near Duke Tower where a platform had been built for the judges. The usual café chairs and tables had been removed as had been the smaller pedestals and life size sculptures. All that remained of the familiar Royal Plaza was Duke Dono's likeness in marble. He looked down on the proceedings from his pedestal near the fountain with a haughty expression in the tilt of his head and clenched jaw. People joked that the empty sockets where his eyes should have been was the feature that resembled him the most.

Alexandra waiting patiently for her chance to sit in her assigned chair had had plenty of time to admire Duke Dono's likeness. She had seen the statue numerous times before but having only given the thing a curious glance in the past, after twenty minutes in its company she determined the artist had captured the idiot's likeness perfectly – a short man with vacant eyes, a fat neck, and a bulging belly. She was seriously getting tired of standing beneath his bulging belly. All she wanted to do was sit as close to Kimberly Lemon as possible.

Poor Kimberly, she thought, watching as her friend sat all alone between the Board of Judge's circular bench and the Protection table. Kimberly throughout the trial would have her back to the witnesses and would be forced to face the High Judge and the Citizen Judges, faces which Alexandra as an audience member found disturbing in their likeness: a pinch of arrogance with a dash of smugness interrupted by moments of boredom. To her dismay, she came to the unhappy conclusion the Citizen Judges, the nine esteemed men and women of the court had already made up their minds about Kimberly Lemon's guilt.

Earlier when Alexandra had emerged from her flat along University Boulevard, she was disappointed to learn she was seated third from the front and closest to the middle aisle. It was as close as she could get. She made a point in the general hubbub and noise to whistle shrilly. Those nearby turned to glare at her including Kimberly. Alexandra felt her cheeks grow warm. She hated to be the center of attention. Kimberly finally noticed Alexandra, her tall slimness and dark hair easily identifiable. It was a good thing Alexandra stood as tall as most men for in the press of people Kimberly might not have seen her.

They exchanged smiles: Alexandra's smile was as radiant with hope as she could manage. Kimberly forced her lips into a half-hearted smile with a trembling hint of gratitude.

A knight made a point of whispering in Alexandra's ear. Forced to sit down she turned to her companion and whispered, "A very good likeness of the Duke don't you think?" Evelyn Lordbuster pressed her long white fingers to her attractive mouth to prevent a rude laugh from escaping. Guinevere Goodbody seated to Evelyn's right leaned forward to glare at them, her plump pale face and speaking eyes chastising them for their unbecoming behavior on such a solemn occasion. Guinevere had no illusions as to the outcome of this trial. It would be a farce from beginning to end.

A stout middle-aged woman wearing her best purple turban had been wise enough to tell her friend to take the Bishop Key around the castle wall, "Let's try Bishop's Gate. We'll have the best view of the gardens."

Indeed, the early crowd who chose Bishop's Gate had an advantage over their neighbors – they had ample time and opportunity to examine the lovely flowers and statues in the garden, stare up at the imposing Duke Tower rising into the sky above their heads, make their way across the stone colonnade near the fountain and finish near the newly built dais where the High Judge's chair stood above them. Below the dais they had time to study the empty benches where the Citizen Judges would sit and the cluttered tables where the Defender and Accuser would sit. Since they were so close, they could also admire the silk Wolfern banner flying in the breeze.

As they shuffled forward, the people had an uninterrupted view of nearly two hundred gold silk upholstered chairs lined up in neat rows along the Royal Plaza. The intermittent groan warned them that once they cleared the chairs they were destined to be shuffled off to the back near the Royal Apartments and forced to stand for the duration of the trial.

Unlike the gawkers, Kimberly Lemon had a perfect view of the High Court Judge's dais and the nine-member Citizen Judges bench. They would determine her innocence or guilt. The judges hadn't arrived yet. But as she sat in the chair assigned to her, she could see the Accuser and the scribe preparing for the trial. It was quite a shock when she recognized the scribe. She would never have guest he would be here as a key part of the trial.

Frank Darknight sat quietly at the scribe table wearing the black robes of a court official. A rumor going around earlier in the morning suggested Roger Merkel's conflict of interest necessitated his expulsion from the case. The Governor, rumor said, forced Roger Merkel to retire early. Beyond the Scribe's bench and beyond the Accuser Phil Potts' black cold eyes Kimberly could see Shehili Swana sitting at the Protector's bench studying her notes. Kimberly had no idea what the next few days would bring.

Shehili seemed confident.

Yet Kimberly, knowing the history of Duke Tower Castle, the City of Blueglennen and Wolfern Province had no such optimism. Close enough to touch stood the curving bench of the Citizen Judges. She should have been happy to be close to members of the community chosen to witness her case and decide her fate. The early pioneers believed until the verdict, the accused still belonged with the pack. After the last spectator was escorted to the back of the plaza and discovered he had to stand on the other side of the gold ropes did the nine members take their seats at the bench. Kimberly frightened realized all of them were strangers.

Anticipating her reaction, her defender jumped up from her chair and whispered in Kimberly's ear, "I insisted on Citizen Judges outside of Wolfern Province."

High Judge Evan Quark, older than old, escorted by several knights made his slow meandering way up the stairs to his chair. When he turned to look out at the crowd of people nearly five hundred in all, he could see the most affluent from their lofty balconies having separated themselves from the rabble, and as always, the one highest above the crowd happened to be the Governor and his family. They were so high up they looked more like tiny specs moving about on the canopied balcony. "Look it's ants on a dunghill," someone whispered in the crowd. Neighbors shared the remark and soon everyone was giggling. The knights looked out at the sea of smiling faces attempting to spot the original jokester. Good luck with that, Alexandra thought.

High Judge Evan Quark looked as if he wanted to send every tourist and witness to the dungeons, and maybe some of the court officials too. Quark had a reputation for swift justice preferring to save the state money by hanging the guilty minutes after his verdict. He did get a kick out of hangings. Public outrage put a stop to Quark's mandate about economizing the court system. The Governor, after years of debate, acquiesced and passed a new rule: public hangings would be postponed until Una was aligned with Shellfargon's halo.

As Quark wished every damned gawkier and tourist and witness to hell, Harry Zany was grateful for the new rule. It meant Kimberly Lemon (if found guilty) would not be executed today. Normally Harry Zany didn't approve of newfangled ideas. Today he was convinced Kimberly was innocent. There was something about the speed of her arrest and trial which made no sense. This was a political move. Yet, he did feel the world was changing too fast. Satellite dishes, computers, televised news and cellphones were making life too complicated. He was of the old Peresus school on Shellfargon's fragility. No drills or probes or mining the hillsides. Keep your bloody hands off the Shell, he thought.

When Gawain heard Roger Merkel had been disqualified as Scribner, he chuckled. Sure buddy – conflict of interest isn't your only crime. The fact your brother Maxwell Merkel may have tried to poison the accused might be another reason for your early retirement including your attempts to delete testimony and exonerate mobsters. Saurus' regime was so corrupt he kept hiring people like himself. Scummy Saurus deserved the Merkels of the world. They were the kind of lowlife who would steal the dentures right out of a grandmother's mouth if they thought they could earn a buck.

As a protector for the accused, Gawain was seated in the second row from the main stage amongst the witnesses. In front of him sat Sylvia Paleone tossing her hair and craning her spine into a pretzel hoping he'd notice her. He appreciated the curves and the soft skin as much as he appreciated the curves and soft skin of a venomous snake – with revulsion. Luella Morrison sat behind Gawain, the unfair comparison circulating in his brain like the words to an old joke, black and white and red all over. Shame on me, he thought.

In contrast to Sylvia Paleone's superficial good looks, Luella was a squat heavyset woman with a perpetual expression of fatigue.

On occasion she had this bizarre beatified rapture on her homely face whenever Sylvia Paleone came into view. Gawain pitied her. Then he wondered if Luella had the hots for Sylvia. If Sylvia realized Luella loved her carnally, oh ho, what a cat fight that would be. Had Luella been the poisoner? Nah. Why would Sylvia bother or Luella risk it? Paleone had bigger fish to catch.

As Gawain watched the crowd, their faces eagerly awaiting the start of the show, he thought about his interrogation of Victoria Lemon. Evidently, Hawk's examination of Maxwell Merkel's movements had led to Saurus' hasty decision to fire the dishwasher. It was well known Saurus employed a taster because he was convinced his enemies would try to poison him. So that left Victoria Lemon, prime poisoner. Victoria wanted the shop and the private suite rented to Antonio Furness. If Kimberly died, Victoria would inherit everything.

Yesterday she'd agreed to meet him. They'd been sitting at a small table belonging to Antonio's Café. "What brought you to Blueglennen, Dela Lemon?" Gawain asked Kimberly's aunt as she thrust her chest at him. She'd agreed to meet him on the grounds lunch would be free. He did his best to ignore her attempts to seduce him. When she wiggled her way toward him through the tables, her large breasts practically spilling out of her tight-fitting cotton blouse, and said, "You, gorgeous man. I can't believe you're a knight? You look more like a movie star." When she extended her hand to be kissed, he started fishing in his backpack for his techno tablet.

A quick study, she dropped the flirtatious behavior. Her sudden transformation made him uncomfortable. She reminded him of a chameleon capable of switching gears in seconds. "I was staying with an old friend in a nearby town and decided to come home to check up on my niece," she said scooping pasta into her generous mouth, absently licking a smear of sauce from the corner.

"I wanted to see the old gang, Lester and Tony. Tony and I used to date, you know. He'd follow me all over town. It got so old," she shrugged. "Blueglennen is just so boring anyway. The same faces, the same streets, the same music. Boring, boring, boring. I decided, it was time to get out. I'm tremendous with numbers, so I started looking for work in banking. I take after my father when it comes to numbers."

He looked down at his techno tablet which happened to be recording their conversation. In a different window he opened his notebook to see a list of arrivals from the train station then a separate Tower list of visitors to the bailey. "You arrived in Blueglennen the day before Star Bridgekeeper went missing. According to your testimony, you claimed Star Bridgekeeper and Kimberly Lemon quarreled on the last day she was seen."

"Yes," she said chugging down the last of her wine and raising her empty glass for a hovering waiter to refill. Gawain hid his annoyance. This lunch was getting expensive.

"Would you elaborate please? What do you mean by, at odds?"

Victoria Lemon sat back in her chair then took a long leisurely look around the café, everywhere but at him. He knew from interrogation training the best liars had no trouble looking him in the eye. Victoria Lemon seemed pleased about something which made him even more suspicious. As an investigator he was familiar with the signs of a natural born liar and situational predator. He marked her complete lack of fear and her growing boredom as indicators she might be a situational predator.

Situation predators were lazy, self-involved and unlikely to waste precious reserves planning a murder. The only inducement would be profit. She'd been working the world with her lies on television. She might covet the shop or the money she thinks Kimberly is hiding. Would she go to all the trouble of kidnapping Star to implicate her niece?

School records showed Victoria to be gifted in the sciences: math and geography while Kimberly excelled in the creative arts: literature and art. Kimberly finished university and took over the shop when her grandfather died. Victoria left school early and had a few brushes with the law. Yet she'd never been arrested and there was no job history. How could she afford to dress and live so lavishly? Idiot. Her job was the oldest one in the world. It was difficult to tell where this woman fit into the picture, difficult to know if she was dangerous or just plain shallow.

The silence stretched on longer than most people found comfortable. When Gawain realized he was being manipulated, a technique he and his fellow interrogators used on criminals, he realized this woman had a level of control unmatched by some of the best investigators in the business. Her technique made him uncomfortable and he didn't like the feeling. He was investigating her. It was his job to make her talk. He forced himself to remain silent and sipped his coffee. The coffee was cold.

A shadow blocked the sun's light for a moment. Gawain looked up in surprise. Victoria hadn't moved a muscle as if she had been aware of someone approaching for quite some time, as if she had been tracking everyone and anyone in their vicinity. Under the circumstances, she seemed amazingly self-possessed. When he recognized D.I. Hawk, he felt relieved and then annoyed for feeling relieved. Did Hawk think he couldn't handle this woman?

"Dela Victoria Lemon, I am D.I. Hawk, chief investigator of Star's murder. May I sit with you?" D.I. Hawk loomed over them for a moment, unexpectedly congenial for Hawk. Gawain wondered if Hawk had been listening in, maybe recording them. Hawk would not have interrupted the questioning unless he believed there was something seriously at stake.

Victoria took her time before agreeing. Unperturbed Hawk sat down next to Gawain. Before Hawk had a chance to question Victoria, Gawain leaned forward and said, "According to our records, Kimberly inherited the Bookworm Emporium. Yet she was the granddaughter of Charles Maxwell and Helena Grace Lemon and you were the daughter. Why would Charles overlook you?"

"Because Kimberly could do no wrong," Victoria said with a sneer. "She was the sweet little baby girl who never did anything wrong."

"There is a rumor that you are the illegitimate daughter of Kimberly's father Alba Coeljukk. That Amber Kimberly Coeljukk raised you as her own and after Amber died, Charles and Helena adopted you. No one in Blueglennen believed Helena could conceive so late in life. But because people liked and respected Charles and Helena, they pretended you were their daughter. There is a record of the Lemons adopting you when you were five years old. It had to hurt that they gave the shop to Kimberly though. You are their legal daughter.

Nothing to say? Alright let's move on. We've tested all the DNA in Kimberly Lemon's private quarters. You and Kimberly are not related. Alba Coeljukk isn't your father. I think you knew that. Kimberly has violet eyes you have brown. Kimberly has reddish blonde hair; your hair is dyed. If I had to guess I'd say you're a brunette. Would it interest you to know who your real father is?"

"Is that a serious question?" Victoria asked pretending confusion.

"Yes. I'm serious. We've tested everyone who spent any time in the shop and compared the DNA to the DNA inside the bin where Star's body was found. And we found a match between you and a male resident of Blueglennen. Would you like to know who your real father is?" Gawain asked.

"No," she said. "Before I left Blueglennen, Charles told me Alba and Helena weren't my parents. I suspected years ago before Helena died. It doesn't matter. Charles told me my father must have been good in math because I did better than anyone in my class. I tested well in every science field."

"Why go into banking," Gawain asked. "When you could have been a doctor or a chemist?

"I'm very sensitive to smells. To tell you the truth, I'm hypersensitive to most enclosed spaces and chemicals. I'm like a bloodhound. One time, I..."

Hawk interrupted her to ask, "Aren't you curious about your real father? Wouldn't you like to know his name? Maybe meet him?"

For the first time the mask of boredom dropped away. Her face contorted into a spasm of hate so intense she looked as if she'd aged a decade. They waited as she got herself under control. Her body trembled for a minute or two. Gawain almost felt sorry for her. Hawk watched her without revealing his thoughts. She dropped her head and unfolded her hands slowly. They saw the droplets of blood on her palms where she had dug her nails deep into her flesh.

"I think I know who he is," she said still mesmerized by the blood. "Before I left Blueglennen he asked me out for a drink. I'd known his family all my life. We'd had drinks together before but back then it was with his wife. And then he got really drunk and tried to seduce me. I kneed him in the groin, and he got so mad he told me I should show him respect since we were related. At first, I didn't believe him and then I began to wonder. His wife found out what I'd done. Stupid cow. She wasn't mad at him for coming on to me. She was pissed I might have damaged his little pecker for life. I wish I had. She sucker-punched me, and I fought back. After the fight, she went limping back to her scum of a husband."

"When was this?" Hawk asked.

"Ten years ago, before Charles died," she said and then looked up at the Cetacea Rampart as if she was remembering something traumatic. "I was three years old, and the Bridgekeepers just dumped me in the street and left me for dead in a foreign country. I was their first born, but they couldn't be bothered. Back then they didn't have the cushy holding in the castle, back then they were just dirty tramps selling garbage. They didn't inherit the holding until after his uncle died."

"You must have hated Sophia and Star," Hawk observed. "They had gotten the love you were denied. Maybe that's why you killed Star to hurt them."

Victoria leaned over. Her long blonde curls hid her face. They waited until she had a chance to compose herself. Then they heard the laughter. It started off soft, barely above a whisper, but soon became a shrieking hysteria which ricocheted off the plaza walls. People sitting in café tables nearby turned to stare. Her laughter wasn't contagious. Her laughter disturbed. Hawk and Bristlecone waited uncomfortably for her to calm down. Bristlecone kept glancing at his watch.

When she stopped laughing, she took out a compact and repaired the damage to her face. Now composed enough to talk, she remarked in a tired voice, "I never envied Sophia or Star. Before I learned the truth, I'd already felt sorry for them. I'd seen firsthand what putrid parents they were. The Bridgekeeper sisters would beg on the street for food or slip into people's homes because they were freezing. Star was in diapers at the time. Their trashy ignorant parents abandoned them the day Sophia could reach the stove and cook their meals.

So, no. I wasn't jealous of the Bridgekeeper sisters. I felt sorry for them. I still hate Charles for leaving me nothing, but I knew I was very, very, lucky the day I met Kimberly's mother. She was the only one on Walrat Island who took me home and fed me. The villagers had seen the Bridgekeepers throw me out of the wagon after they'd picked over the good stuff at the dump.

They heard me crying for days and days and did nothing. But Amber Coeljukk found me and took me home. Her husband Alba tried to throw me out and she threatened to leave him. She was his meal ticket too. Helena was as soft as Amber which was good for me. I landed in a cushy home where I never had to worry about food or a roof over my head.

Until Charles died and Kimberly got the shop. She refused to share the inheritance with me and kicked me out. How's that for familial love?"

Gawain leaned forward, "You robbed the shop and Kimberly kicked you out."

"Did she tell you that?"

"No. Harry Zany told me what happened." Gawain paused when Hawk turned on his com-wave.

The message Hawk sent him made Gawain furious: *Quit treating this witness as a suspect. Let me question her.* Rather than respond Gawain shut his com down and leaned back in his chair.

Hawk changed the subject, "I heard you say Star and your niece were at odds with each other. What did you mean?"

A frown creased Victoria's usually smooth forehead. It was obvious, she didn't like to be interrupted. For a split second, both men wondered if she would ignore his question or evade it as she had with Gawain. Without warning, Victoria's habitual smugness disappeared replaced by inexplicable excitement. She leaned forward and said, "Well, Star was going on and on about the church and telling Kim she was headed for hell if she didn't join the church and Kim told her to get out and Star instead of leaving ran to Kimberly's private quarters looking as if she might cry. Kim hid behind the cash register as cold as the snow on Mount Lordbuster.

When I tried to leave the shop, she bolted the front door with some fancy contraption. Old Timmy Finstickel was in the shop. I could smell him stinking up the place, reeking like some nasty sewer and I told Kim if she didn't let me out, I would scream at the top of my lungs and Timmy would be my witness."

"Why did Dela Kimberly bolt the door in the first place?" Hawk asked.

Victoria shrugged and began cleaning her fingernails with her used napkin.

"She must have had a reason for bolting the door? Why did she bolt the door, Victoria?"

Victoria looked up with a blank expression and said, "Kimberly had this problem with power. She likes to manipulate people. And she was just trying to manipulate me, to see if she could scare me. She's like that, a total control freak." A moment later, she threw her napkin on her empty plate and gathered up her purse. "They're taking too long to get my wine. I'm going to tell Tony the service sucks here."

Gawain jumped up and asked, "You said you came back to Blueglennen to see the old gang and mentioned Art. What is Art's full name?"

As she adjusted her purse on her arm, Victoria looked him in the eye and said matter-of-factly with the insinuation he must be an idiot, "Why Lester Arthur Lucie, of course. And the other member of my entourage was Harry Hanson. He used to be nuts about me. He owns the Shellfargon Seed. You know the one, on Wolfern Promenade?"

Hawk rose to his feet and approached Victoria carefully, "I have just one more question for you Dela Lemon if you'll indulge me."

With a roll of her eyes, she said, "Well? What is it?"

"When you were growing up, did you hear any gossip about the Bridgekeepers' marriage?"

"What do you mean?"

"Did they have an open relationship? Or were there rumors of a divorce?"

For the first time Victoria looked surprised. Hawk's question seemed to puzzle and intrigue her. Gawain could see the synapses firing as she connected with her hippocampus. He wished Shard could be here to see a Delphinid working so hard to answer a simple question. Victoria really wanted to be able to say something inflammatory and he could tell she was debating whether to make up an imaginary lover. In the end she shrugged and said, "Maybe. It wouldn't surprise me. The two trash-eaters deserve each other."

"We appreciate your candor, Dela Victoria."

Long after she'd gone, Gawain wondered why the exchange between Hawk and Victoria Lemon had disturbed him so much. Before he could puzzle out why, Antonio Furness approached their table. Furness watched Victoria leave the plaza before turning to them and asking, "What's she doing here?"

"Just the person I wanted to talk to," Hawk said in an uncharacteristically jovial manner. "Would you mind taking a moment to help us with our investigation?"

Was he trying to recruit these two lowlifes?

Before Antonio sat down, Antonio snapped his fingers and a waiter appeared. He refused to sit until the table was cleared of dirty dishes and empty wine glasses. Hawk leaned back and waited. As Hawk questioned Antonio, Gawain watched the café owner shift in his seat as if he couldn't find a comfortable spot to rest. He wondered if Antonio's uneasiness had more to do with the reputation of his business than Victoria Lemon. He admitted he'd had an affair with Victoria, but their affair was over. He claimed Victoria had a new lover and was presently living with Harry Hanson above his newspaper office.

A blare of trumpets brought Gawain back to the present, back to Kimberly Lemon's trial. He tried to tamp down the despair churning in his gut. They had to find the real killer before this court-of-clowns hung an innocent woman. As he waited for the trial to begin, he reread the interview notes he'd recorded paying close attention to Antonio's testimony:

Sure, Victoria and I used to date. That was nearly twenty years ago. Have you taken a look at her lately? Do you really think I'd start that up again? Hell no. She looks like she's been left on the clothes-line too long. And don't get me started on her sneaky ways. She showed up at my door and told me I had to get out of my apartment?

I told her I'd signed a year's lease and she had no right to throw me out. She went on and on about how the apartment belonged to her family and had been in their family for generations and I told her that Kimberly couldn't afford the taxes on the place and leased the apartment to me. So, if she's trying to get me thrown out, you can tell the controller and the housing committee and even Governor Saurus, I'll go to the highest court in the land before I let that witch move into my home.

His interview with Luella Morrison had been fruitless as well. She was never in the inner circle, never privy to the juicy secrets of the Church of the Holy Centipede or Governor Saurus' regime. She hadn't a clue who the Merkel brothers were either. So far, he could only pin Victoria Lemon on attempted blackmail, Maxwell Merkel on attempted poisoning, and Luella Morrison on being madly in love with Sylvia Paleone. Blackmail and poisoning were crimes in his opinion, being in love with someone of the same sex was not. Unfortunately, Delphi weren't as progressive as members of the UES Albion.

It just seemed too convenient Victoria would show up now followed by Star Bridgekeeper's murder. Her stunned reaction to the news she might be the daughter of the Bridgekeepers had been genuine. She'd wondered but hadn't known for sure. Maybe, the Lemon family hadn't known either. But what about the Bridgekeeper parents? Had they recognized their eldest daughter?

Most parents would have recognized their own flesh-and-blood. The Bridgekeeper parents weren't normal. Their recorded neglect suggested they were too self-involved to wonder about other people's children. That didn't mean Victoria was innocent. She could have killed her half-sister in order to get rid of Kimberly and regain the shop. Someone paid a poisoner to kill Kimberly. Maybe Victoria seduced Merkel?

A hunch wasn't enough for a judge, even these obvious sycophants sitting on the Citizen Judges' bench. Gawain's evidence of conspiracy to commit murder was circumstantial. Merkel claimed the money in his wallet was from a catering job in another town. Merkel's story checked out. But he could have tried to poison Kimberly to keep from going to jail? Wakefield might have blackmailed him thinking he could gain points with Victoria if she knew.

As Kimberly concentrated all her attention on the High Judge's chair, the intricate carvings, the glossy finish, and the massiveness of its material, she managed to avoid the theatrical entrance of the nine robed Delphi. Someone told her later how the Citizen Judges made a spectacle of themselves as they walked past the dais. They were behaving as if they were in a beauty pageant each one trying to outdo the other. Instead of walking single file to the bench as they had for thousands of years, the Citizen Judges sashayed down the aisle, one at a time, smiling and waving and making complete asses of themselves.

They would determine her fate, but they were too busy showing off for the tourists and cameras. Her attempt to concentrate on the High Judge's chair, as if the chair might save her resulted in a tingling shocked surprise when someone sneaked up behind her. The person appeared to loom. It was a bad omen. For a second her brain struggled to accept what her eyes were seeing. Her defender was late. She should have been seated and ready to go before Kimberly arrived. Why was she so late? Did she forget something? Her pen? Her briefcase?

Still attempting to process her bad luck and conscious of the noise, the crowds, the smells of freshly baked bread, cigar smoke, alcohol breath from a passerby including one judge's heavy perfume which made her eyes water, Kimberly looked up at her defender dazed and slightly nauseated. Shehili Swana's large black eyes studied her for approximately thirty seconds without giving any clues away. Kimberly wondered later if she'd just imagined Dela Swana's lips curved in a warm smile. For days she continued to believe Swana's intentions had been good.

Her Defender offered Kimberly the personal techno tablet and said, "Read this." Without another word her Defender turned and walked away. Phil Potts seated at the table to Kimberly's left grinned. Frank Darknight seated at the scribe's table near the witness chair looked alarmed. Sensing danger, Kimberly turned and watched as Shehili Swana walked down the center aisle between the witnesses and the audience. Her Defender walked beyond the gold ropes which separated the poor from the rich with her head held high and her back straight. She turned onto Wolfern Promenade and never looked back.

Kimberly still in a daze looked down at the scribbled note on the screen and read in disbelief the message, *I regret to inform you, Kimberly Amber Lemon, that I can no longer assist you in your defense due to prior commitments. I have left the dossier and the legal documents necessary for your defense on the Protector table. According to Wolfern Law, you are permitted to defend yourself. I am so sorry. I wish you all the best. Stay strong.*

A moment of panic left Kimberly breathless. She gasped for air. The whistling from her dry throat attracted the notice of the citizen judges, as well as, the witnesses seated behind her. One of the witnesses assigned to protect her during the trial moved like an arrow to its target. When Kimberly felt his warm hand on her shoulder, she refused to look up afraid she would burst into tears. Instead Kimberly handed the techno tablet to Knight Bristlecone.

"Is this all the explanation you were given?"

"Yes. What shall I do? What can I do? I'm doomed. I have no law experience. I'm not knowledgeable about court proceedings. The accuser will make a smoothie of me. There'll be nothing left of me but blood and water. What do I do? Oh, hell and damnation."

Gawain leaned forward and in a soothing voice said, "You can request a new defender. When the High Judge is seated, stand up and address the court. Tell them what's happened and beg the court's indulgence. Ask for a new defender or defend yourself. I'll help."

"I can't defend myself," she hissed and when she attempted to swallow her muscles contracted. For a moment she thought she was going to choke on her own tongue. Warm fingers pressed into the back of her neck.

"Breathe, Kimberly. Just breathe. Concentrate on the symbol of your justice system."

"Dono? Why?"

"No, my sweet. Not him. The wolf and her pups. Family. Think of your grandfather. Think of your bookshop. Breathe slowly through your nose."

Desperate to find some peace, she tried to concentrate on the marble pedestal beside the High Judge's chair where the bronze statue of Wolfern Province sat. All her life the wolf and her pups had been a symbol of protection, family, and love. She thought about her grandfather and grandmother. She remembered the picture of her mother in her wedding gown, the picture of her grandmother holding a baby in her arms. That baby had been her. She'd been loved by her grandparents and her mother. A trickle of hope moved down her spine. Instead of feeling alone and afraid she realized she had many friends who wished her only the best.

Swana may have deserted her; yet, Kimberly began to wonder if perhaps Swana's desertion might be a blessing. In the back of her mind, for many days now a niggling worry had been pecking away at her insides, a persistent ache that perhaps things were not right, that Shehili Swana's halfhearted interest in her defense could be a sign of failure. Something had happened between the time Kimberly had been in the catacombs and the time she had been released to prepare for her defense. Her Defender must have discovered new evidence, evidence which pointed to her as the murderer. There could be no other reason to leave her defenseless. Swana wasn't the kind of person to cut and run. What had she learned?

There was no time to wonder what she'd learned. Kimberly must compose herself and prepare a speech asking the court to delay the trial. Separating herself from the pain of Shehili's desertion, Kimberly sent Swana's abdication to her cellphone and turned around to face the first row of chairs on her side of the plaza. She looked into the warm friendly blue eyes of Lynora Reason then at Joanie Fitzhammond. Joanie's keen brown eyes hadn't missed a thing. She nodded as if she knew something, then lifted a book in the air, a book she'd been holding in her lap the entire time. Kimberly recognized the cover. It was one of her grandfather's law books.

Forcing a weak smile Kimberly handed the techno tablet to Lynora Reason because Lynora Reason had the freedom to get up from her chair and walk down the aisle. "This was given to me by mistake. Could you return the tablet to the Unique Boutique?"

Lynora nodded thoughtfully and in a reassuring voice said, "Of course. It won't take a moment." It seemed as if the minutes stretched into hours as Kimberly waited for the High Judge to appear and for Lynora Reason to return. She was curious how Dela Swana would react at receiving the tablet back. Just as the High Judge appeared in his long black robes and his black pointed cap, Lynora returned.

Kimberly turned and asked, "Did you see Shehili?"

Lynora leaned forward and whispered, "No. Her clerk was at the counter. She told me she received an urgent message from her boss. Shehili is on her way to the train station. She ordered the clerk to pack up the merchandise and deliver it to the Albion shuttle. She's going home. The clerk said Dela Swana had given her a generous two-week severance package."

"What about the Cavenymphs? What will happen to them?"

"The Cavenymphs?" Lynora asked turning to Joanie baffled by the question.

Joanie Fitzhammond leaned forward. Soon there were three heads close together in deep whispered conversation. A booming voice interrupted the three women and in an irritated voice told the audience and the court, "All Rise for the High Judge."

Joanie finished her lecture on Cavenymphs with, "Some are bonded to the clerk, others to Swana. The rest are on loan from the Museum of Exotic Creatures."

Lynora Reason hissed, "I'm astonished Dela Swana would desert Kimberly at such a time. Why has she left Kimberly to defend herself alone? It makes no sense."

"The clerk said Dela Swana was on her way to the Albion shuttle. What's that tell you?" Joanie said with a lift of her brow.

Before Kimberly could respond, someone tapped her on the shoulder and she turned in time to see an unfamiliar knight frowning down at her. "Please stand Accused. The court is now in session."

Obediently Kimberly rose to her feet and stood facing the

High Judge known to all in the country of Curl as Farting Quark, a thin stooped-shouldered octogenarian who loved to send people to the gallows based on education or how they smelled. He considered halitosis to be more heinous than murder. His catch phrase: I love a good hanging before bed.

There were no shoppers fingering the merchandise, no customers, no gigglers, no other people in the Boutique but the clerk and upset Cavenymphs on the wall behind her. Shehili Swana set her briefcase and techno tablet on the counter and left the room to fetch her shawl. When she returned, she discovered someone had come in uninvited. She glared at him. Hawk stepped forward.

The expression on his face forced her to take a step back, "What do you want?"

"I told you not to interfere. I warned you. The damage is done. Again. You rush in and take charge and look what happens. Why give up now? Afraid of your father? I doubt that. What's really going on, Swan?"

"She lied. I can't abide a liar."

"How so?"

"It's none of your business."

"It is my business. Tell me now or."

"Or what?" Shehili asked with a scornful sneer. "You'll tell my father and he'll have me court martialed? Don't bother. I've already sent a report to all three captains and they agree with me. Kimberly Lemon can't be trusted."

"I disagree."

"And you say I've lost my objectivity? Hah," she said over her shoulder as she moved closer to her office door, her eyes cold dark pebbles.

"I've sent my findings to the captains," he said. "I believe my reputation as an objective noninterfering ethnographer beats your emotional attachment and sudden aversion. Your behavior endangers us all."

"Then do what you must do," Shehili spat. "I dare you."

"It's not up to me. The captains or the Delphadorturo will decide if we stay."

Shehili Swana shrugged pretending an indifference she didn't feel, "First they tell me I can't defend her. Now when I tell them she's guilty, I'm a troublemaker? Tell them to make up their damned minds. I'm not going back to the Albion. I deserve a vacation. I'm going to travel the world. And I'll tell you again, based on the evidence I've discovered, she's guilty. Why should I waste my time defending a murderess?"

"Good luck finding another post," he warned her as he moved toward the doors. "I nearly forgot." He swung around and looked her in the eye. "Your credentials are suspended. You're no longer a member of our team." He swept out the door and into the sunshine a ferocious smile on his handsome face.

The pretty young clerk watched as Shehili Swana picked up her traveling luggage and set her techno tablet on the counter, "Tell Dela Lemon my opening and closing statements and notes are in here for her defense. The folder marked Defense has everything she'll need. Can you do that for me? Good. Now I must go. It's been a pleasure working with you." Without another word Shehili sailed out of the shop.

The clerk waited a minute or so to be sure she'd really left, and when she was convinced Dela Swana would not return proceeded to dance a jig across the space separating her from the Cavenymphs. Some of the nymphs began to cry and attempted to leap from the wall and follow Swana. Other nymphs, closer to the counter, began to glow their voices rising in unison sending shock waves through the room and simultaneously heart-pounding-mind-tingling music out into the street.

Finally, she could go home. No longer needed as a prop for Dela Swana's masquerade, she could take her Cavenymphs and go home to New Dala. The clerk tried to hug as many of her personal nymphs as her slight body could reach and the nymphs recognizing her love for them began to sing even louder. Outside Unique Boutique the crowd jammed like pebbles on a beach unable to even see Wolfern Promenade, upset they were too far away to hear the trial of the century listened to the nymphs. For a few brief moments they were distracted. Some knew about Cavenymphs and explained to the uninitiated about their history and talent. The Merchant's Row Alliance heard the singing and were uplifted believing the music vindicated Kimberly.

Knight Graceland while stationed on the rampart above Unique Boutique could hear the nymphs singing. His appreciation of the music sparked a brilliant idea. He pulled out his cellphone and called Hawk. Unlike other moments when the knight had what he believed to be a great idea and Hawk stomped on it as too radical or impractical, this time Hawk praised his resourcefulness. Within an hour speakers and video screens were positioned on the ramparts so the people packed on Merchants' Row and the narrow corridor of Wolfern Promenade could watch and hear the trial.

"Look what the knights are doing. They're putting up television screens."

"There's even one on the gatehouse."

Kimberly Lemon rose from her chair to face Judge Quark. Judge Quark was too busy struggling to sit down in his chair with dignity, he never noticed. If circumstances had been normal, Kimberly would have had nothing to say her entire trial; she would have been the body in the chair of the accused, an object they could speculate about with impunity. Nobody wanted to be in her shoes because everyone assumed, she was guilty.

In the country of Curl studies proved poor people committed the majority of crimes, especially crimes of passion. Delphinids believed the crime of passion was the foulest of crimes, committed exclusively by the poor because the middle-class and rich were too gentile and comfortable to bother with such silliness. They all agreed, poor people were often the perpetrators of crimes and tended to murder for the most trivial of reasons. Just the other day, Deletha Child was beaten with a baseball bat. In her terror to avoid a beating, she flung herself off the parapet and onto the rocks below unable to escape Cartel Hill's murderous rampage, all because the two of them were poor.

Kimberly was thinking about Deletha and the poor herself. Her thoughts were moving in a different direction. She noticed how bloodthirsty the crowd was today as they watched the trial. She'd noticed how some of the people when Deletha was running for her life were avidly soaking up the drama and did nothing to stop Cartel. No one had shouted for him to stop or come to her rescue. And now Kimberly could imagine how terrified Deletha had been. She too felt as if she'd been abandoned by her defender and by her neighbors, as if her guilt had already been written in the High Judge's book. For a second, she considered giving up.

No. She wouldn't let them win. She couldn't give up so easily.

Murderers were hung straight after the trial, no use wasting taxpayer money with room and board. Yes. They would kill her straightaway and the thought of the rope around her neck propelled her off her chair so fast she hit her thighs on the tiny table in front of her and nearly dropped the techno tablet. "Your honor," she shouted as a knight continued to fuss with the High Judge's microphone which he was trying to attach to the back of the judge's black robes. She had to call Judge Quark's name several times before he turned his attention to her.

It took him several more minutes to focus his rheumy eyes on Kimberly. He flicked the sleeves of his black robe impatiently back from his scrawny wrists and glared, "The High Court Judge doesn't speak to the accused. Where's your defender?"

"She's gone. I've been left to defend myself, Your Honor."

"Impossible. You must have a defender."

"Give me time to find a replacement, Your Honor."

"No," he said his gray bushy eyebrows meeting, expressing their condemnation of her rudeness and lack of breeding. Without a doubt she looked guilty. Look at her clothes. Rags. Second and third hand rags not fit for an honest person to wear. The sleeve of her sweater looked frayed and dirty. The unclean poor. Revolting.

He rapped on the miniature drum near his elbow for the purpose of calling the court to order. When no one responded he rapped harder petulant in his annoyance. A knight brought him a techno tablet. As the sun rose above the rampart and beat down on the courtroom's head, its warmth reminded the audience of the time. It was noon. Court should have started hours ago. The silence stretched on so long people began to get restless. They stirred in their chairs. Some whispered to their neighbors. Behind the ropes people began to chant, "Let's go. Let's go."

Stubbornly Kimberly remained standing. Judge Quark lifted his head and shouted, his voice sending the microphone into fits which ended in a searing high-pitched squeal. People clamped hands to their heads. The knight whispered in Quark's ear. Everyone in the plaza heard him say, "Sir, the mic can pick up a feather hitting the floor. No need to shout, Your Honor."

Judge Quark shoved the knight aside and rose to his feet. He paused to reflect and in a normal voice spoke to the courtroom, "Is there anyone here willing to defend the accused?"

The silence lasted five minutes. Kimberly refused to look behind her. Then from the corner of her eye she noticed Phil Potts, a man of average height and large belly wearing a blonde hairpiece which fooled no one. He rose to his feet with studied pomp and opened his mouth to answer the judge's question. Before the accuser had a chance to speak, Judge Quark misinterpreting his intentions waved him away. Quark's petulance left him lipless as he said, "You can't be accuser and defender at the same time Potts. Sit down."

"I am fully aware of that fact, Your Honor. I wish to remind you of Curl history. If an accused has no money to pay for a defender, they can defend themselves. If Dela Lemon wishes to defend herself I have no objection."

"We are wasting precious time," Judge Quark announced.

The squeal from the mic tempered his speech. His voice softened when he spoke to the crowd, "The accused may defend herself." Then he looked down at Kimberly. "When you are Defender move to the Protector Arena and sit at the bench, otherwise, at all other times remain seated in that chair. That chair. Do you understand?"

"Yes, Your Honor," Kimberly told him in her best schoolroom voice, teacher to pupil. She collected her belongings and sat down at the Defender bench.

Judge Quark barked, and the squeal from the mic nearly broke the eardrums of those nearby, "Not now, stupid girl."

Kimberly jumped up from the chair, alarmed. Several idiosyncratic thoughts ran through her head before she reached the accused chair: her surprise and delight in discovering how comfortable and plush the defender's chair was compared to the hard and unyielding chair she was approaching, the fleeting smile of encouragement from the newly appointed scribe Frank Darknight and the lovely aroma of richly sugared and baked goods in the attractive gift basket near Phil Potts' bench.

By the time she sat down on the stiff chair of the accused, she remembered where she had seen other such gift baskets and realized with a heavy heart one member of the Merchant's Row Alliance had no love for her. The gift baskets belonged to Bill Anders and Billy Bill Anders of Anders & Son's Pastries. They must think she's guilty. They gave the basket to Phil Potts and wanted to be sure she knew they believed she was a murderess.

For a fraction of a second, she considered turning in her seat and searching for them in the crowd and giving them the stink eye. Why bother? They weren't worth the trouble. After all, Frank believed her innocent and so did Alexandra, Lynora and Joanie, even probably a few of the others. That was good enough for her. Then she heard a familiar voice shout, "Give um hell Kim." She smiled. Harry Zany believed she was innocent too.

Judge Quark beat on his drum, "That will be enough back there. Any more comments from the dung heap and everyone will be removed from the bailey. Understood?" He threw his squinty eyed threat around the plaza then he sat down inch by inch waiting for someone to speak out of turn, so he could make good his threat. When no one did, Judge Quark motioned for Phil Potts to begin opening statements. Familiar with Judge Quark's style, Phil jumped up from his chair and marched over to the Citizen Judges seated in a semi-circle on the ancient, butt warmed and butt polished bench.

Potts was reminded of the numerous citizens of Curl who had planted their various butts for hours on end, sometimes for months at a time on said bench, said bench going back nearly eight hundred years where fellow citizen judges had been known to free a few, send many to prison, and consign an average number to an unlucky death by hanging.

Before Duke Dono absconded with all the treasure of the castle, death had been dealt out by strangulation, guillotine, axe, poison, or stoning. Finally, in this more civilized century expert scientists had concluded death by hanging was the most humane method. If done right, he remembered belatedly. There had been a few unfortunate occasions when the noose had slipped, and the accused had to be hung again.

One of the citizen judges coughed and Potts picked out the trouble maker. The new guy. He might feel sorry for the female. Potts would have to convince him she was a cold-blooded killer. He knew these people better than his own family. He grinned, and a few returned his smile with one of their own. A mouthful of minnow, for sure.

Alexandra S. Montegue seated on a chair three rows back pulled out her cellphone and began frantically typing. Evelyn Lordbuster in the chair next to her bent an attractive head covered in fine gold hair and watched Alexandra's slender fingers flying across the tiny writing board. "Can you send text messages in a court room?" Evelyn asked suddenly concerned for her safety. She didn't want to be sent to prison for breaking the law.

Instead of taking the time to answer, Alexandra ignored Evelyn and typed furiously, her long neck bent to the phone in an urgent posture as if her life depended on sending the message without delay. There was tension in every line of her body, from her feet to her legs to her spine and up her slim arms, all the way to the top of her head. Her thick black hair cut in a romantic bob from a bygone era fell across her white cheek, effectively hiding her expression from her nearest neighbors.

Evelyn leaned back in her chair annoyed. Did Alexandra think she couldn't keep a secret? What was so important she had to text on a day like today?

Phil Potts began his opening statement confident he had no need to persuade the citizen judges or the crowd of the woman's guilt, "I will prove the accused did cold-bloodedly murder poor little Star Bridgekeeper. She had the opportunity, the motive, and the tools. It shall come as no surprise that Kimberly Lemon is a poor wretch who has forsaken our one true god.

Star Bridgekeeper came to her hoping to save her soul. Kimberly brushed the child aside and when Star persevered Kimberly lashed out and killed her. Ashamed of her vile deed, the accused attempted to stuff the body in a garbage bin and hide the evidence in the catacombs. But her crime was discovered. My evidence will prove Kimberly Lemon is guilty of murder."

Until he had been assigned to this case, he'd only had a passing acquaintance with the accused. She made him uncomfortable then. Now he knew why. She didn't play by the rules. On his way back to his chair, Phil heard the tinkling of tiny bells and turned in time to see a striking woman with black hair and brown eyes lift her cellphone closer in order to read the message on the screen. He stopped in his tracks and waited until all eyes were on him. People turned in their seats to stare at the woman. Feeling eyes on her, Alexandra looked up and with twin spots of color between her patrician nose snapped her cellphone shut and stuffed it in her pocket.

Judge Quark pounded the drum by his arm and said, "All cellphones will be shut off immediately. The next person to send a text message or video of this trial will be sent to the dungeons." The rustle of clothing, the frantic opening of purses and carryalls and baggage was deafening as hundreds of people searched for their cellphones and proceeded to shut them down.

Judge Quark pounded the drum which surprised Frank Darknight. "We will have a short recess for lunch," he said as he descended from his chair with the help of a knight.

Those who brought their lunch offered sandwiches to their seated neighbors. Anthony's Café waitstaff could be seen in their black trousers and white aprons weaving through the seated members of the audience taking orders for lattes and pastries. Cher Amie Restaurant took orders from those in the roped arena offering boxed lunches. The Green Monkey offered vegan entrees and desserts.

Guinevere Goodbody seated on the other side of Evelyn offered the two women her vegan wraps made with her family's special sauce. And when Alexandra refused, Guinevere turned to

Harry Zany and offered the soy wrapped sandwich to him. He shook his head in disgust, "No, thank you. I'd rather eat paste."

"But I've been told you love vegetables."

"A lie."

Alexandra stuffed her hands in her pockets and even Harry could see from her expression she'd received good news. It was an odd sight to see the pocket of her stylish black bolero pants undulate as if several worms were cavorting inside which meant her fingers were reading the bumps and dots on her screen. "A Braille screen," Guinevere said in awe. "I thought they weren't out yet. How did you get one?"

A waitstaff from Anthony's Café interrupted Alexandra's response and asked Harry Zany for his order. Once Harry ordered a chicken crepe sandwich, Alexandra pretended she hadn't heard Guinevere's question. Harry placed his box containing his chicken sandwich order on his lap and proceeded to carefully remove the tissue paper, "This is my favorite vegetable."

"Meat is not a vegetable," Guinevere reminded him.

Since Alexandra was familiar with the banter between Guinevere and Harry, she spent the rest of the lunch break thinking about the message she had received from her cousin at Crest Hall. The Delphadorturo was in a meeting but had a three o'clock flight scheduled for New Dala. Her cousin owed her a favor. Would he convince Earl Raker? Would he be in time? She hoped for Kimberly's sake, her cousin's silver tongue moved mountains.

Another twenty minutes passed. In the back beyond the roped area, people had made themselves comfortable on the big blue stones of Wolfern Promenade, some people throwing blankets on the stones and eating their lunch as if they were on a picnic. They pretended the people who refused to sit were looming trees. Their only view was of shoes, ankles, leggings, and butts. Once the trumpets blared, picnickers quickly scrambled to their feet as the High Judge and Citizen Judges returned to the dais. Silence fell. Electricity filled the air. People began to whisper.

Instead of Judge Quark with his cane and petulant lip, a diminutive figure in familiar black robes and gold braid walked briskly up the steps to the High Judge's chair. The new High Judge looked like a lamb shepherded between wolf hounds. The crowd grew excited at the sight of the youngest high judge in the country of Curl appearing in person in their city. The plaza vibrated with excitement as people tried to make sense of this new development. The young woman faced the court and the audience as a knight pinned the mic to the back of her robe. The knight handled the task delicately choosing to snap the mic to her white neck tie.

Once he was finished and had removed himself from the dais, the new High Judge, the youngest member of High Court Judges spoke to the crowd, "Due to unforeseen circumstances, Judge Evan Quark was forced to make an emergency trip to the capital city. As acting High Judge, I, Mercedes Hepplewhite do hereby accept Judge Quark's invitation as surrogate for Case #12345sg10 and will stand in his place for the duration of this trial. I promise to be as fair and thorough as my predecessor. Court is now in session. Please be seated."

E1 Shellfargon Year 5092 NDMP WK 6: UES Albion 4
New high court judge appointed to Kimberly Lemon trial. Request all information on Mercedes Hepplewhite. Commander of Curlecon Forces awaiting confirmation of spook's identity. Special Ops of ISG in route now. Orders are to contain and watch – do not arrest.

E4 Shellfargon Year 5092 NDMP WK 6: UES Albion 4
Urgent request to resume legal counseling of accused Delphinid Kimberly Lemon. Noninterference is a hypocrisy. Do we work for the secret service or for the betterment of the cosmos? By our actions today are we cementing our relationship with the inhabitants as lords or equals? Once our part in this situation is discovered there may be trouble from the Delphadorturo and the Queen of Lacertidae.

Chapter 11

High Judge Mercedes Hepplewhite sat down upon the throne of justice. She looked out across the plaza at the people seated and those bunched together at the back. Knights, arm and arm, kept the crowd from breaking the ropes and squeezing themselves between chairs or making themselves comfortable on the ground between aisles.

She turned to study the Citizen Judges and mentally groaned. For a decade she's seen the same faces, the smug smiles and bored eyeballs as they slept sitting up. Feeling unfriendly eyes on them, like sunflowers they lifted their heads and assumed the appearance of interest. So, there would be a few paid Citizen Judges today. She might be able to discredit them or threaten them with prison time, maybe, even fine some for corruption.

If Mercedes had even a minuscule bit of magical thinking in her body, she would have used prayer right now as a means of protecting the accused. The trial had barely started, and yet the Citizen Judges had already made up their minds. She could see no good coming out of this trial. The accused was doomed.

She would do all she could to make this case a fair one. She refused to be another Judge Quark. This was her chance to be noticed by the 8th Circuit Court or better yet receive the Delphadorturo appointment to the highest court in the land – the Silver Crest Council of Curl or Silver 11 as everyone called the panel. They made the ultimate legal decisions which every Delphi must abide by.

"The Defender may now make her opening statement," Judge Hepplewhite announced, careful to keep her voice at a normal decibel mindful of the microphone attached to her body. To appear impartial, she maintained a neutral expression.

No one moved. Mercedes waited a few more minutes her eyes steady as the woman continued to sit with her hands in her lap upon the chair of the accused. She looked terrified. Poor thing, she thought, examining her with dismay. She looks as if she's been dumped on the side of the road and left to walk home through a particularly nasty bit of woodland. Without a map. Without a lamp. Naked. Oh, stop.

"Dela Lemon. Excuse. Defender Lemon, you may make your opening statement."

People were staring at Kimberly with too much white around

their eyeballs. What were they waiting for? Then from far away she heard someone call her name. She looked around and this time a male voice rang out nearly sending the receiver strapped to Judge Hepplewhite's back into hysterics and surely splitting Kimberly's already fragile confidence into tiny pieces. The knight said something like, "Accused. Stand up before the High Judge or I'll send you to the dungeons for disobedience."

Kimberly sprang up, a fire leaping from her spine up to her neck, a fire she recognized as indignation. The unfairness of the knight's demand rode through her bloodstream like a magical current of electricity. "I am sorry Your Honor. This," she waved her hands about the plaza. "This is all new to me. Shall I stand here and begin my opening statement, or should I move over there?" She pointed at the Defender table.

Mercedes interceded shooting the errant knight a stern look, "As I recall Judge Quark informed you of the correct procedure for so unusual a development. Do you not recall his words?"

"Oh. Yes. Of course. He said something about having to place myself at the Defender's bench when I am playing the part of defense. And, at all other times I'm to sit here on the chair of the accused."

"Yes, well you're half right."

"Sorry Dela. I mean, Your Honor?"

Judge Hepplewhite leaned forward the long sleeves of her robe shifting the papers on her bench, "You are not playing a part, Dela Lemon. Your very life is at stake. I suggest you take this trial seriously."

"I do Your Honor. I do."

"Proceed."

With speed Kimberly shoved back the chair of the accused and made her way to the defender's bench. Just for a millisecond Frank Darknight beamed at her. She took courage from his not so subtle signal. Ignoring the plodding blob of bored resentment to her right, known to the rest of the world as Accuser Phil Potts, Kimberly searched through legal papers, books, and Shehili's briefs with shaky fingers until she finally found the techno tablet hidden under the basket of goods from Ander's Bakery.

She made a point of glaring at Phil Potts who pretended not to notice. Had he read the papers? Had he read the techno tablet? Perhaps. Yet why should she care? To use an Earth term - she was fucked anyway. And then something made her turn around to look behind her and scan the faces of the people seated closest to the front row. In the third row back on her left, she saw Alexandra S. Montague and Harry Zany. Both winked giving her the courage to press on.

Their support provided her with a smidgeon of hope. Not everybody thought she was a murderess.

Yet the unfairness of the situation flooded her body with such burning anger and hatred she wanted so badly to lash out at someone. The idea of thumping Phil Potts on the head with her techno tablet felt so right. For a split second she seriously considered doing just that in front of the whole damned plaza. A few seconds of practical reflection dampened her enthusiasm. All she would do is confirm to the courtroom her enemy's justification for the trial. Instead of hitting him numerous times on his stupid head with its stupid brown curls coiffed like a poodle, she hugged the techno tablet and faced the High Judge. "I'm ready Your Honor."

"Well get on with it then," Judge Hepplewhite said not bothering to hide her impatience.

Kimberly peeked at the words written on the screen. Her former defender's brief message glared back at her. She swept the screen and came to a page marked "Opening Defense."

"We don't have all day Mistress Lemon," the High Judge reminded her. There were a few giggles from the audience. Kimberly ignored them. She had to ignore them, all of them or she would end up gibbering and flailing her arms like a mad woman.

"I will prove that Kimberly Amber Lemon. Uh. Yes. Well. Hum. Right. I will prove that I am innocent of all charges. All of the evidence presented by the accuser is circumstantial and could just as easily be assigned to any citizen of Blueglennen."

And there the words ended. Strange. What? No. No. It can't be. How could she? This wasn't happening to her. She refused to accept this paltry bit of nothing as her only opening statement. Her opening statement must move mountains not sputter to a sad dismal anticlimax. No wonder the defender had given up on her. Either Swana thought Kimberly was guilty, or the Governor threatened her with prison time. Or? Someone close convinced Swana of Kimberly's guilt. Hawk was the most likely one since he'd be believed over anyone else.

With splinters of ice running down her spine, Kimberly dumped the techno tablet on the table and walked away from the Protector Arena out into the open, into the center of the courtroom, exposing herself to the court and the audience. She moved out into the open because something inside insisted she take a stand. The compulsion pressed against her backside propelling her forward. A foreign thought popped into her head, a thought she did not recognize as her own in a voice she'd never heard before. For a moment she thought the Holy Delph had seen fit to help her. *You're on the stage now, the stage of life. Use this moment to move about, let the people see you, let them get to know you, woo them with your presence and your goodness.*

Goodness? My goodness, my ass, Kimberly thought.

No. You're wrong. You must be able to stare into the faces of the high judge, the knight on duty by the high judge's side, the nine citizen judges, the scribe, and the accuser, and most importantly the witnesses – the audience and the television viewers. You must let them see you as a person, as someone vulnerable, scared and alone. If you can get them on your side, you might have a chance, a chance to delay the trial, a chance to find someone as your defender.

Then she felt alone again and realized the other voice was gone. It was as traumatizing as the crowd of people behind her and the Citizen Judges in front of her. By the time she woke up, they were fidgeting in their seats and looking at her with suspicion. Maybe they were just hungry? She'd known there would come a time when she would have to face the crowd eager for her blood and plead for her life. Yet, she didn't have the strength for a test of wills today.

Sure, she could handle a debate, one on one, and argue quite eloquently when her life wasn't at stake. But not now. It had been momentarily reassuring to seek a few friendly faces and latch onto hope in their eyes. But to look out at a hostile crowd, a few morbidly curious, others bored or annoyed would extinguish the little courage she had left. She'd always been painfully shy. Long ago she'd accepted this flaw in her personality. She couldn't do it.

"I beg the indulgence of the court. My Defender defected, and I am unprepared. She left only a few sentences for my opening statement," Kimberly said turning to look at the scribe. Frank Darknight stopped typing when she stopped talking.

Kimberly addressed him, "Would you please strike the last bit from the record Scribe Darknight?"

The Accuser jumped up, "I object."

Judge Hepplewhite tossed his objection aside with a flick of her finger, "May I remind you Accuser Potts that this is the opening statement. There are no rules of engagement for opening statements," and then she leaned forward with a stern expression aimed at Kimberly. "Other than to keep the statement brief. Scribe. Strike the Defender's previous remarks from the court records. Proceed Dela Lemon."

During the few seconds the High Judge Hepplewhite and Accuser Phil Potts ruminated over court protocol, Kimberly had been frantically thinking of an opening line for her defense. Once Darknight deleted her opening remarks and Hepplewhite settled back in her chair, Kimberly had an idea how to begin. The ending, well, the ending, she had no idea about how to end her statement. She would have to speak from the gut. She had read enough court transcripts to know how to proceed. Her grandfather used to read ancient court cases to her at bedtime. She just wished her mind would stop imagining the ending – hung until she died or being tossed from the highest rampart into the Siren River.

Someone from the crowd called out, "We can't hear her. Give her audio. What's the matter with you people?"

Someone poked her in the back and Kimberly turned to find a man handing her an audio cube, the kind a newscaster might hang from his or her neck. Instead of hanging the cube around her neck, Kimberly held the cube at arm's length unsure how her voice would carry. When she cleared her throat, she heard an echo from the speakers. Her voice sounded unnaturally high and phlegmy. She cleared her throat and the squeal made the audience groan.

"Sorry. Sorry folks."

Controlling the volume of her voice, she began, "I will prove to the court and my peers that I am innocent of all charges. I will prove that I had no animosity toward Star Bridgekeeper, that I in fact loved her as a friend and a neighbor, that I only wished the very best for her in the future, that I imagined her as a lovely young woman going to university and someday having children of her own. I could no more hurt her than I could cut off one of my limbs.

I've known Star Bridgekeeper since she was a baby. I watched her grow into a lovely young woman. Before her indoctrination into the Church of the Holy Centipede, Star Bridgekeeper had been a curious, open, sweet-tempered child. Shortly after attending the church, she quarreled with her mother and father, her sister, her neighbors, even her school friends. After attending the church, spending every waking moment in the church or at prayer meetings, she began to shut herself off from everyone.

She began to see herself as a martyr. Due to this fantasy encouraged by the Church of the Holy Centipede, she was ridiculed by her peers and dismissed as a crackpot by her neighbors. Often, she would come to my bookstore and wait until the church opened. I tried to get her to talk to me about her family and friends. Sometimes, I would sense regret as if she wished she could undo her decision to join the church. But after a meeting, she would be even more intransigent obsessing about the need to follow-"

Someone sitting on the rampart shouted, "What's intransigent mean?"

The High Judge, Judge Hepplewhite banged the drum several

times, "Knights arrest that man. While court is in session, there will be no talking from the audience. If there are any further interruptions the Court will adjourn, and the trial will take place in a private setting of my choosing. You may proceed, Defender Lemon."

Kimberly gathered her thoughts and continued, "To follow, um, to follow, yes, to follow the Church of the Holy Centipede because she'd been told if she converted a hundred unbelievers, she would become a saint. She also feared unbelievers would end up in hell if they didn't join the church. I thought if I remained neutral, she might confide in me.

Unhappily, she soon mistrusted everyone but church members. I had hoped that one day she would grow out of her infatuation. I had hoped one day she would stop accusing people of being demons and warning them they would burn in hell if they didn't join the Church of the Holy Centipede. If she'd lived, I truly believe she would have returned to her family and friends and resumed her education."

Kimberly tried to ignore the shocked exclamations and outcries. She suspected they were coming from the Church of the Holy Centipede members. Judge Hepplewhite beat the drum furiously for several minutes until there was silence and announced again, "Silence in the court. Any further outbreak and I'll have all of you removed. Are you finished Dela Lemon?"

"Not quite, Your Honor."

"Proceed."

Kimberly continued, "My condolences go out to the Bridgekeeper family. I can only imagine the pain and suffering you are feeling right now. I am grieving, but I grieve as a neighbor and a friend. It must be horrifying to lose a child. I want to find her killer as much as you do. Over the course of this trial, I will prove to you without a shadow of a doubt, I did not kill Star."

Unable to think of anything else to say, Kimberly walked toward the Defender bench passing Phil Potts who appeared to all intents and purposes desperately bored by her performance, practically asleep. He was slumped over his bench as if he might collapse at any moment with his right arm holding up his head as if finding the job of keeping himself awake onerous. His eyes were glazed. He blinked several times.

Kimberly should have been mortified. Yet, she wasn't, because his acting was so bad and his performance so obvious. He looked like a tool of the Governor and unfit for his job. He was supposed to represent Wolfern Province and prove her a murderer. Yet he acted as if he already knew the verdict. Or maybe this was his strategy - to psych her out and get the Citizen Judges on his side? Whatever his motives, she would do everything possible to prove him wrong.

Straightening her shoulders, she marched back to the Defender's bench with her head held high. She studied the audience trying to guess how her opening statement had gone over with them. Some people were whispering to their neighbors, others watching her with pitying eyes, and a few resembled Phil Potts in their expressions as if they wondered if the trial was a fiction for the benefit of the clueless masses. She sat down in the extremely comfortable Defender's chair and waited for the High Judge to address the court. She felt serene, a feeling she hadn't experienced in a long time.

Mercedes Hepplewhite nodded absently in the direction of the Defender's bench and said to her, "The defense will call its first witness. That means you Dela Lemon."

Kimberly, her fingers flying across the screen searched frantically for the witness list. Then she found the table of contents. After reading the first name, she jumped from her chair and moved to the center of the floor her heart racing. One day, if she survived her own trial, she might want to remember bits and pieces of this terrible day as anecdotes which might or might not amuse her friends. Perhaps if enough time passed, she might even find them funny.

Unbidden an old image from her childhood surfaced. Damned. The picture in her mind's eye of a frightened mole poking his head out of a hole to sniff the air for enemies, then vanishing down the hole in terror must not be her tactic. Forget the mole, she told herself. It would be disastrous if she started laughing hysterically right now. The High Judge certainly wouldn't find the situation amusing.

Kimberly glanced down at the name scrawled on the tablet again just to be sure she'd called the correct person. It was comforting to be able to speed-read Dela Swana's notes: [Character Witness] respectable merchant, never been in trouble, friend to Star. The accused or the witness? Oh shit. I've made a terrible mistake, Kimberly thought. She decided to give the witness a chance. It was a gamble and she could be wrong.

"Your honor, I call Queenie Oppfield of Queenie's Diner to the stand."

As a teenager, Kimberly had been obsessed with courtroom dramas. She was just as familiar with courtroom lingo as she was with her sock drawer — middling familiar. While watching courtroom dramas, she didn't have to pay close attention to what the Defender or the Accuser said, all she had to do was enjoy the show. As a spectator she didn't have a stake in the outcome. As the accused her very life was at stake.

There were no prisons in Wolfern Province like there were in other parts of the country of Curl because if a person was found guilty, the person lost a piece of herself. If convicted of theft, the perpetrator lost his right hand. If convicted of selling stolen property, he or she lost a finger. And if convicted of murder the guilty party was hung or thrown off the ramparts.

Queenie Oppfield took her sweet, ever-loving time making her way to the witness chair. When Queenie settled her considerable bottom down and finished arranging her skirt to her liking, Kimberly stepped closer and opened her mouth to speak. Someone interrupted her before she could get the first word out of her mouth.

"One moment Dela Lemon," the knight guarding the High Judge said as he moved in to stand facing her. He held something in his hand and leaned forward with purpose in his eyes. Before she knew what was happening, he had pinned her. Was this some sort of courting ritual? Were they now betrothed? It was news to her since as far as she knew she'd never met this knight before. She struggled to suppress a giggle. Her indrawn breath came out of the speakers and ricocheted off the plaza walls. She looked down at the tiny microphone on her collar.

Once more beside the witness chair, uncomfortably close to the High Judge's chair, Kimberly turned to address Queenie. With dread Kimberly observed the self-satisfied smirk on Queenie's moon face. Queenie's eyes were a brilliant blue and blazing with self-importance. She was the first witness to be called to the stand and she had never expected to be sitting on the witness chair staring out at a crowd of people, knowing there were millions more watching the trial on their video devices, everyone eager to watch the life and death drama in real time. According to the newscasters some in the crowd had come from as far away as Bojenlac.

"Queenie, Queenie, Queenie," Kimberly's voice bounced off each speaker mounted on the walls and echoed along Wolfern Promenade. A studied look of patience from the High Judge's chair encouraged her to continue, only this time in a more subdued tone.

"Queenie Oppfield, you have lived and worked in Blueglennen all your life and have lived and worked right next door to the Bookworm Emporium. You knew my grandfather and my grandmother. You've known me all my life. Have you ever known me to raise my hand or my voice to anyone?"

With an effort Queenie pulled her eyes away from the crowd and looked at Kimberly with a critical eye, "Not as I know. Most times you'd have your nose in a book and the rest of the time you'd be daydreaming and tripping over things cause you be too busy living in your head."

"What about my relationship with Star Bridgekeeper? Would you say we got along?"

"You and I never did have much to say to each other," Queenie began her words drowned out by a high-pitched screeching. Queenie's normal volume was as if a shepherd on Mount Lordbuster had been calling across the valley to another shepherd on Mount Hellman. When she mercifully stopped talking and the screeching subsided people dropped their hands from their ears.

Queenie tried again turning the volume down which gradually reached a comfortable level. She glanced at the microphone pinned to her best silk blouse in approval. "But after the way the Bridgekeeper family treated poor Star, neglecting her because they assumed the church was taking care of her needs and leaving her to wander the streets at night alone, while they went off to garage sales in neighboring towns, it is a real wonder poor Star had any kind of a decent meal or a place to put her head. By the time her big sister Sophia got home from work late in the evening, she'd be so tired she wouldn't even bother to check if Star was at home. Poor little Star was pretty much on her own most of her life.

Most days, Star spend her after-school hours camped out on the window seat in the Bookworm Emporium. The rest of the time, I'd see her propped up against a store front or taking over a bench seat in the park. Always she'd be reading the Holy Centipede bible. Sometimes she'd be praying for the souls of passersby or making a nuisance of herself on Merchants' Row demanding money.

I did notice you'd took her to Antonio's Café more than my diner. Pretty soon you just stopped bringing her into my diner and bought all her meals at the café. But I don't bear a grudge against you for that since at least the poor kid was getting fed. Nobody else gave a damn, especially not her worthless family. If you hadn't kept an eye on her she might have died of starvation a long time ago. Instead, she died in a garbage bin for lack of air. So yeah, I'd say you treated Star Bridgekeeper a damned sight better than her worthless kin."

Several women in the crowd were booing and hissing. One woman cried out, "Shame on you Brunhildaka and Aldopharoy. Shame. Shame. Shame on you." Kimberly turned and saw some audience members glaring accusingly at the Bridgekeeper family. The family had been placed close to the action, on the raised dais of the outdoor balcony owned by the Green Monkey restaurant. They were seated around the delicate iron table shaded and protected by one of the Green Monkey's signature umbrellas in its neon green and gold colors.

Only Star's parents, Aldoph and Brunie Bridgekeeper were seated at the Green Monkey table. Sophia Bridgekeeper, as witness sat in the first row of the witness annex behind the lawyer Phil Potts who happened to be defending the rights of the deceased Star Bridgekeeper. Sophia's folks were surprised by the crowd's sudden animosity. In typical fashion, Aldoph Bridgekeeper tried to throw his drink on the heads of those booing him below. A waiter caught the glass before the liquid spilled out. Brunie kept her head down and her mouth busy eating. Sophia had to turn all the way around in her seat to watch people in the crowd booing and hissing her parents.

Sophia's smug smile assumed the outrage was directed only at her neglectful parents until she saw the anger directed her way too. The smile vanished when someone yelled, "Run all the Bridgekeepers out of town. That's no way to raise a child. Throw them from the ramparts." Sophia's cheeks turned pink then blue and finally white as she listened to the grumbling from the courtroom. The shades of emotion crept round her neck in sweaty hues that shimmered in the sunlight like a neck scarf on fire. Kimberly with her back to the crowd could still see the action from the gigantic video camera positioned on Governor Saurus' balcony.

For a moment, her stomach lurched in pity at the sight of Sophia's shame. She felt so sorry for her. She'd been unlucky enough to have been born with stupid parents who were too lazy to get off their butts and make sure their children were clean, fed and safe. Their idea of being good parents was to sit on the couch with their computers on their laps and sell cheap ugly junk they'd found in the local dumps.

Sophia was a witness for Phil Potts.

Her sympathy vanished when she remembered Sophia was now Caleb's new girlfriend. As the older sister, maybe, Sophia should have taken better care of Star. Yet that didn't absolve the parents from blame. On the contrary, they were to blame for all the hardship their daughters endured. They'd never been good role models, so how would Sophia have known what good parenting looked like? Although, the Bridgekeeper selfishness didn't mean Aldoph and Brunie deserved to die. Brunhildaka and Aldopharoy. Wow. Who would have thought? She'd never known their birth names until today.

What Kimberly hated was the fact this revelation would devastate Caleb. It might even hurt his future business prospects. Knowing Caleb, she was sure he'd be more upset for Sophia than for his business. When Sophia glared at Kimberly accusingly as if she'd been responsible for the sudden reversal of her family's reputation, all her instincts for self-preservation returned.

"Is there anything else you wish to ask the witness Dela Lemon?" the High Judge Mercedes Hepplewhite asked from the dais.

Kimberly looked away from the video screen where Aldoph and Brunie had tried to hide themselves behind the menus. She turned back to Queenie, desperately running through the questions Shehili might have asked the witness. What Queenie had said was damning information, so why court misfortune by asking a question which might compromise this new direction? It would just be her luck to ask a follow up question and have Queenie find something embarrassing to report about the Lemon family.

What if Queenie had heard the quarrel between Kimberly and Star the day Victoria arrived? Oh. Centipede. Kimberly forced herself to face Queenie. If she so much as moved her eyes in her aunt's direction all would be lost. Kimberly had no illusions about Victoria. If her aunt was prepared to testify against her own niece on behalf of a family she barely knew, Victoria was doing so for her own nefarious reasons.

"No, Your Honor, I have nothing further to ask the witness. Thank you for your testimony Queenie Oppfield," Kimberly said stepping aside as the knight escorted Queenie back to her chair. Queenie milked the moment for all she could by clinging helplessly to the handsome knight all the way to her chair as if she couldn't walk a step without his assistance. Oh. Centipede indeed. Kimberly had seen Queenie lift a grown man above her head once when he refused to pay for his meal.

"Hold on there," Phil Potts declared in an unnecessarily dramatic tone. "I have some questions for the witness."

With a great deal of effort, Accuser Phil Potts pushed himself away from the bench and rose to his feet slowly grimacing in pain. His belly jutted out so far beyond his torso, he looked as if he would birth, at any moment, a monstrous child. Kimberly Lemon wondered if the rumors were true. Could he have dined on orphans and atheists back east? Absurd. Many of his victims believed the rumors were true and wrote down in their wills that they had seen him eat small children before they were hung or thrown off bridges. There was also a rumor he might be descended from gigantic killer whales which once upon a time roamed the ocean floor before they were consumed by serpents.

Phil Potts' unusual physique led Blueglennenites to conclude citizens of the east with their aversion to walking and their obsession with food must all look like Phil Potts. Kimberly knew those rumors were barefaced lies. All she had to do was look behind her at Alexandra and know not all easterners were like Phil Potts. In fact, Bill Anders and Billy Bill Anders Junior were both large men and as different to Potts as seahorse shit is to pudding. Father and son were well known all over Blueglennen for their kindness and generosity. She'd known the Anders all her life and had seen them go out of their way to help people in distress.

And when she glanced over at Phil Potts' side of the bench and noticed the crumbs littering the floor beneath his chair, she realized with a surge of fury while she had been preoccupied doing all she could to save her life as she questioned Queenie, Phil Potts had been busy eating up all the contents inside the box. Her pastries! He'd eaten her pastries which had been a gift from the Merchants' Row Alliance. How dare he! The Bastard.

The knight with a martyred expression escorted Queenie back to the witness chair.

"Dela Oppfield, it has come to our attention you've joined a new organization. Would you tell us a little bit about this organization?"

"What do you mean?" Queenie asked with a suspicious light in her eye and a body poised to pounce from the chair and throttle the questioner.

"Dela Oppfield answer my question. What is this new organization you've joined? Whose idea was it?"

"I have no idea what this man is talking about Your Grace," Queenie said addressing the High Judge on her chair above the witness stand.

"I am not Your Grace, Delus Oppfield. Address me as, Your Honor. Delo Potts be so good as to clarify your question for the witness," Mercedes said, all the while doing her best not to laugh.

"Well, the two of you, better stop calling me Delus Oppfield cause I'm a widow and I done enough changing diapers and bottle washing to earn the title of Delan. So, if you want me to answer your stupid questions, the two of yous better call me Delan," Oppfield warned giving them both the stink eye. A few people giggled. The drums began to beat, and the giggling stopped.

Mercedes Hepplewhite knew where the questioning was headed and wondered how Potts would manage to connect the two. Thin threads are all he really needed. She had seen such nonsense squeezed into the pinholes of the impossible before.

"I am speaking of the Merchants' Row Alliance, Delan Oppfield."

"What of it? I don't understand."

"How was the organization formed, Delan Oppfield? It's an anarchist organization determined to betray the Governor and the City of Blueglennen? You might as well be a member of a terrorist group who plan to blackmail all merchants into joining. Are you not threatening to raise your prices and hold all production to your greedy bosoms forcing citizens to pay outrageous seastar for ordinary everyday items?"

"No. You be wrong. We, we're protecting our living from the greedy paws. The church wants to force us out. They're gonna rezone Merchants' Row so they can sell our shops to some dumbass pilgrims. If that happens, we're homeless. You be dead wrong. We're the victims."

"Who told you such a pack of lies? Who?"

"Lies? You be lying. No. I was there at the meeting. I heard."

"Yes, Delan," Phil Potts said inching closer to her chair. "You were saying?"

"We met in Goodbody's pet store, you know. Well, since you be back east you probably don't know nothing about us. The store's called Life Long Friends. Guinevere Goodbody has the cutest puppies and kittens for sale," Queenie looked out into the crowd and winked. "She's open, all week long, in the afternoons. Before you check out the cute puppies come to my diner, Queenie's Diner for some scrumptious pot pie. My food keeps the shark at bay."

"Delan Oppfield. Stay on topic," Potts demanded.

"Kimberly told us bout Little's wife talking how the church was gonna throw us out of our shops and take over and make our homes into little cells for the pilgrims of the Centipede."

Phil Potts turned to face the audience making sure to include the Citizen Judges in his sweeping gaze with his face expressing disdainful incredulity, "How unfortunate for you, Delan Oppfield. You've been misled. Dela Lemon misheard and spun you a pack of lies, just the way her grandfather used to spin tales out of nothing. You've been bamboozled, my good lady."

"I don't know where you get your information Delphus Potts, but you're so wrong. Dead wrong. I know. I heard it from the horse's mouth. He said bold as you please, right to my face, not the other day the same damned thing I'm trying to get into your noggin. He plans on driving us out of our homes with Saurus' help."

As Potts walked away his face registering his annoyance with Oppfield's slur, he drowned out Queenie's voice, "You're free to go, Delphi Oppfield. We will hear the truth from Bishop Little's lips not hearsay from a third party."

Kimberly jumped up, "Your Honor, is it hearsay if the witness actually heard Bishop Little? If she heard directly from Bishop Little than her testimony isn't third party hearsay."

Phil Potts paused and for such a heavy man managed to spin neatly on his small feet to face the High Judge. Mercedes looked as if she was seriously considering Kimberly's question. Everyone knew as Defender she had the right to question the Accuser's misstatements. Tread carefully Potts, Kimberly thought, don't try your tricks on me. She'd seen enough courtroom dramas to know he was misleading everyone. Did he think everyone in Blueglennen was a hick?

"Will we be hearing Bishop Little's testimony?" Judge Mercedes Hepplewhite asked the Accuser Potts. The surprise on his face annoyed her. The court watched in fascination as the youngest member of the High Judge's circle fenced with the accuser. Her expression warned Potts not to play games with her.

"If you insist, Your Honor."

"I do insist since you brought the subject up and made the subject part of legal record."

When Kimberly moved to sit down, the High Judge spoke again, "You may call your next witness Dela Lemon."

The knight on duty before the High Judge's bench escorted Queenie Oppfield back to her seat a second time and stood in the aisle waiting for Kimberly to call her next witness. Kimberly looked at the next name on the list. She tried to quickly read through the notes and absorbed most of Swana's reasoning. If she'd had a choice, she would have preferred the third witness.

"Quickly, Dela Lemon. Do not keep the court waiting."

"I call Beatrice Bottom to the witness chair, Your Honor."

Queenie was forced to rise and move out into the aisle to make way for Beatrice Bottom. Beatrice maneuvered herself between people and to the witness chair without making a scene. She'd dressed carefully in her best going-to-church print skirt and white blouse with the goat-hair shawl. The shawl caressed her throat and shoulders in all its glorious softness. By afternoon she would be sweltering. Never you mind, Kimberly told herself, you have more serious matters to worry about than Beatrice Bottom's discomfort.

As Beatrice made herself comfortable on the witness chair adjusting her shawl to her liking and Kimberly debated within herself whether to use Shehili Swana's evidence, the crowd beyond the dais grew restless.

Someone shouted, "This is where you ask the witness questions."

Someone else joined in, "Yeah. The suspense is killing us."

Other voices began to chime-in and soon people were laughing and joking amongst themselves. The trial had become notorious by way of social media, newspapers and television soap operas disguised as news channels. Television executives (mostly male) assumed everyone loved a good tragedy about a young beautiful Delphinid girl dying under mysterious circumstances. Never mind another horrific tragedy had occurred, just a few weeks ago, when a young woman had only one recourse but to throw herself off the ramparts to avoid an even more painful death by a crazed stranger.

Why weren't people as outraged by Deletha Child's premature death? Because her family lived in Mudflat Village? Or because she was an immigrant? Or due to her Delphinid, Lacertidae and New Dala DNA? Probably a bit of everything. She'd been pretty but not beautiful. And she was considered ordinary by the snobs who followed the doings of the nobility. The first Bridgekeeper male had been knighted eight-hundred years ago. The family bible listed all the Bridgekeepers up to the present day. Only the locals knew how far the family had fallen in wealth and reputation. They hadn't fallen as low as Finstickel but close enough.

High Judge Mercedes Hepplewhite nodded to the knight on duty and the knight beat a steady rhythm on the drum signaling for silence. The plaza grew quiet. Most Blueglennen knew what the drums meant. Obviously, the rude people in the back were foreigners for they continued to throw out unwanted advice and laugh and joke amongst themselves as if they were on holiday and this was such fun.

Mercedes rose to her feet and her voice through the microphone reverberated off the heavy stone walls, "Silence. One more interruption and I will clear the plaza. Your only source of news will be the newspaper articles about this trial. I warn you, the next person to speak out of turn will be arrested."

The only sound to be heard was a pair of crows quarreling on Knight's Walk, the rampart between the northwest and northeast watchtowers facing the Siren River, the rampart which had the fewest banners fluttering in the breeze. The knights patrolling the walk pretended not to hear the High Court Judge's warning and continued their patrol of the restless crowd on the meadow and the banks of Poison Creek. When a man called up to the knights to ask what was going on, Knight Madas Lively turned to his friend Juleus and Juleus shouted down, "Some jokers in the audience think their funny and the judge thinks their idiots."

Mercedes resumed her place on her throne and nodded to Kimberly, "You may proceed."

Kimberly turned to Beatrice, "Would you tell the court what took place between you and Sophia Bridgekeeper."

Phil Potts jumped up from his chair nearly overturning the table when his belly hit the edge. Frank Darknight steadied the table and managed to rescue his tablet. "Your Honor is Sophia Bridgekeeper on trial here? Why must Dela Lemon continue to drag the grieving Bridgekeeper family through the mud? Is this really important to the case?"

The High Judge Mercedes Hepplewhite looked down upon Dela Kimberly Lemon, "At my side Defender Lemon and Accuser Potts."

When the two of them stood before her bench and looked up, they were astonished at the steeliness of her demeanor. Potts had taken her for a usurper and an easy mark, a tiny insignificant female probably rising quickly through the courts due to her family's wealth and influence. Now he had his doubts. Kimberly had no such prejudices assuming Mercedes Hepplewhite had risen quickly to her rank out of merit not privilege.

Mercedes addressed Kimberly first, "It is rare for the accused to be put in the position of having to defend herself. I have taken your lack of experience into consideration. Yet, Accuser Potts is right. Are you maligning the family for personal reasons or do you have evidence of wrongdoing? I will allow you to question the witness but will stop the questioning, if I sense you're just shoveling more dirt on the Bridgekeeper family knowing you have nothing more to offer."

"I would have preferred calling the third witness but haven't had any time to consider the wisdom of Dela Swana's choice. She wrote down she had reservations. I don't know why. I do know this witness can clear up the reason the family accused me in the first place."

"The testimony of the Bridgekeeper family is not the only evidence provided by the investigation Defender Lemon. Are you wasting the court's time?"

"No, Your Honor. I assure you."

"I will allow the witness to speak if you modify your questions. Proceed. You may be seated Accuser Potts."

Kimberly returned to the witness chair with her heart pounding so loudly in her ears she could barely hear herself think, "Delan Bottom. I appreciate your patience. I'm new to this line of work." A few people chuckled. Their laughter gave her a bit of courage. "It has been established by Queenie Oppfield that Star and I were close and liked each other. Do you know of any reason why the authorities might have thought it strange for us to be friends?"

In her attempt to exclude the Bridgekeepers, she was trying to circle back to her previous question addressed to Queenie. Hopefully, Beatrice would understand what Kimberly was trying to do. Kimberly waited for Beatrice Bottom's answer. "Well, yes, we all did wonder why Star seemed so happy to be at the Bookworm, when the girl should have been with her friends and shopping instead of talking silly stuff about centipedes. But you know, now, that I think back, I wonder if Star and Sophia quarreled because Sophia was jealous. Maybe Star's affection toward you-"

"You mean the Accused," Kimberly cautioned Beatrice. "Pretend I'm not the accused. Think of me as the Defender."

"Strange way to do things but okay. So, let's see. Where was I? Oh, yes. Star's affection toward, ah, Kimberly Lemon became clear to me when I heard Sophia screeching and saying, you're just sweet to that bitch because you know it pisses me off. I know you Star. You don't care about Kimberly Lemon. You're just doing this to make me crazy. I don't care. Go ahead. Drive her nuts with your stupid religious tripe. You'll drive her away too like you've driven Mom and Dad away. Pretty soon there won't be anyone left for you. You'll be all alone."

Kimberly couldn't have asked for better testimony and with gathering excitement began to wonder if perhaps this trial might end sooner than expected. She had a real chance, a real chance to end this nightmare today. She went in for the kill.

"And was there anyone else present when this quarrel took place?"

Beatrice nodded her head her white curls bouncing on her forehead, "Indeed. There were several people on Merchants' Row who couldn't help but hear Sophia screaming at the top of her lungs. There was Harry Zany of Zany Music and Valcinda Moorland of the Children's Playhouse and some other folks, mostly customers window shopping."

"Were any of these customers from Mudflat Village or Greenburg Valley?" Kimberly asked wishing she could find a witness who happened to be a nonmember of the Merchants' Row Alliance.

"Let me think back. I have a good memory for faces. Names give me a problem some of the times. Let me think back. There was a tall fellow with yellow hair down to his ass. Oh yeah, him. Comes to the diner to ogle Queenie's girls. What's his name?"

"Edgar Stipple," a voice shouted out in one of the rows midway between the roped crowd and the witness arena.

High Judge Hepplewhite interrupted the proceedings with a curt command, "Arrest that man Knight Overton."

Several knights posted along the walls of the plaza moved

forward as Knight Overton made his way down the center aisle. No one pointed at the man but those seated near him turned to stare at him which was enough of a clue for the knights. The helpful audience member was summarily escorted from the plaza, well, dragged kicking and screaming until the knights got him near Duke Tower courtyard. The sudden silence was ominous leading everyone to conclude (erroneously people soon discovered) that the unfortunate man had been silenced permanently.

The High Judge unfamiliar with the ways of Governor Saurus' knights called for Knight Overton to return to her side. Knight Overton appeared dragging the young man in tow and everyone saw how the knights had tied his hands behind his back and stuffed his mouth with someone's silk kerchief permanently affixing the kerchief in his mouth by winding a belt around his head. The black leather belt had been tightened so cruelly that the blood could barely circulate in his cheeks.

"Knight Overton untie the man's hands and remove the kerchief immediately. My orders were to arrest him for talking out of turn, not torture him." The confusion on Knight Overton's face would have been comical under ordinary circumstances. No one privy to the young man's white face and trickle of blood from his lips thought the sight funny. It could have been any one of them.

Knight Overton's zealousness reminded the court of the autocrat high above the crowd sitting on a secluded, opulent balcony with his guard around him and his fancy food on the table. The knight had been aware of the governor the whole time and knew he had to show his loyalty by being as brutal as possible.

Saurus who found himself enjoying the trial as if he were at a play watching actors perform for his benefit especially liked the knight's zealotry. The audience below saw the little man with the hairless cheeks and neat well-groomed head sitting comfortably in his iron chair smiling benevolently down upon his kingdom. So, did the video cameras broadcasting the event to the world.

Only the foreign visitors were surprised by the knight's behavior. Saurus owned the media and most Blueglennens were pretty sure anything which cast him in a bad light would be removed. People began to reassess the outcome of the trial. If Kimberly Lemon had been privy to their private thoughts, she would have been extremely afraid because those sitting on chairs and sitting on the ground were beginning to pity her.

All the Blueglennen citizens looked up at the governor trying to assess his mood. Was he unhappy with the young man who had spoken out of turn? Would the young man survive the Governor's displeasure? And what about Edward Stipple? Would he be a witness for the accused, someone outside the Merchants' Row Alliance? If Stipple proved to be a problem would he last the night? Few people had ever witnessed Governor Saurus' brutality. Yet long-time residents had heard rumors and were loath to test the truth of them.

Even some of the tourists were beginning to realize this trial wasn't going to be as fun as they first thought. They noticed how the natives were slumped in their seats hoping to avoid the Governor's attention. Desperately thinking ahead Kimberly Lemon hurried back to the Defender's bench and quickly wrote the name Edgar Stipple down twice, once on her tablet and the second time on a piece of official parchment. She chose from the pile of expensive paper left between the Defender's portion of the table and the Accuser's, realizing belatedly that the parchment might be very old.

As she moved toward the witness chair, she made a stop in front of Frank Darknight who paused in his typing to look up at her. His handsome face might on any other occasion have made her stomach flutter with excitement. He was indeed a beautiful man. But not today. Today her life was on the line. Beautiful men with dark brown eyes and dark brown hair were only fit for dreams and if she were found guilty, she would have no more nights for dreaming.

She handed him the folded parchment and spoke loud enough for the people along Wolfern Promenade and the roped area to hear, "I call Edgar Stipple to the stand. Please have the court present him at the earliest opportunity." It was only after she spoke, she realized she might have just hastened the poor man's death. With that thought, and unbidden, she glanced up at the Governor's balcony in sudden consternation.

The Governor looked down at the crowd with an abstract air. He had no eyes for her. She must look like an ant, an insignificant ant. At least that was the impression he tried to present. Others watching him wondered if he was worried about all this new attention. After a while, even Beatrice Bottom turned in her chair to see what everyone was looking at. Governor Saurus realized everyone was watching him and turned his back on them. A knight stepped up to him with a note and whispered in his ear.

He flicked his fingers impatiently and the knight stepped back, then the Governor leaned over the railing to get a good look at Kimberly Lemon. Did he just give her the finger? What? No. He was too far away. She must have imagined it.

His voice rang out. He had no need of microphones or prompters. For such a small man he had a booming voice. Even though he often couldn't put two words together without prompting, he managed to say, "Knight Overton, I task you with the charge of this big mouth you have in custody and the witness Edgar Stipple. Put them both in a secure location and make sure no harm comes to them while in custody. We are country of laws in Wolfern Province. When Edgar Stipple is called to the witness chair, he will be delivered to the court immediately."

Not wanting to be overshadowed by the Governor's presence in her courtroom, Mercedes Hepplewhite rose to her feet and said, "As the High Court Judge, I call a recess until the witness Edgar Stipple can be brought forth and provide his testimony. We will reconvene in one hour. Court dismissed." Mercedes motioned to Knight Overton who had returned to his post beside her chair and Knight Overton lifted the horn to his lips and blew one quick blast to signify the court's recess.

Drums and horns, Kimberly thought bitterly, such empty traditions of a bygone era. Most states in the country of Curl had moved beyond the pageantry of the dead. Not Blueglennen.

Kimberly Lemon, once again the accused, wrestled with her guard until the High Judge gave her permission to take the tablet and the other documents for her defense back with her to her cell – rather than the dungeons beneath Duke's Tower. She'd been given the locked room facing the courtyard where criminals and their defenders discussed tactics. Opposite the window was another window, a glass window which she knew allowed knights and detectives to watch the interrogations behind protective glass.

As Kimberly spread her papers and the techno tablet on the table, she felt someone watching her. She had no time to worry about who might be spying on her. She had an hour to read Swana's notes and discover where to go next. It seemed as if only a minute or two had passed when a knight appeared to escort her back to the plaza. She gathered her precious documents to her bosom. Jammed between two knights she hurried to keep up.

Once outside among witnesses, the knights allowed her to sit at the Defender's bench. The sun beat down on her head heating up the stone floor and the stone walls until Kimberly thought she would suffocate. She felt as if she were trapped in an oven. She pitied the witnesses and the audience because they'd been stuck in the blazing sun for longer. What if it rained? Would they move the trial inside?

A knight stepped toward her and dropped a scrap of parchment on the table in front of her. She picked up the precious paper and read the note written in old Curl script. *Call your next witness. Edgar Stipple is not fit to testify today.* And the note was signed Honorable Judge, Mercedes Hepplewhite, High Court Judge of Duke Tower City of Blueglennen. Kimberly had anticipated such an event and rose to her feet to address the judge, "Your Honor, I call Tyler Merryweather to the stand. If you please." She added the plea because she suspected all her witnesses would soon find themselves indisposed.

Phil Potts gave her a blank stare. She would have preferred some sort of expressed emotion. Was he at his most dangerous now? Did she give a damned? Her life wasn't worth much anyway. Governor Saurus was in cahoots with Bishop Little and doing his best to undermine her case and throw out Merchants' Row shopkeepers with the rest of the trash. Why? Was it just to make way for the pilgrims? How would the pilgrims serve the Governor? Perhaps things weren't as hopeless as she imagined. Perhaps she had a chance.

A middle-aged man with a bit of a belly and tired eyes stepped up to the podium and stood in front of the witness chair. He lifted his hand and swore to tell the truth. With a sigh of relief, as if he had walked a hundred miles to get here, he settled himself in the witness chair and turned to look at the assembled people. He blinked several times as if amazed at the number of people stuffed inside the bailey. Tyler Merryweather had spent most of his career in the basement of Duke Tower fussing with records and deeds and legal documents. He rarely exchanged two words with the staff much less strangers.

Every so often, he was forced to talk to someone who came in to inquire about zoning districts and property rights. Most of the time though, his clerk dealt with people. Yet a persistent woman, a woman his age had pestered him about the Church of the Holy Centipede's petitions. The church's petition had not yet cleared the Governor's desk and he would say so without hesitation. There had been no need to call him as witness. He blamed the woman for his present circumstances. What was her name? Fitz something.

"Delo Merryweather, thank you for appearing in this court today," Kimberly Lemon began. "It is my understanding you have information about the Church of the Holy Centipede's petition to reinstate the church's former holdings, holdings that took place nearly five-hundred years ago when the cathedral belonged to the old religion of Curl, the Delphadoren religion which worshiped the Holy Delph. Is this true?"

"Which part? The holdings or the new petition?"

"For now, I'm interested in the new petition."

"There is a petition from the Church of the Holy Centipede. Yes. It is still only a petition, not a decree. The Governor has yet to sign the document." There, he had said his piece and now he could go home. He moved as if to rise from the witness chair.

"Where are you going Delo Merryweather? I'm not finished."

Impertinent woman. How dare she address him in such a fashion. He sat back down.

"Do you have this document?"

"Not on me. It's kept in the pending basket at the Bailey Document's Department."

The woman spoke directly to the High Judge Mercedes Hepplewhite, "I wish this document to be included as evidence for the defense."

Mercedes Hepplewhite stared down at her papers reading her notes carefully. After a few tense minutes, she looked up from her papers. "The document should have been requested as evidence before the trial. We will have to accept the witness's testimony as proof of this petition. Proceed Defender Lemon."

"Delo Merryweather as the Duke's Records Clerk you are familiar with zoning laws and laws that have to do with land rights. Is that correct?"

"Yes. I'm familiar with zoning laws and land rights that pertain to Blueglennen, Mudflat Village and Greenburg Valley. I'm also certified for Bitterroot Forest and Mount Lordbuster National Parks and their numerous claims."

"Then tell the court how it's possible all deeds and rights in the last five centuries could become nil and void by this petition? The Church of the Holy Delph closed its doors a century ago, yet the deeds and rights of landlords and shopkeepers have been honored. Wouldn't such a petition set a precedent? Wouldn't there be more petitions reclaiming old rights and wouldn't this set Wolfern Province and the country of Curl itself into confusion and anarchy?"

Merryweather gaped at the High Court Judge for several minutes unable to fathom such a future. He hadn't had time to read the entire petition. The document was controversial, treasonously controversial. He'd sent the petition to the Governor awaiting his decision which would determine the fate of all Curlecons, assured Crest Hall in Delphadore City, as well as, Province House and the Lord's Court would object to its position. The Delphadorturo Raker or the Silver 11 would do something to stop such criminal annexation of land and property.

He opened his mouth and then changed his mind. He wanted so much to turn in his chair and check out the situation on the Governor's balcony. He couldn't help but turn and glance up at the balcony. His life was on the line. His grandchildren's lives were on the line. The cameras revealed Delo Merryweather's uncertainty and unease. The Governor leaned forward in his chair and waved impatiently at Merryweather signally him to proceed.

Merryweather turned back to face Kimberly and said, "When I received the petition from the Church of the Holy Centipede requesting the reassignment of the old church's properties, state properties now occupied by the merchants on Merchants' Row, I knew that such a petition needed to be handled by the Governor.

Under the circumstances such a request might negate present rights and responsibilities of landholders all over the country of Wolfern Province. The Governor has yet to decide whether he will present the petition to the Wolfern State House. Until his determination, the petition will remain in committee, not yet a deed or a law."

"What of redistricting and zoning laws and imminent domain? Those actions can turn what a landholder believes as his or her rights and responsibilities into nothing but useless pieces of paper? Does the Church of the Holy Centipede have the right to rezone Merchants' Row?"

Phil Potts rose from his bench, "How is this pertinent to the case?"

Mercedes addressed Kimberly, "Explain to the court where this is leading Defender Lemon."

Kimberly used her body as a beacon of earnestness desperate to find one friendly face. She looked toward the High Judge, the Citizen Judges, and finally the audience. "It is my intention to prove the Church of the Holy Centipede used Star Bridgekeeper as a means of persuading, annoying, pushing the merchants into giving up their shops to make way for the pilgrim sanctuaries, so the church could profit from the tithings of the pilgrims.

I have witnesses that will testify Star Bridgekeeper went door to door on Merchants' Row evangelizing and pressuring merchants to give up their deeds. There were other converts who also tried to pressure the merchants. Then the Church of the Holy Centipede persuaded Governor Saurus to rezone the Row. I believe Star no longer wanted to be the church's salesperson and the church had a better reason for killing her than me."

Phil Potts moved toward the High Judge's desk and turned to face the audience, "It seems this woman is more likely to prove my case than the other way around. Star Bridgekeeper was an important ally of the church. Why in a Sea Serpent's hell would someone in the church try to harm her? It makes no sense."

"Please return to your seat, Accuser Potts. You'll have a chance for rebuttal," Mercedes ordered waiting until he followed her orders before addressing Kimberly Lemon. "Defender, I am not here as your advisor. The court acknowledges your lack of experience and suggests you find someone who can defend you adequately. Do you understand?"

"I do, Your Honor. Until such time as I can find a defender, may I continue?"

"You may."

"Then I wish to request the Church of the Holy Centipede's petition be placed as evidence with your court."

"Clerk Merryweather, the court requests a copy of the said petition."

"The documents are still in the possession of the Governor, Your Honor," Merryweather reminded her.

As if by magic a knight appeared and stepped toward the High Judge's chair presenting her with a scroll. The scroll had been tied with a silk red ribbon, a custom maintained since before Duke Dono's day. With a curt nod, High Judge Hepplewhite accepted the scroll, untied the ribbon, and briefly scanned the document. The plaza was so quiet Kimberly could hear a bird pecking his way along the rampart wall. When she was satisfied that the scroll contained the information the Defender requested, she motioned for the transcriber to approach the bench.

Frank Darknight jumped up from his chair and accepted the scroll gingerly as if it might break. Once at his desk, he scanned the document, retied the ribbon, handed the scroll back to the knight and returned to his seat. As Kimberly Lemon watched the drama unfold, she worried for her friends. Saurus would attack them once she was gone. The little man on the balcony of Duke Tower had a smug grin on his simple face. Or was his face smug and his grin simple?

"I call Harry Zany of Zany Music to the witness stand, Your Honor," Kimberly announced hoping Harry might assist her in untangling the knots of the Church of the Holy Centipede's plans. She believed Bishop Mark Little had something to do with Star's death or at least knew who might be involved.

Harry Zany made his way to the witness chair smiling and waving as if he were on parade. Once he reached his destination, he plopped himself down on the chair with satisfaction. He seemed eager to do battle. Or was he just nervous? Kimberly worried the Citizen Judges might find Harry's attitude disrespectful. Then she noticed how pale he was, almost white with anxiety. He, also, feared for the Merchants' Row Alliance.

"Delo Zany, according to my former defender's notes you have knowledge of Star Bridgekeeper's position at the Church of the Holy

Centipede. Her duties included proselytizing, encouraging merchants to give up their holdings and recruiting new members. Did Star go door to door and urge the merchants in the bailey to give up their shops and homes for the good of the church?"

Harry Zany looked out upon the sea of faces watching him. He addressed those people primarily. On occasion he would turn and address the High Judge and the Citizen Judges. He seemed especially curious about the cameras. "Well . . . I don't know about proselytizing, unless proselytizing means going door to door and bugging people about your beliefs and demanding money. She demanded money from us every Monday morning before school.

Just to be sure we hadn't forgotten the church's position on the afterlife, she would come back after school to tell us if we didn't give up our shops we would go to hell. She even suggested our ghosts would haunt the streets for eternity."

Kimberly refused to look at the people jammed into the plaza, some of them standing shoulder to shoulder along Wolfern Promenade, others squeezed into the chairs provided for the paying public. The Governor had decreed that since the trial had to take place in the plaza, the restaurant owners and merchants should be compensated for lost revenue.

Would she get a paycheck for her own trial? How ironic that would be. Fighting for her life and after she was hung, a check would arrive in the mail as compensation for her duties as a defender and a shopkeeper. Feeling queasy, she looked at her feet. In her head she began to recite her favorite poem. When she calmed down, she looked up. Should she clasp her hands behind her back? Would she look more imposing if she stabbed the air to emphasize her point the way Potts did. Stupid.

Before she had a chance to respond to Harry's testimony, Potts interrupted, "Your Honor, hearsay is not admissible."

The High Judge spoke, "Your witness is using the word, we, Defender Lemon. He cannot testify for the merchants. He can only testify to his own experience with the deceased."

"Your Honor," Kimberly turned to face her witness. "Harry. I mean Delo Zany, refer only to your personal exchanges with Star Bridgekeeper. How often did Star drop by your store?"

"Like I said, every Monday morning before school and every Monday through Friday after school she'd drop in and wait until I finished with a customer, then announce I should give up my music shop for the good of my soul. And I'd tell her – guess what Star, we have a new release from Dirty Blades of Grass just in, would you like to buy it? And each time I would suggest a music pod or single, she'd tell me she no longer listened to that sort of filth.”

“What was Star like before she joined the Church of the Holy Centipede?”

“Like any other kid, nuts about the opposite sex, giggly, crazy about the latest musical group or movie star. I’d see her, hanging around with a bunch of girls and boys and spending a lot of money on clothes and food. The things kids usually do around here.”

“When did she join the Church of the Holy Centipede?” Kimberly asked reading the list of questions Shehili Swana included on the tablet.

“Just after her best friend Tiffany died?”

“You mean Tiffany Blakely?”

“Yes.”

“Tell the court what happened to Tiffany.”

“Tiffany Blakely was Star Bridgekeeper’s best friend. I remember those two were inseparable, always coming into the music store and standing around pretending to look at music, but really checking out the boys. They had hopes of being discovered by record producers and becoming famous. I have a sound-proof room and they would go in every day after school and sing songs Star had composed. Those of us privileged enough to hear Tiffany sing the songs Star composed figured they would both end up big stars one day.

At the celebration of Wolf Day, a kid skeet-shooting missed the target and hit Tiffany who was riding on the Swizzle Swing twenty-feet above the carnival. Star had been sitting next to Tiffany. The bullet whizzed by Star’s head and hit Tiffany. Tiffany died in Star’s arms. It took a long time before anyone realized what had happened. Girls screaming while riding the Swizzle Swing was part of the excitement of the ride. Star stopped screaming and started to call down to the operator to stop the ride. Her pleas were ignored as well. When the ride ended, the operator realized what happened. But by that time, it was too late. Poor kid, poor, poor kid.”

“Then do you think Star was at her most vulnerable when she joined the Church of the Holy Centipede?” Kimberly asked.

“Yes,” Zany answered.

“Do you think that if Tiffany had lived, she would have joined the church?” Kimberly asked.

“Her folks weren’t church goers. No one had ever seen them in a church anyway. Since Star and Sophia were just little fingerlings, they’ve been fending for themselves. When they weren’t in school or at my music shop, they were begging for money down at Mudflat Village or the train station. I remember when Sophia was only eight years old and she had little Star with her and she’d be asking tourists for money right here in the Royal Plaza. The castle knights put a stop to that right quick. They banned the Bridgekeeper sisters from begging inside the castle for life."

"So, after Tiffany's untimely death with no one to turn to she joined the Church of the Holy Centipede? Or did the church members recruit her? According to testimony by other residents of the castle, the Church of the Holy Centipede promised Star a good paying job if she would join the church and recruit new members. Is that true?"

"Yes. Star told me she'd been offered a good paying job by Bishop Little. It doesn't matter what the church offered Star because there's something else going on you should know about," Harry Zany said leaning forward in his eagerness. "It has to do with something that most of the old timers here in Blueglennen know. It was the day Arthur Darknight and I had lunch and Arthur brought the subject up and I thought, why sure, I remember that."

At first Kimberly wondered if she should stop Harry. What if he told the court something which implicates her? Shouldn't she question him in private and if what he had to say helped her case use it? Would Harry even bring up a topic which might make her appear guilty? She had known Harry all her life. He had a habit of pushing people away by throwing out funny one-liners and joking to defuse serious subjects, but he wasn't an unkind person. He would never deliberately hurt anyone.

"You may proceed, Delo Zany," Kimberly instructed him. "What did you and Arthur Darknight discuss?"

"It's about the secret stair at the Relic shop. Sylvia Paleone's shop, you know?"

"You mean the shop owned by Sylvia Paleone, a member of the Church of the Holy Centipede? Yes. I know she owns the shop called For the Soul Relics and Religious Treasures. What about her shop and a secret stair?"

"Yes. That's it. The shop used to belong to the Finstickel family, back when Duke Dono was alive. The Finstickel family are close cousins to the Duke. In fact, if Wolfern Province had kept their nobility, Tim Finstickel would be our present Duke. He'd be Duke Timothy Finstickel Dono. Imagine what Blueglennen would look like with Timothy Finstickel as our sovereign in the tower," Harry Zany said playing to the crowd. Natives of Blueglennen chuckled.

The idea of crazy old Timothy Finstickel as Blueglennen's ruler boggled everyone's mind. Kimberly thought about the day she'd chased him down the street furious he'd broken into her private quarters and used her bathroom to shower And, then the nasty scene when she discovered he'd washed his dirty underwear in her bathroom sink. And her jewelry box? She still hadn't gotten her jewelry box back. Oh, Holy Delph. Blueglennen would truly be screwed if he was our leader.

Now she realized why the knight treated Finstickel as if he were an honored guest. He'd even ignored the dripping wet underwear draped over the Green Monkey's fancy chair. How could she have forgotten that bit of trivia? Her grandfather used to tell her all the weird stories about the loony Finstickel family and said because they'd been so interbred their progeny had begun to decay physically and mentally.

Finstickel's mother, unlike all the other Finstickel cousins who had intermarried had come from some place back east. In Kimberly's estimation her contribution to the Finstickel line had been too late for the survival of the family. No female anywhere in the world had ever shown the least bit of interest in him, much less interest in marrying or having children with Tim Finstickel. He had no money and lived in an empty suite with no running water.

Then Kimberly remembered Harry had mentioned a secret stair, "Harry, ah, Delo Zany you mentioned a secret stair. Why is a secret stair significant to Star's death?"

"Because the secret stair was the way the Finstickel family traveled from the church to their private quarters at Duke Tower. The stairs provided access without having to mingle with lowly peasants or what Finstickel's great-grandfather referred to as the Smelly-Terminus-Horde. And the secret stair is between the cathedral and Duke Tower where Finstickel's family made their way to church or the tower or Bishop's Garden without ever having to meet the horde. And here's something curious - the passageway still exists and is used today. Arthur Darknight told me when Sylvia rented the shop, she asked Frank..."

At this point Harry Zany stopped talking and turned to look at Frank Darknight busily typing out Harry's testimony. Frank looked at the High Judge. Mercedes Hepplewhite nodded ascent and in unspoken agreement allowed Harry to continue. He finished his testimony by saying, "Sylvia Paleone asked Frank to fix the door leading down to the catacombs because there was a terrible wet draft which creeped into the store room and damaged her artifacts. Frank isn't a carpenter and couldn't help her, so she got someone else to fix the door."

"Was the door sealed?" Kimberly asked suddenly feeling a sliver of hope. Here was another source who could corroborate the existence of the secret stair. Joanie Fitzhammond's testimony now had teeth.

Harry shrugged, "Sorry. I don't know. I think the guy she hired fell down the stairs and broke his neck. At least that was the rumor going round."

Kimberly turned to High Judge Hepplewhite, "Your Honor, with this new evidence, I believe I must call Sylvia Paleone to the witness stand. And in order to expedite the proceedings perhaps your transcriptionist Delo Frank Darknight will confirm Delo Zany's testimony?"

Mercedes Hepplewhite glanced down at the witness Harry Zany and then Frank Darknight, her transcriptionist. This trial was turning into a nightmare. Would Frank Darknight be forced to testify? Perhaps not, if the defense could find the carpenter or paperwork supporting the request to fix the door. "Yes, you may call Sylvia Paleone. She's on your list of witnesses. Let's expediate the current witness Defender. Please continue."

Potts popped up from his chair, "How is this evidence relevant to the case, Your Honor?"

"Dela Lemon?" asked Mercedes to the defender.

Kimberly turned to look at Phil Potts wondering how he might sabotage this new evidence. Could he? How could the tourists, the witnesses, and the Citizen Judges unhear Delo Zany's testimony? Harry Zany's new testimony established doubt. Someone else could have used the secret stair to murder Star Bridgekeeper. It could have been Sylvia Paleone or someone who knew about the secret stair.

That might implicate Joanie Fitzhammond. Kimberly did her best to be surreptitious as she scanned the faces in the crowd pausing only for a second to see how Joanie was dealing with Zany's blockbuster testimony. Joanie smiled, her plain face brightening and appearing younger when she smiled. Her smile reassured and encouraged Kimberly.

Using her need to check Joanie's reaction, Kimberly chose to speak directly to the audience, "The existence of the secret stair establishes doubt as to Kimberly Lemon's guilt. The stair suggests someone else other than me had the means and opportunity to kidnap Star Bridgekeeper and drag her down to the catacombs and kill her. I have a witness who states she heard someone dragging a trash bin through the alley and out onto Wolfern Promenade on the day Star Bridgekeeper disappeared. My witness claims this unknown person was male and she recognized the song he was singing."

"Why?" Phil Potts asked. "Why would this mystery man go to all that trouble? Why use a trash bin in your alley when there are dozens closer?"

"Accuser Potts," Mercedes Hepplewhite cautioned. "Address

Dela Lemon as Defender."

"I will not. She is not a defender."

"Be seated, Accuser Potts. From here on you shall address all your questions and remarks to me or you will be fined and sent to the Department of Justice for twenty-four hours."

Kimberly turned to face Harry Zany doing her best to hide her concern Phil Potts had a point. How could she prove doubt if the actions of the unknown murderer were so bizarre as to defy reason? How many people had known about the secret stair? So far only Arthur Darknight, Frank Darknight, Harry Zany and Sylvia Paleone knew. In order to get Sylvia Paleone to talk she would have to convince Paleone she wasn't a suspect.

"Thank you, Delo Zany, you may step down," she managed to say without revealing her doubts. She turned to the High Judge. "I call Joanie Fitzhammond to the stand."

Joanie Fitzhammond rose slowly to her feet, her shoulders pulled forward as if protecting herself from the stares of the crowd. She kept her head down all the way to the witness chair nearly bumping into Kimberly. Kimberly touched her briefly and murmured in what she hoped was a reassuring voice, "I just have a few questions for you Delan Fitzhammond. Thank you."

Once Kimberly's witness had seated herself in the witness chair, Kimberly gave her a moment to scan the crowd knowing how intimidating it could be to look out upon all those faces, some genuinely concerned, most curious, and a few sneering. It was brave of her to come forward especially when there were factions who would later take out their grievances on someone like her. After Joanie was sworn in and the knight witnessed her identification documents on her cellphone, he said, "The witness is cleared, Your Honor."

Just as Kimberly moved forward to question Joanie, High Judge Mercedes Hepplewhite spoke from the dais, "How many witnesses do you have Defender Lemon?"

Momentarily dismayed, Kimberly had to search in her mind for an image of the witness list. The importance of her answer was not lost on her. Holy Centipede, what if she forgot someone? Her answer, if wrong, could mean life or death.

"Originally I had sixteen witnesses. Now I have seventeen which includes Edgar Stipple."

Mercedes Hepplewhite studied the officiating court appointee with a clinical eye. Her irritation was not lost on the Knight, "Get all the necessary validations ready before the witnesses are called sir. This court is pressed for time. Quickly now."

"We have yet to locate Edgar Stipple, Your Honor," the knight countered.

"Find him."

"Yes, Your Honor."

Once the High Judge motioned for her to continue, Kimberly crossed to the defender's side of the bench and reexamined Shehili Swana's brief notes. *Growthir 12 5092. Duke Dono's portrait. For the Soul Relics and Religious Treasures. Church permits at City Archive.*

When the judge cleared her throat, Kimberly hurried to the witness chair and began her first question. "Joanie, excuse me, Delan Fitzhammond, would you please recite to the court your experiences on Growthir 12 of our good year 5092?"

The witnessed leaned forward, "The whole day?"

Some people in the crowd tittered; Kimberly ignored them.

"During the afternoon of the 12th of Growthir. Where were you and what were you doing?"

"I was at work. I work, worked, at the For the Soul Relics and Religious Treasures for two years in a part-time capacity. My direct supervisor Mary McGirdle had been on vacation and I had been asked to close the shop. The owner, Sylvia Paleone was in her office. I did not know she was even in the shop at the time. She had left by the front door at lunchtime and told me she would not be back. But when I locked up and closed the register, I heard voices coming from the storage room. I was alarmed and went to investigate.

"I discovered Delan Paleone in the storage room. She appeared to be talking to the portrait. But when I opened the door wider to enter the room, I saw the portrait of Duke Dono move as if someone had slipped behind the frame. Delan Paleone didn't give me time to explain why I was in the storage room. She was furious and fired me on the spot. I was shocked. There had been no warning. I wondered if perhaps what I'd seen had been the reason for my firing."

"Before this incident had you received good work reviews from your boss?"

"Yes. Before I was fired, she and Mary McGirdle, the shop manager trusted me enough to leave me alone in the shop and in charge of the money."

"So, what reason did she give for firing you?"

"She didn't give me a reason which made no sense. Mary McGirdle had just given me a glowing review before her vacation and she and Sylvia offered me the temporary management position while Mary McGirdle was absent. If only I could have explained to Delan Paleone I had no idea she was in the shop and entered the storage room simply to collect my personal belongings, my coat and purse, and to lock the storage cabinets as instructed. But she was so furious, she wouldn't let me explain."

"And have you since found employment?" Kimberly asked anticipating the accuser's questioning when he would bring up the subject of Joanie's relationship with Kimberly.

"Yes. You offered me a part-time position at the Bookworm. And later I was elected by the members of the Merchants' Row Alliance to be their accountant, time-keeper and recorder."

This portion of the questioning would be touchy. Kimberly threaded her way carefully through the potential land mines. "As I read Dela Swana's notes, she mentioned City Archive Permits. Were you required to review Church of the Holy Centipede zoning permits in your official capacity as manager of the Merchants' Row Alliance?"

"Yes. I was asked by all the members."

"What did you discover?"

Joanie scooted forward in the large witness chair forgetting for the moment the impertinent and sometimes downright unfriendly stares from the people beyond Kimberly's shoulder, "The president of the Alliance, Harry Zany asked me to check the city map archives and the city permits for the last eight-hundred years to determine whether or not Merchants' Row belongs to the Cathedral or to the merchants."

"And what did you discover?"

"In the year 4280 Duke Dono and the Church of the Holy Delph sold the priests' sleeping quarters to the merchants of Blueglennen. The first shopkeeper who purchased one of the chambers was your five times removed grandfather Silas Lemon. The chamber next to the cathedral, which is now For the Soul Relics and Religious Treasures, was sold to an ancestor of Delo Finstickel.

Until Sylvia Paleone purchased the shop, the rooms had been in the Finstickel family continuously for ten generations. Delo Finstickel's third grandfather asked for a permit to build a private stair down into the catacombs. The records show a permit by Duke Dono for the construction of the stairs."

Kimberly looked up at the High Judge in her chair, then turned to look at the Citizen Judges and finally spun around to face the crowd, "Where does this private staircase lead?" She kept her back to Joanie and watched the Citizen Judges closely.

From their reaction to Joanie's testimony she'd know where she stood with them. She wished she could read minds. From a few Delphi, especially the two on the end of the bench closest to the High Court chair, Joanie's testimony was ancient history. The rest of them expressed interest.

"Exactly between the cathedral and Duke Tower. The door to the private stair is two meters from where the knights found Star Bridgekeeper's body."

"And how long did it take you to research your facts?"

"Four days. Al Pox gathered up the necessary documents for me, documents available to anyone interested in Blueglennen permits. Thanks to Delo Pox I had no trouble finding the maps and permits. He's spent his life organizing, cataloging and storing the documents in hermitically sealed containers at our Blueglennen City Document Retention Office."

"Were they easy to find?"

"Yes and no. Al Pox had no time to go through each individual box. And he had to verify through Governor Saurus whether I could sift through the containers. Saurus allowed me to go through the containers and Al requested I wear gloves. He went through old microfilm and microfiche for anything earlier than 3900."

"Does the Blueglennen City Document Retention Office require citizens to identify themselves when they request city maps and permits?"

"Yes. You must submit a request in writing and the reason for your request first and then when the controller approves the request, a person must sign in and provide identification."

"Do you use a computer to sign in or the old-fashioned way?"

"It's complicated now. You sign your name with pen and ink then the Document Retention Office requires a sample of blood and a photo identification card. The book you sign is a huge leather-bound book. It's the size of a two-year old and remains behind the controller's desk and can only be opened with a key the controller keeps on his person at all time. My signature was the first signature this year."

"How many people have requested records from the Blueglennen City Document Retention Office over the last few years?"

"When I filled out my particular request and signed my name, I noticed above my signature two names in the last four years."

"And those names?"

"Stop Dela Lemon," Judge Mercedes Hepplewhite said with a firmness she had not heard from her until that moment. "You have moved into murky legal territory. We must determine whether these records are under the preview of the court. Submit the names to me and the Citizen Judges at the end of the court day. We will determine whether the names are pertinent to this case."

Accuser Potts jumped up from his seat and began to pace the

floor. Every eye followed him. Kimberly was sure that had been his intention all along. "What purpose does this have with the present trial? I believe Dela Lemon is casting a net over a pond to hunt for sharks. She has nothing, but she's determined to bore us to death with her history lessons. Why is Your Honor allowing this woman to waste our time with foolish questions?"

"Enough, Accuser Potts. Sit down or I will have you removed from court. You'll have your time for cross examination when the defense rests."

Accuser Potts glanced at the crowd in amazement and threw up his hands. What a performance, Kimberly thought. He should be in one of Noble Coral's plays, maybe, as the court jester. Kimberly turned to the High Judge and saw a flicker of annoyance cross her face, annoyance directed at the accuser. Then Mercedes Hepplewhite looked down at Kimberly, "What is the purpose of this questioning?"

"Your Honor, the secret stair establishes reasonable doubt. I've learned that the few who know about it still use it. It is a way of moving between the church and the tower without ever being seen by the public. That is probably why Star was killed and stuffed in a garbage bin and no one noticed. I have lived all my life in Blueglennen and I never knew about the secret stair. My grandfather Charles Lemon was born in the Bookworm Emporium and his family has lived for seven generations in the bailey and never knew about the secret stair. So, those people who are aware of the stair may have some idea who the real killer might be."

"I and the Citizen Judges will determine whether this information can be made available to the general public. Are you finished with this witness?"

"Yes, Your Honor. I had planned to call Al Pox as my next witness. I will postpone his testimony until you and the Citizen Judges make your determination. Instead I call," Kimberly hesitated for a moment her mind blank. Who was next? Oh, Delph. Then she remembered. "I call Joffrey Stu to the stand."

Joffrey Stu, a short portly man with a neat cap of black hair rose from his chair with quiet calm and stood beside it waiting for someone to acknowledge him. His chair had been placed only inches from the Citizen Judges' bench. He squeezed past the other witness Shard Bristlecone and bumped into the former witness Joanie Fitzhammmond, as she made her way blindly toward her chair, her face registering relief. Joffrey Stu was relaxed and ready to testify.

He seemed tickled by the attention. Trials had never been televised in the history of Blueglennen. This was the first. Star's murder was the first in Blueglennen too. Most deaths in Blueglennen, other than the elderly expiring in their beds were due to accidents or overzealous knights interrogating prisoners. As a city employee, knowing what he knew of the inner workings of this corrupt government, he found the whole trial mystifying.

Why would Governor Saurus permit the trial to be televised and allow tourists to jampack the plaza? Did he really think there would be no blow back? There were eight video cameras recording the trial and sending images of his ruthless rule. No other governor needed so many personal guards to protect his precious neck or so many knights to keep the citizens obedient to his whims.

Did he hope other governors in the country of Curl would emulate him and return to the good old days? Or was Saurus attempting to fool the world into thinking he was a progressive leader? Wait. Saurus a mastermind? Saurus a thinker? Hell, no. The man was an idiot. Someone else was doing the thinking and the planning for the governor.

Joffrey suspected deviousness was at the bottom of this farce. Poor child, he thought, as Kimberly Lemon, so thin with her honey-colored hair and foreign violet eyes walked toward him. She had the strangest eyes. He'd never seen a Delphi with such long dark eyelashes. She reminded him of a woodland creature. And as he watched her move closer, he felt a pang of pity for her. She looked so trusting as she rehearsed what she wanted to ask him. He could see her lips moving as she practiced her question. Before turning to the audience, she pressed her lips so tightly he could see fine wrinkles.

How could her defender abandon her to these sharks? What a cruel twist of fate – to be alone facing an army of ruthless people conspiring to blame you for a murder you didn't commit. If Blueglennen citizens were honest, they already knew she was innocent. But what could they do? Everyone knew what happened to those who fought back. One day they disappeared. A terrible thought surfaced, and he tried to quash it. No. She wasn't capable of murder. All signs may lead to her, but he'd known her all his life. She was innocent. He was sure of it.

The Accuser Phil Potts rose to his feet and addressed the High Judge Mercedes Hepplewhite, "If it please your High Judge, may we call a short recess?"

Mercedes motioned for Phil Potts to address her, in private, and beckoned Kimberly Lemon to follow suit. Kimberly glanced at Potts suspiciously. What was he up to?

Mercedes spoke first, "Why should I call for a short recess? We have an hour before dark?"

"It will take an hour just to get all these people out of the bailey, Your Honor," the Accuser said ignoring Kimberly Lemon. Kimberly did her best to ignore the little frog who thought he was a big toad. She did her best to appear calm. She hated the fact he was probably right.

"Return to your seats Accuser Potts and Defender Lemon," Mercedes commanded as she rose to her feet and turned to acknowledge Joffrey Stu. "You may go back to your seat, witness. You will testify tomorrow. We thank you for your service to this court."

The knights on duty ushered the Accuser and Defender to their benches. The High Court Judge Mercedes Hepplewhite still standing banged the drum three times and in a high clear voice, loud enough for even the people packed like sardines on Wolfern Promenade to hear, she announced, "Court is dismissed. We will reconvene at daybreak."

E1 Shellfargon Year 5092 NDMP WK 6: UES Albion 4

Assigned E2 to continue guarding accused. Evidence suggests there will be an attempt on her life again. No help from Gov's staff. Valley Long Gate only permissible entrance now. Delphi scanned at gate by my team. Court Key Gate closed. Knight Graceland apprehended a climber with professional gear at Siren River rampart. Climber is from South Victoria and a Weevil Party member. Claims he has come to rescue Kimberly Lemon. Request Albion security assist. Sheriff's Office compromised.

E3 Shellfargon Year 5092 NDMP Wk. 6: UES Albion 4

As I am a witness for the defense and for the prosecution, I am unable to photograph everyone in Blueglennen. Impossible anyway since thousands of tourists are choking the streets and the train station. Must prepare for trial and gather materials for testimony. E2 will cover Royal Plaza and Sheriff's Office when time permits. Images will be uploaded to Station Com 1.

E4 Shellfargon Year 5092 NDMP WK 6: UES Albion 4

Sending letter from Delphadorturo Raker. Raker signed an executive order permitting foreign agents to defend Delphinids in a court of law if the foreign agents pass the Curlecon Bar Examinations and are in the country legally. Will you permit me to defend the accused Kimberly Lemon tomorrow?

Chapter 12

The High Judge Mercedes Hepplewhite and her court managed to slip out of the Royal Plaza within twenty minutes, escorted by the Governor's knights through Bishop Garden, out through the gate, around the castle's outer bailey along the river side and down into the valley. Instead of residing in the luxurious penthouse of the Governor's mansion at the top of Duke Tower as Judge Evan Quark's replacement, Mercedes chose to remain in the modest home of her Greenburg Valley grandmother near the shores of the Siren River.

The Governor had posted four knights around her grandmother's tiny house. Mingled with the familiar sounds of the Siren waters spilling over rocks, she could hear muffled footsteps as people returned to their homes. She felt sorry for those people still trickling out of the castle's inner bailey at such a late hour. She'd recessed the court before sunset, yet, by her bedside clock and the late newscast the Valley Long Drawbridge was still open, and stragglers were being escorted out of the castle long after midnight.

She was sure the ticket holders would return to the Royal Plaza before sunrise clutching their tickets determined to find better seats. They would be disappointed. Most would be turned away. She'd already received a text of the Governor's displeasure. Due to prior commitments Mercedes' law partner Bertram Jones had no choice but to leave her in Blueglennen and return to their law office in New Enreich. He had sent her a warning text before boarding: *Raker can do nothing. Silver membership uncertain. You want to risk everything on a nobody?*

You mean Saurus has friends in high places and Raker dare not offend them? she typed furiously. Contempt rushed through her body. She followed this question with another: *Shall I forsake my country for a High Court position? You know me better Bertie.* The few hours left before daybreak were spent fruitlessly staring up at her grandmother's plaster ceiling as her eyes mapped out the largest crack. Had she been infected with the same craziness infecting the rest of Blueglennen? Did she smell rebellion in the air?

Gawain Bristlecone escorted Kimberly Lemon back to the Bookworm Emporium by way of the catacombs under Duke Tower. Unable to speak to her privately due to the extra guards on either side of the accused and in his position as lowest ranking knight, Gawain hoped for the best and took the lead carrying his light-stick through the dark passageways. Her guards wouldn't dare harm her with him as witness. He headed north in the direction he knew would lead to the Cathedral of the Holy Centipede.

As they entered the cathedral, he anticipated a confrontation from the Bishop and was surprised when the entourage, once clear of the catacombs, discovered the cathedral brightly lit from a thousand sconces their flames dancing in the drafty air from the gigantic wooden doors. Why had the doors been left open? It was odd that none of the tourists had been curious enough to peek inside the cathedral and take a few pictures on their cellphones. Or maybe pictures from the walls? His nerves were tight as he searched the lofty interior for signs of movement, perhaps someone lurking in the shadows waiting to punish the blasphemer.

The long nave, the transepts, the altar, and the choir were empty of followers, even of the Bishop and his wife. Why had Bishop Little left his precious cathedral open to the elements and to a horde of tourists? As his eye searched for trouble, he spotted something planted on a white plaster buttress, a tracking camera. Then he spotted another one near the massive doors. Of course. the Governor must have placed the cameras in the cathedral.

As if Wakefield knew what he was thinking, he heard the guy say in a condescending voice, "The cathedral is secure Bristlecone since the Bishop allowed the spillover crowd to sit on the pews and watch the trial from the video screen up there." Gawain followed his finger and noticed the massive television screen above the altar. On his ship there were priests who would have been outraged at such sacrilege.

Above the altar were a series of long narrow slits covered in stained-glass depicting brilliantly colored starfish in shades of blue, red, and yellow. Above the starfish, another stained-glass image, much larger and more magnificent overshadowed everything in the cathedral, drawing the eye to it repeatedly. The craftsperson had carved out of the thick granite a crescent-shaped opening and inset a thick piece of stained glass. The image represented the Holy Delph in golden robes with thousands of twinkling stars surrounding his holiness.

The depiction of the Holy Delph floating in space nearly set Gawain off. He struggled to remain respectfully curious. The idea any living creature could survive the vacuum of space was hilarious. An old rumor persisted today on Albion about Murt P. Lano, that he'd been a real person, not just a legend. Had he been a real Earther who bullied and bribed his way onboard? Or was Murt P. Lano just a teaching tool to frightened shipmites?

Supposedly the story started eight generations ago when the first prototype Albion starship embarked from what was left of North America. Among the crew, the scientists and passengers who had been chosen by lottery was a rich dude who bribed the captains to let him board. The rich dude, once he reached the safety of space, announced to the passengers and crew that he was a god. He ordered everyone to bow down to him or face his wrath. When he was ignored and treated like a crackpot, he opened a hatch to prove he was a god.

He lasted a minute in the vacuum of space.

The blood and fluids in his body boiled and then quickly froze and he soon turned into a human pinball bouncing off the starship and space debris until the techs could pull him back inside the ship. Every Albion shipmite grew up shivering in delight over horror stories about Murt P. Lano, the space vampire of Albion 1.

Another oddity about the church was the image above the altar. Gawain was surprised to see the remnants of the Holy Delph in Bishop Little's church. Wasn't the Holy Delph, a myth, and the Holy Centipede, a fact, as witnessed by the first Mark Little? Gawain would have thought the first object to go would be images of the Holy Delph. But perhaps like religions from Gawain's history books about Earth, Bishop Little believed he would attract new believers from the old if he incorporated the old religion into the new.

When Gawain and the Duke's guard exited the cathedral and moved along the empty cobblestone street, Gawain could feel people watching from their windows as the entourage escorted Kimberly Lemon home. He could feel their eyes everywhere, from the ramparts to the basement floors. Curtains twitched, and voices mumbled behind closed doors. The merchants were unhappy. Those who were not on the list of witnesses had been ordered to remain in their shops during the trial. Many merchants chose to lock their doors afraid the crowds might get ugly, maybe steal stuff as mementos or trash shops if the judges declared Kimberly innocent.

Some tourists offered to pay for a view and those willing to pay discovered to their disappointment Merchants' Row had no view. The condos overlooking the plaza were three stories high and Merchants' Row shops were two stories high. Those who paid were no better off than those sitting on Wolfern Promenade's cold stones or the Cetacea stairs.

The Tumbles offered to open their attic trapdoor so paying guests could climb onto their roof. Once on the roof, they discovered they'd been ripped off. They had two views alright: watch and listen to Knight Graceland posted on Knight's Walk Rampart regale the poor along Poison Creek with minute by minute coverage of the trial or watch Governor Saurus and his guests dining and drinking on his balcony. When the Tumbles refused to reimburse the guests, they had the mixed pleasure of standing for hours exposed to the burning rays of the hot afternoon sun.

Those poor suckers even had to pay extra for picnic chairs, wine and cheese. The three couple's unfortunate enough to be accepted at least got to sample a few wines offered by Hadal's Delight. But by the end of the trial, they were broke. Once they hitched rides home, they lied and told everyone they'd been in the thick of the trial. None of them revealed the fact they'd paid an additional 3000 seastars to sleep on the floor of the shop. A small price to pay, one of them said. There would never be such a sight again in the history of Curl. Au contraire mon ami, Gawain thought. You, sorry ass, this trial is nothing compared to what's coming your way.

Gawain reached the Bookworm Emporium first and held out his hand. Kimberly stared at his hand in the blue glow from the wormlight globe, all else was in shadow. When he wiggled his fingers, she realized what he wanted and pulled her key out of her sweater pocket. He gently pushed her aside, opened the shop door, flicked the light on, and closed the door with a decided snap. Wakefield positioned himself next to Kimberly and looked up at Knight's Walk searching the rampart from Valley Long Tower to River View Tower. Knight Lively and Graceland had left hours ago and were with D.I. Hawk at the Department of Justice.

Gawain whispered something in the other knight's ear and Tobias Underwood took his light-stick and walked down the street toward Wolfern Promenade. Kimberly and Gawain heard him say to someone near the bridge gate, "There's nothing to see here. Move on. Didn't you hear the curfew bell? Go on now."

Just as Gawain opened the door and motioned Kimberly and Wakefield inside, a disembodied voice shouted down from the roof above Tumble's shop, "It's her! The accused." Several heads popped into view and Gawain shoved Kimberly inside then ordered Wakefield to follow him. He pointed his light-stick at the gawkers and shouted for his other knight, "Tobias, bring those people down from the roof. Now."

A guard posted inside River View Tower came out to discover what all the commotion was about and to his dismay found people sleeping on Tumble's roof. Someone shined a harsh light in his eyes. "Who goes there?" the knight recognized Bristlecone's voice.

"Guard Snowman, your lordship."

"There are unauthorized people on the Tumble roof. What are you doing up there? Napping?" Snowman watched as two shadows were roughly jerked to their feet by a third person. He recognized Knight Tobias Underwood and then noticed his light-stick hovering over the intruders' heads. Tobias lifted his light-stick threateningly and bellowed, "Off with you now. This is a restricted area." The people on the Tumble roof began to scramble toward the attic door.

"But we paid 3000 seastars," one of the men protested, his voice shrill.

"Tough. Go on now or y'all spend the rest of your days in a dark dank hole in the ground."

Impatiently Gawain raged. These clowns would never survive an attack by Aviangore, not for a minute. Gawain seriously considered going up to the rampart and grabbing himself a hunk of uniform and shaking Snowman until his eyeballs fell out of his skull. He knew reprimanding the idiot would be a futile gesture. The Governor's men were sacrosanct. He had no authority down on the planet. The only person with some clout was D.I. Burhani Hawk.

The tourists came out of the door of the Tumble wine shop grumbling. Tobias Underwood followed them out and shut the door behind him. He threw some paper at the tourists, "Here's your money back. I made the Tumbles open their cash register and reimburse you. What a bunch of slugs. Three-thousand seastars is a lot of money for nothing. You can't see a thing from up there. Come on. Let's find you a warm cozy bed for the night."

"But where will we sleep? The bridge is closed. We've already tried to get rooms in Greenburg Valley. Even Mudflat Village is booked up," a man whined.

"Like I said, we've got a warm cozy bed in one of our deluxe prison cells."

Gawain stopped Underwood, "We'd have to book them and that would take too much time. Take them to the church. They can sleep on the pews."

Underwood led the men toward the Cathedral of the Holy Centipede muttering, "The Bishop's not going to like this."

"I don't care what the Bishop thinks, Underwood. Just do it," Gawain shouted after him. Underwood kept walking and never looked back. Every so often he'd shove one of the tourists. Gawain couldn't wait for the day he could finally wipe the smirk off that squid's face.

While Wakefield sat his lazy butt on the window seat and peered through her curtains to watch the commotion on Tumble's roof, Kimberly slipped into her backroom wishing with all her heart the governor's goons would leave her in peace. She tapped the lamp sitting on a small table near the passageway. The lamp cast enough light to get her down the dark passageway to sanctuary.

Once inside her room, she shut the door and sat on her bed listening. On the other side of the wall, even with a bookshelf between her and the shop, she could hear Gawain reenter her home and order Wakefield to wait outside. When he mentioned in passing that Juleus would be guarding the shop she did a little dance around the room.

These strangers, these aliens from the starship didn't understand Delphi, didn't understand the strong bonds between Delphi pods. They never bothered to ask the most important question of a Delphi – who do you trust above family? Trust had nothing to do with blood or DNA. It had everything to do with instincts beyond the five senses. Juleus Graceland and his family, as well as Harry Zany, Valcinda Moorland, the cousins Guinevere and Dialmere, Reason and Fitzhammmond, Montague and Moth, up to and including Madas Lively belonged to her pod. They were her people, people she trusted with her life.

Wakefield had always belonged to Victoria and Anthony's pod of nincompoops. She'd known from an early age, they couldn't be trusted. Why did Bristlecone keep Wakefield so close? Why did he subject her to that traitor's presence in her own home? Hadn't she already revealed his duplicity? Why couldn't he open his eyes and see the truth? Or were his people so alien they kept enemies close and friends away? One day she hoped to ask Shehili Swana what humans were really like. When she heard the bell chime as the door opened, she knew Wakefield had left for the night.

The silence felt good. She slipped off her shoes and bowed her head unable to decide whether to be terrified or furious. She couldn't seem to work up enough energy even to be sorry for herself. The sound of heavy booted feet marching down her passageway galvanized her into staying awake a bit longer. She planted a fake smile on her face and waited for Gawain to open the door. Instead, he spoke to her through the door, "I've sent Tobias to stand guard in the alley. Knight Graceland will keep watch by the door."

"And where will you be Delo Bristlecone?" she found herself asking suddenly nervous.

"Wakefield and I will be going door to door counting heads and sending unauthorized people to the church for the night. Try to get some sleep Dela Lemon."

"Yes. Yes. I'll try."

She waited until she heard him leave and snuck out to the front of her home in her bare feet. With one hand she flicked the switch which turned off the overhead lights and turned on the outer lights. She walked to the countertop and pressed the secret button. When she heard the bolt click into place, she paused waiting until Juleus jiggled the doorknob and checked the windows. When she was sure he believed she'd gone to bed, she peeked out the window.

The lamplight lit by the glowworms touched the bowed head of Juleus Graceland. He was sitting on the bench beneath her picture window. The blue light shined down on him in such a way, the viewer could almost believe he was holding back the dark. Relieved to know he was close by, she smiled.

He seemed preoccupied with his cellphone which was unusual. Then she heard him say to the other person at the other end, "Hi Mama. Could you keep the fish sandwiches warm for me? Guess what I'm doing? I'm guarding the Emporium. Yeah. Bristlecone asked for me by name. No. I'm not kidding. I know. Don't worry Mama. I'm not going to be stationed on the starship any time soon."

A minute passed as he listened to his mother then he said, "Well, there's still time. I don't know. I'll ask her in the morning. Why don't you just check with one of the other merchants? I can't be a part of this Mama. I pledged to serve and protect Duke Tower, the citizens of Blueglennen, and the rule of law."

Another minute or two passed. As she waited, her feet began to get cold. Then she heard him say, "The wagon will be safe behind the barn."

There was a pause and then he said to his mother, "Nobody's going to steal your wagon."

Another pause followed by his response, "It's too late now, the drawbridge is closed."

Finally, he finished with, "The gate to Bishop's Garden is locked. Then go over to Lively's house if you're scared. I got to go. I'm hanging up now."

Before Knight Graceland caught her eavesdropping, Kimberly walked back to her apartment and tried to lay down on the bed. She knew she had to sleep. It was simple common sense. She must rest before the trial. She had to be sharp. She had to be ready. Yet her body refused to relax. She was doomed. Any sane person would have realized that by now.

With Wakefield beside him Gawain began at the furthest end of Merchants' Row at the door of Unique Boutique. After a dozen hardy knocks on the door and pressing of the doorbell, Gawain shouted up at Shehili's window. He knew she'd come back to town. He knew she'd never intended to leave. Hawk might be fooled but Gawain had his sister Shard who seemed to know everything.

Probably everyone on the street had heard him shouting. With a smirk, he saw the upstairs rooms spring to life followed by the sound of the Cavenymphs singing as if they thought it was morning. Bristlecone waited impatiently for the proprietress to open the damned door. As she stood poised to slam the door in his face, he noticed her fetching silk kimono and a steely look in her eye which promised future vengeance. He wasn't happy with her either and brushed by her and entered the shop calling over his shoulder, "Wakefield stand guard while I check for unlicensed occupants."

Shehili bestowed a stunning smile on Wakefield which probably made his little heart do cartwheels. Once the doors were shut and they were alone, Gawain moved toward the counter and pointed at the wall, "Can you stop their caterwauling?"

She ignored him and marched toward her office. Gawain followed, "We've known each other a long time Themis. You were ordered to return to the ship. Just because your daddy's #1 doesn't mean the other captains can't punish you for being UA. Daedalus told me your license was revoked. So how come you're still here? Are you pretending to be a tourist now?"

"Don't be so sure Ares. As far as we know, I'm still your superior."

"Daedalus is the lead on Shellfargon. I take my orders from him."

When they stopped talking the Cavenymphs stopped singing. Then Gawain found himself saying, unable to contain his anger any longer, "What a nasty trick you pulled on Kimberly. You could have told the captains to go to hell. They have no idea what's really going on down here."

Shehili Swana ignored him. He followed her up the winding stairs to her bedroom, "Where's your clerk?" he asked prepared to grab her arm and make her turn around.

"Ufeeza Wjanebet is at home where she should be, in the K5 suite, a very nice suite with a view of the highway and the woodlands."

"Is that next to Finstickel? The smelly screwball?"

Gawain heard her sigh, "Your sense of direction is terrible. I've often wondered why Daedalus trusts a man who can't even figure out which end is starboard."

Instead of countering her insult, Gawain ran up the stairs ahead of her and began searching her bedroom. Since she was no longer a member of the Blueglennen Ethnography Team he had every right to ignore professional conduct. He opened closet doors, looked under the bed, the sofa, anywhere he thought she might hide someone. The top floor had three rooms, one good sized bathroom and two bedrooms. The largest bedroom faced the Royal Plaza and had the biggest bed.

As Gawain searched her room, Shehili made herself comfortable on the cushioned window seat with an excellent view of the plaza. He was surprised to see a pair of opera glasses resting on top of a techno tablet. In the corner of the bedroom, a small window was open. A cool breeze circulated through the room stirring the gossamer curtains and the skirt of a day gown which Shehili had left hanging on a mannequin.

He stopped below the trapdoor on the ceiling and whirled to face her. She'd moved to the center of the room in a stance he knew well. He thought he'd caught her unawares. For a second, he caught a glimpse of disappointment. Just as quickly boredom returned. They'd been friends since the crib. All four of them had been friends from the day they were born. They'd given each other secret names and as far as he knew had never revealed them to anyone.

"Is someone hiding on your roof Lieutenant Swana?" he asked.

"Don't be silly, Lieutenant Bristlecone. I like my privacy too much. Quit being an idiot. She's turning you into a moonstruck fool."

"Yes, Gawain. Don't be so foolish. We all know Officer Swana so well, don't we?" said a familiar voice. Hawk walked into the room and moved toward Gawain's side. He examined the trapdoor and shook his head.

"Sir," Gawain began.

"Wakefield explained the situation Ares," Hawk said as he took his dark eyes off the trapdoor and turned to scrutinize Swana. "Would you mind continuing your search elsewhere? I'd like to talk to our former team member in private."

Mindful of his position, and the real possibility Themis might become the next captain of the Albion, Gawain made his way to the door. He'd always wondered if Hawk and Swana's relationship was closer than they let on. Like Gawain and his sister Shard, Burhani and Shehili were members of the Seven. The Seven was a term the ship coined to classify their ship's lineage. They were the most recent generation of explorers to leave the Milky Way Galaxy.

Before the Seven, all starship children were raised together in one central nursery protected by heavy shielding walls at the very center of the ship. Their ancestors feared attacks by alien enemies with good reason since the Aviangore had nearly wiped out one starship and another one was missing. They assumed the nursery would be secure since it would be in the center of the ship surrounded by shield walls with guards posted 24/7.

With only one nursery generations were raised from the cradle to the grave, forever in each other's company. Scientists grew alarmed as fewer and fewer shipmites chose to marry, with many disgusted at the idea of procreating with someone they'd known all their lives. When the time came to choose a marriage partner only a handful reluctantly agreed to marry and mate for the good of the ship. It was only when the Albion 4 was headed for extinction, that the ship's captains demanded scientists rethink the pedagogy.

A furious debate over the Westermarck effect, sexual imprinting and incest taboos resulted in the restructuring of the Albion 4. Many people realized the main impediment to procreation stemmed from a lack of choice rather than genetic sexual attraction (GSA), Westermarck effect or incest taboos. For generations, shipmites were treated like prisoners forbidden from moving about freely, confined in a hot noisy crowded cocoon and watched every minute of every day.

After the captains and techs reconfigured the central nursery where past generations had been born and raised, the change was miraculous. Crew members chopped up the central hub and built small attractive living quarters where parents (singles, asexual, bisexual or transsexual) could raise their offspring as they saw fit. The most crucial outcome turned out to be a new rule which allowed shipmites to explore the ship from the command station to the engine room. No longer would children be prisoners on their own ship, allowed free access only when they turned eighteen. Instead they would learn lessons through their failures and triumphs.

Grateful to be a Seven, Gawain walked out of the Unique Boutique and paused on the street. He hesitated thinking back to what Themis had said about his relationship with Kimberly. He stared abstractly at the Bookworm Emporium. Steady Ares, he told himself. You have no business attaching yourself to an alien. There were too many complications.

Yet, if he'd been a Six, he might never have met Kimberly. He knew being so close to her and sharing her troubles endangered them both. He didn't care. His instinct was to trust this Delphinid more than even his family or friends. If he'd been a spook observing her through a vidscreen, he might have been able to maintain an impartial attitude. But he wasn't a spook and didn't like them anyway.

Then he remembered the time he and Hawk nearly lost their chance to join the Albion Special Forces Legion (ASFL). The ASFL were the only members of the Albion crew allowed to explore meteors and planets. The ASFL Corp were made up of soldiers, civil engineers, hull jumpers, rock hounds, fighter pilots, shuttle jocks, and ethnographers. The only way to get on the list was after years of leadership tests.

When he and Hawk were ten years old, they nearly lost the chance to have their names added to the list. Ever since they'd been small, Gawain wanted to be a soldier and Hawk wanted to fly jets. All their dreams might have ended if he and Hawk had panicked while trapped outside the hull. Instead of becoming ethnographers studying the planet of Shellfargon, they might have ended up as space ghoulies floating forevermore in the Andromeda Galaxy.

For his generation the ventilation tubes were the most popular place to play. He and Hawk took the game a bit further by crawling all the way to the docking platform. Unbeknownst to them an unplanned drill was in progress and the docking doors were open. Only a few minutes before the drill, he and Hawk figured out the code to the docking hatch. They let themselves out before the hatch automatically closed behind them.

The vacuum of deep space attacked their bodies immediately. They had a minute of air left. They were trapped between space and the protective canopy. Sirens blared nearly bursting their eardrums. Gawain remembered holding his breath and trying desperately to open the ventilation hatch. Then Hawk grabbed his shoulder and spun him around pointing to the control room. The officers on duty hadn't seen them. They were busy studying the maneuvers on their monitors.

Like Gawain, Hawk's face turned red with the effort to hold in the last of the air in his lungs. With his fingers Hawk signed the words boot, ladybug and shuttle. Incongruously for such a terrifying event, Gawain still remembered Hawk's fingers, long and supple for someone so young.

His hands and feet had started growing long before the rest of him caught up. If events had turned out differently, that insignificant detail about Hawk's long fingers might have been the last thing Gawain remembered before he died. He ripped the cord on his chest pocket and the portable helmet fell to the dock floor. With shaking fingers, he slipped it over his head. It would give them five minutes of oxygen tops.

All shipmites knew the sign for ladybug. While learning to

walk, children were learning the signs that would save their lives, crucial signs which might one day mean life or death, such as boot/ladybug, vacuum, zero-g and acceleration. The boot sign came first, then the ladybug, a short-hand for "take hold." Like ladybugs the boots of every person on the Albion had a dual purpose.

In everyday situations starship boots allowed crew members to move about normally. In ladybug mode, the boots were capable of adhering to any surface. The design kept crew members safe from sudden stops and accelerations. Gawain hit first his right heel then his left turning his boots into sticky feet. The sticky feet held him to the metal dock with a special elastomeric protein everybody called goo.

When Hawk pointed over Gawain's shoulder, Gawain turned and saw a shuttle docked at the end of the hub. It would take them at least three minutes to get to the shuttle and precious more time to open the shuttle hatch, climb inside and get the machine running. Before Gawain had a chance to move, Hawk shoved him toward the hub. Gawain started running down the dock, his progress impeded by the goo. It took all the muscles in his legs to run.

As he hobbled toward life like some demented frog jumping from one lily pad to the next, he felt the dock shake beneath him as the canopy began to eject from its moorings. His lungs were beginning to burn from lack of oxygen. Before he could touch the shuttle door, Hawk tossed him a rebreather and ran past him. He fumbled for the rebreather and with seconds to spare stuck the mask over his nose and mouth. It was later he realized the heavy metal chamber dangling from the mask had hit him in the throat and left a bruise. He never felt the pain. The instant the oxygen entered his lungs, the burning stopped.

Ten seconds later both Hawk and Gawain were inside the shuttle and staring at the console. Any other shipmite would have panicked seeing all those buttons and monitors. Not them. Both Hawk and Gawain had played enough simulations to know what buttons to push. Gawain turned on the engine and got the oxygen flowing while Hawk grabbed the stick. An angry voice blasted in their ears from the shuttle's com and echoed through every speaker on the dock, "What the hell do you think you're doing? Get back to station crewman. ASAP. The canopy is in position."

"Sorry sir," Hawk said. "We got stuck on the dock. We just needed some air."

"Turn off the f'ing engine kid. You want to kill us all?"

Gawain and Hawk put their rebreathers back on and Gawain shut down the engine. They sat in total darkness and cold. He'd been so scared he hadn't noticed the cold. It took an hour for the canopy to cover the docking station and lock into position. They'd been lucky. The shuttle had twelve rebreathers.

They used up ten of them, so it wasn't as if they would die of asphyxiation before the fighters finished their maneuvers. Under the seats they found plenty of blankets and as they covered up, they had ringside seats to the fighters return from 829's moon. It had been the best part of their ordeal to watch the jets swoop through the security gate and back to the docking station. The event made Hawk more determined than ever to be a fighter pilot. Unfortunately, his teachers thought differently. His test scores proved he had the intelligence to fly, but not the split-second reaction required for combat.

What Gawain admired about Hawk was his ability to evolve and move on. They accomplished one part of their dream. They joined the Special Forces Legion in a branch known to only a few — spooks. Between themselves they joked they'd been saved from becoming space ghoulies, so they could be ship spooks instead. Their training was classified and so secret, not even their parents knew what they really did for the ASFL.

Not even Shehili knew what they really did for the captains.

As Gawain looked up at Shehili's window, he wondered if she suspected. She was no dummy. If Hawk and Swana had a thing going, they'd better be careful because there were factions on the Albion who would do everything in their power to separate them. Reese McConnell, 2nd in command was one person who came to mind. If he knew, the 2nd would be so disgusted he'd try to bring back Murt P. Lano and order the dumbass to haunt the lovebirds. Ender Swana's daughter marrying Burhani Hawk would not go down well with any of the captains.

Sure, an ASFL spook and a future 1st captain might outrage old-school elitists. But the 7s didn't give a damn about mixing up the gene pool. It was time to set aside old grudges and prejudices. Albion would benefit from a union between those two. He was sick and tired of bickering captains messing in crew's personal lives. What the two of them did on their own time was nobody's business.

The ship didn't understand the complexities of life when interacting with alien species. In order to blend in, an ethnographer had to set aside preconceived notions and prejudices. Gawain had forged strong friendships with many alien species over the years. He'd even found a few friends on Shellfargon. And maybe a future bride. When he considered his feelings for Kimberly Lemon, he thought about his uncle Captain Trace Bristlecone, 3rd in command. Four decades ago, his uncle was reassigned to Albion 4 because his alien friend was sick, and Albion 3 was on a mission beyond the Milky Way. When she was brought onboard no one on 4 made a fuss. Maybe their lack of concern had something to do with her appearance. She looked human.

It was only when they tried to have children, the meds realized Aunt Zilla was another species. She admitted to the captains that she was a Vulcan and had to go through a series of court trials to prove she wasn't a spook. Gawain's aunt may not have been as exotic looking as Kimberly Lemon; yet, his aunt and uncle were eventually given permission to marry. Their marriage set a precedent for future intermarriages. And contrary to current prejudices Aunt Zilla and Uncle Trace managed to successfully procreate. With the help of modern science, they brought into the Andromeda Galaxy three children and their grandchildren produced children without the requirement of test-tubes or incubators.

The racket from down the street caught his attention. Gawain stepped out of the shadows and moved toward the raised voices and banging. Near the drawbridge, Gawain saw Wakefield hammering on the display window of the Life Long Friend pet shop with both fists. The response to his racket was silence. By now, the menagerie inside should have been going nuts. Wakefield turned when he heard Gawain approach. Simultaneously, a second-story window opened directly above The Children's Playhouse.

Wakefield's shouting and banging agitated the glowworms so much they were slamming against the globe in a frenzy to be free. Normally, the bioluminescent worms would have illuminated only the current section of Merchants' Row. But by now even Knight Graceland standing by the Bookworm Emporium looked as if he'd been splattered with blue paint. From the upstairs window next door to Life Long Friends, the men down below could see an attractive young woman with pale skin and hair the color of midnight lean out. She didn't seem surprised to see them. Resigned to another sleepless night, she rested her arms on the windowsill and peered down at them with a sneer, "Can't you tell by now gentlemen that no one's at home. Guinevere is gone. She left hours ago."

"Where did she go?" Wakefield asked pulling out his notepad and pencil.

How old world of him, Gawain thought with an inner smile, to choose paper and pencil over a techno-pad. He looked up at the lovely lady with what he hoped was a stern expression.

"Answer the question, Dela...?

"Valcinda Moorland."

"Please answer the question, Dela Moorland.

"She's taken the train for Grantport."

"She's a registered witness and due to speak tomorrow," Gawain pointed out. "By leaving she's put her reputation in question and Dela Lemon's life in jeopardy."

"She'll be back before the trial begins," Valcinda assured Gawain. "Don't you worry about her. She's as committed to freeing Kimberly as any of us. She'll be back in a few hours. She's taken the last of her babies down to the Society for Wolfern Critters."

"Why?" asked Gawain.

"Because the banging of drums and megaphones upset the pups and she doesn't trust the crowds to keep their distance. Why aren't you doing something about the disorderly tourists? They bang on our shop doors incessantly day-and-night. They've even woken up my babies and frightened them to death peering in the windows."

"You sell critters too?" asked Gawain.

Wakefield answered for her, "The Children's Playhouse is for our young, not dumb animals."

"Guinevere's pups," Valcinda spit out, "are just as smart as you, smarter even."

"Well, they're not made in the Holy Delph's image," Wakefield responded in kind. "And that's all that should matter, Valcinda Moorland. You're Church of Curl same as me."

"I can be Church of Curl and still think animals have souls," Valcinda shouted over Gawain's attempts to shut them both up. His only recourse was to grab a hunk of Wakefield's shoulder and shake him to get his attention, followed by a rougher shake to remind him who was in charge.

"Enough of this you two. People are trying to sleep." He craned his neck back to get a good look at her. "Wakefield's just doing his job Dela Moorland. We're searching everyone's home for unauthorized occupants."

The street was once again quiet. Valcinda stepped back inside with an oath clearly heard by both men, shut the window and pulled the curtains closed as a final shield against Wakefield's ignorance. Gawain would not be put off and moved toward The Children's Playhouse door rapping smartly on the painted balloons. He heard Wakefield say "Sorry for the commotion, gov. I've known Valcinda since she was a fingerling. She's a stubborn young woman. Too independent for her own good."

"Quit calling me gov. If you must, call me sir. Hold on," Gawain said to Wakefield and turned back to the door as he heard someone draw the bolt. Valcinda stood on the threshold wrapped in a blanket. There was someone standing behind her. He recognized

Valcinda's cousin Caleb and heard Caleb say to her, "Let 'um in Cinda. They're just doing their job."

As Gawain stepped onto the threshold, he thought about the rest of the night. Seven more shops to go, the church, the university dorms and Bishop's Garden. Wait. He'd forgotten the luxury suites above the Royal Plaza. Lovely. He sent a text message to the duty guard at the Tower ordering more knights to search the bailey for unauthorized gate-crashers.

While Gawain and his knights searched the bailey for intruders, Shehili Swana shrugged off Hawk's extended hand and refused to look at him. The breeze from the open window cooled her body yet could not temper her anger or disappointment. She was afraid if she looked at him, she would say something she'd regret. How dare he? How dare he dictate terms to her? The leader of the country of Curl, the Delphadorturo Raker had yet to rescind her law license. If he'd been concerned about her fitness to defend Dela Lemon, he would have ordered her off the planet. Only Albion forbid Swana from defending the accused and ordered her return.

If she did return, would she still outrank the ethnographers? Or would her father and the captains take away her insignias and demote her?

"Look at me Swan," he ordered. He hadn't moved from his place near the door. Maybe, he was afraid she'd throw something at him? Did he think she couldn't hit him from ten-feet away?

She turned from the window to face him, "Don't call me Swan. If you're attempting seduction, your timing sucks."

"We can't save these people," Hawk shouted. With an effort he got his emotions under control. Only with her did he ever show his true self. "It's too late. It was too late the moment we discovered this frigging backwater. Our chemtrail would have led to this outcome eventually, even if we'd left the solar system years ago, and you damn well know it."

"I don't care," she found herself shouting. "We can't leave them defenseless. We've got to warn them, do something to help them. At least let me help one of them. When she's found innocent, I can vouch for her and she can come with us."

"My orders are clear Swan," Hawk told her, his body relaxing and his face resuming his habitual stoicism. "We've got a few months, maybe two to finish our surveys. And then we must leave this solar system."

"It's not up to you. My father is first."

"Your father already made his decision. I'm to get you off this planet and back to the Albion. You've got two days to pack. And no, the Cavenymphs stay here." Without another word Hawk spun on his heel and left the room. In his wake she felt the fury he left behind. As he stomped down the stairs, she heard the front door hit the wall. Beneath her feet, her bedroom floor shook. He was wrong. She would prove him wrong. Running away wouldn't solve anything. They'd been runny for centuries.

The morning sun mocked Kimberly Lemon as she sat at the Defender's Bench and waited for the High Judge to appear. The soft breeze, the sunshine, and the cloudless sky mocked her. There should be storm clouds and lightening. Instead, the squenches were flitting from gargoyle to gargoyle, from potted plant to rampart, pooping on Duke Dono's plastered head and stealing food left unattended. The antics of these birdbrained clowns was a mockery of her trial and her importance in the scheme of things. Long after the noose was removed from her lifeless body and her ashes were placed in an urn, the squenches would remain and they would continue to annoy the living long after she was dead.

The lovely weather and the flora and fauna were telling her life would go on without her. That's what she heard and felt and tasted in the air. Justice would be swift. One of the knights had been kind enough to assure her that women were always given a swift and painless death. How kind. How thoughtful. Yet she wasn't a total idiot. She'd read a few books in her lifetime and the books she'd read were quite graphic about what happened to a person who was hung from the neck until she died. Death might take ten minutes. The hangman might screw up his calculations. Anything was possible.

When the High Court Judge Mercedes Hepplewhite climbed the dais and stepped up to her chair below the Retribution Flag, the flag seemed to be waving farewell, farewell Kimberly Lemon, farewell. She shut her eyes and counted to ten then opened them. The flag was still bowing toward her as if waving adieu, adieu, adieu. She thought she heard the flag say, "You, poor old cow. You've made a right mess of things."

As Hepplewhite stood beside her chair everyone rose to their feet, even the people watching the video from the Church of the Holy

Centipede. In the bottom right hand corner of the big screen set in the stones of the Cetacea Walk, a smaller screen captured the entire city from multiple cameras. Viewers on Merchants' Row were standing. People sitting on rooftops in Mudflat Village were trying to stand.

Along Poison Creek people got up from their blankets and picnic chairs to show their respect. Kimberly turned in time to see the lucky ones behind her, the rich and prosperous from every part of the world stand to show their respect for this young judge.

"The case of Kimberly Lemon versus the City of Blueglennen will resume," Mercedes announced in her high clear voice. As she settled into her chair there was a thunderous rustling of bodies as everyone resumed their seats. Hepplewhite looked at Kimberly Lemon.

"You may resume your questioning of the next witness, Dela Lemon."

"I call Joffrey Stu to the witness chair, Your Honor."

The short portly man with the neat black hair stood up and squeezed his way past Shard Bristlecone, Joanie Fitzhammmond, and Lynora Reason. He glanced at Phil Potts, the Accuser and then quickly away, his distaste evident. His disgust was not lost on Frank Darknight or Mercedes Hepplewhite. Kimberly Lemon was too busy reading Shehili Swana's notes to notice. Just as she rose on shaky legs to question the witness, a familiar voice interrupted her. Surprised Kimberly closed her mouth and turned to look behind her. Everyone's face expressed astonishment.

"If you please, Your Honor. May I beg your indulgence High Judge Hepplewhite?" Shehili Swana shouted.

A familiar knight Gawain Bristlecone had thrust his arm out to prevent Shehili Swana from moving beyond the gold ropes. When he put a hand up to his earpiece, Shehili relaxed. Gawain dropped his arm and listened for a moment. The moment seemed to stretch on for eternity. Finally, Gawain nodded as if he'd been given new orders. He took Dela Swana's arm and escorted her toward the dais.

The two walked abreast down the aisle like some otherworldly bridal couple, one dressed in black leather with sun shades hiding his expression, the other dressed in a tasteful underdress of creamy white cotton accentuated by an overskirt slit down the sides in the brightest of reds. The squenches were the only disruptors heard. They seemed to be quarreling amongst themselves as if they felt aggrieved at the grave injustice perpetuated by this foreign woman.

Even the Citizen Judges and Saurus' guards were struck dumb by this unexpected event. Kimberly watched as Dela Swana climbed the stairs to the dais and approached High Judge Mercedes Hepplewhite. It was difficult to hear their conversation since Hepplewhite had turned off her microphone and Swana wasn't wearing one. When Hepplewhite nodded as if agreeing to Swana's proposal, Shehili Swana walked over to the Defender's Bench where Kimberly stood. Still frozen to her spot feeling the back of her knees pressing against the hot metal of the chair Kimberly opened her mouth and all that came out was "What?"

The woman who had just the day before abandoned her, turned away from the Accuser Phil Potts' burning curiosity and even bigger ears and totally ignored the mumbling crowd behind her. No one was able to read her lips or hear her say. "Kimberly, the High Judge has graciously allowed me to resume my duties as your defender. Don't say no. I can explain everything."

Kimberly felt something pressing into her midriff and looked down at the tablet Shehili offered her. In a wondering daze she heard Shehili say, "Read this. It's for your eyes only. Please Dela Lemon. I had my reasons. This explains everything." Without quite knowing how she had resumed her status as the accused, Kimberly read the words typed on the tablet:

In order to defend you to the best of my ability and to prevent my team of ethnographers from becoming embroiled in this trial, perhaps even imprisoned, I found a way to have my license as an ethnographer revoked. I have received confirmation by my team leader. Now, I can defend you without worrying about involving Albion in your planet's politics. I had no intention of abandoning you. To achieve this objective, I had to keep you out of the loop.

Sincerely, your friend and fellow traveler in this absurdity called life, Lieutenant Major Shehili Swana.

After reading the note a few times, the message finally penetrated her numb brain and Kimberly looked up, caught Shehili's eye, and nodded her head signifying her acceptance of Shehili's offer. Shehili picked up the notes Kimberly had been reading earlier and stepped toward Joffrey Stu who had been sitting in the witness chair for quite some time wondering if he'd be sent away a second time. Shehili stood facing Joffrey Stu her expression serene.

As she leaned forward, she said, "Delo Stu, thank you for your patience. Now that I am once again Dela Lemon's Defender, would you tell us what you witnessed on the evening of Star Bridgekeeper's disappearance."

"Well, you see I was out late that night because someone had mixed up the garbage bins. As the manager of the Waste Disposal Unit, whenever there is a complaint about the bill, it is my job to keep an eye on the bins for a few weeks in case someone's been tampering with dem. That night, I was working my way through the alley, scanning the barcodes and weighing bins. I like to do that before my men empty the bins into the compacters. In the alley behind Merchants' Row, which we call K11b, I found I was way ahead of the compacters. As I turned to go into the K11b I saw someone in a yellow slicker dragging a bin."

"Did you speak with him?"

"No. I thought he was a merchant who'd forgotten to fill his bin before the cart showed up. I figured he was going to return with his bin full."

"Did you get a good look at him?"

"No. It was a foul night, dark and drizzling."

"But you knew it was a man? How?"

"He was about six-feet tall and the smell coming off him was a man smell, if you know what I mean?"

"Please explain to the court what you mean by a man smell?"

"Like a dead carcass in a hot house," Joffrey responded, beaming when he heard a few people chuckle. Then he realized his mistake and added. "I'm not trying to be funny. I don't mean anything cruel. It just popped into my head. Don't think I take this trial lightly. I'm really truly sorry a pretty little girl like Star is dead. It's a real shame."

"No one here believes you take Star Bridgekeeper's death lightly, Delo Stu. Now then. You say you saw this man dragging a bin away from the alley. In which direction did he go?"

"Well, at first, I didn't think nothing of it. I let him by. He grunted. But then he went left instead of right which made no sense. If he had been a shopkeeper from Merchants' Row, he'd have gone right.

Then I wondered if he might be a Royal Plaza merchant, maybe from the Green Monkey or the Cher Amie Restaurant. They sometimes sneak their stuff into the Merchants' Row bins to save money. I know. It's wrong. But we've caught them doing it before. Their bins are supposed to be hidden on the other side of the plaza stairs.

But it was a nasty cold wet night, so I didn't blame the guy."

"And when you were finished scanning the barcodes and weighing the bins, which bin was missing?"

"It was the Bookworm Emporium bin, Dela Defender."

"Thank you Delo Stu. You may step down," Shehili Swana said and then turned to the High Judge. "Your Honor, I will leave Delo Stu's ledger as evidence. It is open to the night of Star Bridgekeeper's disappearance in which Delo Stu has recorded the event."

Mercedes Hepplewhite motioned to her bailiff to accept the ledger. For the first time, the Accuser rose from his seat and spoke to the court, "I would like to cross examine this witness, Your Honor."

Hepplewhite acknowledge his right to do so. Shehili Swana returned to her seat. Phil Potts took her place beside the witness and with his hands behind his back rocked on his heels and studied the man with a critical eye. Joffrey noticed how small the Accuser's feet were in proportion to his large stomach. How did such a big man stay upright on such small feet?

Joffrey grew restless waiting and tried to make himself more comfortable in his seat which was futile because the chair was the most uncomfortable chair, he had ever had the misfortune to plant his behind on. When he'd talked to Shehili Swana a few weeks ago, she'd warned him about cross examinations, that an Accusers job was to make a witness nervous in order to get a witness to slip up and make a mistake.

"On a dark and drizzly night, you can tell the sex of a person just by their smell, ha?"

Joffrey looked up at the man and then out at the people, "A man smells mustier than a woman, I mean muskier like a bear hibernating in a hole for the chill."

"Are you sure Delo Stu? Come now. Even in Blueglennen there are more homeless than ever before. Can you honestly say you can tell the difference between a man and a woman by their smell alone? Why couldn't the person you encountered have been a woman? Think about it. Can you seriously tell this court with a straight face that a homeless woman who has been wearing the same clothes for weeks, hasn't had a shower in as long and sleeps among the garbage bins is going to smell sweeter than a homeless man?"

"I know for a fact that homeless women smell different than homeless men," Joffrey declared, clearly upset with the man's superior attitude. As if he had ever come close to anyone homeless in his life, Joffrey thought with a mental sneer he hoped did not show on his face. "Unlike yourself, I work the streets of Blueglennen and Mudflat Village, Accuser. I come across the homeless every night trying to make themselves warm, both men and women.

There's not much room in the alleys, only enough room for the bins and the compacters, that means we have to squeeze our way down a small corridor, just enough room for one man to get to the bins. So, yeah, after thirty years of working in the Waste Disposal Unit, I can tell real quick what's under my foot, man or a woman, just by their smell."

The Accuser glared down at him for the longest time. Then he stepped back, "We'll have to put you to the test Delo Stu. Right here. Right now. Shall we?"

Shehili Swana rose to her feet, "I protest High Judge Hepplewhite. What sort of test does the Accuser propose? Accuser Potts is wasting our time."

"Give me a day, Your Honor," the Accuser turned to her. "I'll find a man and a woman who are homeless and have this man's nose distinguish their sex for the edification of the court. Remember, Your Honor, Joffrey Stu has claimed he can tell the difference between a man and a woman just by smell alone."

Kimberly looked at the High Judge as she considered his request and began to worry. Then Shehili Swana spoke, "There won't be any need for a test, Your Honor. My next witness will confirm Joffrey Stu's testimony."

"Call your next witness, Defender," Hepplewhite ordered effectively dismissing the Accuser from the floor. Phil Potts returned to his seat and startled everyone when he slammed his fist on the table.

Hepplewhite banged her drum and with a steely eye pointed her mallet at him, "The next outburst from you Accuser and you'll be sent to the Sheriff's office."

"I call Lynora Reason to the witness stand, Your Honor," Shehili said in a sharp clear voice.

Joffrey Stu and Lynora Reason exchanged places. Joffrey, squeezing past the front row seats to sit at the end of the row near the statue of Duke Dono, felt as if the long dead duke was glaring down at him in disfavor. Joffrey gave Duke Dono the stabbing thumb. Only the knight standing by the wall noticed and all he did was laugh under his breath.

The knight stationed near Duke Dono's statue prevented the crowd from speaking to the witnesses. Joffrey had never felt more claustrophobic than he did during this trial. Even down in the dark musty catacombs crawling with vermin, he'd never felt so edgy. At least in the catacombs, he had room to move, stretch his legs, throw out his arms. He watched Lynora Reason raise her hand and swear to tell the truth, the whole truth, and nothing but the truth upon pain of death.

"So help me Great Protector," Lynora finished and dropped her hand as the bailiff wandered back to his post next to the High Judge. He placed the modern edition of the Delphi bible on her desk.

As Mercedes Hepplewhite sat upon the High Judge's chair staring out upon the multitude of faces below her, as if she might have been sitting on a throne in a meadow looking out upon a diverse ecosystem, with people of all colors and shapes and sizes mingling together, and they so brilliant, exotic, and wild as the rarest of grasses and flowers, she felt a momentary uneasiness. They were looking at her as if she were the sun bringing them nourishment and life. Her uneasiness had to do with the pull of such overwhelming power in one person's hand. No wonder after seventy years on the bench Judge Quark had morphed into a monster.

The unnatural quiet brought her back to the moment and she realized, even though she had been distracted, she could see from the ornate golden clock placed on her armrest she'd only been wood-wandering for thirty seconds. Defender Swana waited politely for the High Judge's final word. Mercedes bowed her head and addressed the court, "Yes, Defender, you may proceed." She hoped never to grow so old and vain as to mistake power for justice.

Shehili Swana stepped toward Lynora Reason and asked, "Now Delan Reason, please tell the court exactly where you live and what you were doing the night of Star Bridgekeeper's disappearance."

Lynora Reason lifted her carefully coiffed head. Her gentle blue eyes revealed an uncanny intelligence and sense of humor which translated well on the big screen. She pointed to a balcony above her head and to her right and said "I live in the top floor apartments between the Grand Marshall Suite and the Green Monkey restaurant. On the night of Star Bridgekeeper's disappearance, I had just arrived home from an exciting two-week tour of New Dala's ancient splendors. I arrived at Mudflat Station late in the afternoon of the 24th having spent the Sweat in a miserable bumpy wagon. As has happened before, my luggage chose to stay in New Dala."

People in the audience chuckled. Encouraged by their response, she continued, "They probably hated the idea of having to cross the Serpent Sea in a rickety old boat navigated by an old codger with a little too much spirit under his belt." More people began to laugh also having endured the mixed blessings of travel – its delights, annoyances, and discomforts.

Shehili was thrilled with her witness. Yes. She was a lawyer's dream, the perfect witness: intelligent, honest, and most of all oozing middle-class respectability. The bonus Shehili hadn't expected, having had no time to coach Delan Reason on the perils and intricacies of court testimony was the need to be genuine. She was that and more. She also happened to be a master-storyteller, not only articulate, funny, and composed but honest. Yes!

The tone of Lynora Reason's narrative changed subtly as she continued, from whimsical to more serious, "Once I had a moment to appreciate being home again, I settled myself on my balcony and looked out upon the wonders of the Merchants' Row Alley. If you haven't been privileged to view the alley by night, you've really missed a treat." A few people snickered.

"I'm serious. No, really. My neighbors and I decided years ago to beautify the alley with as many hardy, sweet-smelling, and colorful plants and flowers as we could find. We've built planter boxes along the stone walls and placed a few on either side of our garbage bins to keep the critters from pushing the bins over.

And during Grow and Sweat seasons, we water and feed our plants. In Fallow, we prune and clip off dead flowers, and during Chill, we cover the most delicate plants to protect them from the frost. Yes. All those directly affected by the Row Alley have contributed something to its beautification. On the night of Star Bridgekeeper's disappearance, I sat on my balcony watching the sunset with a cup of coco beside me, happy to be home and hearing nothing untoward below. Then I promptly fell asleep." More people chuckled and were quickly silenced by neighbors eager to hear the rest.

"What woke me was the sound of someone dragging a garbage bin under my balcony. The moon was high, nearly cheek to cheek with the tip of Long Valley Watchtower when the man below my balcony began to sing a familiar anthem. I struggled to remember where I had heard the song last.

You see the melody affected me very deeply. When I heard it, I felt nostalgia and deep sadness. Soon I knew where I'd heard it last. It was the melody to the Battle of Two Rivers. My old school song. My old Annex Preparatory School anthem. When I attended Form Four, back east, all of us sang the Battle of Two Rivers on special days, on days when the Dean read off the list of bowriders who had died while fighting the Lacertidae."

There were only a few in the audience who had never heard of Annex Preparatory School. Most Delphinids were familiar with the reputation of Annex Military School. Only the very young were unfamiliar with the elite school. The school wasn't just for the military. It did prepare future generals, supreme commanders, judges and war heroes. But the school also prepared future law students and teachers for colleges all over the world.

Gawain sitting next to Bracewaddle, a retired former detective inspector, heard Bracewaddle humming a few bars of the school anthem. As a segue to put the man at ease Gawain asked, "From what I know about your school, the Annex is a lot like our West Point Academy on my former planet."

When Bracewaddle turned to look at him, there were unshed

tears in his eyes and Gawain was taken aback. Lynora Reason had touched a nerve with this powerful Shellfargonite.

Shehili Swana anticipating a sudden national fervor asked quickly, "And could you tell the sex of the person singing your school's anthem?"

"Yes, it was very much a man singing, a baritone. I also enjoy the classics and love to listen to Pavropuddy on my music machine at home."

"Thank you, Delan Reason. You may step down. That is all the questioning I have for this witness, Your Honor," Shehili said and moved toward the Defender's bench.

The Accuser Phil Potts addressed the High Judge, "I would like to question the witness, Your Honor. If I may?"

"You may," Mercedes said with an inclination of her head.

Potts strode up to Lynora Reason with a supercilious glint in his eye, "When you provided your name and address, Delan Reason, you neglected to inform us of your rank."

"I have no rank, sir," Lynora began. "I."

"So, you never graduated from Annex Prep?"

"Not at the Annex," she said wishing she could march him out of the court by his big ears and chastise him for his impudence to an elder. But, alas, she was no longer a teacher; and if she were honest, even as a teacher with the most difficult of children, she would never have grabbed them by the ears and dragged them out of the classroom.

"Where did you complete your higher education?" he asked as if he had doubts, she had ever achieved a degree.

"I chose to finish my fifth form in Angland at the Coral Academy of Fine Arts and then went on to a teaching college in Textrus."

"Why did you leave the Annex?"

"My father wanted me to attend the Annex because all my relations, my Bracewaddle relations, attended the school. They've been going to the school for the last two-hundred years. Once at the Annex, I realized my true calling was education. I chose the lower forms hoping to make a difference."

The name Bracewaddle shocked Potts and especially the court, even the Governor. The Governor jumped up from his chair and looked down with his hands braced on the iron rail and stared enigmatically at the witness. Then all eyes turned to see former Detective Inspector Bracewaddle's reaction to the news. Some people even looked curiously at Gawain sitting next to the retired D.I. which made Gawain nervous. Lynora waggled her fingers at George

Bracewaddle, the hero of the Battle of Vespa 1 who had more badges and honors in his private apartments than many a general in the Delphadorturo's military.

"Hi, Uncle George," Lynora couldn't help but say her natural drollery in charge. "Tell Aunt Winifred I'm available for tea tomorrow. Her fish cakes are too good to pass up."

The few chuckles from the Citizen Judges made Shehili Swana's day. Yes, she thought, yes, she had chosen her witnesses well. How would Potts dare disparage the niece of one of the greatest soldiers in Curl history? Potts turned to the High Judge and said, "I have no other questions for the witness, Your Honor."

Potts returned to his seat pointedly ignoring the defender. Humorless bastard, she thought. Invigorated, Shehili pushed her chair back and stood up and addressed the High Judge, "I call my chief investigator and licensed forensic expert to the dais, Shard Bristlecone, Your Honor."

"Accepted, Defense. Make it quick. We break for lunch in thirty minutes," Mercedes reminded her.

Shard Bristlecone who sat next to Joffrey Stu rose to her feet and marched to the witness chair with purpose. Yet paradoxically she appeared to be in an absent-minded funk. A petite dark-haired woman with thick glasses and pale white skin, a paleness due to hours spent indoors with her nose in a book or eyes glued to a microscope, she didn't seem to inspire much confidence in the crowd the way Lynora Reason had with her lively curiosity and bright smile. No, unfortunately, Shard Bristlecone refused to smile for anyone's pleasure least of all her own. The world was a serious place filled with disease, death, and destruction.

If she'd thought much about spending a day amusing herself in an art gallery or attending a Coral play, she would have snorted disparagingly at the idea of wasting a day in silly amusements. She had no time for such foolishness. The world was a serious place and this court was a symbol of the seriousness of a world filled with crime and death. What a circus. What a travesty of justice. Even the Albion had its factions determined to fight each other until there was nothing left of civilized society. So, Albion had its monkey show and Shellfargon had its fishy clowns. Neither one understood the purity of true science.

Couldn't anyone else see the Governor had orchestrated this fishy clown show as a delaying tactic? This travesty of justice was for the benefit of the Delphadorturo at Crest Hall and for dumbass viewers everywhere. The only thing Saurus wanted was to appear benevolent while pillaging and raping his country. But she was determined to get through to these dumbasses the seriousness of the present situation. She would use facts while the foolish took naps. She had been in similar situations before. She had a backup plan.

"Dela Bristlecone, would you state your full name and provide background for the court as to your home and your credentials," Shehili asked her.

"My name is Shard Winthrop Bristlecone. I am an officer on the UES Albion, a descendant of a human species on a planet called Earth, twenty light years from Shellfargon in a galaxy called the Milky Way. I'm a licensed ethnographer assigned to Wolfern Province as an observer.

Recently, I earned a certificate in Shellfargon forensics by the Delphadorturo Earl Raker, having tested with high scores in the 10th percentile. The Supreme Commander has given me permission to do more than just observe the inhabitants of your beautiful planet. I am licensed to perform the duties of coroner. In emergency situations I am also licensed to assist Curlecon medical staff during complicated surgeries.

I am also a certified linguist knowledgeable in twelve languages off-world and three languages on this planet: Curleconese, Lacertinese, and New Dalanese. I am stationed here in the City of Blueglennen as a liaison between the Albion and Wolfern Province. Also, I'm learning the ancient Curlecon language of Delphanese from my native language teacher, Professor Crystova Moth of Duke Tower University."

"Thank you, 2nd Lieutenant Bristlecone. Now, as a licensed forensic expert would you review the evidence you have collected so far."

"The first point I wish to make is that the chain which prevented Star Bridgekeeper from escaping the garbage bin and the lock contained to hold the chain together had no fingerprints on them, not even a partial print. Nor were there any prints on the garbage bin itself. After reviewing Blueglennen's Waste Disposal Unit regulations I have been told their department sends old bins to a refinery to be scrapped. The plastic is melted down into a liquid form to be reused for more garbage bins.

No staff member has ever had the time or inclination to thoroughly scrub a garbage bin down so well that every fingerprint is removed. No one according to the supervisor or the owner would wash the bins for any reason. When bins get old, they're replaced. And since the coded tag matches the Bookworm billing statement, I can safely say the bin was not replaced with a new one. Therefore, whoever kidnapped and murdered Star is a methodical killer who is familiar with the latest forensic science."

"How so?"

"Everyone leaves fingerprints or bodily fluids behind, no matter how hard they might try not to, even when wearing gloves, there are ways to ascertain what make or model of glove a person has worn from the grooves and the whirls and the shapes left behind. There should have been fingerprints on at least one of the links of the chain or numerous fingerprints upon the outer surface of the bin.

The lack of prints on such a large surface leads me to conclude the container where Star Bridgekeeper died had been thoroughly cleaned by the perpetrator. And the perpetrator would have to be someone with expert knowledge of proper cleaning solvents capable of removing all traces of skin tissue and fingerprints. There are only three such solvents on this planet and they are kept under lock and key in the vault at the Coroner's Office. The bin and chain were washed down by this solvent at least a week before our forensic team examined the evidence.

Even though the solvent leaves no trace, there are tests which can determine the approximate time frame of the crime. One test is to replicate the crime scene exactly and measure the accumulation of particles every hour. I used an identical bin and chain and placed them in the same location as the container where Star's body was found. I measured the accumulation of particles generated by the air in the tunnel and the passage of time. That is how I knew Star Bridgekeeper had been inside the garbage bin for a week and three hours.

Also, I discovered something quite curious."

"Continue," Shehili ordered impatiently as Shard paused, her thick black brows meeting as she considered a new thought. "Inside the bin, along the lip of the lid I found a partial index finger print."

With a shrug she continued, "Smudged, I admit but worth further investigation."

"I understand you have more to tell us."

"Yes," Shard stated without expression having long since forgotten her audience in her enthusiasm for her craft. "Upon further investigation, I discovered underneath a large piece of plywood, scraps of dirty cloth, old magazines, candy wrappers, a detonator to a bomb, a pair of reading glasses with one frame bent and the right-hand glass smashed. The dirty scraps of cloth, I soon discovered, were a pair of men's underwear."

Someone in the witness arena giggled and Shehili turned to glare at the perpetrator who happened to be Sylvia Paleone. Sylvia Paleone shrugged and pretended to examine a fingernail. Defender

Swana turned back to face her expert witness, "Go on Professor Bristlecone."

"After using my digital image of the reconstructed underwear and using facial recognition software, I discovered in the archived images a match to the underwear. Since I reconstructed the underwear from pieces I found in the catacomb under the plywood, I wasn't sure of success. But I was in luck. The underwear is Veterhosen worn by men thirty years ago made only in the country of Bojenlac. Thirty years ago, such underwear would have been an extremely expensive luxury item for the average Blueglennen male.

The embargo by Curl against the manufacturers of Bojenlac in 5062 would have made the underwear outrageously expensive. Unless the owner happened to be a member of the upper classes. What is even more interesting is the Veterhosen advertisements are only included in travel magazines from New Dala, Bojenlac, and Angland. I even found one of the Veterhosen adverts in a Vespa 2 pamphlet.

The other evidence I discovered was a pair of reading glasses, black-framed reading glasses with a minor prescription, a plus two-fifty which leads me to believe the owner is nearsighted, perhaps middle-aged or elderly but significantly more likely to be a male. Yes, I'm sure you'll find a few females willing to wear thick black-framed glasses but not a significant sample. There were also travel magazines under the plywood along with the glasses and the shredded underwear. I am confident the Veterhosen and the travel magazines belong to someone with money. In addition, I found candy wrappers, a recent product, made locally, yet unique enough to be exclusively from Pop's Market shop on Merchants' Row.

The most significant find was the detonator. It is from an obsolete bomb used fifteen years previous by the local Blueglennen Militia. Colonel Tremaine identified the detonator for me and concluded it had been used for training purposes by his installation a decade ago and could only have been applied to a SK1000, since the penetration would encompass a mere sixteenth of an acre; therefore, such a device attached to an SK1000 bomb would be useless on the battlefield against bowriders and heat-seeking missiles."

Shehili Swana interrupted Shard noticing the glazed looks of the Citizen Judges and even the scribe Frank Darknight who was madly attempting to keep up with her prolonged testimony, "All the evidence leads to your theory that the person involved in the kidnapping and murder of Star Bridgekeeper was male? Is that what you're trying to tell us?"

Potts shot to his feet, "Your Honor, Defense is leading the

witness."

"I agree Accused. Defense restructure your question please."

"Based on the evidence you uncovered, what is your theory about the murderer?"

"That the cache of materials under the plywood belong to a male between the ages of forty-five and sixty-five who is well-traveled, educated, and a former member of the Blueglennen Militia. He also may have ties to the nobility or hope one day to become a nobleman."

"Could it be simply coincidence that your evidence was in the same area as the garbage bin? Perhaps left by a homeless person sleeping in the catacombs?"

"No. The detonator to the SK1000 disproves such a theory. If the underwear, the old magazines, the candy wrappers, and the broken reading glasses had been the only evidence I found, I might have come to the same conclusion. I have since discovered the catacombs are so frequently used by the Governor's knights and the Church of the Holy Centipede members that a homeless person would have been noticed and booted out of the catacombs without the opportunity to store so many personal items under the plywood.

After checking the nose and throat of the deceased and testing the material found in these cavities, I am confident the underwear was used to drug Star Bridgekeeper. You can see for yourself in Photo 25 the threads of material inside Star Bridgekeeper's mouth which are made of soft cotton. The threads are stuck between the gap in her upper front teeth and wedged in the lower right gum."

There were gasps from the audience and then Sophia Bridgekeeper cried out, "Oh, my sweet sister." When she fell forward, Caleb rushed to catch her before she fell on the person seated in front of her.

Shehili Swana raised her hand to stop Shard from testifying. Mercedes Hepplewhite tapped the drum lightly, "I will ask the audience to remain silent during the testimony please. I understand this is very difficult for Star Bridgekeeper's family. I give you leave to depart from the court if you so desire."

Sophia Bridgekeeper bowed her head and Danny Wakefield awkwardly tried to comfort her by slapping her shoulder. "You may continue with your testimony Shard Bristlecone," Mercedes Hepplewhite ordered nodding encouragingly at Shard and Shehili.

"I found cotton threads on the inside lower right side of Star's mouth and after analysis of the fibers discovered the material had been soaked in a sleeping potion, a concoction requiring expertise with herbs found locally in Bitterroot Forest. I also found hair samples foreign to the deceased clinging to her school jacket. The hairs do not match Dela Lemon's genetic code."

"Do you know who the hairs belong to?" Shehili asked awed by the amount of forensic investigation Shard Bristlecone had discovered so quickly.

"I have yet to ascertain their DNA. I would have to take samples from every member of Blueglennen to determine the owner and that would take – what with the equipment at hand in the Coroner's Office – perhaps – I would guess – six months to a year."

"So, based on the evidence you have currently, the Knight's Guard of Blueglennen should be looking for what type of person? Can you give us anything that might help us find Star's murderer? Height, weight, hair color?"

"As I said, the evidence points to a man between forty-five and sixty-five, well-traveled, well-educated, a former militia soldier with a sweet tooth. In fact, based on the detonator, I would say the man is extremely dangerous. If he's willing to murder a child and cares nothing for innocent bystanders than he is a serious threat to us all."

"Thank you, Professor Bristlecone," Shehili concluded. "I have no further questions for the witness Your Honor."

It was no surprise when Shehili heard Potts' chair scrape against the wooden dais and his voice addressing the High Judge, "I have a few questions for our alien forensic expert."

The lawyers traded places and Shehili Swana confident in Shard's ability to answer the accuser's questions sat down and looked over her notes. While Shard testified, Shehili had been thinking of rearranging her witness testimony for maximum effect.

"Is it possible the evidence could have laid under that plywood for years?" Accuser Potts asked the witness.

"No," Shard answered easily. "Based on the rate of decomposition of the magazines and the evidence accumulated on them, the magazines are thirty years old. Based on other evidence, the magazines were recently removed from their former location within the last few weeks."

"How do you know this?"

"It's called stratification. I also have a degree in anthropology and archeology."

"I don't understand," Potts said glancing at the audience and shrugging his shoulders as if Shard Bristlecone were some sort of magician trying to fool them with her wizardry of words.

Shard ignored his attempts to undermine her testimony and did her best to summarize a complex science in layperson terms. After twenty minutes, Potts threw up his hands and said, "Yes, yes. I get your point Dela Bristlecone. The dust deposited on the evidence indicates they've been moved recently from an attic to the wet dank catacombs and that they belonged to a man. But even with all your great learning, you still haven't answered a question uppermost on my mind. You see, all the evidence points to a man, yet, isn't it possible the accused had help from a man. A co-conspirator could have disposed of Star's body and placed the body in the catacombs?"

"Unlikely."

"Why?"

"Because there is no evidence Kimberly Lemon has ever been in the catacombs, nor is their evidence she hired someone to suffocate Star Bridgekeeper. All evidence points to one person, a man who with premeditation did the deed. He brought chains and a lock and a cleanser along to the murder so that he could remove his fingerprints and skin samples from the garbage bin, the chains and the lock. In addition, he gathered the roots needed for a sleeping potion before the kidnapping took place in order to put Star to sleep. All the evidence indicates the murderer planned his crime meticulously and came prepared with all the materials he would need."

"How so?"

"Because the detonator, the chains and the lock were cleaned with the same solvent. I know for a fact he intended, not only to kill Star, but to set a bomb off where it would do most damage. He isn't just after one person but many innocent people. Star Bridgekeeper may have surprised the man in his attempt to plant a bomb inside the castle. In order to shut her up, he stuffed her in the garbage bin he had previously planned to use as a container for his bomb. He may not have realized by wrapping a chain around the garbage bin he would suffocate her."

Potts moved closer and cocked his head, "What did you say? Did you say – I know for a fact? What bomb are we talking about Dela?" He turned to the audience and threw up his arms. "I've heard nothing about a bomb."

"I am not at liberty to say," Shard answered glaring at the accuser's back. "It is classified."

"Then who can confirm this fantasy?" Potts asked turning back to face her.

"I would have to receive permission from Governor Saurus, Blueglennen's Department of Justice and D.I. Hawk," she told him, never flinching as he tried to stare her down.

"You seem very sure of yourself Dela Bristlecone," Potts stated suspiciously. "It is my understanding from experts that science is never as accurate as scientists would lead us to believe."

Shard leaned forward in her chair and said, "The evidence under the plywood, the evidence on the victim's body, the partial print on the inside of the bin indicate a connection between the contents under the plywood and the evidence found on the chains, lock and garbage bin; thus, in our world Occam's razor suggests that the simplest of competing theories is the most likely to be true.

Are we to seriously believe Kimberly Lemon managed to find a co-conspirator between the ages of forty-five and sixty-five, well-traveled, well-educated, myopic, and a former member of the militia to collaborate with her, a penniless shopkeeper?

What would be his incentive? If she'd hired him to do the deed, where would she have come up with the money to pay him? Records confirm she barely scrapes by on ten yellows a year? On my ship that's equivalent to 10,000 creds a year. Hardly enough money to live on, whatever world you happen to occupy."

"I disagree Madam," Potts insisted. "There are other ways to bribe a person than money. And Kimberly Lemon is young and reasonably attractive. And this Razor you speak of with such awe, well this Razor belittles our world and our citizens. We are far more complicated than some simple riddle. Shellfargonites cannot be defined so easily."

"You misunderstand me, sir. Excuse me, Accuser Potts," Shard replied. "I wasn't referring to people or personalities but of evidence."

High Judge Hepplewhite interceded, "Do you have a question for the witness Accuser? You will have plenty of time to summarize your thoughts in your closing arguments."

"No, your honor," he said. "I have no further questions for the witness."

"We will hear your next witness Defender Swana after a short lunch break," Mercedes said glancing at her clock.

By the time the court returned to the plaza, the sun was overhead turning the plaza into a sizzling skillet. The heat from the sun was nothing to the hate in Shard's heart for that ignorant piece of fish bait. Oh Potts, you, great white poop. She would dearly love to have him on her examination table and see if he had a heart. Not bloody likely.

The heat was making Kimberly just as morose as Shard. She was relieved when Swana returned to defend her, yet the Accuser had had the last word. His accusation that she'd used her feminine wiles to bribe a man old enough to be her grandfather made her sick. What a dirty mind he had. And he'd had the last word. She bet there were people still thinking about that one.

Instead of being escorted back to the Bookworm Emporium for a brief lunch, Kimberly was forced to eat in Duke Tower's cafeteria with knights posted at the door. In the cafeteria with her was a brigade of empty tables and chairs and the sound of voices in the distance. No wonder she had no appetite. Once Kimberly was escorted back to the plaza and the High Judge banged her drum, Shehili Swana rose to her feet and addressed the court, "I call Timothy Finstickel to the witness chair, Your Honor."

The buzz gathered momentum as people watched the extremely tall, emaciated man with the crazy eyes and even crazier hair who had been sitting between Detective Inspector Hawk and the former General George Bracewaddle rise to his feet in confusion looking everywhere but where he should be looking, his eyes following the progress of several white squenches as they circled then dove at the head of Duke Dono. With Hawk's guiding hand under his arm, Finstickel was led to the dais.

Those privileged enough to have a front row seat quickly covered their noses, some coughing and gagging as Finstickel moved past them. Those in the balconies who could not appreciate Finstickel up close leaned forward so far, they were in danger of falling off the balcony and into the arms of the knight guards standing side by side beneath them.

Other people in the crowd trained their binoculars or their opera glasses on the man most Curlecons knew as the last Duke of Blueglennen, properly recorded in the royal registry as the sixteenth Duke Dono of Wolfern, a descendent of the infamous Duke Dono himself. Those unable to see what was going on with their own eyes watched the television screen as the old man shuffled toward the dais.

Someone had donated a new suit to the last surviving member of the Dono family. It had been donated, not loaned, because no one in their right mind wanted the suit back. During the lunch break, he had found the means to slip on his favorite, very much abused, trench coat. His trench coat was torn along one shoulder and accessorized with former meals and escapades of an earthy nature.

His long gray hair newly washed and combed and pulled back into a queue had come unraveled and wisps of hair were sticking up like an angry porcupine's quills. He had had a fit when the Accuser's people had tried to put a new pair of shoes on his feet and the swish, thump, swish, thump he made as he progressed across the dais gradually came to the notice of everyone. The soles of his favorite loafers, circa 5039 were loose. As he plodded his way to the platform, his loafers mocked the audience and the trial as if to say, "This trial is a joke and so are you."

"Would you please give the court your full name, rank, and address Delo Finstickel?" Shehili Swana began. "You have sworn to tell the truth and nothing but the truth, have you not?" Finstickel looked everywhere but at her, his eyes round with terrified confusion.

"Delo Finstickel, please answer the question," Mercedes Hepplewhite ordered sternly.

"My name is Timothy Finstickel. I presently live at the Wolfern Arms suite K3 of the Highway Tower."

"Is that your full name, Delo?"

"My proper name is too long to remember."

"Please Delo Finstickel. Give us your proper name."

"Theodore Archibald Hannibal Timothy Finstickel Dono."

"And are you a descendent of Duke Dono?"

"Yes, he was my seven times removed grandfather on my father's side."

"And are you fifth in line to the Kingship?"

"I suppose so. It means nothing now. The country of Curl belongs to the great unwashed hordes and the City of Blueglennen is owned and operated by the biggest crook of them all, Governor Saurus with the help of his henchmen."

"You are still a part of the royal family, de facto ruler as I understand if the Governor were to fall ill or die while in office?"

"No," Finstickel said with a frown as if she had misunderstood him deliberately. "Wolfern Province belongs to the Governor. If Wolfern Province still belonged to my family, there would be no curfews or."

She waited for him to finish his thought. The minutes ticked by. When the High Judge glanced at the clock, Swana cleared her throat to get his attention. He frowned at her, "Who are you and why are you asking me such impertinent questions young woman? I am a."

Shehili interrupted him, "You have not answered my question sir. Please tell the court your rank Delo Finstickel? Your military rank."

His eyes were glued to the gold trim along her gown, significantly the pattern near her shoulder, "Well, in my youth I was a Corporal 1st Class in the Silver Crest Militia."

"Really? And how long were you in the militia?"

"Seven years, eight months, and twenty days."

"And are you familiar with explosive devices?"

"Of course. I was trained to handle every piece of equipment on the base including incendiary devices."

Potts jumped up and addressed the High Judge, "Your Honor

is this really necessary? Every male and female of age has spent time in the militia. It is compensatory."

"You meant compulsory, of course. Yes. Thank you for that information. Your objection is noted, Accuser. You may sit down," Mercedes Hepplewhite told him.

"Please answer the question, Your Grace," Shehili began and noticed the surprise and confusion in Timothy Finstickel's watery bloodshot blue eyes. When was the last time someone addressed him by that term? Probably only his mother had ever called him Your Grace. "When was the last time you traveled?"

"Travel?"

"Traveled the world, Your Grace?"

His bushy white eyebrows rose adding more wrinkles to his brow, "Well, that was a few years back. 5043 I believe. The grand tour, you see. It was expected."

"By whom?"

"My mother. She insisted I take the Grand Tour even though we could barely afford a trip to Old Town. She found a way. My mother always found a way."

"Tell me about this Grand Tour?"

"Well, it was a long time ago. A foolish notion. Men in my family were expected to be familiar with the art and culture of other countries. Let me tell you. I got enough of art and culture during my tour in the militia. Sand. Nothing but sand, for miles and miles. And critters. Ants bigger than cats. Spiders that can take your head off with one bite of their mighty jaws. Now that was a tour."

"Yes. Yes. I'm familiar with Vespa 2. But what I'm interested in is your grand tour before your militia years."

"The usual," Finstickel said growing increasingly agitated, rocking from side to side and at one point clutching his hair. "New Dala, Angland, Ruska. The Usual. Stupid. Useless. All travel does is prove there are idiots everywhere in the world."

"Do you recognize these travel brochures, Your Grace?" Shehili asked him as she handed him the brochures displayed in individual plastic packets, securely locked against accidental tampering.

"Of course. They're mine."

"All of them?"

"Yes."

"Are you sure?"

"Of course, I am. Why wouldn't I recognize my own stuff."

"Where do you think we found them?"

"Do you think me an imbecile? I heard what your foreign

forensic investigator said. That these travel brochures had been in an attic for twenty years and were found in the catacombs. We have no need for mind games, now do we? You and I know the world better than most. Can't you see my name and address on the labels? It's perfectly clear to me."

Shehili Swana leaned forward and peered at the section where he was pointing, "I see a smudge of dark ink. You can read the inscription? Your eyes must be as good as a high-powered scope on a rifle."

"Don't be silly. I need reading glasses. Yes. You think you're clever. All of you think you're so clever. But you're not. Yes. All the evidence your female monkey found belongs to me. And don't be getting your knickers in a bind because I called your friend a monkey. She's the one that told me your species is descended from primates. We Shellfargonites always knew we were descended from dolphins and lizards. That should tell you which planet is more advanced. And I'll tell you another thing."

Potts and Hepplewhite spoke at the same time. Potts sat down when Mercedes Hepplewhite banged her drum several times.

"Your Honor, this has gone too far," Potts was heard to say before she broke in.

"Silence. Silence in the court. That includes you, Your Grace." Then the High Court Judge turned to look at Finstickel who had a smirk on his face and didn't even bother to hide his enjoyment of the situation. "You need go no further, Your Grace. You cannot incriminate yourself. I am versed in Wolfern Law and know that those of noble birth are excluded from self-incrimination."

Several knights moved forward prompted by the High Judge. They escorted Duke Dono of Wolfern from the dais back to his chair among the witnesses. This time the front row witnesses were prepared and held handkerchiefs to their noses. Hawk jumped up from his seat to allow Finstickel to resume his seat, preoccupied with the message on his cellphone. He read the text message on the screen a second time and then looked at the name of the other person included in the message. Gawain Bristlecone. The message read, "Come quickly both of you. Coroner's Lab."

Once the Duke's Guard returned to the platform, Hawk remained standing and looked in Gawain's direction. Gawain murmured something to Bracewaddle who looked at the two men and nodded. Then to allay Hawk's worries Bracewaddle glanced at the Duke and back to Hawk and then winked. Reassured that Bracewaddle would keep an eye on Finstickel, Hawk moved toward the aisle.

Instead of moving down the center aisle and struggling through the mess around the roped area and the knights standing near the wall, Hawk cut across the row inconveniencing witnesses by stepping on their feet or hitting them in the head with his elbows. Gawain followed close behind. Queenie complained so loudly her gravelly voice carried to the back of the plaza near the Cetacea Stairs, "Hey there, handsome. Mind your big feet. You also, Delo Sweet Thing."

"Beg pardon, Dela," Gawain said with a charming smile, "This is an emergency."

Queenie looked at Gawain's elegant back and fine figure and poked her friend Beatrice in the side, "I'd love some emergency time with him. Wouldn't you?"

Don Tumble shot them both a disgusted look. The women ignored him.

Gawain and Hawk met near the stairs which led to the coroner's laboratory in the basement of the university. "Can we offer any new evidence at this point? Does it matter? It's clear the main suspect can't be tried in a court of law," Hawk said as they rushed down the stairs, through the dimly lit hall.

"Not according to Wolfern Law," Gawain told him as he held the door open for his superior.

They passed an open door and when Gawain peeked inside, he saw Tanny Bright holding a wand, no, a channel changer in her right hand. Hawk kept moving toward the elevator marked basement. Alarmed, Gawain stood on the threshold of her laboratory and noticed Tanny was pointing her wand at the opposite wall. She'd set several objects on the top of a counter which stretched the length of the wall. On the countertop she'd placed a doll dressed in a knight's black uniform holding a tiny LSR7 gun, a life-sized baby carriage, a series of empty soda bottles, and a coffee table.

Where one of the legs to the coffee table used to be there was a huge hole in the wall and a pile of ashes on the countertop. Having only three legs, the coffee table crashed to the floor. The pinhole went completely through the wall to a classroom beyond. "Holy Legs," he shouted. "What the hell are you doing?"

Tanny set her wand on her desk and began to write in a large notebook a series of numbers as foreign to him as his sister's equations. "If I recalculate the anti-matter, I should be able to control the degree of extinction," she told no one in particular. Then she glanced his way, her long dark bangs hiding her eyes. "Oh, go away. Nobody's hurt. They're all watching the trial. Don't worry. I'll be careful. Next time I'll go to the dump. I need a rat anyway. Safety first.

My device must differentiate between animate and inanimate objects or I refuse to continue."

"Is it a state secret Doctor Jekyll?"

"Is that an alien insult?" she asked him as she paused in her writing to throw back her hair to see who was standing by the door. "Oh, it's you. Can't you see I'm busy. Go on now. And shut the door behind you."

From the university basement Gawain heard Hawk calling to him. He ran down a series of stairs and opened the door to the Coroner's Lab, Room 002. Gawain bumped into Hawk as Hawk stopped in his tracks and stared at something on the examination table. Shard stood at the foot of the table. The coroner was in the process of removing his stethoscope from the chest of the young woman sitting upright on the table. Both men heard him say to Shard Bristlecone, "Yes. You are correct. It is extraordinary. A miracle. Impossible."

"If I'm right, it is not a miracle or impossible," Shard replied and turned to her brother and then to her team leader Hawk. "As you can see, the rumors of my death, sorry, poor taste, her death are."

"Never mind," Hawk snapped. "How is this possible?"

Star Bridgekeeper clutched her death shroud closer to her naked body and looked about the room her beautiful eyes clouded with confusion. She was trying to focus on the room and the people pressing close. Her long black hair cascaded down her naked back as did a stream of blood which was trickling down her throat from the coroner's tentative incision.

Shard tried to explain, "Delo Brook asked me to assist him in the autopsy."

"How is this possible?" Hawk demanded looking at first Shard then the coroner. The coroner shrugged and stepped away from the table.

"I'm hungry," Star said. "No. Wait. I'm more thirsty than hungry."

While Gawain went to find a glass and some water, Shard moved in close to assess Star's condition. "May I?" she began as she reached for Star's wrist. "I just want to check your vitals."

Gawain handed Star a paper cup filled with water. She drank it down in one gulp and handed the cup back, "More please."

Hawk watched impatiently as Shard examined Star Bridgekeeper. Dr. Bristlecone looked into the former dead child's eyes, mouth and ears, then listened to her heart with the coroner's stethoscope. After an interminable time, she put down her instruments. She turned to her teammates and declared, "She's a mixture of Delphinid and Lacertidae. I would need to test her DNA to be sure but based on her heart rate and body temperature, I'm pretty sure she's more Lacertidae than Delphinid."

"Hibernation?" Hawk asked.

"Not exactly. I'm guessing she must have been frightened to death. It's my understanding Lacertidae can shut down their metabolism when in danger as a protective survival mechanism."

"Well, what are we waiting for?" Gawain demanded impatiently. "Let's get her upstairs and show her to the world. This means Kimberly is innocent and the trial is over."

The first to see Star Bridgekeeper carried in the arms of Gawain Bristlecone was Harry Hanson. He rose from his chair and stood transfixed with Guinevere Goodbody sitting beside him unaware of the extraordinary event taking place. His curiosity had been fired up by the Albion crew's odd behavior. He'd considered conniving his way into the university with the intention of taking a few photos while no one was looking.

So, with a bit of luck, he was in the perfect spot when Bristlecone marched down the aisle with Star Bridgekeeper in his arms. Harry Hanson lifted his phone to his eye and took the picture which would make him instantly famous all over the world. Within minutes he typed a message and sent the picture out to the world. His first exclusive. His very own award-winning photo with the caption – Victim thought Dead very much Alive.

With Star Bridgekeeper in his arms he paused at the dais, "May it please the court, I would like to present Star Bridgekeeper, very much alive."

"Place her on the witness chair," the High Court Judge ordered.

All eyes were on Gawain as he gently set Star Bridgekeeper on the witness chair and turned to face the High Court Judge Mercedes Hepplewhite, "Coroner Brooks discovered after he cut into Star's throat that she wasn't really dead. The cut you see on her neck was his first incision. He was going to do an autopsy when she woke up. My sister Shard stopped him from doing any further damage.

She believes Bridgekeeper in her terror at being stuffed into a garbage bin, fearing death by asphyxiation went into automatic hibernation. It is something a Lacertidae does involuntarily, just the way you and I breathe. It was her ability to shut down her body's normal functions and go into hibernation that saved her life. On the orders of D.I. Hawk, my sister Dr. Bristlecone tested a sample of Star Bridgekeeper's blood weeks ago and discovered she has Lacertidae DNA. Actually, she's more Lacertidae than Delphinid."

"Thank you, Knight Bristlecone. You may sit down. Young Bridgekeeper, are you well enough to answer some questions for us?"

"I'd love a hamburger if you have one?" she said. The astonished crowd laughed.

"We can arrange that. Anything else?"

"A soda please. An orange soda. And some fries?"

"Of course. And would someone find some clothes for this poor girl?"

After Star Bridgekeeper was properly dressed and had finished her meal, Shehili Swana began the opening questions, "Tell us what happened to you two weeks ago Star?"

"I remember going into the church and falling asleep on a pew. I heard someone in the church and saw someone carrying a box. When I sat up, someone swooped down on me and pressed a cloth to my mouth. I struggled to be free, but he was too strong."

"He?"

"Oh yes. I knew who he was immediately. There's no disguising him not in a million years."

"What do you mean?"

Star Bridgekeeper pointed at Timothy Finstickel, "It was Delo Smelly. Finstickel. The Old Fart. He stuffed me in that old garbage bin and wouldn't let me out. I heard him. I heard him mumbling. I begged him to let me go and he didn't. Why? What did I ever do to him?"

Shehili Swana looked up at the balcony where Governor Saurus and his entourage were watching. The Governor had been standing by the rail transfixed at the sight of Star eating and looking very much alive. He motioned to someone behind him and all the video screens in the castle and outside the castle showed his image.

He looked into the camera and addressed the viewers who were watching the broadcast all over the world, "As a nobleman his Grace Duke Dono cannot be accused of any crimes or incriminate himself. He has ultimate immunity. Kimberly Lemon, on the other hand, has not been proven innocent in the kidnapping and attempted murder of Star Bridgekeeper. The trial will continue."

Mercedes Hepplewhite countered by shouting, "Kimberly Lemon has been charged with murder. There has been no murder, Governor Saurus. As the High Judge, I cannot sanction a continuance of this trial. If I did, I would be in contempt of Curl's Constitution."

"And how do you explain the watch belonging to Kimberly Lemon on Star Bridgekeeper's person?" the Governor snapped, his Textrus accent drawling the words out like a venomous trail of snake slime.

Mercedes turned to Star, "Answer the Governor's question."

Star Bridgekeeper looked down at her hands and then up into Kimberly Lemon's face noticing Kimberly's flushed cheeks, "I saw the pretty watch on Dela Lemon's bed and I thought I'd just take it for the night. It was so unusual. I'm so sorry. I didn't intend to steal it. I just wanted to keep it for a few days. I had every intention of giving it back."

"You see," Shehili Swana said addressing the High Judge. "Your Honor, my client had nothing to do with the missing watch. Star Bridgekeeper admits she stole it. Blueglennen has no case against my client. Will you dismiss the murder charges against my client Kimberly Lemon?"

The voice from the balcony ricocheted off the walls of Duke Tower, the volume unnaturally loud due to the megaphone attached to the Governor's lapel and his impotent rage, "Nothing has been proved. The case will continue."

Mercedes Hepplewhite turned to Star Bridgekeeper, "Due to the unusual nature of these proceedings, the Defender and the Accuser will step down and, I, as the High Judge of Blueglennen will question the victim – which to my knowledge has never occurred in the recorded history of Curl. Darknight please bring the bible to the victim."

No one in the plaza so much as moved a muscle as they strained to hear the victim, who should have been dead, promise to tell the truth and nothing but the truth. When she resumed her seat on the witness chair, the High Judge began to question her, "Answer my questions to the best of your ability Star Bridgekeeper. How is it possible for you to have been pronounced dead and yet be alive and sitting in my courtroom?"

Star turned in her chair, a chair much too big for her and looked up at the High Judge, her startling good looks casting a spell over the crowd. She reminded many viewers of a tragic, romantic heroine from some electronic book cover cowering in terror against a fate worse than death.

Those who knew her well recognized the beginnings of another bout of overzealous dramatic delirium. This was her moment to shine. Having won over death, she was now convinced more than ever the Holy Centipede had saved her for a higher purpose. The world would see the Holy One's miracles at work. She had been given new life, her purpose – to spread the word of the Holy Centipede's awesome miracles.

"I am alive because the Holy Centipede has chosen me as his spokeswoman to spread the word of the gospel, Your Honor. I carry the blessings of the Church of the Holy Centipede and all its numerous miracles. This is but one miracle. After having risen from the dead, it is my destiny to save the souls of the ignorant Shellfargonites whose immortal souls will be damned forever unless they see the true light of his goodness."

"I see," said the High Judge Hepplewhite. "Well, there might be another explanation for this miraculous recovery." The judge looked down at the witness arena and straight at the knight who had carried Star Bridgekeeper to the dais. "Knight Bristlecone, you mentioned that your sister is aware of Star's condition. Where is your sister?"

Shard Bristlecone seated between Joffrey Stu and Joanie Fitzhammond jumped up and said, "I'm here, Your Honor."

"Please come forward Dela Bristlecone and take the witness chair. Star, please sit in the seat vacated by Dela Bristlecone. I will be asking you further questions in a moment."

Once the ladies had switched places, Mercedes bent forward with her hands clasped and began to question Shard, "It is my understanding that you have a degree in medicine? Give me the particulars."

"I have several medical degrees. On my ship, I am a licensed pediatrician, cardiologist, and forensic examiner. Here on Curl, I have recently obtained a degree in Delphinid physiology as well as the physiognomy of the other inhabitant of this planet - Lacertidae."

"That is quite impressive. Then perhaps you can explain how Star Bridgekeeper after having been examined by several doctors and the coroner and declared dead by all three, could come back to life?"

"It was quite astonishing to see the pulse began to beat in her throat just as Dr. Brooks sliced into her skin. After careful examination, I must conclude she inherited the ability to slow her heart rate down so much it is barely discernable. Her body began the hibernation process automatically. It requires less oxygen. It is an involuntary response in most Lacertidae. I'm sure you are familiar with the physiology of the Lacertidae, their evolutionary ability to survive extreme weather conditions due to Vespa 1 & 2's proximity to the sun. Over the millennia they've adapted and are able to survive conditions which would most assuredly kill a Delphinid."

"Yes," Mercedes interjected. "I am familiar with Lacertidae's physiology. What I am curious about is how Star Bridgekeeper can appear to be Delphinid? I thought Delphinids and Lacertidae were incapable of procreation."

Star jumped up from her chair, "It's a sign. It's a miracle. Holy Centipede."

The High Judge banged on her drum and pointed her stick at Star Bridgekeeper with eyes as cold and impersonal as the chair she sat on. All other indications of her wrath remained hidden, only in the rigidity of her jaw did one detect her annoyance with the girl, "Sit down or I will have you removed from this courtroom." For a moment or two no one was sure whether Star would obey the High Judge's order. Perhaps the tugging from Joanie Fitzhammond on Star's arm might have helped persuade her to sit down. With a beaming smile for the people watching, Star reluctantly sat. Mercedes turned back to Shard Bristlecone.

"Please answer my question, Professor Bristlecone," Mercedes commanded.

"Well," Shard looked at Detective Inspector Hawk hesitantly and then back up to the judge, "as an ethnographer I've been curious about the possibility of interspecies procreation especially between reptiles and mammals. After several tests, I can say with confidence Delphinids and Lacertidae are capable of procreation. On Earth, our old planet, the geckos and iguanas give birth to live offspring. Also, some species can change their sex or give birth without a mate. Lacertidae on your planet may all be female but when needs must, they have the capability of changing sex and fertilizing a Delphinid egg."

Mercedes interrupted Shard's testimony, "May I remind you Professor Bristlecone that this case is being televised and there are children in the audience."

"Of course, Your Honor. Yes. Well. It is possible for intermixing of the species."

"How do you know for certain Star Bridgekeeper is mostly Lacertidae?"

"Where Delphinids and Lacertidae are similar is in the fatty tissue surrounding their eyes. Delphinids when they lived in the ocean needed this fat to protect their eyes from debris while swimming. Star also has an unusually rough tongue. Unlike Delphinids, Star can slow down her metabolism and hibernate for long periods of time. In fact, Star has demonstrated she can hibernate longer than any Lacertidae. Her extra eyelid is atrophied due to lack of use. The reason for her degeneration may be because she lives here rather than Vespa 1 & 2."

Mercedes Hepplewhite stood and addressed Shard Bristlecone and the Scribe Frank Darknight, "I would like a detailed medical prognosis from Shard Bristlecone and the other coroners involved in this case with explanations regarding Star Bridgekeeper's hibernation. I also require all notes pertaining to intermixing of species with a copy sent immediately to Delphadorturo Raker. You may step down, Professor Bristlecone."

While Shard Bristlecone made her way back to her chair and Star Bridgekeeper popped up in anticipation of returning to the witness chair, Star shouted out, "You're wrong. I wasn't hibernating. I'm not a dirty Lacertidae. I am a Delphinid and I died, and I was resurrected by the grace and goodness of the Holy Centipede."

Mercedes stopped Star's forward motion with a raised hand and looked out into the crowd addressing those present and those watching their television sets across the world, "All the pertinent facts have been addressed to my satisfaction and it is my judgment Blueglennen vs Kimberly Lemon is a mistrial and closed.

Kimberly Lemon, please stand. It is my judgement that due to the testimony of Timothy Finstickel and the newly awakened Star Bridgekeeper from her hibernation and her admission to the theft of your jewelry, I declare you innocent of kidnapping and murder. You are free to go. Court is adjourned."

"No," the Governor's voice thundered through the microphones sending hands to ears and heads spinning around. People shielded their eyes to stare at the balcony where he stood as tall as he could stretch his diminutive five-feet two-inch frame. His small hands grasped the ledge as he looked down on the little people, his little people.

Then he remembered to smile, "You are in contempt of my laws Dela Hepplewhite. The case will stay open until I'm satisfied with the verdict. We have yet to hear testimony from the Accuser's witnesses and the Citizen Judges have not had a chance to review all the testimony. Since you refuse to obey Wolfern Law, you are in contempt of court and recused from this trial as judge. Quark will resume his duties as High Court Judge. D.I. Hawk escort Dela Hepplewhite and the murderess Kimberly Lemon to the Department of Justice. The trial will resume tomorrow." Once he finished speaking, the Governor left the balcony and reentered his private quarters.

Everyone watched as the former High Court Judge, Dela Mercedes Hepplewhite and the accused Kimberly Lemon were escorted from the dais and marched toward Duke Towers. Most of the court were shocked by the Governor's proclamation, others dismayed, and some like Finstickel delighted. The few who were happy were the Citizen Judges. Even though they were the Governor's cronies and obeyed him without question, now the world knew that in Wolfern Province, Citizen Judges' decisions outweighed a High Court Judge.

So, what if Kimberly was innocent and Finstickel was the one who kidnapped Star Bridgekeeper? Someone had to pay. Clearly ancient laws forbid Finstickel from consideration as kidnapper. So, what if the murder never happened? Kimberly would still be tried for attempted murder. She would also be tried for theft even though Star admitted to stealing the watch. The unfairness of it all reeked from the ramparts to the tower. Yet Delphinids weren't in the least surprised by the Governor's proclamation. The Albion team noticed with misgivings how docile the Delphinids were as they gathered up their belongings and waited patiently for the drawbridge to open.

Shard Bristlecone and her brother Gawain exchanged glances and said nothing as people stood and began collecting their belongings. The Albion siblings approached Shehili Swana and waited patiently as she spoke with the Accuser Phil Potts. Once Phil Potts had collected his papers and the scribe Frank Darknight left with his tablet, Shehili Swana addressed them, "Not here. Come to my private apartments tonight for dinner. We won't be disturbed. I'll make sure of that."

Within an hour of returning Kimberly Lemon to her cell in the catacombs and processing the High Judge Mercedes Hepplewhite, D.I. Hawk had had time to analyze the situation. He had to remind himself he had no authority on this planet, no authority other than what the Governor allowed. Yet the situation had become dire for his team. He refused to accept the present situation without a fight.

His consternation must have shown on his face for Mercedes Hepplewhite said as much when she paused in her pacing of the small cell next to Kimberly's and observed, "I'm sure you think all Curlecons are barbarians. Well, we aren't. This won't stand. It cannot stand. We have laws in Curl, laws the Governor dare not break. You'll see, Detective Inspector. What surprises me is why the Governor would put me down here in this dungeon in the first place."

"He didn't," Hawk said. "I chose to put you down here for your own safety, as well as Dela Lemon's. I don't trust the Department of Justice. There are factions here that don't play by the rules. Gawain Bristlecone is the only person who will be allowed to bring your food. Knight Lively and Graceland are the only knights allowed to stand guard. Between the three of us we'll protect you from the Governor and his mercenaries. We'll do all we can to make you comfortable too. Please excuse me. I'll return shortly."

The women listened to the detective inspector's footsteps fade away and the distant sound of a door closing. Hawk had left behind several glowworm lights. While the High Judge and Hawk had been talking, she emptied the remaining packet of food into the lamps sending the glowworms into a frenzy. She placed two in her room and two in Mercedes' cell. Her prison cell still contained the poster bed and furniture. Mercedes wasn't so lucky. Her cell had a thin mattress on the floor. She asked Lively if Mercedes could stay in her cell and Lively shrugged, "Don't know. I'll check. I have a feeling you won't be in here long anyway."

When Lively did not return and Wakefield showed up to stand guard over the women, Kimberly knew things up top had gone very wrong, seriously wrong. She worried about her friends who had testified on her behalf and would be punished for siding with her. Hours passed, and the women had no idea how long they had been in their cells. For all they knew, it might have been the middle of the night.

Kimberly leaned toward the bars of her cell and called out to the High Judge, "Your Honor."

Mercedes Hepplewhite had been resting her shoulder against the rough stone near the door to the cell. "Call me Mercedes. I'm no longer Your Honor. And yes, Dela Lemon, I believe justice will prevail."

"Maybe back east justice prevails but Blueglennen hasn't seen justice since my grandfather was alive."

Beyond their cells someone chuckled. Both women froze.

E1 Shellfargon Year 5092 NDMP WK 6: UES Albion 4
High Court Judge Hepplewhite arrested. Trial dissolved. Gov Saurus has announced martial law. His knights are removing all tourists and court staff from tower. Merchants' Row members have been placed under house arrest. Two who are native to Blueglennen agreed to courier messages to Delphadorturo Raker. E2 escorted envoys onto last train out. Request immediate evacuation of ethnography team, Hepplewhite and Lemon.

Chapter 13

The chuckle turned into a squawk followed by the sound of something heavy dropping to the dirt-packed floor. Both women tried to see what was going on beyond their cells and soon saw several people moving toward them carrying light-sticks. Kimberly was astonished to see Harry Zany in the lead and Knight Gawain Bristlecone close behind him. Holding a set of keys, obviously stolen from the now unconscious Wakefield, Bristlecone unlocked Kimberly's cell first, "We've come to free you. You're not safe here."

Dela Hepplewhite shouted into the gloom, "What do you mean by free?"

Bristlecone swung Kimberly's cell door open and turned to the judge, "Governor Saurus has declared martial law. We believe this is the day he plans to secede from the Country of Curl. During the trial, his forces stationed themselves around the moat ostensibly to keep order. Once the Governor shut down the trial proceedings, he ordered all non-Blueglennen to leave the castle. He sent all the citizen judges and lawyers down to the valley. They've been told to leave Blueglennen on the morning train. His knights have been loading people onto the trains and sending them out of Wolfern Province. Merchants' Row members are under house arrest.

Saurus ordered a curfew for all citizens of Blueglennen. Knights are patrolling Mudflat Village. The governor claims residents will riot. Horse soldiers are patrolling Greenburg Valley and the Merchants' Row Alliance has been declared a terrorist organization. Saurus' hired thugs are going door to door demanding passports and identification papers.

All castle exits are blocked. The drawbridge is closed. A new order has come down from the Governor, the merchants must take only a suitcase full of personal belongings and gather at the plaza to await the morning train. Their shops have been confiscated by order of the newly commissioned Delphadorturo and Commander of Wolfern Province, Governor Saurus."

"Nonsense. The man is a fool. He'll never get the other provinces to separate from the union," Mercedes said with a sneer.

"You're in just as much danger, Judge Hepplewhite."

"How did you get past the Knights on the mezzanine?" Mercedes asked still suspicious.

"Before Hawk left the tower, he gave me a pass and Harry Zany agreed to be my prisoner. The knights on duty thought I was one of them. They let us go through without even looking at the pass, probably because they recognized Harry. As a member of the Merchants' Row Alliance he's considered a terrorist. They spit on him."

Harry who had been looking down the long dark nether regions of the dungeon turned his head to say, "Gawain stopped them from kicking and beating me."

Gawain continued in a rush, "It was only when we reached the dungeon that I was recognized. I had to knock the man out." He looked contrite, his handsome face drawn and worried.

Kimberly took the keys from Gawain and started to unlock Mercedes Hepplewhite's cell door, "You must come with us. You must get to Delphadore and tell the delphadorturo what's happened here."

"I can be of service to the delphadorturo here rather than run off to New Enreich. How would it look if I deserted my post at such a time as this? Governor Saurus must be told his attempt to secede is futile. The rest of the provinces will fight him. What does he hope to achieve? He'll be surrounded by Curl troops and end up a prisoner in his own dungeon."

"Not so fast, Your Honor," Harry Zany began. "I doubt if he or anyone will end up a prisoner down here."

"Then they can transport him to Delphadore and put him in maximum security," Mercedes countered.

Zany pointed toward the darkness beyond the women's cells at the dirt floor of the passageway which wound through the catacombs. "You don't understand. I don't think there's going to be much left of the dungeon or the castle. Look. Look there, down the steps to the left. Everyone. Just look."

Kimberly saw ahead where the ground was wet. When Zany took three large steps and pointed his light-stick at the substance pooling around his feet, everyone could see what was moving toward them. The stuff reminded Kimberly of lamp oil, only mixed with sand. At first, she thought someone had thrown an old lamp or two on the ground and she was horrified. If the oil ignited, they would be forced to climb the stairs and fight their way passed the iron door and the Governor's hired goons.

From faraway she heard Zany say, "You see the stream of noxious fluid trickling down the passageway. It's a mixture of sand, water, bacteria, decomposing deep sea creatures and poisonous gases our scientists call Hadal's Hellfire. Like all fluids it's following a natural path of least resistance. That nasty stuff is coming from the belly of Shellfargon. If I'm right, we don't have much time. Gawain would you show the ladies to Wolf Inn by way of Poison Creek passage? I'm going to search for the origin and see if I can turn off the taps."

Alarmed, Mercedes and Kimberly rushed toward Harry and stared at the ugly gooey mess trickling toward them. They could feel the air heating up and see the steam rising from the yellow vacuous substance. It reminded Gawain of oozing pus from an open sore. Kimberly spoke first, "Can't we go back up the steps to the mezzanine?"

"There are guards on duty. They don't understand what's going on. They'll kill us all before we can make it to the lobby. The sand is dangerous. Try not to breathe it in," Harry warned pulling his handkerchief out of his pants pocket and holding the cloth to his nose. "I must find the source."

"Why?" Gawain asked. "Come with us."

"No. We need proof," Harry said shaking Gawain's hand off his shoulder. "I'll use my flask. It's made of Dromeda steel like your ship. Don't worry, I plan to take a small sample and get the hell out of here."

Gawain pushed Kimberly Lemon forward. She avoided the hellfire as best she could. Her bare ankles were burning from the steam rising from its fluid. The hard-packed earth near the opposite wall permitted them passage if they moved single file. Without ceremony, Gawain grabbed Hepplewhite by her robe and dragged her along behind them. At a junction Kimberly paused.

Ahead of her were more prison cells. To her left she could see Zany picking his way down a narrow corridor jumping over puddles of hellfire. To her right she could see an opening in the distance and sunshine. She thought she could hear water too. It must be Poison Creek. They were at the bottom of the cliffside below the castle walls and just above the moat. Once they reached the moat, they would have to jump into the stagnant filthy water and swim to the drawbridge. At the same time, they would have to avoid being seen by the guards posted on the watchtowers.

When she refused to go any further, she wasn't thinking about swimming the filthy moat or climbing the bank to the drawbridge. Gawain looked down at her. "See those people," she said pointing at Harry Zany searching for safe footing as he passed locked cells. Prisoners were sticking their arms through the bars and begging him to open their prison doors. "They're watching us. Look Gawain. We can't leave them to die trapped in those cells."

"Some of them could be murderers," he told her trying to grab her arm. She reached out as if to take his hand and then swiped the keys on his belt buckle. Before he could stop her, she was running toward Harry.

Resigned he turned to Mercedes Hepplewhite, "Go on. You must warn Mudflat Villagers and maybe even Greenburg Valley. If Harry can't shut this operation down, none of us inside the castle or within twenty miles will survive. Some fool's been drilling down here. They don't know what the hell their doing."

"What do you mean?" Mercedes asked.

"I think Saurus and his cronies have been secretly drilling below acceptable levels. I'll bet you, there's someone on board the Albion directing this operation, planting traitorous ideas in the little man's head, convincing the greedy idiot they'll pay him a king's ransom for the discovery of new fuels. Our ship needs a special rock to power our engines. Some of our people believe Shellfargon's core has the right type of mineral we need.

Only after the ship's ethnographers insisted on studying your origin story did the captains order the techs to stand-by. They've been doing experimental drilling all over Shellfargon. But once we were permitted to land, the techs were ordered back to the ship. My sister is one of the scientists tasked to find out if drilling might destroy Shellfargon. She's refused to give Captain Lincoln the green light. He's been urging our mining techs to ignore the Delphadorturo and steal the rock. He claims everyone will die if the predators find us and we can't fix our fusion rockets."

"What do you mean? What predators? Have you endangered our world?"

"Please. Just go. Find a way to get through to Raker. Tell him what's happening."

A man in ragged clothes smelling of fear and sweat shot past them. And then another and another prisoner appeared jumping from side to side of the passageway to avoid the stream of toxic fluid. As they ran toward the Poison Creek access the hellfire was close behind. When Gawain realized Kimberly and Harry had been freeing the prisoners, Mercedes nodded and said, "Go on. Help her. I'll find my way to the train station." She threw off her robes and started down the tunnel. Beneath her robes she wore a simple cotton dress. "I'll find a way to reach Raker."

Gawain watched until she dropped down into the moat; then he turned to his left to search for Kimberly. She'd freed all the prisoners from the occupied cells. There were very few prisoners left in the dungeon after Judge Quark's appointment. Unlike Kimberly's televised trial, his trials had been done in secret and the moment he made his decision to hang the prisoner, the knights took the poor soul to the hangman. When Kimberly disappeared around a corner, he broke into a run. There were no more cells where she was headed.

The splatter from a puddle of hellfire burned a hole in the hem of his pant leg. Even though he was desperate to keep up with her, he was forced to watch where he walked. The liquid was congealing, and noxious fumes were making it harder to breathe. He threw off his shirt and tied the sleeves around the lower half of his face. His eyes were burning. He wondered how Kimberly could stand the fumes and then remembered – she was a delphinid. She had a protective coating of fat around her eyes which kept the fumes from burning the delicate membranes.

No wonder she and Harry Zany were able to move so fast through the smoky toxic passageway. They were native to the planet and capable of surviving conditions he could not. As he felt the passageway descend to lower chambers taking him beyond the castle walls and into the bedrock, he had to slow down even more realizing the trickle of foul ooze was fast becoming a creek. He had no idea what the liquid would do to him. It might burn the flesh and muscle right down to the bones.

Then he saw Kimberly. And beyond Kimberly, he saw Zany. They had stopped at the shores of a yellow foul-smelling pool. Zany and Kimberly were separated by the creek of hellfire moving toward Gawain. Gawain was forced to walk a tightrope of bedrock left untouched by the hellfire. Once he was near Kimberly, he paused to look up and realized he was standing in a huge cavern, bigger than the Royal Plaza. The crystals covering the ceiling distorted the image of the pool of yellow hellfire and hot geysers below. He looked down at the pool horrified by the sight. Saurus couldn't have done this without the Albion's help.

In the center of the sludge he could see buttresses from the mast and a portion of the gigantic mud pump still visible. The bottom half of the mud pump was dissolving in the poisonous yellow hellfire. The pump was made from the same material as the ship's hull. Yet the hellfire had already burned away the thick outer coating. Soon the hellfire shooting up from the center of the pool like a geyser from a gigantic dragon would fill the cavern and drown them all.

Harry had been kneeling near the edge of the pool. He rose to his feet and waited for the droplets around the lip of the flask to cool before screwing the top on. He saw Gawain first. Kimberly turned to look at Gawain. She looked so pale and sick with despair.

"We've got to find a better container for this monstrous mess," Harry said holding the flask away from his body as if it might bite him.

"I don't think you're going to need a sample because I have a feeling this stuff is on its way up to the surface real soon," Gawain shouted, furious with them both.

"What do you mean?" Harry asked. Why was Harry surprised by Gawain's anger?

"We can't stay here. It's dangerous. We are standing on a volcano. Do you understand? Hot gases and lava are going to pressurize this chamber and send this shit through the roof."

"I don't understand," Kimberly said moving toward Gawain. "What is a volcano?"

"We've got to get the hell out of here. Now," he told her. His anxiety must have finally gotten through to her. He held back from dragging her out of the chamber. Still shocked Kimberly followed him out. He heard Zany following close behind them. By the time they reached the junction, the liquid had found its level and was flowing straight out into the moat. They were forced to run for the iron door. The knight on duty had deserted his post.

As the three of them ran past Kimberly's cell they could see her bed floating in the hot yellow goo and slowly dissolving into a rainbow of colors as the coverlet burned. The iron door leading to the mezzanine was open. The knights who had been on duty were lying on the floor. Gawain threw up his arm in time to prevent a heavy vase from knocking him out. The vase fell to the floor and shattered into small pieces as Valcinda and Alexandra stepped back.

Before the women could embrace Kimberly, Gawain spoke, "We need to get the hell out of the castle and as far away from the flash point as possible. Once the hot gases and lava reach a certain pressure point this castle will turn into a gigantic chimney."

"What's he talking about?" Valcinda asked Kimberly.

Harry Zany held out his flask holding the flask with the lips of his steel gloved thumb and finger, "I have a sample of the stuff in here. Go ahead touch the flask."

Valcinda hesitated and then with one finger touched the side. "Hellhounds," she swore. "What do you have in there? Liquid fire?"

"Something like," Gawain said. "We don't have time for a lecture. Let's go to the plaza."

"Goodbody's guarding the tower doors. She hasn't come back, and we're worried. Something's wrong. She might have been seen and arrested. We saw Saurus and his cronies running down she stairs to the catacombs. They're probably trying to get to the Church of the Holy Centipede. They may know a way out we haven't discovered yet."

"What about Bishop's Garden, the gate leads to the river side of the castle?" Harry suggested.

"It's locked," Alexandra told him. "The knights locked

Bishop's Key and pulled up the drawbridge. We're trapped."

As Gawain ran across the mezzanine floor, the others followed. They met Goodbody perched on a bench watching the water cascading down the tiers of the fountain. She jumped up when she saw them. "We're trapped," she told them. "There's no way out. I saw the last of Saurus' knights disappear inside the church. We tried to open the church doors. They won't let us in."

Gawain saw many Merchants' Row shopkeepers clutching their belongings. Some were sitting at the café tables. Some looked terrified, others resigned. A sound startled everyone. People looked up into the sky terrified to see a flying object above them. Some were convinced the alien ship had planned the whole thing and they were all going to die.

When Gawain recognized the object hovering over their heads, he relaxed and began to wave. "It's Hawk. He's brought the shuttle pod. Come with me." People began to trickle behind him up the Cetacea Steps to the rampart walk. Now, they assumed the shuttle pod had arrived to rescue them. Merchants began to gather up their belongings.

A collective groan went up when the first to arrive on the walk looked down. He saw a pod no bigger than a wagon perched on the shelf of rocks near the bottom of the castle walls. The shuttle pod's hatch opened, and D.I. Burhani Hawk climbed out. He gestured to Gawain and pointed at his ear. In all the excitement Gawain had forgotten about his chip. He activated his chip and heard Hawk's voice inside his head: *Judge Hepplewhite contacted me a few minutes ago, she told me about some sort of hellfire beneath the castle. She thinks you're all in danger. Is there a way to open the drawbridge?*

Gawain turned to look for Harry Zany. Since he was the tallest person in the group, he wasn't hard to find. "Is there a way for us to open the bridge?"

As Gawain watched Harry shake his head sadly back and forth then say, "Need the password and key," other Blueglennens were talking at the same time.

"Saurus, the seahorse shit-droppings made sure only his men knew the password."

"We tried everything," someone else said.

"The drawbridge gate is made of heavy steel and the drawbridge is six feet thick."

Gawain sent Hawk a thought wave: *No luck. They've tried to open the gate but Saurus made sure only he and his men knew the password. It takes a key too. No way we can break through in time.*

Gawain heard Hawk's reply: *End transmission.* Gawain shut down his chip.

Hawk shouted up to Gawain, "We can take four at a time. No room for personal belongings. Do you have a rope ladder? I can't land on the rampart or in the plaza. The fuel from the pod might ignite the gasses from the lava."

Hawk was smiling which made Gawain real nervous. He wasn't fooling anybody, "I don't know. We'll look around and see if we can find something. We don't have much time. The hellfire is spilling into the moat. You'll be trapped too."

"We know. We've been watching from above," Hawk told him.

"Saurus has been drilling in the dungeons below the castle. He's managed to get deep enough to disturb a reserve of super-heated lava. It's like nothing we've got back home. This stuff can burn through steel plating. It's just a matter of time before it blows."

Several people screamed. Fearing a panic Gawain shouted, "Control your people, Harry. We don't have time for hysterics."

Harry and Queenie with the help of Knights Graceland and Lively managed to drag the hysterical ones down the steps and ordered them to sit at the café tables. Luella Morrison and Sylvia Paleone were the worst offenders. Don Tumble managed to gather up his manhood and wipe the tears from his cheeks. Forever afterward, he would be known as Don the Dewy Drip behind his back. His wife Diane, as she stood on the rampart avoided looking anywhere but down, pretending to be studying Hawk's shuttle pod even though her cheeks were a blue flame.

Darknight who was standing behind his elderly parents at the very back of the rampart spoke up, "We've got the shop ladder. It might reach the shuttle pod. I need some help carrying it though."

Valcinda Moorland shook her head and threw up her hands, "No. No. Your ladder won't work. Not even the wine shop ladder will reach the rocks. You need something better. It's in my bedroom on the third floor. Guinevere helped me make it. It's a chute ladder made of ropes and heavy sailing cloth. I'll need at least five people to help me carry it down."

Frank and Valcinda ran down the steps to the plaza. Before Harry could move, Queenie stopped him, "You keep those hysterical ones quiet. I'll go help Valcinda and Frank."

Beatrice made as if to follow her and Knight Graceland held her back, "You stay. My Mom would be spit eels if something happened to you. I'll help them."

Bill Anders and Billy Bill Anders offered to help. The volunteers disappeared down Wolfern Promenade. From the Cetacea

Stairs Kimberly could see the train station. A red umbrella attracted her eye and then she remembered someone she knew who carried such an umbrella – her aunt Victoria Lemon. Standing beside her was the tall svelte dark-haired chef Antonio Furness. There were no guards at the train station only Blueglennen attempting to get on the last train.

Alexandra turned in the direction she was looking and murmured, "Rats leaving a sinking ship. No surprise."

"Oh, Holy Legs! Where's Lynora Reason and Joanie Fitzhammond? Have you seen them?" Kimberly asked.

Guinevere leaned forward and whispered, "They took the first train out of town."

Alexandra tapped her on the arm, "They left right after the trial when the High Judge was arrested. They told me they were going straight to Delphadore. Joanie knows some people in the Secret Service. Fancy that, huh? Sweet little old Joanie knowing spies. Lynora Reason's going to talk to the High Sheriff. She was already suspicious of the Governor and when he declared martial law, she knew she couldn't use her cellphone or any local transmission for fear Saurus would intercept her call."

"So, they're off to save Blueglennen, unaware Blueglennen will be long gone by the time they return," Kimberly said. "The tower might become a gigantic geyser, Gawain says."

"Yes," Gawain interrupted. "Duke Tower might be the conduit for a natural geyser. It might spew hot gasses, tar and ash. But we'll be long gone by then. Don't worry. We've still got time before the pyroclastic cloud destroys everything for miles around.

The cloud will crush every tree in the Bitterroot Forest and bury all the homes for miles. When Reason and Fitzhammond return to Blueglennen, they'll be coming home to a huge crater where the castle used to be, and towns buried under the debris."

"How do you know what's really going to happen, Knight Bristlecone? You've never witnessed hellfire eruptions or any kind of natural disaster on our planet? Your describing some event from your ship's archives. There must be something we can do?" a woman asked. Kimberly and the others turned to look at the person who'd asked the question. Tanny Bright was sitting on the top Cetacea Stair holding Papa Darknight's bony freckled hand.

"What can you possibly do?" Diane screamed, her face beet red from the heat and flames as the hot lava moved to the mezzanine and began to set wooden posts and furniture aflame.

Tanny Bright ignored her and jumped to her feet, "What's your ship's outer hull made of?"

Kimberly poked Gawain in the arm. Oblivious to hysteria, Gawain had been watching the activity below as his team members piled rocks against the tower wall. He looked at Kimberly in surprise when she slapped his arm. "Tanny's asking you a question, Gawain. What's your ship's hull made of?"

"His ship?" Alexandra asked. "Are you telling me he's from Albion?"

Kimberly looked up into Alexandra's incredulous face aware she'd made a mistake. Then she saw rivulets of yellow hellfire trickling into Bishop's Garden. What did secrecy matter if they were all going to die? "Yes. He's here to study us. You must have realized he wasn't Delphi? Look at his eyes. His eyes are nothing like ours."

Alexandra rubbed her forehead which meant she was scared and upset, "I thought he'd had plastic surgery. Back east everyone wants to look like the aliens."

Tanny Bright pushed through the crowd and nearly sent Alexandra sailing off the rampart onto a café table but for Gawain's quick reflexes, "We don't have time for this." She gasped and took hold of Alexandra's arm. "Sorry. I didn't mean to push you. Are you alright?"

With a rueful smile Alexandra shook her head and Tanny turned back to Gawain still intent on getting an answer, "I've got something that can take care of our current threat. I wanted to test my invention on one of your ship's proton torpedoes though. That's not going to happen now. Still my baby turned your cheesy cellphones into sand and metal splinters. So, what's your hull made of really?"

"Space ships used to be made of titanium alloys and ceramic tiles. Now we have an even stronger material called Dromeda."

"You're lying," Tanny said with a suspicious frown and crossed her arms as if to separate herself from his lies. "The cellphones you've given us are made of carbon graphite, gold, copper, silver, lithium and aluminum alloys. But they've been repurposed so many times the elements are compromised. You've added unknown minerals to prevent degradation. My sensors guesstimate your cellphones are centuries old. Your hull is probably centuries old too."

"No. The hull is new. We nearly lost the ship a few decades ago. I can't tell you anymore. It's classified. Yes, Dela. You're right, the cellphones we've given your people are repurposed cellphones from decades ago. But I'm not lying about Dromeda. The UES Albion is made of materials collected from the Andromeda Galaxy. Most of the material comes from asteroids."

"Is it stronger than your puny gold?"

"A hundred times stronger than our diamonds."

"I have no concept of diamonds so your reference means nothing to me. We'll just have to test the WHIP on the hellfire," she said as she reached into an inside pocket of her leather shirt. When she took out her invention everyone groaned. It looked like a channel changer. Still those who knew her best moved in closer to get a good look. She pointed the WHIP at the closest person and Kimberly dropped to the ground and began to crawl toward the stairs.

"Don't worry Kimberly. I'm not going to hurt you. I've tested this baby on rats. It won't hurt a living organism, not even a piece of lettuce. Although lettuce isn't sentient, and not in the same category as delphinids...never mind. We don't have time to debate whether lettuce feels pain and is in the same category.

Just rest assured, the WHIP won't harm lettuce. Now, everybody move back. Let's see what she can do," Tanny shouted at the end. She turned to face Duke Tower and the columns holding up the courtyard. The hellfire had risen several feet undulating at the base of the granite columns like a writhing yellow monster. Soon the hellfire would reach their water source.

Tanny held the device in her hand as if she planned to switch on a television. Blueglennen's brainiest Delphinid was looking at a small black screen above a series of buttons. Symbols in bright red and white were running across the black background. When she smiled people took further precautions and started inching down the Cetacea Stairs. Tanny pressed a button on the side of the WHIP and the people nearby were reminded of the sound a squench makes when upset. With her left hand she dug in her pants pocket and took out her cellphone.

No one exclaimed over Tanny's cellphone which surprised Gawain. It looked nothing like the ancient ones his technicians constantly repaired and resold to Shellfargon consumers. Her cellphone was made of minerals he'd never seen before. After entering a series of codes, he heard a piercing whine emit from the WHIP far more piercing than a squench. Tanny aimed the WHIP at a concrete planter near the fountain. Within seconds the planter crumbled into particles of calcium, silicon, aluminum, slag, and tiny stones.

Gawain moved closer, "Let me try. I'm a better shot."

"I wasn't aiming at the hellfire. I wanted to be sure the WHIP is operational. Move away now," she told him and dropped to the rampart floor inching her way toward the tower. The heat radiating off the burning roof of the dormitory could be felt by everyone, even ten yards away. Tanny, her thoughts concentrated solely on success didn't feel the heat. With a steady hand she pushed the launch codes and aimed the WHIP at the edge of the hellfire flow.

The WHIP tore through the hellfire and the slate creating a two-foot crevice across the plaza floor. The onlookers watched in awe as the WHIP rearranged the molecules in the paving stones and the hellfire. The apparatus effectively rearranged both back to their original molecular structure. Her test was a success. Yet. The hellfire still flowed building up behind the crevice and once reaching the gap spilled into it. And that was the beauty of the WHIP. Her baby had generated enough power to carve a deep hole through the paving stones and the substructure giving them time to escape.

She jumped to her feet and began shrieking excitedly, "It works. Oh, Holy Delph. It works."

"Can that thing disintegrate all the hellfire inside the Tower?" Gawain shouted.

Tanny shook her head dismally, "No. I've got only a few energy pellets left. It's not enough to stop this monster. Only when the hellfire cools can the WHIP rearrange its molecules."

A few people groaned and then someone shouted hurray. The merchants on the rampart watched as Valcinda, Frank, and the others began to climb the stairs each with a section of the chute ladder under their arms. It seemed like hours before the end of the chute was lowered down to the impatient Hawk and Swana who'd managed to set up a platform near the shuttle pod. Each ethnographer held a side of the chute in preparation for the first person to slide down. No one on the rampart spoke or so much as twitched.

"I'll go first, you bunch of polyps," Tanny said still exuberant over her WHIP's performance.

"No," Gawain ordered. "Someone else should go first."

Diane Tumble scowled, "Why? She's offered to test the chute."

Gawain pulled his gun from its scabbard to emphasize his point, "I said no."

Suddenly people were looking at him differently. He'd metamorphized from a gallant knight into a sea serpent. Months of preparation and socializing and he'd become an alien with one thoughtless move. He didn't care. His instincts screamed caution.

Frank Darknight stepped forward and began to weave his way through the people. His grandmother cried out. He ignored her pleas. "I'll test the chute," he told Gawain with a reserved expression and then turned to the crowd. "See you at the bottom." He had to squeeze between the Anders, father and son, as they sat on either side of the chute while others held the top steady. The father and son's combined weight kept the chute from plunging down the wall.

As Gawain watched Frank's progress, from the moment he

entered the chute to the time he spent tumbling toward the bottom where Hawk and Shehili waited, he made calculations. He saw more than the others because he was the tallest of them all. He, Zany and the Anders felt the pull when Frank panicked and tried to grab hold of the ropes. The pull nearly sent all four men over the rampart. "Hold tight. Don't let go," Gawain shouted to the Anders, Lively and Graceland.

During his descent Frank Darknight hit the tower wall several times before he got to the bottom. The granite rocks piled up against the castle wall couldn't have helped much either. He saw Hawk duck inside the chute and drag Frank out by his legs. With Shehili's help they managed to get Frank upright. He limped his way to the cruiser. Gawain hoped it was nothing worse than a sprain.

After getting Darknight strapped into his seat inside the cruiser, Hawk gave Gawain a thumb's up. Gawain turned to the others. "Go slow. Crawl if you must. Tanny's next."

Diane snorted, "Now she gets to go. After we see Frank limping."

"Another word out of you and you'll go to the end of the line," he told her in a fierce whisper.

By the time the cruiser had five passengers strapped in, those on the rampart watched anxiously as the sun began to set over Mount Lordbuster. Hawk chose to fly over the plaza as he took the evacuees to safer ground. He probably wanted to judge whether he had a chance of getting the cruiser down on the plaza floor. Shehili Swana remained on the rock shelf waiting for the next person to descend. Once all the women were at the bottom, bruised and bloody, Queenie discovered she'd dislocated her elbow. Her profanity was so eloquent and memorable, Alexandra vowed to retell the choicest ones at her next dinner party.

The next ones to descend the chute were the smallest and lightest men. Once they were safely down, there were five men left on the rampart: father and son Anders, Bristlecone, Lively and Graceland. Graceland insisted his friend Lively go next. It turned out to be the best idea since Lively was a big Delphinid. It took all four of them to hold the chute steady as Lively tumbled down to the waiting shuttle pod. Once Lively was safe, Knight Graceland went next. He smiled gently and slipped inside holding his crossed arms close to his chest. At the bottom he climbed out and helped Shehili hold the chute steady for the next passenger.

When father and son Anders began to quarrel about which one would go down, Gawain drew his gun again and pointed the weapon at Junior's chest. "Get going. Your Dad will follow."

During Junior's descent his father cried and continually asked Gawain, "Did he make it? Is he alive?"

It was a relief to finally be able to tell Senior his son had made it down to the bottom without injury. As Gawain returned his gun to its scabbard, he felt someone's thick strong hand pull him to the cold granite walk and the popping of vertebrae as father Anders shoved him down the chute. Unprepared, he desperately tried to slow his descent. Hoping to avoid cracking his skull he tried to pull against the forces of gravity and get his head between his legs. It felt like hours before he reached the half way point with his knees tucked close to his chest. Just as he tasted hope, his head hit something hard and everything went black.

When he woke, he found himself laid out on the ground on his backside looking up at the moon. It was a crescent moon. Beneath his body he felt soft ground and smelled grass. A face obscured his view of the moon. It was Kimberly Lemon. She wiped the tears from her cheeks and tried to smile, "You're alive. I didn't believe Shehili. She claims she's a nurse. How many skills do you guys have on Albion?"

"Dozens, Dela Lemon."

"You saved our lives. I don't care what the others say, you're a hero."

"What about my Dad?" he heard Junior say.

"Of course, he's a hero Billy."

"What happened to Senior?" Gawain asked.

"He died saving his son's life. In retrospect, he saved all your lives," he heard Shehili Swana say. "The Albion sent shuttle pods here with tow-lines and a Dromeda capstone. They managed to contain the hellfire before it reached the promenade. Merchants' Row is safe. Tanny's been sent to the Albion. Our technicians are working on improving her device. The eruption was heard on Walrat Island. They claim there's ash over most of the eastern shore. We have a lot of work ahead of us Gawain. Rest and get your strength back. That's an order from Hawk and the captains."

E1 Shellfargon Year 5092 NDMP WK 6: UES Albion 4

Orders Confirmed. E2 hurt. Request medical on shuttle dock stat. Sending full report of Blueglennen evacuation. Request private audience: bridge only.

Chapter 14

On the cobblestone street of Merchants' Row, the glow worms swim round and round their containers illuminating the night. Most of the shopkeepers are fast asleep minus one. Only a sliver of cool blue light seeps between the velvet curtains which conceals most of the interior from curious eyes. All that a passerby might see is the big bay window and a newly stenciled inscription in frosted white letters: Bookworm Emporium. The sliver of light is coming from inside the dark room. A single lamp sits on the wood floor. Near the lamp someone has thrown down a red and black wool picnic blanket. On top of the blanket is a wicker basket with its contents spread out between the two adults.

After two months without any word from Gawain, Kimberly can hardly contain her curiosity. Before Gawain had a chance to bite into his shrimp penne, Kimberly asked, "I'd rather know what happened to you and Hawk on the Albion than go over news from Blueglennen. I'm sure you've heard all about what's been happening here from Blueglennen 84."

"Only general information. Like the fact the Duke Tower Blowout nearly destroyed Mudflat Village and Old Town, but Albion techs and the university's engineers tapped the geyser in time and with hundreds of Bright's WHIPs cleared away the crystalized Saurus Brimstone from the castle and the outlying areas. I would have chosen a better name than Saurus for the Brimstone but what the hell.

Dela Hepplewhite is acting Governor until Wolfern Province's special election and Governor Saurus was discovered hiding in a Mudflat Village cellar. His bodyguard deserted him. No surprise. Channel 84 reports the big news, I want to hear about you and your neighbors. I see there's no damage to the Emporium. Tell me what I missed."

Kimberly took a sip of her wine before speaking, "The funeral for Bill Anders was a few weeks ago. He was awarded the Medal of Honor by Raker. Billy Bill accepted the medal from Governor Hepplewhite at a private ceremony in the newly renovated plaza. You arrived too late to see the renovations. The plaza and promenade look so beautiful."

"It was a relief to discover the bridge was down when I arrived."

"Oh yes. Valley Long Drawbridge is to remain down every hour of every day, never to be closed again. The engineers will be removing the metal gates next week. And there are plans to create an additional exit on the Highway Tower side of the castle."

"How did Saurus escape? Every exit had been closed to us."

Before answering Kimberly grabbed a shrimp and popped it in her mouth. Gawain waited patiently for her to swallow the tasty treat. "You're never going to believe this but Saurus had Bishop Little cut through the floor of the church under the altar. A series of winding stairs leads out the River View wall. Saurus had artisans create a door which looks like a part of the castle. That's how Saurus and his bodyguard escaped. Before the trial ended, Bishop Little sent his family away. Many believe he knew what Saurus was up to and claim he is a traitor. If you stand on the opposite bank of the Siren River you can't tell there's a door. It's quite remarkable. Sadly, the artisans were murdered by Governor Saurus' bodyguard.

And guess what, the committee agreed to remove Duke Dono's statue including some of the other statues representing medieval maleficence. They're being stored in the university basement until the new museum is finished. Greenburg Valley wants the statues for their history museum. I hear Finstickel is delighted. Ironic, huh? Finstickel is in prison for kidnapping Star Bridgekeeper and murdering her and still feels vindicated by Greenburg? I say to Greenburg, just go ahead and perpetuate Dono's past crimes but we're gonna remind future generations of his crimes. Oh yeah. We've."

"Why is Bishop Little in jail?" Gawain interrupted. "Was he involved in seceding from Curl too?"

"Oh, no. He'd been bribing Governor Saurus and when Saurus made a plea deal he told the knights about Bishop Little's creative accounting. He'd been using most of the Church of the Holy Centipede's donations to purchase property in Hemway and build himself a villa. He claimed eventually there would be funds for a new church celebrating the Holy Centipede. But then the accountants discovered other creative ways he redirected donations."

"But I saw scaffolding all over the cathedral's entrance and what appears to be a lot of reconstruction going on inside the chapel. What's that about?"

"Sylvia Paleone had hoped to take over the ministry of the church, but she won't have time now because she's desperately trying to defend herself against accusations involving crimes against the country of Curl and espionage with a foreign entity. That would be your ship the Albion, I think. Something to do with one of your captains. Anyway, since there is no other chapter in Curl worshipping the Holy Centipede, the citizens of Blueglennen, Mudflat Village, and

Greenburg Valley are going to use the cathedral as a place of worship for all faiths.

Everyone has agreed to make the cathedral a public place where all are welcome. Tourism will generate funds and people can come and admire the stained-glass windows and lovely architecture. We even have a rich patron formerly connected with the Church of the Holy Delph donating several pieces of priceless artwork and paintings. When I found out who this benefactor was, I was stunned. I'd had no idea Alexandra came from money. She seems so normal.

It seems she's from old money and happens to be the last remaining heir of the Montagues. She was so grateful to us for saving her life, she's decided to make Blueglennen her home. Yes. I'm not kidding. She's bought the Finstickel suite, you know. It was hard for Finstickel to give up his private apartments but he's desperate for money to pay his lawyers. In just a few weeks her new home will be fumigated and ready for occupation. Isn't that marvelous? I'm so happy for her and for myself since she'll be one of my neighbors."

"You should finish your shrimp Kimberly, it's getting cold," Gawain told her finishing off his wine and setting his empty plate in the basket near her. "What about Star? Is she still living with you?" His look around the bookshop wasn't lost on her. Kimberly's entire body from her head to her toes began to tingle. After all they had been through together, she had picked up on numerous cues from his posture to his guarded expressions and believed she could read his body language with one-hundred percent accuracy. Tonight would be a very special night. It was already special since he'd come straight from the ship to her.

To mollify him she took several bites of her shrimp sandwich and emptied her wine glass, then turned to face him. He'd made himself comfortable on the blanket, his long lean body draped full length on the floor facing her. His right arm supported the weight of his upper body and his clenched fist supported his head. He looked like he was posing for a fashion magazine.

She couldn't help but admire his lean muscled body, his beautiful auburn hair and handsome eyes. He waited patiently for her to speak reminding her again of how lucky she was to find such a kindred spirit. On the outside he looked like a film star. On the inside he was one of the sweetest, most sensitive and honorable people she'd ever met. How many men were as patient as this one? Here she'd been prattling on and on about little stuff and he continued to behave as if her every word was a fountain of wisdom.

She had to look away from him in order to answer his question with any cogency, "I offered her my home and she stayed for a few days then left in a rage when I refused to accept the centipede as my savior. She returned to her parents and soon quarreled with them, after her mother confessed her affair with a Lacertidae. It is sad to see her old friends and my neighbors continue to shun her. She ran away again.

Knight Graceland found her living with Caleb and her half-sister Sophia. Graceland's mother called her son to tell him she'd seen Star in the neighborhood. Caleb is such a sweet guy and so patient with Star. I think she's finally found a home. When she needs extra money, she works for Caleb. Just yesterday they were fixing the cracks by the altar and I heard her telling Caleb all about the Holy Centipede. He let her talk and just kept on working.

Oh, and I forgot the most important thing. I hope someone reported the information to your ship. It has to do with Harry Zany's discovery. Did you hear about his picture from his cellphone – the one with the registration plate on the pump? It implicates a certain drilling company Saurus used to illegally drill below the castle."

As she spoke Gawain kept nodding his head and when she finished, he said, "Yes. Harry's picture helped us track down the people involved in the illegal drilling. The people involved are in the Albion brig and due to face a court martial. I'd wondered why Harry put himself in danger just to retrieve a sample which wasn't necessary since the whole castle would be engulfed in the nasty stuff in a few hours. He not only put himself in danger but you."

Throwing down her sandwich, she told him in a firm voice, "He did not. I followed him because I believed there were more people locked away. And I wanted to see for myself what Governor Saurus was doing. When I saw those poor people in peril from the poisonous gases and hellfire, I knew I couldn't run away. With Harry's pictures of the mud pump and the plate and the hellfire, he has proven the myth is not a myth. He's saved Shellfargon. Historians are even now writing about what happened here. Enough about that day, I want to hear what's been going on with you. It's been months since I heard from you."

Gawain sat up, crossed his legs and didn't settle down until he had positioned himself just right so that he could look directly into her eyes. The determination in his eyes and the grim set of his mouth worried her. He acted as if his news would shock her, "In my father's day, we made mistakes, tragic mistakes. When we made first contact with a species in the Andromeda Galaxy, we were clueless to the damage we would cause. Our past mistakes have resulted in stricter laws regarding first contact and interspecies conduct. Because of our mistakes, we have laws forbidding fraternization until both parties have been vetted."

"I don't understand," she told him. The discomfort on his face made her blush.

"Well, ah. You know. Hell. For one thing, we might not even be compatible in that way."

"Are you talking about procreation? If you are, I can say for sure that I don't plan to have children until Curl has made peace with Vespa 1 & 2. You can forget about that part of our future conduct."

"Really?" he asked frowning. "But the war between your countries has been going on for nearly a century?"

"Why should I have children if my children will die in some stupid war overseas?"

"I see. But you wouldn't exist if your parents thought the same way you do."

"We can get back to that subject later. If I understand you correctly, you're telling me a bunch of strangers will make the decision whether you and I can have sex tonight."

Gawain leaned back and looked out the window. The curtains were drawn, so there was no point in searching for eavesdroppers unless he thought someone might be listening to their private conversation. Was the room bugged? Was someone watching them with hidden cameras? Why was Gawain behaving so oddly? The man she'd known a few months ago had been confident, assured, gallant and amusing. Now, after months spent on his ship, he seemed jumpy, almost paranoid.

"Yes. If any of us do anything inappropriate we will be arrested and perhaps face a court martial. If found guilty by a tribunal of the captains, the guilty person would be stripped of his rank and spend the rest of his days on the ship," he said in an acid tone so unlike himself. He looked into her eyes his expression unhappy. "Which doesn't mean I like this situation any better than you do. I've come here tonight to spend a few precious hours with you, not to fight. I've had enough of fighting."

"What do you mean?" she asked moving a bit closer. He didn't push her away which was a good sign.

"Shehili didn't tell you?"

"I've barely seen Shehili the last few weeks. She's at Crest Hall. She, Joanie Fitzhammmond, my friends Crystova Moth and Lynora Reason have been in numerous private meetings with the Delphadorturo and his cabinet. Did you know Joanie used to be a spook? She must have been damned good because no one suspected. I heard she gave up her career because she refused to follow unethical orders which she believed were made by traitors. Those people tried to get her killed and lied to their superiors about her. It sounds so covert and deadly."

"I knew Shehili was a part of the Wolfern Delegation advising the Delphadorturo. Our permit to continue the Shellfargon Project is due to expire. I had no idea Fitzhammond, Moth and Reason were a part of the delegation. How are they involved?"

"I don't know. I'm as surprised as you are. I've often wondered if Lynora's travels included more than just museums and natural wonders. She meets all sorts of people on her travels which means she has plenty of opportunity to see what's really going on in the world.

Perhaps Raker believes my friends have insights into Shellfargon very few do. And, of course, the university staff are routinely invited to Crest Hall what with the Albion orbiting our planet. Didn't Raker agree to work with your captains? From the text messages I get from Lynora and Crystova that's the impression I get. They're due to arrive on the morning train tomorrow. If you have any questions you can ask Tanny. She's been conferencing with Governor Hepplewhite."

"Tanny Bright is an impressive young person," Gawain said absently, glancing around the shop as if contemplating the walls for more priceless manuscripts. "Some of our scientists are hoping to work down here and learn from her. That's an endorsement of her intellectual gifts, you know. We have some smart people too, but she beats them all to hell and back."

"You still haven't answered my question. What happened on the ship?"

His handsome eyes returned to the contemplation of her face and she did her best to control her impulse to grab his face and plant a big wet kiss on his lips. His ship's captains and their stupid rules were ruining all her plans. Something in his manner chilled her. She sat back and waited for him to speak.

"What happened when our team returned to the Albion after Governor Saurus' arrest is confidential. I'm sorry. I can't say more. Let's just say ... problems were fixed, and all is well."

Unable to pretend any longer, Kimberly jumped to her feet and walked toward the cash register. In one of the cubbyholes she grabbed a pocket mirror and returned to the picnic blanket. She handed the mirror to Gawain and said, "Then you'd better do something about the burn on your neck because your collar has droplets of fresh blood on it from your skin rubbing up against the scar. I'm assuming someone shot you with one of your fancy space guns like the one you were threating the merchants with on the

Cetacea Rampart. Or maybe someone hit you with a hot poker."

He gazed into the mirror and studied the blood on his collar then handed the pocket mirror back to Kimberly, "Those fancy space guns like the LSR7 were designed and manufactured by your people, Kimberly. Don't worry about my wound. It will heal and so will my ship. My people have more pressing concerns right now."

As Kimberly opened her mouth to respond to his cryptic remark someone banged urgently on her shop door and a familiar voice shouted, "Kimberly. I know you're in there. I can see your lamp on the floor. Is someone with you? Are they holding you prisoner?"

Before Kimberly had a chance to respond Gawain jumped to his feet. It took him three steps to reach the door, unbolt the lock and fling the door open. Tanny Bright stood under the lantern's light, the lantern Caleb and Sophie had assembled and set in the wall above the door. Tanny looked as if she'd been combing her hair with a dust mob. It was the rest of her that alarmed Kimberly the most. Her familiar leather apron was thick with yellow globs that even from the middle of the room reminded Kimberly of noxious toxic hellfire from the geyser which had nearly destroyed Duke Tower and her home.

"What's the matter Tanny?" Kimberly asked struggling to stand, all sorts of possible disasters running through her head. Tanny had discovered the hellfire was cancerous and they would all die? Gawain, with his body blocking her entry lifted his arms and held onto the door lintels in a futile attempt to discourage Tanny from entering. She simply slipped under his arm and ran toward Kimberly nearly knocking her over in her agitation.

Without ceremony she told Kimberly, "We must talk. Privately. It's urgent." Then she looked over her shoulder at Gawain. "He must go."

Surprise and hurt registered on Gawain's face but was quickly gone. His reaction to Tanny's rudeness bothered her the most. He was holding something back. She took Tanny's hand and said, "We can talk in my private quarters."

"No. Lieutenant Gawain must go."

"Lieutenant? He's still a knight. Hepplewhite wants him here in Blueglennen to restructure her new security detail and sheriff's department."

"He's an advisor, not a knight. And his real title is Lieutenant Commander. He's next in line to the succession. Swana, Hawk, and Bristlecone are all vetted to be the next Captains of the Albion. Bristlecone has seniority over Hawk and yet he declined the captaincy giving Hawk his spot. Shard is taking over the science officers post. Hawk has just been made 2nd replacing Reese McConnell who has been sent to the brig. It's a prison like the dungeon at Duke Tower."

"It's nothing like the cell Kimberly stayed in," Gawain said slamming the door behind him and striding toward the women doing his best to contain his irritation. "You signed an oath Dela Bright. You've just betrayed that oath and will no longer have clearance to receive any more intelligence briefings."

Tanny ignored Gawain and looked only at Kimberly, "They made me sign a document giving the Albion my solemn promise not to reveal any details about the ship, its classified information, or the events that took place last month. But since then I have felt I can no longer trust the Albion. The Albion has lied to our people Kimberly. They aren't here to help us. They're here to gather up all the supplies they need before leaving this galaxy. They're pirates Kimberly.

Like the serpents they have no loyalty to anyone or anything. They did something horrendous in the Andromeda Galaxy. I've gathered from their archives they nearly wiped out an entire civilization. Captain Reese McConnell was bribing Governor Saurus with money and power, so he could drill for the rock which will fuel their ship. They need our planet's wealth.

And when they have the rock and the supplies they need, they plan to run away before the Aviangore come for them. Right now, they're helpless without our resources, with very little fuel and food. A ship's coming for them. It's a Dromeda prison ship. The Aviangore claim these humans from the Albion starship are destroyers of worlds. I've already sent all the documents I've found in their archive to Hepplewhite and Raker."

Then she turned to face Gawain, "He's our enemy. We must hold him here until the knights can take him away."

"She's got it all wrong Kimberly," Gawain said holding his hands up. It was a strange thing for him to do.

"That's what humans do to show they don't have a weapon. They hold out their arms and show their empty palms," Tanny explained to her.

"You've got it all wrong. I don't know where you obtained your information but that's not what happened. And to be clear, I am not a pirate and none of our people on the Albion are pirates. I wasn't even born until after our ship left the Andromeda Galaxy. None of us on the ship were born at the time of first contact with the Aviangore. Yes, our ancestors made mistakes. Yes. They met with aliens without the proper protocols. How were they to know? They paid for their mistakes. Yet the Aviangore continue to punish us," he told Kimberly, his eyes beseeching her to understand.

Tanny interrupted him, "You make it seem so simple. But it

wasn't simple. It was ugly. It was stupid. I've seen your archives. I've seen how you destroyed your own planet and then thought you could rape other planets and other species. Well the Aviangore are on their way and from what I've learned they are far worse than humans. You've led them straight to us. We don't have your technology or your fire power. We're the Mudflat Villagers facing off against the knights of Delphadore. We can't protect ourselves from a far superior force which can with a flick of a button destroy us all with one nuclear blast. Oh yes. I've read your history. I know."

'We had no intention of staying here. We had plans just to trade our technology for food and fuel. We thought we had plenty of time, plenty of time."

Tanny shook her head and then in her frustration grabbed a dusty lock and began to twist the curl tighter and tighter until the blood stopped flowing through the tip of her finger, "You've been watching us for years and now you come down and promise us so much and all we'll get in return is a dead planet. There'll be nothing left alive. Don't you understand? Nothing. Shellfargon will be an asteroid circling the sun, nothing but a hunk of rock. You're filth. All your kind are filth, garbage, the cockroaches of the galaxy."

"We have three years," he said trying to peer over Tanny's head to see Kimberly's face.

"Projected. Not confirmed," Tanny told him using her sore finger to jab the air.

"If we leave your solar system in a year, they'll never know we've been here."

"With every household on Shellfargon including Vespa in possession of your alien technology? You can't confiscate everyone's cellphone or everyone's computer. Those devices can certainly be traced directly to your culture?"

Kimberly stepped between Gawain and Tanny, "That must be why Lynora, Joanie, Crystova, and Shehili are in private talks with Raker and his cabinet. They're trying to come up with a plan, a way we can protect our planet. Are the Lacertidae aware of what's coming?"

Tanny shrugged, her expression desolated. Gawain had told Kimberly about a person called Santa Claus. She'd told him about a fictional character every child grew up to believe was real – the beautiful seastar named Silver who left the children of Shellfargon packages of treasure and candy under their beds.

The despair on Tanny's face from her dusty hair, desolate expression, and slumped shoulders reminded Kimberly of the crushing disappointment children experience when they learn Silver is not a magical creature, a special envoy of the Holy Delph but a fiction created by parents to control children on St Delph Day.

At that precise moment Kimberly's cellphone buzzed. She looked at the others and then down at the phone. "Go on answer it," Gawain urged.

"What do we have to lose anyway?" Tanny said walking over to the window seat and throwing herself onto the pillows.

She didn't recognize the number. "Hello" she said tentatively.

"Dela Kimberly Lemon?"

"Yes. This is Dela Lemon."

"How do you do Dela Lemon. A pleasure. This is Eden Marshall from the UES Albion. I am the Science Officer on the Albion. I want you to know before we continue that you are on speaker phone and my captains are in the room. They can hear everything we say. You know Burhani Hawk. He is now 2nd Captain. Our 1st Captain is Endor Swana. And Trace Bristlecone, Lieutenant Gawain's aunt is our 3rd Captain."

Kimberly watched Gawain's face and tried unsuccessfully to figure out what he might be thinking as his ship's Science Officer continued, "Would you set your phone on speaker so that we might talk to Tanny Bright and the Lieutenant Commander?"

Shrugging, Kimberly set the phone on speaker and held the phone midway between all three standing in her book shop. They heard the Albion's science officer say, "Lieutenant Bristlecone. Would you do us the honor of escorting Tanny Bright and Kimberly Lemon to the Governor's private suite. The Interim Governor has set up an interstellar conference.

We will be interlinked with Raker in New Enreich, Vespa 1 & 2 leaders, and the Albion. Our conference will be secure and private. It will be up to each country to decide whether to televise the video. At present, we wish to avoid hysteria and the possibility of anarchy."

"I'll be happy to escort the ladies to Duke Tower," Gawain said.

"Why should I trust your man?" Tanny asked frowning up at Gawain.

"I have trusted Bristlecone in the past, Officer Marshall," Kimberly said leaning toward the cellphone to be sure she was heard. "He saved my city and my friends. I think I'll be safe to walk with him to Duke Tower. And Tanny will be with me. I'm pretty sure she wouldn't want to be left out of this discussion. The country of Curl needs her now more than ever."

Without waiting for an answer, Kimberly shut off her cellphone and stuck the device in her sweater pocket. Avoiding their eyes, she walked into the back room. She was grateful when they didn't try to follow her. She dressed quickly in clothes she hoped made her look confident, a confidence she wasn't feeling.

When she returned to the shop with her purse slung over her shoulder the blanket had been folded and placed on the window seat next to the basket. All the crumbs had been swept into the bin near the door. The room looked the same as it had this morning. She looked toward the lizard clock in the corner and a fear, not for herself but for history turned her body icy cold. Should she text Crystova and tell her where to find the illuminated manuscript? All she had learned tonight made her sick with worry. She didn't want another burden. The manuscript must go.

Gawain looked up from his contemplation of the maps on the table. His smile dissolved when he saw her expression. Before moving toward the door, she told him, "Make sure all the listening devices in my book shop and in my private quarters are removed."

He didn't even bother to argue with her; he'd already come to the same conclusion. "We have three years. We can fix this. If we all pull together. We can fix this."

Something broke inside and unable to speak, she headed blindly toward Wolfern Promenade. Tanny linked arms with her. Some sense returned, and she slowed her pace. From far away she thought she heard Tanny say, "The door locks automatically now. You'd better hurry up or we'll leave you behind."

As he ran up to them and fell into step, Kimberly punched him in the gut with her elbow, "Don't ever speak to me again. I no longer trust you or your ship. You had a chance to be honest with us and present us with the facts, years ago when we might have had a fighting chance. If you and your ship survive, which I suspect you will because that's the kind of irony the cosmos deals out, and my planet doesn't, your people will have another debt to pay.

I don't believe in a God, but I do believe in consequences. There have been plenty of species who've gone extinct for one reason or another. From what I can tell from the little you've told me about your planet you're the kind of species that has a self-destructive button built into your DNA."

"We have three years. Anything is possible," Gawain told her unable to hide his own despair.

A deeply held honesty forced Kimberly to say, "We've been fighting a never-ending war with the Lacertidae. We have no reason to feel superior. But we haven't destroyed someone's planet. Are you sure the Aviangore are coming to our solar system?"

At the fountain in the courtyard of Duke Tower, Gawain

stopped. Kimberly looked up into his face. Tanny ignoring them marched past the fountain and toward the glass doors. A knight swung the glass door open for her and said something into his earpiece. Kimberly waited for Gawain to answer her question thinking about all the millions of people on her planet unaware of their imminent destruction. She heard him say, "They've been tracking us for three centuries. I guarantee, they will find us."

As Kimberly followed Gawain and the other security detail up to the penthouse of Duke Tower, she thought about all her friends and all the people preparing for bed or waking up in anticipation of starting their day. At last census, there were about three million Shellfargons, hundreds of Serpents, millions of species in the air and in the sea, and thousands of humans on the Albion. Could one ship be so dangerous? Then she walked into the conference room and on the wall between the picture windows which faced the plaza was a television screen.

Governor Hepplewhite stood behind her desk. Her cabinet stood on either side of her looking up at the huge video screen. In a small group near the entrance was Shehili Swana, Burhani Hawk, Shard Bristlecone and several Albion officers. One of them must be the science officer Eden Marshall. She learned later that 1st Captain Ender Swana and 3rd captain Trace Bristlecone were not present, that there always had to be at least two captains on the starship.

Even though she stood next to her, Shehili Swana sounded a million miles away as she whispered in Kimberly's ear, "We made a powerful enemy on a planet we call Taurus. Over thousands of years of evolution made us immune to many deadly diseases. We did our best to protect any new lifeforms we met during our travels. Yet a fateful meeting between the United Earth Starship Albion 2 and a few Aviangore resulted in millions of deaths on their planet.

On the planet of Taurus, ten percent survived. Most survivors from Taurus were belters working in the asteroid fields on the other side of a dead moon. We're not sure how they survived when so many died. It could have something to do with their adaption to space and the minerals they mined. All we know is that they formed a collective and soon after this devastation they began hunting for the Albion 2.

They found Albion 2 and destroyed it. Then they went after Albion 3. And when they found our planet Earth, they showed no mercy. We had nearly destroyed Earth all on our own. We were working to fix what we'd nearly broken and then the Aviangore found us. I am so sorry we involved your people in our troubles. I'm so very, very sorry."

"Why did you build the ships in the first place? Why do you

call your ship Albion 4?" Kimberly asked absently, finding herself suddenly unable to focus. She looked away from the screen her stomach lurching, threatening to throw up the delicious food she and Gawain shared only an hour ago. It was worse than she thought, much worse.

"We knew our planet was dying. We tried to repair what we'd done to our oceans and air, but we'd waited so long. As a contingency plan, several countries joined forces and worked together to build ships. We hoped to find an exoplanet which could support us. Albion 1 left first, decades before the Aviangore reached our solar system. The Aviangore destroyed all the ships that didn't make it off the docking ring. We were one of five ships that survived the attack. We had been stationed on Mars collecting material for our fusion rockets. We have yet to find the other four ships and Albion 1 is still missing."

"Why are you apologizing?" Kimberly asked suddenly frightened, stepping away from her friend and the man she thought she loved and moving closer to Governor Hepplewhite and her people.

In less than an hour she had her answer. The starship Albion 4 showed the delegates in New Enreich, Blueglennen, Walrat Island, Moorland, Textus, North and South Victoria, Angland, Hemway, Bojenlac, New Dala and Vespas 1 & 2 the last ten minutes of historical footage captured by their starship's cameras of the final destruction of their home world called Earth.